Collected Stories of
WILLIAM FAULKNER

Collected Stories
of
WILLIAM FAULKNER

VINTAGE BOOKS

A Division of Random House

New York

VINTAGE BOOKS EDITION, FEBRUARY 1977
Copyright, 1934, 1950, by Random House, Inc. Copyright, 1930, 1931, 1932, 1933, 1934, 1935, 1939, 1943, 1948, by William Faulkner. Copyright, 1930, by *Forum.* Copyright, 1930, 1932, 1934, 1941, 1942, 1943, by Curtis Publishing Company. Copyright renewed 1957, 1958, 1959, 1960, 1961, 1962 by William Faulkner. Copyright renewed 1962, 1963, 1967, 1969, 1970, 1971 by Estelle Faulkner and Jill Faulkner Summers. Copyright renewed 1976 by Jill Faulkner Summers.

All rights reserved under International and Pan-American Copyright Conventions. Published in the United States by Random House, Inc., New York, and simultaneously in Canada by Random House of Canada Limited, Toronto. Originally published by Random House, Inc., in 1950.

Acknowledgment is here made to the following magazines, in which some of the stories included in this volume first appeared: *The American Mercury, Forum, Harper's Magazine, The Saturday Evening Post, Scribner's Magazine* and *The Sewanee Review.*

Library of Congress Cataloging in Publication Data
Faulkner, William, 1897-1962.
Collected stories of William Faulkner.
[PZ3.F272Co7] [PS3511.A86] 813'.5'2 76-40938
ISBN 0-394-72257-4
Manufactured in the United States of America

3579B864

Contents

Contents

I · THE COUNTRY

Barn Burning

THE STORE in which the Justice of the Peace's court was sitting smelled of cheese. The boy, crouched on his nail keg at the back of the crowded room, knew he smelled cheese, and more: from where he sat he could see the ranked shelves close-packed with the solid, squat, dynamic shapes of tin cans whose labels his stomach read, not from the lettering which meant nothing to his mind but from the scarlet devils and the silver curve of fish—this, the cheese which he knew he smelled and the hermetic meat which his intestines believed he smelled coming in intermittent gusts momentary and brief between the other constant one, the smell and sense just a little of fear because mostly of despair and grief, the old fierce pull of blood. He could not see the table where the Justice sat and before which his father and his father's enemy (*our enemy* he thought in that despair; *ourn! mine and hisn both! He's my father!*) stood, but he could hear them, the two of them that is, because his father had said no word yet:

"But what proof have you, Mr. Harris?"

"I told you. The hog got into my corn. I caught it up and sent it back to him. He had no fence that would hold it. I told him so, warned him. The next time I put the hog in my pen. When he came to get it I gave him enough wire to patch up his pen. The next time I put the hog up and kept it. I rode down to his house and saw the wire I gave him still rolled on

3

to the spool in his yard. I told him he could have the hog when he paid me a dollar pound fee. That evening a nigger came with the dollar and got the hog. He was a strange nigger. He said, 'He say to tell you wood and hay kin burn.' I said, 'What?' 'That whut he say to tell you,' the nigger said. 'Wood and hay kin burn.' That night my barn burned. I got the stock out but I lost the barn."

"Where is the nigger? Have you got him?"

"He was a strange nigger, I tell you. I don't know what became of him."

"But that's not proof. Don't you see that's not proof?"

"Get that boy up here. He knows." For a moment the boy thought too that the man meant his older brother until Harris said, "Not him. The little one. The boy," and, crouching, small for his age, small and wiry like his father, in patched and faded jeans even too small for him, with straight, uncombed, brown hair and eyes gray and wild as storm scud, he saw the men between himself and the table part and become a lane of grim faces, at the end of which he saw the Justice, a shabby, collarless, graying man in spectacles, beckoning him. He felt no floor under his bare feet; he seemed to walk beneath the palpable weight of the grim turning faces. His father, stiff in his black Sunday coat donned not for the trial but for the moving, did not even look at him. *He aims for me to lie*, he thought, again with that frantic grief and despair. *And I will have to do hit.*

"What's your name, boy?" the Justice said.

"Colonel Sartoris Snopes," the boy whispered.

"Hey?" the Justice said. "Talk louder. Colonel Sartoris? I reckon anybody named for Colonel Sartoris in this country can't help but tell the truth, can they?" The boy said nothing. *Enemy! Enemy!* he thought; for a moment he could not even see, could not see that the Justice's face was kindly nor discern that his voice was troubled when he spoke to the man named Harris: "Do you want me to question this boy?" But he could hear, and during those subsequent long seconds while there was absolutely no sound in the crowded little room save that of quiet and intent breathing it was as if he had swung outward at the end of a grape vine, over a ravine, and at the top of the swing had been caught in a prolonged instant of mesmerized gravity, weightless in time.

"No!" Harris said violently, explosively. "Damnation! Send him out of here!" Now time, the fluid world, rushed beneath him again, the voices coming to him again through the smell of cheese and sealed meat, the fear and despair and the old grief of blood:

"This case is closed. I can't find against you, Snopes, but I can give you advice. Leave this country and don't come back to it."

His father spoke for the first time, his voice cold and harsh, level, without emphasis: "I aim to. I don't figure to stay in a country among people who . . ." he said something unprintable and vile, addressed to no one.

"That'll do," the Justice said. "Take your wagon and get out of this country before dark. Case dismissed."

His father turned, and he followed the stiff black coat, the wiry figure walking a little stiffly from where a Confederate provost's man's musket ball had taken him in the heel on a stolen horse thirty years ago, followed the two backs now, since his older brother had appeared from somewhere in the crowd, no taller than the father but thicker, chewing tobacco steadily, between the two lines of grim-faced men and out of the store and across the worn gallery and down the sagging steps and among the dogs and half-grown boys in the mild May dust, where as he passed a voice hissed:

"Barn burner!"

Again he could not see, whirling; there was a face in a red haze, moonlike, bigger than the full moon, the owner of it half again his size, he leaping in the red haze toward the face, feeling no blow, feeling no shock when his head struck the earth, scrabbling up and leaping again, feeling no blow this time either and tasting no blood, scrabbling up to see the other boy in full flight and himself already leaping into pursuit as his father's hand jerked him back, the harsh, cold voice speaking above him: "Go get in the wagon."

It stood in a grove of locusts and mulberries across the road. His two hulking sisters in their Sunday dresses and his mother and her sister in calico and sunbonnets were already in it, sitting on and among the sorry residue of the dozen and more movings which even the boy could remember—the battered stove, the broken beds and chairs, the clock inlaid with mother-of-pearl, which would not run, stopped at some fourteen minutes past two o'clock of a dead and forgotten day and time, which had been his mother's dowry. She was crying, though when she saw him she drew her sleeve across her face and began to descend from the wagon. "Get back," the father said.

"He's hurt. I got to get some water and wash his . . ."

"Get back in the wagon," his father said. He got in too, over the tail-gate. His father mounted to the seat where the older brother already sat and struck the gaunt mules two savage blows with the peeled willow, but without heat. It was not even sadistic; it was exactly that same quality which in later years would cause his descendants to over-run the engine before putting a motor car into motion, striking and reining back in the same movement. The wagon went on, the store with its quiet crowd of grimly watching men dropped behind; a curve in the road hid it. *Forever* he thought. *Maybe he's done satisfied now, now that he has . . .* stopping himself, not to say it aloud even to himself. His mother's hand touched his shoulder.

"Does hit hurt?" she said.

"Naw," he said. "Hit don't hurt. Lemme be."

"Can't you wipe some of the blood off before hit dries?"

"I'll wash to-night," he said. "Lemme be, I tell you."

The wagon went on. He did not know where they were going. None of them ever did or ever asked, because it was always somewhere, always a house of sorts waiting for them a day or two days or even three days away. Likely his father had already arranged to make a crop on another farm before he . . . Again he had to stop himself. He (the father) always did. There was something about his wolflike independence and even courage when the advantage was at least neutral which impressed strangers, as if they got from his latent ravening ferocity not so much a sense of dependability as a feeling that his ferocious conviction in the rightness of his own actions would be of advantage to all whose interest lay with his.

That night they camped, in a grove of oaks and beeches where a spring ran. The nights were still cool and they had a fire against it, of a rail lifted from a nearby fence and cut into lengths—a small fire, neat, niggard almost, a shrewd fire; such fires were his father's habit and custom always, even in freezing weather. Older, the boy might have remarked this and wondered why not a big one; why should not a man who had not only seen the waste and extravagance of war, but who had in his blood an inherent voracious prodigality with material not his own, have burned everything in sight? Then he might have gone a step farther and thought that that was the reason: that niggard blaze was the living fruit of nights passed during those four years in the woods hiding from all men, blue or gray, with his strings of horses (captured horses, he called them). And older still, he might have divined the true reason: that the element of fire spoke to some deep mainspring of his father's being, as the element of steel or of powder spoke to other men, as the one weapon for the preservation of integrity, else breath were not worth the breathing, and hence to be regarded with respect and used with discretion.

But he did not think this now and he had seen those same niggard blazes all his life. He merely ate his supper beside it and was already half asleep over his iron plate when his father called him, and once more he followed the stiff back, the stiff and ruthless limp, up the slope and on to the starlit road where, turning, he could see his father against the stars but without face or depth—a shape black, flat, and bloodless as though cut from tin in the iron folds of the frockcoat which had not been made for him, the voice harsh like tin and without heat like tin:

"You were fixing to tell them. You would have told him." He didn't answer. His father struck him with the flat of his hand on the side of the head, hard but without heat, exactly as he had struck the two mules at the store, exactly as he would strike either of them with any stick in order to kill a horse fly, his voice still without heat or anger: "You're getting to be a man. You got to learn. You got to learn to stick to your own blood or you ain't going to have any blood to stick to you. Do you think either of them, any man there this morning, would? Don't you know all they wanted was a chance to get at me because they knew I had them beat? Eh?" Later, twenty years later, he was to tell himself, "If I had said they wanted only truth, justice, he would have hit me again." But now he said nothing. He was not crying. He just stood there. "Answer me," his father said.

"Yes," he whispered. His father turned.

"Get on to bed. We'll be there tomorrow."

To-morrow they were there. In the early afternoon the wagon stopped before a paintless two-room house identical almost with the dozen others it had stopped before even in the boy's ten years, and again, as on the other dozen occasions, his mother and aunt got down and began to unload the wagon, although his two sisters and his father and brother had not moved.

"Likely hit ain't fitten for hawgs," one of the sisters said.

"Nevertheless, fit it will and you'll hog it and like it," his father said. "Get out of them chairs and help your Ma unload."

The two sisters got down, big, bovine, in a flutter of cheap ribbons; one of them drew from the jumbled wagon bed a battered lantern, the other a worn broom. His father handed the reins to the older son and began to climb stiffly over the wheel. "When they get unloaded, take the team to the barn and feed them." Then he said, and at first the boy thought he was still speaking to his brother: "Come with me."

"Me?" he said.

"Yes," his father said. "You."

"Abner," his mother said. His father paused and looked back—the harsh level stare beneath the shaggy, graying, irascible brows.

"I reckon I'll have a word with the man that aims to begin to-morrow owning me body and soul for the next eight months."

They went back up the road. A week ago—or before last night, that is—he would have asked where they were going, but not now. His father had struck him before last night but never before had he paused afterward to explain why; it was as if the blow and the following calm, outrageous voice still rang, repercussed, divulging nothing to him save the terrible handicap of being young, the light weight of his few years, just heavy enough to prevent his soaring free of the world as it seemed to be ordered but not heavy enough to keep him footed solid in it, to resist it and try to change the course of its events.

Presently he could see the grove of oaks and cedars and the other flowering trees and shrubs where the house would be, though not the house yet. They walked beside a fence massed with honeysuckle and Cherokee roses and came to a gate swinging open between two brick pillars, and now, beyond a sweep of drive, he saw the house for the first time and at that instant he forgot his father and the terror and despair both, and even when he remembered his father again (who had not stopped) the terror and despair did not return. Because, for all the twelve movings, they had sojourned until now in a poor country, a land of small farms and fields and houses, and he had never seen a house like this before. *Hit's big as a courthouse* he thought quietly, with a surge of peace and joy whose reason he could not have thought into words, being too young for that: *They are safe from him. People whose lives are a part of this peace and dignity are beyond his touch, he no more to them than a buzzing wasp: capable of stinging for a little moment but that's all; the spell of this peace and dignity rendering even the barns and stable and cribs which belong to it impervious to the puny flames he might contrive* . . . this, the peace and joy, ebbing for an instant as he looked again at the stiff black back, the stiff and implacable limp of the figure which was not dwarfed by the house, for the reason that it had never looked big anywhere and which now, against the serene columned backdrop, had more than ever that impervious quality of something cut ruthlessly from tin, depthless, as though, sidewise to the sun, it would cast no shadow. Watching him, the boy remarked the absolutely undeviating course which his father held and saw the stiff foot come squarely down in a pile of fresh droppings where a horse had stood in the drive and which his father could have avoided by a simple change of stride. But it ebbed only for a moment, though he could not have thought this into words either, walking on in the spell of the house, which he could ever want but without envy, without sorrow, certainly never with that ravening and jealous rage which unknown to him walked in the ironlike black coat before him: *Maybe he will feel it too. Maybe it will even change him now from what maybe he couldn't help but be.*

They crossed the portico. Now he could hear his father's stiff foot as it came down on the boards with clocklike finality, a sound out of all proportion to the displacement of the body it bore and which was not dwarfed either by the white door before it, as though it had attained to a sort of vicious and ravening minimum not to be dwarfed by anything—the flat, wide, black hat, the formal coat of broadcloth which had once been black but which had now that friction-glazed greenish cast of the bodies of old house flies, the lifted sleeve which was too large, the lifted hand like a curled claw. The door opened so promptly that the boy knew the Negro must have been watching them all the time, an old man with neat grizzled hair, in a linen jacket, who stood barring the door with his body, saying, "Wipe yo foots, white man, fo you come in here. Major ain't home nohow."

"Get out of my way, nigger," his father said, without heat too, flinging the door back and the Negro also and entering, his hat still on his head. And now the boy saw the prints of the stiff foot on the doorjamb and saw them appear on the pale rug behind the machinelike deliberation of the foot which seemed to bear (or transmit) twice the weight which the body compassed. The Negro was shouting "Miss Lula! Miss Lula!" somewhere behind them, then the boy, deluged as though by a warm wave by a suave turn of carpeted stair and a pendant glitter of chandeliers and a mute gleam of gold frames, heard the swift feet and saw her too, a lady—perhaps he had never seen her like before either— in a gray, smooth gown with lace at the throat and an apron

tied at the waist and the sleeves turned back, wiping cake or
biscuit dough from her hands with a towel as she came up
the hall, looking not at his father at all but at the tracks on
the blond rug with an expression of incredulous amazement.
"I tried," the Negro cried. "I tole him to . . ."
"Will you please go away?" she said in a shaking voice.
"Major de Spain is not at home. Will you please go away?"
His father had not spoken again. He did not speak again.
He did not even look at her. He just stood stiff in the center
of the rug, in his hat, the shaggy iron-gray brows twitching
slightly above the pebble-colored eyes as he appeared to
examine the house with brief deliberation. Then with the
same deliberation he turned; the boy watched him pivot on
the good leg and saw the stiff foot drag round the arc of
the turning, leaving a final long and fading smear. His father
never looked at it, he never once looked down at the rug.
The Negro held the door. It closed behind them, upon the
hysteric and indistinguishable woman-wail. His father
stopped at the top of the steps and scraped his boot clean on
the edge of it. At the gate he stopped again. He stood for
a moment, planted stiffly on the stiff foot, looking back at
the house. "Pretty and white, ain't it?" he said. "That's
sweat. Nigger sweat. Maybe it ain't white enough yet to
suit him. Maybe he wants to mix some white sweat with it."
    Two hours later the boy was chopping wood behind the
house within which his mother and aunt and the two sisters
(the mother and aunt, not the two girls, he knew that; even
at this distance and muffled by walls the flat loud voices of
the two girls emanated an incorrigible idle inertia) were
setting up the stove to prepare a meal, when he heard the
hooves and saw the linen-clad man on a fine sorrel mare,
whom he recognized even before he saw the rolled rug in
front of the Negro youth following on a fat bay carriage
horse—a suffused, angry face vanishing, still at full gallop,

beyond the corner of the house where his father and brother were sitting in the two tilted chairs; and a moment later, almost before he could have put the axe down, he heard the hooves again and watched the sorrel mare go back out of the yard, already galloping again. Then his father began to shout one of the sisters' names, who presently emerged backward from the kitchen door dragging the rolled rug along the ground by one end while the other sister walked behind it.

"If you ain't going to tote, go on and set up the wash pot," the first said.

"You, Sarty!" the second shouted. "Set up the wash pot!" His father appeared at the door, framed against that shabbiness, as he had been against that other bland perfection, impervious to either, the mother's anxious face at his shoulder.

"Go on," the father said. "Pick it up." The two sisters stooped, broad, lethargic; stooping, they presented an incredible expanse of pale cloth and a flutter of tawdry ribbons.

"If I thought enough of a rug to have to git hit all the way from France I wouldn't keep hit where folks coming in would have to tromp on hit," the first said. They raised the rug.

"Abner," the mother said. "Let me do it."

"You go back and git dinner," his father said. "I'll tend to this."

From the woodpile through the rest of the afternoon the boy watched them, the rug spread flat in the dust beside the bubbling wash-pot, the two sisters stooping over it with that profound and lethargic reluctance, while the father stood over them in turn, implacable and grim, driving them though never raising his voice again. He could smell the harsh homemade lye they were using; he saw his mother come to the door once and look toward them with an expression not anxious now but very like despair; he saw his father turn, and he fell to with the axe and saw from the corner of his eye his father raise from the ground a flattish fragment of field stone and examine it and return to the pot, and this time his mother actually spoke: "Abner. Abner. Please don't. Please, Abner."

Then he was done too. It was dusk; the whippoorwills had already begun. He could smell coffee from the room where they would presently eat the cold food remaining from the mid-afternoon meal, though when he entered the house he realized they were having coffee again probably because there was a fire on the hearth, before which the rug now lay spread over the backs of the two chairs. The tracks of his father's foot were gone. Where they had been were now long, water-cloudy scoriations resembling the sporadic course of a lilliputian mowing machine.

It still hung there while they ate the cold food and then went to bed, scattered without order or claim up and down the two rooms, his mother in one bed, where his father would later lie, the older brother in the other, himself, the aunt, and the two sisters on pallets on the floor. But his father was not in bed yet. The last thing the boy remembered was the depthless, harsh silhouette of the hat and coat bending over the rug and it seemed to him that he had not even closed his eyes when the silhouette was standing over him, the fire almost dead behind it, the stiff foot prodding him awake. "Catch up the mule," his father said.

When he returned with the mule his father was standing in the black door, the rolled rug over his shoulder. "Ain't you going to ride?" he said.

"No. Give me your foot."

He bent his knee into his father's hand, the wiry, surprising power flowed smoothly, rising, he rising with it, on to the mule's bare back (they had owned a saddle once; the boy could remember it though not when or where) and with the same effortlessness his father swung the rug up in front of him. Now in the starlight they retraced the afternoon's path, up the dusty road rife with honeysuckle, through the gate and up the black tunnel of the drive to the lightless house, where he sat on the mule and felt the rough warp of the rug drag across his thighs and vanish.

"Don't you want me to help?" he whispered. His father did not answer and now he heard again that stiff foot striking the hollow portico with that wooden and clocklike deliberation, that outrageous overstatement of the weight it carried. The rug, hunched, not flung (the boy could tell that even in the darkness) from his father's shoulder struck the angle of wall and floor with a sound unbelievably loud, thunderous, then the foot again, unhurried and enormous; a light came on in the house and the boy sat, tense, breathing steadily and quietly and just a little fast, though the foot itself did not increase its beat at all, descending the steps now; now the boy could see him.

"Don't you want to ride now?" he whispered. "We kin both ride now," the light within the house altering now, flaring up and sinking. *He's coming down the stairs now*, he thought. He had already ridden the mule up beside the horse block; presently his father was up behind him and he doubled the reins over and slashed the mule across the neck, but before the animal could begin to trot the hard, thin arm came round him, the hard, knotted hand jerking the mule back to a walk.

In the first red rays of the sun they were in the lot, putting plow gear on the mules. This time the sorrel mare was in the lot before he heard it at all, the rider collarless and even bareheaded, trembling, speaking in a shaking voice as the woman in the house had done, his father merely looking up

once before stooping again to the hame he was buckling, so
that the man on the mare spoke to his stooping back:

"You must realize you have ruined that rug. Wasn't there
anybody here, any of your women . . ." he ceased, shaking,
the boy watching him, the older brother leaning now in the
stable door, chewing, blinking slowly and steadily at nothing
apparently. "It cost a hundred dollars. But you never had a
hundred dollars. You never will. So I'm going to charge you
twenty bushels of corn against your crop. I'll add it in your
contract and when you come to the commissary you can
sign it. That won't keep Mrs. de Spain quiet but maybe it
will teach you to wipe your feet off before you enter her
house again."

Then he was gone. The boy looked at his father, who still
had not spoken or even looked up again, who was now ad-
justing the logger-head in the hame.

"Pap," he said. His father looked at him—the inscrutable
face, the shaggy brows beneath which the gray eyes glinted
coldly. Suddenly the boy went toward him, fast, stopping
as suddenly. "You done the best you could!" he cried. "If
he wanted hit done different why didn't he wait and tell
you how? He won't git no twenty bushels! He won't git
none! We'll gether hit and hide hit! I kin watch . . ."

"Did you put the cutter back in that straight stock like
I told you?"

"No, sir," he said.

"Then go do it."

That was Wednesday. During the rest of that week he
worked steadily, at what was within his scope and some
which was beyond it, with an industry that did not need to
be driven nor even commanded twice; he had this from his
mother, with the difference that some at least of what he
did he liked to do, such as splitting wood with the half-size
axe which his mother and aunt had earned, or saved money

somehow, to present him with at Christmas. In company
with the two older women (and on one afternoon, even one
of the sisters), he built pens for the shoat and the cow which
were a part of his father's contract with the landlord, and
one afternoon, his father being absent, gone somewhere on
one of the mules, he went to the field.

They were running a middle buster now, his brother
holding the plow straight while he handled the reins, and
walking beside the straining mule, the rich black soil shear-
ing cool and damp against his bare ankles, he thought *Maybe
this is the end of it. Maybe even that twenty bushels that
seems hard to have to pay for just a rug will be a cheap price
for him to stop forever and always from being what he used
to be;* thinking, dreaming now, so that his brother had to
speak sharply to him to mind the mule: *Maybe he even
won't collect the twenty bushels. Maybe it will all add up
and balance and vanish—corn, rug, fire; the terror and grief,
the being pulled two ways like between two teams of horses
—gone, done with for ever and ever.*

Then it was Saturday; he looked up from beneath the
mule he was harnessing and saw his father in the black coat
and hat. "Not that," his father said. "The wagon gear."
And then, two hours later, sitting in the wagon bed behind
his father and brother on the seat, the wagon accomplished
a final curve, and he saw the weathered paintless store with
its tattered tobacco- and patent-medicine posters and the
tethered wagons and saddle animals below the gallery. He
mounted the gnawed steps behind his father and brother,
and there again was the lane of quiet, watching faces for the
three of them to walk through. He saw the man in spectacles sitting at the plank table and he did not need to be
told this was a Justice of the Peace; he sent one glare of
fierce, exultant, partisan defiance at the man in collar and
cravat now, whom he had seen but twice before in his life,

and that on a galloping horse, who now wore on his face
an expression not of rage but of amazed unbelief which the
boy could not have known was at the incredible circumstance of being sued by one of his own tenants, and came
and stood against his father and cried at the Justice: "He
ain't done it! He ain't burnt . . ."

"Go back to the wagon," his father said.

"Burnt?" the Justice said. "Do I understand this rug was
burned too?"

"Does anybody here claim it was?" his father said. "Go
back to the wagon." But he did not, he merely retreated to
the rear of the room, crowded as that other had been, but
not to sit down this time, instead, to stand pressing among
the motionless bodies, listening to the voices:

"And you claim twenty bushels of corn is too high for
the damage you did to the rug?"

"He brought the rug to me and said he wanted the tracks
washed out of it. I washed the tracks out and took the rug
back to him."

"But you didn't carry the rug back to him in the same
condition it was in before you made the tracks on it."

His father did not answer, and now for perhaps half a
minute there was no sound at all save that of breathing, the
faint, steady suspiration of complete and intent listening.

"You decline to answer that, Mr. Snopes?" Again his
father did not answer. "I'm going to find against you, Mr.
Snopes. I'm going to find that you were responsible for the
injury to Major de Spain's rug and hold you liable for it.
But twenty bushels of corn seems a little high for a man in
your circumstances to have to pay. Major de Spain claims it
cost a hundred dollars. October corn will be worth about
fifty cents. I figure that if Major de Spain can stand a ninety-
five dollar loss on something he paid cash for, you can stand
a five-dollar loss you haven't earned yet. I hold you in dam-

ages to Major de Spain to the amount of ten bushels of corn over and above your contract with him, to be paid to him out of your crop at gathering time. Court adjourned."

It had taken no time hardly, the morning was but half begun. He thought they would return home and perhaps back to the field, since they were late, far behind all other farmers. But instead his father passed on behind the wagon, merely indicating with his hand for the older brother to follow with it, and crossed the road toward the blacksmith shop opposite, pressing on after his father, overtaking him, speaking, whispering up at the harsh, calm face beneath the weathered hat: "He won't git no ten bushels neither. He won't git one. We'll . . ." until his father glanced for an instant down at him, the face absolutely calm, the grizzled eyebrows tangled above the cold eyes, the voice almost pleasant, almost gentle:

"You think so? Well, we'll wait till October anyway."

The matter of the wagon—the setting of a spoke or two and the tightening of the tires—did not take long either, the business of the tires accomplished by driving the wagon into the spring branch behind the shop and letting it stand there, the mules nuzzling into the water from time to time, and the boy on the seat with the idle reins, looking up the slope and through the sooty tunnel of the shed where the slow hammer rang and where his father sat on an upended cypress bolt, easily, either talking or listening, still sitting there when the boy brought the dripping wagon up out of the branch and halted it before the door.

"Take them on to the shade and hitch," his father said. He did so and returned. His father and the smith and a third man squatting on his heels inside the door were talking, about crops and animals; the boy, squatting too in the ammoniac dust and hoof-parings and scales of rust, heard his father tell a long and unhurried story out of the time before

the birth of the older brother even when he had been a professional horsetrader. And then his father came up beside
him where he stood before a tattered last year's circus poster
on the other side of the store, gazing rapt and quiet at the
scarlet horses, the incredible poisings and convolutions of
tulle and tights and the painted leers of comedians, and said,
"It's time to eat."

But not at home. Squatting beside his brother against the
front wall, he watched his father emerge from the store and
produce from a paper sack a segment of cheese and divide it
carefully and deliberately into three with his pocket knife
and produce crackers from the same sack. They all three
squatted on the gallery and ate, slowly, without talking;
then in the store again, they drank from a tin dipper tepid
water smelling of the cedar bucket and of living beech trees.
And still they did not go home. It was a horse lot this time,
a tall rail fence upon and along which men stood and sat
and out of which one by one horses were led, to be walked
and trotted and then cantered back and forth along the road
while the slow swapping and buying went on and the sun
began to slant westward, they—the three of them—watching and listening, the older brother with his muddy eyes and
his steady, inevitable tobacco, the father commenting now
and then on certain of the animals, to no one in particular.

It was after sundown when they reached home. They ate
supper by lamplight, then, sitting on the doorstep, the boy
watched the night fully accomplish, listening to the whippoorwills and the frogs, when he heard his mother's voice:
"Abner! No! No! Oh, God. Oh, God. Abner!" and he rose,
whirled, and saw the altered light through the door where
a candle stub now burned in a bottle neck on the table and
his father, still in the hat and coat, at once formal and burlesque as though dressed carefully for some shabby and
ceremonial violence, emptying the reservoir of the lamp

back into the five-gallon kerosene can from which it had been filled, while the mother tugged at his arm until he shifted the lamp to the other hand and flung her back, not savagely or viciously, just hard, into the wall, her hands flung out against the wall for balance, her mouth open and in her face the same quality of hopeless despair as had been in her voice. Then his father saw him standing in the door.

"Go to the barn and get that can of oil we were oiling the wagon with," he said. The boy did not move. Then he could speak.

"What . . ." he cried. "What are you . . ."

"Go get that oil," his father said. "Go."

Then he was moving, running, outside the house, toward the stable: this the old habit, the old blood which he had not been permitted to choose for himself, which had been bequeathed him willy nilly and which had run for so long (and who knew where, battening on what of outrage and savagery and lust) before it came to him. *I could keep on,* he thought. *I could run on and on and never look back, never need to see his face again. Only I can't. I can't,* the rusted can in his hand now, the liquid sploshing in it as he ran back to the house and into it, into the sound of his mother's weeping in the next room, and handed the can to his father.

"Ain't you going to even send a nigger?" he cried. "At least you sent a nigger before!"

This time his father didn't strike him. The hand came even faster than the blow had, the same hand which had set the can on the table with almost excruciating care flashing from the can toward him too quick for him to follow it, gripping him by the back of his shirt and on to tiptoe before he had seen it quit the can, the face stooping at him in breathless and frozen ferocity, the cold, dead voice speaking over him to the older brother who leaned against the table.

chewing with that steady, curious, sidewise motion of cows:

"Empty the can into the big one and go on. I'll catch up with you."

"Better tie him up to the bedpost," the brother said.

"Do like I told you," the father said. Then the boy was moving, his bunched shirt and the hard, bony hand between his shoulder-blades, his toes just touching the floor, across the room and into the other one, past the sisters sitting with spread heavy thighs in the two chairs over the cold hearth, and to where his mother and aunt sat side by side on the bed, the aunt's arms about his mother's shoulders.

"Hold him," the father said. The aunt made a startled movement. "Not you," the father said. "Lennie. Take hold of him. I want to see you do it." His mother took him by the wrist. "You'll hold him better than that. If he gets loose don't you know what he is going to do? He will go up yonder." He jerked his head toward the road. "Maybe I'd better tie him."

"I'll hold him," his mother whispered.

"See you do then." Then his father was gone, the stiff foot heavy and measured upon the boards, ceasing at last.

Then he began to struggle. His mother caught him in both arms, he jerking and wrenching at them. He would be stronger in the end, he knew that. But he had no time to wait for it. "Lemme go!" he cried. "I don't want to have to hit you!"

"Let him go!" the aunt said. "If he don't go, before God, I am going up there myself!"

"Don't you see I can't?" his mother cried. "Sarty! Sarty! No! No! Help me, Lizzie!"

Then he was free. His aunt grasped at him but it was too late. He whirled, running, his mother stumbled forward on to her knees behind him, crying to the nearer sister: "Catch him, Net! Catch him!" But that was too late too, the sister (the sisters were twins, born at the same time, yet either of them now gave the impression of being, encompassing as much living meat and volume and weight as any other two of the family) not yet having begun to rise from the chair, her head, face, alone merely turned, presenting to him in the flying instant an astonishing expanse of young female features untroubled by any surprise even, wearing only an expression of bovine interest. Then he was out of the room, out of the house, in the mild dust of the starlit road and the heavy rifeness of honeysuckle, the pale ribbon unspooling with terrific slowness under his running feet, reaching the gate at last and turning in, running, his heart and lungs drumming, on up the drive toward the lighted house, the lighted door. He did not knock, he burst in, sobbing for breath, incapable for the moment of speech; he saw the astonished face of the Negro in the linen jacket without knowing when the Negro had appeared.

"De Spain!" he cried, panted. "Where's . . ." then he saw the white man too emerging from a white door down the hall. "Barn!" he cried. "Barn!"

"What?" the white man said. "Barn?"

"Yes!" the boy cried. "Barn!"

"Catch him!" the white man shouted.

But it was too late this time too. The Negro grasped his shirt, but the entire sleeve, rotten with washing, carried away, and he was out that door too and in the drive again, and had actually never ceased to run even while he was screaming into the white man's face.

Behind him the white man was shouting, "My horse! Fetch my horse!" and he thought for an instant of cutting across the park and climbing the fence into the road, but he did not know the park nor how high the vine-massed fence might be and he dared not risk it. So he ran on down the drive, blood and breath roaring; presently he was in the road again though he could not see it. He could not hear either: the galloping mare was almost upon him before he heard her, and even then he held his course, as if the very urgency of his wild grief and need must in a moment more find him wings, waiting until the ultimate instant to hurl himself aside and into the weed-choked roadside ditch as the horse thundered past and on, for an instant in furious silhouette against the stars, the tranquil early summer night sky which, even before the shape of the horse and rider vanished, stained abruptly and violently upward: a long, swirling roar incredible and soundless, blotting the stars, and he springing up and into the road again, running again, knowing it was too late yet still running even after he heard the shot and, an instant later, two shots, pausing now without knowing he had ceased to run, crying "Pap! Pap!", running again before he knew he had begun to run, stumbling, tripping over something and scrabbling up again without ceasing to run, looking backward over his shoulder at the glare as he got up, running on among the invisible trees, panting, sobbing, "Father! Father!"

At midnight he was sitting on the crest of a hill. He did not know it was midnight and he did not know how far he had come. But there was no glare behind him now and he sat now, his back toward what he had called home for four days anyhow, his face toward the dark woods which he would enter when breath was strong again, small, shaking steadily in the chill darkness, hugging himself into the remainder of his thin, rotten shirt, the grief and despair now no longer terror and fear but just grief and despair. *Father. My father*, he thought. "He was brave!" he cried suddenly, aloud but not loud, no more than a whisper: "He was! He was in the war! He was in Colonel Sartoris' cav'ry!" not knowing that his father had gone to that war a private in the fine old European sense, wearing no uniform, admitting the authority of and giving fidelity to no man or army or flag, going to war as Malbrouck himself did: for booty—it meant nothing and less than nothing to him if it were enemy booty or his own.

The slow constellations wheeled on. It would be dawn and then sun-up after a while and he would be hungry. But that would be to-morrow and now he was only cold, and walking would cure that. His breathing was easier now and he decided to get up and go on, and then he found that he had been asleep because he knew it was almost dawn, the night almost over. He could tell that from the whippoor-wills. They were everywhere now among the dark trees below him, constant and inflectioned and ceaseless, so that, as the instant for giving over to the day birds drew nearer and nearer, there was no interval at all between them. He got up. He was a little stiff, but walking would cure that too as it would the cold, and soon there would be the sun. He went on down the hill, toward the dark woods within which the liquid silver voices of the birds called unceasing —the rapid and urgent beating of the urgent and quiring heart of the late spring night. He did not look back.

Shingles for the Lord

Pap got up a good hour before daylight and caught the mule and rid down to Killegrews' to borrow the froe and maul. He ought to been back with it in forty minutes. But the sun had rose and I had done milked and fed and was eating my breakfast when he got back, with the mule not only in a lather but right on the edge of the thumps too.

"Fox hunting," he said. "Fox hunting. A seventy-year-old man, with both feet and one knee, too, already in the grave, squatting all night on a hill and calling himself listening to a fox race that he couldn't even hear unless they had come right up onto the same log he was setting on and bayed into his ear trumpet. Give me my breakfast," he told maw. "Whitfield is standing there right this minute, straddle of that board tree with his watch in his hand."

And he was. We rid on past the church, and there was not only Solon Quick's school-bus truck but Reverend Whitfield's old mare too. We tied the mule to a sapling and hung our dinner bucket on a limb, and with pap toting Killegrew's froe and maul and the wedges and me toting our ax, we went on to the board tree where Solon and Homer Bookwright, with their froes and mauls and axes and wedges, was setting on two upended cuts, and Whitfield was standing jest like pap said, in his boiled shirt and his black hat and pants and necktie, holding his watch in his hand. It was gold and in the morning sunlight it looked big as a full-growed squash. "You're late," he said.

So pap told again about how Old Man Killegrew had been off fox hunting all night, and nobody at home to lend him the froe but Mrs. Killegrew and the cook. And naturally, the cook wasn't going to lend none of Killegrew's tools out, and Mrs. Killegrew was worser deaf than even Killegrew. If you was to run in and tell her the house was afire, she would jest keep on rocking and say she thought so, too, unless she began to holler back to the cook to turn the dogs loose before you could even open your mouth.

"You could have gone yesterday and borrowed the froe," Whitfield said. "You have known for a month now that you had promised this one day out of a whole summer toward putting a roof on the house of God."

"We ain't but two hours late," pap said. "I reckon the Lord will forgive it. He ain't interested in time, nohow. He's interested in salvation."

Whitfield never even waited for pap to finish. It looked to me like he even got taller, thundering down at pap like a cloudburst. "He ain't interested in neither! Why should He be, when He owns them both? And why He should turn around for the poor, mizzling souls of men that can't even borrow tools in time to replace the shingles on His church, I don't know either. Maybe it's just because He made them. Maybe He just said to Himself: 'I made them; I don't know why. But since I did, I Godfrey, I'll roll My sleeves up and drag them into glory whether they will or no!' "

But that wasn't here nor there either now, and I reckon he knowed it, jest like he knowed there wasn't going to be nothing atall here as long as he stayed. So he put the watch back into his pocket and motioned Solon and Homer up, and we all taken off our hats except him while he stood there with his face raised into the sun and his eyes shut and his eyebrows looking like a big iron-gray caterpillar lying along the edge of a cliff. "Lord," he said, "make them good straight shingles to lay smooth, and let them split out easy; they're for You," and opened his eyes and looked at us again, mostly at pap, and went and untied his mare and clumb up slow and stiff, like old men do, and rid away.

Pap put down the froe and maul and laid the three wedges in a neat row on the ground and taken up the ax.

"Well, men," he said, "let's get started. We're already late."

"Me and Homer ain't," Solon said. "We was here." This time him and Homer didn't set on the cuts. They squatted on their heels. Then I seen that Homer was whittling on a stick. I hadn't noticed it before. "I make it two hours and a little over," Solon said. "More or less."

Pap was still about half stooped over, holding the ax. "It's nigher one," he said. "But call it two for the sake of the argument. What about it?"

"What argument?" Homer said.

"All right," pap said. "Two hours then. What about it?"

"Which is three man-hour units a hour, multiplied by two hours," Solon said. "Or a total of six work units." When the WPA first come to Yoknapatawpha County and started to giving out jobs and grub and mattresses, Solon went in to Jefferson to get on it. He would drive his school-bus truck the twenty-two miles in to town every morning and come back that night. He done that for almost a week before he found out he would not only have to sign his farm off into somebody else's name, he couldn't even own and run the school bus that he had built himself. So he come back that night and never went back no more, and since then hadn't nobody better mention WPA to him unless they aimed to fight, too, though every now and then he would turn up with something all figured down into work units like he done now. "Six units short."

"Four of which you and Homer could have already worked out while you was setting here waiting on me," pap said.

"Except that we didn't," Solon said. "We promised Whitfield two units of twelve three-unit hours toward getting some new shingles on the church roof. We been here ever since sunup, waiting for the third unit to show up, so we could start. You don't seem to kept up with these modern ideas about work that's been flooding and uplifting the country in the last few years."

"What modren ideas?" pap said. "I didn't know there was but one idea about work—until it is done, it ain't done, and when it is done, it is."

Homer made another long, steady whittle on the stick. His knife was sharp as a razor.

Solon taken out his snuffbox and filled the top and tilted the snuff into his lip and offered the box to Homer, and Homer shaken his head, and Solon put the top back on the box and put the box back into his pocket.

"So," pap said, "jest because I had to wait two hours for a old seventy-year man to get back from fox hunting that never had no more business setting out in the woods all night than he would 'a' had setting all night in a highway juke joint, we all three have got to come back here tomorrow to finish them two hours that you and Homer ——"

"I ain't," Solon said. "I don't know about Homer. I promised Whitfield one day. I was here at sunup to start it. When the sun goes down, I will consider I have done finished it."

"I see," pap said. "I see. It's me that's got to come back. By myself. I got to break into a full morning to make up them two hours that you and Homer spent resting. I got to spend two hours of the next day making up for the two hours of the day before that you and Homer never even worked."

"It's going to more than jest break into a morning," Solon

said. "It's going to wreck it. There's six units left over. Six one-man-hour units. Maybe you can work twice as fast as me and Homer put together and finish them in four hours, but I don't believe you can work three times as fast and finish in two."

Pap was standing up now. He was breathing hard. We could hear him. "So," he said. "So." He swung the ax and druv the blade into one of the cuts and snatched it up onto its flat end, ready to split. "So I'm to be penalized a half a day of my own time, from my own work that's waiting for me at home right this minute, to do six hours more work than the work you fellers lacked two hours of even doing atall, purely and simply because I am jest a average hard-working farmer trying to do the best he can, instead of a durn froe-owning millionaire named Quick or Bookwright."

They went to work then, splitting the cuts into bolts and riving the bolts into shingles for Tull and Snopes and the others that had promised for tomorrow to start nailing onto the church roof when they finished pulling the old shingles off. They set flat on the ground in a kind of circle, with their legs spraddled out on either side of the propped-up bolt, Solon and Homer working light and easy and steady as two clocks ticking, but pap making every lick of hisn like he was killing a moccasin. If he had jest swung the maul half as fast as he swung it hard, he would have rove as many shingles as Solon and Homer together, swinging the maul up over his head and holding it there for what looked like a whole minute sometimes and then swinging it down onto the blade of the froe, and not only a shingle flying off every lick but the froe going on into the ground clean up to the helve eye, and pap setting there wrenching at it slow and steady and hard, like he jest wished it would try to hang on a root or a rock and stay there.

"Here, here," Solon said. "If you don't watch out you

won't have nothing to do neither during them six extra units tomorrow morning but rest."

Pap never even looked up. "Get out of the way," he said. And Solon done it. If he hadn't moved the water bucket, pap would have split it, too, right on top of the bolt, and this time the whole shingle went whirling past Solon's shin jest like a scythe blade.

"What you ought to do is to hire somebody to work out them extra overtime units," Solon said.

"With what?" Pap said. "I ain't had no WPA experience in dickering over labor. Get out of the way."

But Solon had already moved this time. Pap would have had to change his whole position or else made this one curve. So this one missed Solon, too, and pap set there wrenching the froe, slow and hard and steady, back out of the ground.

"Maybe there's something else besides cash you might be able to trade with," Solon said. "You might use that dog."

That was when pap actually stopped. I didn't know it myself then either, but I found it out a good long time before Solon did. Pap set there with the maul up over his head and the blade of the froe set against the block for the next lick, looking up at Solon. "The dog?" he said.

It was a kind of mixed hound, with a little bird dog and some collie and maybe a considerable of almost anything else, but it would ease through the woods without no more noise than a hant and pick up a squirrel's trail on the ground and bark jest once, unless it knowed you was where you could see it, and then tiptoe that trail out jest like a man and never make another sound until it treed, and only then when it knowed you hadn't kept in sight of it. It belonged to pap and Vernon Tull together. Will Varner give it to Tull as a puppy, and pap raised it for a half interest; me and him trained it and it slept in my bed with me until it got so big maw finally run it out of the house, and for the last six months

Solon had been trying to buy it. Him and Tull had agreed on two dollars for Tull's half of it, but Solon and pap was still six dollars apart on ourn, because pap said it was worth ten dollars of anybody's money and if Tull wasn't going to collect his full half of that, he was going to collect it for him.

"So that's it," pap said. "Them things wasn't work units atall. They was dog units."

"Jest a suggestion," Solon said. "Jest a friendly offer to keep them runaway shingles from breaking up your private business for six hours tomorrow morning. You sell me your half of that trick overgrown fyce and I'll finish these shingles for you."

"Naturally including them six extra units of one dollars," pap said.

"No, no," Solon said. "I'll pay you the same two dollars for your half of that dog that me and Tull agreed on for his half of it. You meet me here tomorrow morning with the dog and you can go on back home or wherever them urgent private affairs are located, and forget about that church roof."

For about ten seconds more, pap set there with the maul up over his head, looking at Solon. Then for about three seconds he wasn't looking at Solon or at nothing else. Then he was looking at Solon again. It was jest exactly like after about two and nine-tenths seconds he found out he wasn't looking at Solon, so he looked back at him as quick as he could. "Hah," he said. Then he began to laugh. It was laughing all right, because his mouth was open and that's what it sounded like. But it never went no further back than his teeth and it never come nowhere near reaching as high up as his eyes. And he never said "Look out" this time neither. He jest shifted fast on his hips and swung the maul down, the froe done already druv through the bolt and into the ground

while the shingle was still whirling off to slap Solon across
the shin.

Then they went back at it again. Up to this time I could
tell pap's licks from Solon's and Homer's, even with my back
turned, not because they was louder or steadier, because
Solon and Homer worked steady, too, and the froe never
made no especial noise jest going into the ground, but because
they was so infrequent; you would hear five or six of Solon's
and Homer's little polite chipping licks before you would
hear pap's froe go "chug!" and know that another shingle
had went whirling off somewhere. But from now on pap's
sounded jest as light and quick and polite as Solon's or
Homer's either, and, if anything, even a little faster, with the
shingles piling up steadier than I could stack them, almost;
until now there was going to be more than a plenty of them
for Tull and the others to shingle with tomorrow, right on
up to noon, when we heard Armstid's farm bell, and Solon
laid his froe and maul down and looked at his watch too. And
I wasn't so far away neither, but by the time I caught up with
pap he had untied the mule from the sapling and was already
on it. And maybe Solon and Homer thought they had pap,
and maybe for a minute I did, too, but I jest wish they could
have seen his face then. He reached our dinner bucket down
from the limb and handed it to me.

"Go on and eat," he said. "Don't wait for me. Him and
his work units. If he wants to know where I went, tell him
I forgot something and went home to get it. Tell him I had
to go back home to get two spoons for us to eat our dinner
with. No, don't tell him that. If he hears I went somewhere
to get something I needed to use, even if it's jest a tool to eat
with, he will refuse to believe I jest went home, for the reason
that I don't own anything there that even I would borrow."
He hauled the mule around and heeled him in the flank.
Then he pulled up again. "And when I come back, no matter

what I say, don't pay no attention to it. No matter what happens, don't you say nothing. Don't open your mouth a-tall, you hear?"

Then he went on, and I went back to where Solon and Homer was setting on the running board of Solon's school-bus truck, eating, and sho enough Solon said jest exactly what pap said he was going to.

"I admire his optimism, but he's mistaken. If it's something he needs that he can't use his natural hands and feet for, he's going somewhere else than jest his own house."

We had jest went back to the shingles when pap rid up and got down and tied the mule back to the sapling and come and taken up the ax and snicked the blade into the next cut.

"Well, men," he said, "I been thinking about it. I still don't think it's right, but I still ain't thought of anything to do about it. But somebody's got to make up for them two hours nobody worked this morning, and since you fellers are two to one against me, it looks like it's going to be me that makes them up. But I got work waiting at home for me tomorrow. I got corn that's crying out loud for me right now. Or maybe that's jest a lie too. Maybe the whole thing is, I don't mind admitting here in private that I been outfigured, but I be dog if I'm going to set here by myself tomorrow morning admitting it in public. Anyway, I ain't. So I'm going to trade with you, Solon. You can have the dog."

Solon looked at pap. "I don't know as I want to trade now," he said.

"I see," pap said. The ax was still stuck in the cut. He began to pump it up and down to back it out.

"Wait," Solon said. "Put that durn ax down." But pap held the ax raised for the lick, looking at Solon and waiting. "You're swapping me half a dog for a half a day's work," Solon said.

"Your half of the dog for that half a day's work you still owe on these shingles."

"And the two dollars," pap said. "That you and Tull agreed on. I sell you half the dog for two dollars, and you come back here tomorrow and finish the shingles. You give me the two dollars now, and I'll meet you here in the morning with the dog, and you can show me the receipt from Tull for his half then."

"Me and Tull have already agreed," Solon said.

"All right," pap said. "Then you can pay Tull his two dollars and bring his receipt with you without no trouble."

"Tull will be at the church tomorrow morning, pulling off them old shingles," Solon said.

"All right," pap said. "Then it won't be no trouble at all for you to get a receipt from him. You can stop at the church when you pass. Tull ain't named Grier. He won't need to be off somewhere borrowing a crowbar."

So Solon taken out his purse and paid pap the two dollars and they went back to work. And now it looked like they really was trying to finish that afternoon, not jest Solon, but even Homer, that didn't seem to be concerned in it nohow, and pap, that had already swapped a half a dog to get rid of whatever work Solon claimed would be left over. I quit trying to stay up with them; I jest stacked shingles.

Then Solon laid his froe and maul down. "Well, men," he said, "I don't know what you fellers think, but I consider this a day."

"All right," pap said. "You are the one to decide when to quit, since whatever elbow units you consider are going to be shy tomorrow will be yourn."

"That's a fact," Solon said. "And since I am giving a day and a half to the church instead of jest a day, like I started out doing, I reckon I better get on home and tend to a little of my own work." He picked up his froe and maul and ax and went to his truck and stood waiting for Homer to come and get in.

"I'll be here in the morning with the dog," pap said.

"Sholy," Solon said. It sounded like he had forgot about the dog, or that it wasn't no longer any importance. But he stood there again and looked hard and quiet at pap for about a second. "And a bill of sale from Tull for his half of it. As you say, it won't be no trouble a-tall to get that from him." Him and Homer got into the truck and he started the engine. You couldn't say jest what it was. It was almost like Solon was hurrying himself, so pap wouldn't have to make any excuse or pretense toward doing or not doing anything. "I have always understood the fact that lightning don't have to hit twice is one of the reasons why they named it lightning. So getting lightning-struck is a mistake that might happen to any man. The mistake I seem to made is, I never realized in time that what I was looking at was a cloud. I'll see you in the morning."

"With the dog," pap said.

"Certainly," Solon said, again like it had slipped his mind completely. "With the dog."

Then him and Homer drove off. Then pap got up.

"What?" I said. "What? You swapped him your half of Tull's dog for that half a day's work tomorrow. Now what?"

"Yes," pap said. "Only before that I had already swapped Tull a half a day's work pulling off them old shingles tomorrow, for Tull's half of that dog. Only we ain't going to wait until tomorrow. We're going to pull them shingles off tonight, and without no more racket about it than is necessary. I don't aim to have nothing on my mind tomorrow but watching Mr. Solon Work-Unit Quick trying to get a bill of sale for two dollars or ten dollars either on the other half of that dog. And we'll do it tonight. I don't want him jest to find out at sunup tomorrow that he is too late. I want him to find out then that even when he laid down to sleep he was already too late."

So we went back home and I fed and milked while pap went down to Killegrews' to carry the froe and maul back and to borrow a crowbar. But of all places in the world and doing what under the sun with it, Old Man Killegrew had went and lost his crowbar out of a boat into forty feet of water. And pap said how he come within a inch of going to Solon's and borrowing his crowbar out of pure poetic justice, only Solon might have smelled the rat jest from the idea of the crowbar. So pap went to Armstid's and borrowed hisn and come back and we et supper and cleaned and filled the lantern while maw still tried to find out what we was up to that couldn't wait till morning.

We left her still talking, even as far as the front gate, and come on back to the church, walking this time, with the rope and crowbar and a hammer for me, and the lantern still dark. Whitfield and Snopes was unloading a ladder from Snopes' wagon when we passed the church on the way home before dark, so all we had to do was to set the ladder up against the church. Then pap clumb up onto the roof with the lantern and pulled off shingles until he could hang the lantern inside behind the decking, where it could shine out through the cracks in the planks, but you couldn't see it unless you was passing in the road, and by that time anybody would 'a' already heard us. Then I clumb up with the rope, and pap reached it through the decking and around a rafter and back and tied the ends around our waists, and we started. And we went at it. We had them old shingles jest raining down, me using the claw hammer and pap using the crowbar, working the bar under a whole patch of shingles at one time and then laying back on the bar like in one more lick or if the crowbar ever happened for one second to get a solid holt, he would tilt up that whole roof at one time like a hinged box lid.

That's exactly what he finally done. He laid back on the bar and this time it got a holt. It wasn't jest a patch of shingles, it was a whole section of decking, so that when he lunged back he snatched that whole section of roof from around the lantern like you would shuck a corn nubbin. The lantern was hanging on a nail. He never even moved the nail, he jest pulled the board off of it, so that it looked like for a whole minute I watched the lantern, and the crowbar, too, setting there in the empty air in a little mess of floating shingles, with the empty nail still sticking through the bail of the lantern, before the whole thing started down into the church. It hit the floor and bounced once. Then it hit the floor again, and this time the whole church jest blowed up into a pit of yellow jumping fire, with me and pap hanging over the edge of it on two ropes.

I don't know what become of the rope nor how we got out of it. I don't remember climbing down. Jest pap yelling behind me and pushing me about halfway down the ladder and then throwing me the rest of the way by a handful of my overhalls, and then we was both on the ground, running for the water barrel. It set under the gutter spout at the side, and Armstid was there then; he had happened to go out to his lot about a hour back and seen the lantern on the church roof, and it stayed on his mind until finally he come up to see what was going on, and got there jest in time to stand yelling back and forth with pap across the water barrel. And I believe we still would have put it out. Pap turned and squatted against the barrel and got a holt of it over his shoulder and stood up with that barrel that was almost full and run around the corner and up the steps of the church and hooked his toe on the top step and come down with the barrel busting on top of him and knocking him cold out as a wedge.

So we had to drag him back first, and maw was there then, and Mrs. Armstid about the same time, and me and Armstid

run with the two fire buckets to the spring, and when we got
back there was a plenty there, Whitfield, too, with more
buckets, and we done what we could, but the spring was two
hundred yards away and ten buckets emptied it and it taken
five minutes to fill again, and so finally we all jest stood
around where pap had come to again with a big cut on his
head and watched it go. It was a old church, long dried out,
and full of old colored-picture charts that Whitfield had accumulated for more than fifty years, that the lantern had lit
right in the middle of when it finally exploded. There was a
special nail where he would keep a old long nightshirt he
would wear to baptize in. I would use to watch it all the time
during church and Sunday school, and me and the other boys
would go past the church sometimes jest to peep in at it,
because to a boy of ten it wasn't jest a cloth garment or even
a iron armor; it was the old strong Archangel Michael his
self, that had fit and strove and conquered sin for so long
that it finally had the same contempt for the human beings
that returned always to sin as hogs and dogs done that the old
strong archangel his self must have had.

For a long time it never burned, even after everything else
inside had. We could watch it, hanging there among the fire,
not like it had knowed in its time too much water to burn
easy, but like it had strove and fit with the devil and all the
hosts of hell too long to burn in jest a fire that Res Grier
started, trying to beat Solon Quick out of half a dog. But at
last it went, too, not in a hurry still, but jest all at once, kind
of roaring right on up and out against the stars and the far
dark spaces. And then there wasn't nothing but jest pap,
drenched and groggy-looking, on the ground, with the rest
of us around him, and Whitfield like always in his boiled shirt
and his black hat and pants, standing there with his hat on,
too, like he had strove too long to save what hadn't ought to
been created in the first place, from the damnation it didn't

even want to escape, to bother to need to take his hat off in any presence. He looked around at us from under it; we was all there now, all that belonged to that church and used it to be born and marry and die from—us and the Armstids and Tulls, and Bookwright and Quick and Snopes.

"I was wrong," Whitfield said. "I told you we would meet here tomorrow to roof a church. We'll meet here in the morning to raise one."

"Of course we got to have a church," pap said. "We're going to have one. And we're going to have it soon. But there's some of us done already give a day or so this week, at the cost of our own work. Which is right and just, and we're going to give more, and glad to. But I don't believe that the Lord ——"

Whitfield let him finish. He never moved. He jest stood there until pap finally run down of his own accord and hushed and set there on the ground mostly not looking at maw, before Whitfield opened his mouth.

"Not you," Whitfield said. "Arsonist."

"Arsonist?" pap said.

"Yes," Whitfield said. "If there is any pursuit in which you can engage without carrying flood and fire and destruction and death behind you, do it. But not one hand shall you lay to this new house until you have proved to us that you are to be trusted again with the powers and capacities of a man." He looked about at us again. "Tull and Snopes and Armstid have already promised for tomorrow. I understand that Quick had another half day he intended ——"

"I can give another day," Solon said.

"I can give the rest of the week," Homer said.

"I ain't rushed neither," Snopes said.

"That will be enough to start with, then," Whitfield said. "It's late now. Let us all go home."

He went first. He didn't look back once, at the church or

at us. He went to the old mare and clumb up slow and stiff and powerful, and was gone, and we went too, scattering. But I looked back at it. It was jest a shell now, with a red and fading core, and I had hated it at times and feared it at others, and I should have been glad. But there was something that even that fire hadn't even touched. Maybe that's all it was—jest indestructibility, endurability—that old man that could plan to build it back while its walls was still fire-fierce and then calmly turn his back and go away because he knowed that the men that never had nothing to give toward the new one but their work would be there at sunup tomorrow, and the day after that, and the day after that, too, as long as it was needed, to give that work to build it back again. So it hadn't gone a-tall; it didn't no more care for that little fire and flood than Whitfield's old baptizing gown had done. Then we was home. Maw had left so fast the lamp was still lit, and we could see pap now, still leaving a puddle where he stood, with a cut across the back of his head where the barrel had busted and the blood-streaked water soaking him to the waist.

"Get them wet clothes off," maw said.

"I don't know as I will or not," pap said. "I been publicly notified that I ain't fitten to associate with white folks, so I publicly notify them same white folks and Methodists, too, not to try to associate with me, or the devil can have the hindmost."

But maw hadn't even listened. When she come back with a pan of water and a towel and the liniment bottle, pap was already in his nightshirt.

"I don't want none of that neither," he said. "If my head wasn't worth busting, it ain't worth patching." But she never paid no mind to that neither. She washed his head off and dried it and put the bandage on and went out again, and pap went and got into bed.

"Hand me my snuff; then you get out of here and stay out too," he said.

But before I could do that maw come back. She had a glass of hot toddy, and she went to the bed and stood there with it, and pap turned his head and looked at it.

"What's that?" he said.

But maw never answered, and then he set up in bed and drawed a long, shuddering breath—we could hear it—and after a minute he put out his hand for the toddy and set there holding it and drawing his breath, and then he taken a sip of it.

"I Godfrey, if him and all of them put together think they can keep me from working on my own church like ary other man, he better be a good man to try it." He taken another sip of the toddy. Then he taken a long one. "Arsonist," he said. "Work units. Dog units. And now arsonist. I Godfrey, what a day!"

The Tall Men

THEY PASSED THE DARK bulk of the cotton gin. Then they saw the lamplit house and the other car, the doctor's coupé, just stopping at the gate, and they could hear the hound baying.

"Here we are," the old deputy marshal said.

"What's that other car?" the younger man said, the stranger, the state draft investigator.

"Doctor Schofield's," the marshal said. "Lee McCallum asked me to send him out when I telephoned we were coming."

"You mean you warned them?" the investigator said. "You telephoned ahead that I was coming out with a warrant for these two evaders? Is this how you carry out the orders of the United States Government?"

The marshal was a lean, clean old man who chewed tobacco, who had been born and lived in the county all his life.

"I understood all you wanted was to arrest these two McCallum boys and bring them back to town," he said.

"It was!" the investigator said. "And now you have warned them, given them a chance to run. Possibly put the Government to the expense of hunting them down with troops. Have you forgotten that you are under a bond yourself?"

"I ain't forgot it," the marshal said. "And ever since we

left Jefferson I been trying to tell you something for you not to forget. But I reckon it will take these McCallums to impress that on you. . . . Pull in behind the other car. We'll try to find out first just how sick whoever it is that is sick is."

The investigator drew up behind the other car and switched off and blacked out his lights. "These people," he said. Then he thought, *But this doddering, tobacco-chewing old man is one of them, too, despite the honor and pride of his office, which should have made him different.* So he didn't speak it aloud, removing the keys and getting out of the car, and then locking the car itself, rolling the windows up first, thinking, *These people who lie about and conceal the ownership of land and property in order to hold relief jobs which they have no intention of performing, standing on their constitutional rights against having to work, who jeopardize the very job itself through petty and transparent subterfuge to acquire a free mattress which they intend to attempt to sell; who would relinquish even the job, if by so doing they could receive free food and a place, any rathole, in town to sleep in; who, as farmers, make false statements to get seed loans which they will later misuse, and then react in loud vituperative outrage and astonishment when caught at it. And then, when at long last a suffering and threatened Government asks one thing of them in return, one thing simply, which is to put their names down on a selective-service list, they refuse to do it.*

The old marshal had gone on. The investigator followed, through a stout paintless gate in a picket fence, up a broad brick walk between two rows of old shabby cedars, toward the rambling and likewise paintless sprawl of the two-story house in the open hall of which the soft lamplight glowed and the lower story of which, as the investigator now perceived, was of logs.

He saw a hall full of soft lamplight beyond a stout paintless gallery running across the log front, from beneath which the same dog which they had heard, a big hound, came booming again, to stand foursquare facing them in the walk, bellowing, until a man's voice spoke to it from the house. He followed the marshal up the steps onto the gallery. Then he saw the man standing in the door, waiting for them to approach—a man of about forty-five, not tall, but blocky, with a brown, still face and horseman's hands, who looked at him once, brief and hard, and then no more, speaking to the marshal, "Howdy, Mr. Gombault. Come in."

"Howdy, Rafe," the marshal said. "Who's sick?"

"Buddy," the other said. "Slipped and caught his leg in the hammer mill this afternoon."

"Is it bad?" the marshal said.

"It looks bad to me," the other said. "That's why we sent for the doctor instead of bringing him in to town. We couldn't get the bleeding stopped."

"I'm sorry to hear that," the marshal said. "This is Mr. Pearson." Once more the investigator found the other looking at him, the brown eyes still, courteous enough in the brown face, the hand he offered hard enough, but the clasp quite limp, quite cold. The marshal was still speaking. "From Jackson. From the draft board." Then he said, and the investigator could discern no change whatever in his tone: "He's got a warrant for the boys."

The investigator could discern no change whatever anywhere. The limp hard hand merely withdrew from his, the still face now looking at the marshal. "You mean we have declared war?"

"No," the marshal said.

"That's not the question, Mr. McCallum," the investigator said. "All required of them was to register. Their numbers might not even be drawn this time; under the law of

averages, they probably would not be. But they refused—
failed, anyway—to register."

"I see," the other said. He was not looking at the investigator. The investigator couldn't tell certainly if he was even
looking at the marshal, although he spoke to him, "You
want to see Buddy? The doctor's with him now."

"Wait," the investigator said. "I'm sorry about your
brother's accident, but I——" The marshal glanced back
at him for a moment, his shaggy gray brows beetling, with
something at once courteous yet a little impatient about the
glance, so that during the instant the investigator sensed
from the old marshal the same quality which had been in
the other's brief look. The investigator was a man of better
than average intelligence; he was already becoming aware
of something a little different here from what he had expected. But he had been in relief work in the state several
years, dealing almost exclusively with country people, so he
still believed he knew them. So he looked at the old marshal,
thinking, *Yes. The same sort of people, despite the office,
the authority and responsibility which should have changed
him*. Thinking again, *These people. These people*. "I intend to take the night train back to Jackson," he said. "My
reservation is already made. Serve the warrant and we
will -——"

"Come along," the old marshal said. "We are going to
have plenty of time."

So he followed—there was nothing else to do—fuming
and seething, attempting in the short length of the hall to
regain control of himself in order to control the situation,
because he realized now that if the situation were controlled,
it would devolve upon him to control it; that if their departure with their prisoners were expedited, it must be himself and not the old marshal who would expedite it. He had
been right. The doddering old officer was not only at bot-

tom one of these people, he had apparently been corrupted
anew to his old, inherent, shiftless sloth and unreliability
merely by entering the house. So he followed in turn, down
the hall and into a bedroom; whereupon he looked about
him not only with amazement but with something very like
terror. The room was a big room, with a bare unpainted
floor, and besides the bed, it contained only a chair or two
and one other piece of old-fashioned furniture. Yet to the
investigator it seemed so filled with tremendous men cast
in the same mold as the man who had met them that the
very walls themselves must bulge. Yet they were not big,
not tall, and it was not vitality, exuberance, because they
made no sound, merely looking quietly at him where he
stood in the door, with faces bearing an almost identical
stamp of kinship—a thin, almost frail old man of about
seventy, slightly taller than the others; a second one, white-
haired, too, but otherwise identical with the man who had
met them at the door; a third one about the same age as
the man who had met them, but with something delicate in
his face and something tragic and dark and wild in the same
dark eyes; the two absolutely identical blue-eyed youths;
and lastly the blue-eyed man on the bed over which the
doctor, who might have been any city doctor, in his neat
city suit, leaned—all of them turning to look quietly at him
and the marshal as they entered. And he saw, past the doctor,
the slit trousers of the man on the bed and the exposed,
bloody, mangled leg, and he turned sick, stopping just inside the door under that quiet, steady regard while the
marshal went up to the man who lay on the bed, smoking
a cob pipe, a big, old-fashioned, wicker-covered demijohn,
such as the investigator's grandfather had kept his whisky
in, on the table beside him.

"Well, Buddy," the marshal said, "this is bad."

"Ah, it was my own damn fault," the man on the bed

said. "Stuart kept warning me about that frame I was using."

"That's correct," the second old one said.

Still the others said nothing. They just looked steadily and quietly at the investigator until the marshal turned slightly and said, "This is Mr. Pearson. From Jackson. He's got a warrant for the boys."

Then the man on the bed said, "What for?"

"That draft business, Buddy," the marshal said.

"We're not at war now," the man on the bed said.

"No," the marshal said. "It's that new law. They didn't register."

"What are you going to do with them?"

"It's a warrant, Buddy. Swore out."

"That means jail."

"It's a warrant," the old marshal said. Then the investigator saw that the man on the bed was watching him, puffing steadily at the pipe.

"Pour me some whisky, Jackson," he said.

"No," the doctor said. "He's had too much already."

"Pour me some whisky, Jackson," the man on the bed said. He puffed steadily at the pipe, looking at the investigator. "You come from the Government?" he said.

"Yes," the investigator said. "They should have registered. That's all required of them yet. They did not——" His voice ceased, while the seven pairs of eyes contemplated him, and the man on the bed puffed steadily.

"We would have still been here," the man on the bed said. "We wasn't going to run." He turned his head. The two youths were standing side by side at the foot of the bed. "Anse, Lucius," he said.

To the investigator it sounded as if they answered as one, "Yes, father."

"This gentleman has come all the way from Jackson to

say the Government is ready for you. I reckon the quickest place to enlist will be Memphis. Go upstairs and pack."

The investigator started, moved forward. "Wait!" he cried.

But Jackson, the eldest, had forestalled him. He said, "Wait," also, and now they were not looking at the investigator. They were looking at the doctor.

"What about his leg?" Jackson said.

"Look at it," the doctor said. "He almost amputated it himself. It won't wait. And he can't be moved now. I'll need my nurse to help me, and some ether, provided he hasn't had too much whisky to stand the anesthetic too. One of you can drive to town in my car. I'll telephone ——"

"Ether?" the man on the bed said. "What for? You just said yourself it's pretty near off now. I could whet up one of Jackson's butcher knives and finish it myself, with another drink or two. Go on. Finish it."

"You couldn't stand any more shock," the doctor said. "This is whisky talking now."

"Shucks," the other said. "One day in France we was running through a wheat field and I saw the machine gun, coming across the wheat, and I tried to jump it like you would jump a fence rail somebody was swinging at your middle, only I never made it. And I was on the ground then, and along toward dark that begun to hurt, only about that time something went whang on the back of my helmet, like when you hit a anvil, so I never knowed nothing else until I woke up. There was a heap of us racked up along a bank outside a field dressing station, only it took a long time for the doctor to get around to all of us, and by that time it was hurting bad. This here ain't hurt none to speak of since I got a-holt of this johnny-jug. You go on and finish it. If it's help you need, Stuart and Rafe will help you. . . . Pour me a drink, Jackson."

This time the doctor raised the demijohn and examined the level of the liquor. "There's a good quart gone," he said. "If you've drunk a quart of whisky since four o'clock, I doubt if you could stand the anesthetic. Do you think you could stand it if I finished it now?"

"Yes, finish it. I've ruined it; I want to get shut of it."

The doctor looked about at the others, at the still, identical faces watching him. "If I had him in town, in the hospital, with a nurse to watch him, I'd probably wait until he got over this first shock and got the whisky out of his system. But he can't be moved now, and I can't stop the bleeding like this, and even if I had ether or a local anesthetic ——"

"Shucks," the man on the bed said. "God never made no better local nor general comfort or anesthetic neither than what's in this johnny-jug. And this ain't Jackson's leg nor Stuart's nor Rafe's nor Lee's. It's mine. I done started it; I reckon I can finish cutting it off any way I want to."

But the doctor was still looking at Jackson. "Well, Mr. McCallum?" he said. "You're the oldest."

But it was Stuart who answered. "Yes," he said. "Finish it. What do you want? Hot water, I reckon."

"Yes," the doctor said. "Some clean sheets. Have you got a big table you can move in here?"

"The kitchen table," the man who had met them at the door said. "Me and the boys ——"

"Wait," the man on the bed said. "The boys won't have time to help you." He looked at them again. "Anse, Lucius," he said.

Again it seemed to the investigator that they answered as one, "Yes, father."

"This gentleman yonder is beginning to look impatient. You better start. Come to think of it, you won't need to pack. You will have uniforms in a day or two. Take the truck. There won't be nobody to drive you to Memphis and

bring the truck back, so you can leave it at the Gayoso
Feed Company until we can send for it. I'd like for you to
enlist into the old Sixth Infantry, where I used to be. But I
reckon that's too much to hope, and you'll just have to
chance where they send you. But it likely won't matter,
once you are in. The Government done right by me in my
day, and it will do right by you. You just enlist wherever
they want to send you, need you, and obey your sergeants
and officers until you find out how to be soldiers. Obey
them, but remember your name and don't take nothing from
no man. You can go now."

"Wait!" the investigator cried again; again he started,
moved forward into the center of the room. "I protest this!
I'm sorry about Mr. McCallum's accident. I'm sorry about
the whole business. But it's out of my hands and out of his
hands now. This charge, failure to register according to law,
has been made and the warrant issued. It cannot be evaded
this way. The course of the action must be completed before
any other step can be taken. They should have thought of
this when these boys failed to register. If Mr. Gombault
refuses to serve this warrant, I will serve it myself and take
these men back to Jefferson with me to answer this charge
as made. And I must warn Mr. Gombault that he will be
cited for contempt!"

The old marshal turned, his shaggy eyebrows beetling
again, speaking down to the investigator as if he were a
child, "Ain't you found out yet that me or you neither ain't
going nowhere for a while?"

"What?" the investigator cried. He looked about at the
grave faces once more contemplating him with that remote
and speculative regard. "Am I being threatened?" he cried.

"Ain't anybody paying any attention to you at all," the
marshal said. "Now you just be quiet for a while, and you
will be all right, and after a while we can go back to town."

So he stopped again and stood while the grave, contemplative faces freed him once more of that impersonal and unbearable regard, and saw the two youths approach the bed and bend down in turn and kiss their father on the mouth, and then turn as one and leave the room, passing him without even looking at him. And sitting in the lamplit hall beside the old marshal, the bedroom door closed now, he heard the truck start up and back and turn and go down the road, the sound of it dying away, ceasing, leaving the still, hot night—the Mississippi Indian summer, which had already outlasted half of November—filled with the loud last shrilling of the summer's cicadas, as though they, too, were aware of the imminent season of cold weather and of death.

"I remember old Anse," the marshal said pleasantly, chatily, in that tone in which an adult addresses a strange child. "He's been dead fifteen-sixteen years now. He was about sixteen when the old war broke out, and he walked all the way to Virginia to get into it. He could have enlisted and fought right here at home, but his ma was a Carter, so wouldn't nothing do him but to go all the way back to Virginia to do his fighting, even though he hadn't never seen Virginia before himself; walked all the way back to a land he hadn't never even seen before and enlisted in Stonewall Jackson's army and stayed in it all through the Valley, and right up to Chancellorsville, where them Carolina boys shot Jackson by mistake, and right on up to that morning in 'Sixty-five when Sheridan's cavalry blocked the road from Appomattox to the Valley, where they might have got away again. And he walked back to Mississippi with just about what he had carried away with him when he left, and he got married and built the first story of this house—this here log story we're in right now—and started getting them boys —Jackson and Stuart and Raphael and Lee and Buddy.

"Buddy come along late, late enough to be in the other war, in France in it. You heard him in there. He brought back two medals, an American medal and a French one, and no man knows till yet how he got them, just what he done. I don't believe he even told Jackson and Stuart and them. He hadn't hardly got back home, with them numbers on his uniform and the wound stripes and them two medals, before he had found him a girl, found her right off, and a year later them twin boys was born, the livin', spittin' image of old Anse McCallum. If old Anse had just been about seventy-five years younger, the three of them might have been thriblets. I remember them—two little critters exactly alike, and wild as spikehorn bucks, running around here day and night both with a pack of coon dogs until they got big enough to help Buddy and Stuart and Lee with the farm and the gin, and Rafe with the horses and mules, when he would breed and raise and train them and take them to Memphis to sell, right on up to three, four years back, when they went to the agricultural college for a year to learn more about whiteface cattle.

"That was after Buddy and them had quit raising cotton. I remember that too. It was when the Government first begun to interfere with how a man farmed his own land, raised his cotton. Stabilizing the price, using up the surplus, they called it, giving a man advice and help, whether he wanted it or not. You may have noticed them boys in yonder tonight; curious folks almost, you might call them. That first year, when county agents was trying to explain the new system to farmers, the agent come out here and tried to explain it to Buddy and Lee and Stuart, explaining how they would cut down the crop, but that the Government would pay farmers the difference, and so they would actually be better off than trying to farm by themselves.

" 'Why, we're much obliged,' Buddy says. 'But we don't

need no help. We'll just make the cotton like we always done; if we can't make a crop of it, that will just be our lookout and our loss, and we'll try again.'

"So they wouldn't sign no papers nor no cards nor nothing. They just went on and made the cotton like old Anse had taught them to; it was like they just couldn't believe that the Government aimed to help a man whether he wanted help or not, aimed to interfere with how much of anything he could make by hard work on his own land, making the crop and ginning it right here in their own gin, like they had always done, and hauling it to town to sell, hauling it all the way into Jefferson before they found out they couldn't sell it because, in the first place, they had made too much of it and, in the second place, they never had no card to sell what they would have been allowed. So they hauled it back. The gin wouldn't hold all of it, so they put some of it under Rafe's mule shed and they put the rest of it right here in the hall where we are setting now, where they would have to walk around it all winter and keep themselves reminded to be sho and fill out that card next time.

"Only next year they didn't fill out no papers neither. It was like they still couldn't believe it, still believed in the freedom and liberty to make or break according to a man's fitness and will to work, guaranteed by the Government that old Anse had tried to tear in two once and failed, and admitted in good faith he had failed and taken the consequences, and that had give Buddy a medal and taken care of him when he was far away from home in a strange land and hurt.

"So they made that second crop. And they couldn't sell it to nobody neither because they never had no cards. This time they built a special shed to put it under, and I remember how in that second winter Buddy come to town one day to see Lawyer Gavin Stevens. Not for legal advice how to sue

the Government or somebody into buying the cotton, even
if they never had no card for it, but just to find out why. 'I
was for going ahead and signing up for it,' Buddy says. 'If
that's going to be the new rule. But we talked it over, and
Jackson ain't no farmer, but he knowed father longer than
the rest of us, and he said father would have said no, and I
reckon now he would have been right.'

"So they didn't raise any more cotton; they had a plenty
of it to last a while—twenty-two bales, I think it was. That
was when they went into whiteface cattle, putting old Anse's
cotton land into pasture, because that's what he would have
wanted them to do if the only way they could raise cotton
was by the Government telling them how much they could
raise and how much they could sell it for, and where, and
when, and then pay them for not doing the work they didn't
do. Only even when they didn't raise cotton, every year the
county agent's young fellow would come out to measure
the pasture crops they planted so he could pay them for that,
even if they never had no not-cotton to be paid for. Except
that he never measured no crop on this place. 'You're wel-
come to look at what we are doing,' Buddy says. 'But don't
draw it down on your map.'

" 'But you can get money for this,' the young fellow says.
'The Government wants to pay you for planting all this.'

" 'We are aiming to get money for it,' Buddy says. 'When
we can't, we will try something else. But not from the Government. Give that to them that want to take it. We can
make out.'

"And that's about all. Them twenty-two bales of orphan
cotton are down yonder in the gin right now, because
there's room for it in the gin now because they ain't using
the gin no more. And them boys grew up and went off a year
to the agricultural college to learn right about whiteface
cattle, and then come back to the rest of them—these here

curious folks living off here to themselves, with the rest of the world all full of pretty neon lights burning night and day both, and easy, quick money scattering itself around everywhere for any man to grab a little, and every man with a shiny new automobile already wore out and throwed away and the new one delivered before the first one was even paid for, and everywhere a fine loud grabble and snatch of AAA and WPA and a dozen other three-letter reasons for a man not to work. Then this here draft comes along, and these curious folks ain't got around to signing that neither, and you come all the way up from Jackson with your paper all signed and regular, and we come out here, and after a while we can go back to town. A man gets around, don't he?"

"Yes," the investigator said. "Do you suppose we can go back to town now?"

"No," the marshal told him in that same kindly tone, "not just yet. But we can leave after a while. Of course you will miss your train. But there will be another one tomorrow."

He rose, though the investigator had heard nothing. The investigator watched him go down the hall and open the bedroom door and enter and close it behind him. The investigator sat quietly, listening to the night sounds and looking at the closed door until it opened presently and the marshal came back, carrying something in a bloody sheet, carrying it gingerly.

"Here," he said. "Hold it a minute."

"It's bloody," the investigator said.

"That's all right," the marshal said. "We can wash when we get through." So the investigator took the bundle and stood holding it while he watched the old marshal go back down the hall and on through it and vanish and return presently with a lighted lantern and a shovel. "Come along," he said. "We're pretty near through now."

The investigator followed him out of the house and across

the yard, carrying gingerly the bloody, shattered, heavy bundle in which it still seemed to him he could feel some warmth of life, the marshal striding on ahead, the lantern swinging against his leg, the shadow of his striding scissoring and enormous along the earth, his voice still coming back over his shoulder, chatty and cheerful, "Yes, sir. A man gets around and he sees a heap; a heap of folks in a heap of situations. The trouble is, we done got into the habit of confusing the situations with the folks. Take yourself, now," he said in that same kindly tone, chatty and easy; "you mean all right. You just went and got yourself all fogged up with rules and regulations. That's our trouble. We done invented ourselves so many alphabets and rules and recipes that we can't see anything else; if what we see can't be fitted to an alphabet or a rule, we are lost. We have come to be like critters doctor folks might have created in laboratories, that have learned how to slip off their bones and guts and still live, still be kept alive indefinite and forever maybe even without even knowing the bones and the guts are gone. We have slipped our backbone; we have about decided a man don't need a backbone any more; to have one is old-fashioned. But the groove where the backbone used to be is still there, and the backbone has been kept alive, too, and someday we're going to slip back onto it. I don't know just when nor just how much of a wrench it will take to teach us, but someday."

They had left the yard now. They were mounting a slope; ahead of them the investigator could see another clump of cedars, a small clump, somehow shaggily formal against the starred sky. The marshal entered it and stopped and set the lantern down and, following with the bundle, the investigator saw a small rectangle of earth enclosed by a low brick coping. Then he saw the two graves, or the headstones— two plain granite slabs set upright in the earth.

"Old Anse and Mrs. Anse," the marshal said. "Buddy's wife wanted to be buried with her folks. I reckon she would have been right lonesome up here with just McCallums. Now, let's see." He stood for a moment, his chin in his hand; to the investigator he looked exactly like an old lady trying to decide where to set out a shrub. "They was to run from left to right, beginning with Jackson. But after the boys was born, Jackson and Stuart was to come up here by their pa and ma, so Buddy could move up some and make room. So he will be about here." He moved the lantern nearer and took up the shovel. Then he saw the investigator still holding the bundle. "Set it down," he said. "I got to dig first."

"I'll hold it," the investigator said.

"Nonsense, put it down." the marshal said. "Buddy won't mind."

So the investigator put the bundle down on the brick coping and the marshal began to dig, skillfully and rapidly, still talking in that cheerful, interminable voice, "Yes, sir. We done forgot about folks. Life has done got cheap, and life ain't cheap. Life's a pretty durn valuable thing. I don't mean just getting along from one WPA relief check to the next one, but honor and pride and discipline that make a man worth preserving, make him of any value. That's what we got to learn again. Maybe it takes trouble, bad trouble, to teach it back to us; maybe it was the walking to Virginia because that's where his ma come from, and losing a war and then walking back, that taught it to old Anse. Anyway, he seems to learned it, and to learned it good enough to bequeath it to his boys. Did you notice how all Buddy had to do was to tell them boys of his it was time to go, because the Government had sent them word? And how they told him good-by? Growned men kissing one another without hiding and without shame. Maybe that's what I am trying to say. . . . There." he said. "That's big enough."

He moved quickly, easily; before the investigator could stir, he had lifted the bundle into the narrow trench and was covering it, covering it as rapidly as he had dug, smoothing the earth over it with the shovel. Then he stood up and raised the lantern—a tall, lean old man, breathing easily and lightly.

"I reckon we can go back to town now," he said.

A Bear Hunt

RATLIFF IS TELLING THIS. He is a sewing-machine agent; time was when he traveled about our county in a light, strong buckboard drawn by a sturdy, wiry, mismatched team of horses; now he uses a model T Ford, which also carries his demonstrator machine in a tin box on the rear, shaped like a dog kennel and painted to resemble a house.

Ratliff may be seen anywhere without surprise—the only man present at the bazaars and sewing bees of farmers' wives; moving among both men and women at all-day singings at country churches, and singing, too, in a pleasant barytone. He was even at this bear hunt of which he speaks, at the annual hunting camp of Major de Spain in the river bottom twenty miles from town, even though there was no one there to whom he might possibly have sold a machine, since Mrs. de Spain doubtless already owned one, unless she had given it to one of her married daughters, and the other man—the man called Lucius Provine—with whom he became involved, to the violent detriment of his face and other members, could not have bought one for his wife even if he would, without Ratliff sold it to him on indefinite credit.

Provine is also a native of the county. But he is forty now and most of his teeth are gone, and it is years now since he and his dead brother and another dead and forgotten contemporary named Jack Bonds were known as the Provine gang and terrorized our quiet town after the unimaginative fashion of wild youth by letting off pistols on the square late Saturday nights or galloping their horses down scurrying and screaming lanes of churchgoing ladies on Sunday morning. Younger citizens of the town do not know him at all save as a tall, apparently strong and healthy man who loafs in a brooding, saturnine fashion wherever he will be allowed, never exactly accepted by any group, and who makes no effort whatever to support his wife and three children.

There are other men among us now whose families are in want; men who, perhaps, would not work anyway, but who now, since the last few years, cannot find work. These all attain and hold to a certain respectability by acting as agents for the manufacturers of minor articles like soap and men's toilet accessories and kitchen objects, being seen constantly about the square and the streets carrying small black sample cases. One day, to our surprise, Provine also appeared with such a case, though within less than a week the town officers discovered that it contained whisky in pint bottles. Major de Spain extricated him somehow, as it was Major de Spain who supported his family by eking out the money which Mrs. Provine earned by sewing and such—perhaps as a Roman gesture of salute and farewell to the bright figure which Provine had been before time whipped him.

For there are older men who remember the Butch—he has even lost somewhere in his shabby past the lusty dare-deviltry of the nickname—Provine of twenty years ago; that youth without humor, yet with some driving, inarticulate zest for breathing which has long since burned out of him, who performed in a fine frenzy, which was, perhaps, mostly alcohol, certain outrageous and spontaneous deeds, one of which was the Negro-picnic business. The picnic was at a Negro church a few miles from town. In the midst of it, the two Provines and Jack Bonds, returning from a dance in the country, rode up with drawn pistols and freshly lit cigars; and taking the Negro men one by one, held the burning cigar ends to the popular celluloid collars of the day, leaving each victim's neck ringed with an abrupt and faint and painless ring of carbon. This is he of whom Ratliff is talking.

But there is one thing more which must be told here in order to set the stage for Ratliff. Five miles farther down the river from Major de Spain's camp, and in an even wilder part of the river's jungle of cane and gum and pin oak, there is an Indian mound. Aboriginal, it rises profoundly and darkly enigmatic, the only elevation of any kind in the wild, flat jungle of river bottom. Even to some of us—children though we were, yet we were descended of literate, town-bred people—it possessed inferences of secret and violent blood, of savage and sudden destruction, as though the yells and hatchets which we associated with Indians through the hidden and secret dime novels which we passed among ourselves were but trivial and momentary manifestations of what dark power still dwelled or lurked there, sinister, a little sardonic, like a dark and nameless beast lightly and lazily slumbering with bloody jaws—this, perhaps, due to the fact that a remnant of a once powerful clan of the Chickasaw tribe still lived beside it under Government protection. They now had American names and they lived as the sparse white people who surrounded them in turn lived.

Yet we never saw them, since they never came to town, having their own settlement and store. When we grew older we realized that they were no wilder or more illiterate than the white people, and that probably their greatest deviation from the norm—and this, in our country, no especial deviation—was the fact that they were a little better than suspect to manufacture moonshine whisky back in the swamps. Yet to us, as children, they were a little fabulous, their swamp-hidden lives inextricable from the life of the dark mound,

which some of us had never seen, yet of which we had all
heard, as though they had been set by the dark powers to be
guardians of it.

As I said, some of us had never seen the mound, yet all of
us had heard of it, talked of it as boys will. It was as much a
part of our lives and background as the land itself, as the lost
Civil War and Sherman's march, or that there were Negroes
among us living in economic competition who bore our
family names; only more immediate, more potential and alive.
When I was fifteen, a companion and I, on a dare, went into
the mound one day just at sunset. We saw some of those Indians for the first time; we got directions from them and
reached the top of the mound just as the sun set. We had
camping equipment with us, but we made no fire. We didn't
even make down our beds. We just sat side by side on that
mound until it became light enough to find our way back to
the road. We didn't talk. When we looked at each other in
the gray dawn, our faces were gray, too, quiet, very grave.
When we reached town again, we didn't talk either. We just
parted and went home and went to bed. That's what we
thought, felt, about the mound. We were children, it is true,
yet we were descendants of people who read books and who
were—or should have been—beyond superstition and impervious to mindless fear.

Now Ratliff tells about Lucius Provine and his hiccup.

When I got back to town, the first fellow I met says,
"What happened to your face, Ratliff? Was De Spain using
you in place of his bear hounds?"

"No, boys," I says. "Hit was a cattymount."

"What was you trying to do to hit, Ratliff?" a fellow says.

"Boys," I says, "be dog if I know."

And that was the truth. Hit was a good while after they
had done hauled Luke Provine offen me that I found that

out. Because I never knowed who Old Man Ash was, no more than Luke did. I just knowed that he was Major's nigger, a-helping around camp. All I knowed, when the whole thing started, was what I thought I was aiming to do—to maybe help Luke sho enough, or maybe at the outside to just have a little fun with him without hurting him, or even maybe to do Major a little favor by getting Luke outen camp for a while. And then hyer hit is about midnight and that durn fellow comes swurging outen the woods wild as a skeered deer, and runs in where they are setting at the poker game, and I says, "Well, you ought to be satisfied. You done run clean out from under them." And he stopped dead still and give me a kind of glare of wild astonishment; he didn't even know that they had quit; and then he swurged all over me like a barn falling down.

Hit sho stopped that poker game. Hit taken three or four of them to drag him offen me, with Major turned in his chair with a set of threes in his hand, a-hammering on the table and hollering cusses. Only a right smart of the helping they done was stepping on my face and hands and feet. Hit was like a fahr—the fellows with the water hose done the most part of the damage.

"What the tarnation hell does this mean?" Major hollers, with three or four fellows holding Luke, and him crying like a baby.

"He set them on me!" Luke says. "He was the one sent me up there, and I'm a-going to kill him!"

"Set who on you?" Major says.

"Them Indians!" Luke says, crying. Then he tried to get at me again, flinging them fellows holding his arms around like they was rag dolls, until Major pure cussed him quiet. He's a man yet. Don't let hit fool you none because he claims he ain't strong enough to work. Maybe hit's because he ain't never wore his strength down toting around one of them

little black satchels full of pink galluses and shaving soap.
Then Major asked me what hit was all about, and I told him
how I had just been trying to help Luke get shed of them
hiccups.

Be dog if I didn't feel right sorry for him. I happened to
be passing out that way, and so I just thought I would drop
in on them and see what luck they was having, and I druv up
about sundown, and the first fellow I see was Luke. I wasn't
surprised, since this here would be the biggest present gathering of men in the county, let alone the free eating and
whisky, so I says, "Well, this is a surprise." And he says:

"Hic-uh! Hic-ow! Hic-oh! Hic—oh, God!" He had done
already had them since nine o'clock the night before; he had
been teching the jug ever' time Major offered him one and
ever' time he could get to hit when Old Man Ash wasn't
looking; and two days before Major had killed a bear, and I
reckon Luke had already et more possum-rich bear pork—
let alone the venison they had, with maybe a few coons and
squirls throwed in for seasoning—than he could have hauled
off in a waggin. So here he was, going three times to the minute, like one of these here clock bombs; only hit was bear
meat and whisky instead of dynamite, and so he couldn't explode and put himself outen his misery.

They told me how he had done already kept ever'body
awake most of the night before, and how Major got up mad
anyway, and went off with his gun and Ash to handle them
two bear hounds, and Luke following—outen pure misery, I
reckon, since he hadn't slept no more than nobody else—
walking along behind Major, saying, "Hic-ah! Hic-ow! Hic-
oh! Hic—oh, Lord!" until Major turns on him and says:

"Get to hell over yonder with them shotgun fellows on
the deer stands. How do you expect me to walk up on a bear
or even hear the dogs when they strike? I might as well be
riding a motorcycle."

So Luke went on back to where the deer standers was along the log-line levee. I reckon he never so much went away as he kind of died away in the distance like that ere motorcycle Major mentioned. He never tried to be quiet. I reckon he knowed hit wouldn't be no use. He never tried to keep to the open, neither. I reckon he thought that any fool would know from his sound that he wasn't no deer. No. I reckon he was so mizzable by then that he hoped somebody would shoot him. But nobody never, and he come to the first stand, where Uncle Ike McCaslin was, and set down on a log behind Uncle Ike with his elbows on his knees and his face in his hands, going, "Hic-uh! Hic-uh! Hic-uh! Hic-uh!" until Uncle Ike turns and says:

"Confound you, boy; get away from here. Do you reckon any varmint in the world is going to walk up to a hay baler? Go drink some water."

"I done already done that," Luke says, without moving. "I been drinking water since nine o'clock last night. I done already drunk so much water that if I was to fall down I would gush like a artesian well."

"Well, go away anyhow," Uncle Ike says. "Get away from here."

So Luke gets up and kind of staggers away again, kind of dying away again like he was run by one of these hyer one-cylinder gasoline engines, only a durn sight more often and regular. He went on down the levee to where the next stand was, and they druv him way from there, and he went on toward the next one. I reckon he was still hoping that somebody would take pity on him and shoot him, because now he kind of seemed to give up. Now, when he come to the "oh, God" part of hit, they said you could hyear him clean back to camp. They said he would echo back from the canebrake across the river like one of these hyer loud-speakers down in a well. They said that even the dogs on the trail quit baying, and so they all come up and made him come back to camp. That's where he was when I come in. And Old Man Ash was there, too, where him and Major had done come in so Major could take a nap, and neither me nor Luke noticing him except as just another nigger around.

That was hit. Neither one of us knowed or even thought about him. I be dog if hit don't look like sometimes that when a fellow sets out to play a joke, hit ain't another fellow he's playing that joke on; hit's a kind of big power laying still somewhere in the dark that he sets out to prank with without knowing hit, and hit all depends on whether that ere power is in the notion to take a joke or not, whether or not hit blows up right in his face like this one did in mine. Because I says, "You done had them since nine o'clock yesterday? That's nigh twenty-four hours. Seems like to me you'd 'a' done something to try to stop them." And him looking at me like he couldn't make up his mind whether to jump up and bite my head off or just to try and bite hisn off, saying "Hic-uh! Hic-uh!" slow and regular. Then he says,

"I don't want to get shed of them. I like them. But if you had them, I would get shed of them for you. You want to know how?"

"How?" I says.

"I'd just tear your head off. Then you wouldn't have nothing to hiccup with. They wouldn't worry you then. I'd be glad to do hit for you."

"Sho now," I says, looking at him setting there on the kitchen steps—hit was after supper, but he hadn't et none, being as his throat had done turned into a one-way street on him, you might say—going "Hic-uh! Hic-oh! Hic-oh! Hic-uh!" because I reckon Major had done told him what would happen to him if he taken to hollering again. I never meant no harm. Besides, they had done already told me how he had kept everybody awake all night the night before and had done skeered all the game outen that part of the bottom, and besides, the walk might help him to pass his own time. So I says, "I believe I know how you might get shed of them. But, of course, if you don't want to get shed of them ——"

And he says, "I just wish somebody would tell me how. I'd pay ten dollars just to set here for one minute without saying 'hic' ——" Well, that set him off sho enough. Hit was like up to that time his insides had been satisfied with going "hic-uh" steady, but quiet, but now, when he reminded himself, hit was like he had done opened a cut-out, because right away he begun hollering, "Hic—oh, God!" like when them fellows on the deer stands had made him come back to camp, and I heard Major's feet coming bup-bup-bup across the floor. Even his feet sounded mad, and I says quick,

"Sh-h-h-h! You don't want to get Major mad again, now."

So he quieted some, setting there on the kitchen steps, with Old Man Ash and the other niggers moving around inside the kitchen, and he says, "I will try anything you can sujest. I done tried ever'thing I knowed and ever'thing anybody else told me to. I done held my breath and drunk water until I feel just like one of these hyer big automobile tahrs they use to advertise with, and I hung by my knees offen that limb yonder for fifteen minutes and drunk a pint bottle full of water upside down, and somebody said to swallow a buckshot and I done that. And still I got them. What do you know that I can do?"

"Well," I says, "I don't know what you would do. But if hit was me that had them, I'd go up to the mound and get old John Basket to cure me."

Then he set right still, and then he turned slow and looked at me; I be dog if for a minute he didn't even hiccup. "John Basket?" he says.

"Sho," I says. "Them Indians knows all sorts of dodges that white doctors ain't hyeard about yet. He'd be glad to do that much for a white man, too, them pore aboriginees would, because the white folks have been so good to them—not only letting them keep that ere hump of dirt that don't nobody want noways, but letting them use names like ourn and selling them flour and sugar and farm tools at not no more than a fair profit above what they would cost a white man. I hyear tell how pretty soon they are even going to start letting them come to town once a week. Old Basket would be glad to cure them hiccups for you."

"John Basket," he says; "them Indians," he says, hiccuping slow and quiet and steady. Then he says right sudden, "I be dog if I will!" Then I be dog if hit didn't sound like he was crying. He jumped up and stood there cussing, sounding like he was crying. "Hit ain't a man hyer has got any mercy on me, white or black. Hyer I done suffered and suffered more than twenty-four hours without food or sleep, and not a sonabitch of them has any mercy or pity on me!"

"Well, I was trying to," I says. "Hit ain't me that's got them. I just thought, seeing as how you had done seemed to got to the place where couldn't no white man help you. But hit ain't no law making you go up there and get shed of them." So I made like I was going away. I went back around the corner of the kitchen and watched him set down on the steps again, going "Hic-uh! Hic-uh!" slow and quiet again; and then I seen, through the kitchen window, Old Man Ash standing just inside the kitchen door, right still, with his head bent like he was listening. But still I never suspected nothing. Not even did I suspect nothing when, after a while, I watched Luke get up again, sudden but quiet, and stand for a minute looking at the window where the poker game and the folks was, and then look off into the dark towards the road that went down the bottom. Then he went into the house, quiet, and come out a minute later with a lighted lantrun and a shotgun. I don't know whose gun hit was and I don't reckon he did, nor cared neither. He just come out kind of quiet and determined, and went on down the road. I could see the lantrun, but I could hyear him a long time after the lantrun had done disappeared. I had come back around the kitchen then and I was listening to him dying away down the bottom, when old Ash says behind me:

"He gwine up dar?"

"Up where?" I says.

"Up to de mound," he says.

"Why, I be dog if I know," I says. "The last time I talked to him he never sounded like he was fixing to go nowhere. Maybe he just decided to take a walk. Hit might do him some good; make him sleep tonight and help him get up a appetite for breakfast maybe. What do you think?"

But Ash never said nothing. He just went on back into the kitchen. And still I never suspected nothing. How could I? I hadn't never even seen Jefferson in them days. I hadn't never even seen a pair of shoes, let alone two stores in a row or a arc light.

So I went on in where the poker game was, and I says, "Well, gentlemen, I reckon we might get some sleep tonight." And I told them what had happened, because more than like he would stay up there until daylight rather than walk them five miles back in the dark, because maybe them Indians wouldn't mind a little thing like a fellow with hiccups, like white folks would. And I be dog if Major didn't rear up about hit.

"Dammit, Ratliff," he says, "you ought not to done that."

"Why, I just sujested hit to him, Major, for a joke," I says. "I just told him about how old Basket was a kind of doctor. I never expected him to take hit serious. Maybe he ain't even going up there. Maybe's he's just went out after a coon."

But most of them felt about hit like I did. "Let him go," Mr. Fraser says. "I hope he walks around all night. Damn if

I slept a wink for him all night long. . . . Deal the cards,
Uncle Ike."

"Can't stop him now, noways," Uncle Ike says, dealing
the cards. "And maybe John Basket can do something for
his hiccups. Durn young fool, eating and drinking himself to
where he can't talk nor swallow neither. He set behind me
on a log this morning, sounding just like a hay baler. I thought
once I'd have to shoot him to get rid of him. . . . Queen bets
a quarter, gentlemen."

So I set there watching them, thinking now and then about
that durn fellow with his shotgun and his lantrun stumbling
and blundering along through the woods, walking five miles
in the dark to get shed of his hiccups, with the varmints all
watching him and wondering just what kind of a hunt this
was and just what kind of a two-leg varmint hit was that
made a noise like that, and about them Indians up at the
mound when he would come walking in, and I would have
to laugh until Major says, "What in hell are you mumbling
and giggling at?"

"Nothing," I says. "I was just thinking about a fellow
I know."

"And damn if you hadn't ought to be out there with him,"
Major says. Then he decided hit was about drink time and he
begun to holler for Ash. Finally I went to the door and hollered for Ash towards the kitchen, but hit was another one
of the niggers that answered. When he come in with the
demijohn and fixings, Major looks up and says "Where's
Ash?"

"He done gone," the nigger says.

"Gone?" Major says. "Gone where?"

"He say he gwine up to'ds de mound," the nigger says.
And still I never knowed, never suspected. I just thought to
myself, "That old nigger has turned powerful tender-hearted
all of a sudden, being skeered for Luke Provine to walk

around by himself in the dark. Or maybe Ash likes to listen to them hiccups," I thought to myself.

"Up to the mound?" Major says. "By dad, if he comes back here full of John Basket's bust-skull whisky I'll skin him alive."

"He ain't say what he gwine fer," the nigger says. "All he tell me when he left, he gwine up to'ds de mound and he be back by daylight."

"He better be," Major says. "He better be sober too."

So we set there and they went on playing and me watching them like a durn fool, not suspecting nothing, just thinking how hit was a shame that that durned old nigger would have to come in and spoil Luke's trip, and hit come along towards eleven o'clock and they begun to talk about going to bed, being as they was all going out on stand tomorrow, when we hyeard the sound. Hit sounded like a drove of wild horses coming up that road, and we hadn't no more than turned towards the door, a-asking one another what in tarnation hit could be, with Major just saying, "What in the name of ——" when hit come across the porch like a harrycane and down the hall, and the door busted open and there Luke was. He never had no gun and lantrun then, and his clothes was nigh tore clean offen him, and his face looked wild as ere a man in the Jackson a-sylum. But the main thing I noticed was that he wasn't hiccuping now. And this time, too, he was nigh crying.

"They was fixing to kill me!" he says. "They was going to burn me to death! They had done tried me and tied me onto the pile of wood, and one of them was coming with the fahr when I managed to bust loose and run!"

"Who was?" Major says. "What in the tarnation hell are you talking about?"

"Them Indians!" Luke says. "They was fixing to ——"

"What?" Major hollers. "Damn to blue blazes, what?"

And that was where I had to put my foot in hit. He hadn't never seen me until then. "At least they cured your hiccups," I says.

Hit was then that he stopped right still. He hadn't never even seen me, but he seen me now. He stopped right still and looked at me with that ere wild face that looked like hit had just escaped from Jackson and had ought to be took back there quick.

"What?" he says.

"Anyway, you done run out from under them hiccups," I says.

Well, sir, he stood there for a full minute. His eyes had done gone blank, and he stood there with his head cocked a little, listening to his own insides. I reckon hit was the first time he had took time to find out that they was gone. He stood there right still for a full minute while that ere kind of shocked astonishment come onto his face. Then he jumped on me. I was still setting in my chair, and I be dog if for a minute I didn't think the roof had done fell in.

Well, they got him offen me at last and got him quieted down, and then they washed me off and give me a drink, and I felt better. But even with that drink I never felt so good but what I felt hit was my duty to my honor to call him outen the back yard, as the fellow says. No, sir. I know when I done made a mistake and guessed wrong; Major de Spain wasn't the only man that caught a bear on that hunt; no, sir. I be dog, if it had been daylight, I'd a hitched up my Ford and taken out of there. But hit was midnight, and besides, that nigger, Ash, was on my mind then. I had just begun to suspect that hit was more to this business than met the nekkid eye. And hit wasn't no good time then to go back to the kitchen then and ask him about hit, because Luke was using the kitchen. Major had give him a drink, too, and he was back there, making up for them two days he hadn't et, talk-

ing a right smart about what he aimed to do to such and such
a sonabitch that would try to play his durn jokes on him, not
mentioning no names; but mostly laying himself in a new set
of hiccups, though I ain't going back to see.

So I waited until daylight, until I hyeard the niggers stirring around in the kitchen; then I went back there. And
there was old Ash, looking like he always did, oiling Major's
boots and setting them behind the stove and then taking up
Major's rifle and beginning to load the magazine. He just
looked once at my face when I come in, and went on shoving
ca'tridges into the gun.

"So you went up to the mound last night," I says. He
looked up at me again, quick, and then down again. But he
never said nothing, looking like a durned old frizzle-headed
ape. "You must know some of them folks up there," I says.

"I knows some of um," he says, shoving ca'tridges into
the gun.

"You know old John Basket?" I says.

"I knows some of um," he says, not looking at me.

"Did you see him last night?" I says. He never said nothing at all. So then I changed my tone, like a fellow has to do
to get anything outen a nigger. "Look here," I says. "Look
at me." He looked at me. "Just what did you do up there
last night?"

"Who, me?" he says.

"Come on," I says. "Hit's all over now. Mr. Provine has
done got over his hiccups and we done both forgot about
anything that might have happened when he got back last
night. You never went up there just for fun last night. Or
maybe hit was something you told them up there, told old
man Basket. Was that hit?" He had done quit looking at me,
but he never stopped shoving ca'tridges into that gun. He
looked quick to both sides. "Come on," I says. "Do you want
to tell me what happened up there, or do you want me to

mention to Mr. Provine that you was mixed up in hit some way?" He never stopped loading the rifle and he never looked at me, but I be dog if I couldn't almost see his mind working. "Come on," I says. "Just what was you doing up there last night?"

Then he told me. I reckon he knowed hit wasn't no use to try to hide hit then; that if I never told Luke, I could still tell Major. "I jest dodged him and got dar first en told um he was a new revenue agent coming up dar tonight, but dat he warn't much en dat all dey had to do was to give um a good skeer en likely he would go away. En dey did en he did."

"Well!" I says. "Well! I always thought I was pretty good at joking folks," I says, "but I take a back seat for you. What happened?" I says. "Did you see hit?"

"Never much happened," he says. "Dey jest went down de road a piece en atter a while hyer he come a-hickin' en a-blumpin' up de road wid de lant'un en de gun. They took de lant'un en de gun away frum him en took him up pon topper de mound en talked de Injun language at him fer a while. Den dey piled up some wood en fixed him on hit so he could git loose in a minute, en den one of dem come up de hill wid de fire, en he done de rest."

"Well!" I says. "Well, I'll be eternally durned!" And then all on a sudden hit struck me. I had done turned and was going out when hit struck me, and I stopped and I says, "There's one more thing I want to know. Why did you do hit?"

Now he set there on the wood box, rubbing the gun with his hand, not looking at me again. "I wuz jest helping you kyo him of dem hiccups."

"Come on," I says. "That wasn't your reason. What was hit? Remember, I got a right smart I can tell Mr. Provine and Major both now. I don't know what Major will do, but I know what Mr. Provine will do if I was to tell him."

And he set there, rubbing that ere rifle with his hand. He was kind of looking down, like he was thinking. Not like he was trying to decide whether to tell me or not, but like he was remembering something from a long time back. And that's exactly what he was doing, because he says:

"I ain't skeered for him to know. One time dey was a picnic. Hit was a long time back, nigh twenty years ago. He was a young man den, en in de middle of de picnic, him en he brother en nudder white man—I fergit he name—dey rid up wid dey pistols out en cotch us niggers one at a time en burned our collars off. Hit was him dat burnt mine."

"And you waited all this time and went to all this trouble, just to get even with him?" I says.

"Hit warn't dat," he says, rubbing the rifle with his hand. "Hit wuz de collar. Back in dem days a top nigger hand made two dollars a week. I paid fo' bits fer dat collar. Hit wuz blue, wid a red picture of de race betwixt de Natchez en de Robert E. Lee running around hit. He burnt hit up. I makes ten dollars a week now. En I jest wish I knowed where I could buy another collar like dat un fer half of hit. I wish I did."

Two Soldiers

ME AND PETE would go down to Old Man Killegrew's and listen to his radio. We would wait until after supper, after dark, and we would stand outside Old Man Killegrew's parlor window, and we could hear it because Old Man Killegrew's wife was deaf, and so he run the radio as loud as it would run, and so me and Pete could hear it plain as Old Man Killegrew's wife could, I reckon, even standing outside with the window closed.

And that night I said, "What? Japanese? What's a pearl harbor?" and Pete said, "Hush."

And so we stood there, it was cold, listening to the fellow in the radio talking, only I couldn't make no heads nor tails neither out of it. Then the fellow said that would be all for a while, and me and Pete walked back up the road to home, and Pete told me what it was. Because he was nigh twenty and he had done finished the Consolidated last June and he knowed a heap: about them Japanese dropping bombs on Pearl Harbor and that Pearl Harbor was across the water.

"Across what water?" I said. "Across that Government reservoy up at Oxford?"

"Naw," Pete said. "Across the big water. The Pacific Ocean."

We went home. Maw and pap was already asleep, and me

and Pete laid in the bed, and I still couldn't understand where it was, and Pete told me again—the Pacific Ocean.

"What's the matter with you?" Pete said. "You're going on nine years old. You been in school now ever since September. Ain't you learned nothing yet?"

"I reckon we ain't got as fer as the Pacific Ocean yet," I said.

We was still sowing the vetch then that ought to been all finished by the fifteenth of November, because pap was still behind, just like he had been ever since me and Pete had knowed him. And we had firewood to git in, too, but every night me and Pete would go down to Old Man Killegrew's and stand outside his parlor window in the cold and listen to his radio; then we would come back home and lay in the bed and Pete would tell me what it was. That is, he would tell me for a while. Then he wouldn't tell me. It was like he didn't want to talk about it no more. He would tell me to shut up because he wanted to go to sleep, but he never wanted to go to sleep.

He would lay there, a heap stiller than if he was asleep, and it would be something, I could feel it coming out of him, like he was mad at me even, only I knowed he wasn't thinking about me, or like he was worried about something, and it wasn't that neither, because he never had nothing to worry about. He never got behind like pap, let alone stayed behind. Pap give him ten acres when he graduated from the Consolidated, and me and Pete both reckoned pap was durn glad to get shut of at least ten acres, less to have to worry with himself; and Pete had them ten acres all sowed to vetch and busted out and bedded for the winter, and so it wasn't that. But it was something. And still we would go down to Old Man Killegrew's every night and listen to his radio, and they was at it in the Philippines now, but General MacArthur was holding um. Then we would come back home and lay in the bed, and Pete wouldn't tell me nothing or talk at all. He would just lay there still as a ambush and when I would touch him, his side or his leg would feel hard and still as iron, until after a while I would go to sleep.

Then one night—it was the first time he had said nothing to me except to jump on me about not chopping enough wood at the wood tree where we was cutting—he said, "I got to go."

"Go where?" I said.

"To that war," Pete said.

"Before we even finish gettin' in the firewood?"

"Firewood, hell," Pete said.

"All right," I said. "When we going to start?"

But he wasn't even listening. He laid there, hard and still as iron in the dark. "I got to go," he said. "I jest ain't going to put up with no folks treating the Unity States that way."

"Yes," I said. "Firewood or no firewood, I reckon we got to go."

This time he heard me. He laid still again, but it was a different kind of still.

"You?" he said. "To a war?"

"You'll whup the big uns and I'll whup the little uns," I said.

Then he told me I couldn't go. At first I thought he just never wanted me tagging after him, like he wouldn't leave me go with him when he went sparking them girls of Tull's. Then he told me the Army wouldn't leave me go because I was too little, and then I knowed he really meant it and that I couldn't go nohow noways. And somehow I hadn't believed until then that he was going himself, but now I knowed he was and that he wasn't going to leave me go with him a-tall.

"I'll chop the wood and tote the water for you-all then!" I said. "You got to have wood and water!"

Anyway, he was listening to me now. He wasn't like iron now.

He turned onto his side and put his hand on my chest because it was me that was laying straight and hard on my back now.

"No," he said. "You got to stay here and help pap."

"Help him what?" I said. "He ain't never caught up nohow. He can't get no further behind. He can sholy take care of this little shirttail of a farm while me and you are whupping them Japanese. I got to go too. If you got to go, then so have I."

"No," Pete said. "Hush now. Hush." And he meant it, and I knowed he did. Only I made sho from his own mouth. I quit.

"So I just can't go then," I said.

"No," Pete said. "You just can't go. You're too little, in the first place, and in the second place ——"

"All right," I said. "Then shut up and leave me go to sleep."

So he hushed then and laid back. And I laid there like I was already asleep, and pretty soon he was asleep and I knowed it was the wanting to go to the war that had worried him and kept him awake, and now that he had decided to go, he wasn't worried any more.

The next morning he told maw and pap. Maw was all right. She cried.

"No," she said, crying, "I don't want him to go. I would rather go myself in his place, if I could. I don't want to save the country. Them Japanese could take it and keep it, so long as they left me and my family and my children alone. But I remember my brother Marsh in that other war. He had to go to that one when he wasn't but nineteen, and our mother couldn't understand it then any more than I can now. But she told Marsh if he had to go, he had to go. And so, if Pete's got to go to this one, he's got to go to it. Jest don't ask me to understand why."

But pap was the one. He was the feller. "To the war?" he said. "Why, I just don't see a bit of use in that. You ain't old enough for the draft, and the country ain't being invaded. Our President in Washington, D. C., is watching the conditions and he will notify us. Besides, in that other war your ma just mentioned, I was drafted and sent clean to Texas and was held there nigh eight months until they finally quit fighting. It seems to me that that, along with your Uncle Marsh who received a actual wound on the battlefields of France, is enough for me and mine to have to do to protect the country, at least in my lifetime. Besides, what'll I do for help on the farm with you gone? It seems to me I'll get mighty far behind."

"You been behind as long as I can remember," Pete said. "Anyway, I'm going. I got to."

"Of course he's got to go," I said. "Them Japanese ——"

"You hush your mouth!" maw said, crying. "Nobody's talking to you! Go and get me a armful of wood! That's what you can do!"

So I got the wood. And all the next day, while me and Pete and pap was getting in as much wood as we could in that time because Pete said how pap's idea of plenty of wood was one more stick laying against the wall that maw ain't put on the fire yet, Maw was getting Pete ready to go. She washed and mended his clothes and cooked him a shoe box of vittles. And that night me and Pete laid in the bed and listened to her packing his grip and crying, until after a while Pete got up in his nightshirt and went back there, and I could hear them talking, until at last maw said, "You got to go, and so I want you to go. But I don't understand it, and I won't never, and so don't expect me to." And Pete come back and got into the bed again and laid again still and hard as iron on his back, and then ne said, and he wasn't talking to me, he wasn't talking to nobody: "I got to go. I just got to."

"Sho you got to," I said. "Them Japanese ——" He turned over hard, he kind of surged over onto his side, looking at me in the dark.

"Anyway, you're all right," he said. "I expected to have more trouble with you than with all the rest of them put together."

"I reckon I can't help it neither," I said. "But maybe it will run a few years longer and I can get there. Maybe someday I will jest walk in on you."

"I hope not," Pete said. "Folks don't go to wars for fun. A man don't leave his maw crying just for fun."

"Then why are you going?" I said.

"I got to," he said. "I just got to. Now you go on to sleep. I got to ketch that early bus in the morning."

"All right," I said. "I hear tell Memphis is a big place. How will you find where the Army's at?"

"I'll ask somebody where to go to join it," Pete said. "Go on to sleep now."

"Is that what you'll ask for? Where to join the Army?" I said.

"Yes," Pete said. He turned onto his back again. "Shut up and go to sleep."

We went to sleep. The next morning we et breakfast by lamplight because the bus would pass at six o'clock. Maw wasn't crying now. She jest looked grim and busy, putting breakfast on the table while we et it. Then she finished packing Pete's grip, except he never wanted to take no grip to the war, but maw said decent folks never went nowhere, not even to a war, without a change of clothes and something to tote them in. She put in the shoe box of fried chicken and biscuits and she put the Bible in, too, and then it was time to go. We didn't know until then that maw wasn't going to the bus. She jest brought Pete's cap and overcoat, and still she didn't cry no more, she jest stood with her hands on Pete's shoulders and she didn't move, but somehow, and just holding Pete's shoulders, she looked as hard and fierce as when Pete had turned toward me in the bed last night and tole me that anyway I was all right.

"They could take the country and keep the country, so long as they never bothered me and mine," she said. Then she said, "Don't never forget who you are. You ain't rich and the rest of the world outside of Frenchman's Bend never heard of you. But your blood is good as any blood anywhere, and don't you never forget it."

Then she kissed him, and then we was out of the house, with pap toting Pete's grip whether Pete wanted him to or not. There wasn't no dawn even yet, not even after we had stood on the highway by the mailbox, a while. Then we seen the lights of the bus coming and I was watching the bus until it come up and Pete flagged it, and then, sho enough, there was daylight—it had started while I wasn't watching. And now me and Pete expected pap to say something else foolish, like he done before, about how Uncle Marsh getting wounded in France and that trip to Texas pap taken in 1918 ought to be enough to save the Unity States in 1942, but he never. He done all right too. He jest said, "Good-by, son. Always remember what your ma told you and write her whenever you find the time." Then he shaken Pete's hand, and Pete looked at me a minute and put his hand on my head and rubbed my head durn nigh hard enough to wring my neck off and jumped into the bus, and the feller wound the door shut and the bus began to hum; then it was moving, humming and grinding and whining louder and louder; it was going fast, with two little red lights behind it that never seemed to get no littler, but just seemed to be running to, gether until pretty soon they would touch and jest be one light. But they never did, and then the bus was gone, and even like it was, I could have pretty nigh busted out crying, nigh to nine years old and all.

Me and pap went back to the house. All that day we worked at the wood tree, and so I never had no good chance until about middle of the afternoon. Then I taken my slingshot and I would have liked to took all my bird eggs, too, because Pete had give me his collection and he holp me with mine, and he would like to git the box out and look at them as good as I would, even if he was nigh twenty years old. But the box was too big to tote a long ways and have to worry with, so I just taken the shikepoke egg, because it was the best un, and wropped it up good into a matchbox and hid it and the slingshot under the corner of the barn. Then we et supper and went to bed, and I thought then how if I would 'a' had to stayed in that room and that bed like that even for one more night, I jest couldn't 'a' stood it. Then I could hear pap snoring, but I never heard no sound from maw, whether she was asleep or not, and I don't reckon she was. So I taken my shoes and drapped them out the window, and then I clumb out like I used to watch Pete do when he was still jest seventeen and pap held that he was too young yet to be tom-catting around at night, and wouldn't leave him out, and I put on my shoes and went to the barn and got the slingshot and the shikepoke egg and went to the highway.

It wasn't cold, it was jest durn confounded dark, and that highway stretched on in front of me like, without nobody using it, it had stretched out half again as fer just like a man does when he lays down, so that for a time it looked like full sun was going to ketch me before I had finished them twenty-two miles to Jefferson. But it didn't. Daybreak was jest starting when I walked up the hill into town. I could smell breakfast cooking in the cabins and I wished I had thought to brought me a cold biscuit, but that was too late now. And Pete had told me Memphis was a piece beyond Jefferson, but I never knowed it was no eighty miles. So I stood there on that empty square, with daylight coming and coming and the street lights still burning and that Law looking down at me, and me still eighty miles from Memphis, and it had took me all night to walk jest twenty-two miles, and so, by the time I got to Memphis at that rate, Pete would 'a' done already started for Pearl Harbor.

"Where do you come from?" the Law said.

And I told him again. "I got to get to Memphis. My brother's there."

"You mean you ain't got any folks around here?" the Law said. "Nobody but that brother? What are you doing way off down here and your brother in Memphis?"

And I told him again, "I got to get to Memphis. I ain't got no time to waste talking about it and I ain't got time to walk it. I got to git there today."

"Come on here," the Law said.

We went down another street. And there was the bus, just like when Pete got into it yestiddy morning, except there wasn't no lights on it now and it was empty. There was a regular bus dee-po like a railroad dee-po, with a ticket counter and a feller behind it, and the Law said, "Set down over there," and I set down on the bench, and the Law said, "I want to use your telephone," and he talked in the telephone a minute and put it down and said to the feller behind the ticket counter, "Keep your eye on him. I'll be back as soon as Mrs. Habersham can arrange to get herself up and dressed." He went out. I got up and went to the ticket counter.

"I want to go to Memphis," I said.

"You bet," the feller said. "You set down on the bench now. Mr. Foote will be back in a minute."

"I don't know no Mr. Foote," I said. "I want to ride that bus to Memphis."

"You got some money?" he said. "It'll cost you seventy-two cents."

I taken out the matchbox and unwropped the shikepoke egg. "I'll swap you this for a ticket to Memphis," I said.

"What's that?" he said.

"It's a shikepoke egg," I said. "You never seen one before. It's worth a dollar. I'll take seventy-two cents fer it."

"No," he said, "the fellers that own that bus insist on a cash basis. If I started swapping tickets for bird eggs and livestock and such, they would fire me. You go and set down on the bench now, like Mr. Foote ———"

I started for the door, but he caught me, he put one hand on the ticket counter and jumped over it and caught up with me and reached his hand out to ketch my shirt. I whupped out my pocketknife and snapped it open.

"You put a hand on me and I'll cut it off," I said.

I tried to dodge him and run at the door, but he could move quicker than any grown man I ever see, quick as Pete almost. He cut me off and stood with his back against the door and one foot raised a little, and there wasn't no other way to get out. "Get back on that bench and stay there," he said.

And there wasn't no other way out. And he stood there with his back against the door. So I went back to the bench. And then it seemed like to me that dee-po was full of folks. There was that Law again, and there was two ladies in fur coats and their faces already painted. But they still looked like they had got up in a hurry and they still never liked it, a old one and a young one, looking down at me.

"He hasn't got a overcoat!" the old one said. "How in the world did he ever get down here by himself?"

"I ask you," the Law said. "I couldn't get nothing out of

him except his brother is in Memphis and he wants to get back up there."

"That's right," I said. "I got to git to Memphis today."

"Of course you must," the old one said. "Are you sure you can find your brother when you get to Memphis?"

"I reckon I can," I said. "I ain't got but one and I have knowed him all my life. I reckon I will know him again when I see him."

The old one looked at me. "Somehow he doesn't look like he lives in Memphis," she said.

"He probably don't," the Law said. "You can't tell though. He might live anywhere, overhalls or not. This day and time they get scattered overnight from he—— hope to breakfast; boys and girls, too, almost before they can walk good. He might have been in Missouri or Texas either yestiddy, for all we know. But he don't seem to have any doubt his brother is in Memphis. All I know to do is send him up there and leave him look."

"Yes," the old one said.

The young one set down on the bench by me and opened a hand satchel and taken out a artermatic writing pen and some papers.

"Now, honey," the old one said, "we're going to see that you find your brother, but we must have a case history for our files first. We want to know your name and your brother's name and where you were born and when your parents died."

"I don't need no case history neither," I said. "All I want is to get to Memphis. I got to get there today."

"You see?" the Law said. He said it almost like he enjoyed it. "That's what I told you."

"You're lucky, at that, Mrs. Habersham," the bus feller said. "I don't think he's got a gun on him, but he can open that knife da—— I mean, fast enough to suit any man."

But the old one just stood there looking at me.

"Well," she said. "Well. I really don't know what to do."

"I do," the bus feller said. "I'm going to give him a ticket out of my own pocket, as a measure of protecting the company against riot and bloodshed. And when Mr. Foote tells the city board about it, it will be a civic matter and they will not only reimburse me, they will give me a medal too. Hey, Mr. Foote?"

But never nobody paid him no mind. The old one still stood looking down at me. She said "Well," again. Then she taken a dollar from her purse and give it to the bus feller. "I suppose he will travel on a child's ticket, won't he?"

"Wellum," the bus feller said, "I just don't know what the regulations would be. Likely I will be fired for not crating him and marking the crate Poison. But I'll risk it."

Then they were gone. Then the Law come back with a sandwich and give it to me.

"You're sure you can find that brother?" he said.

"I ain't yet convinced why not," I said. "If I don't see Pete first, he'll see me. He knows me too."

Then the Law went out for good, too, and I et the sandwich. Then more folks come in and bought tickets, and then the bus feller said it was time to go, and I got into the bus just like Pete done, and we was gone.

I seen all the towns. I seen all of them. When the bus got to going good, I found out I was jest about wore out for sleep. But there was too much I hadn't never saw before. We run out of Jefferson and run past fields and woods, then we would run into another town and out of that un and past fields and woods again, and then into another town with stores and gins and water tanks, and we run along by the railroad for a spell and I seen the signal arm move, and then I seen the train and then some more towns, and I was jest about plumb wore out for sleep, but I couldn't resk it. Then

Memphis begun. It seemed like, to me, it went on for miles. We would pass a patch of stores and I would think that was sholy it and the bus would even stop. But it wouldn't be Memphis yet and we would go on again past water tanks and smokestacks on top of the mills, and if they was gins and sawmills, I never knowed there was that many and I never seen any that big, and where they got enough cotton and logs to run um I don't know.

Then I see Memphis. I knowed I was right this time. It was standing up into the air. It looked like about a dozen whole towns bigger than Jefferson was set up on one edge in a field, standing up into the air higher than ara hill in all Yoknapatawpha County. Then we was in it, with the bus stopping ever' few feet, it seemed like to me, and cars rushing past on both sides of it and the street crowded with folks from ever'where in town that day, until I didn't see how there could 'a' been nobody left in Mis'sippi a-tall to even sell me a bus ticket, let alone write out no case histories. Then the bus stopped. It was another bus dee-po, a heap bigger than the one in Jefferson. And I said, "All right. Where do folks join the Army?"

"What?" the bus feller said.

And I said it again, "Where do folks join the Army?"

"Oh," he said. Then he told me how to get there. I was afraid at first I wouldn't ketch on how to do in a town big as Memphis. But I caught on all right. I never had to ask but twice more. Then I was there, and I was durn glad to git out of all them rushing cars and shoving folks and all that racket for a spell, and I thought, It won't be long now, and I thought how if there was any kind of a crowd there that had done already joined the Army, too, Pete would likely see me before I seen him. And so I walked into the room. And Pete wasn't there.

He wasn't even there. There was a soldier with a big arrerhead on his sleeve, writing, and two fellers standing in front of him, and there was some more folks there, I reckon. It seems to me I remember some more folks there.

I went to the table where the soldier was writing, and I said, "Where's Pete?" and he looked up and I said, "My brother. Pete Grier. Where is he?"

"What?" the soldier said. "Who?"

And I told him again. "He joined the Army yestiddy. He's going to Pearl Harbor. So am I. I want to ketch him. Where you all got him?" Now they were all looking at me, but I never paid them no mind. "Come on," I said. "Where is he?"

The soldier had quit writing. He had both hands spraddled out on the table. "Oh," he said. "You're going, too, hah?"

"Yes," I said. "They got to have wood and water. I can chop it and tote it. Come on. Where's Pete?"

The soldier stood up. "Who let you in here?" he said. "Go on. Beat it."

"Durn that," I said. "You tell me where Pete ——"

I be dog if he couldn't move faster than the bus feller even. He never come over the table, he come around it, he was on me almost before I knowed it, so that I jest had time to jump back and whup out my pocket-knife and snap it open and hit one lick, and he hollered and jumped back and grabbed one hand with the other and stood there cussing and hollering.

One of the other fellers grabbed me from behind, and I hit at him with the knife, but I couldn't reach him.

Then both of the fellers had me from behind, and then another soldier come out of a door at the back. He had on a belt with a britching strop over one shoulder.

"What the hell is this?" he said.

"That little son cut me with a knife!" the first sol dier hollered. When he said that I tried to get at him again but both them fellers was holding me, two against one, and the soldier with the backing strop said, "Here, here. Put your knife up, feller. None of us are armed. A man don't knife-fight folks that are barehanded." I could begin to hear him then. He sounded jest like Pete talked to me. "Let him go," he said. They let me go. "Now what's all the trouble about?" And I told him. "I see," he said. "And you come up to see if he was all right before he left."

"No," I said. "I came to——"

But he had already turned to where the first soldier was wropping a handkerchief around his hand.

"Have you got him?" he said. The first soldier went back to the table and looked at some papers.

"Here he is," he said. "He enlisted yestiddy. He's in a detachment leaving this morning for Little Rock." He had a watch stropped on his arm. He looked at it. "The train leaves in about fifty minutes. If I know country boys, they're probably all down there at the station right now."

"Get him up here," the one with the backing strop said. "Phone the station. Tell the porter to get him a cab. And you come with me," he said.

It was another office behind that un, with jest a table and some chairs. We set there while the soldier smoked, and it wasn't long; I knowed Pete's feet soon as I heard them. Then the first soldier opened the door and Pete come in. He never had no soldier clothes on. He looked jest like he did when he got on the bus yestiddy morning, except it seemed to me like it was at least a week, so much had happened, and I had done had to do so much traveling. He come in and there he was, looking at me like he hadn't never left home, except that here we was in Memphis, on the way to Pearl Harbor.

"What in durnation are you doing here?" he said.

And I told him, "You got to have wood and water to cook with. I can chop it and tote it for you-all."

"No," Pete said. "You're going back home."

"No, Pete," I said. "I got to go too. I got to. It hurts my heart, Pete."

"No," Pete said. He looked at the soldier. "I jest don't know what could have happened to him, lootenant," he said. "He never drawed a knife on anybody before in his life." He looked at me. "What did you do it for?"

"I don't know," I said. "I jest had to. I jest had to git here. I jest had to find you."

"Well, don't you never do it again, you hear?" Pete said. "You put that knife in your pocket and you keep it there. If I ever again hear of you drawing it on anybody, I'm coming back from wherever I am at and whup the fire out of you. You hear me?"

"I would pure cut a throat if it would bring you back to stay," I said. "Pete," I said. "Pete."

"No," Pete said. Now his voice wasn't hard and quick no more, it was almost quiet, and I knowed now I wouldn't never change him. "You must go home. You must look after maw, and I am depending on you to look after my ten acres. I want you to go back home. Today. Do you hear?"

"I hear," I said.

"Can he get back home by himself?" the soldier said.

"He come up here by himself," Pete said.

"I can get back, I reckon," I said. "I don't live in but one place. I don't reckon it's moved."

Pete taken a dollar out of his pocket and give it to me. "That'll buy your bus ticket right to our mailbox," he said. "I want you to mind the lootenant. He'll send you to the bus. And you go back home and you take care of maw and look after my ten acres and keep that durn knife in your pocket. You hear me?"

"Yes, Pete," I said.

"All right," Pete said. "Now I got to go." He put his hand

on my head again. But this time he never wrung my neck.
He just laid his hand on my head a minute. And then I be
dog if he didn't lean down and kiss me, and I heard his feet
and then the door, and I never looked up and that was all,
me setting there, rubbing the place where Pete kissed me
and the soldier throwed back in his chair, looking out the
window and coughing. He reached into his pocket and
handed something to me without looking around. It was a
piece of chewing gum.

"Much obliged," I said. "Well, I reckon I might as well
start back. I got a right fer piece to go."

"Wait," the soldier said. Then he telephoned again and I
said again I better start back, and he said again, "Wait. Remember what Pete told you."

So we waited, and then another lady come in, old, too, in
a fur coat, too, but she smelled all right, she never had no
artermatic writing pen nor no case history neither. She come
in and the soldier got up, and she looked around quick until
she saw me, and come and put her hand on my shoulder light
and quick and easy as maw herself might 'a' done it.

"Come on," she said. "Let's go home to dinner."

"Nome," I said. "I got to ketch the bus to Jefferson."

"I know. There's plenty of time. We'll go home and eat
dinner first."

She had a car. And now we was right down in the middle
of all them other cars. We was almost under the busses, and
all them crowds of people on the street close enough to
where I could have talked to them if I had knowed who
they was. After a while she stopped the car. "Here we are,"
she said, and I looked at it, and if all that was her house, she
sho had a big family. But all of it wasn't. We crossed a hall
with trees growing in it and went into a little room without
nothing in it but a nigger dressed up in a uniform a heap
shinier than them soldiers had, and the nigger shut the door,

and then I hollered, "Look out!" and grabbed, but it was all right; that whole little room jest went right on up and stopped and the door opened and we was in another hall, and the lady unlocked a door and we went in, and there was another soldier, a old feller, with a britching strop, too, and a silver-colored bird on each shoulder.

"Here we are," the lady said. "This is Colonel McKellogg. Now, what would you like for dinner?"

"I reckon I'll jest have some ham and eggs and coffee," I said.

She had done started to pick up the telephone. She stopped. "Coffee?" she said. "When did you start drinking coffee?"

"I don't know," I said. "I reckon it was before I could remember."

"You're about eight, aren't you?" she said.

"Nome," I said. "I'm eight and ten months. Going on eleven months."

She telephoned then. Then we set there and I told them how Pete had jest left that morning for Pearl Harbor and I had aimed to go with him, but I would have to go back home to take care of maw and look after Pete's ten acres, and she said how they had a little boy about my size, too, in a school in the East. Then a nigger, another one, in a short kind of shirttail coat, rolled a kind of wheelbarrer in. It had my ham and eggs and a glass of milk and a piece of pie, too, and I thought I was hungry. But when I taken the first bite I found out I couldn't swallow it, and I got up quick.

"I got to go," I said.

"Wait," she said.

"I got to go," I said.

"Just a minute," she said. "I've already telephoned for the car. It won't be but a minute now. Can't you drink the milk even? Or maybe some of your coffee?"

"Nome," I said. "I ain't hungry. I'll eat when I git home." Then the telephone rung. She never even answered it.

"There," she said. "There's the car." And we went back down in that 'ere little moving room with the dressed-up nigger. This time it was a big car with a soldier driving it. I got into the front with him. She give the soldier a dollar. "He might get hungry," she said. "Try to find a decent place for him."

"O.K., Mrs. McKellogg," the soldier said.

Then we was gone again. And now I could see Memphis good, bright in the sunshine, while we was swinging around it. And first thing I knowed, we was back on the same highway the bus run on this morning—the patches of stores and them big gins and sawmills, and Memphis running on for miles, it seemed like to me, before it begun to give out. Then we was running again between the fields and woods, running fast now, and except for that soldier, it was like I hadn't never been to Memphis a-tall. We was going fast now. At this rate, before I knowed it we would be home again, and I thought about me riding up to Frenchman's Bend in this big car with a soldier running it, and all of a sudden I begun to cry. I never knowed I was fixing to, and I couldn't stop it. I set there by that soldier, crying. We was going fast.

Shall Not Perish

WHEN THE MESSAGE came about Pete, Father and I had already gone to the field. Mother got it out of the mailbox after we left and brought it down to the fence, and she already knew beforehand what it was because she didn't even have on her sunbonnet, so she must have been watching from the kitchen window when the carrier drove up. And I already knew what was in it too. Because she didn't speak. She just stood at the fence with the little pale envelope that didn't even need a stamp on it in her hand, and it was me that hollered at Father, from further away across the field than he was, so that he reached the fence first where Mother waited even though I was already running. "I know what it is," Mother said. "But can't open it. Open it."

"No it ain't!" I hollered, running. "No it ain't!" Then I was hollering, "No, Pete! No, Pete!" Then I was hollering, "God damn them Japs! God damn them Japs!" and then I was the one Father had to grab and hold, trying to hold me, having to wrastle with me like I was another man instead of just nine.

And that was all. One day there was Pearl Harbor. And the next week Pete went to Memphis, to join the army and go there and help them; and one morning Mother stood at the field fence with a little scrap of paper not even big enough to start a fire with, that didn't even need a stamp on the envelope, saying, *A ship was. Now it is not. Your son was one of them.* And we allowed ourselves one day to grieve, and that was all. Because it was April, the hardest middle push of planting time, and there was the land, the seventy acres which were our bread and fire and keep, which had outlasted the Griers before us because they had done right by it, and had outlasted Pete because while he was here he had done his part to help and would outlast Mother and Father and me if we did ours.

Then it happened again. Maybe we had forgotten that it could and was going to, again and again, to people who loved sons and brothers as we loved Pete, until the day finally came when there would be an end to it. After that day when we saw Pete's name and picture in the Memphis paper, Father would bring one home with him each time he went to town. And we would see the pictures and names of soldiers and sailors from other counties and towns in Mississippi and Arkansas and Tennessee, but there wasn't another from ours, and so after a while it did look like Pete was going to be all.

Then it happened again. It was late July, a Friday. Father had gone to town early on Homer Bookwright's cattletruck and now it was sundown. I had just come up from the field with the light sweep and I had just finished stalling the mule and come out of the barn when Homer's truck stopped at the mailbox and Father got down and came up the lane, with a sack of flour balanced on his shoulder and a package under his arm and the folded newspaper in his hand. And I took one look at the folded paper and then no more. Because I knew it too, even if he always did have one when he came back from town. Because it was bound to happen sooner or later; it would not be just us out of all Yoknapatawpha County who had loved enough to have sole right to grief. So I just met him and took part of the load and turned beside him, and we entered the kitchen together where our cold supper waited on the table and Mother sat in the last of sunset in the open door, her hand and arm strong and steady on the dasher of the churn.

When the message came about Pete, Father never touched her. He didn't touch her now. He just lowered the flour onto the table and went to the chair and held out the folded paper. "It's Major de Spain's boy," he said. "In town. The av-aytor. That was home last fall in his officer uniform. He run his airplane into a Japanese battleship and blowed it up. So they knowed where he was at." And Mother didn't stop the churn for a minute either, because even I could tell that the butter had almost come. Then she got up and went to the sink and washed her hands and came back and sat down again.

"Read it," she said.

So Father and I found out that Mother not only knew all the time it was going to happen again, but that she already knew what she was going to do when it did, not only this time but the next one too, and the one after that and the one after that, until the day finally came when all the grieving about the earth, the rich and the poor too, whether they lived with ten nigger servants in the fine big painted houses in town or whether they lived on and by seventy acres of not extra good land like us or whether all they owned was the right to sweat today for what they would eat tonight, could say, *At least this there was some point to why we grieved.*

We fed and milked and came back and ate the cold supper, and I built a fire in the stove and Mother put on the kettle and whatever else would heat enough water for two, and I fetched in the washtub from the back porch, and while Mother washed the dishes and cleaned up the kitchen, Father and I sat on the front steps. This was about the time of day that Pete and I would walk the two miles down to Old Man Killegrew's house last December, to listen to the radio tell about Pearl Harbor and Manila. But more than Pearl Harbor

and Manila has happened since then, and Pete don't make one
to listen to it. Nor do I: it's like, since nobody can tell us
exactly where he was when he stopped being *is*, instead of
just becoming *was* at some single spot on the earth where
the people who loved him could weight him down with a
stone, Pete still *is* everywhere about the earth, one among all
the fighters forever, *was* or *is* either. So Mother and Father
and I don't need a little wooden box to catch the voices of
them that saw the courage and the sacrifice. Then Mother
called me back to the kitchen. The water smoked a little in
the washtub, beside the soap dish and my clean nightshirt and
the towel Mother made out of our worn-out cotton sacks,
and I bathe and empty the tub and leave it ready for her, and
we lie down.

Then morning, and we rose. Mother was up first, as always. My clean white Sunday shirt and pants were waiting,
along with the shoes and stockings I hadn't even seen since
frost was out of the ground. But in yesterday's overalls still
I carried the shoes back to the kitchen where Mother stood
in yesterday's dress at the stove where not only our breakfast
was cooking but Father's dinner too, and set the shoes beside
her Sunday ones against the wall and went to the barn, and
Father and I fed and milked and came back and sat down and
ate while Mother moved back and forth between the table
and the stove till we were done, and she herself sat down.
Then I got out the blacking-box, until Father came and took
it away from me—the polish and rag and brush and the four
shoes in succession. "De Spain is rich," he said. "With a
monkey nigger in a white coat to hold the jar up each time
he wants to spit. You shine all shoes like you aimed yourself
to wear them: just the parts that you can see yourself by
looking down."

Then we dressed. I put on my Sunday shirt and the pants
so stiff with starch that they would stand alone, and carried

my stockings back to the kitchen just as Mother entered, carrying hers, and dressed too, even her hat, and took my stockings from me and put them with hers on the table beside the shined shoes, and lifted the satchel down from the cupboard shelf. It was still in the cardboard box it came in, with the colored label of the San Francisco drugstore where Pete bought it—a round, square-ended, water-proof satchel with a handle for carrying, so that as soon as Pete saw it in the store he must have known too that it had been almost exactly made for exactly what we would use it for, with a zipper opening that Mother had never seen before nor Father either. That is, we had all three been in the drugstore and the ten-cent-store in Jefferson but I was the only one who had been curious enough to find out how one worked, even though even I never dreamed we would ever own one. So it was me that zipped it open, with a pipe and a can of tobacco in it for Father and a hunting cap with a carbide headlight for me and for Mother the satchel itself, and she zipped it shut and then open and then Father tried it, running the slide up and down the little clicking track until Mother made him stop before he wore it out; and she put the satchel, still open, back into the box and I fetched in from the barn the empty quart bottle of cattle-dip and she scalded the bottle and cork and put them and the clean folded towel into the satchel and set the box onto the cupboard shelf, the zipper still open because when we came to need it we would have to open it first and so we would save that much wear on the zipper too. She took the satchel from the box and the bottle from the satchel and filled the bottle with clean water and corked it and put it back into the satchel with the clean towel and put our shoes and stockings in and zipped the satchel shut, and we walked to the road and stood in the bright hot morning beside the mailbox until the bus came up and stopped.

It was the school bus, the one I rode back and forth to

Frenchman's Bend to school in last winter, and that Pete rode
in every morning and evening until he graduated, but going
in the opposite direction now, in to Jefferson, and only on
Saturday, seen for a long time down the long straight stretch
of Valley road while other people waiting beside other mailboxes got into it. Then it was our turn. Mother handed the
two quarters to Solon Quick, who built it and owned it and
drove it, and we got in too and it went on, and soon there was
no more room for the ones that stood beside the mailboxes
and signalled and then it went fast, twenty miles then ten
then five then one, and up the last hill to where the concrete
streets began, and we got out and sat on the curb and Mother
opened the satchel and took our shoes and the bottle of water
and the towel and we washed our feet and put on our shoes
and stockings and Mother put the bottle and towel back and
shut the bag.

And we walked beside the iron picket fence long enough
to front a cotton patch; we turned into the yard which was
bigger than farms I had seen and followed the gravel drive
wider and smoother than roads in Frenchman's Bend, on to
the house that to me anyway looked bigger than the courthouse, and mounted the steps between the stone columns
and crossed the portico that would have held our whole
house, galleries and all, and knocked at the door. And then
it never mattered whether our shoes were shined at all or
not: the whites of the monkey nigger's eyes for just a second
when he opened the door for us, the white of his coat for
just a second at the end of the hall before it was gone too,
his feet not making any more noise than a cat's leaving us
to find the right door by ourselves, if we could. And we
did—the rich man's parlor that any woman in Frenchman's
Bend and I reckon in the rest of the county too could have
described to the inch but which not even the men who would
come to Major de Spain after bank-hours or on Sunday to

ask to have a note extended, had ever seen, with a light
hanging in the middle of the ceiling the size of our whole
washtub full of chopped-up ice and a gold-colored harp
that would have blocked our barn door and a mirror that
a man on a mule could have seen himself and the mule both
in, and a table shaped like a coffin in the middle of the floor
with the Confederate flag spread over it and the photograph
of Major de Spain's son and the open box with the medal in
it and a big blue automatic pistol weighting down the flag,
and Major de Spain standing at the end of the table with his
hat on until after a while he seemed to hear and recognize
the name which Mother spoke;—not a real major but just
called that because his father had been a real one in the old
Confederate war, but a banker powerful in money and
politics both, that Father said had made governors and senators too in Mississippi;—an old man, too old you would have
said to have had a son just twenty-three; too old anyway
to have had that look on his face.

"Ha," he said. "I remember now. You too were advised
that your son poured out his blood on the altar of unpre-
paredness and inefficiency. What do you want?"

"Nothing," Mother said. She didn't even pause at the
door. She went on toward the table. "We had nothing to
bring you. And I don't think I see anything here we would
want to take away."

"You're wrong," he said. "You have a son left. Take what
they have been advising to me: go back home and pray.
Not for the dead one: for the one they have so far left you,
that something somewhere, somehow will save him!" She
wasn't even looking at him. She never had looked at him
again. She just went on across that barn-sized room exactly
as I have watched her set mine and Father's lunch pail into
the fence corner when there wasn't time to stop the plows
to eat, and turn back toward the house.

"I can tell you something simpler than that," she said. "Weep." Then she reached the table. But it was only her body that stopped, her hand going out so smooth and quick that his hand only caught her wrist, the two hands locked together on the big blue pistol, between the photograph and the little hunk of iron medal on its colored ribbon, against that old flag that a heap of people I knew had never seen and a heap more of them wouldn't recognize if they did, and over all of it the old man's voice that ought not to have sounded like that either.

"For his country! He had no country: this one I too repudiate. His country and mine both was ravaged and polluted and destroyed eighty years ago, before even I was born. His forefathers fought and died for it then, even though what they fought and lost for was a dream. He didn't even have a dream. He died for an illusion. In the interests of usury, by the folly and rapacity of politicians, for the glory and aggrandisement of organized labor!"

"Yes," Mother said. "Weep."

"The fear of elective servants for their incumbencies! The subservience of misled workingmen for the demagogues who misled them! Shame? Grief? How can poltroonery and rapacity and voluntary thralldom know shame or grief?"

"All men are capable of shame," Mother said. "Just as all men are capable of courage and honor and sacrifice. And grief too. It will take time, but they will learn it. It will take more grief than yours and mine, and there will be more. But it will be enough."

"When? When all the young men are dead? What will there be left then worth the saving?"

"I know," Mother said. "I know. Our Pete was too young too to have to die." Then I realized that their hands were no longer locked, that he was erect again and that the pistol was hanging slack in Mother's hand against her side, and for a minute I thought she was going to unzip the satchel and take the towel out of it. But she just laid the pistol back on the table and stepped up to him and took the handkerchief from his breast pocket and put it into his hand and stepped back. "That's right," she said. "Weep. Not for him: for us, the old, who don't know why. What is your Negro's name?"

But he didn't answer. He didn't even raise the handkerchief to his face. He just stood there holding it, like he hadn't discovered yet that it was in his hand, or perhaps even what it was Mother had put there. "For us, the old," he said. "You believe. You have had three months to learn again, to find out why; mine happened yesterday. Tell me."

"I don't know," Mother said. "Maybe women are not supposed to know why their sons must die in battle; maybe all they are supposed to do is just to grieve for them. But my son knew why And my brother went to the war when I was a girl, and our mother didn't know why either, but he did. And my grandfather was in that old one there too, and I reckon his mother didn't know why either, but I reckon he did. And my son knew why he had to go to this one, and he knew I knew he did even though I didn't, just as he knew that this child here and I both knew he would not come back. But he knew why, even if I didn't, couldn't, never can. So it must be all right, even if I couldn't understand it. Because there is nothing in him that I or his father didn't put there. What is your Negro's name?"

He called the name then. And the nigger wasn't so far away after all, though when he entered Major de Spain had already turned so that his back was toward the door. He didn't look around. He just pointed toward the table with the hand Mother had put the handkerchief into, and the nigger went to the table without looking at anybody and without making any more noise on the floor than a cat and he didn't stop at all; it looked to me like he had already turned and started back before he even reached the table: one flick of the black hand and the white sleeve and the pistol vanished without me even seeing him touch it and when he passed me again going out, I couldn't see what he had done with it. So Mother had to speak twice before I knew she was talking to me.

"Come," she said.

"Wait," said Major de Spain. He had turned again, facing us. "What you and his father gave him. You must know what that was."

"I know it came a long way," Mother said. "So it must have been strong to have lasted through all of us. It must have been all right for him to be willing to die for it after that long time and coming that far. Come," she said again.

"Wait," he said. "Wait. Where did you come from?"

Mother stopped. "I told you: Frenchman's Bend."

"I know. How? By wagon? You have no car."

"Oh," Mother said. "We came in Mr. Quick's bus. He comes in every Saturday."

"And waits until night to go back. I'll send you back in my car." He called the nigger's name again. But Mother stopped him. "Thank you," she said. "We have already paid Mr. Quick. He owes us the ride back home."

There was an old lady born and raised in Jefferson who died rich somewhere in the North and left some money to the town to build a museum with. It was a house like a church, built for nothing else except to hold the pictures she picked out to put in it—pictures from all over the United States, painted by people who loved what they had seen or where they had been born or lived enough to want to paint pictures of it so that other people could see it too; pictures of men and women and children, and the houses and streets and cities and the woods and fields and streams where they worked or lived or pleasured, so that all the people who wanted to, people like us from Frenchman's Bend or from littler places even than Frenchman's Bend in our county or beyond our state too, could come without charge into the cool and the quiet and look without let at the pictures of men and women and children who were the same people that we were even if their houses and barns were different and their fields worked different, with different things growing in them. So it was already late when we left the museum, and later still when we got back to where the bus waited, and later still more before we got started, although at least we could get into the bus and take our shoes and stockings back off. Because Mrs. Quick hadn't come yet and so Solon had to wait for her, not because she was his wife but because he made her pay a quarter out of her egg-money to ride to town and back on Saturday, and he wouldn't go off and leave anybody who had paid him. And so, even though the bus ran fast again, when the road finally straightened out into the long Valley stretch, there was only the last sunset spoking out across the sky, stretching all the way across America from the Pacific ocean, touching all the places that the men and women in the museum whose names we didn't even know had loved enough to paint pictures of them, like a big soft fading wheel.

And I remembered how Father used to always prove any point he wanted to make to Pete and me, by Grandfather. It didn't matter whether it was something he thought we ought to have done and hadn't, or something he would have stopped us from doing if he had just known about it in time. "Now, take your Grandpap," he would say. I could remember him too: Father's grandfather even, old, so old you just wouldn't believe it, so old that it would seem to me he must have gone clean back to the old fathers in Genesis and Exodus that talked face to face with God, and Grandpap outlived them all except him. It seemed to me he must have been too old even to have actually fought in the old Confederate war, although that was about all he talked about, not only when we thought that maybe he was awake but even when we knew he must be asleep, until after a while we had to admit that we never knew which one he really was. He would sit in his chair under the mulberry in the yard or on the sunny end of the front gallery or in his corner by the hearth; he would start up out of the chair and we still wouldn't know which one he was, whether he never had been asleep or whether he hadn't ever waked even when he jumped up, hollering, "Look out! Look out! Here they come!" He wouldn't even always holler the same name; they wouldn't even always be on the same side or even soldiers: Forrest, or Morgan, or Abe Lincoln, or Van Dorn, or Grant or Colonel Sartoris himself, whose people still lived in our county, or Mrs. Rosa Millard, Colonel Sartoris's mother-in-law who stood off the Yankees and carpetbaggers too for the whole four years of the war until Colonel Sartoris could get back home. Pete thought it was just funny. Father and I were ashamed. We didn't know what Mother thought nor even what it was, until the afternoon at the picture show.

It was a continued picture, a Western; it seemed to me that it had been running every Saturday afternoon for years. Pete and Father and I would go in to town every Saturday to see it, and sometimes Mother would go too, to sit there in the dark while the pistols popped and snapped and the horses galloped and each time it would look like they were going to catch him but you knew they wouldn't quite, that there would be some more of it next Saturday and the one after that and the one after that, and always the week in between for me and Pete to talk about the villain's pearl-handled pistol that Pete wished was his and the hero's spotted horse that I wished was mine. Then one Saturday Mother decided to take Grandpap. He sat between her and me,

already asleep again, so old now that he didn't even have
to snore, until the time came that you could have set a watch
by every Saturday afternoon: when the horses all came
plunging down the cliff and whirled around and came boiling up the gully until in just one more jump they would
come clean out of the screen and go galloping among the
little faces turned up to them like corn shucks scattered
across a lot. Then Grandpap waked up. For about five
seconds he sat perfectly still. I could even feel him sitting
still, he sat so still so hard. Then he said, "Cavalry!" Then
he was on his feet. "Forrest!" he said. "Bedford Forrest! Get
out of here! Get out of the way!" clawing and scrabbling
from one seat to the next one whether there was anybody
in them or not, into the aisle with us trying to follow and
catch him, and up the aisle toward the door still hollering,
"Forrest! Forrest! Here he comes! Get out of the way!"
and outside at last, with half the show behind us and Grandpap blinking and trembling at the light and Pete propped
against the wall by his arms like he was being sick, laughing,
and father shaking Grandpap's arm and saying, "You old
fool! You old fool!" until Mother made him stop. And we
half carried him around to the alley where the wagon was
hitched and helped him in and Mother got in and sat by him,
holding his hand until he could begin to stop shaking. "Go
get him a bottle of beer," she said.

"He don't deserve any beer," Father said. "The old fool,
having the whole town laughing. . . ."

"Go get him some beer!" Mother said. "He's going to sit
right here in his own wagon and drink it. Go on!" And
Father did, and Mother held the bottle until Grandpap got
a good hold on it, and she sat holding his hand until he got
a good swallow down him. Then he begun to stop shaking.
He said, "Ah-h-h," and took another swallow and said,

"Ah-h-h," again and then he even drew his other hand out
of Mother's and he wasn't trembling now but just a little,
taking little darting sips at the bottle and saying "Hah!" and
taking another sip and saying "Hah!" again, and not just
looking at the bottle now but looking all around, and his
eyes snapping a little when he blinked. "Fools yourselves!"
Mother cried at Father and Pete and me. "He wasn't running
from anybody! He was running in front of them, hollering
at all clods to look out because better men than they were
coming, even seventy-five years afterwards, still powerful,
still dangerous, still coming!"

And I knew them too. I had seen them too, who had
never been further from Frenchman's Bend than I could
return by night to sleep. It was like the wheel, like the sunset itself, hubbed at that little place that don't even show
on a map, that not two hundred people out of all the earth
know is named Frenchman's Bend or has any name at all,
and spoking out in all the directions and touching them all,
never a one too big for it to touch, never a one too little to
be remembered:—the places that men and women have
lived in and loved whether they had anything to paint pictures of them with or not, all the little places quiet enough
to be lived in and loved and the names of them before they
were quiet enough, and the names of the deeds that made
them quiet enough and the names of the men and the women
who did the deeds, who lasted and endured and fought the
battles and lost them and fought again because they didn't
even know they had been whipped, and tamed the wilder-
ness and overpassed the mountains and deserts and died and
still went on as the shape of the United States grew and
went on. I knew them too: the men and women still powerful seventy-five years and twice that and twice that again
afterward, still powerful and still dangerous and still com-

ing, North and South and East and West, until the name of
what they did and what they died for became just one single
word, louder than any thunder. It was America, and it
covered all the western earth.

II · THE VILLAGE

A Rose for Emily

I

WHEN Miss Emily Grierson died, our whole town went to her funeral: the men through a sort of respectful affection for a fallen monument, the women mostly out of curiosity to see the inside of her house, which no one save an old man-servant—a combined gardener and cook—had seen in at least ten years.

It was a big, squarish frame house that had once been white, decorated with cupolas and spires and scrolled balconies in the heavily lightsome style of the seventies, set on what had once been our most select street. But garages and cotton gins had encroached and obliterated even the august names of that neighborhood; only Miss Emily's house was left, lifting its stubborn and coquettish decay above the cotton wagons and the gasoline pumps—an eyesore among eyesores. And now Miss Emily had gone to join the representatives of those august names where they lay in the cedar-bemused cemetery among the ranked and anonymous graves of Union and Confederate soldiers who fell at the battle of Jefferson.

Alive, Miss Emily had been a tradition, a duty, and a care; a sort of hereditary obligation upon the town, dating from that day in 1894 when Colonel Sartoris, the mayor—he who fathered the edict that no Negro woman should appear on the streets without an apron—remitted her taxes, the dispensation dating from the death of her father on into perpetuity. Not that Miss Emily would have accepted charity. Colonel Sartoris invented an involved tale to the effect that Miss Emily's father had loaned money to the town, which the town, as a matter of business, preferred this way of repaying. Only a man of Colonel Sartoris' generation and thought could have invented it, and only a woman could have believed it.

When the next generation, with its more modern ideas, became mayors and aldermen, this arrangement created some little dissatisfaction. On the first of the year they mailed her a tax notice. February came, and there was no reply. They wrote her a formal letter, asking her to call at the sheriff's office at her convenience. A week later the mayor wrote her himself, offering to call or to send his car for her, and received in reply a note on paper of an archaic shape, in a thin, flowing calligraphy in faded ink, to the effect that she no longer went out at all. The tax notice was also enclosed, without comment.

They called a special meeting of the Board of Aldermen. A deputation waited upon her, knocked at the door through which no visitor had passed since she ceased giving china-painting lessons eight or ten years earlier. They were admitted by the old Negro into a dim hall from which a stairway mounted into still more shadow. It smelled of dust and disuse—a close, dank smell. The Negro led them into the parlor. It was furnished in heavy, leather-covered furniture. When the Negro opened the blinds of one window, they could see that the leather was cracked; and when they sat down, a faint dust rose sluggishly about their thighs, spinning with slow motes in the single sun-ray. On a tarnished gilt easel before the fireplace stood a crayon portrait of Miss Emily's father.

They rose when she entered—a small, fat woman in black, with a thin gold chain descending to her waist and vanishing into her belt, leaning on an ebony cane with a tarnished gold head. Her skeleton was small and spare; perhaps that was why what would have been merely plumpness in another was obesity in her. She looked bloated, like a body long submerged in motionless water, and of that pallid hue. Her eyes, lost in the fatty ridges of her face, looked like two small pieces of coal pressed into a lump of dough as they moved from one face to another while the visitors stated their errand.

She did not ask them to sit. She just stood in the door and listened quietly until the spokesman came to a stumbling halt. Then they could hear the invisible watch ticking at the end of the gold chain.

Her voice was dry and cold. "I have no taxes in Jefferson. Colonel Sartoris explained it to me. Perhaps one of you can gain access to the city records and satisfy yourselves."

"But we have. We are the city authorities, Miss Emily. Didn't you get a notice from the sheriff, signed by him?"

"I received a paper, yes," Miss Emily said. "Perhaps he considers himself the sheriff . . . I have no taxes in Jefferson."

"But there is nothing on the books to show that, you see We must go by the—"

"See Colonel Sartoris. I have no taxes in Jefferson."

"But, Miss Emily—"

"See Colonel Sartoris." (Colonel Sartoris had been dead almost ten years.) "I have no taxes in Jefferson. Tobe!" The Negro appeared. "Show these gentlemen out."

II

So SHE vanquished them, horse and foot, just as she had vanquished their fathers thirty years before about the smell.

That was two years after her father's death and a short time
after her sweetheart—the one we believed would marry her
—had deserted her. After her father's death she went out
very little; after her sweetheart went away, people hardly
saw her at all. A few of the ladies had the temerity to call,
but were not received, and the only sign of life about the
place was the Negro man—a young man then—going in
and out with a market basket.

"Just as if a man—any man—could keep a kitchen properly," the ladies said; so they were not surprised when the
smell developed. It was another link between the gross,
teeming world and the high and mighty Griersons.

A neighbor, a woman, complained to the mayor, Judge
Stevens, eighty years old.

"But what will you have me do about it, madam?" he said.

"Why, send her word to stop it," the woman said. "Isn't
there a law?"

"I'm sure that won't be necessary," Judge Stevens said.
"It's probably just a snake or a rat that nigger of hers killed
in the yard. I'll speak to him about it."

The next day he received two more complaints, one from
a man who came in diffident deprecation. "We really must
do something about it, Judge. I'd be the last one in the world
to bother Miss Emily, but we've got to do something." That
night the Board of Aldermen met—three graybeards and
one younger man, a member of the rising generation.

"It's simple enough," he said. "Send her word to have her
place cleaned up. Give her a certain time to do it in, and if
she don't . . ."

"Dammit, sir," Judge Stevens said, "will you accuse a
lady to her face of smelling bad?"

So the next night, after midnight, four men crossed Miss
Emily's lawn and slunk about the house like burglars, sniffing
along the base of the brickwork and at the cellar openings

while one of them performed a regular sowing motion with his hand out of a sack slung from his shoulder. They broke open the cellar door and sprinkled lime there, and in all the outbuildings. As they recrossed the lawn, a window that had been dark was lighted and Miss Emily sat in it, the light behind her, and her upright torso motionless as that of an idol. They crept quietly across the lawn and into the shadow of the locusts that lined the street. After a week or two the smell went away.

That was when people had begun to feel really sorry for her. People in our town, remembering how old lady Wyatt, her great-aunt, had gone completely crazy at last, believed that the Griersons held themselves a little too high for what they really were. None of the young men were quite good enough for Miss Emily and such. We had long thought of them as a tableau, Miss Emily a slender figure in white in the background, her father a spraddled silhouette in the foreground, his back to her and clutching a horsewhip, the two of them framed by the back-flung front door. So when she got to be thirty and was still single, we were not pleased exactly, but vindicated; even with insanity in the family she wouldn't have turned down all of her chances if they had really materialized.

When her father died, it got about that the house was all that was left to her; and in a way, people were glad. At last they could pity Miss Emily. Being left alone, and a pauper, she had become humanized. Now she too would know the old thrill and the old despair of a penny more or less.

The day after his death all the ladies prepared to call at the house and offer condolence and aid, as is our custom. Miss Emily met them at the door, dressed as usual and with no trace of grief on her face. She told them that her father was not dead. She did that for three days, with the ministers calling on her, and the doctors, trying to persuade her to let them dispose of the body. Just as they were about to resort to law and force, she broke down, and they buried her father quickly.

We did not say she was crazy then. We believed she had to do that. We remembered all the young men her father had driven away, and we knew that with nothing left, she would have to cling to that which had robbed her, as people will.

I I I

SHE WAS SICK for a long time. When we saw her again, her hair was cut short, making her look like a girl, with a vague resemblance to those angels in colored church windows— sort of tragic and serene.

The town had just let the contracts for paving the side-walks, and in the summer after her father's death they began the work. The construction company came with niggers and mules and machinery, and a foreman named Homer Barron, a Yankee—a big, dark, ready man, with a big voice and eyes lighter than his face. The little boys would follow in groups to hear him cuss the niggers, and the niggers singing in time to the rise and fall of picks. Pretty soon he knew every-body in town. Whenever you heard a lot of laughing any-where about the square, Homer Barron would be in the center of the group. Presently we began to see him and Miss Emily on Sunday afternoons driving in the yellow-wheeled buggy and the matched team of bays from the livery stable.

At first we were glad that Miss Emily would have an interest, because the ladies all said, "Of course a Grierson would not think seriously of a Northerner, a day laborer." But there were still others, older people, who said that even grief could not cause a real lady to forget *noblesse oblige*—

without calling it *noblesse oblige*. They just said, "Poor Emily. Her kinsfolk should come to her." She had some kin in Alabama; but years ago her father had fallen out with them over the estate of old lady Wyatt, the crazy woman, and there was no communication between the two families. They had not even been represented at the funeral.

And as soon as the old people said, "Poor Emily," the whispering began. "Do you suppose it's really so?" they said to one another. "Of course it is. What else could . . ." This behind their hands; rustling of craned silk and satin behind jalousies closed upon the sun of Sunday afternoon as the thin, swift clop-clop-clop of the matched team passed: "Poor Emily."

She carried her head high enough—even when we believed that she was fallen. It was as if she demanded more than ever the recognition of her dignity as the last Grierson; as if it had wanted that touch of earthiness to reaffirm her imperviousness. Like when she bought the rat poison, the arsenic. That was over a year after they had begun to say "Poor Emily," and while the two female cousins were visiting her.

"I want some poison," she said to the druggist. She was over thirty then, still a slight woman, though thinner than usual, with cold, haughty black eyes in a face the flesh of which was strained across the temples and about the eye-sockets as you imagine a lighthouse-keeper's face ought to look. "I want some poison," she said.

"Yes, Miss Emily. What kind? For rats and such? I'd recom—"

"I want the best you have. I don't care what kind."

The druggist named several. "They'll kill anything up to an elephant. But what you want is—"

"Arsenic," Miss Emily said. "Is that a good one?"

"Is . . . arsenic? Yes, ma'am. But what you want—"

"I want arsenic."

The druggist looked down at her. She looked back at him, erect, her face like a strained flag. "Why, of course," the druggist said. "If that's what you want. But the law requires you to tell what you are going to use it for."

Miss Emily just stared at him, her head tilted back in order to look him eye for eye, until he looked away and went and got the arsenic and wrapped it up. The Negro delivery boy brought her the package; the druggist didn't come back. When she opened the package at home there was written on the box, under the skull and bones: "For rats."

I V

So THE NEXT day we all said, "She will kill herself"; and we said it would be the best thing. When she had first begun to be seen with Homer Barron, we had said, "She will marry him." Then we said, "She will persuade him yet," because Homer himself had remarked—he liked men, and it was known that he drank with the younger men in the Elks' Club—that he was not a marrying man. Later we said, "Poor Emily" behind the jalousies as they passed on Sunday afternoon in the glittering buggy, Miss Emily with her head high and Homer Barron with his hat cocked and a cigar in his teeth, reins and whip in a yellow glove.

Then some of the ladies began to say that it was a disgrace to the town and a bad example to the young people. The men did not want to interfere, but at last the ladies forced the Baptist minister—Miss Emily's people were Episcopal—to call upon her. He would never divulge what happened during that interview, but he refused to go back again. The next Sunday they again drove about the streets, and the following day the minister's wife wrote to Miss Emily's relations in Alabama.

So she had blood-kin under her roof again and we sat back to watch developments. At first nothing happened. Then we were sure that they were to be married. We learned that Miss Emily had been to the jeweler's and ordered a man's toilet set in silver, with the letters H. B. on each piece. Two days later we learned that she had bought a complete outfit of men's clothing, including a nightshirt, and we said, "They are married." We were really glad. We were glad because the two female cousins were even more Grierson than Miss Emily had ever been.

So we were not surprised when Homer Barron—the streets had been finished some time since—was gone. We were a little disappointed that there was not a public blowing-off, but we believed that he had gone on to prepare for Miss Emily's coming, or to give her a chance to get rid of the cousins. (By that time it was a cabal, and we were all Miss Emily's allies to help circumvent the cousins.) Sure enough, after another week they departed. And, as we had expected all along, within three days Homer Barron was back in town. A neighbor saw the Negro man admit him at the kitchen door at dusk one evening.

And that was the last we saw of Homer Barron. And of Miss Emily for some time. The Negro man went in and out with the market basket, but the front door remained closed. Now and then we would see her at a window for a moment, as the men did that night when they sprinkled the lime, but for almost six months she did not appear on the streets. Then we knew that this was to be expected too; as if that quality of her father which had thwarted her woman's life so many times had been too virulent and too furious to die.

When we next saw Miss Emily, she had grown fat and her hair was turning gray. During the next few years it grew grayer and grayer until it attained an even pepper-and salt iron-gray, when it ceased turning. Up to the day of her death at seventy-four it was still that vigorous iron-gray, like the hair of an active man.

From that time on her front door remained closed, save for a period of six or seven years, when she was about forty, during which she gave lessons in china-painting. She fitted up a studio in one of the downstairs rooms, where the daughters and granddaughters of Colonel Sartoris' contemporaries were sent to her with the same regularity and in the same spirit that they were sent to church on Sundays with a twenty-five-cent piece for the collection plate. Meanwhile her taxes had been remitted.

Then the newer generation became the backbone and the spirit of the town, and the painting pupils grew up and fell away and did not send their children to her with boxes of color and tedious brushes and pictures cut from the ladies' magazines. The front door closed upon the last one and remained closed for good. When the town got free postal delivery, Miss Emily alone refused to let them fasten the metal numbers above her door and attach a mailbox to it. She would not listen to them.

Daily, monthly, yearly we watched the Negro grow grayer and more stooped, going in and out with the market basket. Each December we sent her a tax notice, which would be returned by the post office a week later, unclaimed. Now and then we would see her in one of the downstairs windows— she had evidently shut up the top floor of the house—like the carven torso of an idol in a niche, looking or not looking at us, we could never tell which. Thus she passed from generation to generation—dear, inescapable, impervious, tranquil, and perverse.

And so she died. Fell ill in the house filled with dust and shadows, with only a doddering Negro man to wait on her. We did not even know she was sick; we had long since given up trying to get any information from the Negro.

He talked to no one, probably not even to her, for his voice
had grown harsh and rusty, as if from disuse.

She died in one of the downstairs rooms, in a heavy
walnut bed with a curtain, her gray head propped on a pillow
yellow and moldy with age and lack of sunlight.

V

The Negro met the first of the ladies at the front door and
let them in, with their hushed, sibilant voices and their quick,
curious glances, and then he disappeared. He walked right
through the house and out the back and was not seen again.

The two female cousins came at once. They held the
funeral on the second day, with the town coming to look
at Miss Emily beneath a mass of bought flowers, with the
crayon face of her father musing profoundly above the bier
and the ladies sibilant and macabre; and the very old men
—some in their brushed Confederate uniforms—on the porch
and the lawn, talking of Miss Emily as if she had been a contemporary of theirs, believing that they had danced with
her and courted her perhaps, confusing time with its math-
ematical progression, as the old do, to whom all the past is
not a diminishing road but, instead, a huge meadow which
no winter ever quite touches, divided from them now by the
narrow bottle-neck of the most recent decade of years.

Already we knew that there was one room in that region
above stairs which no one had seen in forty years, and which
would have to be forced. They waited until Miss Emily
was decently in the ground before they opened it.

The violence of breaking down the door seemed to fill
this room with pervading dust. A thin, acrid pall as of the
tomb seemed to lie everywhere upon this room decked and
furnished as for a bridal: upon the valance curtains of faded
rose color, upon the rose-shaded lights, upon the dressing

table, upon the delicate array of crystal and the man's toilet
things backed with tarnished silver, silver so tarnished that
the monogram was obscured. Among them lay a collar and
tie, as if they had just been removed, which, lifted, left upon
the surface a pale crescent in the dust. Upon a chair hung
the suit, carefully folded; beneath it the two mute shoes
and the discarded socks.

The man himself lay in the bed.

For a long while we just stood there, looking down at the
profound and fleshless grin. The body had apparently once
lain in the attitude of an embrace, but now the long sleep
that outlasts love, that conquers even the grimace of love,
had cuckolded him. What was left of him, rotted beneath
what was left of the nightshirt, had become inextricable
from the bed in which he lay; and upon him and upon the
pillow beside him lay that even coating of the patient and
biding dust.

Then we noticed that in the second pillow was the inden-
tation of a head. One of us lifted something from it, and
leaning forward, that faint and invisible dust dry and acrid
in the nostrils, we saw a long strand of iron-gray hair.

Hair

I

THIS GIRL, this Susan Reed, was an orphan. She lived with a family named Burchett, that had some more children, two or three more. Some said that Susan was a niece or a cousin or something; others cast the usual aspersions on the character of Burchett and even of Mrs. Burchett: you know. Women mostly, these were.

She was about five when Hawkshaw first came to town. It was his first summer behind that chair in Maxey's barber shop that Mrs Burchett brought Susan in for the first time. Maxey told me about how him and the other barbers watched Mrs Burchett trying for three days to get Susan (she was a thin little girl then, with big scared eyes and this straight, soft hair not blonde and not brunette) into the shop. And Maxey told how at last it was Hawkshaw that went out into the street and worked with the girl for about fifteen minutes until he got her into the shop and into his chair—him that hadn't never said more than Yes or No to any man or woman in the town that anybody ever saw. "Be durn if it didn't look like Hawkshaw had been waiting for her to come along," Maxey told me.

That was her first haircut. Hawkshaw gave it to her, and her sitting there under the cloth like a little scared rabbit. But six months after that she was coming to the shop by

herself and letting Hawkshaw cut her hair, still looking like
a little old rabbit, with her scared face and those big eyes
and that hair without any special name showing above the
cloth. If Hawkshaw was busy, Maxey said she would come
in and sit on the waiting bench close to his chair with her
legs sticking straight out in front of her until Hawkshaw
got done. Maxey says they considered her Hawkshaw's client
the same as if she had been a Saturday night shaving customer. He says that one time the other barber, Matt Fox,
offered to wait on her, Hawkshaw being busy, and that
Hawkshaw looked up like a flash. "I'll be done in a minute,"
he says. "I'll tend to her." Maxey told me that Hawkshaw
had been working for him for almost a year then, but that
was the first time he ever heard him speak positive about
anything.

That fall the girl started to school. She would pass the
barber shop each morning and afternoon. She was still shy,
walking fast like little girls do, with that yellow-brown head
of hers passing the window level and fast like she was on
skates. She was always by herself at first, but pretty soon
her head would be one of a clump of other heads, all talking,
not looking toward the window at all, and Hawkshaw standing there in the window, looking out. Maxey said him and
Matt would not have to look at the clock at all to tell when
five minutes to eight and to three o'clock came, because they
could tell by Hawkshaw. It was like he would kind of drift
up to the window without watching himself do it, and be
looking out about the time for the school children to begin
to pass. When she would come to the shop for a haircut,
Hawkshaw would give her two or three of those peppermints where he would give the other children just one,
Maxey told me.

No; it was Matt Fox, the other barber, told me that. He
was the one who told me about the doll Hawkshaw gave her

on Christmas. I don't know how he found it out. Hawkshaw never told him. But he knew some way; he knew more about Hawkshaw than Maxey did. He was a married man himself, Matt was. A kind of fat, flabby fellow, with a pasty face and eyes that looked tired or sad—something. A funny fellow, and almost as good a barber as Hawkshaw. He never talked much either, and I don't know how he could have known so much about Hawkshaw when a talking man couldn't get much out of him. I guess maybe a talking man hasn't got the time to ever learn much about anything except words.

Anyway, Matt told me about how Hawkshaw gave her a present every Christmas, even after she got to be a big girl. She still came to him, to his chair, and him watching her every morning and afternoon when she passed to and from school. A big girl, and she wasn't shy any more.

You wouldn't have thought she was the same girl. She got grown fast. Too fast. That was the trouble. Some said it was being an orphan and all. But it wasn't that. Girls are different from boys. Girls are born weaned and boys don't ever get weaned. You see one sixty years old, and be damned if he won't go back to the perambulator at the bat of an eye.

It's not that she was bad. There's not any such thing as a woman born bad, because they are all born bad, born with the badness in them. The thing is, to get them married before the badness comes to a natural head. But we try to make them conform to a system that says a woman can't be married until she reaches a certain age. And nature don't pay any attention to systems, let alone women paying any attention to them, or to anything. She just grew up too fast. She reached the point where the badness came to a head before the system said it was time for her to. I think they can't help it. I have a daughter of my own, and I say that.

So there she was. Matt told me they figured up and she

couldn't have been more than thirteen when Mrs Burchett
whipped her one day for using rouge and paint, and during
that year, he said, they would see her with two or three
other girls giggling and laughing on the street at all hours
when they should have been in school; still thin, with that
hair still not blonde and not brunette, with her face caked
with paint until you would have thought it would crack
like dried mud when she laughed, with the regular simple
gingham and such dresses that a thirteen-year-old child
ought to wear pulled and dragged to show off what she
never had yet to show off, like the older girls did with their
silk and crepe and such.

Matt said he watched her pass one day, when all of a
sudden he realized she never had any stockings on. He said
he thought about it and he said he could not remember that
she ever did wear stockings in the summer, until he realized
that what he had noticed was not the lack of stockings, but
that her legs were like a woman's legs: female. And her only
thirteen.

I say she couldn't help herself. It wasn't her fault. And
it wasn't Burchett's fault, either. Why, nobody can be as
gentle with them, the bad ones, the ones that are unlucky
enough to come to a head too soon, as men. Look at the
way they—all the men in town—treated Hawkshaw. Even
after folks knew, after all the talk began, there wasn't a man
of them talked before Hawkshaw. I reckon they thought
he knew too, had heard some of the talk, but whenever they
talked about her in the shop, it was while Hawkshaw was
not there. And I reckon the other men were the same, because there was not a one of them that hadn't seen Hawkshaw at the window, looking at her when she passed, or
looking at her on the street; happening to kind of be passing
the picture show when it let out and she would come out
with some fellow, having begun to go with them before she

was fourteen. Folks said how she would have to slip out and meet them and slip back into the house again with Mrs Burchett thinking she was at the home of a girl friend.

They never talked about her before Hawkshaw. They would wait until he was gone, to dinner, or on one of those two-weeks' vacations of his in April that never anybody could find out about; where he went or anything. But he would be gone, and they would watch the girl slipping around, skirting trouble, bound to get into it sooner or later, even if Burchett didn't hear something first. She had quit school a year ago. For a year Burchett and Mrs Burchett thought that she was going to school every day, when she hadn't been inside the building even. Somebody—one of the high-school boys maybe, but she never drew any lines: schoolboys, married men, anybody—would get her a report card every month and she would fill it out herself and take it home for Mrs Burchett to sign. It beats the devil how the folks that love a woman will let her fool them.

So she quit school and went to work in the ten-cent store. She would come to the shop for a haircut, all painted up, in some kind of little flimsy off-color clothes that showed her off, with her face watchful and bold and discreet all at once, and her hair gummed and twisted about her face. But even the stuff she put on it couldn't change that brown-yellow color. Her hair hadn't changed at all. She wouldn't always go to Hawkshaw's chair. Even when his chair was empty, she would sometimes take one of the others, talking to the barbers, filling the whole shop with noise and perfume and her legs sticking out from under the cloth. Hawkshaw wouldn't look at her then. Even when he wasn't busy, he had a way of looking the same: intent and down-looking like he was making out to be busy, hiding behind the making-out.

That was how it was when he left two weeks ago on that

April vacation of his, that secret trip that folks had given up
trying to find where he went ten years ago. I made Jefferson
a couple of days after he left, and I was in the shop. They
were talking about him and her.

"Is he still giving her Christmas presents?" I said.

"He bought her a wrist watch two years ago," Matt Fox
said. "Paid sixty dollars for it."

Maxey was shaving a customer. He stopped, the razor in
his hand, the blade loaded with lather. "Well, I'll be durned,"
he said. "Then he must— You reckon he was the first one,
the one that—"

Matt hadn't looked around. "He aint give it to her yet,"
he said.

"Well, durn his tight-fisted time," Maxey said. "Any old
man that will fool with a young girl, he's pretty bad. But a
fellow that will trick one and then not even pay her nothing—"

Matt looked around now; he was shaving a customer too.
"What would you say if you heard that the reason he aint
give it to her is that he thinks she is too young to receive
jewelry from anybody that aint kin to her?"

"You mean, he dont *know?* He dont know what everybody else in this town except maybe Mr and Mrs Burchett
has knowed for three years?"

Matt went back to work again, his elbow moving steady,
the razor moving in little jerks. "How would he know?
Aint anybody but a woman going to tell him. And he dont
know any women except Mrs Cowan. And I reckon she
thinks he's done heard."

"That's a fact," Maxey says.

That was how things were when he went off on his vacation two weeks ago. I worked Jefferson in a day and a half,
and went on. In the middle of the next week I reached

Division. I didn't hurry. I wanted to give him time. It was on a Wednesday morning I got there.

II

IF THERE HAD BEEN love once, a man would have said that Hawkshaw had forgotten her. Meaning love, of course. When I first saw him thirteen years ago (I had just gone on the road then, making North Mississippi and Alabama with a line of work shirts and overalls) behind a chair in the barber shop in Porterfield, I said, "Here is a bachelor born. Here is a man who was born single and forty years old."

A little, sandy-complected man with a face you would not remember and would not recognize again ten minutes later, in a blue serge suit and a black bow tie, the kind that snaps together in the back, that you buy already tied in the store. Maxey told me he was still wearing that serge suit and tie when he got off the south-bound train in Jefferson a year later, carrying one of these imitation leather suitcases. And when I saw him again in Jefferson in the next year, behind a chair in Maxey's shop, if it had not been for the chair I wouldn't have recognized him at all. Same face, same tie; be damned if it wasn't like they had picked him up, chair, customer and all, and set him down sixty miles away without him missing a lick. I had to look back out the window at the square to be sure I wasn't in Porterfield myself any time a year ago. And that was the first time I realized that when I had made Porterfield about six weeks back, he had not been there.

It was three years after that before I found out about him. I would make Division about five times a year—a store and four or five houses and a sawmill on the State line between Mississippi and Alabama. I had noticed a house there. It was a good house, one of the best there, and it was always closed.

When I would make Division in the late spring or the early summer there would always be signs of work around the house. The yard would be cleaned up of weeds, and the flower beds tended to and the fences and roof fixed. Then when I would get back to Division along in the fall or the winter, the yard would be grown up in weeds again, and maybe some of the pickets gone off the fence where folks had pulled them off to mend their own fences or maybe for firewood; I dont know. And the house would be always closed; never any smoke at the kitchen chimney. So one day I asked the storekeeper about it and he told me.

It had belonged to a man named Starnes, but the family was all dead. They were considered the best folks, because they owned some land, mortgaged. Starnes was one of these lazy men that was satisfied to be a landowner as long as he had enough to eat and a little tobacco. They had one daughter that went and got herself engaged to a young fellow, son of a tenant farmer. The mother didn't like the idea, but Starnes didn't seem to object. Maybe because the young fellow (his name was Stribling) was a hard worker; maybe because Starnes was just too lazy to object. Anyway, they were engaged and Stribling saved his money and went to Birmingham to learn barbering. Rode part of the way in wagons and walked the rest, coming back each summer to see the girl.

Then one day Starnes died, sitting in his chair on the porch; they said that he was too lazy to keep on breathing, and they sent for Stribling. I heard he had built up a good trade of his own in the Birmingham shop, saving his money; they told me he had done picked out the apartment and paid down on the furniture and all, and that they were to be married that summer. He came back. All Starnes had ever raised was a mortgage, so Stribling paid for the burial. It cost a right smart, more than Starnes was worth, but Mrs

Starnes had to be suited. So Stribling had to start saving again.

But he had already leased the apartment and paid down on the furniture and the ring and he had bought the wedding license when they sent for him again in a hurry. It was the girl this time. She had some kind of fever. These backwoods folks: you know how it is. No doctors, or veterinaries, if they are. Cut them and shoot them: that's all right. But let them get a bad cold and maybe they'll get well or maybe they'll die two days later of cholera. She was delirious when Stribling got there. They had to cut all her hair off. Stribling did that, being an expert you might say; a professional in the family. They told me she was one of these thin, unhealthy girls anyway, with a lot of straight hair not brown and not yellow.

She never knew him, never knew who cut off her hair. She died so, without knowing anything about it, without knowing even that she died, maybe. She just kept on saying, "Take care of maw. The mortgage. Paw wont like it to be left so. Send for Henry (That was him: Henry Stribling; Hawkshaw: I saw him the next year in Jefferson. "So you're Henry Stribling," I said). The mortgage. Take care of maw. Send for Henry. The mortgage. Send for Henry." Then she died. There was a picture of her, the only one they had. Hawkshaw sent it, with a lock of the hair he had cut off, to an address in a farm magazine, to have the hair made into a frame for the picture. But they both got lost, the hair and the picture, in the mail somehow. Anyway he never got either of them back.

He buried the girl too, and the next year (he had to go back to Birmingham and get shut of the apartment which he had engaged and let the furniture go so he could save again) he put a headstone over her grave. Then he went away again and they heard how he had quit the Birmingham shop.

He just quit and disappeared, and they all saying how in time he would have owned the shop. But he quit, and next April, just before the anniversary of the girl's death, he showed up again. He came to see Mrs Starnes and went away again in two weeks.

After he was gone they found out how he had stopped at the bank at the county seat and paid the interest on the mortgage. He did that every year until Mrs Starnes died. She happened to die while he was there. He would spend about two weeks cleaning up the place and fixing it so she would be comfortable for another year, and she letting him, being as she was better born than him; being as he was one of these parveynoos. Then she died too. "You know what Sophie said to do," she says. "That mortgage. Mr Starnes will be worried when I see him."

So he buried her too. He bought another headstone, to suit her. Then he begun to pay the principal on the mortgage. Starnes had some kin in Alabama. The folks in Division expected the kin to come and claim the place. But maybe the kin were waiting until Hawkshaw had got the mortgage cleared. He made the payment each year, coming back and cleaning up the place. They said he would clean up that house inside like a woman, washing and scrubbing it. It would take him two weeks each April. Then he would go away again, nobody knew where, returning each April to make the payment at the bank and clean up that empty house that never belonged to him.

He had been doing that for about five years when I saw him in Maxey's shop in Jefferson, the year after I saw him in a shop in Porterfield, in that serge suit and that black bow tie. Maxey said he had them on when he got off the south-bound train that day in Jefferson, carrying that paper suitcase. Maxey said they watched him for two days about the square, him not seeming to know anybody or to have any business or to be in any hurry; just walking about the square like he was just looking around.

It was the young fellows, the loafers that pitch dollars all day long in the clubhouse yard, waiting for the young girls to come giggling down to the post office and the soda fountain in the late afternoon, working their hips under their dresses, leaving the smell of perfume when they pass, that gave him his name. They said he was a detective, maybe because that was the last thing in the world anybody would suspect him to be. So they named him Hawkshaw, and Hawkshaw he remained for the twelve years he stayed in Jefferson, behind that chair in Maxey's shop. He told Maxey he was from Alabama.

"What part?" Maxey said. "Alabama's a big place. Birmingham?" Maxey said, because Hawkshaw looked like he might have come from almost anywhere in Alabama except Birmingham.

"Yes," Hawkshaw said. "Birmingham."

And that was all they ever got out of him until I happened to notice him behind the chair and to remember him back in Porterfield.

"Porterfield?" Maxey said. "My brother-in-law owns that shop. You mean you worked in Porterfield last year?"

"Yes," Hawkshaw said. "I was there."

Maxey told me about the vacation business. How Hawkshaw wouldn't take his summer vacation; said he wanted two weeks in April instead. He wouldn't tell why. Maxey said April was too busy for vacations, and Hawkshaw offered to work until then, and quit. "Do you want to quit then?" Maxey said that was in the summer, after Mrs Burchett had brought Susan Reed to the shop for the first time.

"No," Hawkshaw said. "I like it here. I just want two weeks off in April."

"On business?" Maxey said.

"On business," Hawkshaw said.

When Maxey took his vacation, he went to Porterfield to visit his brother-in-law; maybe shaving his brother-in-law's customers, like a sailor will spend his vacation in a rowboat on an artificial lake. The brother-in-law told him Hawkshaw had worked in his shop, would not take a vacation until April, went off and never came back. "He'll quit you the same way," the brother-in-law said. "He worked in a shop in Bolivar, Tennessee, and in one in Florence, Alabama, for a year and quit the same way. He wont come back. You watch and see."

Maxey said he came back home and he finally got it out of Hawkshaw how he had worked for a year each in six or eight different towns in Alabama and Tennessee and Mississippi. "Why did you quit them?" Maxey said. "You are a good barber; one of the best children's barbers I ever saw. Why did you quit?"

"I was just looking around," Hawkshaw said.

Then April came, and he took his two weeks. He shaved himself and packed up that paper suitcase and took the north-bound train.

"Going on a visit, I reckon," Maxey said.

"Up the road a piece," Hawkshaw said.

So he went away, in that serge suit and black bow tie. Maxey told me how, two days later, it got out how Hawkshaw had drawn from the bank his year's savings. He boarded at Mrs Cowan's and he had joined the church and he spent no money at all. He didn't even smoke. So Maxey and Matt and I reckon everybody else in Jefferson thought that he had saved up steam for a year and was now bound on one of these private sabbaticals among the fleshpots of Memphis. Mitch Ewing, the depot freight agent, lived at Mrs Cowan's too. He told how Hawkshaw had bought his ticket only to the junction-point. "From there he can go to either Memphis or Birmingham or New Orleans," Mitch said.

"Well, he's gone, anyway," Maxey said. "And mark my words, that's the last you'll see of that fellow in this town."

And that's what everybody thought until two weeks later. On the fifteenth day Hawkshaw came walking into the shop at his regular time, like he hadn't even been out of town, and took off his coat and begun to hone his razors. He never told anybody where he had been. Just up the road a piece.

Sometimes I thought I would tell them. I would make Jefferson and find him there behind that chair. He didn't change, grow any older in the face, any more than that Reed girl's hair changed, for all the gum and dye she put on it. But there he would be, back from his vacation "up the road a piece," saving his money for another year, going to church on Sunday, keeping that sack of peppermints for the children that came to him to be barbered, until it was time to take that paper suitcase and his year's savings and go back to Division to pay on the mortgage and clean up the house.

Sometimes he would be gone when I got to Jefferson, and Maxey would tell me about him cutting that Reed girl's hair, snipping and snipping it and holding the mirror up for her to see like she was an actress. "He dont charge her," Matt Fox said. "He pays the quarter into the register out of his own pocket."

"Well, that's his business," Maxey said. "All I want is the quarter. I dont care where it comes from."

Five years later maybe I would have said, "Maybe that's her price." Because she got in trouble at last. Or so they said. I dont know, except that most of the talk about girls, women, is envy or retaliation by the ones that dont dare to and the ones that failed to. But while he was gone one April they were whispering how she had got in trouble at last and had tried to doctor herself with turpentine and was bad sick.

Anyhow, she was off the streets for about three months; some said in a hospital in Memphis, and when she came into the shop again she took Matt's chair, though Hawkshaw's was empty at the time, like she had already done before to devil him, maybe. Maxey said she looked like a painted ghost, gaunt and hard, for all her bright dress and such, sitting there in Matt's chair, filling the whole shop with her talking and her laughing and her perfume and her long, naked-looking legs, and Hawkshaw making out he was busy at his empty chair.

Sometimes I thought I would tell them. But I never told anybody except Gavin Stevens. He is the district attorney, a smart man: not like the usual pedagogue lawyer and office holder. He went to Harvard, and when my health broke down (I used to be a bookkeeper in a Gordonville bank and my health broke down and I met Stevens on a Memphis train when I was coming home from the hospital) it was him that suggested I try the road and got me my position with this company. I told him about it two years ago. "And now the girl has gone bad on him, and he's too old to hunt up another one and raise her," I said. "And some day he'll have the place paid out and those Alabama Starnes can come and take it, and he'll be through. Then what do you think he will do?"

"I dont know," Stevens said.

"Maybe he'll just go off and die," I said.

"Maybe he will," Stevens said.

"Well," I said, "he wont be the first man to tilt at windmills."

"He wont be the first man to die, either," Stevens said.

III

So LAST WEEK I went on to Division. I got there on a Wednesday. When I saw the house, it had just been painted. The storekeeper told me that the payment Hawkshaw had made was the last one; that Starnes' mortgage was clear. "Them Alabama Starnes can come and take it now," he said.

"Anyway, Hawkshaw did what he promised her, promised Mrs Starnes," I said.

"Hawkshaw?" he said. "Is that what they call him? Well, I'll be durned. Hawkshaw. Well, I'll be durned."

It was three months before I made Jefferson again. When I passed the barber shop I looked in without stopping. And there was another fellow behind Hawkshaw's chair, a young fellow. "I wonder if Hawk left his sack of peppermints," I said to myself. But I didn't stop. I just thought, 'Well, he's gone at last,' wondering just where he would be when old age got him and he couldn't move again; if he would probably die behind a chair somewhere in a little three-chair country shop, in his shirt sleeves and that black tie and those serge pants.

I went on and saw my customers and had dinner, and in the afternoon I went to Stevens' office. "I see you've got a new barber in town," I said.

"Yes," Stevens said. He looked at me a while, then he said, "You haven't heard?"

"Heard what?" I said. Then he quit looking at me.

"I got your letter," he said, "that Hawkshaw had paid off the mortgage and painted the house. Tell me about it."

So I told him how I got to Division the day after Hawkshaw had left. They were talking about him on the porch of the store, wondering just when those Alabama Starnes would come in. He had painted the house himself, and he had cleaned up the two graves; I dont reckon he wanted to disturb Starnes by cleaning his. I went up to see them. He had even scrubbed the headstones, and he had set out an apple shoot over the girl's grave. It was in bloom, and what with the folks all talking about him, I got curious too, to see the inside of that house. The storekeeper had the key, and he said he reckoned it would be all right with Hawkshaw.

It was clean inside as a hospital. The stove was polished and the woodbox filled. The storekeeper told me Hawkshaw did that every year, filled the woodbox before he left. "Those Alabama kinsfolk will appreciate that," I said. We went on back to the parlor. There was a melodeon in the corner, and a lamp and a Bible on the table. The lamp was clean, the bowl empty and clean too; you couldn't even smell oil on it. That wedding license was framed, hanging above the mantel like a picture. It was dated April 4, 1905.

"Here's where he keeps that mortgage record," the storekeeper (his name is Bidwell) said. He went to the table and opened the Bible. The front page was the births and deaths, two columns. The girl's name was Sophie. I found her name in the birth column, and on the death side it was next to the last one. Mrs Starnes had written it. It looked like it might have taken her ten minutes to write it down. It looked like this:

Sofy starnes Dide april 16 th 1905

Hawkshaw wrote the last one himself; it was neat and well written, like a bookkeeper's hand:

Mrs Will Starnes. April 23, 1916.

"The record will be in the back," Bidwell said.

We turned to the back. It was there, in a neat column, in Hawkshaw's hand. It began with April 16, 1917, $200.00. The next one was when he made the next payment at the bank: April 16, 1918, $200.00; and April 16, 1919, $200.00; and April 16, 1920, $200.00; and on to the last one: April 16, 1930, $200.00. Then he had totaled the column and written under it:

"Paid in full. April 16, 1930."

It looked like a sentence written in a copy book in the old-time business colleges, like it had flourished, the pen had, in spite of him. It didn't look like it was written boastful; it just flourished somehow, the end of it, like it had run out of the pen somehow before he could stop it.

"So he did what he promised her he would," Stevens said.

"That's what I told Bidwell," I said.

Stevens went on like he wasn't listening to me much.

"So the old lady could rest quiet. I guess that's what the pen was trying to say when it ran away from him: that now she could lie quiet. And he's not much over forty-five. Not so much anyway. Not so much but what, when he wrote 'Paid in full' under that column, time and despair rushed as slow and dark under him as under any garlanded boy or crownless and crestless girl."

"Only the girl went bad on him," I said. "Forty-five's pretty late to set out to find another. He'll be fifty-five at least by then."

Stevens looked at me then. "I didn't think you had heard," he said.

"Yes," I said. "That is, I looked in the barber shop when I passed. But I knew he would be gone. I knew all the time he would move on, once he had that mortgage cleared. Maybe he never knew about the girl, anyway. Or likely he knew and didn't care."

"You think he didn't know about her?"

"I dont see how he could have helped it. But I dont know. What do you think?"

"I dont know. I dont think I want to know. I know something so much better than that."

"What's that?" I said. He was looking at me. "You keep on telling me I haven't heard the news. What is it I haven't heard?"

"About the girl," Stevens said. He looked at me.

"On the night Hawkshaw came back from his last vacation, they were married. He took her with him this time."

Centaur in Brass

IN OUR TOWN Flem Snopes now has a monument to himself, a monument of brass, none the less enduring for the fact that, though it is constantly in sight of the whole town and visible from three or four points miles out in the country, only four people, two white men and two Negroes, know that it is his monument, or that it is a monument at all.

He came to Jefferson from the country, accompanied by his wife and infant daughter and preceded by a reputation for shrewd and secret dealing. There lives in our county a sewing-machine agent named Suratt, who used to own a half interest in a small back-street restaurant in town—himself no mean hand at that technically unassailable opportunism which passes with country folks—and town folks, too—for honest shrewdness.

He travels about the county steadily and constantly, and it was through him that Snope's doings first came to our ears: how first, a clerk in a country store, Snopes one day and to everyone's astonishment was married to the store owner's daughter, a young girl who was the belle of the countryside. They were married suddenly, on the same day upon which three of the girl's erstwhile suitors left the county and were seen no more.

Soon after the wedding Snopes and his wife moved to Texas, from where the wife returned a year later with a well-grown baby. A month later Snopes himself returned, accompanied by a broad-hatted stranger and a herd of half-wild mustang ponies, which the stranger auctioned off, collected the money, and departed. Then the purchasers discovered that none of the ponies had ever had a bridle on. But they never learned if Snopes had had any part in the business, or had received any part of the money.

The next we heard of him was when he appeared one day in a wagon laden with his family and household goods, and with a bill-of-sale for Suratt's half of the restaurant. How he got the bill-of-sale, Suratt never told, and we never learned more than that there was somehow involved in the affair a worthless piece of land which had been a portion of Mrs. Snopes's dowry. But what the business was even Suratt, a humorous, talkative man who was as ready to laugh at a joke on himself as at one on anyone else, never told. But when he mentioned Snopes's name after that, it was in a tone of savage and sardonic and ungrudging admiration.

"Yes, sir," he said, "Flem Snopes outsmarted me. And the man that can do that, I just wish I was him, with this whole State of Mississippi to graze on."

In the restaurant business Snopes appeared to prosper. That is, he soon eliminated his partner, and presently he was out of the restaurant himself, with a hired manager to run it, and we began to believe in the town that we knew what was the mainspring of his rise and luck. We believed that it was his wife; we accepted without demur the evil which such little lost towns like ours seem to foist even upon men who are of good thinking despite them. She helped in the restaurant at first. We could see her there behind the wooden counter worn glass-smooth by elbows in their eating generations: young, with the rich coloring of a calendar; a face smooth, unblemished by any thought or by anything else: an appeal immediate and profound and without calculation or shame, with (because of its unblemishment and not its size) something of that vast, serene, impervious beauty of a snowclad virgin mountain flank, listening and not smiling while Major Hoxey, the town's lone rich middle-aged bachelor, graduate of Yale and soon to be mayor of the town, incongruous there among the collarless shirts and the overalls and the grave, country-eating faces, sipped his coffee and talked to her.

Not impregnable: impervious. That was why it did not need gossip when we watched Snopes's career mount beyond the restaurant and become complement with Major Hoxey's in city affairs, until less than six months after Hoxey's inauguration Snopes, who had probably never been close to any piece of machinery save a grindstone until he moved to town, was made superintendent of the municipal power plant. Mrs. Snopes was born one of those women the deeds and fortunes of whose husbands alone are the barometers of their good name; for to do her justice, there was no other handle for gossip save her husband's rise in Hoxey's administration.

But there was still that intangible thing: partly something in her air, her face; partly what we had already heard about Flem Snopes's methods. Or perhaps what we knew or believed about Snopes was all; perhaps what we thought to be her shadow was merely his shadow falling upon her. But anyway, when we saw Snopes and Hoxey together we would think of them and of adultery in the same instant, and we would think of the two of them walking and talking in amicable cuckoldry. Perhaps, as I said, this was the fault of the town. Certainly it was the fault of the town that the idea of their being on amicable terms outraged us more than the idea of the adultery itself. It seemed foreign, decadent, perverted: we could have accepted, if not condoned, the adultery had they only been natural and logical and enemies.

But they were not. Yet neither could they have been called

friends. Snopes had no friends; there was no man nor woman among us, not even Hoxey or Mrs. Snopes, who we believed could say, "I know his thought"—least of all, those among whom we saw him now and then, sitting about the stove in the rear of a certain smelly, third-rate grocery, listening and not talking, for an hour or so two or three nights a week. And so we believed that, whatever his wife was, she was not fooling him. It was another woman who did that: a Negro woman, the new young wife of Tom-Tom, the day fireman in the power plant.

Tom-Tom was black: a big bull of a man weighing two hundred pounds and sixty years old and looking about forty. He had been married about a year to his third wife, a young woman whom he kept with the strictness of a Turk in a cabin two miles from town and from the power plant where he spent twelve hours a day with shovel and bar.

One afternoon he had just finished cleaning the fires and he was sitting in the coal-bunker, resting and smoking his pipe, when Snopes, his superintendent, employer and boss, came in. The fires were clean and the steam was up again, and the safety valve on the middle boiler was blowing off.

Snopes entered: a potty man of no particular age, broad and squat, in a clean though collarless white shirt and a plaid cap. His face was round and smooth, either absolutely impenetrable or absolutely empty. His eyes were the color of stagnant water; his mouth was a tight, lipless seam. Chewing steadily, he looked up at the whistling safety valve.

"How much does that whistle weigh?" he said after a time.

"Must weight ten pound, anyway," Tom-Tom said.

"Is it solid brass?"

"If it ain't, I ain't never seed no brass what *is* solid," Tom-Tom said.

Snopes had not once looked at Tom-Tom. He continued to look upward toward the thin, shrill, excruciating sound of the valve. Then he spat, and turned and left the boiler-room.

II

HE BUILT HIS monument slowly. But then, it is always strange to what involved and complex methods a man will resort in order to steal something. It's as though there were some intangible and invisible social force that mitigates against him, confounding his own shrewdness with his own cunning, distorting in his judgment the very value of the object of his greed, which in all probability, had he but picked it up and carried it openly away, nobody would have remarked or cared. But then, that would not have suited Snopes, since he apparently had neither the high vision of a confidence man nor the unrecking courage of a brigand.

His vision at first, his aim, was not even that high; it was no higher than that of a casual tramp who pauses in passing to steal three eggs from beneath a setting hen. Or perhaps he was merely not certain yet that there really was a market for brass. Because his next move was five months after Harker, the night engineer, came on duty one evening and found the three safety whistles gone and the vents stopped with one-inch steel screw plugs capable of a pressure of a thousand pounds.

"And them three boiler heads you could poke a hole through with a soda straw!" Harker said. "And that damn black night fireman, Turl, that couldn't even read a clock face, still throwing coal into them! When I looked at the gauge on the first boiler, I never believed I would get to the last boiler in time to even reach the injector.

"So when I finally got it into Turl's head that that 100 on that dial meant where Turl would not only lose his job, he would lose it so good they wouldn't even be able to find the job to give it to the next misbegotten that believed that live steam was something you blowed on a window pane in cold weather, I got settled down enough to ask him where them safety valves had gone to.

" 'Mr. Snopes took um off,' Turl says.

" 'What in the hell for?'

" 'I don't know. I just telling you what Tom-Tom told me. He say Mr. Snopes say the shut-off float in the water tank ain't heavy enough. Say that tank start leaking some day, and so he going to fasten them three safety valves on the float and make it heavier.'

" 'You mean—' I says. That's as far as I could get: 'You mean ——'

" 'That what Tom-Tom say. I don't know nothing about it.'

"But they were gone. Up to that night, me and Turl had been catching forty winks or so now and then when we got caught up and things was quiet. But you can bet we never slept none that night. Me and him spent that whole night, time about, on that coal pile, where we could watch them three gauges. And from midnight on, after the load went off, we never had enough steam in all three of them boilers put together to run a peanut parcher. And even when I was in bed, at home, I couldn't sleep. Time I shut my eyes I would begin to see a steam gauge about the size of a washtub, with a red needle big as a shovel moving up toward a hundred pounds, and I would wake myself up hollering and sweating."

But even that wore away after a while, and then Turl and Harker were catching their forty winks or so again. Perhaps they decided that Snopes had stolen his three eggs and was done. Perhaps they decided that he had frightened himself with the ease with which he had got the eggs. Because it was five months before the next act took place.

Then one afternoon, with his fires cleaned and steam up again, Tom-Tom, smoking his pipe on the coal pile, saw Snopes enter, carrying in his hand an object which Tom-Tom said later he thought was a mule shoe. He watched

Snopes retire into a dim corner behind the boilers, where there had accumulated a miscellaneous pile of metal junk, all covered with dirt: fittings, valves, rods and bolts and such, and, kneeling there, begin to sort the pieces, touching them one by one with the mule shoe and from time to time removing one piece and tossing it behind him, into the runway. Tom-Tom watched him try with the magnet every loose piece of metal in the boiler-room, sorting out the iron from the brass: then Snopes ordered Tom-Tom to gather up the segregated pieces of brass and bring them in to his office.

Tom-Tom gathered the pieces into a box. Snopes was waiting in the office. He glanced once into the box, then he spat. "How do you and Turl get along?" he said. Turl, I had better repeat, was the night fireman; a Negro too, though he was saddle-colored where Tom-Tom was black, and in place of Tom-Tom's two hundred pounds Turl, even with his laden shovel, would hardly have tipped a hundred and fifty.

"I tends to my business," Tom-Tom said. "What Turl does wid hisn ain't no trouble of mine."

"That ain't what Turl thinks," Snopes said, chewing, watching Tom-Tom, who looked at Snopes as steadily in turn; looked down at him. "Turl wants me to give him your day shift. He says he's tired firing at night."

"Let him fire here long as I is, and he can have it," Tom-Tom said.

"Turl don't want to wait that long," Snopes said, chewing, watching Tom-Tom's face. Then he told Tom-Tom how Turl was planning to steal some iron from the plant and lay it at Tom-Tom's door and so get Tom-Tom fired. And Tom-Tom stood there, huge, hulking, with his hard round little head. "That's what he's up to," Snopes said. "So I want you to take this stuff out to your house and hide it where Turl can't find it. And as soon as I get enough evidence on Turl, I'm going to fire him."

Tom-Tom waited until Snopes had finished, blinking his eyes slowly. Then he said immediately: "I knows a better way than that."

"What way?" Snopes said. Tom-Tom didn't answer. He stood, big, humorless, a little surly; quiet; more than a little implacable though heatless. "No, no," Snopes said. "That won't do. You have any trouble with Turl, and I'll fire you both. You do like I say, unless you are tired of your job and want Turl to have it. Are you tired of it?"

"Ain't no man complained about my pressure yet," Tom-Tom said sullenly.

"Then you do like I say. You take that stuff out home with you tonight. Don't let nobody see you; not even your wife. And if you don't want to do it, just say so. I reckon I can get somebody that will do it."

And that's what Tom-Tom did. And he kept his own counsel too, even when afterward, as discarded fittings and such accumulated again, he would watch Snopes test them one by one with the magnet and sort him out another batch to take out home and hide. Because he had been firing those boilers for forty years, ever since he was a man. At that time there was but one boiler, and he had got twelve dollars a month for firing it, but now there were three, and he got sixty dollars a month; and now he was sixty, and he owned his little cabin and a little piece of corn, and a mule and a wagon in which he rode into town to church twice each Sunday, with his new young wife beside him and a gold watch and chain.

And Harker didn't know then, either, even though he would watch the junked metal accumulate in the corner and then disappear over night until it came to be his nightly joke to enter with his busy, bustling air and say to Turl: "Well, Turl, I notice that little engine is still running. There's a right smart of brass in them bushings and wrist pins, but I reckon it's moving too fast to hold that magnet against it." Then more soberly; quite soberly, in fact, without humor or irony at all, since there was some of Suratt in Harker too: "That durn fellow! I reckon he'd sell the boilers too, if he knowed of any way you and Tom-Tom could keep steam up without them."

And Turl didn't answer. Because by that time Turl had his own private temptations and worries, the same as Tom-Tom, of which Harker was also unaware.

In the meantime, the first of the year came and the city was audited.

"They come down here," Harker said, "two of them, in glasses. They went over the books and they poked around everywhere, counting everything in sight and writing it down. Then they went back to the office and they was still there at six o'clock when I come on. It seems that there was something wrong; it seems like there was some old brass parts wrote down in the books, only the brass seemed to be missing or something. It was on the books all right, and the new valves and things it had been replaced with was there. But be durn if they could find a one of them old pieces except one busted bib that had got mislaid under the work-bench someway or other. It was right strange. So I went back with them and held the light while they looked again in all the corners, getting a right smart of soot and grease on them, but that brass just naturally seemed to be plumb missing. So they went away.

"And the next morning early they come back. They had the city clerk with them this time and they beat Mr. Snopes down here and so they had to wait till he come in in his check cap and his chew, chewing and looking at them while they told him. They was right sorry; they hemmed and hawed a right smart, being sorry. But it wasn't nothing else they could do except to come back on him, long as he was the superin-

tendent; and did he want me and Turl and Tom-Tom
arrested right now, or would tomorrow do? And him standing there, chewing, with them eyes like two gobs of cup
grease on a hunk of raw dough, and them still telling him
how sorry they was.

"'How much does it come to?' he says.

"'Three hundred and four dollars and fifty-two cents, Mr.
Snopes.'

"'Is that the full amount?'

"'We checked our figures twice, Mr. Snopes.'

"'All right,' he says. And he reaches down and hauls out
the money and pays them the three hundred and four dollars
and fifty-two cents in cash, and asks for a receipt."

III

THEN THE NEXT Summer came, with Harker still laughing at
and enjoying what he saw, and seeing so little, thinking how
they were all fooling one another while he looked on, when
it was him who was being fooled. For in that Summer the
thing ripened, came to a head. Or maybe Snopes just decided
to cut his first hay crop; clean the meadow for reseeding. Because he could never have believed that on the day when he
sent for Turl, he had set the capital on his monument and
had started to tear the scaffolding down.

It was in the evening; he returned to the plant after supper
and sent for Turl; again two of them, white man and Negro,
faced one another in the office.

"What's this about you and Tom-Tom?" Snopes said.

"'Bout me and which?" Turl said. "If Tom-Tom depending on me for his trouble, he sho' done quit being a fireman
and turned waiter. It take two folks to have trouble, and
Tom-Tom ain't but one, I don't care how big he is."

Snopes watched Turl. "Tom-Tom thinks you want to fire
the day shift."

Turl looked down. He looked briefly at Snopes's face; at
the still eyes, the slow unceasing jaw, and down again. "I
can handle as much coal as Tom-Tom," he said.

Snopes watched him: the smooth, brown, aside-looking
face. "Tom-Tom knows that, too. He knows he's getting
old. But he knows there ain't nobody else can crowd him but
you." Then, watching Turl's face, Snopes told him how for
two years Tom-Tom had been stealing brass from the plant,
in order to lay it on Turl and get him fired; how only that
day Tom-Tom had told him that Turl was the thief.

Turl looked up. "That's a lie," he said. "Can't no nigger
accuse me of stealing when I ain't, I don't care how big he
is."

"Sho'," Snopes said. "So the thing to do is to get that brass
back."

"If Tom-Tom got it, I reckon Mr. Buck Conner the man
to get it back," Turl said. Buck Conner was the city marshal.

"Then you'll go to jail, sure enough. Tom-Tom'll say he
didn't know it was there. You'll be the only one that knew
it was there. So what you reckon Buck Conner'll think?
You'll be the one that knew where it was hid at, and Buck
Conner'll know that even a fool has got more sense than to
steal something and hide it in his corn-crib. The only thing
you can do is to get that brass back. Go out there in the
daytime, while Tom-Tom is at work, and get it and bring it
to me and I'll put it away somewhere to use as evidence on
Tom-Tom. Unless maybe you don't want that day shift. Just
say so, if you don't. I reckon I can find somebody else that
does."

And Turl agreed to do that. He hadn't fired any boilers
for forty years. He hadn't done anything at all for as long as
forty years, since he was just past thirty. But even if he were

a hundred, no man could ever accuse him of having done anything that would aggregate forty years net. "Unless Turl's night prowling might add up that much," Harker said. "If Turl ever gets married, he wan't need no front door a-tall; he wouldn't know what it was for. If he couldn't come tom-catting in through the back window, he wouldn't know what he come after. Would you, Turl?"

So from here on it is simple enough, since a man's mistakes, like his successes, usually are simple. Particularly the success. Perhaps that's why it is so often missed: it was just over-looked.

"His mistake was in picking out Turl to pull his chestnuts," Harker said. "But even Turl wasn't as bad as the second mistake he made at the same time without knowing it. And that was, when he forgot about that high yellow wife of Tom-Tom's. When I found out how he had picked out Turl, out of all the niggers in Jefferson, that's prowled at least once (or tried to) every gal within ten miles of town, to go out to Tom-Tom's house knowing all the time how Tom-Tom would be down here wrastling coal until seven o'clock and then have two miles to walk home, and expect Turl to spend his time out there hunting for anything that ain't hid in Tom-Tom's bed, and when I would think about Tom-Tom down here, wrastling them boilers with this same amical cuckoldry like the fellow said about Mr. Snopes and Colonel Hoxey, stealing brass so he can keep Turl from getting his job away from him, and Turl out yonder tending to Tom-Tom's home business at the same time, sometimes I think I will die.

"It was bound to not last. The question was, which would happen first: if Tom-Tom would catch Turl, or if Mr. Snopes would catch Turl, or if I would bust a blood vessel laughing some night. Well, it was Turl. He seemed to be having too much trouble locating that brass; he had been hunting it for three weeks already, coming in a little late almost every night now, with Tom-Tom having to wait until Turl come before he could start home. Maybe that was it. Or maybe Mr. Snopes was out there himself one day, hid in the bushes too, waiting for it to get along toward dark (it was already April then); him on one side of Tom-Tom's house and Turl creeping up through the corn patch on the other. Anyway, he come back down here one night and he was waiting when Turl come in about a half hour late, as usual, and Tom-Tom all ready to go home soon as Turl got here. Mr. Snopes sent for Turl and asked him if he had found it.

" 'Find it when?' Turl says.

" 'While you was out there hunting for it about dusk to-night,' Mr. Snopes says. And there's Turl, wondering just how much Mr. Snopes knows, and if he can risk saying how he has been at home in bed since six-thirty this morning, or maybe up to Mottstown on business. 'Maybe you are still looking for it in the wrong place,' Mr. Snopes says, watching Turl, and Turl not looking at Mr. Snopes except maybe now and then. 'If Tom-Tom had hid that iron in his bed, you ought to done found it three weeks ago,' Mr. Snopes says. 'So suppose you look in that corn-crib where I told you to look.'

"So Turl went out to look one more time. But he couldn't seem to find it in the corn-crib neither. Leastways, that's what he told Mr. Snopes when Mr. Snopes finally run him down back here about nine o'clock one night. Turl was on a kind of a spot, you might say. He would have to wait until along toward dark to go up to the house, and already Tom-Tom had been grumbling some about how Turl was getting later and later about coming to work every night. And once he found that brass, he would have to begin getting back to the plant at seven o'clock, and the days getting longer all the time.

"So 'Turl goes back to give one more go-round for that brass evidence. But still he can't find it. He must have looked under every shuck and thread in Tom-Tom's bed tick, but without no more success than them two audits had. He just couldn't seem to find that evidence nohow. So then Mr. Snopes says he will give Turl one more chance, and if he don't find that evidence this time, Mr. Snopes is going to tell Tom-Tom how there is a strange tom-cat on his back fence. And whenever a nigger husband in Jefferson hears that, he finds out where Turl is at before he even sharpens his razor: ain't that so, Turl?

"So the next evening Turl goes out to look again. To do or die this time. He comes creeping up out of the woods about sundown, the best time of day for brass hunting, specially as there is a moon that night. So here he comes, creeping up through the corn patch to the back porch, where the cot is, and pretty soon he can make out somebody in a white nightgown laying on the cot. But Turl don't rise up and walk even then; that ain't Turl's way. Turl plays by the rules. He creeps up—it's dust-dark by then, and the moon beginning to shine a little—all careful and quiet, and tom-cats up on to the back porch and stoops over the cot and puts his hand on nekkid meat and says, 'Honeybunch, papa's done arrived.' "

IV

IN THE VERY QUIET hearing of it I seemed to partake for the instant of Turl's horrid surprise. Because it was Tom-Tom on the cot; Tom-Tom, whom Turl believed to be at the moment two miles away, waiting for Turl to come and take over from him at the power plant.

The night before, on his return home Tom-Tom had brought with him a last year's watermelon which the local butcher had kept all Winter in cold storage and which he had given to Tom-Tom, being himself afraid to eat it, and a pint of whiskey. Tom-Tom and his wife consumed them and went to bed, where an hour later she waked Tom-Tom by her screaming. She was violently ill, and she was afraid that she was dying. She was too frightened to let Tom-Tom go for help, and while he dosed her as he could, she confessed to him about herself and Turl. As soon as she told it she became easier and went off to sleep, either before she had time to realize the enormity of what she had done, or while she was still too occupied in being alive to care.

But Tom-Tom wasn't. The next morning, after he convinced himself that she was all right, he reminded her of it. She wept some, and tried to retract; she ran the gamut of tears to anger, through denial and cajolery back to tears again. But she had Tom-Tom's face to look at all the while, and so after a time she hushed and she just lay there, watching him as he went methodically about cooking breakfast, her own and his, saying no word, apparently oblivious of even her presence. Then he fed her, made her eat, with the same detachment, implacable and without heat. She was waiting for him to leave for work; she was doubtless then and had been all the while inventing and discarding practical expedients; so busy that it was mid-morning before she realized that he had no intention of going to town, though she did not know that he had arranged to get word to the plant by seven that morning that he would take the day off.

So she lay there in the bed, quite quiet, her eyes a little wide, still as an animal, while he cooked their dinner and fed her again with that clumsy and implacable care. And just before sundown he locked her in the bedroom, she still saying no word, not asking him what he was about, just watching with her quiet, still eyes the door until it closed and the key clicked. Then Tom-Tom put on one of her nightgowns and with a naked butcher knife beside him, he lay down on the

cot on the back porch. And there he was, without having
moved for almost an hour, when Turl crept on to the porch
and touched him.

In the purely reflex action of Turl's turning to flee, Tom-
Tom rose, clutching the knife, and sprang at Turl. He leaped
astride of Turl's neck and shoulders; his weight was the impetus which sent Turl off the porch, already running when
his feet touched earth, carrying with him on the retina of his
fear a single dreadful glint of moonlight on the blade of the
lifted knife, as he crossed the back lot and, with Tom-Tom
on his back, entered the trees—the two of them a strange
and furious beast with two heads and a single pair of legs like
an inverted centaur speeding phantomlike just ahead of the
boardlike streaming of Tom-Tom's shirt-tail and just beneath
the silver glint of the lifted knife, through the moony April
woods.

"Tom-Tom big buck man," Turl said. "Make three of me.
But I sho' toted him. And whenever I would see the moon
glint that butcher knife, I could a picked up two more like
him without even stopping." He said that at first he just ran;
it was only when he found himself among the trees that it
occurred to him that his only hope was to rake Tom-Tom off
against a tree trunk. "But he helt on so tight with that one
arm that whenever I busted him into a tree, I had to bust into
the tree too. And then we'd bounce off and I'd catch that
moonglint in that nekkid knife, and I could a picked up two
more Tom-Toms.

" 'Bout that time was when Tom-Tom started squalling.
He was holding on with both hands then, so I knowed that I
had done outrun that butcher knife anyhow. But I was good
started then; my feets never paid Tom-Tom no more mind
when he started squalling to stop and let him off than they
did me. Then Tom-Tom grabbed my head with both hands
and begun to haul it around like I was a runaway bareback

mule, and then I seed the ditch. It was about forty foot deep and it looked a solid mile across, but it was too late then. My feets never even slowed up. They run far as from here to that door yonder out into nekkid air before us even begun to fall. And they was still clawing that moonlight when me and Tom-Tom hit the bottom."

The first thing I wanted to know was, what Tom-Tom used in lieu of the butcher knife which he had dropped. He didn't use anything. He and Turl just sat there in the ditch and talked. Because there is a sanctuary beyond despair for any beast which has dared all, which even its mortal enemy respects. Or maybe it was just nigger nature. Anyway, it was perfectly plain to both of them as they sat there, perhaps panting a little while they talked, that Tom-Tom's home had been outraged, not by Turl, but by Flem Snopes; that Turl's life and limbs had been endangered, not by Tom-Tom, but by Flem Snopes.

That was so plain to them that they sat there quietly in the ditch, getting their wind back, talking a little without heat like two acquaintances meeting in the street; so plain that they made their concerted plan without recourse to definite words on the subject. They merely compared notes; perhaps they laughed a little at themselves. Then they climbed out of the ditch and returned to Tom-Tom's cabin, where Tom-Tom unlocked his wife, and he and Turl sat before the hearth while the woman prepared a meal for them, which they ate as quietly but without loss of time: the two grave, scratched faces leaned to the same lamp, above the same dishes, while in the background the woman watched them, shadowy and covert and unspeaking.

Tom-Tom took her to the barn with them to help load the brass into the wagon, where Turl spoke for the first time since they climbed together out of the ditch in Harker's "amical" cuckoldry: "Great God, man, how long did it take you to tote all this stuff out here?"

"Not long," Tom-Tom said. "Been working at it 'bout two years."

It required four trips in the wagon; it was daybreak when the last load was disposed of, and the sun was rising when Turl entered the power plant, eleven hours late.

"Where in hell you been?" Harker said.

Turl glanced up at the three gauges, his scratched face wearing an expression of monkeylike gravity. "Been helping a friend of mine."

"Helping what friend of yours?"

"Boy named Turl," Turl said, squinting at the gauges.

V

"AND THAT WAS all he said," Harker said. "And me looking at that scratched face of hisn, and at the mate of it that Tom-Tom brought in at six o'clock. But Turl didn't tell me then. And I ain't the only one he never told nothing that morning. Because Mr. Snopes got there before six o'clock, before Turl had got away. He sent for Turl and asked him if he had found that brass and Turl told him no.

" 'Why didn't you find it?' Mr. Snopes said.

"Turl didn't look away, this time. 'Because it ain't no brass there. That's the main reason.'

" 'How do you know there ain't?' Mr. Snopes says.

"And Turl looked him straight in them eyes. 'Because Tom-Tom say it ain't,' Turl says.

"Maybe he ought to knew then. But a man will go to any length to fool himself; he will tell himself stuff and believe it that he would be downright mad with a fellow he had done trimmed for believing it. So now he sends for Tom-Tom.

" 'I ain't got no brass,' Tom-Tom says.

" 'Where is it, then?'

" 'It's where you said you wanted it.'

" 'Where I said I wanted it when?'

" 'When you took them whistle valves off the boilers,' Tom-Tom says.

"That's what whipped him. He didn't dare to fire neither one of them, you see. And so he'd have to see one of them there all day long every day, and know that the other one was there all night long every night; he would have to know that during every twenty-four hours that passed, one or the other of them was there, getting paid—paid, mind you, by the hour—for living half their lives right there under that tank with them four loads of brass in it that now belonged to him by right of purchase and which he couldn't claim now because now he had done waited too late.

"It sure was too late. But next New Year it got later. Come New Year's and the town got audited again; again them two spectacled fellows come down here and checked the books and went away and come back with not only the city clerk, but with Buck Conner too, with a warrant for Turl and Tom-Tom. And there they were, hemming and hawing, being sorry again, pushing one another in front to talk. It seems how they had made a mistake two years ago, and instead of three-hundred-and-four-fifty-two of this here evaporating brass, there was five-hundred-and-twenty-five dollars worth, leaving a net of over two-hundred-and-twenty dollars. And there was Buck Conner with the warrant, all ready to arrest Turl and Tom-Tom when he give the word, and it so happening that Turl and Tom-Tom was both in the boiler-room at that moment, changing shifts.

"So Snopes paid them. Dug down and hauled out the money and paid them the two-hundred-and-twenty and got his receipt. And about two hours later I happened to pass through the office. At first I didn't see nobody, because the

light was off. So I thought maybe the bulb was burned out,
seeing as that light burned all the time. But it wasn't burned
out; it was just turned out. Only before I turned it on I saw
him, setting there. So I didn't turn the light on. I just went
on out and left him setting there, setting right still."

VI

IN THOSE DAYS Snopes lived in a new little bungalow on the
edge of town, and, when shortly after that New Year he
resigned from the power plant, as the weather warmed into
Spring they would see him quite often in his tiny grassless
and treeless side yard. It was a locality of such other hopeless
little houses inhabited half by Negroes, and washed clay gul-
lies and ditches filled with scrapped automobiles and tin cans,
and the prospect was not pleasing. Yet he spent quite a lot
of his time there, sitting on the steps, not doing anything.
And so they wondered what he could be looking at there,
since there was nothing to see above the massed trees which
shaded the town itself except the low smudge of the power
plant, and the water tank. And it too was condemned now,
for the water had suddenly gone bad two years ago and the
town now had a new reservoir underground. But the tank
was a stout one and the water was still good to wash the
streets with, and so the town let it stand, refusing at one time
a quite liberal though anonymous offer to purchase and remove it.

So they wondered what Snopes was looking at. They
didn't know that he was contemplating his monument: that
shaft taller than anything in sight and filled with transient and
symbolical liquid that was not even fit to drink, but which,
for the very reason of its impermanence, was more enduring
through its fluidity and blind renewal than the brass which
poisoned it, than columns of basalt or of lead.

Dry September

I

THROUGH THE BLOODY September twilight, aftermath of
sixty-two rainless days, it had gone like a fire in dry grass—
the rumor, the story, whatever it was. Something about Miss
Minnie Cooper and a Negro. Attacked, insulted, frightened:
none of them, gathered in the barber shop on that Saturday
evening where the ceiling fan stirred, without freshening it,
the vitiated air, sending back upon them, in recurrent surges
of stale pomade and lotion, their own stale breath and odors,
knew exactly what had happened.

"Except it wasn't Will Mayes," a barber said. He was a
man of middle age; a thin, sand-colored man with a mild
face, who was shaving a client. "I know Will Mayes. He's
a good nigger. And I know Miss Minnie Cooper, too."

"What do you know about her?" a second barber said.

"Who is she?" the client said. "A young girl?"

"No," the barber said. "She's about forty, I reckon. She
aint married. That's why I dont believe—"

"Believe, hell!" a hulking youth in a sweat-stained silk
shirt said. "Wont you take a white woman's word before a
nigger's?"

"I dont believe Will Mayes did it," the barber said. "I
know Will Mayes."

"Maybe you know who did it, then. Maybe you already got him out of town, you damn niggerlover."

"I dont believe anybody did anything. I dont believe anything happened. I leave it to you fellows if them ladies that get old without getting married dont have notions that a man cant—"

"Then you are a hell of a white man," the client said. He moved under the cloth. The youth had sprung to his feet.

"You dont?" he said. "Do you accuse a white woman of lying?"

The barber held the razor poised above the half-risen client. He did not look around.

"It's this durn weather," another said. "It's enough to make a man do anything. Even to her."

Nobody laughed. The barber said in his mild, stubborn tone: "I aint accusing nobody of nothing. I just know and you fellows know how a woman that never—"

"You damn niggerlover!" the youth said.

"Shut up, Butch," another said. "We'll get the facts in plenty of time to act."

"Who is? Who's getting them?" the youth said. "Facts, hell! I—"

"You're a fine white man," the client said. "Aint you?" In his frothy beard he looked like a desert rat in the moving pictures. "You tell them, Jack," he said to the youth. "If there aint any white men in this town, you can count on me, even if I aint only a drummer and a stranger."

"That's right, boys," the barber said. "Find out the truth first. I know Will Mayes."

"Well, by God!" the youth shouted. "To think that a white man in this town—"

"Shut up, Butch," the second speaker said. "We got plenty of time."

The client sat up. He looked at the speaker. "Do you

claim that anything excuses a nigger attacking a white woman? Do you mean to tell me you are a white man and you'll stand for it? You better go back North where you came from. The South dont want your kind here."

"North what?" the second said. "I was born and raised in this town."

"Well, by God!" the youth said. He looked about with a strained, baffled gaze, as if he was trying to remember what it was he wanted to say or to do. He drew his sleeve across his sweating face. "Damn if I'm going to let a white woman—"

"You tell them, Jack," the drummer said. "By God, if they—"

The screen door crashed open. A man stood in the floor, his feet apart and his heavy-set body poised easily. His white shirt was open at the throat; he wore a felt hat. His hot, bold glance swept the group. His name was McLendon. He had commanded troops at the front in France and had been decorated for valor.

"Well," he said, "are you going to sit there and let a black son rape a white woman on the streets of Jefferson?"

Butch sprang up again. The silk of his shirt clung flat to his heavy shoulders. At each armpit was a dark halfmoon. "That's what I been telling them! That's what I—"

"Did it really happen?" a third said. "This aint the first man scare she ever had, like Hawkshaw says. Wasn't there something about a man on the kitchen roof, watching her undress, about a year ago?"

"What?" the client said. "What's that?" The barber had been slowly forcing him back into the chair; he arrested himself reclining, his head lifted, the barber still pressing him down.

McLendon whirled on the third speaker. "Happen? What

the hell difference does it make? Are you going to let the black sons get away with it until one really does it?"

"That's what I'm telling them!" Butch shouted. He cursed, long and steady, pointless.

"Here, here," a fourth said. "Not so loud. Dont talk so loud."

"Sure," McLendon said; "no talking necessary at all. I've done my talking. Who's with me?" He poised on the balls of his feet, roving his gaze.

The barber held the drummer's face down, the razor poised. "Find out the facts first, boys. I know Willy Mayes. It wasn't him. Let's get the sheriff and do this thing right."

McLendon whirled upon him his furious, rigid face. The barber did not look away. They looked like men of different races. The other barbers had ceased also above their prone clients. "You mean to tell me," McLendon said, "that you'd take a nigger's word before a white woman's? Why, you damn niggerloving—"

The third speaker rose and grasped McLendon's arm; he too had been a soldier. "Now, now. Let's figure this thing out. Who knows anything about what really happened?"

"Figure out hell!" McLendon jerked his arm free. "All that're with me get up from there. The ones that aint—" He roved his gaze, dragging his sleeve across his face.

Three men rose. The drummer in the chair sat up. "Here," he said, jerking at the cloth about his neck; "get this rag off me. I'm with him. I dont live here, but by God, if our mothers and wives and sisters—" He smeared the cloth over his face and flung it to the floor. McLendon stood in the floor and cursed the others. Another rose and moved toward him. The remainder sat uncomfortable, not looking at one another, then one by one they rose and joined him.

The barber picked the cloth from the floor. He began to

fold it neatly. "Boys, dont do that. Will Mayes never done it. I know."

"Come on," McLendon said. He whirled. From his hip pocket protruded the butt of a heavy automatic pistol. They went out. The screen door crashed behind them reverberant in the dead air.

The barber wiped the razor carefully and swiftly, and put it away, and ran to the rear, and took his hat from the wall. "I'll be back as soon as I can," he said to the other barbers. "I cant let—" He went out, running. The two other barbers followed him to the door and caught it on the rebound, leaning out and looking up the street after him. The air was flat and dead. It had a metallic taste at the base of the tongue.

"What can he do?" the first said. The second one was saying "Jees Christ, Jees Christ" under his breath. "I'd just as lief be Will Mayes as Hawk, if he gets McLendon riled."

"Jees Christ, Jees Christ," the second whispered.

"You reckon he really done it to her?" the first said.

II

SHE WAS thirty-eight or thirty-nine. She lived in a small frame house with her invalid mother and a thin, sallow, unflagging aunt, where each morning between ten and eleven she would appear on the porch in a lace-trimmed boudoir cap, to sit swinging in the porch swing until noon. After dinner she lay down for a while, until the afternoon began to cool. Then, in one of the three or four new voile dresses which she had each summer, she would go downtown to spend the afternoon in the stores with the other ladies, where they would handle the goods and haggle over the prices in cold, immediate voices, without any intention of buying.

She was of comfortable people—not the best in Jefferson,

but good people enough—and she was still on the slender side of ordinary looking, with a bright, faintly haggard manner and dress. When she was young she had had a slender, nervous body and a sort of hard vivacity which had enabled her for a time to ride upon the crest of the town's social life as exemplified by the high school party and church social period of her contemporaries while still children enough to be unclassconscious.

She was the last to realize that she was losing ground; that those among whom she had been a little brighter and louder flame than any other were beginning to learn the pleasure of snobbery—male—and retaliation—female. That was when her face began to wear that bright, haggard look. She still carried it to parties on shadowy porticoes and summer lawns, like a mask or a flag, with that bafflement of furious repudiation of truth in her eyes. One evening at a party she heard a boy and two girls, all schoolmates, talking. She never accepted another invitation.

She watched the girls with whom she had grown up as they married and got homes and children, but no man ever called on her steadily until the children of the other girls had been calling her "aunty" for several years, the while their mothers told them in bright voices about how popular Aunt Minnie had been as a girl. Then the town began to see her driving on Sunday afternoons with the cashier in the bank. He was a widower of about forty—a high-colored man, smelling always faintly of the barber shop or of whisky. He owned the first automobile in town, a red runabout; Minnie had the first motoring bonnet and veil the town ever saw. Then the town began to say: "Poor Minnie." "But she is old enough to take care of herself," others said. That was when she began to ask her old schoolmates that their children call her "cousin" instead of "aunty."

It was twelve years now since she had been relegated into

adultery by public opinion, and eight years since the cashier had gone to a Memphis bank, returning for one day each Christmas, which he spent at an annual bachelors' party at a hunting club on the river. From behind their curtains the neighbors would see the party pass, and during the over-the-way Christmas day visiting they would tell her about him, about how well he looked, and how they heard that he was prospering in the city, watching with bright, secret eyes her haggard, bright face. Usually by that hour there would be the scent of whisky on her breath. It was supplied her by a youth, a clerk at the soda fountain: "Sure; I buy it for the old gal. I reckon she's entitled to a little fun."

Her mother kept to her room altogether now; the gaunt aunt ran the house. Against that background Minnie's bright dresses, her idle and empty days, had a quality of furious unreality. She went out in the evenings only with women now, neighbors, to the moving pictures. Each afternoon she dressed in one of the new dresses and went downtown alone, where her young "cousins" were already strolling in the late afternoons with their delicate, silken heads and thin, awkward arms and conscious hips, clinging to one another or shrieking and giggling with paired boys in the soda fountain when she passed and went on along the serried store fronts, in the doors of which the sitting and lounging men did not even follow her with their eyes any more.

III

THE BARBER WENT SWIFTLY up the street where the sparse lights, insect-swirled, glared in rigid and violent suspension in the lifeless air. The day had died in a pall of dust; above the darkened square, shrouded by the spent dust, the sky was as clear as the inside of a brass bell. Below the east was a rumor of the twice-waxed moon.

When he overtook them McLendon and three others were getting into a car parked in an alley. McLendon stooped his thick head, peering out beneath the top. "Changed your mind, did you?" he said. "Damn good thing; by God, to-morrow when this town hears about how you talked to-night—"

"Now, now," the other ex-soldier said. "Hawkshaw's all right. Come on, Hawk; jump in."

"Will Mayes never done it, boys," the barber said. "If anybody done it. Why, you all know well as I do there aint any town where they got better niggers than us. And you know how a lady will kind of think things about men when there aint any reason to, and Miss Minnie anyway—"

"Sure, sure," the soldier said. "We're just going to talk to him a little; that's all."

"Talk hell!" Butch said. "When we're through with the—"

"Shut up, for God's sake!" the soldier said. "Do you want everybody in town—"

"Tell them, by God!" McLendon said. "Tell every one of the sons that'll let a white woman—"

"Let's go; let's go: here's the other car." The second car slid squealing out of a cloud of dust at the alley mouth. McLendon started his car and took the lead. Dust lay like fog in the street. The street lights hung nimbused as in water. They drove on out of town.

A rutted lane turned at right angles. Dust hung above it too, and above all the land. The dark bulk of the ice plant, where the Negro Mayes was night watchman, rose against the sky. "Better stop here, hadn't we?" the soldier said. McLendon did not reply. He hurled the car up and slammed to a stop, the headlights glaring on the blank wall.

"Listen here, boys," the barber said; "if he's here, dont that prove he never done it? Dont it? If it was him, he

would run. Dont you see he would?" The second car came
up and stopped. McLendon got down; Butch sprang down
beside him. "Listen, boys," the barber said.

"Cut the lights off!" McLendon said. The breathless dark
rushed down. There was no sound in it save their lungs as
they sought air in the parched dust in which for two months
they had lived; then the diminishing crunch of McLendon's
and Butch's feet, and a moment later McLendon's voice:

"Will! . . . Will!"

Below the east the wan hemorrhage of the moon increased.
It heaved above the ridge, silvering the air, the dust, so that
they seemed to breathe, live, in a bowl of molten lead. There
was no sound of nightbird nor insect, no sound save their
breathing and a faint ticking of contracting metal about the
cars. Where their bodies touched one another they seemed
to sweat dryly, for no more moisture came. "Christ!" a
voice said; "let's get out of here."

But they didn't move until vague noises began to grow
out of the darkness ahead; then they got out and waited
tensely in the breathless dark. There was another sound: a
blow, a hissing expulsion of breath and McLendon cursing
in undertone. They stood a moment longer, then they ran
forward. They ran in a stumbling clump, as though they
were fleeing something. "Kill him, kill the son," a voice
whispered. McLendon flung them back.

"Not here," he said. "Get him into the car." "Kill him,
kill the black son!" the voice murmured. They dragged the
Negro to the car. The barber had waited beside the car. He
could feel himself sweating and he knew he was going to be
sick at the stomach.

"What is it, captains?" the Negro said. "I aint done nothing. 'Fore God, Mr John." Someone produced handcuffs.
They worked busily about the Negro as though he were a
post, quiet, intent, getting in one another's way. He sub-

mitted to the handcuffs, looking swiftly and constantly from
dim face to dim face. "Who's here, captains?" he said, leaning to peer into the faces until they could feel his breath
and smell his sweaty reek. He spoke a name or two. "What
you all say I done, Mr John?"

McLendon jerked the car door open. "Get in!" he said.

The Negro did not move. "What you all going to do with
me, Mr John? I aint done nothing. White folks, captains, I
aint done nothing: I swear 'fore God." He called another
name.

"Get in!" McLendon said. He struck the Negro. The
others expelled their breath in a dry hissing and struck him
with random blows and he whirled and cursed them, and
swept his manacled hands across their faces and slashed the
barber upon the mouth, and the barber struck him also.
"Get him in there," McLendon said. They pushed at him.
He ceased struggling and got in and sat quietly as the others
took their places. He sat between the barber and the soldier,
drawing his limbs in so as not to touch them, his eyes going
swiftly and constantly from face to face. Butch clung to the
running board. The car moved on. The barber nursed his
mouth with his handkerchief.

"What's the matter, Hawk?" the soldier said.

"Nothing," the barber said. They regained the highroad
and turned away from town. The second car dropped back
out of the dust. They went on, gaining speed; the final
fringe of houses dropped behind.

"Goddamn, he stinks!" the soldier said.

"We'll fix that," the drummer in front beside McLendon
said. On the running board Butch cursed into the hot rush
of air. The barber leaned suddenly forward and touched
McLendon's arm.

"Let me out, John," he said.

"Jump out, niggerlover," McLendon said without turning

his head. He drove swiftly. Behind them the sourceless lights
of the second car glared in the dust. Presently McLendon
turned into a narrow road. It was rutted with disuse. It led
back to an abandoned brick kiln—a series of reddish mounds
and weed- and vine-choked vats without bottom. It had been
used for pasture once, until one day the owner missed one
of his mules. Although he prodded carefully in the vats with
a long pole, he could not even find the bottom of them.

"John," the barber said.

"Jump out, then," McLendon said, hurling the car along
the ruts. Beside the barber the Negro spoke:

"Mr Henry."

The barber sat forward. The narrow tunnel of the road
rushed up and past. Their motion was like an extinct furnace
blast: cooler, but utterly dead. The car bounded from rut
to rut.

"Mr Henry," the Negro said.

The barber began to tug furiously at the door. "Look out,
there!" the soldier said, but the barber had already kicked
the door open and swung onto the running board. The
soldier leaned across the Negro and grasped at him, but he
had already jumped. The car went on without checking
speed.

The impetus hurled him crashing through dust-sheathed
weeds, into the ditch. Dust puffed about him, and in a thin,
vicious crackling of sapless stems he lay choking and retch-
ing until the second car passed and died away. Then he rose
and limped on until he reached the highroad and turned
toward town, brushing at his clothes with his hands. The
moon was higher, riding high and clear of the dust at last,
and after a while the town began to glare beneath the dust.
He went on, limping. Presently he heard cars and the glow
of them grew in the dust behind him and he left the road
and crouched again in the weeds until they passed. Mc-

Lendon's car came last now. There were four people in it
and Butch was not on the running board.

They went on; the dust swallowed them; the glare and
the sound died away. The dust of them hung for a while,
but soon the eternal dust absorbed it again. The barber
climbed back onto the road and limped on toward town.

IV

As SHE DRESSED for supper on that Saturday evening, her
own flesh felt like fever. Her hands trembled among the
hooks and eyes, and her eyes had a feverish look, and her
hair swirled crisp and crackling under the comb. While she
was still dressing the friends called for her and sat while she
donned her sheerest underthings and stockings and a new
voile dress. "Do you feel strong enough to go out?" they
said, their eyes bright too, with a dark glitter. "When you
have had time to get over the shock, you must tell us what
happened. What he said and did; everything."

In the leafed darkness, as they walked toward the square,
she began to breathe deeply, something like a swimmer preparing to dive, until she ceased trembling, the four of them
walking slowly because of the terrible heat and out of
solicitude for her. But as they neared the square she began
to tremble again, walking with her head up, her hands
clenched at her sides, their voices about her murmurous, also
with that feverish, glittering quality of their eyes.

They entered the square, she in the center of the group,
fragile in her fresh dress. She was trembling worse. She
walked slower and slower, as children eat ice cream, her
head up and her eyes bright in the haggard banner of her
face, passing the hotel and the coatless drummers in chairs
along the curb looking around at her: "That's the one: see?
The one in pink in the middle." "Is that her? What did they

do with the nigger? Did they—?" "Sure. He's all right."
"All right, is he?" "Sure. He went on a little trip." Then the
drug store, where even the young men lounging in the doorway tipped their hats and followed with their eyes the
motion of her hips and legs when she passed.

They went on, passing the lifted hats of the gentlemen,
the suddenly ceased voices, deferent, protective. "Do you
see?" the friends said. Their voices sounded like long, hovering sighs of hissing exultation. "There's not a Negro on the
square. Not one."

They reached the picture show. It was like a miniature
fairyland with its lighted lobby and colored lithographs of
life caught in its terrible and beautiful mutations. Her lips
began to tingle. In the dark, when the picture began, it
would be all right; she could hold back the laughing so it
would not waste away so fast and so soon. So she hurried on
before the turning faces, the undertones of low astonishment, and they took their accustomed places where she could
see the aisle against the silver glare and the young men and
girls coming in two and two against it.

The lights flicked away; the screen glowed silver, and
soon life began to unfold, beautiful and passionate and sad,
while still the young men and girls entered, scented and
sibilant in the half dark, their paired backs in silhouette delicate and sleek, their slim, quick bodies awkward, divinely
young, while beyond them the silver dream accumulated,
inevitably on and on. She began to laugh. In trying to sup-
press it, it made more noise than ever; heads began to turn.
Still laughing, her friends raised her and led her out, and
she stood at the curb, laughing on a high, sustained note,
until the taxi came up and they helped her in.

They removed the pink voile and the sheer underthings
and the stockings, and put her to bed, and cracked ice for
her temples, and sent for the doctor. He was hard to locate,

so they ministered to her with hushed ejaculations, renew-
ing the ice and fanning her. While the ice was fresh and
cold she stopped laughing and lay still for a time, moaning
only a little. But soon the laughing welled again and her
voice rose screaming.

"Shhhhhhhhhhh! Shhhhhhhhhhhhhh!" they said, freshening the icepack, smoothing her hair, examining it for gray;
"poor girl!" Then to one another: "Do you suppose anything really happened?" their eyes darkly aglitter, secret and
passionate. "Shhhhhhhhhh! Poor girl! Poor Minnie!"

V

It was midnight when McLendon drove up to his neat new
house. It was trim and fresh as a birdcage and almost as
small, with its clean, green-and-white paint. He locked the
car and mounted the porch and entered. His wife rose from
a chair beside the reading lamp. McLendon stopped in the
floor and stared at her until she looked down.

"Look at that clock," he said, lifting his arm, pointing.
She stood before him, her face lowered, a magazine in her
hands. Her face was pale, strained, and weary-looking.
"Haven't I told you about sitting up like this, waiting to
see when I come in?"

"John," she said. She laid the magazine down. Poised on
the balls of his feet, he glared at her with his hot eyes, his
sweating face.

"Didn't I tell you?" He went toward her. She looked up
then. He caught her shoulder. She stood passive, looking at
him.

"Don't, John. I couldn't sleep . . . The heat; something.
Please, John. You're hurting me."

"Didn't I tell you?" He released her and half struck, half
flung her across the chair, and she lay there and watched
him quietly as he left the room.

He went on through the house, ripping off his shirt, and on the dark, screened porch at the rear he stood and mopped his head and shoulders with the shirt and flung it away. He took the pistol from his hip and laid it on the table beside the bed, and sat on the bed and removed his shoes, and rose and slipped his trousers off. He was sweating again already, and he stooped and hunted furiously for the shirt. At last he found it and wiped his body again, and, with his body pressed against the dusty screen, he stood panting. There was no movement, no sound, not even an insect. The dark world seemed to lie stricken beneath the cold moon and the lidless stars.

Death Drag

THE AIRPLANE appeared over town with almost the abruptness of an apparition. It was travelling fast; almost before we knew it was there it was already at the top of a loop; still over the square, in violation of both city and government ordinance. It was not a good loop either, performed viciously and slovenly and at top speed, as though the pilot were either a very nervous man or in a hurry, or (and this queerly: there is in our town an ex-army aviator. He was coming out of the post office when the airplane appeared going south; he watched the hurried and ungraceful loop and he made the comment) as though the pilot were trying to make the minimum of some specified manœuvre in order to save gasoline. The airplane came over the loop with one wing down, as though about to make an Immelmann turn. Then it did a half roll, the loop three-quarters complete, and without any break in the whine of the full-throttled engine and still at top speed and with that apparition-like suddenness, it disappeared eastward toward our airport. When the first small boys reached the field, the airplane was on the ground, drawn up into a fence corner at the end of the field. It was motionless and empty. There was no one in sight at all. Resting there, empty and dead, patched and shabby and painted awkwardly with a single thin coat of dead black, it gave again that illusion of ghostliness, as though it might have flown there and made that loop and landed by itself.

Our field is still in an embryonic state. Our town is built upon hills, and the field, once a cotton field, is composed of forty acres of ridge and gully, upon which, by means of grading and filling, we managed to build an X-shaped runway into the prevailing winds. The runways are long enough in themselves, but the field, like our town, is controlled by men who were of middle age when younger men first began to fly, and so the clearance is not always good. On one side is a grove of trees which the owner will not permit to be felled; on another is the barnyard of a farm: sheds and houses, a long barn with a roof of rotting shingles, a big hay-cock. The airplane had come to rest in the fence corner near the barn. The small boys and a Negro or two and a white man, descended from a halted wagon in the road, were standing quietly about it when two men in helmets and lifted goggles emerged suddenly around the corner of the barn. One was tall, in a dirty coverall. The other was quite short, in breeches and puttees and a soiled, brightly patterned overcoat which looked as if he had got wet in it and it had shrunk on him. He walked with a decided limp.

They had stopped at the corner of the barn. Without appearing to actually turn their heads, they seemed to take in at one glance the entire scene, quickly. The tall man spoke. "What town is this?"

One of the small boys told him the name of the town.

"Who lives here?" the tall man said.

"Who lives here?" the boy repeated.

"Who runs this field? Is it a private field?"

"Oh. It belongs to the town. They run it."

"Do they all live here? The ones that run it?"

The white man, the Negroes, the small boys, all watched the tall man.

"What I mean, is there anybody in this town that flies, that owns a ship? Any strangers here that fly?"

"Yes," the boy said. "There's a man lives here that flew in the war, the English army."

"Captain Warren was in the Royal Flying Corps," a second boy said.

"That's what I said," the first boy said.

"You said the English army," the second boy said.

The second man, the short one with the limp, spoke. He spoke to the tall man, quietly, in a dead voice, in the diction of Weber and Fields in vaudeville, making his *wh*'s into *v*'s and his *th*'s into *d*'s. "What does that mean?" he said.

"It's all right," the tall man said. He moved forward. "I think I know him." The short man followed, limping, terrific, crablike. The tall man had a gaunt face beneath a two-days' stubble. His eyeballs looked dirty, too, with a strained, glaring expression. He wore a dirty helmet of cheap, thin cloth, though it was January. His goggles were worn, but even we could tell that they were good ones. But then everybody quit looking at him to look at the short man; later, when we older people saw him, we said among ourselves that he had the most tragic face we had ever seen; an expression of outraged and convinced and indomitable despair, like that of a man carrying through choice a bomb which, at a certain hour each day, may or may not explode. He had a nose which would have been out of proportion to a man six feet tall. As shaped by his close helmet, the entire upper half of his head down to the end of his nose would have fitted a six-foot body. But below that, below a lateral line bisecting his head from the end of his nose to the back of his skull, his jaw, the rest of his face, was not two inches deep. His jaw was a long, flat line clapping-to beneath his nose like the jaw of a shark, so that the tip of his nose and the tip of his jaw almost touched. His goggles were merely flat pieces of window-glass held in felt frames. His helmet was leather. Down the back of it, from the top to the hem, was a long savage tear, held together top and bottom by strips of adhesive tape almost black with dirt and grease.

From around the corner of the barn there now appeared a third man, again with that abrupt immobility, as though he had materialized there out of thin air; though when they saw him he was already moving toward the group. He wore an overcoat above a neat civilian suit; he wore a cap. He was a little taller than the limping man, and broad, heavily built. He was handsome in a dull, quiet way; from his face, a man of infrequent speech. When he came up the spectators saw that he, like the limping man, was also a Jew. That is, they knew at once that two of the strangers were of a different race from themselves, without being able to say what the difference was. The boy who had first spoken probably revealed by his next speech what they thought the difference was. He, as well as the other boys, was watching the man who limped.

"Were you in the war?" the boy said. "In the air war?"

The limping man did not answer. Both he and the tall man were watching the gate. The spectators looked also and saw a car enter the gate and come down the edge of the field toward them. Three men got out of the car and approached. Again the limping man spoke quietly to the tall man: "Is that one?"

"No," the tall man said, without looking at the other. He watched the newcomers, looking from face to face. He spoke to the oldest of the three. "Morning," he said. "You run this field?"

"No," the newcomer said. "You want the secretary of the Fair Association. He's in town."

"Any charge to use it?"

"I don't know. I reckon they'll be glad to have you use it."

"Go on and pay them," the limping man said.

The three newcomers looked at the airplane with that blank, knowing, respectful air of groundlings. It reared on its muddy wheels, the propeller motionless, rigid, with a quality immobile and poised and dynamic. The nose was big with engine, the wings taut, the fuselage streaked with oil behind the rusting exhaust pipes. "Going to do some business here?" the oldest one said.

"Put you on a show," the tall man said.

"What kind of show?"

"Anything you want. Wing-walking; death-drag."

"What's that? Death-drag?"

"Drop a man onto the top of a car and drag him off again. Bigger the crowd, the more you'll get."

"You will get your money's worth," the limping man said.

The boys still watched him. "Were you in the war?" the first boy said.

The third stranger had not spoken up to this time. He now said: "Let's get on to town."

"Right," the tall man said. He said generally, in his flat, dead voice, the same voice which the three strangers all seemed to use, as though it were their common language: "Where can we get a taxi? Got one in town?"

"We'll take you to town," the men who had come up in the car said.

"We'll pay," the limping man said.

"Glad to do it," the driver of the car said. "I won't charge you anything. You want to go now?"

"Sure," the tall man said. The three strangers got into the back seat, the other three in front. Three of the boys followed them to the car.

"Lemme hang on to town, Mr. Black?" one of the boys said.

"Hang on," the driver said. The boys got onto the running boards. The car returned to town. The three in front could hear the three strangers talking in the back. They talked quietly, in low, dead voices, somehow quiet and urgent, discussing something among themselves, the tall man and the handsome one doing most of the talking. The three in front heard only one speech from the limping man: "I won't take less . . ."

"Sure," the tall man said. He leaned forward and raised his voice a little: "Where'll I find this Jones, this secretary?"

The driver told him.

"Is the newspaper or the printing shop near there? I want some handbills."

"I'll show you," the driver said. "I'll help you get fixed up."

"Fine," the tall man said. "Come out this afternoon and I'll give you a ride, if I have time."

The car stopped at the newspaper office. "You can get your handbills here," the driver said.

"Good," the tall man said. "Is Jones's office on this street?"

"I'll take you there, too," the driver said.

"You see about the editor," the tall man said. "I can find Jones, I guess." They got out of the car. "I'll come back here," the tall man said. He went on down the street, swiftly, in his dirty coverall and helmet. Two other men had joined the group before the newspaper office. They all entered, the limping man leading, followed by the three boys.

"I want some handbills," the limping man said. "Like this one." He took from his pocket a folded sheet of pink paper. He opened it; the editor, the boys, the five men, leaned to see it. The lettering was black and bold:

DEMON DUNCAN
DAREDEVIL OF THE AIR
DEATH DEFYING SHOW WILL BE GIVEN
UNDER THE AUSPICES OF . . . .
THIS P.M. AT TWO P.M.
COME ONE COME ALL AND SEE DEMON DUNCAN
DEFY DEATH IN DEATH DROP & DRAG OF DEATH

"I want them in one hour," the limping man said.

"What you want in this blank space?" the editor said.

"What you got in this town?"

"What we got?"

"What auspices? American Legion? Rotary Club? Chamber of Commerce?"

"We got all of them."

"I'll tell you which one in a minute, then," the limping man said. "When my partner gets back."

"You have to have a guarantee before you put on the show, do you?" the editor said.

"Why, sure. Do you think I should put on a daredevil without auspices? Do you think I should for a nickel maybe jump off the airplane?"

"Who's going to jump?" one of the later comers said; he was a taxi-driver.

The limping man looked at him. "Don't you worry about that," he said. "Your business is just to pay the money. We will do all the jumping you want, if you pay enough."

"I just asked which one of you all was the jumper."

"Do I ask you whether you pay me in silver or in greenbacks?" the limping man said. "Do I ask you?"

"No," the taxi-driver said.

"About these bills," the editor said. "You said you wanted them in an hour."

"Can't you begin on them, and leave that part out until my partner comes back?"

"Suppose he don't come before they are finished?"

"Well, that won't be my fault, will it?"

"All right," the editor said. "Just so you pay for them."

"You mean, I should pay without a auspices on the handbill?"

"I ain't in this business for fun," the editor said.

"We'll wait," the limping man said.

They waited.

"Were you a flyer in the war, Mister?" the boy said.

The limping man turned upon the boy his long, misshapen, tragic face. "The war? Why should I fly in a war?"

"I thought maybe because of your leg. Captain Warren limps, and he flew in the war. I reckon you just do it for fun?"

"For fun? What for fun? Fly? Gruss Gott. I hate it, I wish the man what invented them was here; I would put him into that machine yonder and I would print on his back, Do not do it, one thousand times."

"Why do you do it, then?" the man who had entered with the taxi-driver said.

"Because of that Republican Coolidge. I was in business, and that Coolidge ruined business; ruined it. That's why. For fun? Gruss Gott."

They looked at the limping man. "I suppose you have a license?" the second late-comer said.

The limping man looked at him. "A license?"

"Don't you have to have a license to fly?"

"Oh; a license. For the airplane to fly; sure, I understand. Sure. We got one. You want to see it?"

"You're supposed to show it to anybody that wants to see it, aren't you?"

"Why, sure. You want to see it?"

"Where is it?"

"Where should it be? It's nailed to the airplane, where the government put it. Did you thought maybe it was nailed to me? Did you thought maybe I had a engine on me and maybe wings? It's on the airplane. Call a taxi and go to the airplane and look at it."

"I run a taxi," the driver said.

"Well, run it. Take this gentleman out to the field where he can look at the license on the airplane."

"It'll be a quarter," the driver said. But the limping man was not looking at the driver. He was leaning against the counter. They watched him take a stick of gum from his pocket and peel it. They watched him put the gum into his mouth. "I said it'll be a quarter, Mister," the driver said.

"Was you talking to me?" the limping man said.

"I thought you wanted a taxi out to the airport."

"Me? What for? What do I want to go out to the airport for? I just come from there. I ain't the one that wants to see that license. I have already seen it. I was there when the government nailed it onto the airplane."

II

CAPTAIN WARREN, the ex-army flyer, was coming out of the store, where he met the tall man in the dirty coverall. Captain Warren told about it in the barber shop that night, when the airplane was gone.

"I hadn't seen him in fourteen years, not since I left England for the front in '17. 'So it was you that rolled out of that loop with two passengers and a twenty model Hisso smokepot?' I said.

"'Who else saw me?' he said. So he told me about it, standing there, looking over his shoulder every now and then. He was sick; a man stopped behind him to let a couple of ladies pass, and Jock whirled like he might have shot the man if he'd had a gun, and while we were in the café some one slammed a door at the back and I thought he would come out of his monkey suit. 'It's a little nervous trouble I've got,' he told me. 'I'm all right.' I had tried to get him to come out home with me for dinner, but he wouldn't. He said that he had to kind of jump himself and eat before he knew it, sort of. We had started down the street and we were passing the restaurant when he said: 'I'm going to eat,' and he turned

and ducked in like a rabbit and sat down with his back to
the wall and told Vernon to bring him the quickest thing he
had. He drank three glasses of water and then Vernon
brought him a milk bottle full and he drank most of that
before the dinner came up from the kitchen. When he took off
his helmet, I saw that his hair was pretty near white, and he
is younger than I am. Or he was, up there when we were in
Canada training. Then he told me what the name of his
nervous trouble was. It was named Ginsfarb. The little one;
the one that jumped off the ladder."

"What was the trouble?" we asked. "What were they
afraid of?"

"They were afraid of inspectors," Warren said. "They
had no licenses at all."

"There was one on the airplane."

"Yes. But it did not belong to that airplane. That one had
been grounded by an inspector when Ginsfarb bought it.
The license was for another airplane that had been wrecked,
and some one had helped Ginsfarb compound another felony
by selling the license to him. Jock had lost his license about
two years ago when he crashed a big plane full of Fourth-
of-July holidayers. Two of the engines quit, and he had to
land. The airplane smashed up some and broke a gas line,
but even then they would have been all right if a passenger
hadn't got scared (it was about dusk) and struck a match.
Jock was not so much to blame, but the passengers all burned
to death, and the government is strict. So he couldn't get a
license, and he couldn't make Ginsfarb even pay to take out
a parachute rigger's license. So they had no license at all; if
they were ever caught, they'd all go to the penitentiary."

"No wonder his hair was white," some one said.

"That wasn't what turned it white," Warren said. "I'll
tell you about that. So they'd go to little towns like this one,
fast, find out if there was anybody that might catch them,

and if there wasn't, they'd put on the show and then clear out and go to another town, staying away from the cities. They'd come in and get handbills printed while Jock and the other one would try to get underwritten by some local organization. They wouldn't let Ginsfarb do this part, because he'd stick out for his price too long and they'd be afraid to risk it. So the other two would do this, get what they could, and if they could not get what Ginsfarb told them to, they'd take what they could and then try to keep Ginsfarb fooled until it was too late. Well, this time Ginsfarb kicked up. I guess they had done it too much on him.

"So I met Jock on the street. He looked bad; I offered him a drink, but he said he couldn't even smoke any more. All he could do was drink water; he said he usually drank about a gallon during the night, getting up for it.

" 'You look like you might have to jump yourself to sleep, too,' I said.

" 'No, I sleep fine. The trouble is, the nights aren't long enough. I'd like to live at the North Pole from September to April, and at the South Pole from April to September. That would just suit me.'

" 'You aren't going to last long enough to get there,' I said.

" 'I guess so. It's a good engine. I see to that.'

" 'I mean, you'll be in jail.'

"Then he said: 'Do you think so? Do you guess I could?'

"We went on to the café. He told me about the racket, and showed me one of those Demon Duncan handbills. 'Demon Duncan?' I said.

" 'Why not? Who would pay to see a man named Ginsfarb jump from a ship?'

" 'I'd pay to see that before I'd pay to see a man named Duncan do it,' I said.

"He hadn't thought of that. Then he began to drink water,

and he told me that Ginsfarb had wanted a hundred dollars
for the stunt, but that he and the other fellow only got sixty.

" 'What are you going to do about it?' I said.

" 'Try to keep him fooled and get this thing over and get
to hell away from here,' he said.

" 'Which one is Ginsfarb?' I said. 'The little one that looks
like a shark?'

"Then he began to drink water. He emptied my glass too
at one shot and tapped it on the table. Vernon brought him
another glass. 'You must be thirsty,' Vernon said.

" 'Have you got a pitcher of it?' Jock said.

" 'I could fill you a milk bottle.'

" 'Let's have it,' Jock said. 'And give me another glass
while I'm waiting.' Then he told me about Ginsfarb, why
his hair had turned gray.

" 'How long have you been doing this?' I said.

" 'Ever since the 26th of August.'

" 'This is just January,' I said.

" 'What about it?'

" 'The 26th of August is not six months past.' "

He looked at me. Vernon brought the bottle of water.
Jock poured a glass and drank it. He began to shake, sitting
there, shaking and sweating, trying to fill the glass again.
Then he told me about it, talking fast, filling the glass and
drinking.

"Jake (the other one's name is Jake something; the good-
looking one) drives the car, the rented car. Ginsfarb swaps
onto the car from the ladder. Jock said he would have to fly
the ship into position over a Ford or a Chevrolet running on
three cylinders, trying to keep Ginsfarb from jumping from
twenty or thirty feet away in order to save gasoline in the
ship and in the rented car. Ginsfarb goes out on the bottom
wing with his ladder, fastens the ladder onto a strut, hooks
himself into the other end of the ladder, and drops off; everybody on the ground thinks that he has done what they all

came to see: fallen off and killed himself. That's what he
calls his death-drop. Then he swaps from the ladder onto the
top of the car, and the ship comes back and he catches the
ladder and is dragged off again. That's his death-drag.

"Well, up till the day when Jock's hair began to turn
white, Ginsfarb, as a matter of economy, would do it all at
once; he would get into position above the car and drop off
on his ladder and then make contact with the car, and sometimes Jock said the ship would not be in the air three minutes. Well, on this day the rented car was a bum or something; anyway, Jock had to circle the field four or five times
while the car was getting into position, and Ginsfarb, seeing
his money being blown out the exhaust pipes, finally refused
to wait for Jock's signal and dropped off anyway. It was all
right, only the distance between the ship and the car was not
as long as the rope ladder. So Ginsfarb hit on the car, and
Jock had just enough soup to zoom and drag Ginsfarb, still
on the ladder, over a high-power electric line, and he held
the ship in that climb for twenty minutes while Ginsfarb
climbed back up the ladder with his leg broken. He held the
ship in a climb with his knees, with the throttle wide open
and the engine revving about eleven hundred, while he
reached back and opened that cupboard behind the cockpit
and dragged out a suitcase and propped the stick so he could
get out on the wing and drag Ginsfarb back into the ship.
He got Ginsfarb in the ship and on the ground again and
Ginsfarb says: 'How far did we go?' and Jock told him they
had flown with full throttle for thirty minutes and Ginsfarb
says: 'Will you ruin me yet?'"

III

THE REST of this is composite. It is what we (groundlings,
dwellers in and backbone of a small town interchangeable
with and duplicate of ten thousand little dead clottings of

human life about the land) saw, refined and clarified by the expert, the man who had himself seen his own lonely and scudding shadow upon the face of the puny and remote earth.

The three strangers arrived at the field, in the rented car. When they got out of the car, they were arguing in tense, dead voices, the pilot and the handsome man against the man who limped. Captain Warren said they were arguing about the money.

"I want to see it," Ginsfarb said. They stood close; the handsome man took something from his pocket.

"There. There it is. See?" he said.

"Let me count it myself," Ginsfarb said.

"Come on, come on," the pilot hissed, in his dead, tense voice. "We tell you we got the money! Do you want an inspector to walk in and take the money and the ship too and put us in jail? Look at all these people waiting."

"You fooled me before," Ginsfarb said.

"All right," the pilot said. "Give it to him. Give him his ship too. And he can pay for the car when he gets back to town. We can get a ride in; there's a train out of here in fifteen minutes."

"You fooled me once before," Ginsfarb said.

"But we're not fooling you now. Come on. Look at all these people."

They moved toward the airplane, Ginsfarb limping ter-rifically, his back stubborn, his face tragic, outraged, cold. There was a good crowd: country people in overalls; the men a general dark clump against which the bright dresses of the women, the young girls, showed. The small boys and several men were already surrounding the airplane. We watched the limping man begin to take objects from the body of it: a parachute, a rope ladder. The handsome man went to the propeller. The pilot got into the back seat.

"Off!" he said, sudden and sharp. "Stand back, folks. We're going to wring the old bird's neck."

They tried three times to crank the engine.

"I got a mule, Mister," a countryman said. "How much'll you pay for a tow?"

The three strangers did not laugh. The limping man was busy attaching the rope ladder to one wing.

"You can't tell me," a countrywoman said. "Even he ain't that big a fool."

The engine started then. It seemed to lift bodily from the ground a small boy who stood behind it and blow him aside like a leaf. We watched it turn and trundle down the field.

"You can't tell me that thing's flying," the countrywoman said. "I reckon the Lord give me eyes. I can see it ain't flying. You folks have been fooled."

"Wait," another voice said. "He's got to turn into the wind."

"Ain't there as much wind right there or right here as there is down yonder?" the woman said. But it did fly. It turned back toward us; the noise became deafening. When it came broadside on to us, it did not seem to be going fast, yet we could see daylight beneath the wheels and the earth. But it was not going fast; it appeared rather to hang gently just above the earth until we saw that. beyond and beneath it, trees and earth in panorama were fleeing backward at dizzy speed, and then it tilted and shot skyward with a noise like a circular saw going into a white oak log. "There ain't nobody in it!" the countrywoman said. "You can't tell me!"

The third man, the handsome one in the cap, had got into the rented car. We all knew it: a battered thing which the owner would rent to any one who would make a deposit of ten dollars. He drove to the end of the field, faced down the runway, and stopped. We looked back at the airplane. It was high, coming back toward us; some one cried suddenly, his voice puny and thin: "There! Out on the wing! See?"

"It ain't!" the countrywoman said. "I don't believe it!"

"You saw them get in it," some one said.

"I don't believe it!" the woman said.

Then we sighed; we said, "Aaahhhhhhh"; beneath the wing of the airplane there was a falling dot. We knew it was a man. Some way we knew that that lonely, puny, falling shape was that of a living man like ourselves. It fell. It seemed to fall for years, yet when it checked suddenly up without visible rope or cord, it was less far from the airplane than was the end of the delicate pen-slash of the profiled wing.

"It ain't a man!" the woman shrieked.

"You know better," the man said. "You saw him get in it."

"I don't care!" the woman cried. "It ain't a man! You take me right home this minute!"

The rest is hard to tell. Not because we saw so little; we saw everything that happened, but because we had so little in experience to postulate it with. We saw that battered rented car moving down the field, going faster, jouncing in the broken January mud, then the sound of the airplane blotted it, reduced it to immobility; we saw the dangling ladder and the shark-faced man swinging on it beneath the death-colored airplane. The end of the ladder raked right across the top of the car, from end to end, with the limping man on the ladder and the capped head of the handsome man leaning out of the car. And the end of the field was coming nearer, and the airplane was travelling faster than the car, passing it. And nothing happened. "Listen!" some one cried. "They are talking to one another!"

Captain Warren told us what they were talking about, the two Jews yelling back and forth at one another: the shark-faced man on the dangling ladder that looked like a cobweb, the other one in the car; the fence, the end of the field, coming closer.

"Come on!" the man in the car shouted.

"What did they pay?"

"Jump!"

"If they didn't pay that hundred, I won't do it."

Then the airplane zoomed, roaring, the dangling figure on the gossamer ladder swinging beneath it. It circled the field twice while the man got the car into position again. Again the car started down the field; again the airplane came down with its wild, circular-saw drone which died into a splutter as the ladder and the clinging man swung up to the car from behind; again we heard the two puny voices shrieking at one another with a quality at once ludicrous and horrible: the one coming out of the very air itself, shrieking about something sweated out of the earth and without value anywhere else:

"How much did you say?"

"Jump!"

"What? How much did they pay?"

"Nothing! Jump!"

"Nothing?" the man on the ladder wailed in a fading, outraged shriek. "Nothing?" Again the airplane was dragging the ladder irrevocably past the car, approaching the end of the field, the fences, the long barn with its rotting roof. Suddenly we saw Captain Warren beside us; he was using words we had never heard him use.

"He's got the stick between his knees," Captain Warren said. "Exalted suzerain of mankind; saccharine and sacred symbol of eternal rest." We had forgot about the pilot, the man still in the airplane. We saw the airplane, tilted upward, the pilot standing upright in the back seat, leaning over the side and shaking both hands at the man on the ladder. We could hear him yelling now as again the man on the ladder was dragged over the car and past it, shrieking:

"I won't do it! I won't do it!" He was still shrieking when the airplane zoomed; we saw him, a diminishing and shrieking spot against the sky above the long roof of the barn: "I won't do it! I won't do it!" Before, when the speck left the airplane, falling, to be snubbed up by the ladder, we knew that it was a living man; again, when the speck left the ladder, falling, we knew that it was a living man, and we knew that there was no ladder to snub him up now. We saw him falling against the cold, empty January sky until the silhouette of the barn absorbed him; even from here, his attitude froglike, outraged, implacable. From somewhere in the crowd a woman screamed, though the sound was blotted out by the sound of the airplane. It reared skyward with its wild, tearing noise, the empty ladder swept backward beneath it. The sound of the engine was like a groan, a groan of relief and despair.

IV

CAPTAIN WARREN told us in the barber shop on that Saturday night.

"Did he really jump off, onto that barn?" we asked him.

"Yes. He jumped. He wasn't thinking about being killed, or even hurt. That's why he wasn't hurt. He was too mad, too in a hurry to receive justice. He couldn't wait to fly back down. Providence knew that he was too busy and that he deserved justice, so Providence put that barn there with the rotting roof. He wasn't even thinking about hitting the barn; if he'd tried to, let go of his belief in a cosmic balance to bother about landing, he would have missed the barn and killed himself."

It didn't hurt him at all, save for a long scratch on his face that bled a lot, and his overcoat was torn completely down the back, as though the tear down the back of the helmet had run on down the overcoat. He came out of the barn running before we got to it. He hobbled right among us, with his bloody face, his arms waving, his coat dangling from either shoulder.

"Where is that secretary?" he said.

"What secretary?"

"That American Legion secretary." He went on, limping fast, toward where a crowd stood about three women who had fainted. "You said you would pay a hundred dollars to see me swap to that car. We pay rent on the car and all, and now you would—"

"You got sixty dollars," some one said.

The man looked at him. "Sixty? I said one hundred. Then you would let me believe it was one hundred and it was just sixty; you would see me risk my life for sixty dollars. . . ." The airplane was down; none of us were aware of it until the pilot sprang suddenly upon the man who limped. He jerked the man around and knocked him down before we could grasp the pilot. We held the pilot, struggling, crying, the tears streaking his dirty, unshaven face. Captain Warren was suddenly there, holding the pilot.

"Stop it!" he said. "Stop it!"

The pilot ceased. He stared at Captain Warren, then he slumped and sat on the ground in his thin, dirty garment, with his unshaven face, dirty, gaunt, with his sick eyes, crying. "Go away," Captain Warren said. "Let him alone for a minute."

We went away, back to the other man, the one who limped. They had lifted him and he drew the two halves of his overcoat forward and looked at them. Then he said: "I want some chewing gum."

Some one gave him a stick. Another offered him a ciga-

rette. "Thanks," he said. "I don't burn up no money. I ain't
got enough of it yet." He put the gum into his mouth. "You
would take advantage of me. If you thought I would risk
my life for sixty dollars, you fool yourself."

"Give him the rest of it," some one said. "Here's my
share."

The limping man did not look around. "Make it up to
a hundred, and I will swap to the car like on the handbill,"
he said.

Somewhere a woman screamed behind him. She began
to laugh and to cry at the same time. "Don't . . ." she said,
laughing and crying at the same time. "Don't let . . ." until
they led her away. Still the limping man had not moved.
He wiped his face on his cuff and he was looking at his
bloody sleeve when Captain Warren came up.

"How much is he short?" Warren said. They told Warren.
He took out some money and gave it to the limping man.

"You want I should swap to the car?" he said.

"No," Warren said. "You get that crate out of here quick
as you can."

"Well, that's your business," the limping man said. "I got
witnesses I offered to swap." He moved; we made way and
watched him, in his severed and dangling overcoat, approach
the airplane. It was on the runway, the engine running. The
third man was already in the front seat. We watched the
limping man crawl terrifically in beside him. They sat there,
looking forward.

The pilot began to get up. Warren was standing beside
him. "Ground it," Warren said. "You are coming home
with me."

"I guess we'd better get on," the pilot said. He did not
look at Warren. Then he put out his hand. "Well . . ." he
said.

Warren did not take his hand. "You come on home with
me," he said.

"Who'd take care of that bastard?"

"Who wants to?"

"I'll get him right, some day. Where I can beat hell out of him."

"Jock," Warren said.

"No," the other said.

"Have you got an overcoat?"

"Sure I have."

"You're a liar." Warren began to pull off his overcoat.

"No," the other said; "I don't need it." He went on toward the machine. "See you some time," he said over his shoulder. We watched him get in, heard an airplane come to life, come alive. It passed us, already off the ground. The pilot jerked his hand once, stiffly; the two heads in the front seat did not turn nor move. Then it was gone, the sound was gone.

Warren turned. "What about that car they rented?" he said.

"He give me a quarter to take it back to town," a boy said.

"Can you drive it?"

"Yes, sir. I drove it out here. I showed him where to rent it."

"The one that jumped?"

"Yes, sir." The boy looked a little aside. "Only I'm a little scared to take it back. I don't reckon you could come with me."

"Why, scared?" Warren said.

"That fellow never paid nothing down on it, like Mr. Harris wanted. He told Mr. Harris he might not use it, but if he did use it in his show, he would pay Mr. Harris twenty dollars for it instead of ten like Mr. Harris wanted. He told me to take it back and tell Mr. Harris he never used the car. And I don't know if Mr. Harris will like it. He might get mad."

Elly

Bordering the sheer drop of the precipice, the wooden railing looked like a child's toy. It followed the curving road in thread-like embrace, passing the car in a flimsy blur. Then it flicked behind and away like a taut ribbon cut with scissors.

Then they passed the sign, the first sign, *Mills City. 6 mi* and Elly thought, with musing and irrevocable astonishment, 'Now we are almost there. It is too late now'; looking at Paul beside her, his hands on the wheel, his face in profile as he watched the fleeing road. She said, "Well. What can I do to make you marry me, Paul?" thinking 'There was a man plowing in that field, watching us when we came out of those woods with Paul carrying the motor-robe, and got back into the car,' thinking this quietly, with a certain detachment and inattention, because there was something else about to obliterate it. 'Something dreadful that I have forgotten about,' she thought, watching the swift and increasing signs which brought Mills City nearer and nearer. 'Something terrible that I shall remember in a minute,' saying aloud, quietly: "There's nothing else I can do now, is there?"

Still Paul did not look at her. "No," he said. "There's nothing else you can do."

Then she remembered what it was she had forgotten. She remembered her grandmother, thinking of the old woman

with her dead hearing and her inescapable cold eyes waiting
at Mills City, with amazed and quiet despair: 'How could
I have ever forgot about her? How could I have? How
could I?'

She was eighteen. She lived in Jefferson, two hundred
miles away, with her father and mother and grandmother,
in a biggish house. It had a deep veranda with screening
vines and no lights. In this shadow she half lay almost nightly
with a different man—youths and young men of the town
at first, but later with almost anyone, any transient in the
small town whom she met by either convention or by
chance, provided his appearance was decent. She would
never ride in their cars with them at night, and presently
they all believed that they knew why, though they did not
always give up hope at once—until the courthouse clock
struck eleven. Then for perhaps five minutes longer they
(who had been practically speechless for an hour or more)
would talk in urgent whispers:

"You must go now."

"No. Not now."

"Yes. Now."

"Why?"

"Because. I'm tired. I want to go to bed."

"I see. So far, and no mother. Is that it?"

"Maybe." In the shadow now she would be alert, cool,
already fled, without moving, beyond some secret reserve
of laughter. And he would leave, and she would enter the
dark house and look up at the single square of light which
fell upon the upper hallway, and change completely. Wearily
now, with the tread almost of an old woman, she would
mount the stairs and pass the open door of the lighted room
where her grandmother sat, erect, an open book in her
hands, facing the hall. Usually she did not look into the
room when she passed. But now and then she did. Then

for an instant they would look full at one another: the old woman cold, piercing; the girl weary, spent, her face, her dark dilated eyes, filled with impotent hatred. Then she would go on and enter her own room and lean for a time against the door, hearing the grandmother's light click off presently, sometimes crying silently and hopelessly, whispering, "The old bitch. The old bitch." Then this would pass. She would undress and look at her face in the mirror, examining her mouth now pale of paint and heavy, flattened (so she would believe) and weary and dulled with kissing, thinking 'My God. Why do I do it? What is the matter with me?' thinking of how tomorrow she must face the old woman again with the mark of last night upon her mouth like bruises, with a feeling of the pointlessness and emptiness of life more profound than the rage or the sense of persecution.

Then one afternoon at the home of a girl friend she met Paul de Montigny. After he departed the two girls were alone. Now they looked at one another quietly, like two swordsmen, with veiled eyes.

"So you like him, do you?" the friend said. "You've got queer taste, haven't you?"

"Like who?" Elly said. "I don't know who you are talking about."

"Oh yeah?" the friend said. "You didn't notice his hair then. Like a knitted cap. And his lips. Blubber, almost." Elly looked at her.

"What are you talking about?" Elly said.

"Nothing," the other said. She glanced toward the hall, then she took a cigarette from the front of her dress and lit it. "I don't know anything about it. I just heard it, too. How his uncle killed a man once that accused him of having nigger blood."

"You're lying," Elly said.

The other expelled smoke. "All right. Ask your grand-mother about his family. Didn't she used to live in Louisiana too?"

"What about you?" Elly said. "You invited him into your house."

"I wasn't hid in the cloak closet, kissing him, though."

"Oh, yeah?" Elly said. "Maybe you couldn't."

"Not till you got your face out of the way, anyhow," the other said.

That night she and Paul sat on the screened and shadowed veranda. But at eleven o'clock it was she who was urgent and tense: "No! No! Please. Please."

"Oh, come on. What are you afraid of?"

"Yes. I'm afraid. Go, please. Please."

"Tomorrow, then?"

"No. Not tomorrow or any time."

"Yes. Tomorrow."

This time she did not look in when she passed her grand-mother's door. Neither did she lean against her own door to cry. But she was panting, saying aloud against the door in thin exultation: "A nigger. A nigger. I wonder what she would say if she knew about that."

The next afternoon Paul walked up onto the veranda. Elly was sitting in the swing, her grandmother in a chair nearby. She rose and met Paul at the steps. "Why did you come here?" she said. "Why did you?" Then she turned and seemed to watch herself walking before him toward the thin old woman sitting bolt upright, sitting bolt and impla-cably chaste in that secret place, peopled with ghosts, very likely to Elly at any given moment uncountable and un-namable, who might well have owned one single mouth. She leaned down, screaming: "This is Mr. de Montigny, Grandmother!"

"What?"

"Mr. de Montigny! From Louisiana!" she screamed, and saw the grandmother, without moving below the hips, start violently backward as a snake does to strike. That was in the afternoon. That night Elly quitted the veranda for the first time. She and Paul were in a close clump of shrubbery on the lawn; in the wild close dark for that instant Elly was lost, her blood aloud with desperation and exultation and vindication too, talking inside her at the very brink of surrender loud as a voice: "I wish she were here to see! I wish she were here to see!" when something—there had been no sound—shouted at her and she made a mad awkward movement of recovery. The grandmother stood just behind and above them. When she had arrived, how long she had been there, they did not know. But there she stood, saying nothing, in the long anti-climax while Paul departed without haste and Elly stood, thinking stupidly, 'I am caught in sin without even having time to sin.' Then she was in her room, leaning against the door, trying to still her breathing, listening for the grandmother to mount the stairs and go to her father's room. But the old woman's footsteps ceased at her own door. Elly went to her bed and lay upon it without undressing, still panting, the blood still aloud. 'So,' she thought, 'it will be tomorrow. She will tell him in the morning.' Then she began to writhe, to toss lightly from side to side. 'I didn't even have a chance to sin,' she thought, with panting and amazed regret. 'She thinks I did and she will tell that I did, yet I am still virgin. She drove me to it, then prevented me at the last moment.' Then she was lying with the sun in her eyes still fully dressed. 'So it will be this morning, today,' she thought dully. 'My God. How could I. How could I. I don't want any man, anything.'

She was waiting in the dining-room when her father came down to breakfast. He said nothing, apparently knew nothing. 'Maybe it's mother she told,' Elly thought. But after a while her mother, too, appeared and departed for town also, saying nothing. 'So it has not been yet,' she thought, mounting the stairs. Her grandmother's door was closed. When she opened it, the old woman was sitting up in bed, reading a newspaper; she looked up, cold, still, implacable, while Elly screamed at her in the empty house: "What else can I do, in this little dead, hopeless town? I'll work. I don't want to be idle. Just find me a job—anything, anywhere, so that it's so far away that I'll never have to hear the word Jefferson again." She was named for the grandmother—Ailanthia, though the old woman had not heard her own name or her granddaughter's or anyone else's in almost fifteen years save when it was screamed at her as Elly now screamed: "It hadn't even happened last night! Won't you believe me? That's it. It hadn't even happened! At least, I would have had something, something . . ." with the other watching her with that cold, fixed, immobile, inescapable gaze of the very deaf. "All right!" Elly cried. "I'll get married then! Will you be satisfied then?"

That afternoon she met Paul downtown. "Was everything all right last night?" he said. "Why, what is it? Did they—"

"No. Paul, marry me." They were in the rear of the drugstore, partially concealed by the prescription counter, though anyone might appear behind it at any moment. She leaned against him, her face wan, tense, her painted mouth like a savage scar upon it. "Marry me. Or it will be too late, Paul."

"I don't marry them," Paul said. "Here. Pull yourself together."

She leaned against him, rife with promise. Her voice was wan and urgent. "We almost did last night. If you'll marry me, I will."

"You will, eh? Before or after?"

"Yes. Now. Any time."

"I'm sorry," he said.

"Not even if I will now?"

"Come on, now. Pull yourself together."

"Oh, I can hear you. But I don't believe you. And I am afraid to try and find out." She began to cry. He spoke in thin and mounting annoyance:

"Stop it, I tell you!"

"Yes. All right. I've stopped. You won't, then? I tell you, it will be too late."

"Hell, no. I don't marry them, I tell you."

"All right. Then it's good-bye. Forever."

"That's O.K. by me, too. If that's how you feel. If I ever see you again, you know what it will mean. But no marrying. And I'll see next time that we don't have any audience."

"There won't be any next time," Elly said.

The next day he was gone. A week later, her engagement was in the Memphis papers. It was to a young man whom she had known from childhood. He was assistant cashier in the bank, who they said would be president of it some day. He was a grave, sober young man of impeccable character and habits, who had been calling on her for about a year with a kind of placid formality. He took supper with the family each Sunday night, and when infrequent road shows came to town he always bought tickets for himself and Elly and her mother. When he called on her, even after the engagement was announced, they did not sit in the dark swing. Perhaps he did not know that anyone had ever sat in it in the darkness. No one sat in it at all now, and Elly passed the monotonous round of her days in a kind of dull peace. Sometimes at night she cried a little, though not often; now and then she examined her mouth in the glass and cried quietly, with quiet despair and resignation. 'Anyway I can live quietly now,' she thought. 'At least I can live out the rest of my dead life as quietly as if I were already dead.'

Then one day, without warning, as though she, too, had

accepted the armistice and the capitulation, the grandmother
departed to visit her son in Mills City. Her going seemed to
leave the house bigger and emptier than it had ever been,
as if the grandmother had been the only other actually living
person in it. There were sewing women in the house daily
now, making the trousseau, yet Elly seemed to herself to
move quietly and aimlessly, in a hiatus without thought or
sense, from empty room to empty room giving upon an
identical prospect too familiar and too peaceful to be even
saddening any longer. For long hours now she would stand
at her mother's bedroom window, watching the slow and
infinitesimal clematis tendrils as they crept and overflowed
up the screen and onto the veranda roof with the augmenting summer. Two months passed so; she would be married
in three weeks. Then one day her mother said, "Your grandmother wants to come home Sunday. Why don't you and
Philip drive down to Mills City and spend Saturday night
with your uncle, and bring her back Sunday?" Five minutes
later, at the mirror, Elly looked at her reflection as you look
at someone who has just escaped a fearful danger. 'God,'
she thought, 'what was I about to do? *What was I about
to do?*'

Within the hour she had got Paul on the telephone, leaving home to do it, taking what precautions for secrecy her
haste would afford her.

"Saturday morning?" he said.

"Yes. I'll tell mother Phi . . . he wants to leave early, at
daylight. They won't recognize you or the car. I'll be ready
and we can get away quick."

"Yes." She could hear the wire, distance; she had a feeling
of exultation, escape. "But you know what it means. If I
come back. What I told you."

"I'm not afraid. I still don't believe you, but I am not
afraid to try it now."

Again she could hear the wire. "I'm not going to marry you, Elly."

"All right, darling. I tell you I'm not afraid to try it any more. Exactly at daylight. I'll be waiting."

She went to the bank. After a time Philip was free and came to her where she waited, her face tense and wan beneath the paint, her eyes bright and hard. "There is something you must do for me. It's hard to ask, and I guess it will be hard to do."

"Of course I'll do it. What is it?"

"Grandmother is coming home Sunday. Mother wants you and me to drive down Saturday and bring her back."

"All right. I can get away Saturday."

"Yes. You see, I told you it would be hard. I don't want you to go."

"Don't want me to . . ." He looked at her bright, almost haggard face. "You want to go alone?" She didn't answer, watching him. Suddenly she came and leaned against him with a movement practiced, automatic. She took one of his arms and drew it around her. "Oh," he said. "I see. You want to go with someone else."

"Yes. I can't explain now. But I will later. But mother will never understand. She won't let me go unless she thinks it is you."

"I see." His arm was without life; she held it about her. "It's another man you want to go with."

She laughed, not loud, not long. "Don't be foolish. Yes. There's another man in the party. People you don't know and that I don't expect to see again before I am married. But mother won't understand. That's why I must ask you. Will you do it?"

"Yes. It's all right. If we can't trust one another, we haven't got any business marrying."

"Yes. We must trust one another." She released his arm.

She looked at him intently, speculatively, with a cold and curious contempt. "And you'll let mother believe . . ."

"You can trust me. You know that."

"Yes. I'm sure I can." Suddenly she held out her hand. "Good-bye."

"Good-bye?"

She leaned against him again. She kissed him. "Careful," he said. "Somebody might . . ."

"Yes. Until later, then. Until I explain." She moved back, looked at him absently, speculatively. "This is the last trouble I'll ever give you, I expect. Maybe this will be worth that to you. Good-bye."

That was Thursday afternoon. On Saturday morning, at dawn, when Paul stopped his car before the dark house, she seemed to materialize at once, already running across the lawn. She sprang into the car before he could descend and open the door, swirling down into the seat, leaning forward and taut with urgency and flight like an animal. "Hurry!" she said. "Hurry! Hurry! Hurry!"

But he held the car a moment longer. "Remember. I told you what it meant if I came back. O.K.?"

"I heard you. I tell you I'm not afraid to risk it now. Hurry! Hurry!"

And then, ten hours later, with the Mills City signs increasing with irrevocable diminishment, she said, "So you won't marry me? You won't?"

"I told you that all the time."

"Yes. But I didn't believe you. I didn't believe you. I thought that when I—after— And now there is nothing else I can do, is there?"

"No," he said.

"No," she repeated. Then she began to laugh, her voice beginning to rise.

"Elly!" he said. "Stop it, now!"

"All right," she said. "I just happened to think about my grandmother. I had forgotten her."

Pausing at the turn of the stair, Elly could hear Paul and her uncle and aunt talking in the living-room below. She stood quite still, in an attitude almost pensive, nun-like, virginal, as though posing, as though she had escaped for the moment into a place where she had forgotten where she came from and where she intended to go. Then a clock in the hall struck eleven, and she moved. She went on up the stairs quietly and went to the door of her cousin's room, which she was to occupy for the night, and entered. The grandmother sat in a low chair beside the dressing table littered with the frivolous impedimenta of a young girl . . . bottles, powder puffs, photographs, a row of dance programs stuck into the mirror frame. Elly paused. They looked at one another for a full moment before the old woman spoke: "Not contented with deceiving your parents and your friends, you must bring a Negro into my son's house as a guest."

"Grandmother!" Elly said.

"Having me sit down to table with a negro man."

"Grandmother!" Elly cried in that thin whisper, her face haggard and grimaced. She listened. Feet, voices were coming up the stairs, her aunt's voice and Paul's. "Hush!" Elly cried. "Hush!"

"What? What did you say?"

Elly ran to the chair and stooped and laid her fingers on the old woman's thin and bloodless lips and, one furiously importunate and the other furiously implacable, they glared eye to eye across the hand while the feet and the voices passed the door and ceased. Elly removed her hand. From the row of them in the mirror frame she jerked one of the cards with its silken cord and tiny futile pencil. She wrote

on the back of the card. *He is not a negro he went to Va.
and Harvard and everywhere.*

The grandmother read the card. She looked up. "I can
understand Harvard, but not Virginia. Look at his hair, his
fingernails, if you need proof. I don't. I know the name
which his people have borne for four generations." She returned the card. "That man must not sleep under this roof."

Elly took another card and scrawled swiftly. *He shall. He
is my guest. I asked him here. You are my grandmother you
would not have me treat any guest that way not even a dog.*

The grandmother read it. She sat with the card in her
hand. "He shall not drive me to Jefferson. I will not put a foot
in that car, and you shall not. We will go home on the train.
No blood of mine shall ride with him again."

Elly snatched another card, scrawled furiously. *I will.
You cannot stop me. Try and stop me.*

The grandmother read it. She looked at Elly. They glared
at one another. "Then I will have to tell your father."

Already Elly was writing again. She thrust the card at her
grandmother almost before the pencil had ceased; then in the
same motion she tried to snatch it back. But the grandmother
had already grasped the corner of it and now they glared
at one another, the card joining them like a queer umbilical
cord. "Let go!" Elly cried. "Let it go!"

"Turn loose," the grandmother said.

"Wait," Elly cried thinly, whispering, tugging at the card,
twisting it. "I made a mistake. I—" With an astonishing
movement, the grandmother bent the card up as Elly tried to
snatch it free.

"Ah," she said, then she read aloud: *Tell him. What do
you know.* "So. You didn't finish it, I see. What do I know?"

"Yes," Elly said. Then she began to speak in a fierce whisper: "Tell him! Tell him we went into a clump of trees
this morning and stayed there two hours. Tell him!" The

grandmother folded the card carefully and quietly. She rose. "Grandmother!" Elly cried.

"My stick," the grandmother said. "There; against the wall."

When she was gone Elly went to the door and turned the latch and recrossed the room. She moved quietly, getting a robe of her cousin's from the closet, and undressed, slowly, pausing to yawn terrifically. "God, I'm tired," she said aloud, yawning. She sat down at the dressing table and began to manicure her nails with the cousin's equipment. There was a small ivory clock on the dressing table. She glanced at it now and then.

Then the clock below stairs struck midnight. She sat for a moment longer with her head above her glittering nails, listening to the final stroke. Then she looked at the ivory one beside her. 'I'd hate to catch a train by you,' she thought. As she looked at it her face began again to fill with the weary despair of the afternoon. She went to the door and passed into the dark hall. She stood in the darkness, on her naked feet, her head bent, whimpering quietly to herself with bemused and childish self-pity. 'Everything's against me,' she thought. 'Everything.' When she moved, her feet made no sound. She walked with her arms extended into the darkness. She seemed to feel her eyeballs turning completely and blankly back into her skull with the effort to see. She entered the bathroom and locked the door. Then haste and urgency took her again. She ran to the angle of the wall beyond which the guest room was and stooped, cupping her voice into the angle with her hands. "Paul!" she whispered, "Paul!" holding her breath while the dying and urgent whisper failed against the cold plaster. She stooped, awkward in the borrowed robe, her blind eyes unceasing in the darkness with darting despair. She ran to the lavatory, found the tap in the darkness and tempered the drip of water to a minor but penetrating monotony. Then she opened the door and stood just within it. She heard the clock below stairs strike the half hour. She had not stirred, shaking slowly as with cold, when it struck one.

She heard Paul as soon as he left the guest room. She heard him come down the hall; she heard his hand seek the switch. When it clicked on, she found that her eyes were closed.

"What's this?" Paul said. He wore a suit of her uncle's pajamas. "What the devil—"

"Lock the door," she whispered.

"Like hell. You fool. You damned fool."

"Paul!" She held him as though she expected him to flee. She shut the door behind him and fumbled for the latch when he caught her wrist.

"Let me out of here!" he whispered.

She leaned against him, shaking slowly, holding him. Her eyes showed no iris at all. "She's going to tell daddy. She's going to tell daddy to-morrow, Paul!" Between the whispers the water dripped its unhurried minor note.

"Tell what? What does she know?"

"Put your arms around me, Paul."

"Hell, no. Let go. Let's get out of here."

"Yes. You can help it. You can keep her from telling daddy."

"How help it? Damn it, let me go!"

"She will tell, but it won't matter then. Promise. Paul. Say you will."

"Marry you? Is that what you are talking about? I told you yesterday I wouldn't. Let me go, I tell you."

"All right. All right." She spoke in an eager whisper. "I believe you now. I didn't at first, but I do now. You needn't marry me, then. You can help it without marrying me." She clung to him, her hair, her body, rich with voluptuous and fainting promise. "You won't have to marry me. Will you do it?"

"Do what?"

"Listen. You remember that curve with the little white fence, where it is so far down to the bottom? Where if a car went through that little fence. . . ."

"Yes. What about it?"

"Listen. You and she will be in the car. She won't know, won't have time to suspect. And that little old fence wouldn't stop anything and they will all say it was an accident. She is old; it wouldn't take much; maybe even the shock and you are young and maybe it won't even . . . Paul! Paul!" With each word her voice seemed to faint and die, speaking with a dying cadence out of urgency and despair while he looked down at her blanched face, at her eyes filled with desperate and voluptuous promise. "Paul!"

"And where will you be all this time?" She didn't stir, her face like a sleepwalker's. "Oh. I see. You'll go home on the train. Is that it?"

"Paul!" she said in that prolonged and dying whisper. "Paul!"

In the instant of striking her his hand, as though refusing of its own volition the office, opened and touched her face in a long, shuddering motion almost a caress. Again, gripping her by the back of the neck, he assayed to strike her; again his hand, something, refused. When he flung her away she stumbled backward into the wall. Then his feet ceased and then the water began to fill the silence with its steady and unhurried sound. After a while the clock below struck two, and she moved wearily and heavily and closed the tap.

But that did not seem to stop the sound of the water. It seemed to drip on into the silence where she lay rigid on her back in bed, not sleeping, not even thinking. It dripped on while behind the frozen grimace of her aching face she got through the ritual of breakfast and of departure, the grandmother between Paul and herself in the single seat. Even the sound of the car could not drown it out, until suddenly she realized what it was. 'It's the signboards,' she thought, watching them as they diminished in retrograde. 'I even remember that one; now it's only about two miles. I'll wait until the next one; then I will . . . now. Now.' "Paul," she said. He didn't look at her. "Will you marry me?"

"No." Neither was she looking at his face. She was watching his hands as they jockeyed the wheel slightly and constantly. Between them the grandmother sat, erect, rigid beneath the archaic black bonnet, staring straight ahead like a profile cut from parchment.

"I'm going to ask you just once more. Then it will be too late. I tell you it will be too late then, Paul . . . Paul?"

"No, I tell you. You don't love me. I don't love you. We've never said we did."

"All right. Not love, then. Will you marry me without it? Remember, it will be too late."

"No. I will not."

"But why? Why, Paul?" He didn't answer. The car fled on. Now it was the first sign which she had noticed; she thought quietly, 'We must be almost there now. It is the next curve.' She said aloud, speaking across the deafness of the old woman between them: "Why not, Paul? If it's that story about nigger blood, I don't believe it. I don't care." 'Yes,' she thought, 'this is the curve.' The road entered the curve, descending. She sat back, and then she found her grandmother looking full at her. But she did not try now to veil her face, her eyes, any more than she would have tried to conceal her voice: "Suppose I have a child?"

"Suppose you do? I can't help it now. You should have thought of that. Remember, you sent for me; I didn't ask to come back."

"No. You didn't ask. I sent for you. I made you. And this is the last time. Will you? Quick!"

"No."

"All right," she said. She sat back; at that instant the road seemed to poise and pause before plunging steeply downward beside the precipice; the white fence began to flicker past. As Elly flung the robe aside she saw her grandmother still watching her; as she lunged forward across the old woman's knees they glared eye to eye—the haggard and desperate girl and the old woman whose hearing had long since escaped everything and whose sight nothing escaped —for a profound instant of despairing ultimatum and implacable refusal. "Then die!" she cried into the old woman's face; "die!" grasping at the wheel as Paul tried to fling her back. But she managed to get her elbow into the wheel spokes with all her weight on it, sprawling across her grandmother's body, holding the wheel hard over as Paul struck her on the mouth with his fist. "Oh," she screamed, "you hit me. You *hit* me!" When the car struck the railing it flung her free, so that for an instant she lay lightly as an alighting bird upon Paul's chest, her mouth open, her eyes round with shocked surprise. "You hit me!" she wailed. Then she was falling free, alone in a complete and peaceful silence like a vacuum. Paul's face, her grandmother, the car, had disappeared, vanished as though by magic; parallel with her eyes the shattered ends of white railing, the crumbling edge of the precipice where dust whispered and a faint gout of it hung like a toy balloon, rushed mutely skyward.

Overhead somewhere a sound passed, dying away—the snore of an engine, the long hissing of tires in gravel, then the wind sighed in the trees again, shivering the crests against the sky. Against the bole of one of them the car lay in an inextricable and indistinguishable mass, and Elly sat in a litter of broken glass, staring dully at it. "Something happened," she whimpered. "He hit me. And now they are dead; it's me that's hurt, and nobody will come." She moaned a little, whimpering. Then with an air of dazed astonish-

ment she raised her hand. The palm was red and wet. She
sat whimpering quietly, digging stupidly at her palm.
"There's glass all in it and I can't even see it," she said, whimpered, gazing at her palm while the warm blood stained
slowly down upon her skirt. Again the sound rushed steadily
past high overhead, and died away. She looked up, following
it. "There goes another one," she whimpered. "They won't
even stop to see if I am hurt."

Uncle Willy

I KNOW what they said. They said I didn't run away from home but that I was tolled away by a crazy man who, if I hadn't killed him first, would have killed me inside another week. But if they had said that the women, the good women in Jefferson had driven Uncle Willy out of town and I followed him and did what I did because I knew that Uncle Willy was on his last go-round and this time when they got him again it would be for good and forever, they would have been right. Because I wasn't tolled away and Uncle Willy wasn't crazy, not even after all they had done to him. I didn't have to go; I didn't have to go any more than Uncle Willy had to invite me instead of just taking it for granted that I wanted to come. I went because Uncle Willy was the finest man I ever knew, because even women couldn't beat him, because in spite of them he wound up his life getting fun out of being alive and he died doing the thing that was the most fun of all because I was there to help him. And that's something that most men and even most women too don't get to do, not even the women that call meddling with other folks' lives fun.

He wasn't anybody's uncle, but all of us, and grown people too, called him (or thought of him) as Uncle Willy. He didn't have any kin at all except a sister in Texas married to an oil millionaire. He lived by himself in a little old neat

white house where he had been born on the edge of town,
he and an old nigger named Job Wylie that was older than
he was even, that cooked and kept the house and was the
porter at the drugstore which Uncle Willy's father had
established and which Uncle Willy ran without any other
help than old Job; and during the twelve or fourteen years
(the life of us as children and then boys), while he just used
dope, we saw a lot of him. We liked to go to his store because
it was always cool and dim and quiet inside because he never
washed the windows; he said the reason was that he never
had to bother to dress them because nobody could see in
anyway, and so the heat couldn't get in either. And he never
had any customers except country people buying patent
medicines that were already in bottles, and niggers buying
cards and dice, because nobody had let him fill a prescription
in forty years I reckon, and he never had any soda fountain
trade because it was old Job who washed the glasses and
mixed the syrups and made the ice cream ever since Uncle
Willy's father started the business in eighteen-fifty-some-
thing and so old Job couldn't see very well now, though
papa said he didn't think that old Job took dope too, it was
from breathing day and night the air which Uncle Willy
had just exhaled.

But the ice cream tasted all right to us, especially when we
came in hot from the ball games. We had a league of three
teams in town and Uncle Willy would give the prize, a ball
or a bat or a mask, for each game though he would never
come to see us play, so after the game both teams and maybe
all three would go to the store to watch the winner get the
prize. And we would eat the ice cream and then we would
all go behind the prescription case and watch Uncle Willy
light the little alcohol stove and fill the needle and roll his
sleeve up over the little blue myriad punctures starting at
his elbow and going right on up into his shirt. And the next

day would be Sunday and we would wait in our yards and
fall in with him as he passed from house to house and go on
to Sunday school, Uncle Willy with us, in the same class
with us, sitting there while we recited. Mr. Barbour from the
Sunday school never called on him. Then we would finish
the lesson and we would talk about baseball until the bell
rang and Uncle Willy still not saying anything, just sitting
there all neat and clean, with his clean collar and no tie and
weighing about a hundred and ten pounds and his eyes
behind his glasses kind of all run together like broken eggs.
Then we would all go to the store and eat the ice cream
that was left over from Saturday and then go behind the
prescription case and watch him again: the little stove and
his Sunday shirt rolled up and the needle going slow into
his blue arm and somebody would say, "Don't it hurt?" and
he would say, "No. I like it."

II

THEN THEY made him quit dope. He had been using it for
forty years, he told us once, and now he was sixty and he
had about ten years more at the outside, only he didn't tell
us that because he didn't need to tell even fourteen-year-old
boys that. But they made him quit. It didn't take them long.
It began one Sunday morning and it was finished by the
next Friday; we had just sat down in our class and Mr. Barbour had just begun, when all of a sudden Reverend Schultz,
the minister, was there, leaning over Uncle Willy and already
hauling him out of his seat when we looked around, hauling
him up and saying in that tone in which preachers speak to
fourteen-year-old boys that I don't believe even pansy boys
like: "Now, Brother Christian, I know you will hate to
leave Brother Barbour's class, but let's you and I go in and
join Brother Miller and the men and hear what he can tell

us on this beautiful and heartwarming text," and Uncle
Willy still trying to hold back and looking around at us
with his run-together eyes blinking and saying plainer than
if he had spoke it: "What's this? What's this, fellows? What
are they fixing to do to me?"

We didn't know any more than he did. We just finished
the lesson; we didn't talk any baseball that day; and we
passed the alcove where Mr. Miller's men's Bible class met,
with Reverend Schultz sitting in the middle of them like he
did every Sunday, like he was just a plain man like the rest
of them yet kind of bulging out from among the others like
he didn't have to move or speak to keep them reminded that
he wasn't a plain man; and I would always think about April
Fool's one year when Miss Callaghan called the roll and then
stepped down from her desk and said, "Now I'm going to
be a pupil today," and took a vacant seat and called out a
name and made them go to her desk and hold the lesson and
it would have been fun if you could have just quit remembering that tomorrow wouldn't be April Fool's and the day
after that wouldn't be either. And Uncle Willy was sitting
by Reverend Schultz looking littler than ever, and I thought
about one day last summer when they took a country man
named Bundren to the asylum at Jackson but he wasn't too
crazy not to know where he was going, sitting there in the
coach window handcuffed to a fat deputy sheriff that was
smoking a cigar.

Then Sunday school was over and we went out to wait
for him, to go to the store and eat the ice cream. And he
didn't come out. He didn't come out until church was over
too, the first time that he had ever stayed for church that
any of us knew of—that anybody knew of, papa told me
later—coming out with Mrs. Merridew on one side of him
and Reverend Schultz on the other still holding him by the
arm and he looking around at us again with his eyes saying

again only desperate now: "Fellows, what's this? What's this, fellows?" and Reverend Schultz shoving him into Mrs. Merridew's car and Mrs. Merridew saying, loud, like she was in the pulpit: "Now, Mr. Christian, I'm going to take you right out to my house and I'm going to fix you a nice glass of cool lemonade and then we will have a nice chicken dinner and then you are going to take a nice nap in my hammock and then Brother and Sister Schultz are coming out and we will have some nice ice cream," and Uncle Willy saying, "No. Wait, ma'am, wait! Wait! I got to go to the store and fill a prescription I promised this morning—"

So they shoved him into the car and him looking back at us where we stood there; he went out of sight like that, sitting beside Mrs. Merridew in the car like Darl Bundren and the deputy on the train, and I reckon she was holding his wrist and I reckon she never needed any handcuffs and Uncle Willy giving us that single look of amazed and desperate despair.

Because now he was already an hour past the time for his needle and that afternoon when he finally slipped away from Mrs. Merridew he was five hours past it and so he couldn't even get the key into the lock, and so Mrs. Merridew and Reverend Schultz caught him and this time he wasn't talking or looking either: he was trying to get away like a half-wild cat tries to get away. They took him to his home and Mrs. Merridew telegraphed his sister in Texas and Uncle Willy didn't come to town for three days because Mrs. Merridew and Mrs. Hovis took turn about staying in the house with him day and night until his sister could get there. That was vacation then and we played the game on Monday and that afternoon the store was still locked and Tuesday it was still locked, and so it was not until Wednesday afternoon and Uncle Willy was running fast.

He didn't have any shirt on and he hadn't shaved and he

could not get the key into the lock at all, panting and whimpering and saying, "She went to sleep at last; she went to
sleep at last," until one of us took the key and unlocked the
door. We had to light the little stove too and fill the needle
and this time it didn't go into his arm slow, it looked like
he was trying to jab it clean through the bone. He didn't go
back home. He said he wouldn't need anything to sleep on
and he gave us the money and let us out the back door and
we bought the sandwiches and the bottle of coffee from the
café and we left him there.

Then the next day, it was Mrs. Merridew and Reverend
Schultz and three more ladies; they had the marshal break in
the door and Mrs. Merridew holding Uncle Willy by the
back of the neck and shaking him and kind of whispering,
"You little wretch! You little wretch! Slip off from *me*, will
you?" and Reverend Schultz saying, "Now, Sister; now,
Sister; control yourself," and the other ladies hollering Mr.
Christian and Uncle Willy and Willy, according to how old
they were or how long they had lived in Jefferson. It didn't
take them long.

The sister got there from Texas that night and we would
walk past the house and see the ladies on the front porch or
going in and out, and now and then Reverend Schultz kind
of bulging out from among them like he would out of Mr.
Miller's Bible class, and we could crawl up behind the hedge
and hear them through the window, hear Uncle Willy crying and cussing and fighting to get out of the bed and the
ladies saying, "Now, Mr. Christian; now, Uncle Willy,"
and "Now, Bubber," too, since his sister was there; and
Uncle Willy crying and praying and cussing. And then it
was Friday, and he gave up. We could hear them holding
him in the bed; I reckon this was his last go-round, because
none of them had time to talk now; and then we heard him,
his voice weak but clear and his breath going in and out.

"Wait," he said. "Wait! I will ask it one more time. Won't you please quit? Won't you please go away? Won't you please go to hell and just let me come on at my own gait?"

"No, Mr. Christian," Mrs. Merridew said. "We are doing this to save you."

For a minute we didn't hear anything. Then we heard Uncle Willy lay back in the bed, kind of flop back.

"All right," he said. "All right."

It was like one of those sheep they would sacrifice back in the Bible. It was like it had climbed up onto the altar itself and flopped onto its back with its throat held up and said: "All right. Come on and get it over with. Cut my damn throat and go away and let me lay quiet in the fire."

III

HE WAS SICK for a long time. They took him to Memphis and they said that he was going to die. The store stayed locked all the time now, and after a few weeks we didn't even keep up the league. It wasn't just the balls and the bats. It wasn't that. We would pass the store and look at the big old lock on it and at the windows you couldn't even see through, couldn't even see inside where we used to eat the ice cream and tell him who beat and who made the good plays and him sitting there on his stool with the little stove burning and the dope boiling and bubbling and the needle waiting in his hand, looking at us with his eyes blinking and all run together behind his glasses so you couldn't even tell where the pupil was like you can in most eyes. And the niggers and the country folks that used to trade with him coming up and looking at the lock too, and asking us how he was and when he would come home and open up again. Because even after the store opened again, they would not trade with the clerk that Mrs. Merridew and Reverend

Schultz put in the store. Uncle Willy's sister said not to
bother about the store, to let it stay shut because she would
take care of Uncle Willy if he got well. But Mrs. Merridew
said no, she not only aimed to cure Uncle Willy, she was
going to give him a complete rebirth, not only into real
Christianity but into the practical world too, with a place
in it waiting for him so he could hold up his head not only
with honor but pride too among his fellow men; she said
that at first her only hope had been to fix it so he would not
have to face his Maker slave body and soul to morphine,
but now since his constitution was stronger than anybody
could have believed, she was going to see that he assumed
that position in the world which his family's name entitled
him to before he degraded it.

She and Reverend Schultz found the clerk. He had
been in Jefferson about six months. He had letters
to the church, but nobody except Reverend Schultz and
Mrs. Merridew knew anything about him. That is, they
made him the clerk in Uncle Willy's store; nobody else
knew anything about him at all. But Uncle Willy's old
customers wouldn't trade with him. And we didn't either.
Not that we had much trade to give him and we certainly
didn't expect him to give us any ice cream and I don't
reckon we would have taken it if he had offered it to us.
Because it was not Uncle Willy, and pretty soon it wasn't
even the same ice cream because the first thing the clerk
did after he washed the windows was to fire old Job, only
old Job refused to quit. He stayed around the store anyhow, mumbling to himself and the clerk would run him
out the front door and old Job would go around to the
back and come in and the clerk would find him again and
cuss him, whispering, cussing old Job good even if he did
have letters to the church; he went and swore out a warrant and the marshal told old Job he would have to stay out

of the store. Then old Job moved across the street. He would sit on the curb all day where he could watch the door and every time the clerk came in sight old Job would holler, "I ghy tell um! I ghy do hit!" So we even quit passing the store. We would cut across the corner not to pass it, with the windows clean now and the new town trade the clerk had built up—he had a lot of trade now—going in and out, just stopping long enough to ask old Job about Uncle Willy, even though we had already got what news came from Memphis about him every day and we knew that old Job would not know, would not be able to get it straight even if someone told him, since he never did believe that Uncle Willy was sick, he just believed that Mrs. Merridew had taken him away somewhere by main force and was holding him in another bed somewhere so he couldn't get up and come back home; and old Job sitting on the curb and blinking up at us with his little watery red eyes like Uncle Willy would and saying, "I ghy tell um! Holting him up dar whilst whipper-snappin' trash makin' free wid Marse Hoke Christian's sto. I ghy tell um!"

IV

UNCLE WILLY didn't die. One day he came home with his skin the color of tallow and weighing about ninety pounds now and with his eyes like broken eggs still but dead eggs, eggs that had been broken so long now that they didn't even smell dead any more—until you looked at them and saw that they were anything in the world except dead. That was after he got to know us again. I don't mean that he had forgotten about us exactly. It was like he still liked us as boys, only he had never seen us before and so he would have to learn our names and which faces the names belonged to. His sister had gone back to Texas now, because Mrs. Merridew was going to look after him until he was completely recovered, completely cured. Yes. Cured.

I remember that first afternoon when he came to town and we walked into the store and Uncle Willy looked at the clean windows that you could see through now and at the town customers that never had traded with him, and at the clerk and said, "You're my clerk, hey?" and the clerk begun to talk about Mrs. Merridew and Reverend Schultz and Uncle Willy said, "All right, all right," and now he ate some ice cream too, standing at the counter with us like he was a customer too and still looking around the store while he ate the ice cream, with those eyes that were not dead at all and he said, "Looks like you been getting more work out of my damned old nigger than I could," and the clerk began to say something else about Mrs. Merridew and Uncle Willy said, "All right, all right. Just get a holt of Job right away and tell him I am going to expect him to be here every day and that I want him to keep this store looking like this from now on." Then we went on behind the prescription case, with Uncle Willy looking around here too, at how the clerk had it neated up, with a big new lock on the cabinet where the drugs and such were kept, with those eyes that wouldn't anybody call dead, I don't care who he was, and said, "Step up there and tell that fellow I want my keys." But it wasn't the stove and the needle. Mrs. Merridew had busted both of them that day. But it wasn't that anyway, because the clerk came back and begun to talk about Mrs. Merridew and Reverend Schultz, and Uncle Willy listening and saying, "All right, all right," and we never had seen him laugh before and his face didn't change now but we knew that he was laughing behind it. Then we went out. He turned sharp off the square, down Nigger Row to Sonny Barger's store and I took the money and bought the Jamaica ginger from Sonny and caught up with them and we went home with

Uncle Willy and we sat in the pasture while he drank the Jamaica ginger and practiced our names some more.

And that night we met him where he said. He had the wheelbarrow and the crowbar and we broke open the back door and then the cabinet with the new lock on it and got the can of alcohol and carried it to Uncle Willy's and buried it in the barn. It had almost three gallons in it and he didn't come to town at all for four weeks and he was sick again, and Mrs. Merridew storming into the house, jerking out drawers and flinging things out of closets and Uncle Willy lying in the bed and watching her with those eyes that were a long way from being dead. But she couldn't find anything because it was all gone now, and besides she didn't know what it was she was looking for because she was looking for a needle. And the night Uncle Willy was up again we took the crowbar and went back to the store and when we went to the cabinet we found that it was already open and Uncle Willy's stool sitting in the door and a quart bottle of alcohol on the stool in plain sight, and that was all. And then I knew that the clerk knew who got the alcohol before but I didn't know why he hadn't told Mrs. Merridew until two years later.

I didn't know that for two years, and Uncle Willy a year now going to Memphis every Saturday in the car his sister had given him. I wrote the letter with Uncle Willy looking over my shoulder and dictating, about how his health was improving but not as fast as the doctor seemed to want and that the doctor said he ought not to walk back and forth to the store and so a car, not an expensive car, just a small car that he could drive himself or maybe find a negro boy to drive for him if his sister thought he ought not to: and she sent the money and he got a burr-headed nigger boy about my size named Secretary to drive it for him. That is, Secretary said he could drive a car; certainly he and Uncle Willy

both learned on the night trips they would make back into
the hill country to buy corn whisky and Secretary learned to
drive in Memphis pretty quick, too, because they went every
Saturday, returning Monday morning with Uncle Willy
insensible on the back seat, with his clothes smelling of that
smell whose source I was not to discover at first hand for
some years yet, and two or three half-empty bottles and a
little notebook full of telephone numbers and names like
Lorine and Billie and Jack. I didn't know it for two years,
not until that Monday morning when the sheriff came and
padlocked and sealed what was left of Uncle Willy's stock
and when they tried to find the clerk they couldn't even
find out what train he had left town on; a hot morning in
July and Uncle Willy sprawled out on the back seat, and on
the front seat with Secretary a woman twice as big as Uncle
Willy, in a red hat and a pink dress and a dirty white fur
coat over the back of the seat and two straw suitcases on the
fenders, with hair the color of a brand new brass hydrant
bib and her cheeks streaked with mascara and caked powder
where she had sweated.

It was worse than if he had started dope again. You would
have thought he had brought smallpox to town. I remember
how when Mrs. Merridew telephoned Mamma that afternoon you could hear her from away out at her house, over
the wire, clean out to the back door and the kitchen: "Married! *Married!* Whore! Whore! *Whore!*" like the clerk used
to cuss old Job, and so maybe the church can go just so
far and maybe the folks that are in it are the ones that know
the best or are entitled to say when to disconnect religion
for a minute or two. And Papa was cussing too, not cussing
anybody; I knew he was not cussing Uncle Willy or even
Uncle Willy's new wife, just like I knew that I wished Mrs.
Merridew could have been there to hear him. Only I reckon
if she had been there she couldn't have heard anything be-

cause they said she still had on a house dress when she went
and snatched Reverend Schultz into her car and went out
to Uncle Willy's, where he was still in bed like always on
Monday and Tuesday, and his new wife run Mrs. Merridew
and Reverend Schultz out of the house with the wedding
license like it was a gun or a knife. And I remember how all
that afternoon—Uncle Willy lived on a little quiet side
street where the other houses were all little new ones that
country people who had moved to town within the last fifteen years, like mail carriers and little storekeepers, lived—
how all that afternoon mad-looking ladies with sun-bonnets
on crooked came busting out of that little quiet street
dragging the little children and the grown girls with them,
heading for the mayor's office and Reverend Schultz's house,
and how the young men and the boys that didn't work and
some of the men that did would drive back and forth past
Uncle Willy's house to look at her sitting on the porch smoking cigarettes and drinking something out of a glass; and how
she came down town the next day to shop, in a black hat
now and a red-and-white striped dress so that she looked
like a great big stick of candy and three times as big as
Uncle Willy now, walking along the street with men popping
out of the stores when she passed like she was stepping on
a line of spring triggers and both sides of her behind kind
of pumping up and down inside the dress until somebody
hollered, threw back his head and squalled: "YIPPEEE!"
like that and she kind of twitched her behind without even
stopping and then they hollered sure enough.

And the next day the wire came from his sister, and Papa
for the lawyer and Mrs. Merridew for the witness went out
there and Uncle Willy's wife showed them the license and
told them to laugh that off, that Manuel Street or not she
was married as good and tight as any high-nosed bitch in
Jefferson or anywhere else and Papa saying, "Now, Mrs.

Merridew; now, Mrs. Christian," and he told Uncle Willy's wife how Uncle Willy was bankrupt now and might even lose the house too, and his wife said how about that sister in Texas, was Papa going to tell her that the oil business was bankrupt too and not to make her laugh. So they telegraphed the sister again and the thousand dollars came and they had to give Uncle Willy's wife the car too. She went back to Memphis that same afternoon, driving across the square with the straw suitcases, in a black lace dress now and already beginning to sweat again under her new makeup because it was still hot, and stopping where the men were waiting at the post office for the afternoon mail and she said, "Come on up to Manuel Street and see me sometime and I will show you hicks what you and this town can do to yourselves and one another."

And that afternoon Mrs. Merridew moved back into Uncle Willy's house and Papa said the letter she wrote Uncle Willy's sister had eleven pages to it because Papa said she would never forgive Uncle Willy for getting bankrupted. We could hear her from behind the hedge: "You're crazy, Mr. Christian; crazy. I have tried to save you and make something out of you besides a beast but now my patience is exhausted. I am going to give you one more chance. I am going to take you to Keeley and if that fails, I am going to take you myself to your sister and force her to commit you to an asylum." And the sister sent papers from Texas declaring that Uncle Willy was incompetent and making Mrs. Merridew his guardian and trustee, and Mrs. Merridew took him to the Keeley in Memphis. And that was all.

V

THAT IS, I reckon they thought that that was all, that this time Uncle Willy would surely die. Because even Papa thought that he was crazy now because even Papa said that if it hadn't been for Uncle Willy I would not have run away, and therefore I didn't run away, I was tolled away by a lunatic; it wasn't Papa, it was Uncle Robert that said that he wasn't crazy because any man who could sell Jefferson real estate for cash while shut up in a Keeley institute wasn't crazy or even drunk. Because they didn't even know that he was out of Keeley, even Mrs. Merridew didn't know it until he was gone two days and they couldn't find him. They never did find him or find out how he got out and I didn't either until I got the letter from him to take the Memphis bus on a certain day and he would meet me at a stop on the edge of Memphis. I didn't even realize that I had not seen Secretary or old Job either in two weeks. But he didn't toll me away. I went because I wanted to, because he was the finest man I ever knew, because he had had fun all his life in spite of what they had tried to do to him or with him, and I hoped that maybe if I could stay with him a while I could learn how to, so I could still have fun too when I had to get old. Or maybe I knew more than that, without knowing it, like I knew that I would do anything he asked me to do, no matter what it was, just like I helped him break into the store for the alcohol when he took it for granted that I would without asking me to at all and then helped him hide it from Mrs. Merridew. Maybe I even knew what old Job was going to do. Not what he did do, but that he would do it if the occasion arose, and that this would have to be Uncle Willy's last go-round and if I wasn't there it would be just him against all the old terrified and timid clinging to dull and rule-ridden breathing which Jefferson was to him and which, even though he had escaped Jefferson, old Job still represented.

So I cut some grass that week and I had almost two dollars. I took the bus on the day he said and he was waiting for me

at the edge of town, in a Ford now without any top on it and
you could still read the chalk letters, $85 *cash* on the wind-
shield, and a brand new tent folded up in the back of it and
Uncle Willy and old Job in the front seat, and Uncle Willy
looked fine with a checked cap new except for a big oil
stain, with the bill turned round behind and a pair of goggles
cocked up on the front of it and his celluloid collar freshly
washed and no tie in it and his nose peeling with sunburn
and his eyes bright behind his glasses. I would have gone
with him anywhere; I would do it over again right now,
knowing what was going to happen. He would not have to
ask me now any more than he did then. So I got on top of the
tent and we didn't go toward town, we went the other way.
I asked where we were going but he just said wait, rushing
the little car along like he couldn't get there quick enough
himself, and I could tell from his voice that this was fine, this
was the best yet, better than anybody else could have thought
about doing, and old Job hunched down in the front seat,
holding on with both hands and yelling at Uncle Willy about
going so fast. Yes. Maybe I knew from old Job even then
that Uncle Willy may have escaped Jefferson but he had
just dodged it; he hadn't gotten away.

Then we came to the sign, the arrow that said Airport, and
we turned and I said: "What? What is it?" but Uncle Willy
just said: "Wait; just wait," like he couldn't hardly wait
himself, hunched over the wheel with his white hair blowing under his cap and his collar riding up behind so you
could see his neck between the collar and the shirt; and old
Job saying (Oh yes, I could tell even then): "He got hit, all
right. He done done hit. But I done tole him. Nemmine.
I done warned him." Then we came to the airport and Uncle
Willy stopped quick and pointed up without even getting
out and said, "Look."

It was an airplane flying around and Uncle Willy running

up and down the edge of the field waving his handkerchief until it saw him and came down and landed and rolled up to us, a little airplane with a two-cylinder engine. It was Secretary, in another new checked cap and goggles like Uncle Willy's and they told me how Uncle Willy had bought one for old Job too but old Job wouldn't wear it. And that night —we stayed in a little tourist camp about two miles away and he had a cap and goggles all ready for me too; and then I knew why they hadn't been able to find him—Uncle Willy told me how he had bought the airplane with some of the money he had sold his house for after his sister saved it because she had been born in it too, but that Captain Bean at the airport wouldn't teach him to run it himself because he would need a permit from a doctor ("By God," Uncle Willy said, "damn if these Republicans and Democrats and XYZ's ain't going to have it soon where a man can't even flush the toilet in his own bathroom.") and he couldn't go to the doctor because the doctor might want to send him back to the Keeley or tell Mrs. Merridew where he was. So he just let Secretary learn to run it first and now Secretary had been running it for two weeks, which was almost fourteen days longer than he had practiced on the car before they started out with it. So Uncle Willy bought the car and tent and camping outfit yesterday and tomorrow we were going to start. We would go first to a place named Renfro where nobody knew us and where there was a big pasture that Uncle Willy had found out about and we would stay there a week while Secretary taught Uncle Willy to run the airplane. Then we would head west. When we ran out of the house money we would stop at a town and take up passengers and make enough to buy gasoline and food to get to the next town, Uncle Willy and Secretary in the airplane and me and old Job in the car; and old Job sitting in a chair against the wall, blinking at Uncle Willy with his little weak

red sullen eyes, and Uncle Willy reared up on the cot with
his cap and goggles still on and his collar without any tie (it
wasn't fastened to his shirt at all: just buttoned around his
neck) sometimes sideways and sometimes even backward
like an Episcopal minister's, and his eyes bright behind his
glasses and his voice bright and fine. "And by Christmas we
will be in California!" he said. "Think of that. California!"

VI

So how could they say that I had to be tolled away? How
could they? I suppose I knew then that it wouldn't work,
couldn't work, that it was too fine to be true. I reckon I even
knew how it was going to end just from the glum way Secretary acted whenever Uncle Willy talked about learning to
run the airplane himself, just as I knew from the way old Job
looked at Uncle Willy, not what he did of course, but what
he would do if the occasion arose. Because I was the other
white one. I was white, even if old Job and Secretary were
both older than me, so it would be all right; I could do it all
right. It was like I knew even then that, no matter what
might happen to him, he wouldn't ever die and I thought
that if I could just learn to live like he lived, no matter what
might happen to me I wouldn't ever die either.

So we left the next morning, just after daylight because
there was another fool rule that Secretary would have to
stay in sight of the field until they gave him a license to go
away. We filled the airplane with gas and Secretary went
up in it just like he was going up to practice. Then Uncle
Willy got us into the car quick because he said the airplane
could make sixty miles an hour and so Secretary would be
at Renfro a long while before we got there. But when we
got to Renfro Secretary wasn't there and we put the tent up
and ate dinner and he still didn't come and Uncle Willy

beginning to cuss and we ate supper and dark came but Secretary didn't and Uncle Willy was cussing good now. He didn't come until the next day. We heard him and ran out and watched him fly right over us, coming from the opposite direction of Memphis, going fast and us all hollering and waving. But he went on, with Uncle Willy jumping up and down and cussing, and we were loading the tent into the car to try to catch him when he came back. We didn't hear him at all now and we could see the propeller because it wasn't running and it looked like Secretary wasn't even going to light in the pasture but he was going to light in some trees on the edge of it. But he skinned by them and kind of bumped down and we ran up and found him still sitting in the airplane with his eyes closed and his face the color of wood ashes and he said, "Captin, will you please tell me where to find Ren——" before he even opened his eyes to see who we were. He said he had landed seven times yesterday and it wouldn't be Renfro and they would tell him how to get to Renfro and he would go there and that wouldn't be Renfro either and he had slept in the airplane last night and he hadn't eaten since we left Memphis because he had spent the three dollars Uncle Willy gave him for gasoline and if he hadn't run out of gas when he did he wouldn't never have found us.

Uncle Willy wanted me to go to town and get some more gas so he could start learning to run it right away but Secretary wouldn't. He just refused. He said the airplane belonged to Uncle Willy and he reckoned he belonged to Uncle Willy too, leastways until he got back home, but that he had flown all he could stand for a while. So Uncle Willy started the next morning.

I thought for a while that I would have to throw old Job down and hold him and him hollering, "Don't you git in dat thing!" and still hollering, "I ghy tell um! I ghy tell um!"

while we watched the airplane with Secretary and Uncle Willy in it kind of jump into the air and then duck down like Uncle Willy was trying to take the short cut to China and then duck up again and get to going pretty straight at last and fly around the pasture and then turn down to land, and every day old Job hollering at Uncle Willy and field hands coming up out of the fields and folks in wagons and walking stopping in the road to watch them and the airplane coming down, passing us with Uncle Willy and Secretary side by side and looking exactly alike, I don't mean in the face but exactly alike like two tines of a garden fork look exactly like just before they chop into the ground; we could see Secretary's eyes and his mouth run out so you could almost hear him saying, "Hooooooooo!" and Uncle Willy's glasses shining and his hair blowing from under his cap and his celluloid collar that he washed every night before he went to bed and no tie in it and they would go by, fast, and old Job hollering, "You git outer dar! You git outer dat thing!" and we could hear Secretary too: "Turn hit loose, Unker Willy! Turn hit *loose!*" and the airplane would go on, ducking up one second and down the next and with one wing higher than the other one second and lower the next and then it would be traveling sideways and maybe it would hit the ground sideways the first time, with a kind of crashing sound and the dust spurting up and then bounce off again and Secretary hollering, "Unker Willy! *Turn loose!*" and at night in the tent Uncle Willy's eyes would still be shining and he would be too excited to stop talking and go to sleep and I don't believe he even remembered that he had not taken a drink since he first thought about buying the airplane.

Oh yes, I know what they said about me after it was all over, what Papa said when he and Mrs. Merridew got there that morning, about me being the white one, almost a man, and Secretary and old Job just irresponsible niggers, yet it was old Job and Secretary who tried to prevent him. Because that was it; that was what they couldn't understand.

I remember the last night and Secretary and old Job both working on him, when old Job finally made Secretary tell Uncle Willy that he would never learn to fly, and Uncle Willy stopped talking and stood up and looked at Secretary. "Didn't you learn to run it in two weeks?" he said. Secretary said yes. "You, a damn, trifling, worthless, ignorant, burr-headed nigger?" and Secretary said yes. "And me that graduated from a university and ran a fifteen-thousand-dollar business for forty years, yet you tell me I can't learn to run a damn little fifteen-hundred-dollar airplane?" Then he looked at me. "Don't you believe I can run it?" he said. And I looked at him and I said, "Yes. I believe you can do anything."

VII

AND NOW I can't tell them. I can't say it. Papa told me once that somebody said that if you know it you can say it. Or maybe the man that said that didn't count fourteen-year-old boys. Because I must have known it was going to happen. And Uncle Willy must have known it too, known that the moment would come. It was like we both had known it and we didn't even have to compare notes, tell one another that we did: he not needing to say that day in Memphis, "Come with me so you will be there when I will need you," and me not needing to say, "Let me come so I can be there when you will."

Because old Job telephoned Mrs. Merridew. He waited until we were asleep and slipped out and walked all the way to town and telephoned her; he didn't have any money and he probably never telephoned in his life before, yet he tele-

phoned her and the next morning he came up running in the
dew (the town, the telephone, was five miles away) just as
Secretary was getting the engine started and I knew what he
had done even before he got close enough to holler, running
and stumbling along slow across the pasture, hollering, "Holt
um! Holt um! Dey'll be here any minute! Jest holt um ten
minutes en dey'll be here," and I knew and I ran and met him
and now I did hold him and him fighting and hitting at me
and still hollering at Uncle Willy in the airplane. "You telephoned?" I said. "Her? *Her?* Told her where he is?"

"Yes," Uncle Job hollered. "En she say she gonter git yo
pappy and start right away and be here by six o'clock," and
me holding him; he felt like a handful of scrawny dried sticks
and I could hear his lungs wheezing and I could feel his heart,
and Secretary came up running too and old Job begun to
holler at Secretary, "Git him outer dar! Dey comin! Dey be
here any minute if you can jest holt um!" and Secretary
saying, "Which? Which?" and old Job hollered at him to
run and hold the airplane and Secretary turned and I tried to
grab his leg but I couldn't and I could see Uncle Willy looking toward us and Secretary running toward the airplane
and I got onto my knees and waved and I was hollering too.
I don't reckon Uncle Willy could hear me for the engine.
But I tell you he didn't need to, because we knew, we both
knew; and so I knelt there and held old Job on the ground
and we saw the airplane start, with Secretary still running
after it, and jump into the air and duck down and then jump
up again and then it looked like it had stopped high in the
air above the trees where we thought Secretary was fixing to
land that first day before it ducked down beyond them and
went out of sight and Secretary was already running and so
it was only me and Uncle Job that had to get up and start.

Oh, yes, I know what they said about me; I knew it all that
afternoon while we were going home with the hearse in front

and Secretary and old Job in the Ford next and Papa and me in our car coming last and Jefferson getting nearer and nearer; and then all of a sudden I began to cry. Because the dying wasn't anything, it just touched the outside of you that you wore around with you for comfort and convenience like you do your clothes: it was because the old garments, the clothes that were not worth anything had betrayed one of the two of us and the one betrayed was me, and Papa with his other arm around my shoulders now, saying, "Now, now; I didn't mean that. You didn't do it. Nobody blames you."

You see? That was it. I did help Uncle Willy. He knows I did. He knows he couldn't have done it without me. He knows I did; we didn't even have to look at one another when he went. That's it.

And now they will never understand, not even Papa, and there is only me to try to tell them and how can I ever tell them, and make them understand? How can I?

Mule in the Yard

It was a gray day in late January, though not cold because of the fog. Old Het, just walked in from the poorhouse, ran down the hall toward the kitchen, shouting in a strong, bright, happy voice. She was about seventy probably, though by her own counting, calculated from the ages of various housewives in the town from brides to grandmothers whom she claimed to have nursed in infancy, she would have to be around a hundred and at least triplets. Tall, lean, fog-beaded, in tennis shoes and a long rat-colored cloak trimmed with what forty or fifty years ago had been fur, a modish though not new purple toque set upon her headrag and carrying (time was when she made her weekly rounds from kitchen to kitchen carrying a brocaded carpetbag though since the advent of the ten-cent stores the carpetbag became an endless succession of the convenient paper receptacles with which they supply their customers for a few cents) the shopping-bag, she ran into the kitchen and shouted with strong and childlike pleasure: "Miss Mannie! Mule in de yard!"

Mrs. Hait, stooping to the stove, in the act of drawing from it a scuttle of live ashes, jerked upright; clutching the scuttle, she glared at old Het, then she too spoke at once, strong too, immediate. "Them sons of bitches," she said. She left the kitchen, not running exactly, yet with a kind of outraged celerity, carrying the scuttle—a compact woman of forty-odd, with an air of indomitable yet relieved bereavement, as though that which had relicted her had been a woman and a not particularly valuable one at that. She wore a calico wrapper and a sweater coat, and a man's felt hat which they in the town knew had belonged to her ten years' dead husband. But the man's shoes had not belonged to him. They were high shoes which buttoned, with toes like small tulip bulbs, and in the town they knew that she had bought them new for herself. She and old Het ran down the kitchen steps and into the fog. That's why it was not cold: as though there lay supine and prisoned between earth and mist the long winter night's suspiration of the sleeping town in dark, close rooms—the slumber and the rousing; the stale waking thermostatic, by re-heating heat-engendered: it lay like a scum of cold grease upon the steps and the wooden entrance to the basement and upon the narrow plank walk which led to a shed building in the corner of the yard: upon these planks, running and still carrying the scuttle of live ashes, Mrs. Hait skated viciously.

"Watch out!" old Het, footed securely by her rubber soles, cried happily. "Dey in de front!" Mrs. Hait did not fall. She did not even pause. She took in the immediate scene with one cold glare and was running again when there appeared at the corner of the house and apparently having been born before their eyes of the fog itself, a mule. It looked taller than a giraffe. Longheaded, with a flying halter about its scissorlike ears, it rushed down upon them with violent and apparitionlike suddenness.

"Dar hit!" old Het cried, waving the shopping-bag. "Hoo!" Mrs. Hait whirled. Again she skidded savagely on the greasy planks as she and the mule rushed parallel with one another toward the shed building, from whose open doorway there now projected the static and astonished face of a cow. To the cow the fog-born mule doubtless looked

taller and more incredibly sudden than a giraffe even, and
apparently bent upon charging right through the shed as
though it were made of straw or were purely and simply
mirage. The cow's head likewise had a quality transient and
abrupt and unmundane. It vanished, sucked into invisibility
like a match flame, though the mind knew and the reason
insisted that she had withdrawn into the shed, from which,
as proof's burden, there came an indescribable sound of
shock and alarm by shed and beast engendered, analogous to
a single note from a profoundly struck lyre or harp. Toward
this sound Mrs. Hait sprang, immediately, as if by pure reflex,
as though in invulnerable compact of female with female
against a world of mule and man. She and the mule converged upon the shed at top speed, the heavy scuttle poised
lightly in her hand to hurl. Of course it did not take this
long, and likewise it was the mule which refused the gambit.
Old Het was still shouting "Dar hit! Dar hit!" when it
swerved and rushed at her where she stood tall as a stove
pipe, holding the shopping-bag which she swung at the beast
as it rushed past her and vanished beyond the other corner
of the house as though sucked back into the fog which had
produced it, profound and instantaneous and without any
sound.

With that unhasteful celerity Mrs. Hait turned and set
the scuttle down on the brick coping of the cellar entrance
and she and old Het turned the corner of the house in time to
see the now wraithlike mule at the moment when its course
converged with that of a choleric-looking rooster and eight
Rhode Island Red hens emerging from beneath the house.
Then for an instant its progress assumed the appearance and
trappings of an apotheosis: hell-born and hell-returning, in
the act of dissolving completely into the fog, it seemed to rise
vanishing into a sunless and dimensionless medium borne
upon and enclosed by small winged goblins.

"Dey's mo in de front!" old Het cried.

"Them sons of bitches," Mrs. Hait said, again in that grim, prescient voice without rancor or heat. It was not the mules to which she referred; it was not even the owner of them. It was her whole town-dwelling history as dated from that April dawn ten years ago when what was left of Hait had been gathered from the mangled remains of five mules and several feet of new Manila rope on a blind curve of the railroad just out of town; the geographical hap of her very home; the very components of her bereavement—the mules, the defunct husband, and the owner of them. His name was Snopes; in the town they knew about him too—how he bought his stock at the Memphis market and brought it to Jefferson and sold it to farmers and widows and orphans black and white, for whatever he could contrive—down to a certain figure; and about how (usually in the dead season of winter) teams and even small droves of his stock would escape from the fenced pasture where he kept them and, tied one to another with sometimes quite new hemp rope (and which item Snopes included in the subsequent claim), would be annihilated by freight trains on the same blind curve which was to be the scene of Hait's exit from this world; once a town wag sent him through the mail a printed train schedule for the division. A squat, pasty man perennially tieless and with a strained, harried expression, at stated intervals he passed athwart the peaceful and somnolent life of the town in dust and uproar, his advent heralded by shouts and cries, his passing marked by a yellow cloud filled with tossing jug-shaped heads and clattering hooves and the same forlorn and earnest cries of the drovers; and last of all and well back out of the dust, Snopes himself moving at a harried and panting trot, since it was said in the town that he was deathly afraid of the very beasts in which he cleverly dealt.

The path which he must follow from the railroad station

to his pasture crossed the edge of town near Hait's home; Hait and Mrs. Hait had not been in the house a week before they waked one morning to find it surrounded by galloping mules and the air filled with the shouts and cries of the drovers. But it was not until that April dawn some years later, when those who reached the scene first found what might be termed foreign matter among the mangled mules and the savage fragments of new rope, that the town suspected that Hait stood in any closer relationship to Snopes and the mules than that of helping at periodical intervals to drive them out of his front yard. After that they believed that they knew; in a three days' recess of interest, surprise, and curiosity they watched to see if Snopes would try to collect on Hait also.

But they learned only that the adjuster appeared and called upon Mrs. Hait and that a few days later she cashed a check for eight thousand five hundred dollars, since this was back in the old halcyon days when even the companies considered their southern branches and divisions the legitimate prey of all who dwelt beside them. She took the cash: she stood in her sweater coat and the hat which Hait had been wearing on the fatal morning a week ago and listened in cold, grim silence while the teller counted the money and the president and the cashier tried to explain to her the virtues of a bond, then of a savings account, then of a checking account, and departed with the money in a salt sack under her apron; after a time she painted her house: that serviceable and time-defying color which the railroad station was painted, as though out of sentiment or (as some said) gratitude.

The adjuster also summoned Snopes into conference, from which he emerged not only more harried-looking than ever, but with his face stamped with a bewildered dismay which it was to wear from then on, and that was the last time his pasture fence was ever to give inexplicably away at dead of night upon mules coupled in threes and fours by adequate rope even though not always new. And then it seemed as though the mules themselves knew this, as if, even while haltered at the Memphis block at his bid, they sensed it somehow as they sensed that he was afraid of them. Now, three or four times a year and as though by fiendish concord and as soon as they were freed of the box car, the entire uproar—the dust cloud filled with shouts earnest, harried, and dismayed, with plunging demoniac shapes—would become translated in a single burst of perverse and uncontrollable violence, without any intervening contact with time, space, or earth, across the peaceful and astonished town and into Mrs. Hait's yard, where, in a certain hapless despair which abrogated for the moment even physical fear, Snopes ducked and dodged among the thundering shapes about the house (for whose very impervious paint the town believed that he felt he had paid and whose inmate lived within it a life of idle and queen-like ease on money which he considered at least partly his own) while gradually that section and neighborhood gathered to look on from behind adjacent window curtains and porches screened and not, and from the sidewalks and even from halted wagons and cars in the street—housewives in the wrappers and boudoir caps of morning, children on the way to school, casual Negroes and casual whites in static and entertained repose.

They were all there when, followed by old Het and carrying the stub of a worn-out broom, Mrs. Hait ran around the next corner and onto the handkerchief-sized plot of earth which she called her front yard. It was small; any creature with a running stride of three feet could have spanned it in two paces, yet at the moment, due perhaps to the myopic and distortive quality of the fog, it seemed to be as incredibly full of mad life as a drop of water beneath the microscope. Yet again she did not falter. With the broom clutched in her hand and apparently with a kind of sublime faith in her own invulnerability, she rushed on after the haltered mule which was still in that arrested and wraithlike process of vanishing furiously into the fog, its wake indicated by the tossing and dispersing shapes of the nine chickens like so many jagged scraps of paper in the dying air blast of an automobile, and the madly dodging figure of a man. The man was Snopes; beaded too with moisture, his wild face gaped with hoarse shouting and the two heavy lines of shaven beard descending from the corners of it as though in alluvial retrospect of years of tobacco, he screamed at her: "Fore God, Miz Hait! I done everything I could!" She didn't even look at him.

"Ketch that big un with the bridle on," she said in her cold, panting voice. "Git that big un outen here."

"Sho!" Snopes shrieked. "Jest let um take their time. Jest don't git um excited now."

"Watch out!" old Het shouted. "He headin fer de back again!"

"Git the rope," Mrs. Hait said, running again. Snopes glared back at old Het.

"Fore God, where is ere rope?" he shouted.

"In de cellar fo God!" old Het shouted, also without pausing. "Go roun de udder way en head um." Again she and Mrs. Hait turned the corner in time to see again the still-vanishing mule with the halter once more in the act of floating lightly onward in its cloud of chickens with which, they being able to pass under the house and so on the chord of a circle while it had to go around on the arc, it had once more coincided. When they turned the next corner they were in the back yard again.

"Fo God!" old Het cried. "He fixin to misuse de cow!" For they had gained on the mule now, since it had stopped. In fact, they came around the corner on a tableau. The cow now stood in the centre of the yard. She and the mule faced one another a few feet apart. Motionless, with lowered heads and braced forelegs, they looked like two book ends from two distinct pairs of a general pattern which some one of amateurly bucolic leanings might have purchased, and which some child had salvaged, brought into idle juxtaposition and then forgotten; and, his head and shoulders projecting above the back-flung slant of the cellar entrance where the scuttle still sat, Snopes standing as though buried to the armpits for a Spanish-Indian-American suttee. Only again it did not take this long. It was less than tableau; it was one of those things which later even memory cannot quite affirm. Now and in turn, man and cow and mule vanished beyond the next corner, Snopes now in the lead, carrying the rope, the cow next with her tail rigid and raked slightly like the stern staff of a boat. Mrs. Hait and old Het ran on, passing the open cellar gaping upon its accumulation of human necessities and widowed womanyears—boxes for kindling wood, old papers and magazines, the broken and outworn furniture and utensils which no woman ever throws away; a pile of coal and another of pitch pine for priming fires—and ran on and turned the next corner to see man and cow and mule all vanishing now in the wild cloud of ubiquitous chickens which had once more crossed beneath the house and emerged. They ran on, Mrs. Hait in grim and unflagging silence, old Het with the eager and happy amazement of a child. But when they gained the front again they saw only Snopes. He lay flat on his stomach, his head and shoulders upreared by his outstretched arms, his coat tail swept forward by its own arrested momentum about his head so that from beneath it his slack-jawed face mused in wild repose like that of a burlesqued nun.

"Whar'd dey go?" old Het shouted at him. He didn't answer.

"Dey tightenin' on de curves!" she cried. "Dey already in de back again!" That's where they were. The cow made a feint at running into her shed, but deciding perhaps that her speed was too great, she whirled in a final desperation of despair-like valor. But they did not see this, nor see the mule, swerving to pass her, crash and blunder for an instant at the open cellar door before going on. When they arrived, the mule was gone. The scuttle was gone too, but they did not notice it; they saw only the cow standing in the centre of the yard as before, panting, rigid, with braced forelegs and lowered head facing nothing, as if the child had returned and removed one of the book ends for some newer purpose or game. They ran on. Mrs. Hait ran heavily now, her mouth too open, her face putty-colored and one hand pressed to her side. So slow was their progress that the mule in its third circuit of the house overtook them from behind and soared past with undiminished speed, with brief demon thunder and a keen ammonia-sweet reek of sweat sudden and sharp as a jeering cry, and was gone. Yet they ran doggedly on around the next corner in time to see it succeed at last in vanishing into the fog; they heard its hoofs, brief, staccato, and derisive, on the paved street, dying away.

"Well!" old Het said, stopping. She panted, happily. "Gentlemen, hush! Ain't we had—" Then she became stone still; slowly her head turned, high-nosed, her nostrils pulsing; perhaps for the instant she saw the open cellar door as they had last passed it, with no scuttle beside it. "Fo God I smells smoke!" she said. "Chile, run, git yo money."

That was still early, not yet ten o'clock. By noon the house had burned to the ground. There was a farmers' supply store where Snopes could be usually found; more than one had made a point of finding him there by that time. They told him about how when the fire engine and the crowd reached the scene, Mrs. Hait, followed by old Het carrying her shopping-bag in one hand and a framed portrait of Mr. Hait in the other, emerged with an umbrella and wearing a new, dun-colored, mail-order coat, in one pocket of which lay a fruit jar filled with smoothly rolled banknotes and in the other a heavy, nickel-plated pistol, and crossed the street to the house opposite, where with old Het beside her in another rocker, she had been sitting ever since on the veranda, grim, inscrutable, the two of them rocking steadily, while hoarse and tireless men hurled her dishes and furniture and bedding up and down the street.

"What are you telling me for?" Snopes said. "Hit warn't me that set that ere scuttle of live fire where the first thing that passed would knock hit into the cellar."

"It was you that opened the cellar door, though."

"Sho. And for what? To git that rope, her own rope, where she told me to git it."

"To catch your mule with, that was trespassing on her property. You can't get out of it this time, I. O. There ain't a jury in the county that won't find for her."

"Yes. I reckon not. And just because she is a woman. That's why. Because she is a durn woman. All right. Let her go to her durn jury with hit. I can talk too; I reckon hit's a few things I could tell a jury myself about—" He ceased. They were watching him.

"What? Tell a jury about what?"

"Nothing. Because hit ain't going to no jury. A jury between her and me? Me and Mannie Hait? You boys don't know her if you think she's going to make trouble over a pure acci-dent couldn't nobody help. Why, there ain't a fairer, finer woman in the county than Miz Mannie Hait. I just wisht I had a opportunity to tell her so." The opportunity came at once. Old Het was behind her, carrying the shopping-bag. Mrs. Hait looked once, quietly, about at the faces, making no response to the murmur of curious salutation, then not again. She didn't look at Snopes long either, nor talk to him long.

"I come to buy that mule," she said.

"What mule?" They looked at one another. "You'd like to own that mule?" She looked at him. "Hit'll cost you a hundred and fifty, Miz Mannie."

"You mean dollars?"

"I don't mean dimes nor nickels neither, Miz Mannie."

"Dollars," she said. "That's more than mules was in Hait's time."

"Lots of things is different since Hait's time. Including you and me."

"I reckon so," she said. Then she went away. She turned without a word, old Het following.

"Maybe one of them others you looked at this morning would suit you," Snopes said. She didn't answer. Then they were gone.

"I don't know as I would have said that last to her," one said.

"What for?" Snopes said. "If she was aiming to law something outen me about that fire, you reckon she would have come and offered to pay me money for hit?" That was about one o'clock. About four o'clock he was shouldering his way through a throng of Negroes before a cheap grocery store when one called his name. It was old Het, the now bulging shopping-bag on her arm, eating bananas from a paper sack.

"Fo God I wuz jest dis minute huntin fer you," she said. She handed the banana to a woman beside her and delved and fumbled in the shopping-bag and extended a greenback. "Miz Mannie gimme dis to give you; I wuz jest on de way to de sto whar you stay at. Here." He took the bill.

"What's this? From Miz Hait?"

"Fer de mule." The bill was for ten dollars. "You don't need to gimme no receipt. I kin be de witness I give hit to you."

"Ten dollars? For that mule? I told her a hundred and fifty dollars."

"You'll have to fix dat up wid her yo'self. She jest gimme dis to give ter you when she sot out to fetch de mule."

"Set out to fetch— She went out there herself and taken my mule outen my pasture?"

"Lawd, chile," old Het said, "Miz Mannie ain't skeered of no mule. Ain't you done foun dat out?"

And then it became late, what with the yet short winter days; when she came in sight of the two gaunt chimneys against the sunset, evening was already finding itself. But she could smell the ham cooking before she came in sight of the cow shed even, though she could not see it until she came around in front where the fire burned beneath an iron skillet set on bricks and where nearby Mrs. Hait was milking the cow. "Well," old Het said, "you is settled down, ain't you?" She looked into the shed, neated and raked and swept even, and floored now with fresh hay. A clean new lantern burned on a box, beside it a pallet bed was spread neatly on the straw and turned neatly back for the night. "Why, you is fixed up," she said with pleased astonishment. Within the door was a kitchen chair. She drew it out and sat down beside the skillet and laid the bulging shopping-bag beside her.

"I'll tend dis meat whilst you milks. I'd offer to strip dat cow fer you ef I wuzn't so wo out wid all dis excitement we been had." She looked around her. "I don't believe I sees yo new mule, dough." Mrs. Hait grunted, her head against the cow's flank. After a moment she said,

"Did you give him that money?"

"I give um ter him. He ack surprise at first, lak maybe he think you didn't aim to trade dat quick. I tole him to settle de details wid you later. He taken de money, dough. So I reckin dat's offen his mine en yo'n bofe." Again Mrs. Hait grunted. Old Het turned the ham in the skillet. Beside it the coffee pot bubbled and steamed. "Cawfee smell good too," she said. "I ain't had no appetite in years now. A bird couldn't live on de vittles I eats. But jest lemme git a whiff er cawfee en seem lak hit always whets me a little. Now, ef you jest had nudder little piece o dis ham, now— Fo God, you got company aready." But Mrs. Hait did not even look up until she had finished. Then she turned without rising from the box on which she sat.

"I reckon you and me better have a little talk," Snopes said. "I reckon I got something that belongs to you and I hear you got something that belongs to me." He looked about, quickly, ceaselessly, while old Het watched him. He turned to her. "You go away, aunty. I don't reckon you want to set here and listen to us."

"Lawd, honey," old Het said. "Don't you mind me. I done already had so much troubles myself dat I kin set en listen to udder folks' widout hit worryin me a-tall. You gawn talk whut you came ter talk; I jest set here en tend de ham." Snopes looked at Mrs. Hait.

"Ain't you going to make her go away?" he said.

"What for?" Mrs. Hait said. "I reckon she ain't the first critter that ever come on this yard when hit wanted and went or stayed when hit liked." Snopes made a gesture, brief, fretted, restrained.

"Well," he said. "All right. So you taken the mule."

"I paid you for it. She give you the money."

"Ten dollars. For a hundred-and-fifty-dollar mule. Ten dollars."

"I don't know anything about hundred-and-fifty-dollar mules. All I know is what the railroad paid." Now Snopes looked at her for a full moment.

"What do you mean?"

"Them sixty dollars a head the railroad used to pay you for mules back when you and Hait——"

"Hush," Snopes said; he looked about again, quick, ceaseless. "All right. Even call it sixty dollars. But you just sent me ten."

"Yes. I sent you the difference." He looked at her, perfectly still. "Between that mule and what you owed Hait."

"What I owed——"

"For getting them five mules onto the tr——"

"Hush!" he cried. "Hush!" Her voice went on, cold, grim, level.

"For helping you. You paid him fifty dollars each time, and the railroad paid you sixty dollars a head for the mules. Ain't that right?" He watched her. "The last time you never paid him. So I taken that mule instead. And I sent you the ten dollars difference."

"Yes," he said in a tone of quiet, swift, profound bemusement; then he cried: "But look! Here's where I got you. Hit was our agreement that I wouldn't never owe him nothing until after the mules was——"

"I reckon you better hush yourself," Mrs. Hait said.

"—until hit was over. And this time, when over had come, I never owed nobody no money because the man hit would have been owed to wasn't nobody," he cried triumphantly. "You see?" Sitting on the box, motionless, downlooking, Mrs. Hait seemed to muse. "So you just take your ten dollars back and tell me where my mule is and we'll just go back good friends to where we started at. Fore God, I'm as sorry as ere a living man about that fire——"

"Fo God!" old Het said, "hit was a blaze, wuzn't it?"

"—but likely with all that ere railroad money you still got, you just been wanting a chance to build new, all along. So here. Take hit." He put the money into her hand. "Where's my mule?" But Mrs. Hait didn't move at once.

"You want to give it back to me?" she said.

"Sho. We been friends all the time; now we'll just go back to where we left off being. I don't hold no hard feelings and don't you hold none. Where you got the mule hid?"

"Up at the end of that ravine ditch behind Spilmer's," she said.

"Sho. I know. A good, sheltered place, since you ain't got nere barn. Only if you'd a just left hit in the pasture, hit would a saved us both trouble. But hit ain't no hard feelings though. And so I'll bid you goodnight. You're all fixed up, I see. I reckon you could save some more money by not building no house a-tall."

"I reckon I could," Mrs. Hait said. But he was gone.

"Whut did you leave de mule dar fer?" old Het said.

"I reckon that's far enough," Mrs. Hait said.

"Fer enough?" But Mrs. Hait came and looked into the skillet, and old Het said, "Wuz hit me er you dat mentioned something erbout er nudder piece o dis ham?" So they were both eating when in the not-quite-yet accomplished twilight Snopes returned. He came up quietly and stood, holding his hands to the blaze as if he were quite cold. He did not look at any one now.

"I reckon I'll take that ere ten dollars," he said.

"What ten dollars?" Mrs. Hait said. He seemed to muse upon the fire. Mrs. Hait and old Het chewed quietly, old Het alone watching him.

"You ain't going to give hit back to me?" he said.

"You was the one that said to let's go back to where we started," Mrs. Hait said.

"Fo God you wuz, en dat's de fack," old Het said. Snopes mused upon the fire; he spoke in a tone of musing and amazed despair:

"I go to the worry and the risk and the agoment for years and years and I get sixty dollars. And you, one time, without no trouble and no risk, without even knowing you are going to git it, git eighty-five hundred dollars. I never begrudged hit to you; can't nere a man say I did, even if hit did seem a little strange that you should git it all when he wasn't working for you and you never even knowed where he was at and what doing; that all you done to git it was to be married to him. And now, after all these ten years of not begrudging you hit, you taken the best mule I had and you ain't even going to pay me ten dollars for hit. Hit ain't right. Hit ain't justice."

"You got de mule back, en you ain't satisfried yit," old Het said. "Whut does you want?" Now Snopes looked at Mrs. Hait.

"For the last time I ask hit," he said. "Will you or won't you give hit back?"

"Give what back?" Mrs. Hait said. Snopes turned. He stumbled over something—it was old Het's shopping-bag— and recovered and went on. They could see him in silhouette, as though framed by the two blackened chimneys against the dying west; they saw him fling up both clenched hands in a gesture almost Gallic, of resignation and impotent despair. Then he was gone. Old Het was watching Mrs. Hait.

"Honey," she said. "Whut did you do wid de mule?" Mrs. Hait leaned forward to the fire. On her plate lay a stale biscuit. She lifted the skillet and poured over the biscuit the grease in which the ham had cooked.

"I shot it," she said.

"You which?" old Het said. Mrs. Hait began to eat the biscuit. "Well," old Het said, happily, "de mule burnt de house en you shot de mule. Dat's whut I calls justice." It was getting dark fast now, and before her was still the three-mile walk to the poorhouse. But the dark would last a long time in January, and the poorhouse too would not move at once. She sighed with weary and happy relaxation "Gentlemen, hush! Ain't we had a day!"

That Will Be Fine

WE COULD HEAR the water running into the tub. We looked at the presents scattered over the bed where mamma had wrapped them in the colored paper, with our names on them so Grandpa could tell who they belonged to easy when he would take them off the tree. There was a present for everybody except Grandpa because mamma said that Grandpa is too old to get presents any more.

"This one is yours," I said.

"Sho now," Rosie said. "You come on and get in that tub like your mamma tell you."

"I know what's in it," I said. "I could tell you if I wanted to."

Rosie looked at her present. "I reckon I kin wait twell hit be handed to me at the right time," she said.

"I'll tell you what's in it for a nickel," I said.

Rosie looked at her present. "I ain't got no nickel," she said. "But I will have Christmas morning when Mr. Rodney give me that dime."

"You'll know what's in it anyway then and you won't pay me," I said. "Go and ask mamma to lend you a nickel."

Then Rosie grabbed me by the arm. "You come on and get in that tub," she said. "You and money! If you ain't rich time you twenty-one, hit will be because the law done abolished money or done abolished you."

So I went and bathed and came back, with the presents all scattered out across mamma's and papa's bed and you could almost smell it and tomorrow night they would begin to shoot the fireworks and then you could hear it too. It would be just tonight and then tomorrow we would get on the train, except papa, because he would have to stay at the livery stable until after Christmas Eve, and go to Grandpa's, and then tomorrow night and then it would be Christmas and Grandpa would take the presents off the tree and call out our names, and the one from me to Uncle Rodney that I bought with my own dime and so after a while Uncle Rodney would prize open Grandpa's desk and take a dose of Grandpa's tonic and maybe he would give me another quarter for helping him, like he did last Christmas, instead of just a nickel, like he would do last summer while he was visiting mamma and us and we were doing business with Mrs. Tucker before Uncle Rodney went home and began to work for the Compress Association, and it would be fine. Or maybe even a half a dollar and it seemed to me like I just couldn't wait.

"Jesus, I can't hardly wait," I said.

"You which?" Rosie hollered. "Jesus?" she hollered. "Jesus? You let your mamma hear you cussing and I bound you'll wait. You talk to me about a nickel! For a nickel I'd tell her just what you said."

"If you'll pay me a nickel I'll tell her myself," I said.

"Get into that bed!" Rosie hollered. "A seven-year-old boy, cussing!"

"If you will promise not to tell her, I'll tell you what's in your present and you can pay me the nickel Christmas morning," I said.

"Get in that bed!" Rosie hollered. "You and your nickel! I bound if I thought any of you all was fixing to buy even a dime present for your grandpa, I'd put in a nickel of hit myself."

"Grandpa don't want presents," I said. "He's too old."

"Hah," Rosie said. "Too old, is he? Suppose everybody decided you was too young to have nickels: what would you think about that? Hah?"

So Rosie turned out the light and went out. But I could still see the presents by the firelight: the ones for Uncle Rodney and Grandma and Aunt Louisa and Aunt Louisa's husband Uncle Fred, and Cousin Louisa and Cousin Fred and the baby and Grandpa's cook and our cook, that was Rosie, and maybe somebody ought to give Grandpa a present only maybe it ought to be Aunt Louisa because she and Uncle Fred lived with Grandpa, or maybe Uncle Rodney ought to because he lived with Grandpa too. Uncle Rodney always gave mamma and papa a present but maybe it would be just a waste of his time and Grandpa's time both for Uncle Rodney to give Grandpa a present, because one time I asked mamma why Grandpa always looked at the present Uncle Rodney gave her and papa and got so mad, and papa began to laugh and mamma said papa ought to be ashamed, that it wasn't Uncle Rodney's fault if his generosity was longer than his pocket book, and papa said Yes, it certainly wasn't Uncle Rodney's fault, he never knew a man to try harder to get money than Uncle Rodney did, that Uncle Rodney had tried every known plan to get it except work, and that if mamma would just think back about two years she would remember one time when Uncle Rodney could have thanked his stars that there was one man in the connection whose generosity, or whatever mamma wanted to call it, was at least five hundred dollars shorter than his pocket book, and mamma said she defied papa to say that Uncle Rodney stole the money, that it had been malicious persecution and papa knew it, and that papa and most other men were prejudiced against Uncle Rodney, why she didn't know, and that if papa begrudged having lent Uncle Rodney the five hundred dollars when the family's good name was

at stake to say so and Grandpa would raise it somehow and
pay papa back, and then she began to cry and papa said
All right, all right, and mamma cried and said how Uncle
Rodney was the baby and that must be why papa hated
him and papa said All right, all right; for God's sake, all
right.

Because mamma and papa didn't know that Uncle Rodney
had been handling his business all the time he was visiting
us last summer, any more than the people in Mottstown
knew that he was doing business last Christmas when I
worked for him the first time and he paid me the quarter.
Because he said that if he preferred to do business with
ladies instead of men it wasn't anybody's business except his,
not even Mr. Tucker's. He said how I never went around
telling people about papa's business and I said how everybody knew papa was in the livery-stable business and so I
didn't have to tell them, and Uncle Rodney said Well,
that was what half of the nickel was for and did I want to
keep on making the nickels or did I want him to hire somebody else? So I would go on ahead and watch through Mr.
Tucker's fence until he came out to go to town and I would
go along behind the fence to the corner and watch until
Mr. Tucker was out of sight and then I would put my hat
on top of the fence post and leave it there until I saw Mr.
Tucker coming back. Only he never came back while I
was there because Uncle Rodney would always be through
before then, and he would come up and we would walk
back home and he would tell mamma how far we had
walked that day and mamma would say how good that was
for Uncle Rodney's health. So he just paid me a nickel at
home. It wasn't as much as the quarter when he was in
business with the other lady in Mottstown Christmas, but
that was just one time and he visited us all summer and so
by that time I had a lot more than a quarter. And besides

the other time was Christmas and he took a dose of Grandpa's tonic before he paid me the quarter and so maybe this time it might be even a half a dollar. I couldn't hardly wait.

II

BUT IT GOT TO BE daylight at last and I put on my Sunday suit, and I would go to the front door and watch for the hack and then I would go to the kitchen and ask Rosie if it wasn't almost time and she would tell me the train wasn't even due for two hours yet. Only while she was telling me we heard the hack, and so I thought it was time for us to go and get on the train and it would be fine, and then we would go to Grandpa's and then it would be tonight and then tomorrow and maybe it would be a half a dollar this time and Jesus it would be fine. Then mamma came running out without even her hat on and she said how it was two hours yet and she wasn't even dressed and John Paul said Yessum but papa sent him and papa said for John Paul to tell mamma that Aunt Louisa was here and for mamma to hurry. So we put the basket of presents into the hack and I rode on the box with John Paul and mamma hollering from inside the hack about Aunt Louisa, and John Paul said that Aunt Louisa had come in a hired buggy and papa took her to the hotel to eat breakfast because she left Mottstown before daylight even. And so maybe Aunt Louisa had come to Jefferson to help mamma and papa get a present for Grandpa.

"Because we have one for everybody else," I said, "I bought one for Uncle Rodney with my own money."

Then John Paul began to laugh and I said Why? and he said it was at the notion of me giving Uncle Rodney anything that he would want to use, and I said Why? and John Paul said because I was shaped like a man, and I said

Why? and John Paul said he bet papa would like to give
Uncle Rodney a present without even waiting for Christmas,
and I said What? and John Paul said A job of work. And I
told John Paul how Uncle Rodney had been working all the
time he was visiting us last summer, and John Paul quit
laughing and said Sho, he reckoned anything a man kept
at all the time, night and day both, he would call it work
no matter how much fun it started out to be, and I said
Anyway Uncle Rodney works now, he works in the office
of the Compress Association, and John Paul laughed good
then and said it would sholy take a whole association to
compress Uncle Rodney. And then mamma began to holler
to go straight to the hotel, and John Paul said Nome, papa
said to come straight to the livery stable and wait for him.
And so we went to the hotel and Aunt Louisa and papa
came out and papa helped Aunt Louisa into the hack and
Aunt Louisa began to cry and mamma hollering Louisa!
Louisa! What is it? What has happened? and papa saying
Wait now. Wait. Remember the nigger, and that meant
John Paul, and so it must have been a present for Grandpa
and it didn't come.

And then we didn't go on the train after all. We went to
the stable and they already had the light road hack hitched
up and waiting, and mamma was crying now and saying
how papa never even had his Sunday clothes and papa
cussing now and saying Damn the clothes; if we didn't get
to Uncle Rodney before the others caught him, papa would
just wear the clothes Uncle Rodney had on now. So we got
into the road hack fast and papa closed the curtains and then
mamma and Aunt Louisa could cry all right and papa hollered to John Paul to go home and tell Rosie to pack his
Sunday suit and take her to the train; anyway that would be
fine for Rosie. So we didn't go on the train but we went
fast, with papa driving and saying Didn't anybody know

where he was? and Aunt Louisa quit crying a while and said how Uncle Rodney didn't come to supper last night, but right after supper he came in and how Aunt Louisa had a terrible feeling as soon as she heard his step in the hall and how Uncle Rodney wouldn't tell her until they were in his room and the door closed and then he said he must have two thousand dollars and Aunt Louisa said where in the world could she get two thousand dollars? and Uncle Rodney said Ask Fred, that was Aunt Louisa's husband, and George, that was papa; tell them they would have to dig it up, and Aunt Louisa said she had that terrible feeling and she said Rodney! Rodney! What—and Uncle Rodney begun to cuss and say Dammit, don't start sniveling and crying now, and Aunt Louisa said Rodney, what have you done now? and then they both heard the knocking at the door and how Aunt Louisa looked at Uncle Rodney and she knew the truth before she even laid eyes on Mr. Pruitt and the sheriff, and how she said Don't tell pa! Keep it from pa! It will kill him. . . .

"Who?" papa said. "Mister who?"

"Mr. Pruitt," Aunt Louisa said, crying again. "The president of the Compress Association. They moved to Mottstown last spring. You don't know him."

So she went down to the door and it was Mr. Pruitt and the sheriff. And how Aunt Louisa begged Mr. Pruitt for Grandpa's sake and how she gave Mr. Pruitt her oath that Uncle Rodney would stay right there in the house until papa could get there, and Mr. Pruitt said how he hated it to happen at Christmas too and so for Grandpa's and Aunt Louisa's sake he would give them until the day after Christmas if Aunt Louisa would promise him that Uncle Rodney would not try to leave Mottstown. And how Mr. Pruitt showed her with her own eyes the check with Grandpa's name signed to it and how even Aunt Louisa could see that

Grandpa's name had been—and then mamma said Louisa!
Louisa! Remember Georgie! and that was me, and papa
cussed too, hollering How in damnation do you expect
to keep it from him? By hiding the newspapers? and Aunt
Louisa cried again and said how everybody was bound to
know it, that she didn't expect or hope that any of us could
ever hold our heads up again, that all she hoped for was to
keep it from Grandpa because it would kill him. She cried
hard then and papa had to stop at a branch and get down
and soak his handkerchief for mamma to wipe Aunt Louisa's
face with it and then papa took the bottle of tonic out of the
dash pocket and put a few drops on the handkerchief, and
Aunt Louisa smelled it and then papa took a dose of the
tonic out of the bottle and mamma said George! and papa
drank some more of the tonic and then made like he was
handing the bottle back for mamma and Aunt Louisa to
take a dose too and said, "I don't blame you. If I was a
woman in this family I'd take to drink too. Now let me get
this bond business straight."

"It was those road bonds of ma's," Aunt Louisa said.

We were going fast again now because the horses had
rested while papa was wetting the handkerchief and taking
the dose of tonic, and papa was saying All right, what about
the bonds? when all of a sudden he jerked around in the
seat and said, "Road bonds? Do you mean he took that
damn screw driver and prized open your mother's desk too?"

Then mamma said George! how can you? only Aunt
Louisa was talking now, quick now, not crying now, not
yet, and papa with his head turned over his shoulder and
saying Did Aunt Louisa mean that that five hundred papa
had to pay out two years ago wasn't all of it? And Aunt
Louisa said it was twenty-five hundred, only they didn't
want Grandpa to find it out, and so Grandma put up her
road bonds for security on the note, and how they said now

that Uncle Rodney had redeemed Grandma's note and the road bonds from the bank with some of the Compress Association's bonds out of the safe in the Compress Association office, because when Mr. Pruitt found the Compress Association's bonds were missing he looked for them and found them in the bank and when he looked in the Compress Association's safe all he found was the check for two thousand dollars with Grandpa's name signed to it, and how Mr. Pruitt hadn't lived in Mottstown but a year but even he knew that Grandpa never signed that check and besides he looked in the bank again and Grandpa never had two thousand dollars in it, and how Mr. Pruitt said how he would wait until the day after Christmas if Aunt Louisa would give him her sworn oath that Uncle Rodney would not go away, and Aunt Louisa did it and then she went back upstairs to plead with Uncle Rodney to give Mr. Pruitt the bonds and she went into Uncle Rodney's room where she had left him, and the window was open and Uncle Rodney was gone.

"Damn Rodney!" papa said. "The bonds! You mean, nobody knows where the bonds are?"

Now we were going fast because we were coming down the last hill and into the valley where Mottstown was. Soon we would begin to smell it again; it would be just today and then tonight and then it would be Christmas, and Aunt Louisa sitting there with her face white like a whitewashed fence that has been rained on and papa said Who in hell ever gave him such a job anyway, and Aunt Louisa said Mr. Pruitt, and papa said how even if Mr. Pruitt had only lived in Mottstown a few months, and then Aunt Louisa began to cry without even putting her handkerchief to her face this time and mamma looked at Aunt Louisa and she began to cry too and papa took out the whip and hit the team a belt with it even if they were going fast and he cussed.

"Damnation to hell," papa said. "I see. Pruitt's married."

Then we could see it too. There were holly wreaths in the windows like at home in Jefferson, and I said, "They shoot fireworks in Mottstown too like they do in Jefferson."

Aunt Louisa and mamma were crying good now, and now it was papa saying Here, here; remember Georgie, and that was me, and Aunt Louisa said, "Yes, yes! Painted common thing, traipsing up and down the streets all afternoon alone in a buggy, and the one and only time Mrs. Church called on her, and that was because of Mr. Pruitt's position alone, Mrs. Church found her without corsets on and Mrs. Church told me she smelled liquor on her breath."

And papa saying Here, here, and Aunt Louisa crying good and saying how it was Mrs. Pruitt that did it because Uncle Rodney was young and easy led because he never had had opportunities to meet a nice girl and marry her, and papa was driving fast toward Grandpa's house and he said, "Marry? Rodney marry? What in hell pleasure would he get out of slipping out of his own house and waiting until after dark and slipping around to the back and climbing up the gutter and into a room where there wasn't anybody in it but his own wife."

And so mamma and Aunt Louisa were crying good when we got to Grandpa's.

III

AND UNCLE RODNEY wasn't there. We came in, and Grandma said how Mandy, that was Grandpa's cook, hadn't come to cook breakfast and when Grandma sent Emmeline, that was Aunt Louisa's baby's nurse, down to Mandy's cabin in the back yard, the door was locked on the inside but Mandy wouldn't answer and then Grandma went down there herself and Mandy wouldn't answer and so Cousin

Fred climbed in the window and Mandy was gone and Uncle Fred had just got back from town then and he and papa both hollered, "Locked? on the inside? and nobody in it?"

And then Uncle Fred told papa to go in and keep Grandpa entertained and he would go and then Aunt Louisa grabbed papa and Uncle Fred both and said she would keep Grandpa quiet and for both of them to go and find him, find him, and papa said if only the fool hasn't tried to sell them to some-body, and Uncle Fred said Good God, man, don't you know that check was dated ten days ago? And so we went in where Grandpa was reared back in his chair and saying how he hadn't expected papa until tomorrow but by God he was glad to see somebody at last because he waked up this morning and his cook had quit and Louisa had chased off somewhere before daylight and now he couldn't even find Uncle Rodney to go down and bring his mail and a cigar or two back, and so thank God Christmas never came but once a year and so be damned if he wouldn't be glad when it was over, only he was laughing now because when he said that about Christmas before Christmas he always laughed, it wasn't until after Christmas that he didn't laugh when he said that about Christmas. Then Aunt Louisa got Grandpa's keys out of his pocket herself and opened the desk where Uncle Rodney would prize it open with a screw driver, and took out Grandpa's tonic and then mamma said for me to go and find Cousin Fred and Cousin Louisa.

So Uncle Rodney wasn't there. Only at first I thought maybe it wouldn't be a quarter even, it wouldn't be nothing this time, so at first all I had to think about was that anyway it would be Christmas and that would be something anyway. Because I went on around the house, and so after a while papa and Uncle Fred came out, and I could see them through the bushes knocking at Mandy's door and calling, "Rodney, Rodney," like that. Then I had to get back in the bushes because Uncle Fred had to pass right by me to go to the woodshed to get the axe to open Mandy's door. But they couldn't fool Uncle Rodney. If Mr. Tucker couldn't fool Uncle Rodney in Mr. Tucker's own house, Uncle Fred and papa ought to known they couldn't fool him right in his own papa's back yard. So I didn't even need to hear them. I just waited until after a while Uncle Fred came back out the broken door and came to the woodshed and took the axe and pulled the lock and hasp and steeple off the woodhouse door and went back and then papa came out of Mandy's house and they nailed the woodhouse lock onto Mandy's door and locked it and they went around behind Mandy's house, and I could hear Uncle Fred nailing the windows up. Then they went back to the house. But it didn't matter if Mandy was in the house too and couldn't get out, because the train came from Jefferson with Rosie and papa's Sunday clothes on it and so Rosie was there to cook for Grandpa and us and so that was all right too.

But they couldn't fool Uncle Rodney. I could have told them that. I could have told them that sometimes Uncle Rodney even wanted to wait until after dark to even begin to do business. And so it was all right even if it was late in the afternoon before I could get away from Cousin Fred and Cousin Louisa. It was late; soon they would begin to shoot the fireworks downtown, and then we would be hearing it too, so I could just see his face a little between the slats where papa and Uncle Fred had nailed up the back window; I could see his face where he hadn't shaved, and he was asking me why in hell it took me so long because he had heard the Jefferson train come before dinner, before eleven o'clock, and laughing about how papa and Uncle Fred had nailed him up in the house to keep him when that was exactly what he wanted, and that I would have to slip out right after supper somehow and did I reckon I could

manage it? And I said how last Christmas it had been a
quarter, but I didn't have to slip out of the house that time,
and he laughed, saying Quarter? Quarter? did I ever see ten
quarters all at once? and I never did, and he said for me to
be there with the screw driver right after supper and I
would see ten quarters, and to remember that even God
didn't know where he is and so for me to get the hell away
and stay away until I came back after dark with the screw
driver.

And they couldn't fool me either. Because I had been
watching the man all afternoon, even when he thought I
was just playing and maybe because I was from Jefferson
instead of Mottstown and so I wouldn't know who he was.
But I did, because once when he was walking past the back
fence and he stopped and lit his cigar again and I saw the
badge under his coat when he struck the match and so I
knew he was like Mr. Watts at Jefferson that catches the
niggers. So I was playing by the fence and I could hear him
stopping and looking at me and I played and he said,
"Howdy, son. Santy Claus coming to see you tomorrow?"

"Yes, sir," I said.

"You're Miss Sarah's boy, from up at Jefferson, ain't you?"
he said.

"Yes, sir," I said.

"Come to spend Christmas with your grandpa, eh?" he
said. "I wonder if your Uncle Rodney's at home this afternoon."

"No, sir," I said.

"Well, well, that's too bad," he said. "I wanted to see him
a minute. He's downtown, I reckon?"

"No, sir," I said.

"Well, well," he said. "You mean he's gone away on a
visit, maybe?"

"Yes, sir," I said.

"Well, well," he said. "That's too bad. I wanted to see him on a little business. But I reckon it can wait." Then he looked at me and then he said, "You're sure he's out of town, then?"

"Yes, sir," I said.

"Well, that was all I wanted to know," he said. "If you happen to mention this to your Aunt Louisa or your Uncle Fred you can tell them that was all I wanted to know."

"Yes, sir," I said. So he went away. And he didn't pass the house any more. I watched for him, but he didn't come back. So he couldn't fool me either.

IV

THEN IT BEGAN to get dark and they started to shoot the fireworks downtown. I could hear them, and soon we would be seeing the Roman candles and skyrockets and I would have the ten quarters then and I thought about the basket full of presents and I thought how maybe I could go on downtown when I got through working for Uncle Rodney and buy a present for Grandpa with a dime out of the ten quarters and give it to him tomorrow and maybe, because nobody else had given him a present, Grandpa might give me a quarter too instead of the dime tomorrow, and that would be twenty-one quarters, except for the dime, and that would be fine sure enough. But I didn't have time to do that. We ate supper, and Rosie had to cook that too, and mamma and Aunt Louisa with powder on their faces where they had been crying, and Grandpa; it was papa helping him take a dose of tonic every now and then all afternoon while Uncle Fred was downtown, and Uncle Fred came back and papa came out in the hall and Uncle Fred said he had looked everywhere, in the bank and in the Compress, and how Mr. Pruitt had helped him but they couldn't find a sign either of them or of the money, because Uncle Fred was afraid because one night last week Uncle Rodney hired a rig and went somewhere and Uncle Fred found out Uncle Rodney drove over to the main line at Kingston and caught the fast train to Memphis, and papa said Damnation, and Uncle Fred said By God we will go down there after supper and sweat it out of him, because at least we have got him. I told Pruitt that and he said that if we hold to him, he will hold off and give us a chance.

So Uncle Fred and papa and Grandpa came in to supper together, with Grandpa between them saying Christmas don't come but once a year, thank God, so hooray for it, and papa and Uncle Fred saying Now you are all right, pa; straight ahead now, pa, and Grandpa would go straight ahead awhile and then begin to holler Where in hell is that damn boy? and that meant Uncle Rodney, and that Grandpa was a good mind to go downtown himself and haul Uncle Rodney out of that damn pool hall and make him come home and see his kinfolks. And so we ate supper and mamma said she would take the children upstairs and Aunt Louisa said No, Emmeline could put us to bed, and so we went up the back stairs, and Emmeline said how she had done already had to cook breakfast extra today and if folks thought she was going to waste all her Christmas doing extra work they never had the sense she give them credit for and that this looked like to her it was a good house to be away from nohow, and so we went into the room and then after a while I went back down the back stairs and I remembered where to find the screw driver too. Then I could hear the firecrackers plain from downtown, and the moon was shining now but I could still see the Roman candles and the skyrockets running up the sky. Then Uncle Rodney's hand came out of the crack in the shutter and took the screw driver. I couldn't see his face now and it wasn't laughing exactly, it didn't sound exactly like laughing, it was just the way he breathed behind the shutter.

Because they couldn't fool him. "All right," he said. "Now that's ten quarters. But wait. Are you sure nobody knows where I am?"

"Yes, sir," I said. "I waited by the fence until he come and asked me."

"Which one?" Uncle Rodney said.

"The one that wears the badge," I said.

Then Uncle Rodney cussed. But it wasn't mad cussing. It sounded just like it sounded when he was laughing except the words.

"He said if you were out of town on a visit, and I said Yes sir," I said.

"Good," Uncle Rodney said. "By God, some day you will be as good a business man as I am. And I won't make you a liar much longer, either. So now you have got ten quarters, haven't you?"

"No," I said. "I haven't got them yet."

Then he cussed again, and I said, "I will hold my cap up and you can drop them in it and they won't spill then."

Then he cussed hard, only it wasn't loud. "Only I'm not going to give you ten quarters," he said, and I begun to say You said—and Uncle Rodney said, "Because I am going to give you twenty."

And I said Yes, sir, and he told me how to find the right house, and what to do when I found it. Only there wasn't any paper to carry this time because Uncle Rodney said how this was a twenty-quarter job, and so it was too important to put on paper and besides I wouldn't need a paper because I would not know them anyhow, and his voice coming hissing down from behind the shutter where I couldn't see him and still sounding like when he cussed while he was saying how papa and Uncle Fred had done him a favor by nailing up the door and window and they didn't even have sense enough to know it.

"Start at the corner of the house and count three windows. Then throw the handful of gravel against the window. Then when the window opens—never mind who it will be, you won't know anyway—just say who you are and then say 'He will be at the corner with the buggy in ten minutes. Bring the jewelry.' Now you say it," Uncle Rodney said.

"He will be at the corner with the buggy in ten minutes. Bring the jewelry," I said.

"Say 'Bring all the jewelry,'" Uncle Rodney said.

"Bring all the jewelry," I said.

"Good," Uncle Rodney said. Then he said, "Well? What are you waiting on?"

"For the twenty quarters," I said.

Uncle Rodney cussed again. "Do you expect me to pay you before you have done the work?" he said.

"You said about a buggy," I said. "Maybe you will forget to pay me before you go and you might not get back until after we go back home. And besides, that day last summer when we couldn't do any business with Mrs. Tucker because she was sick and you wouldn't pay me the nickel because you said it wasn't your fault Mrs. Tucker was sick."

Then Uncle Rodney cussed hard and quiet behind the crack and then he said, "Listen. I haven't got the twenty quarters now. I haven't even got one quarter now. And the only way I can get any is to get out of here and finish this business. And I can't finish this business tonight unless you do your work. See? I'll be right behind you. I'll be waiting right there at the corner in the buggy when you come back. Now, go on. Hurry."

V

So I went on across the yard, only the moon was bright now and I walked behind the fence until I got to the street.

And I could hear the firecrackers and I could see the Roman candles and skyrockets sliding up the sky, but the fireworks were all downtown, and so all I could see along the street was the candles and wreaths in the windows. So I came to the lane, went up the lane to the stable, and I could hear the horse in the stable, but I didn't know whether it was the right stable or not; but pretty soon Uncle Rodney kind of jumped around the corner of the stable and said Here you are, and he showed me where to stand and listen toward the house and he went back into the stable. But I couldn't hear anything but Uncle Rodney harnessing the horse, and then he whistled and I went back and he had the horse already hitched to the buggy and I said Whose horse and buggy is this; it's a lot skinnier than Grandpa's horse? And Uncle Rodney said It's my horse now, only damn this moonlight to hell. Then I went back down the lane to the street and there wasn't anybody coming so I waved my arm in the moonlight, and the buggy came up and I got in and we went fast. The side curtains were up and so I couldn't see the skyrockets and Roman candles from town, but I could hear the firecrackers and I thought maybe we were going through town and maybe Uncle Rodney would stop and give me some of the twenty quarters and I could buy Grandpa a present for tomorrow, but we didn't; Uncle Rodney just raised the side curtain without stopping and then I could see the house, the two magnolia trees, but we didn't stop until we came to the corner.

"Now," Uncle Rodney said, "when the window opens, say 'He will be at the corner in ten minutes. Bring *all* the jewelry.' Never mind who it will be. You don't want to know who it is. You want to even forget what house it is. See?"

"Yes, sir," I said. "And then you will pay me the——"

"Yes!" he said, cussing. "Yes! Get out of here quick!"

So I got out and the buggy went on and I went back up the street. And the house was dark all right except for one light, so it was the right one, besides the two trees. So I went across the yard and counted the three windows and I was just about to throw the gravel when a lady ran out from behind a bush and grabbed me. She kept on trying to say something, only I couldn't tell what it was, and besides she never had time to say very much anyhow because a man ran out from behind another bush and grabbed us both. Only he grabbed her by the mouth, because I could tell that from the kind of slobbering noise she made while she was fighting to get loose.

"Well, boy?" he said. "What is it? Are you the one?"

"I work for Uncle Rodney," I said.

"Then you're the one," he said. Now the lady was fighting and slobbering sure enough, but he held her by the mouth. "All right. What is it?"

Only I didn't know Uncle Rodney ever did business with men. But maybe after he began to work in the Compress Association he had to. And then he had told me I would not know them anyway, so maybe that was what he meant.

"He says to be at the corner in ten minutes," I said. "And to bring all the jewelry. He said for me to say that twice. Bring all the jewelry."

The lady was slobbering and fighting worse than ever now, so maybe he had to turn me loose so he could hold her with both hands.

"Bring all the jewelry," he said, holding the lady with both hands now. "That's a good idea. That's fine. I don't blame him for telling you to say that twice. All right. Now you go back to the corner and wait and when he comes, tell him this: 'She says to come and help carry it.' Say that to him twice, too. Understand?"

"Then I'll get my twenty quarters," I said.

"Twenty quarters, hah?" the man said, holding the lady. "That's what you are to get, is it? That's not enough. You tell him this, too: 'She says to give you a piece of the jewelry.' Understand?"

"I just want my twenty quarters," I said.

Then he and the lady went back behind the bushes again and I went on, too, back toward the corner, and I could see the Roman candles and skyrockets again from toward town and I could hear the firecrackers, and then the buggy came back and Uncle Rodney was hissing again behind the curtain like when he was behind the slats on Mandy's window.

"Well?" he said.

"She said for you to come and help carry it," I said.

"What?" Uncle Rodney said. "She said he's not there?"

"No, sir. She said for you to come and help carry it. For me to say that twice." Then I said, "Where's my twenty quarters?" because he had already jumped out of the buggy and jumped across the walk into the shadow of some bushes. So I went into the bushes too and said, "You said you would give——"

"All right; all right!" Uncle Rodney said. He was kind of squatting along the bushes; I could hear him breathing. "I'll give them to you tomorrow. I'll give you thirty quarters tomorrow. Now you get to hell on home. And if they have been down to Mandy's house, you don't know anything. Run, now. Hurry."

"I'd rather have the twenty quarters tonight," I said.

He was squatting fast along in the shadow of the bushes, and I was right behind him, because when he whirled around he almost touched me, but I jumped back out of the bushes in time and he stood there cussing at me and then he stooped down and I saw it was a stick in his hand and I turned and ran. Then he went on, squatting along in the shadow, and then I went back to the buggy, because the day after Christmas we would go back to Jefferson, and so if Uncle Rodney didn't get back before then I would not see him again until next summer and then maybe he would be in business with another lady and my twenty quarters would be like my nickel that time when Mrs. Tucker was sick. So I waited by the buggy and I could watch the skyrockets and the Roman candles and I could hear the firecrackers from town, only it was late now and so maybe all the stores would be closed and so I couldn't buy Grandpa a present, even when Uncle Rodney came back and gave me my twenty quarters. So I was listening to the firecrackers and thinking about how maybe I could tell Grandpa that I had wanted to buy him a present and so maybe he might give me fifteen cents instead of a dime anyway, when all of a sudden they started shooting firecrackers back at the house where Uncle Rodney had gone. Only they just shot five of them fast, and when they didn't shoot any more I thought that maybe in a minute they would shoot the skyrockets and Roman candles too. But they didn't. They just shot the five firecrackers right quick and then stopped, and I stood by the buggy and then folks began to come out of the houses and holler at one another and then I began to see men running toward the house where Uncle Rodney had gone, and then a man came out of the yard fast and went up the street toward Grandpa's and I thought at first it was Uncle Rodney and that he had forgotten the buggy, until I saw that it wasn't.

But Uncle Rodney never came back and so I went on toward the yard to where the men were, because I could still watch the buggy too and see Uncle Rodney if he came back out of the bushes, and I came to the yard and I saw six men carrying something long and then two other men ran up and stopped me and one of them said Hell-fire, it's one of those kids, the one from Jefferson. And I could see then that what the men were carrying was a window blind with something wrapped in a quilt on it and so I thought at first that they had come to help Uncle Rodney carry the jewelry, only I didn't see Uncle Rodney anywhere, and then one of the men said, "Who? One of the kids? Hell-fire, somebody take him on home."

So the man picked me up, but I said I had to wait on Uncle Rodney, and the man said that Uncle Rodney would be all right, and I said But I wanted to wait for him here, and then one of the men behind us said Damn it, get him on out of here, and we went on. I was riding on the man's back and then I could look back and see the six men in the moonlight carrying the blind with the bundle on it, and I said Did it belong to Uncle Rodney? and the man said No, if it belonged to anybody now it belonged to Grandpa. And so then I knew what it was.

"It's a side of beef," I said. "You are going to take it to Grandpa." Then the other man made a funny sound and the one I was riding on said Yes, you might call it a side of beef, and I said, "It's a Christmas present for Grandpa. Who is it going to be from? Is it from Uncle Rodney?"

"No," the man said. "Not from him. Call it from the men of Mottstown. From all the husbands in Mottstown."

VI

THEN WE CAME in sight of Grandpa's house. And now the lights were all on, even on the porch, and I could see folks in the hall, I could see ladies with shawls over their heads, and some more of them going up the walk toward the porch, and then I could hear somebody in the house that sounded like singing and then papa came out of the house and came down the walk to the gate and we came up and the man put me down and I saw Rosie waiting at the gate too. Only it didn't sound like singing now because there wasn't any music with it, and so maybe it was Aunt Louisa again and so maybe she didn't like Christmas now any better than Grandpa said he didn't like it.

"It's a present for Grandpa," I said.

"Yes," papa said. "You go on with Rosie and go to bed. Mamma will be there soon. But you be a good boy until she comes. You mind Rosie. All right, Rosie. Take him on. Hurry."

"You don't need to tell me that," Rosie said. She took my hand. "Come on."

Only we didn't go back into the yard, because Rosie came out the gate and we went up the street. And then I thought maybe we were going around the back to dodge the people and we didn't do that, either. We just went on up the street, and I said, "Where are we going?"

And Rosie said, "We gonter sleep at a lady's house name Mrs. Jordon."

So we went on. I didn't say anything. Because papa had forgotten to say anything about my slipping out of the house yet and so maybe if I went on to bed and stayed quiet he would forget about it until tomorrow too. And besides, the main thing was to get a holt of Uncle Rodney and get my twenty quarters before we went back home, and so maybe that would be all right tomorrow too. So we went on and Rosie said Yonder's the house, and we went in the yard and then all of a sudden Rosie saw the possum. It was in a persimmon tree in Mrs. Jordon's yard and I could see it against the moonlight too, and I hollered, "Run! Run and get Mrs. Jordon's ladder!"

And Rosie said, "Ladder my foot! You going to bed!"

But I didn't wait. I began to run toward the house, with Rosie running behind me and hollering You, Georgie! You come back here! But I didn't stop. We could get the ladder and get the possum and give it to Grandpa along with the

side of meat and it wouldn't cost even a dime and then maybe
Grandpa might even give me a quarter too, and then when I
got the twenty quarters from Uncle Rodney I would have
twenty-one quarters and that will be fine.

That Evening Sun

I

MONDAY IS NO DIFFERENT from any other weekday in Jefferson now. The streets are paved now, and the telephone and electric companies are cutting down more and more of the shade trees—the water oaks, the maples and locusts and elms —to make room for iron poles bearing clusters of bloated and ghostly and bloodless grapes, and we have a city laundry which makes the rounds on Monday morning, gathering the bundles of clothes into bright-colored, specially-made motor cars: the soiled wearing of a whole week now flees apparitionlike behind alert and irritable electric horns, with a long diminishing noise of rubber and asphalt like tearing silk, and even the Negro women who still take in white people's washing after the old custom, fetch and deliver it in automobiles.

But fifteen years ago, on Monday morning the quiet, dusty, shady streets would be full of Negro women with, balanced on their steady, turbaned heads, bundles of clothes tied up in sheets, almost as large as cotton bales, carried so without touch of hand between the kitchen door of the white house and the blackened washpot beside a cabin door in Negro Hollow.

Nancy would set her bundle on the top of her head, then upon the bundle in turn she would set the black straw sailor hat which she wore winter and summer. She was tall, with a high, sad face sunken a little where her teeth were missing. Sometimes we would go a part of the way down the lane and across the pasture with her, to watch the balanced bundle and the hat that never bobbed nor wavered, even when she walked down into the ditch and up the other side and stooped through the fence. She would go down on her hands and knees and crawl through the gap, her head rigid, uptilted, the bundle steady as a rock or a balloon, and rise to her feet again and go on.

Sometimes the husbands of the washing women would fetch and deliver the clothes, but Jesus never did that for Nancy, even before father told him to stay away from our house, even when Dilsey was sick and Nancy would come to cook for us.

And then about half the time we'd have to go down the lane to Nancy's cabin and tell her to come on and cook breakfast. We would stop at the ditch, because father told us to not have anything to do with Jesus—he was a short black man, with a razor scar down his face—and we would throw rocks at Nancy's house until she came to the door, leaning her head around it without any clothes on.

"What yawl mean, chunking my house?" Nancy said. "What you little devils mean?"

"Father says for you to come on and get breakfast," Caddy said. "Father says it's over a half an hour now, and you've got to come this minute."

"I aint studying no breakfast," Nancy said. "I going to get my sleep out."

"I bet you're drunk," Jason said. "Father says you're drunk. Are you drunk, Nancy?"

"Who says I is?" Nancy said. "I got to get my sleep out. I aint studying no breakfast."

So after a while we quit chunking the cabin and went back home. When she finally came, it was too late for me to go to school. So we thought it was whisky until that day they arrested her again and they were taking her to jail and they passed Mr Stovall. He was the cashier in the bank and a deacon in the Baptist church, and Nancy began to say:

"When you going to pay me, white man? When you going to pay me, white man? It's been three times now since you paid me a cent—" Mr Stovall knocked her down, but she kept on saying, "When you going to pay me, white man? It's been three times now since—" until Mr Stovall kicked her in the mouth with his heel and the marshal caught Mr Stovall back, and Nancy lying in the street, laughing. She turned her head and spat out some blood and teeth and said, "It's been three times now since he paid me a cent."

That was how she lost her teeth, and all that day they told about Nancy and Mr Stovall, and all that night the ones that passed the jail could hear Nancy singing and yelling. They could see her hands holding to the window bars, and a lot of them stopped along the fence, listening to her and to the jailer trying to make her stop. She didn't shut up until almost daylight, when the jailer began to hear a bumping and scraping upstairs and he went up there and found Nancy hanging from the window bar. He said that it was cocaine and not whisky, because no nigger would try to commit suicide unless he was full of cocaine, because a nigger full of cocaine wasn't a nigger any longer.

The jailer cut her down and revived her; then he beat her, whipped her. She had hung herself with her dress. She had fixed it all right, but when they arrested her she didn't have on anything except a dress and so she didn't have anything to tie her hands with and she couldn't make her hands let go of the window ledge. So the jailer heard the noise and ran up there and found Nancy hanging from the window, stark naked, her belly already swelling out a little, like a little balloon.

When Dilsey was sick in her cabin and Nancy was cooking for us, we could see her apron swelling out; that was before father told Jesus to stay away from the house. Jesus was in the kitchen, sitting behind the stove, with his razor scar on his black face like a piece of dirty string. He said it was a watermelon that Nancy had under her dress.

"It never come off of your vine, though," Nancy said.

"Off of what vine?" Caddy said.

"I can cut down the vine it did come off of," Jesus said.

"What makes you want to talk like that before these chillen?" Nancy said. "Whyn't you go on to work? You done et. You want Mr Jason to catch you hanging around his kitchen, talking that way before these chillen?"

"Talking what way?" Caddy said. "What vine?"

"I cant hang around white man's kitchen," Jesus said. "But white man can hang around mine. White man can come in my house, but I cant stop him. When white man want to come in my house, I aint got no house. I cant stop him, but he cant kick me outen it. He cant do that."

Dilsey was still sick in her cabin. Father told Jesus to stay off our place. Dilsey was still sick. It was a long time. We were in the library after supper.

"Isn't Nancy through in the kitchen yet?" mother said. "It seems to me that she has had plenty of time to have finished the dishes."

"Let Quentin go and see," father said. "Go and see if Nancy is through, Quentin. Tell her she can go on home."

I went to the kitchen. Nancy was through. The dishes were put away and the fire was out. Nancy was sitting in a chair, close to the cold stove. She looked at me.

"Mother wants to know if you are through," I said.

"Yes," Nancy said. She looked at me. "I done finished." She looked at me.

"What is it?" I said. "What is it?"

"I aint nothing but a nigger," Nancy said. "It aint none of my fault."

She looked at me, sitting in the chair before the cold stove, the sailor hat on her head. I went back to the library. It was the cold stove and all, when you think of a kitchen being warm and busy and cheerful. And with a cold stove and the dishes all put away, and nobody wanting to eat at that hour.

"Is she through?" mother said.

"Yessum," I said.

"What is she doing?" mother said.

"She's not doing anything. She's through."

"I'll go and see," father said.

"Maybe she's waiting for Jesus to come and take her home," Caddy said.

"Jesus is gone," I said. Nancy told us how one morning she woke up and Jesus was gone.

"He quit me," Nancy said. "Done gone to Memphis, I reckon. Dodging them city *po*-lice for a while, I reckon."

"And a good riddance," father said. "I hope he stays there."

"Nancy's scaired of the dark," Jason said.

"So are you," Caddy said.

"I'm not," Jason said.

"Scairy cat," Caddy said.

"I'm not," Jason said.

"You, Candace!" mother said. Father came back.

"I am going to walk down the lane with Nancy," he said. "She says that Jesus is back."

"Has she seen him?" mother said.

"No. Some Negro sent her word that he was back in town. I wont be long."

"You'll leave me alone, to take Nancy home?" mother said. "Is her safety more precious to you than mine?"

"I wont be long," father said.

"You'll leave these children unprotected, with that Negro about?"

"I'm going too," Caddy said. "Let me go, Father."

"What would he do with them, if he were unfortunate enough to have them?" father said.

"I want to go, too," Jason said.

"Jason!" mother said. She was speaking to father. You could tell that by the way she said the name. Like she believed that all day father had been trying to think of doing the thing she wouldn't like the most, and that she knew all the time that after a while he would think of it. I stayed quiet, because father and I both knew that mother would want him to make me stay with her if she just thought of it in time. So father didn't look at me. I was the oldest. I was nine and Caddy was seven and Jason was five.

"Nonsense," father said. "We wont be long."

Nancy had her hat on. We came to the lane. "Jesus always been good to me," Nancy said. "Whenever he had two dollars, one of them was mine." We walked in the lane. "If I can just get through the lane," Nancy said, "I be all right then."

The lane was always dark. "This is where Jason got scared on Hallowe'en," Caddy said.

"I didn't," Jason said.

"Cant Aunt Rachel do anything with him?" father said. Aunt Rachel was old. She lived in a cabin beyond Nancy's, by herself. She had white hair and she smoked a pipe in the door, all day long; she didn't work any more. They said she was Jesus' mother. Sometimes she said she was and sometimes she said she wasn't any kin to Jesus.

"Yes, you did," Caddy said. "You were scairder than Frony. You were scairder than T.P. even. Scairder than niggers."

"Cant nobody do nothing with him," Nancy said. "He say

I done woke up the devil in him and aint but one thing going to lay it down again."

"Well, he's gone now," father said. "There's nothing for you to be afraid of now. And if you'd just let white men alone."

"Let what white men alone?" Caddy said. "How let them alone?"

"He aint gone nowhere," Nancy said. "I can feel him. I can feel him now, in this lane. He hearing us talk, every word, hid somewhere, waiting. I aint seen him, and I aint going to see him again but once more, with that razor in his mouth. That razor on that string down his back, inside his shirt. And then I aint going to be even surprised."

"I wasn't scaired," Jason said.

"If you'd behave yourself, you'd have kept out of this," father said. "But it's all right now. He's probably in St. Louis now. Probably got another wife by now and forgot all about you."

"If he has, I better not find out about it," Nancy said. "I'd stand there right over them, and every time he wropped her, I'd cut that arm off. I'd cut his head off and I'd slit her belly and I'd shove—"

"Hush," father said.

"Slit whose belly, Nancy?" Caddy said.

"I wasn't scaired," Jason said. "I'd walk right down this lane by myself."

"Yah," Caddy said. "You wouldn't dare to put your foot down in it if we were not here too."

II

DILSEY WAS STILL SICK, so we took Nancy home every night until mother said, "How much longer is this going on? I to

be left alone in this big house while you take home a frightened Negro?"

We fixed a pallet in the kitchen for Nancy. One night we
waked up, hearing the sound. It was not singing and it was
not crying, coming up the dark stairs. There was a light in
mother's room and we heard father going down the hall,
down the back stairs, and Caddy and I went into the hall.
The floor was cold. Our toes curled away from it while we
listened to the sound. It was like singing and it wasn't like
singing, like the sounds that Negroes make.

Then it stopped and we heard father going down the back
stairs, and we went to the head of the stairs. Then the sound
began again, in the stairway, not loud, and we could see
Nancy's eyes halfway up the stairs, against the wall. They
looked like cat's eyes do, like a big cat against the wall,
watching us. When we came down the steps to where she
was, she quit making the sound again, and we stood there
until father came back up from the kitchen, with his pistol in
his hand. He went back down with Nancy and they came
back with Nancy's pallet.

We spread the pallet in our room. After the light in
mother's room went off, we could see Nancy's eyes again.
"Nancy," Caddy whispered, "are you asleep, Nancy?"

Nancy whispered something. It was oh or no, I dont know
which. Like nobody had made it, like it came from nowhere
and went nowhere, until it was like Nancy was not there at
all; that I had looked so hard at her eyes on the stairs that
they had got printed on my eyeballs, like the sun does when
you have closed your eyes and there is no sun. "Jesus,"
Nancy whispered. "Jesus."

"Was it Jesus?" Caddy said. "Did he try to come into the
kitchen?"

"Jesus," Nancy said. Like this: Jeeeeeeeeeeeeeeeesus, until
the sound went out, like a match or a candle does.

"It's the other Jesus she means," I said.

"Can you see us, Nancy?" Caddy whispered. "Can you see our eyes too?"

"I aint nothing but a nigger," Nancy said. "God knows. God knows."

"What did you see down there in the kitchen?" Caddy whispered. "What tried to get in?"

"God knows," Nancy said. We could see her eyes. "God knows."

Dilsey got well. She cooked dinner. "You'd better stay in bed a day or two longer," father said.

"What for?" Dilsey said. "If I had been a day later, this place would be to rack and ruin. Get on out of here now, and let me get my kitchen straight again."

Dilsey cooked supper too. And that night, just before dark, Nancy came into the kitchen.

"How do you know he's back?" Dilsey said. "You aint seen him."

"Jesus is a nigger," Jason said.

"I can feel him," Nancy said. "I can feel him laying yonder in the ditch."

"Tonight?" Dilsey said. "Is he there tonight?"

"Dilsey's a nigger too," Jason said.

"You try to eat something," Dilsey said.

"I dont want nothing," Nancy said.

"I aint a nigger," Jason said.

"Drink some coffee," Dilsey said. She poured a cup of coffee for Nancy. "Do you know he's out there tonight? How come you know it's tonight?"

"I know," Nancy said. "He's there, waiting. I know. I done lived with him too long. I know what he is fixing to do fore he know it himself."

"Drink some coffee," Dilsey said. Nancy held the cup to her mouth and blew into the cup. Her mouth pursed out

like a spreading adder's, like a rubber mouth, like she had
blown all the color out of her lips with blowing the coffee.

"I aint a nigger," Jason said. "Are you a nigger, Nancy?"

"I hellborn, child," Nancy said. "I wont be nothing soon.
I going back where I come from soon."

III

SHE BEGAN TO DRINK the coffee. While she was drinking, holding the cup in both hands, she began to make the sound again.
She made the sound into the cup and the coffee sploshed out
onto her hands and her dress. Her eyes looked at us and she
sat there, her elbows on her knees, holding the cup in both
hands, looking at us across the wet cup, making the sound.
"Look at Nancy," Jason said. "Nancy cant cook for us now.
Dilsey's got well now."

"You hush up," Dilsey said. Nancy held the cup in both
hands, looking at us, making the sound, like there were two
of them: one looking at us and the other making the sound.
"Whyn't you let Mr Jason telefoam the marshal?" Dilsey
said. Nancy stopped then, holding the cup in her long brown
hands. She tried to drink some coffee again, but it sploshed
out of the cup, onto her hands and her dress, and she put the
cup down. Jason watched her.

"I cant swallow it," Nancy said. "I swallows but it wont
go down me."

"You go down to the cabin," Dilsey said. "Frony will fix
you a pallet and I'll be there soon."

"Wont no nigger stop him," Nancy said.

"I aint a nigger," Jason said. "Am I, Dilsey?"

"I reckon not," Dilsey said. She looked at Nancy. "I dont
reckon so. What you going to do, then?"

Nancy looked at us. Her eyes went fast, like she was afraid

there wasn't time to look, without hardly moving at all. She looked at us, at all three of us at one time. "You member that night I stayed in yawls' room?" she said. She told about how we waked up early the next morning, and played. We had to play quiet, on her pallet, until father woke up and it was time to get breakfast. "Go and ask your maw to let me stay here tonight," Nancy said. "I wont need no pallet. We can play some more."

Caddy asked mother. Jason went too. "I cant have Negroes sleeping in the bedrooms," mother said. Jason cried. He cried until mother said he couldn't have any dessert for three days if he didn't stop. Then Jason said he would stop if Dilsey would make a chocolate cake. Father was there.

"Why dont you do something about it?" mother said. "What do we have officers for?"

"Why is Nancy afraid of Jesus?" Caddy said. "Are you afraid of father, mother?"

"What could the officers do?" father said. "If Nancy hasn't seen him, how could the officers find him?"

"Then why is she afraid?" mother said.

"She says he is there. She says she knows he is there tonight."

"Yet we pay taxes," mother said. "I must wait here alone in this big house while you take a Negro woman home."

"You know that I am not lying outside with a razor," father said.

"I'll stop if Dilsey will make a chocolate cake," Jason said. Mother told us to go out and father said he didn't know if Jason would get a chocolate cake or not, but he knew what Jason was going to get in about a minute. We went back to the kitchen and told Nancy.

"Father said for you to go home and lock the door, and you'll be all right," Caddy said. "All right from what, Nancy? Is Jesus mad at you?" Nancy was holding the coffee cup in her hands again, her elbows on her knees and her hands holding the cup between her knees. She was looking into the cup. "What have you done that made Jesus mad?" Caddy said. Nancy let the cup go. It didn't break on the floor, but the coffee spilled out, and Nancy sat there with her hands still making the shape of the cup. She began to make the sound again, not loud. Not singing and not unsinging. We watched her.

"Here," Dilsey said. "You quit that, now. You get aholt of yourself. You wait here. I going to get Versh to walk home with you." Dilsey went out.

We looked at Nancy. Her shoulders kept shaking, but she quit making the sound. We watched her. "What's Jesus going to do to you?" Caddy said. "He went away."

Nancy looked at us. "We had fun that night I stayed in yawls' room, didn't we?"

"I didn't," Jason said. "I didn't have any fun."

"You were asleep in mother's room," Caddy said. "You were not there."

"Let's go down to my house and have some more fun," Nancy said.

"Mother wont let us," I said. "It's too late now."

"Dont bother her," Nancy said. "We can tell her in the morning. She wont mind."

"She wouldn't let us," I said.

"Dont ask her now," Nancy said. "Dont bother her now."

"She didn't say we couldn't go," Caddy said.

"We didn't ask," I said.

"If you go, I'll tell," Jason said.

"We'll have fun," Nancy said. "They won't mind, just to my house. I been working for yawl a long time. They won't mind."

"I'm not afraid to go," Caddy said. "Jason is the one that's afraid. He'll tell."

"I'm not," Jason said.

"Yes, you are," Caddy said. "You'll tell."

"I won't tell," Jason said. "I'm not afraid."

"Jason ain't afraid to go with me," Nancy said. "Is you, Jason?"

"Jason is going to tell," Caddy said. The lane was dark. We passed the pasture gate. "I bet if something was to jump out from behind that gate, Jason would holler."

"I wouldn't," Jason said. We walked down the lane. Nancy was talking loud.

"What are you talking so loud for, Nancy?" Caddy said.

"Who; me?" Nancy said. "Listen at Quentin and Caddy and Jason saying I'm talking loud."

"You talk like there was five of us here," Caddy said. "You talk like father was here too."

"Who; me talking loud, Mr Jason?" Nancy said.

"Nancy called Jason 'Mister,' " Caddy said.

"Listen how Caddy and Quentin and Jason talk," Nancy said.

"We're not talking loud," Caddy said. "You're the one that's talking like father—"

"Hush," Nancy said; "hush, Mr Jason."

"Nancy called Jason 'Mister' aguh—"

"Hush," Nancy said. She was talking loud when we crossed the ditch and stooped through the fence where she used to stoop through with the clothes on her head. Then we came to her house. We were going fast then. She opened the door. The smell of the house was like the lamp and the smell of Nancy was like the wick, like they were waiting for one another to begin to smell. She lit the lamp and closed the door and put the bar up. Then she quit talking loud, looking at us.

"What're we going to do?" Caddy said.

"What do yawl want to do?" Nancy said.

"You said we would have some fun," Caddy said.

There was something about Nancy's house; something you could smell besides Nancy and the house. Jason smelled it, even. "I don't want to stay here," he said. "I want to go home."

"Go home, then," Caddy said.

"I don't want to go by myself," Jason said.

"We're going to have some fun," Nancy said.

"How?" Caddy said.

Nancy stood by the door. She was looking at us, only it was like she had emptied her eyes, like she had quit using them. "What do you want to do?" she said.

"Tell us a story," Caddy said. "Can you tell a story?"

"Yes," Nancy said.

"Tell it," Caddy said. We looked at Nancy. "You don't know any stories."

"Yes," Nancy said. "Yes, I do."

She came and sat in a chair before the hearth. There was a little fire there. Nancy built it up, when it was already hot inside. She built a good blaze. She told a story. She talked like her eyes looked, like her eyes watching us and her voice talking to us did not belong to her. Like she was living somewhere else, waiting somewhere else. She was outside the cabin. Her voice was inside and the shape of her, the Nancy that could stoop under a barbed wire fence with a bundle of clothes balanced on her head as though without weight, like a balloon, was there. But that was all. "And so this here queen come walking up to the ditch, where that bad man was hiding. She was walking up to the ditch, and she say, 'If I can just get past this here ditch,' was what she say . . ."

"What ditch?" Caddy said. "A ditch like that one out there? Why did a queen want to go into a ditch?"

"To get to her house," Nancy said. She looked at us. "She

had to cross the ditch to get into her house quick and bar the door."

"Why did she want to go home and bar the door?" Caddy said.

IV

NANCY LOOKED at us. She quit talking. She looked at us. Jason's legs stuck straight out of his pants where he sat on Nancy's lap. "I don't think that's a good story," he said. "I want to go home."

"Maybe we had better," Caddy said. She got up from the floor. "I bet they are looking for us right now." She went toward the door.

"No," Nancy said. "Don't open it." She got up quick and passed Caddy. She didn't touch the door, the wooden bar.

"Why not?" Caddy said.

"Come back to the lamp," Nancy said. "We'll have fun. You don't have to go."

"We ought to go," Caddy said. "Unless we have a lot of fun." She and Nancy came back to the fire, the lamp.

"I want to go home," Jason said. "I'm going to tell."

"I know another story," Nancy said. She stood close to the lamp. She looked at Caddy, like when your eyes look up at a stick balanced on your nose. She had to look down to see Caddy, but her eyes looked like that, like when you are balancing a stick.

"I won't listen to it," Jason said. "I'll bang on the floor."

"It's a good one," Nancy said. "It's better than the other one."

"What's it about?" Caddy said. Nancy was standing by the lamp. Her hand was on the lamp, against the light, long and brown.

"Your hand is on that hot globe," Caddy said. "Don't it feel hot to your hand?"

Nancy looked at her hand on the lamp chimney. She took her hand away, slow. She stood there, looking at Caddy, wringing her long hand as though it were tied to her wrist with a string.

"Let's do something else," Caddy said.

"I want to go home," Jason said.

"I got some popcorn," Nancy said. She looked at Caddy and then at Jason and then at me and then at Caddy again. "I got some popcorn."

"I don't like popcorn," Jason said. "I'd rather have candy."

Nancy looked at Jason. "You can hold the popper." She was still wringing her hand; it was long and limp and brown.

"All right," Jason said. "I'll stay a while if I can do that. Caddy can't hold it. I'll want to go home again if Caddy holds the popper."

Nancy built up the fire. "Look at Nancy putting her hands in the fire," Caddy said. "What's the matter with you, Nancy?"

"I got popcorn," Nancy said. "I got some." She took the popper from under the bed. It was broken. Jason began to cry.

"Now we can't have any popcorn," he said.

"We ought to go home, anyway," Caddy said. "Come on, Quentin."

"Wait," Nancy said; "wait. I can fix it. Don't you want to help me fix it?"

"I don't think I want any," Caddy said. "It's too late now."

"You help me, Jason," Nancy said. "Don't you want to help me?"

"No," Jason said. "I want to go home."

"Hush," Nancy said; "hush. Watch. Watch me. I can fix it so Jason can hold it and pop the corn." She got a piece of wire and fixed the popper.

"It won't hold good," Caddy said.

"Yes, it will," Nancy said. "Yawl watch. Yawl help me shell some corn."

The popcorn was under the bed too. We shelled it into the popper and Nancy helped Jason hold the popper over the fire.

"It's not popping," Jason said. "I want to go home."

"You wait," Nancy said. "It'll begin to pop. We'll have fun then." She was sitting close to the fire. The lamp was turned up so high it was beginning to smoke.

"Why don't you turn it down some?" I said.

"It's all right," Nancy said. "I'll clean it. Yawl wait. The popcorn will start in a minute."

"I don't believe it's going to start," Caddy said. "We ought to start home, anyway. They'll be worried."

"No," Nancy said. "It's going to pop. Dilsey will tell um yawl with me. I been working for yawl long time. They won't mind if yawl at my house. You wait, now. It'll start popping any minute now."

Then Jason got some smoke in his eyes and he began to cry. He dropped the popper into the fire. Nancy got a wet rag and wiped Jason's face, but he didn't stop crying.

"Hush," she said. "Hush." But he didn't hush. Caddy took the popper out of the fire.

"It's burned up," she said. "You'll have to get some more popcorn, Nancy."

"Did you put all of it in?" Nancy said.

"Yes," Caddy said. Nancy looked at Caddy. Then she took the popper and opened it and poured the cinders into her apron and began to sort the grains, her hands long and brown, and we watching her.

"Haven't you got any more?" Caddy said.

"Yes," Nancy said; "yes. Look. This here ain't burnt. All we need to do is—"

"I want to go home," Jason said. "I'm going to tell."

"Hush," Caddy said. We all listened. Nancy's head was already turned toward the barred door, her eyes filled with red lamplight. "Somebody is coming," Caddy said.

Then Nancy began to make that sound again, not loud, sitting there above the fire, her long hands dangling between her knees; all of a sudden water began to come out on her face in big drops, running down her face, carrying in each one a little turning ball of firelight like a spark until it dropped off her chin. "She's not crying," I said.

"I ain't crying," Nancy said. Her eyes were closed. "I ain't crying. Who is it?"

"I don't know," Caddy said. She went to the door and looked out. "We've got to go now," she said. "Here comes father."

"I'm going to tell," Jason said. "Yawl made me come."

The water still ran down Nancy's face. She turned in her chair. "Listen. Tell him. Tell him we going to have fun. Tell him I take good care of yawl until in the morning. Tell him to let me come home with yawl and sleep on the floor. Tell him I won't need no pallet. We'll have fun. You member last time how we had so much fun?"

"I didn't have fun," Jason said. "You hurt me. You put smoke in my eyes. I'm going to tell."

V

FATHER CAME IN. He looked at us. Nancy did not get up.

"Tell him," she said.

"Caddy made us come down here," Jason said. "I didn't want to."

Father came to the fire. Nancy looked up at him. "Can't you go to Aunt Rachel's and stay?" he said. Nancy looked up at father, her hands between her knees. "He's not here," father said. "I would have seen him. There's not a soul in sight."

"He in the ditch," Nancy said. "He waiting in the ditch yonder."

"Nonsense," father said. He looked at Nancy. "Do you know he's there?"

"I got the sign," Nancy said.

"What sign?"

"I got it. It was on the table when I come in. It was a hog-bone, with blood meat still on it, laying by the lamp. He's out there. When yawl walk out that door, I gone."

"Gone where, Nancy?" Caddy said.

"I'm not a tattletale," Jason said.

"Nonsense," father said.

"He out there," Nancy said. "He looking through that window this minute, waiting for yawl to go. Then I gone."

"Nonsense," father said. "Lock up your house and we'll take you on to Aunt Rachel's."

" 'Twont do no good," Nancy said. She didn't look at father now, but he looked down at her, at her long, limp, moving hands. "Putting it off wont do no good."

"Then what do you want to do?" father said.

"I don't know," Nancy said. "I can't do nothing. Just put it off. And that don't do no good. I reckon it belong to me. I reckon what I going to get ain't no more than mine."

"Get what?" Caddy said. "What's yours?"

"Nothing," father said. "You all must get to bed."

"Caddy made me come," Jason said.

"Go on to Aunt Rachel's," father said.

"It won't do no good," Nancy said. She sat before the fire, her elbows on her knees, her long hands between her knees. "When even your own kitchen wouldn't do no good. When even if I was sleeping on the floor in the room with your chillen, and the next morning there I am, and blood—"

"Hush," father said. "Lock the door and put out the lamp and go to bed."

"I scared of the dark," Nancy said. "I scared for it to happen in the dark."

"You mean you're going to sit right here with the lamp lighted?" father said. Then Nancy began to make the sound again, sitting before the fire, her long hands between her knees. "Ah, damnation," father said. "Come along, chillen. It's past bedtime."

"When yawl go home, I gone," Nancy said. She talked quieter now, and her face looked quiet, like her hands. "Anyway, I got my coffin money saved up with Mr. Lovelady." Mr. Lovelady was a short, dirty man who collected the Negro insurance, coming around to the cabins or the kitchens every Saturday morning, to collect fifteen cents. He and his wife lived at the hotel. One morning his wife committed suicide. They had a child, a little girl. He and the child went away. After a week or two he came back alone. We would see him going along the lanes and the back streets on Saturday mornings.

"Nonsense," father said. "You'll be the first thing I'll see in the kitchen tomorrow morning."

"You'll see what you'll see, I reckon," Nancy said. "But it will take the Lord to say what that will be."

VI

WE LEFT HER sitting before the fire.

"Come and put the bar up," father said. But she didn't move. She didn't look at us again, sitting quietly there between the lamp and the fire. From some distance down the lane we could look back and see her through the open door.

"What, Father?" Caddy said. "What's going to happen?"

"Nothing," father said. Jason was on father's back, so

Jason was the tallest of all of us. We went down into the ditch. I looked at it, quiet. I couldn't see much where the moonlight and the shadows tangled.

"If Jesus is hid here, he can see us, cant he?" Caddy said.

"He's not there," father said. "He went away a long time ago."

"You made me come," Jason said, high; against the sky it looked like father had two heads, a little one and a big one. "I didn't want to."

We went up out of the ditch. We could still see Nancy's house and the open door, but we couldn't see Nancy now, sitting before the fire with the door open, because she was tired. "I just done got tired," she said. "I just a nigger. It ain't no fault of mine."

But we could hear her, because she began just after we came up out of the ditch, the sound that was not singing and not unsinging. "Who will do our washing now, Father?" I said.

"I'm not a nigger," Jason said, high and close above father's head.

"You're worse," Caddy said, "you are a tattletale. If something was to jump out, you'd be scairder than a nigger."

"I wouldn't," Jason said.

"You'd cry," Caddy said.

"Caddy," father said.

"I wouldn't!" Jason said.

"Scairy cat," Caddy said.

"Candace!" father said.

III · THE WILDERNESS

Red Leaves

I

THE TWO INDIANS crossed the plantation toward the slave quarters. Neat with whitewash, of baked soft brick, the two rows of houses in which lived the slaves belonging to the clan, faced one another across the mild shade of the lane marked and scored with naked feet and with a few home-made toys mute in the dust. There was no sign of life.

"I know what we will find," the first Indian said.

"What we will not find," the second said. Although it was noon, the lane was vacant, the doors of the cabins empty and quiet; no cooking smoke rose from any of the chinked and plastered chimneys.

"Yes. It happened like this when the father of him who is now the Man, died."

"You mean, of him who was the Man."

"Yao."

The first Indian's name was Three Basket. He was perhaps sixty. They were both squat men, a little solid, burgher-like; paunchy, with big heads, big, broad, dust-colored faces of a certain blurred serenity like carved heads on a ruined wall in Siam or Sumatra, looming out of a mist. The sun had done it, the violent sun, the violent shade. Their hair looked like sedge grass on burnt-over land. Clamped through one ear Three Basket wore an enameled snuffbox.

"I have said all the time that this is not the good way. In the old days there were no quarters, no Negroes. A man's time was his own then. He had time. Now he must spend most of it finding work for them who prefer sweating to do."

"They are like horses and dogs."

"They are like nothing in this sensible world. Nothing contents them save sweat. They are worse than the white people."

"It is not as though the Man himself had to find work for them to do."

"You said it. I do not like slavery. It is not the good way. In the old days, there was the good way. But not now."

"You do not remember the old way either."

"I have listened to them who do. And I have tried this way. Man was not made to sweat."

"That's so. See what it has done to their flesh."

"Yes. Black. It has a bitter taste, too."

"You have eaten of it?"

"Once. I was young then, and more hardy in the appetite than now. Now it is different with me."

"Yes. They are too valuable to eat now."

"There is a bitter taste to the flesh which I do not like."

"They are too valuable to eat, anyway, when the white men will give horses for them."

They entered the lane. The mute, meager toys—the fetish-shaped objects made of wood and rags and feathers—lay in the dust about the patinaed doorsteps, among bones and broken gourd dishes. But there was no sound from any cabin, no face in any door; had not been since yesterday, when Issetibbeha died. But they already knew what they would find.

It was in the central cabin, a house a little larger than the others, where at certain phases of the moon the Negroes would gather to begin their ceremonies before removing after nightfall to the creek bottom, where they kept the drums. In this room they kept the minor accessories, the cryptic ornaments, the ceremonial records which consisted of sticks daubed with red clay in symbols. It had a hearth in the center of the floor, beneath a hole in the roof, with a few cold wood ashes and a suspended iron pot. The window shutters were closed; when the two Indians entered, after the abashless sunlight they could distinguish nothing with the eyes save a movement, shadow, out of which eyeballs rolled, so that the place appeared to be full of Negroes. The two Indians stood in the doorway.

"Yao," Basket said. "I said this is not the good way."

"I don't think I want to be here," the second said.

"That is black man's fear which you smell. It does not smell as ours does."

"I don't think I want to be here."

"Your fear has an odor too."

"Maybe it is Issetibbeha which we smell."

"Yao. He knows. He knows what we will find here. He knew when he died what we should find here today." Out of the rank twilight of the room the eyes, the smell, of Negroes rolled about them. "I am Three Basket, whom you know," Basket said into the room. "We are come from the Man. He whom we seek is gone?" The Negroes said nothing. The smell of them, of their bodies, seemed to ebb and flux in the still hot air. They seemed to be musing as one upon something remote, inscrutable. They were like a single octopus. They were like the roots of a huge tree uncovered, the earth broken momentarily upon the writhen, thick, fetid tangle of its lightless and outraged life. "Come," Basket said. "You know our errand. Is he whom we seek gone?"

"They are thinking something," the second said. "I do not want to be here."

"They are knowing something," Basket said.

"They are hiding him, you think?"

"No. He is gone. He has been gone since last night. It happened like this before, when the grandfather of him who is now the Man died. It took us three days to catch him. For three days Doom lay above the ground, saying 'I see my horse and my dog. But I do not see my slave. What have you done with him that you will not permit me to lie quiet?'"

"They do not like to die."

"Yao. They cling. It makes trouble for us, always. A people without honor and without decorum. Always a trouble."

"I do not like it here."

"Nor do I. But then, they are savages; they cannot be expected to regard usage. That is why I say that this way is a bad way."

"Yao. They cling. They would even rather work in the sun than to enter the earth with a chief. But he is gone."

The Negroes had said nothing, made no sound. The white eyeballs rolled, wild, subdued; the smell was rank, violent. "Yes, they fear," the second said. "What shall we do now?"

"Let us go and talk with the Man."

"Will Moketubbe listen?"

"What can he do? He will not like to. But he is the Man now."

"Yao. He is the Man. He can wear the shoes with the red heels all the time now." They turned and went out. There was no door in the door frame. There were no doors in any of the cabins.

"He did that anyway," Basket said.

"Behind Issetibbeha's back. But now they are his shoes, since he is the Man."

"Yao. Issetibbeha did not like it. I have heard. I know that

he said to Moketubbe: 'When you are the Man, the shoes
will be yours. But until then, they are my shoes.' But now
Moketubbe is the Man; he can wear them."

"Yao," the second said. "He is the Man now. He used to
wear the shoes behind Issetibbeha's back, and it was not
known if Issetibbeha knew this or not. And then Issetibbeha
became dead, who was not old, and the shoes are Moketubbe's, since he is the Man now. What do you think of that?"

"I don't think about it," Basket said. "Do you?"

"No," the second said.

"Good," Basket said. "You are wise."

II

THE HOUSE sat on a knoll, surrounded by oak trees. The
front of it was one story in height, composed of the deck
house of a steamboat which had gone ashore and which
Doom, Issetibbeha's father, had dismantled with his slaves
and hauled on cypress rollers twelve miles home overland. It
took them five months. His house consisted at the time of one
brick wall. He set the steamboat broadside on to the wall,
where now the chipped and flaked gilding of the rococo
cornices arched in faint splendor above the gilt lettering of
the stateroom names above the jalousied doors.

Doom had been born merely a subchief, a Mingo, one of
three children on the mother's side of the family. He made
a journey—he was a young man then and New Orleans was
a European city—from north Mississippi to New Orleans
by keel boat, where he met the Chevalier Sœur Blonde de
Vitry, a man whose social position, on its face, was as
equivocal as Doom's own. In New Orleans, among the
gamblers and cutthroats of the river front, Doom, under the
tutelage of his patron, passed as the chief, the Man, the hereditary owner of that land which belonged to the male side

of the family; it was the Chevalier de Vitry who called him *du homme*, and hence Doom.

They were seen everywhere together—the Indian, the squat man with a bold, inscrutable, underbred face, and the Parisian, the expatriate, the friend, it was said, of Carondelet and the intimate of General Wilkinson. Then they disappeared, the two of them, vanishing from their old equivocal haunts and leaving behind them the legend of the sums which Doom was believed to have won, and some tale about a young woman, daughter of a fairly well-to-do West Indian family, the son and brother of whom sought Doom with a pistol about his old haunts for some time after his disappearance.

Six months later the young woman herself disappeared, boarding the St. Louis packet, which put in one night at a wood landing on the north Mississippi side, where the woman, accompanied by a Negro maid, got off. Four Indians met her with a horse and wagon, and they traveled for three days, slowly, since she was already big with child, to the plantation, where she found that Doom was now chief. He never told her how he accomplished it, save that his uncle and his cousin had died suddenly. At that time the house consisted of a brick wall built by shiftless slaves, against which was propped a thatched lean-to divided into rooms and littered with bones and refuse, set in the center of ten thousand acres of matchless parklike forest where deer grazed like domestic cattle. Doom and the woman were married there a short time before Issetibbeha was born, by a combination itinerant minister and slave trader who arrived on a mule, to the saddle of which was lashed a cotton umbrella and a three-gallon demijohn of whisky. After that, Doom began to acquire more slaves and to cultivate some of his land, as the white people did. But he never had enough for them to do. In utter idleness the majority of them led lives transplanted whole out of African jungles, save on the occasions when, entertaining guests, Doom coursed them with dogs.

When Doom died, Issetibbeha, his son, was nineteen. He became proprietor of the land and of the quintupled herd of blacks for which he had no use at all. Though the title of Man rested with him, there was a hierarchy of cousins and uncles who ruled the clan and who finally gathered in squatting conclave over the Negro question, squatting profoundly beneath the golden names above the doors of the steamboat.

"We cannot eat them," one said.

"Why not?"

"There are too many of them."

"That's true," a third said. "Once we started, we should have to eat them all. And that much flesh diet is not good for man."

"Perhaps they will be like deer flesh. That cannot hurt you."

"We might kill a few of them and not eat them," Issetibbeha said.

They looked at him for a while. "What for?" one said.

"That is true," a second said. "We cannot do that. They are too valuable; remember all the bother they have caused us, finding things for them to do. We must do as the white men do."

"How is that?" Issetibbeha said.

"Raise more Negroes by clearing more land to make corn to feed them, then sell them. We will clear the land and plant it with food and raise Negroes and sell them to the white men for money."

"But what will we do with this money?" a third said.

They thought for a while.

"We will see," the first said. They squatted, profound, grave.

"It means work," the third said.

"Let the Negroes do it," the first said.

"Yao. Let them. To sweat is bad. It is damp. It opens the pores."

"And then the night air enters."

"Yao. Let the Negroes do it. They appear to like sweating."

So they cleared the land with the Negroes and planted it in grain. Up to that time the slaves had lived in a huge pen with a lean-to roof over one corner, like a pen for pigs. But now they began to build quarters, cabins, putting the young Negroes in the cabins in pairs to mate; five years later Issetibbeha sold forty head to a Memphis trader, and he took the money and went abroad upon it, his maternal uncle from New Orleans conducting the trip. At that time the Chevalier Sœur Blonde de Vitry was an old man in Paris, in a toupee and a corset, with a careful toothless old face fixed in a grimace quizzical and profoundly tragic. He borrowed three hundred dollars from Issetibbeha and in return he introduced him into certain circles; a year later Issetibbeha returned home with a gilt bed, a pair of girandoles by whose light it was said that Pompadour arranged her hair while Louis smirked at his mirrored face across her powdered shoulder, and a pair of slippers with red heels. They were too small for him, since he had not worn shoes at all until he reached New Orleans on his way abroad.

He brought the slippers home in tissue paper and kept them in the remaining pocket of a pair of saddlebags filled with cedar shavings, save when he took them out on occasion for his son, Moketubbe, to play with. At three years of age Moketubbe had a broad, flat, Mongolian face that appeared to exist in a complete and unfathomable lethargy, until confronted by the slippers.

Moketubbe's mother was a comely girl whom Issetibbeha had seen one day working in her shift in a melon patch. He stopped and watched her for a while—the broad, solid thighs, the sound back, the serene face. He was on his way to the creek to fish that day, but he didn't go any farther; perhaps while he stood there watching the unaware girl he may have remembered his own mother, the city woman, the fugitive with her fans and laces and her Negro blood, and all the tawdry shabbiness of that sorry affair. Within the year Moketubbe was born; even at three he could not get his feet into the slippers. Watching him in the still, hot afternoons as he struggled with the slippers with a certain monstrous repudiation of fact, Issetibbeha laughed quietly to himself. He laughed at Moketubbe and the shoes for several years, because Moketubbe did not give up trying to put them on until he was sixteen. Then he quit. Or Issetibbeha thought he had. But he had merely quit trying in Issetibbeha's presence. Issetibbeha's newest wife told him that Moketubbe had stolen and hidden the shoes. Issetibbeha quit laughing then, and he sent the woman away, so that he was alone. "Yao," he said. "I too like being alive, it seems." He sent for Moketubbe. "I give them to you," he said.

Moketubbe was twenty-five then, unmarried. Issetibbeha was not tall, but he was taller by six inches than his son and almost a hundred pounds lighter. Moketubbe was already diseased with flesh, with a pale, broad, inert face and dropsical hands and feet. "They are yours now," Issetibbeha said, watching him. Moketubbe had looked at him once when he entered, a glance brief, discreet, veiled.

"Thanks," he said.

Issetibbeha looked at him. He could never tell if Moketubbe saw anything, looked at anything. "Why will it not be the same if I give the slippers to you?"

"Thanks," Moketubbe said. Issetibbeha was using snuff at the time; a white man had shown him how to put the powder

into his lip and scour it against his teeth with a twig of gum
or of alphea.

"Well," he said, "a man cannot live forever." He looked
at his son, then his gaze went blank in turn, unseeing, and
he mused for an instant. You could not tell what he was
thinking, save that he said half aloud: "Yao. But Doom's
uncle had no shoes with red heels." He looked at his son
again, fat, inert. "Beneath all that, a man might think of
doing anything and it not be known until too late." He sat
in a splint chair hammocked with deer thongs. "He cannot
even get them on; he and I are both frustrated by the same
gross meat which he wears. He cannot even get them on.
But is that my fault?"

He lived for five years longer, then he died. He was sick
one night, and though the doctor came in a skunk-skin vest
and burned sticks, he died before noon.

That was yesterday; the grave was dug, and for twelve
hours now the People had been coming in wagons and carriages and on horseback and afoot, to eat the baked dog and
the succotash and the yams cooked in ashes and to attend
the funeral.

III

"It will be three days," Basket said, as he and the other
Indian returned to the house. "It will be three days and the
food will not be enough; I have seen it before."

The second Indian's name was Louis Berry. "He will
smell too, in this weather."

"Yao. They are nothing but a trouble and a care."

"Maybe it will not take three days."

"They run far. Yao. We will smell this Man before he
enters the earth. You watch and see if I am not right."

They approached the house.

"He can wear the shoes now," Berry said. "He can wear them now in man's sight."

"He cannot wear them for a while yet," Basket said. Berry looked at him. "He will lead the hunt."

"Moketubbe?" Berry said. "Do you think he will? A man to whom even talking is travail?"

"What else can he do? It is his own father who will soon begin to smell."

"That is true," Berry said. "There is even yet a price he must pay for the shoes. Yao. He has truly bought them. What do you think?"

"What do you think?"

"What do you think?"

"I think nothing."

"Nor do I. Issetibbeha will not need the shoes now. Let Moketubbe have them; Issetibbeha will not care."

"Yao. Man must die."

"Yao. Let him; there is still the Man."

The bark roof of the porch was supported by peeled cypress poles, high above the texas of the steamboat, shading an unfloored banquette where on the trodden earth mules and horses were tethered in bad weather. On the forward end of the steamboat's deck sat an old man and two women. One of the women was dressing a fowl, the other was shelling corn. The old man was talking. He was barefoot, in a long linen frock coat and a beaver hat.

"This world is going to the dogs," he said. "It is being ruined by white men. We got along fine for years and years, before the white men foisted their Negroes upon us. In the old days the old men sat in the shade and ate stewed deer's flesh and corn and smoked tobacco and talked of honor and grave affairs; now what do we do? Even the old wear themselves into the grave taking care of them that like sweating." When Basket and Berry crossed the deck he ceased and looked up at them. His eyes were querulous, bleared; his face was myriad with tiny wrinkles. "He is fled also," he said.

"Yes," Berry said, "he is gone."

"I knew it. I told them so. It will take three weeks, like when Doom died. You watch and see."

"It was three days, not three weeks," Berry said.

"Were you there?"

"No," Berry said. "But I have heard."

"Well, I was there," the old man said. "For three whole weeks, through the swamps and the briers—" They went on and left him talking.

What had been the saloon of the steamboat was now a shell, rotting slowly; the polished mahogany, the carving glinting momentarily and fading through the mold in figures cabalistic and profound; the gutted windows were like cataracted eyes. It contained a few sacks of seed or grain, and the fore part of the running gear of a barouche, to the axle of which two C-springs rusted in graceful curves, supporting nothing. In one corner a fox cub ran steadily and soundlessly up and down a willow cage; three scrawny gamecocks moved in the dust, and the place was pocked and marked with their dried droppings.

They passed through the brick wall and entered a big room of chinked logs. It contained the hinder part of the barouche, and the dismantled body lying on its side, the window slatted over with willow withes, through which protruded the heads, the still, beady, outraged eyes and frayed combs of still more game chickens. It was floored with packed clay; in one corner leaned a crude plow and two hand-hewn boat paddles. From the ceiling, suspended by four deer thongs, hung the gilt bed which Issetibbeha had fetched from Paris. It had neither mattress nor springs, the frame crisscrossed now by a neat hammocking of thongs.

Issetibbeha had tried to have his newest wife, the young one, sleep in the bed. He was congenitally short of breath himself, and he passed the nights half reclining in his splint chair. He would see her to bed and, later, wakeful, sleeping as he did but three or four hours a night, he would sit in the darkness and simulate slumber and listen to her sneak infinitesimally from the gilt and ribboned bed, to lie on a quilt pallet on the floor until just before daylight. Then she would enter the bed quietly again and in turn simulate slumber, while in the darkness beside her Issetibbeha quietly laughed and laughed.

The girandoles were lashed by thongs to two sticks propped in a corner where a ten-gallon whisky keg lay also. There was a clay hearth; facing it, in the splint chair, Moketubbe sat. He was maybe an inch better than five feet tall, and he weighed two hundred and fifty pounds. He wore a broadcloth coat and no shirt, his round, smooth copper balloon of belly swelling above the bottom piece of a suit of linen underwear. On his feet were the slippers with the red heels. Behind his chair stood a stripling with a punkah-like fan made of fringed paper. Moketubbe sat motionless, with his broad, yellow face with its closed eyes and flat nostrils, his flipperlike arms extended. On his face was an expression profound, tragic, and inert. He did not open his eyes when Basket and Berry came in.

"He has worn them since daylight?" Basket said.

"Since daylight," the stripling said. The fan did not cease. "You can see."

"Yao," Basket said. "We can see." Moketubbe did not move. He looked like an effigy, like a Malay god in frock coat, drawers, naked chest, the trivial scarlet-heeled shoes.

"I wouldn't disturb him, if I were you," the stripling said.

"Not if I were you," Basket said. He and Berry squatted. The stripling moved the fan steadily. "O Man," Basket said, "listen." Moketubbe did not move. "He is gone," Basket said.

"I told you so," the stripling said. "I knew he would flee. I told you."

"Yao," Basket said. "You are not the first to tell us afterward what we should have known before. Why is it that some of you wise men took no steps yesterday to prevent this?"

"He does not wish to die," Berry said.

"Why should he not wish it?" Basket said.

"Because he must die some day is no reason," the stripling said. "That would not convince me either, old man."

"Hold your tongue," Berry said.

"For twenty years," Basket said, "while others of his race sweat in the fields, he served the Man in the shade. Why should he not wish to die, since he did not wish to sweat?"

"And it will be quick," Berry said. "It will not take long."

"Catch him and tell him that," the stripling said.

"Hush," Berry said. They squatted, watching Moketubbe's face. He might have been dead himself. It was as though he were cased so in flesh that even breathing took place too deep within him to show.

"Listen, O Man," Basket said. "Issetibbeha is dead. He waits. His dog and his horse we have. But his slave has fled. The one who held the pot for him, who ate of his food, from his dish, is fled. Issetibbeha waits."

"Yao," Berry said.

"This is not the first time," Basket said. "This happened when Doom, thy grandfather, lay waiting at the door of the earth. He lay waiting three days, saying, 'Where is my Negro?' And Issetibbeha, thy father, answered, 'I will find him. Rest; I will bring him to you so that you may begin the journey.'"

"Yao," Berry said.

Moketubbe had not moved, had not opened his eyes.

"For three days Issetibbeha hunted in the bottom," Basket said. "He did not even return home for food, until the Negro was with him; then he said to Doom, his father, 'Here is thy dog, thy horse, thy Negro; rest.' Issetibbeha, who is dead since yesterday, said it. And now Issetibbeha's Negro is fled. His horse and his dog wait with him, but his Negro is fled."

"Yao," Berry said.

Moketubbe had not moved. His eyes were closed; upon his supine monstrous shape there was a colossal inertia, something profoundly immobile, beyond and impervious to flesh. They watched his face, squatting.

"When thy father was newly the Man, this happened," Basket said. "And it was Issetibbeha who brought back the slave to where his father waited to enter the earth." Moketubbe's face had not moved, his eyes had not moved. After a while Basket said, "Remove the shoes."

The stripling removed the shoes. Moketubbe began to pant, his bare chest moving deep, as though he were rising from beyond his unfathomed flesh back into life, like up from the water, the sea. But his eyes had not opened yet.

Berry said, "He will lead the hunt."

"Yao," Basket said. "He is the Man. He will lead the hunt."

IV

ALL THAT DAY the Negro, Issetibbeha's body servant, hidden in the barn, watched Issetibbeha's dying. He was forty, a Guinea man. He had a flat nose, a close, small head; the inside corners of his eyes showed red a little, and his prominent gums were a pale bluish red above his square, broad teeth. He had been taken at fourteen by a trader off Kam-

erun, before his teeth had been filed. He had been Issetibbeha's body servant for twenty-three years.

On the day before, the day on which Issetibbeha lay sick,
he returned to the quarters at dusk. In that unhurried hour
the smoke of the cooking fires blew slowly across the street
from door to door, carrying into the opposite one the smell
of the identical meat and bread. The women tended them;
the men were gathered at the head of the lane, watching him
as he came down the slope from the house, putting his naked
feet down carefully in a strange dusk. To the waiting men
his eyeballs were a little luminous.

"Issetibbeha is not dead yet," the headman said.

"Not dead," the body servant said. "Who not dead?"

In the dusk they had faces like his, the different ages, the
thoughts sealed inscrutable behind faces like the death masks
of apes. The smell of the fires, the cooking, blew sharp and
slow across the strange dusk, as from another world, above
the lane and the pickaninnies naked in the dust.

"If he lives past sundown, he will live until daybreak,"
one said.

"Who says?"

"Talk says."

"Yao. Talk says. We know but one thing." They looked
at the body servant as he stood among them, his eyeballs
a little luminous. He was breathing slow and deep. His chest
was bare; he was sweating a little. "He knows. He knows it."

"Let us let the drums talk."

"Yao. Let the drums tell it."

The drums began after dark. They kept them hidden in
the creek bottom. They were made of hollowed cypress
knees, and the Negroes kept them hidden; why, none knew.
They were buried in the mud on the bank of a slough; a
lad of fourteen guarded them. He was undersized, and a
mute; he squatted in the mud there all day, clouded over

with mosquitoes, naked save for the mud with which he coated himself against the mosquitoes, and about his neck a fiber bag containing a pig's rib to which black shreds of flesh still adhered, and two scaly barks on a wire. He slobbered onto his clutched knees, drooling; now and then Indians came noiselessly out of the bushes behind him and stood there and contemplated him for a while and went away, and he never knew it.

From the loft of the stable where he lay hidden until dark and after, the Negro could hear the drums. They were three miles away, but he could hear them as though they were in the barn itself below him, thudding and thudding. It was as though he could see the fire too, and the black limbs turning into and out of the flames in copper gleams. Only there would be no fire. There would be no more light there than where he lay in the dusty loft, with the whispering arpeggios of rat feet along the warm and immemorial ax-squared rafters. The only fire there would be the smudge against mosquitoes where the women with nursing children crouched, their heavy sluggish breasts nippled full and smooth into the mouths of men children; contemplative, oblivious of the drumming, since a fire would signify life.

There was a fire in the steamboat, where Issetibbeha lay dying among his wives, beneath the lashed girandoles and the suspended bed. He could see the smoke, and just before sunset he saw the doctor come out, in a waistcoat made of skunk skins, and set fire to two clay-daubed sticks at the bows of the boat deck. "So he is not dead yet," the Negro said into the whispering gloom of the loft, answering himself; he could hear the two voices, himself and himself:

"Who not dead?"

"You are dead."

"Yao, I am dead," he said quietly. He wished to be where the drums were. He imagined himself springing out of the bushes, leaping among the drums on his bare, lean, greasy, invisible limbs. But he could not do that, because man leaped past life, into where death was; he dashed into death and did not die, because when death took a man, it took him just this side of the end of living. It was when death overran him from behind, still in life. The thin whisper of rat feet died in fainting gusts along the rafters. Once he had eaten rat. He was a boy then, but just come to America. They had lived ninety days in a three-foot-high 'tween-deck in tropic latitudes, hearing from topside the drunken New England captain intoning aloud from a book which he did not recognize for ten years afterward to be the Bible. Squatting in the stable so, he had watched the rat, civilized, by association with man reft of its inherent cunning of limb and eye; he had caught it without difficulty, with scarce a movement of his hand, and he ate it slowly, wondering how any of the rats had escaped so long. At that time he was still wearing the single white garment which the trader, a deacon in the Unitarian church, had given him, and he spoke then only his native tongue.

He was naked now, save for a pair of dungaree pants bought by Indians from white men, and an amulet slung on a thong about his hips. The amulet consisted of one half of a mother-of-pearl lorgnon which Issetibbeha had brought back from Paris, and the skull of a cottonmouth moccasin. He had killed the snake himself and eaten it, save the poison head. He lay in the loft, watching the house, the steamboat, listening to the drums, thinking of himself among the drums.

He lay there all night. The next morning he saw the doctor come out, in his skunk vest, and get on his mule and ride away, and he became quite still and watched the final dust from beneath the mule's delicate feet die away, and then he found that he was still breathing and it seemed strange to him that he still breathed air, still needed air. Then he lay and watched quietly, waiting to move, his eyeballs a little luminous, but with a quiet light, and his breathing light and regular, and saw Louis Berry come out and look at the sky. It was good light then, and already five Indians squatted in their Sunday clothes along the steamboat deck; by noon there were twenty-five there. That afternoon they dug the trench in which the meat would be baked, and the yams; by that time there were almost a hundred guests—decorous, quiet, patient in their stiff European finery—and he watched Berry lead Issetibbeha's mare from the stable and tie her to a tree, and then he watched Berry emerge from the house with the old hound which lay beside Issetibbeha's chair. He tied the hound to the tree too, and it sat there, looking gravely about at the faces. Then it began to howl. It was still howling at sundown, when the Negro climbed down the back wall of the barn and entered the spring branch, where it was already dusk. He began to run then. He could hear the hound howling behind him, and near the spring, already running, he passed another Negro. The two men, the one motionless and the other running, looked for an instant at each other as though across an actual boundary between two different worlds. He ran on into full darkness, mouth closed, fists doubled, his broad nostrils bellowing steadily.

He ran on in the darkness. He knew the country well, because he had hunted it often with Issetibbeha, following on his mule the course of the fox or the cat beside Issetibbeha's mare; he knew it as well as did the men who would pursue him. He saw them for the first time shortly before sunset of the second day. He had run thirty miles then, up the creek bottom, before doubling back; lying in a pawpaw thicket he saw the pursuit for the first time. There were two of them, in shirts and straw hats, carrying their neatly rolled trousers under their arms, and they had no weapons. They were middle-aged, paunchy, and they could not have moved very fast anyway; it would be twelve hours before they could return to where he lay watching them. "So I will have until midnight to rest," he said. He was near enough to the plantation to smell the cooking fires, and he thought how he ought to be hungry, since he had not eaten in thirty hours. "But it is more important to rest," he told himself. He continued to tell himself that, lying in the pawpaw thicket, because the effort of resting, the need and the haste to rest, made his heart thud the same as the running had done. It was as though he had forgot how to rest, as though the six hours were not long enough to do it in, to remember again how to do it.

As soon as dark came he moved again. He had thought to keep going steadily and quietly through the night, since there was nowhere for him to go, but as soon as he moved he began to run at top speed, breasting his panting chest, his broad-flaring nostrils through the choked and whipping darkness. He ran for an hour, lost by then, without direction, when suddenly he stopped, and after a time his thudding heart unraveled from the sound of the drums. By the sound they were not two miles away; he followed the sound until he could smell the smudge fire and taste the acrid smoke. When he stood among them the drums did not cease; only the headman came to him where he stood in the drifting smudge, panting, his nostrils flaring and pulsing, the hushed glare of his ceaseless eyeballs in his mud-daubed face as though they were worked from lungs.

"We have expected thee," the headman said. "Go, now."

"Go?"

"Eat, and go. The dead may not consort with the living; thou knowest that."

"Yao. I know that." They did not look at one another. The drums had not ceased.

"Wilt thou eat?" the headman said.

"I am not hungry. I caught a rabbit this afternoon, and ate while I lay hidden."

"Take some cooked meat with thee, then."

He accepted the cooked meat, wrapped in leaves, and entered the creek bottom again; after a while the sound of the drums ceased. He walked steadily until daybreak. "I have twelve hours," he said. "Maybe more, since the trail was followed by night." He squatted and ate the meat and wiped his hands on his thighs. Then he rose and removed the dungaree pants and squatted again beside a slough and coated himself with mud—face, arms, body and legs—and squatted again, clasping his knees, his head bowed. When it was light enough to see, he moved back into the swamp and squatted again and went to sleep so. He did not dream at all. It was well that he moved, for, waking suddenly in broad daylight and the high sun, he saw the two Indians. They still carried their neatly rolled trousers; they stood opposite the place where he lay hidden, paunchy, thick, soft-looking, a little ludicrous in their straw hats and shirt tails.

"This is wearying work," one said.

"I'd rather be at home in the shade myself," the other said. "But there is the Man waiting at the door to the earth."

"Yao." They looked quietly about; stooping, one of them removed from his shirt tail a clot of cockleburs. "Damn that Negro," he said.

"Yao. When have they ever been anything but a trial and a care to us?"

In the early afternoon, from the top of a tree, the Negro looked down into the plantation. He could see Issetibbeha's body in a hammock between the two trees where the horse and the dog were tethered, and the concourse about the steamboat was filled with wagons and horses and mules, with carts and saddle-horses, while in bright clumps the women and the smaller children and the old men squatted about the long trench where the smoke from the barbecuing meat blew slow and thick. The men and the big boys would all be down there in the creek bottom behind him, on the trail, their Sunday clothes rolled carefully up and wedged into tree crotches. There was a clump of men near the door to the house, to the saloon of the steamboat, though, and he watched them, and after a while he saw them bring Moketubbe out in a litter made of buckskin and persimmon poles; high hidden in his leafed nook the Negro, the quarry, looked quietly down upon his irrevocable doom with an expression as profound as Moketubbe's own. "Yao," he said quietly. "He will go then. That man whose body has been dead for fifteen years, he will go also."

In the middle of the afternoon he came face to face with an Indian. They were both on a footlog across a slough—the Negro gaunt, lean, hard, tireless and desperate; the Indian thick, soft-looking, the apparent embodiment of the ultimate and the supreme reluctance and inertia. The Indian made no move, no sound; he stood on the log and watched the Negro plunge into the slough and swim ashore and crash away into the undergrowth.

Just before sunset he lay behind a down log. Up the log in slow procession moved a line of ants. He caught them and ate them slowly, with a kind of detachment, like that of a dinner guest eating salted nuts from a dish. They too had a salt taste, engendering a salivary reaction out of all proportion. He ate them slowly, watching the unbroken line move up the log and into oblivious doom with a steady and terrific undeviation. He had eaten nothing else all day; in his caked mud mask his eyes rolled in reddened rims. At sunset, creeping along the creek bank toward where he had spotted a frog, a cottonmouth moccasin slashed him suddenly across the forearm with a thick, sluggish blow. It struck clumsily, leaving two long slashes across his arm like two razor slashes, and half sprawled with its own momentum and rage, it appeared for the moment utterly helpless with its own awkwardness and choleric anger. "Olé, grandfather," the Negro said. He touched its head and watched it slash him again across his arm, and again, with thick, raking, awkward blows. "It's that I do not wish to die," he said. Then he said it again—"It's that I do not wish to die"—in a quiet tone, of slow and low amaze, as though it were something that, until the words had said themselves, he found that he had not known, or had not known the depth and extent of his desire.

V

MOKETUBBE TOOK the slippers with him. He could not wear them very long while in motion, not even in the litter where he was slung reclining, so they rested upon a square of fawnskin upon his lap—the cracked, frail slippers a little shapeless now, with their scaled patent-leather surfaces and buckleless tongues and scarlet heels, lying upon the supine obese shape just barely alive, carried through swamp and brier by swinging relays of men who bore steadily all day long the crime and its object, on the business of the slain. To Moketubbe it must have been as though, himself immortal, he were being carried rapidly through hell by doomed spirits which, alive, had contemplated his disaster, and, dead, were oblivious partners to his damnation.

After resting for a while, the litter propped in the center of the squatting circle and Moketubbe motionless in it, with closed eyes and his face at once peaceful for the instant and filled with inescapable foreknowledge, he could wear the slippers for a while. The stripling put them on him, forcing his big, tender, dropsical feet into them; whereupon into his face came again that expression tragic, passive and profoundly attentive, which dyspeptics wear. Then they went

on. He made no move, no sound, inert in the rhythmic litter
out of some reserve of inertia, or maybe of some kingly
virtue such as courage or fortitude. After a time they set the
litter down and looked at him, at the yellow face like that
of an idol, beaded over with sweat. Then Three Basket or
Had-Two-Fathers would say: "Take them off. Honor has
been served." They would remove the shoes. Moketubbe's
face would not alter, but only then would his breathing become perceptible, going in and out of his pale lips with a
faint ah-ah-ah sound, and they would squat again while the
couriers and the runners came up.

"Not yet?"

"Not yet. He is going east. By sunset he will reach Mouth
of Tippah. Then he will turn back. We may take him
tomorrow."

"Let us hope so. It will not be too soon."

"Yao. It has been three days now."

"When Doom died, it took only three days."

"But that was an old man. This one is young."

"Yao. A good race. If he is taken tomorrow, I will win a
horse."

"May you win it."

"Yao. This work is not pleasant."

That was the day on which the food gave out at the plantation. The guests returned home and came back the next
day with more food, enough for a week longer. On that day
Issetibbeha began to smell; they could smell him for a long
way up and down the bottom when it got hot toward noon
and the wind blew. But they didn't capture the Negro on
that day, nor on the next. It was about dusk on the sixth
day when the couriers came up to the litter; they had found
blood. "He has injured himself."

"Not bad, I hope," Basket said. "We cannot send with
Issetibbeha one who will be of no service to him."

"Nor whom Issetibbeha himself will have to nurse and care for," Berry said.

"We do not know," the courier said. "He has hidden himself. He has crept back into the swamp. We have left pickets."

They trotted with the litter now. The place where the Negro had crept into the swamp was an hour away. In the hurry and excitement they had forgotten that Moketubbe still wore the slippers; when they reached the place Moketubbe had fainted. They removed the slippers and brought him to.

With dark, they formed a circle about the swamp. They squatted, clouded over with gnats and mosquitoes; the evening star burned low and close down the west, and the constellations began to wheel overhead. "We will give him time," they said. "Tomorrow is just another name for today."

"Yao. Let him have time." Then they ceased, and gazed as one into the darkness where the swamp lay. After a while the noise ceased, and soon the courier came out of the darkness.

"He tried to break out."

"But you turned him back?"

"He turned back. We feared for a moment, the three of us. We could smell him creeping in the darkness, and we could smell something else, which we did not know. That was why we feared, until he told us. He said to slay him there, since it would be dark and he would not have to see the face when it came. But it was not that which we smelled; he told us what it was. A snake had struck him. That was two days ago. The arm swelled, and it smelled bad. But it was not that which we smelled then, because the swelling had gone down and his arm was no larger than that of a child. He showed us. We felt the arm, all of us did; it was no larger than that of a child. He said to give him a hatchet so he could chop the arm off. But tomorrow is today also."

"Yao. Tomorrow is today."

"We feared for a while. Then he went back into the swamp."

"That is good."

"Yao. We feared. Shall I tell the Man?"

"I will see," Basket said. He went away. The courier squatted, telling again about the Negro. Basket returned. "The Man says that it is good. Return to your post."

The courier crept away. They squatted about the litter; now and then they slept. Sometime after midnight the Negro waked them. He began to shout and talk to himself, his voice coming sharp and sudden out of the darkness, then he fell silent. Dawn came; a white crane flapped slowly across the jonquil sky. Basket was awake. "Let us go now," he said. "It is today."

Two Indians entered the swamp, their movements noisy. Before they reached the Negro they stopped, because he began to sing. They could see him, naked and mud-caked, sitting on a log, singing. They squatted silently a short distance away, until he finished. He was chanting something in his own language, his face lifted to the rising sun. His voice was clear, full, with a quality wild and sad. "Let him have time," the Indians said, squatting, patient, waiting. He ceased and they approached. He looked back and up at them through the cracked mud mask. His eyes were bloodshot, his lips cracked upon his square short teeth. The mask of mud appeared to be loose on his face, as if he might have lost flesh since he put it there; he held his left arm close to his breast. From the elbow down it was caked and shapeless with black mud. They could smell him, a rank smell. He watched them quietly until one touched him on the arm. "Come," the Indian said. "You ran well. Do not be ashamed."

VI

As THEY NEARED the plantation in the tainted bright morning, the Negro's eyes began to roll a little, like those of a horse. The smoke from the cooking pit blew low along the earth and upon the squatting and waiting guests about the yard and upon the steamboat deck, in their bright, stiff, harsh finery; the women, the children, the old men. They had sent couriers along the bottom, and another on ahead, and Issetibbeha's body had already been removed to where the grave waited, along with the horse and the dog, though they could still smell him in death about the house where he had lived in life. The guests were beginning to move toward the grave when the bearers of Moketubbe's litter mounted the slope.

The Negro was the tallest there, his high, close, mud-caked head looming above them all. He was breathing hard, as though the desperate effort of the six suspended and desperate days had catapulted upon him at once; although they walked slowly, his naked scarred chest rose and fell above the close-clutched left arm. He looked this way and that continuously, as if he were not seeing, as though sight never quite caught up with the looking. His mouth was open a little upon his big white teeth; he began to pant. The already moving guests halted, pausing, looking back, some with pieces of meat in their hands, as the Negro looked about at their faces with his wild, restrained, unceasing eyes.

"Will you eat first?" Basket said. He had to say it twice.

"Yes," the Negro said. "That's it. I want to eat."

The throng had begun to press back toward the center; the word passed to the outermost: "He will eat first."

They reached the steamboat. "Sit down," Basket said. The Negro sat on the edge of the deck. He was still panting, his chest rising and falling, his head ceaseless with its white

eyeballs, turning from side to side. It was as if the inability
to see came from within, from hopelessness, not from
absence of vision. They brought food and watched quietly
as he tried to eat it. He put the food into his mouth and
chewed it, but chewing, the half-masticated matter began
to emerge from the corners of his mouth and to drool down
his chin, onto his chest, and after a while he stopped chewing
and sat there, naked, covered with dried mud, the plate on
his knees, and his mouth filled with a mass of chewed food,
open, his eyes wide and unceasing, panting and panting.
They watched him, patient, implacable, waiting.

"Come," Basket said at last.

"It's water I want," the Negro said. "I want water."

The well was a little way down the slope toward the
quarters. The slope lay dappled with the shadows of noon,
of that peaceful hour when, Issetibbeha napping in his chair
and waiting for the noon meal and the long afternoon to
sleep in, the Negro, the body servant, would be free. He
would sit in the kitchen door then, talking with the women
who prepared the food. Beyond the kitchen the lane between
the quarters would be quiet, peaceful, with the women talking to one another across the lane and the smoke of the
dinner fires blowing upon the pickaninnies like ebony toys
in the dust.

"Come," Basket said.

The Negro walked among them, taller than any. The
guests were moving on toward where Issetibbeha and the
horse and the dog waited. The Negro walked with his high
ceaseless head, his panting chest. "Come," Basket said. "You
wanted water."

"Yes," the Negro said. "Yês." He looked back at the
house, then down to the quarters, where today no fire
burned, no face showed in any door, no pickaninny in the
dust, panting. "It struck me here, raking me across this arm;
once, twice, three times. I said, 'Olé, Grandfather.'"

"Come now," Basket said. The Negro was still going through the motion of walking, his knee action high, his head high, as though he were on a treadmill. His eyeballs had a wild, restrained glare, like those of a horse. "You wanted water," Basket said. "Here it is."

There was a gourd in the well. They dipped it full and gave it to the Negro, and they watched him try to drink. His eyes had not ceased as he tilted the gourd slowly against his caked face. They could watch his throat working and the bright water cascading from either side of the gourd, down his chin and breast. Then the water stopped. "Come," Basket said.

"Wait," the Negro said. He dipped the gourd again and tilted it against his face, beneath his ceaseless eyes. Again they watched his throat working and the unswallowed water sheathing broken and myriad down his chin, channeling his caked chest. They waited, patient, grave, decorous, implacable; clansman and guest and kin. Then the water ceased, though still the empty gourd tilted higher and higher, and still his black throat aped the vain motion of his frustrated swallowing. A piece of water-loosened mud carried away from his chest and broke at his muddy feet, and in the empty gourd they could hear his breath: ah-ah-ah.

"Come," Basket said, taking the gourd from the Negro and hanging it back in the well.

A Justice

I

UNTIL GRANDFATHER DIED, we would go out to the farm every Saturday afternoon. We would leave home right after dinner in the surrey, I in front with Roskus, and Grandfather and Caddy and Jason in the back. Grandfather and Roskus would talk, with the horses going fast, because it was the best team in the county. They would carry the surrey fast along the levels and up some of the hills even. But this was in north Mississippi, and on some of the hills Roskus and I could smell Grandfather's cigar.

The farm was four miles away. There was a long, low house in the grove, not painted but kept whole and sound by a clever carpenter from the quarters named Sam Fathers, and behind it the barns and smokehouses, and further still, the quarters themselves, also kept whole and sound by Sam Fathers. He did nothing else, and they said he was almost a hundred years old. He lived with the Negroes and they— the white people; the Negroes called him a blue-gum— called him a Negro. But he wasn't a Negro. That's what I'm going to tell about.

When we got there, Mr. Stokes, the manager, would send a Negro boy with Caddy and Jason to the creek to fish, because Caddy was a girl and Jason was too little, but I wouldn't go with them. I would go to Sam Fathers' shop, where he would be making breast-yokes or wagon wheels, and I would always bring him some tobacco. Then he would stop working and he would fill his pipe—he made them himself, out of creek clay with a reed stem—and he would tell me about the old days. He talked like a nigger—that is, he said his words like niggers do, but he didn't say the same words—and his hair was nigger hair. But his skin wasn't quite the color of a light nigger and his nose and his mouth and chin were not nigger nose and mouth and chin. And his shape was not like the shape of a nigger when he gets old. He was straight in the back, not tall, a little broad, and his face was still all the time, like he might be somewhere else all the while he was working or when people, even white people, talked to him, or while he talked to me. It was just the same all the time, like he might be away up on a roof by himself, driving nails. Sometimes he would quit work with something half-finished on the bench, and sit down and smoke. And he wouldn't jump up and go back to work when Mr. Stokes or even Grandfather came along.

So I would give him the tobacco and he would stop work and sit down and fill his pipe and talk to me.

"These niggers," he said. "They call me Uncle Blue-Gum. And the white folks, they call me Sam Fathers."

"Isn't that your name?" I said.

"No. Not in the old days. I remember. I remember how I never saw but one white man until I was a boy big as you are; a whisky trader that came every summer to the Plantation. It was the Man himself that named me. He didn't name me Sam Fathers, though."

"The Man?" I said.

"He owned the Plantation, the Negroes, my mammy too. He owned all the land that I knew of until I was grown. He was a Choctaw chief. He sold my mammy to your great-grandpappy. He said I didn't have to go unless I wanted to, because I was a warrior too then. He was the one who named me Had-Two-Fathers."

"Had-Two-Fathers?" I said. "That's not a name. That's not anything."

"It was my name once. Listen."

II

THIS IS HOW Herman Basket told it when I was big enough to hear talk. He said that when Doom came back from New Orleans, he brought this woman with him. He brought six black people, though Herman Basket said they already had more black people in the Plantation than they could find use for. Sometimes they would run the black men with dogs, like you would a fox or a cat or a coon. And then Doom brought six more when he came home from New Orleans. He said he won them on the steamboat, and so he had to take them. He got off the steamboat with the six black people, Herman Basket said, and a big box in which something was alive, and the gold box of New Orleans salt about the size of a gold watch. And Herman Basket told how Doom took a puppy out of the box in which something was alive, and how he made a bullet of bread and a pinch of the salt in the gold box, and put the bullet into the puppy and the puppy died.

That was the kind of a man that Doom was, Herman Basket said. He told how, when Doom got off the steamboat that night, he wore a coat with gold all over it, and he had three gold watches, but Herman Basket said that even after seven years, Doom's eyes had not changed. He said that Doom's eyes were just the same as before he went away, before his name was Doom, and he and Herman Basket and my pappy were sleeping on the same pallet and talking at night, as boys will.

Doom's name was Ikkemotubbe then, and he was not born to be the Man, because Doom's mother's brother was the Man, and the Man had a son of his own, as well as a brother. But even then, and Doom no bigger than you are, Herman Basket said that sometimes the Man would look at Doom and he would say: "O Sister's Son, your eye is a bad eye, like the eye of a bad horse."

So the Man was not sorry when Doom got to be a young man and said that he would go to New Orleans, Herman Basket said. The Man was getting old then. He used to like to play mumble-peg and to pitch horseshoes both, but now he just liked mumble-peg. So he was not sorry when Doom went away, though he didn't forget about Doom. Herman Basket said that each summer when the whisky-trader came, the Man would ask him about Doom. "He calls himself David Callicoat now," the Man would say. "But his name is Ikkemotubbe. You haven't heard maybe of a David Callicoat getting drowned in the Big River, or killed in the white man's fight at New Orleans?"

But Herman Basket said they didn't hear from Doom at all until he had been gone seven years. Then one day Herman Basket and my pappy got a written stick from Doom to meet him at the Big River. Because the steamboat didn't come up our river any more then. The steamboat was still in our river, but it didn't go anywhere any more. Herman Basket told how one day during the high water, about three years after Doom went away, the steamboat came and crawled up on a sand-bar and died.

That was how Doom got his second name, the one before Doom. Herman Basket told how four times a year the steamboat would come up our river, and how the People would go to the river and camp and wait to see the steamboat pass, and he said that the white man who told the steamboat where to swim was named David Callicoat. So when Doom told Herman Basket and pappy that he was going to New Orleans, he said, "And I'll tell you something else. From now on, my name is not Ikkemotubbe. It's David Callicoat. And some day I'm going to own a steamboat, too." That was the kind of man that Doom was, Herman Basket said.

So after seven years he sent them the written stick and Herman Basket and pappy took the wagon and went to meet Doom at the Big River, and Doom got off the steamboat with the six black people. "I won them on the steamboat," Doom said. "You and Craw-ford (my pappy's name was Crawfishford, but usually it was Craw-ford) can divide them."

"I don't want them," Herman Basket said that pappy said.

"Then Herman can have them all," Doom said.

"I don't want them either," Herman Basket said.

"All right," Doom said. Then Herman Basket said he asked Doom if his name was still David Callicoat, but instead of answering, Doom told one of the black people something in the white man's talk, and the black man lit a pine knot. Then Herman Basket said they were watching Doom take the puppy from the box and make the bullet of bread and the New Orleans salt which Doom had in the little gold box, when he said that pappy said:

"I believe you said that Herman and I were to divide these black people."

Then Herman Basket said he saw that one of the black people was a woman.

"You and Herman don't want them," Doom said.

"I wasn't thinking when I said that," pappy said. "I will take the lot with the woman in it. Herman can have the other three."

"I don't want them," Herman Basket said.

"You can have four, then," pappy said. "I will take the woman and one other."

"I don't want them," Herman Basket said.

"I will take only the woman," pappy said. "You can have the other five."

"I don't want them," Herman Basket said.

"You don't want them, either," Doom said to pappy. "You said so yourself."

Then Herman Basket said that the puppy was dead. "You didn't tell us your new name," he said to Doom.

"My name is Doom now," Doom said. "It was given me by a French chief in New Orleans. In French talking, Doo-um; in our talking, Doom."

"What does it mean?" Herman Basket said.

He said how Doom looked at him for a while. "It means the Man," Doom said.

Herman Basket told how they thought about that. He said they stood there in the dark, with the other puppies in the box, the ones that Doom hadn't used, whimpering and scuffing, and the light of the pine knot shining on the eyeballs of the black people and on Doom's gold coat and on the puppy that had died.

"You cannot be the Man," Herman Basket said. "You are only on the sister's side. And the Man has a brother and a son."

"That's right," Doom said. "But if I were the Man, I would give Craw-ford those black people. I would give Herman something, too. For every black man I gave Craw-ford, I would give Herman a horse, if I were the Man."

"Craw-ford only wants this woman," Herman Basket said.

"I would give Herman six horses, anyway," Doom said. "But maybe the Man has already given Herman a horse."

"No," Herman Basket said. "My ghost is still walking."

It took them three days to reach the Plantation. They camped on the road at night. Herman Basket said that they did not talk.

They reached the Plantation on the third day. He said

that the Man was not very glad to see Doom, even though
Doom brought a present of candy for the Man's son. Doom
had something for all his kinsfolk, even for the Man's
brother. The Man's brother lived by himself in a cabin by
the creek. His name was Sometimes-Wakeup. Sometimes
the People took him food. The rest of the time they didn't
see him. Herman Basket told how he and pappy went with
Doom to visit Sometimes-Wakeup in his cabin. It was at
night, and Doom told Herman Basket to close the door.
Then Doom took the puppy from pappy and set it on the
floor and made a bullet of bread and the New Orleans salt
for Sometimes-Wakeup to see how it worked. When they
left, Herman Basket said how Sometimes-Wakeup burned a
stick and covered his head with the blanket.

That was the first night that Doom was at home. On the
next day Herman Basket told how the Man began to act
strange at his food, and died before the doctor could get there
and burn sticks. When the Willow-Bearer went to fetch the
Man's son to be the Man, they found that he had acted
strange and then died too.

"Now Sometimes-Wakeup will have to be the Man,"
pappy said.

So the Willow-Bearer went to fetch Sometimes-Wakeup
to come and be the Man. The Willow-Bearer came back
soon. "Sometimes-Wakeup does not want to be the Man,"
the Willow-Bearer said. "He is sitting in his cabin with his
head in his blanket."

"Then Ikkemotubbe will have to be the Man," pappy
said.

So Doom was the Man. But Herman Basket said that
pappy's ghost would not be easy. Herman Basket said he
told pappy to give Doom a little time. "I am still walking,"
Herman Basket said.

"But this is a serious matter with me," pappy said.

He said that at last pappy went to Doom, before the Man and his son had entered the earth, before the eating and the horse-racing were over. "What woman?" Doom said.

"You said that when you were the Man," pappy said. Herman Basket said that Doom looked at pappy but that pappy was not looking at Doom.

"I think you don't trust me," Doom said. Herman Basket said how pappy did not look at Doom. "I think you still believe that that puppy was sick," Doom said. "Think about it."

Herman Basket said that pappy thought.

"What do you think now?" Doom said.

But Herman Basket said that pappy still did not look at Doom. "I think it was a well dog," pappy said.

III

AT LAST the eating and the horse-racing were over and the Man and his son had entered the earth. Then Doom said, "Tomorrow we will go and fetch the steamboat." Herman Basket told how Doom had been talking about the steamboat ever since he became the Man, and about how the House was not big enough. So that evening Doom said, "Tomorrow we will go and fetch the steamboat that died in the river."

Herman Basket said how the steamboat was twelve miles away, and that it could not even swim in the water. So the next morning there was no one in the Plantation except Doom and the black people. He told how it took Doom all that day to find the People. Doom used the dogs, and he found some of the People in hollow logs in the creek bottom. That night he made all the men sleep in the House. He kept the dogs in the House, too.

Herman Basket told how he heard Doom and pappy talking in the dark. "I don't think you trust me," Doom said.

"I trust you," pappy said.

"That is what I would advise," Doom said.

"I wish you could advise that to my ghost," pappy said.

The next morning they went to the steamboat. The women and the black people walked. The men rode in the wagons, with Doom following behind with the dogs.

The steamboat was lying on its side on the sand-bar. When they came to it, there were three white men on it. "Now we can go back home," pappy said.

But Doom talked to the white men. "Does this steamboat belong to you?" Doom said.

"It does not belong to you," the white men said. And though they had guns, Herman Basket said they did not look like men who would own a boat.

"Shall we kill them?" he said to Doom. But he said that Doom was still talking to the men on the steamboat.

"What will you take for it?" Doom said.

"What will you give for it?" the white men said.

"It is dead," Doom said. "It's not worth much."

"Will you give ten black people?" the white men said.

"All right," Doom said. "Let the black people who came with me from the Big River come forward." They came forward, the five men and the woman. "Let four more black people come forward." Four more came forward. "You are now to eat of the corn of those white men yonder," Doom said. "May it nourish you." The white men went away, the ten black people following them. "Now," Doom said, "let us make the steamboat get up and walk."

Herman Basket said that he and pappy did not go into the river with the others, because pappy said to go aside and talk. They went aside. Pappy talked, but Herman Basket said that he said he did not think it was right to kill white men, but pappy said how they could fill the white men with rocks and sink them in the river and nobody would find them. So Herman Basket said they overtook the three white men and the ten black people, then they turned back toward the boat. Just before they came to the steamboat, pappy said to the black men: "Go on to the Man. Go and help make the steamboat get up and walk. I will take this woman on home."

"This woman is my wife," one of the black men said. "I want her to stay with me."

"Do you want to be arranged in the river with rocks in your inside too?" pappy said to the black man.

"Do you want to be arranged in the river yourself?" the black man said to pappy. "There are two of you, and nine of us."

Herman Basket said that pappy thought. Then pappy said, "Let us go to the steamboat and help the Man."

They went to the steamboat. But Herman Basket said that Doom did not notice the ten black people until it was time to return to the Plantation. Herman Basket told how Doom looked at the black people, then looked at pappy. "It seems that the white men did not want these black people," Doom said.

"So it seems," pappy said.

"The white men went away, did they?" Doom said.

"So it seems," pappy said.

Herman Basket told how every night Doom would make all the men sleep in the House, with the dogs in the House too, and how each morning they would return to the steamboat in the wagons. The wagons would not hold everybody, so after the second day the women stayed at home. But it was three days before Doom noticed that pappy was staying at home too. Herman Basket said that the woman's husband may have told Doom. "Craw-ford hurt his back lifting the steamboat," Herman Basket said he told Doom. "He said he would stay ɪt the Plantation and sit with his feet in the Hot Spring so that the sickness in his back could return to the earth."

"That is a good idea," Doom said. "He has been doing this for three days, has he? Then the sickness should be down in his legs by now."

When they returned to the Plantation that night, Doom sent for pappy. He asked pappy if the sickness had moved. Pappy said how the sickness moved very slow. "You must sit in the Spring more," Doom said.

"That is what I think," pappy said.

"Suppose you sit in the Spring at night too," Doom said.

"The night air will make it worse," pappy said.

"Not with a fire there," Doom said. "I will send one of the black people with you to keep the fire burning."

"Which one of the black people?" pappy said.

"The husband of the woman which I won on the steamboat," Doom said.

"I think my back is better," pappy said.

"Let us try it," Doom said.

"I know my back is better," pappy said.

"Let us try it, anyway," Doom said. Just before dark Doom sent four of the People to fix pappy and the black man at the Spring. Herman Basket said the People returned quickly. He said that as they entered the House, pappy entered also.

"The sickness began to move suddenly," pappy said. "It has reached my feet since noon today."

"Do you think it will be gone by morning?" Doom said.

"I think so," pappy said.

"Perhaps you had better sit in the Spring tonight and make sure," Doom said.

"I know it will be gone by morning," pappy said.

IV

Wʜᴇɴ ɪᴛ ɢᴏᴛ to be summer, Herman Basket said that the
steamboat was out of the river bottom. It had taken them
five months to get it out of the bottom, because they had to
cut down the trees to make a path for it. But now he said
the steamboat could walk faster on the logs. He told how
pappy helped. Pappy had a certain place on one of the ropes
near the steamboat that nobody was allowed to take, Herman
Basket said. It was just under the front porch of the steamboat where Doom sat in his chair, with a boy with a branch
to shade him and another boy with a branch to drive away
the flying beasts. The dogs rode on the boat too.

In the summer, while the steamboat was still walking, Herman Basket told how the husband of the woman came to
Doom again. "I have done what I could for you," Doom
said. "Why don't you go to Craw-ford and adjust this matter
yourself?"

The black man said that he had done that. He said that
pappy said to adjust it by a cock-fight, pappy's cock against
the black man's, the winner to have the woman, the one
who refused to fight to lose by default. The black man said
he told pappy he did not have a cock, and that pappy said
that in that case the black man lost by default and that the
woman belonged to pappy. "And what am I to do?" the
black man said.

Doom thought. Then Herman Basket said that Doom
called to him and asked him which was pappy's best cock
and Herman Basket told Doom that pappy had only one.
"That black one?" Doom said. Herman Basket said he told
Doom that was the one. "Ah," Doom said. Herman Basket
told how Doom sat in his chair on the porch of the steamboat while it walked, looking down at the People and
the black men pulling the ropes, making the steamboat walk.

"Go and tell Craw-ford you have a cock," Doom said to the black man. "Just tell him you will have a cock in the pit. Let it be tomorrow morning. We will let the steamboat sit down and rest." The black man went away. Then Herman Basket said that Doom was looking at him, and that he did not look at Doom. Because he said there was but one better cock in the Plantation than pappy's, and that one belonged to Doom. "I think that that puppy was not sick," Doom said. "What do you think?"

Herman Basket said that he did not look at Doom. "That is what I think," he said.

"That is what I would advise," Doom said.

Herman Basket told how the next day the steamboat sat and rested. The pit was in the stable. The People and the black people were there. Pappy had his cock in the pit. Then the black man put his cock into the pit. Herman Basket said that pappy looked at the black man's cock.

"This cock belongs to Ikkemotubbe," pappy said.

"It is his," the People told pappy. "Ikkemotubbe gave it to him with all to witness."

Herman Basket said that pappy had already picked up his cock. "This is not right," pappy said. "We ought not to let him risk his wife on a cock-fight."

"Then you withdraw?" the black man said.

"Let me think," pappy said. He thought. The People watched. The black man reminded pappy of what he had said about defaulting. Pappy said he did not mean to say that and that he withdrew it. The People told him that he could only withdraw by forfeiting the match. Herman Basket said that pappy thought again. The People watched. "All right," pappy said. "But I am being taken advantage of."

The cocks fought. Pappy's cock fell. Pappy took it up quickly. Herman Basket said it was like pappy had been waiting for his cock to fall so he could pick it quickly up. "Wait," he said. He looked at the People. "Now they have fought. Isn't that true?" The People said that it was true. "So that settles what I said about forfeiting."

Herman Basket said that pappy began to get out of the pit. "Aren't you going to fight?" the black man said.

"I don't think this will settle anything," pappy said. "Do you?"

Herman Basket told how the black man looked at pappy. Then he quit looking at pappy. He was squatting. Herman Basket said the People looked at the black man looking at the earth between his feet. They watched him take up a clod of dirt, and then they watched the dust come out between the black man's fingers. "Do you think that this will settle anything?" pappy said.

"No," the black man said. Herman Basket said that the People could not hear him very good. But he said that pappy could hear him.

"Neither do I," pappy said. "It would not be right to risk your wife on a cock-fight."

Herman Basket told how the black man looked up, with the dry dust about the fingers of his hand. He said the black man's eyes looked red in the dark pit, like the eyes of a fox. "Will you let the cocks fight again?" the black man said.

"Do you agree that it doesn't settle anything?" pappy said.

"Yes," the black man said.

Pappy put his cock back into the ring. Herman Basket said that pappy's cock was dead before it had time to act strange, even. The black man's cock stood upon it and started to crow, but the black man struck the live cock away and he jumped up and down on the dead cock until it did not look like a cock at all, Herman Basket said.

Then it was fall, and Herman Basket told how the steamboat came to the Plantation and stopped beside the House and died again. He said that for two months they had been in sight of the Plantation, making the steamboat walk on the logs, but now the steamboat was beside the House and the House was big enough to please Doom. He gave an eating. It lasted a week. When it was over, Herman Basket told how the black man came to Doom a third time. Herman Basket said that the black man's eyes were red again, like those of a fox, and that they could hear his breathing in the room. "Come to my cabin," he said to Doom. "I have something to show you."

"I thought it was about that time," Doom said. He looked about the room, but Herman Basket told Doom that pappy had just stepped out. "Tell him to come also," Doom said. When they came to the black man's cabin, Doom sent two of the People to fetch pappy. Then they entered the cabin. What the black man wanted to show Doom was a new man.

"Look," the black man said. "You are the Man. You are to see justice done."

"What is wrong with this man?" Doom said.

"Look at the color of him," the black man said. He began to look around the cabin. Herman Basket said that his eyes went red and then brown and then red, like those of a fox. He said they could hear the black man's breathing. "Do I get justice?" the black man said. "You are the Man."

"You should be proud of a fine yellow man like this," Doom said. He looked at the new man. "I don't see that justice can darken him any," Doom said. He looked about the cabin also. "Come forward, Craw-ford," he said. "This is a man, not a copper snake; he will not harm you." But Herman Basket said that pappy would not come forward. He said the black man's eyes went red and then brown and then red when he breathed. "Yao," Doom said, "this is not right. Any man is entitled to have his melon patch protected from these wild bucks of the woods. But first let us name this man." Doom thought. Herman Basket said the black man's eyes went quieter now, and his breath went quieter too. "We will call him Had-Two-Fathers," Doom said.

V

SAM FATHERS lit his pipe again. He did it deliberately, rising and lifting between thumb and forefinger from his forge a coal of fire. Then he came back and sat down. It was getting late. Caddy and Jason had come back from the creek, and I could see Grandfather and Mr. Stokes talking beside the carriage, and at that moment, as though he had felt my gaze, Grandfather turned and called my name.

"What did your pappy do then?" I said.

"He and Herman Basket built the fence," Sam Fathers said. "Herman Basket told how Doom made them set two posts into the ground, with a sapling across the top of them. The nigger and pappy were there. Doom had not told them about the fence then. Herman Basket said it was just like when he and pappy and Doom were boys, sleeping on the same pallet, and Doom would wake them at night and make them get up and go hunting with him, or when he would make them stand up with him and fight with their fists, just for fun, until Herman Basket and pappy would hide from Doom.

"They fixed the sapling across the two posts and Doom said to the nigger: 'This is a fence. Can you climb it?'

"Herman Basket said the nigger put his hand on the sapling and sailed over it like a bird.

"Then Doom said to pappy: 'Climb this fence.'

" 'This fence is too high to climb,' pappy said.

" 'Climb this fence, and I will give you the woman,' Doom said.

"Herman Basket said pappy looked at the fence a while. 'Let me go under this fence.' he said.

" 'No,' Doom said.

"Herman Basket told me how pappy began to sit down on the ground. 'It's not that I don't trust you,' pappy said.

" 'We will build the fence this high,' Doom said.

" 'What fence?' Herman Basket said.

" 'The fence around the cabin of this black man,' Doom said.

" 'I can't build a fence I couldn't climb,' pappy said.

" 'Herman will help you,' Doom said.

"Herman Basket said it was just like when Doom used to wake them and make them go hunting. He said the dogs found him and pappy about noon the next day, and that they began the fence that afternoon. He told me how they had to cut the saplings in the creek bottom and drag them in by hand, because Doom would not let them use the wagon. So sometimes one post would take them three or four days. 'Never mind,' Doom said. 'You have plenty of time. And the exercise will make Craw-ford sleep at night.'

"He told me how they worked on the fence all that winter and all the next summer, until after the whisky trader had come and gone. Then it was finished. He said that on the day they set the last post, the nigger came out of the cabin and put his hand on the top of a post (it was a palisade fence, the posts set upright in the ground) and flew out like a bird. 'This is a good fence,' the nigger said. 'Wait,' he said. 'I have something to show you.' Herman Basket said he flew back over the fence again and went into the cabin and came back. Herman Basket said that he was carrying a new man and that he held the new man up so they could see it above the fence. 'What do you think about this for color?' he said."

Grandfather called me again. This time I got up. The sun was already down beyond the peach orchard. I was just twelve then, and to me the story did not seem to have got anywhere, to have had point or end. Yet I obeyed Grandfather's voice, not that I was tired of Sam Fathers' talking, but with that immediacy of children with which they flee temporarily something which they do not quite understand; that, and the instinctive promptness with which we all obeyed Grandfather, not from concern of impatience or reprimand, but because we all believed that he did fine things, that his waking life passed from one fine (if faintly grandiose) picture to another.

They were in the surrey, waiting for me. I got in; the horses moved at once, impatient too for the stable. Caddy had one fish, about the size of a chip, and she was wet to the waist. We drove on, the team already trotting. When we passed Mr. Stokes' kitchen we could smell ham cooking. The smell followed us on to the gate. When we turned onto the road home it was almost sundown. Then we couldn't smell the cooking ham any more. "What were you and Sam talking about?" Grandfather said.

We went on, in that strange, faintly sinister suspension of twilight in which I believed that I could still see Sam Fathers back there, sitting on his wooden block, definite, immobile, and complete, like something looked upon after a long time in a preservative bath in a museum. That was it. I was just twelve then, and I would have to wait until I had passed on and through and beyond the suspension of twilight. Then I knew that I would know. But then Sam Fathers would be dead.

"Nothing, sir," I said. "We were just talking."

A Courtship

THIS IS HOW it was in the old days, when old Issetibbeha was still the Man, and Ikkemotubbe, Issetibbeha's nephew, and David Hogganbeck, the white man who told the steamboat where to walk, courted Herman Basket's sister.

The People all lived in the Plantation now. Issetibbeha and General Jackson met and burned sticks and signed a paper, and now a line ran through the woods, although you could not see it. It ran straight as a bee's flight among the woods, with the Plantation on one side of it, where Issetibbeha was the Man, and America on the other side, where General Jackson was the Man. So now when something happened on one side of the line, it was a bad fortune for some and a good fortune for others, depending on what the white man happened to possess, as it had always been. But merely by occurring on the other side of that line which you couldn't even see, it became what the white men called a crime punishable by death if they could just have found who did it. Which seemed foolish to us. There was one uproar which lasted off and on for a week, not that the white man had disappeared, because he had been the sort of white man which even other white men did not regret, but because of a delusion that he had been eaten. As if any man, no matter how hungry, would risk eating the flesh of a coward or thief in this country where even in winter there is always something to be found to eat;—this land for which, as Issetibbeha used to say after he had become so old that nothing more was required of him except to sit in the sun and criticise the degeneration of the People and the folly and rapacity of politicians, the Great Spirit has done more and man less than for any land he ever heard of. But it was a free country, and if the white man wished to make a rule even that foolish in their half of it, it was all right with us.

Then Ikkemotubbe and David Hogganbeck saw Herman Basket's sister. As who did not, sooner or later, young men and old men too, bachelors and widowers too, and some who were not even widowers yet, who for more than one reason within the hut had no business looking anywhere else, though who is to say what age a man must reach or just how unfortunate he must have been in his youthful compliance, when he shall no longer look at the Herman Basket's sisters of this world and chew his bitter thumbs too, aihee. Because she walked in beauty. Or she sat in it, that is, because she did not walk at all unless she had to. One of the earliest sounds in the Plantation would be the voice of Herman Basket's aunt crying to know why she had not risen and gone to the spring for water with the other girls, which she did not do sometimes until Herman Basket himself rose and made her, or in the afternoon crying to know why she did not go to the river with the other girls and women to wash, which she did not do very often either. But she did not need to. Anyone who looks as Herman Basket's sister did at seventeen and eighteen and nineteen does not need to wash.

Then one day Ikkemotubbe saw her, who had known her all his life except during the first two years. He was Issetibbeha's sister's son. One night he got into the steamboat with David Hogganbeck and went away. And suns passed and then moons and then three high waters came and went and old Issetibbeha had entered the earth a year and his son Moketubbe was the Man when Ikkemotubbe returned, named Doom now, with the white friend called the Chevalier Sœur-Blonde de Vitry and the eight new slaves which we did not need either, and his gold-laced hat and cloak and the little gold box of strong salt and the wicker wine hamper containing the four other puppies which were still alive, and within two days Moketubbe's little son was dead and within three Ikkemotubbe whose name was Doom now was himself the Man. But he was not Doom yet. He was still just Ikkemotubbe, one of the young men, the best one, who rode the hardest and fastest and danced the longest and got the drunkest and was loved the best, by the young men and the girls and the older women too who should have had other things to think about. Then one day he saw Herman Basket's sister, whom he had known all his life except for the first two years.

After Ikkemotubbe looked at her, my father and Owl-by-Night and Sylvester's John and the other young men looked away. Because he was the best of them and they loved him then while he was still just Ikkemotubbe. They would hold the other horse for him as, stripped to the waist, his hair and body oiled with bear's grease as when racing (though with honey mixed into the bear's grease now) and with only a rope hackamore and no saddle as when racing, Ikkemotubbe would ride on his new racing pony past the gallery where Herman Basket's sister sat shelling corn or peas into the silver wine pitcher which her aunt had inherited from her second cousin by marriage's great-aunt who was old David Colbert's wife, while Log-in-the-Creek (one of the young men too, though nobody paid any attention to him. He raced no horses and fought no cocks and cast no dice, and even when forced to, he would not even dance fast enough to keep out of the other dancers' way, and disgraced both himself and the others each time by becoming sick after only five or six horns of what was never even his whisky) leaned against one of the gallery posts and blew into his harmonica. Then one of the young men held the racing pony, and on his gaited mare now and wearing his flower-painted weskit and pigeon-tailed coat and beaver hat in which he looked handsomer than a steamboat gambler and richer even than the whisky-trader, Ikkemotubbe would ride past the gallery where Herman Basket's sister shelled another pod of peas into the pitcher and Log-in-the-Creek sat with his back against the post and blew into the harmonica. Then another of the young men would take the mare too and Ikkemotubbe would walk to Herman Basket's and sit on the gallery too in his fine clothes while Herman Basket's sister shelled another pod of peas perhaps into the silver pitcher and Log-in-the-Creek lay on his back on the floor, blowing into the harmonica. Then the whisky-trader came and Ikkemotubbe and the young men invited Log-in-the-Creek into the woods until they became tired of carrying him. And although a good deal wasted outside, as usual Log-in-the-Creek became sick and then asleep after seven or eight horns, and Ikkemotubbe returned to Herman Basket's gallery, where for a day or two at least he didn't have to not listen to the harmonica.

Finally Owl-at-Night made a suggestion. "Send Herman Basket's aunt a gift." But the only thing Ikkemotubbe owned which Herman Basket's aunt didn't, was the new racing pony. So after a while Ikkemotubbe said, "So it seems I want this girl even worse than I believed," and sent Owl-at-Night to tie the racing pony's hackamore to Herman Basket's kitchen door handle. Then he thought how Herman Basket's aunt could not even always make Herman Basket's sister just get up and go to the spring for water. Besides, she was the second cousin by marriage to the grand-niece of the wife of old David Colbert, the chief Man of all the Chickasaws in our section, and she looked upon Issetibbeha's whole family and line as mushrooms.

"But Herman Basket has been known to make her get up and go to the spring," my father said. "And I never heard him claim that old Dave Colbert's wife or his wife's niece or anybody else's wife or niece or aunt was any better than anybody else. Give Herman the horse."

"I can beat that," Ikkemotubbe said. Because there was no horse in the Plantation or America either between Natchez and Nashville whose tail Ikkemotubbe's new pony ever looked at. "I will run Herman a horse-race for his influence," he said. "Run," he told my father. "Catch Owl-at-Night before he reaches the house." So my father brought the pony back in time. But just in case Herman Basket's aunt had been watching from the kitchen window or something, Ikkemotubbe sent Owl-at-Night and Sylvester's John home for his crate of gamecocks, though he expected little from this since Herman Basket's aunt already owned the best cocks in the Plantation and won all the money every Sunday morning anyway. And then Herman Basket declined to commit himself, so a horse-race would have been merely for pleasure and money. And Ikkemotubbe said how money could not help him, and with that damned girl on his mind day and night his tongue had forgotten the savor of pleasure. But the whisky-trader always came, and so for a day or two at least he wouldn't have to not listen to the harmonica.

Then David Hogganbeck also looked at Herman Basket's sister, whom he too had been seeing once each year since the steamboat first walked to the Plantation. After a while even winter would be over and we would begin to watch the mark which David Hogganbeck had put on the landing to show us when the water would be tall enough for the steamboat to walk in. Then the river would reach the mark, and

sure enough within two suns the steamboat would cry in
the Plantation. Then all the People—men and women and
children and dogs, even Herman Basket's sister because
Ikkemotubbe would fetch a horse for her to ride and so
only Log-in-the-Creek would remain, not inside the house
even though it was still cold, because Herman Basket's aunt
wouldn't let him stay inside the house where she would
have to step over him each time she passed, but squatting in
his blanket on the gallery with an old cooking-pot of fire
inside the blanket with him—would stand on the landing,
to watch the upstairs and the smokestack moving among the
trees and hear the puffing of the smokestack and its feet
walking fast in the water too when it was not crying. Then
we would begin to hear David Hogganbeck's fiddle, and
then the steamboat would come walking up the last of the
river like a race-horse, with the smoke rolling black and its
feet flinging the water aside as a running horse flings dirt,
and Captain Studenmare who owned the steamboat chewing
tobacco in one window and David Hogganbeck playing his
fiddle in the other, and between them the head of the boy
slave who turned the wheel, who was not much more than
half as big as Captain Studenmare and not even a third as
big as David Hogganbeck. And all day long the trading
would continue, though David Hogganbeck took little part
in this. And all night long the dancing would continue, and
David Hogganbeck took the biggest part in this. Because he
was bigger than any two of the young men put together
almost, and although you would not have called him a man
built for dancing or running either, it was as if that very
double size which could hold twice as much whisky as any
other, could also dance twice as long, until one by one the
young men fell away and only he was left. And there was
horse-racing and eating, and although David Hogganbeck
had no horses and did not ride one since no horse could

have carried him and run fast too, he would eat a match
each year for money against any two of the young men
whom the People picked, and David Hogganbeck always
won. Then the water would return toward the mark he had
made on the landing, and it would be time for the steamboat
to leave while there was still enough water in the river for it
to walk in.

And then it did not go away. The river began to grow
little, yet still David Hogganbeck played his fiddle on
Herman Basket's gallery while Herman Basket's sister stirred
something for cooking into the silver wine pitcher and
Ikkemotubbe sat against a post in his fine clothes and his
beaver hat and Log-in-the-Creek lay on his back on the
floor with the harmonica cupped in both hands to his mouth,
though you couldn't hear now whether he was blowing into
it or not. Then you could see the mark which David Hogganbeck had marked on the landing while he still played his
fiddle on Herman Basket's gallery where Ikkemotubbe had
brought a rocking chair from his house to sit in until David
Hogganbeck would have to leave in order to show the steamboat the way back to Natchez. And all that afternoon the
People stood along the landing and watched the steamboat's
slaves hurling wood into its stomach for steam to make it
walk; and during most of that night, while David Hogganbeck drank twice as much and danced twice as long as even
David Hogganbeck, so that he drank four times as much
and danced four times as long as even Ikkemotubbe, even
an Ikkemotubbe who at last had looked at Herman Basket's
sister or at least had looked at someone else looking at her,
the older ones among the People stood along the landing and
watched the slaves hurling wood into the steamboat's stomach, not to make it walk but to make its voice cry while
Captain Studenmare leaned out of the upstairs with the end
of the crying-rope tied to the door-handle. And the next

day Captain Studenmare himself came onto the gallery and
grasped the end of David Hogganbeck's fiddle.

"You're fired," he said.

"All right," David Hogganbeck said. Then Captain
Studenmare grasped the end of David Hogganbeck's fiddle.

"We will have to go back to Natchez where I can get
money to pay you off," he said.

"Leave the money at the saloon," David Hogganbeck
said. "I'll bring the boat back out next spring."

Then it was night. Then Herman Basket's aunt came out
and said that if they were going to stay there all night, at
least David Hogganbeck would have to stop playing his
fiddle so other people could sleep. Then she came out and
said for Herman Basket's sister to come in and go to bed.
Then Herman Basket came out and said, "Come on now,
fellows. Be reasonable." Then Herman Basket's aunt came
out and said that the next time she was going to bring Herman Basket's dead uncle's shotgun. So Ikkemotubbe and
David Hogganbeck left Log-in-the-Creek lying on the floor
and stepped down from the gallery. "Goodnight," David
Hogganbeck said.

"I'll walk home with you," Ikkemotubbe said. So they
walked across the Plantation to the steamboat. It was dark
and there was no fire in its stomach now because Captain
Studenmare was still asleep under Issetibbeha's back porch.
Then Ikkemotubbe said, "Goodnight."

"I'll walk home with you," David Hogganbeck said. So
they walked back across the Plantation to Ikkemotubbe's
house. But David Hogganbeck did not have time to say
goodnight now because Ikkemotubbe turned as soon as they
reached his house and started back toward the steamboat.
Then he began to run, because David Hogganbeck still did
not look like a man who could run fast. But he had not
looked like a man who could dance a long time either, so

when Ikkemotubbe reached the steamboat and turned and ran again, he was only a little ahead of David Hogganbeck. And when they reached Ikkemotubbe's house he was still only a little ahead of David Hogganbeck when he stopped, breathing fast but only a little fast, and held the door open for David Hogganbeck to enter.

"My house is not very much house," he said. "But it is yours." So they both slept in Ikkemotubbe's bed in his house that night. And the next afternoon, although Herman Basket would still do no more than wish him success, Ikkemotubbe sent my father and Sylvester's John with his saddle mare for Herman Basket's aunt to ride on, and he and Herman Basket ran the horse-race. And he rode faster than anyone had ever ridden in the Plantation. He won by lengths and lengths and, with Herman Basket's aunt watching, he made Herman Basket take all the money, as though Herman Basket had won, and that evening he sent Owl-at-Night to tie the racing pony's hackamore to the door-handle of Herman Basket's kitchen. But that night Herman Basket's aunt did not even warn them. She came out the first time with Herman Basket's dead uncle's gun, and hardly a moment had elapsed before Ikkemotubbe found out that she meant him too. So he and David Hogganbeck left Log-in-the-Creek lying on the gallery and they stopped for a moment at my father's house on the first trip between Ikkemotubbe's house and the steamboat, though when my father and Owl-at-Night finally found Ikkemotubbe to tell him that Herman Basket's aunt must have sent the racing pony far into the woods and hidden it because they had not found it yet, Ikkemotubbe and David Hogganbeck were both asleep in David Hogganbeck's bed in the steamboat.

And the next morning the whisky-trader came, and that afternoon Ikkemotubbe and the young men invited Log-in-the-Creek into the woods and my father and Sylvester's

John returned for the whisky-trader's buckboard and, with
my father and Sylvester's John driving the buckboard and
Log-in-the-Creek lying on his face on top of the little house
on the back of the buckboard where the whisky-kegs rode
and Ikkemotubbe standing on top of the little house, wearing the used general's coat which General Jackson gave
Issetibbeha, with his arms folded and one foot advanced
onto Log-in-the-Creek's back, they rode slow past the gallery where David Hogganbeck played his fiddle while
Herman Basket's sister stirred something for cooking into
the silver wine pitcher. And when my father and Owl-at-
Night found Ikkemotubbe that night to tell him they still
had not found where Herman Basket's aunt had hidden the
pony, Ikkemotubbe and David Hogganbeck were at Ikkemotubbe's house. And the next afternoon Ikkemotubbe and
the young men invited David Hogganbeck into the woods
and it was a long time this time and when they came out,
David Hogganbeck was driving the buckboard while the
legs of Ikkemotubbe and the other young men dangled from
the open door of the little whisky-house like so many strands
of vine hay and Issetibbeha's general's coat was tied by its
sleeves about the neck of one of the mules. And nobody
hunted for the racing pony that night, and when Ikkemotubbe waked up, he didn't know at first even where he was.
And he could already hear David Hogganbeck's fiddle before he could move aside enough of the young men to get
out of the little whisky-house, because that night neither
Herman Basket's aunt nor Herman Basket and then finally
Herman Basket's dead uncle's gun could persuade David
Hogganbeck to leave the gallery and go away or even to
stop playing the fiddle.

So the next morning Ikkemotubbe and David Hogganbeck squatted in a quiet place in the woods while the young
men, except Sylvester's John and Owl-by-Night who were

still hunting for the horse, stood on guard. "We could fight for her then," David Hogganbeck said.

"We could fight for her," Ikkemotubbe said. "But white men and the People fight differently. We fight with knives, to hurt good and to hurt quickly. That would be all right, if I were to lose. Because I would wish to be hurt good. But if I am to win, I do not wish you to be hurt good. If I am to truly win, it will be necessary for you to be there to see it. On the day of the wedding, I wish you to be present, or at least present somewhere, not lying wrapped in a blanket on a platform in the woods, waiting to enter the earth." Then my father said how Ikkemotubbe put his hand on David Hogganbeck's shoulder and smiled at him. "If that could satisfy me, we would not be squatting here discussing what to do. I think you see that."

"I think I do," David Hogganbeck said.

Then my father said how Ikkemotubbe removed his hand from David Hogganbeck's shoulder. "And we have tried whisky," he said.

"We have tried that," David Hogganbeck said.

"Even the racing pony and the general's coat failed me," Ikkemotubbe said. "I had been saving them, like a man with two hole-cards."

"I wouldn't say that the coat completely failed," David Hogganbeck said. "You looked fine in it."

"Aihee," Ikkemotubbe said. "So did the mule." Then my father said how he was not smiling either as he squatted beside David Hogganbeck, making little marks in the earth with a twig. "So there is just one other thing," he said. "And I am already beaten at that too before we start."

So all that day they ate nothing. And that night when they left Log-in-the-Creek lying on Herman Basket's gallery, instead of merely walking for a while and then running for a while back and forth between Ikkemotubbe's house

and the steamboat, they began to run as soon as they left
Herman Basket's. And when they lay down in the woods
to sleep, it was where they would not only be free of temp-
tation to eat but of opportunity too, and from which it
would take another hard run as an appetiser to reach the
Plantation for the match. Then it was morning and they ran
back to where my father and the young men waited on
horses to meet them and tell Ikkemotubbe that they still
hadn't found where under the sun Herman Basket's aunt
could have hidden the pony and to escort them back across
the Plantation to the race-course, where the People waited
around the table, with Ikkemotubbe's rocking chair from
Herman Basket's gallery for Issetibbeha and a bench behind
it for the judges. First there was a recess while a ten-year-old
boy ran once around the race-track, to let them recover
breath. Then Ikkemotubbe and David Hogganbeck took
their places on either side of the table, facing each other
across it, and Owl-at-Night gave the word.

First, each had that quantity of stewed bird chitterlings
which the other could scoop with two hands from the pot.
Then each had as many wild turkey eggs as he was old,
Ikkemotubbe twenty-two and David Hogganbeck twenty-
three, though Ikkemotubbe refused the advantage and said
he would eat twenty-three too. Then David Hogganbeck
said he was entitled to one more than Ikkemotubbe so he
would eat twenty-four, until Issetibbeha told them both to
hush and get on, and Owl-at-Night tallied the shells. Then
there was the tongue, paws and melt of a bear, though for
a little while Ikkemotubbe stood and looked at his half of
it while David Hogganbeck was already eating. And at the
half-way he stopped and looked at it again while David
Hogganbeck was finishing. But it was all right; there was a
faint smile on his face such as the young men had seen on
it at the end of a hard running when he was going from

now on not on the fact that he was still alive but on the fact that he was Ikkemotubbe. And he went on, and Owl-at-Night tallied the bones, and the women set the roasted shote on the table and Ikkemotubbe and David Hogganbeck moved back to the tail of the shote and faced one another across it and Owl-at-Night had even given the word to start until he gave another word to stop. "Give me some water," Ikkemotubbe said. So my father handed him the gourd and he even took a swallow. But the water returned as though it had merely struck the back of his throat and bounced, and Ikkemotubbe put the gourd down and raised the tail of his shirt before his bowed face and turned and walked away as the People opened aside to let him pass.

And that afternoon they did not even go to the quiet place in the woods. They stood in Ikkemotubbe's house while my father and the others stood quietly too in the background. My father said that Ikkemotubbe was not smiling now. "I was right yesterday," he said. "If I am to lose to thee, we should have used the knives. You see," he said, and now my father said he even smiled again, as at the end of the long hard running when the young men knew that he would go on, not because he was still alive but because he was Ikkemotubbe; "—you see, although I have lost, I still cannot reconcile."

"I had you beat before we started," David Hogganbeck said. "We both knew that."

"Yes," Ikkemotubbe said. "But I suggested it."

"Then what do you suggest now?" David Hogganbeck said. And now my father said how they loved David Hogganbeck at that moment as they loved Ikkemotubbe; that they loved them both at that moment while Ikkemotubbe stood before David Hogganbeck with the smile on his face and his right hand flat on David Hogganbeck's chest, because there were men in those days.

"Once more then, and then no more," Ikkemotubbe said. "The Cave." Then he and David Hogganbeck stripped and my father and the others oiled them, body and hair too, with bear's grease mixed with mint, not just for speed this time but for lasting too, because the Cave was a hundred and thirty miles away, over in the country of old David Colbert—a black hole in the hill which the spoor of wild creatures merely approached and then turned away and which no dog could even be beaten to enter and where the boys from among all the People would go to lie on their first Night-away-from-Fire to prove if they had the courage to become men, because it had been known among the People from a long time ago that the sound of a whisper or even the disturbed air of a sudden movement would bring parts of the roof down and so all believed that not even a very big movement or sound or maybe none at all at some time would bring the whole mountain into the cave. Then Ikkemotubbe took the two pistols from the trunk and drew the loads and reloaded them. "Whoever reaches the Cave first can enter it alone and fire his pistol," he said. "If he comes back out, he has won."

"And if he does not come back out?" David Hogganbeck said.

"Then you have won," Ikkemotubbe said.

"Or you," David Hogganbeck said.

And now my father said how Ikkemotubbe smiled again at David Hogganbeck. "Or me," he said. "Though I think I told you yesterday that such as that for me will not be victory." Then Ikkemotubbe put another charge of powder, with a wadding and bullet, into each of two small medicine bags, one for himself and one for David Hogganbeck, just in case the one who entered the Cave first should not lose quick enough, and, wearing only their shirts and shoes and each with his pistol and medicine bag looped on a cord

around his neck, they emerged from Ikkemotubbe's house
and began to run.

It was evening then. Then it was night, and since David
Hogganbeck did not know the way, Ikkemotubbe continued
to set the pace. But after a time it was daylight again and
now David Hogganbeck could run by the sun and the landmarks which Ikkemotubbe described to him while they
rested beside a creek, if he wished to go faster. So sometimes David Hogganbeck would run in front and sometimes
Ikkemotubbe, then David Hogganbeck would pass Ikkemotubbe as he sat beside a spring or a stream with his feet in
the water and Ikkemotubbe would smile at David Hogganbeck and wave his hand. Then he would overtake David
Hogganbeck and the country was open now and they would
run side by side in the prairies with his hand lying lightly
on David Hogganbeck's shoulder, not on the top of the
shoulder but lightly against the back of it until after a while
he would smile at David Hogganbeck and draw ahead. But
then it was sundown, and then it was dark again so Ikkemotubbe slowed and then stopped until he heard David Hogganbeck and knew that David Hogganbeck could hear him
and then he ran again so that David Hogganbeck could follow the sound of his running. So when David Hogganbeck
fell, Ikkemotubbe heard it and went back and found David
Hogganbeck in the dark and turned him onto his back and
found water in the dark and soaked his shirt in it and returned and wrung the water from the shirt into David Hogganbeck's mouth. And then it was daylight and Ikkemotubbe
waked also and found a nest containing five unfledged birds
and ate and brought the other three to David Hogganbeck
and then he went on until he was just this side of where
David Hogganbeck could no longer see him and sat down
again until David Hogganbeck got up onto his feet.

And he gave David Hogganbeck the landmarks for that

day too, talking back to David Hogganbeck over his shoulder as they ran, though David Hogganbeck did not need them because he never overtook Ikkemotubbe again. He never came closer than fifteen or twenty paces, although it looked at one time like he was. Because this time it was Ikkemotubbe who fell. And the country was open again so Ikkemotubbe could lie there for a long time and watch David Hogganbeck coming. Then it was sunset again, and then it was dark again, and he lay there listening to David Hogganbeck coming for a long time until it was time for Ikkemotubbe to get up and he did and they went on slowly in the dark with David Hogganbeck at least a hundred paces behind him, until he heard David Hogganbeck fall and then he lay down too. Then it was day again and he watched David Hogganbeck get up onto his feet and come slowly toward him and at last he tried to get up too but he did not and it looked like David Hogganbeck was going to come up with him. But he got up at last while David Hogganbeck was still four or five paces away and they went on until David Hogganbeck fell, and then Ikkemotubbe thought he was just watching David Hogganbeck fall until he found that he had fallen too but he got up onto his hands and knees and crawled still another ten or fifteen paces before he too lay down. And there in the sunset before him was the hill in which the Cave was, and there through the night, and there still in the sunrise.

So Ikkemotubbe ran into the Cave first, with his pistol already cocked in his hand. He told how he stopped perhaps for a second at the entrance, perhaps to look at the sun again or perhaps just to see where David Hogganbeck had stopped. But David Hogganbeck was running too and he was still only that fifteen or twenty paces behind, and besides, because of that damned sister of Herman Basket's, there had been no light nor heat either in that sun for moons

and moons. So he ran into the Cave and turned and saw
David Hogganbeck also running into the Cave and he cried,
"Back, fool!" But David Hogganbeck still ran into the Cave
even as Ikkemotubbe pointed his pistol at the roof and fired.
And there was a noise, and a rushing, and a blackness and a
dust, and Ikkemotubbe told how he thought, *Aihee. It
comes.* But it did not, and even before the blackness he saw
David Hogganbeck cast himself forward onto his hands and
knees, and there was not a complete blackness either because
he could see the sunlight and air and day beyond the tunnel
of David Hogganbeck's arms and legs as, still on his hands
and knees, David Hogganbeck held the fallen roof upon
his back. "Hurry," David Hogganbeck said. "Between my
legs. I can't—"

"Nay, brother," Ikkemotubbe said. "Quickly thyself,
before it crushes thee. Crawl back."

"Hurry," David Hogganbeck said behind his teeth.
"Hurry, damn you." And Ikkemotubbe did, and he remembered David Hogganbeck's buttocks and legs pink in the
sunrise and the slab of rock which supported the fallen roof
pink in the sunrise too across David Hogganbeck's back.
But he did not remember where he found the pole nor how
he carried it alone into the Cave and thrust it into the hole
beside David Hogganbeck and stooped his own back under
it and lifted until he knew that some at least of the weight
of the fallen roof was on the pole.

"Now," he said. "Quickly."

"No," David Hogganbeck said.

"Quickly, brother," Ikkemotubbe said. "The weight is
off thee."

"Then I can't move," David Hogganbeck said. But Ikkemotubbe couldn't move either, because now he had to hold
the fallen roof up with his back and legs. So he reached one
hand and grasped David Hogganbeck by the meat and

jerked him backward out of the hole until he lay face-down
upon the earth. And maybe some of the weight of the fallen
roof was on the pole before, but now all of the weight was
on it and Ikkemotubbe said how he thought, *This time surely
aihee*. But it was the pole and not his back which snapped
and flung him face-down too across David Hogganbeck like
two flung sticks, and a bright gout of blood jumped out of
David Hogganbeck's mouth.

But by the second day David Hogganbeck had quit
vomiting blood, though Ikkemotubbe had run hardly forty
miles back toward the Plantation when my father met him
with the horse for David Hogganbeck to ride. Presently my
father said, "I have a news for thee."

"So you found the pony," Ikkemotubbe said. "All right.
Come on. Let's get that damned stupid fool of a white
man—"

"No, wait, my brother," my father said. "I have a news
for thee."

And presently Ikkemotubbe said, "All right."

But when Captain Studenmare borrowed Issetibbeha's
wagon to go back to Natchez in, he took the steamboat
slaves too. So my father and the young men built a fire in
the steamboat's stomach to make steam for it to walk, while
David Hogganbeck sat in the upstairs and drew the crying-
rope from time to time to see if the steam was strong enough
yet, and at each cry still more of the People came to the
landing until at last all the People in the Plantation except
old Issetibbeha perhaps stood along the bank to watch the
young men hurl wood into the steamboat's stomach:—a
thing never before seen in our Plantation at least. Then the
steam was strong and the steamboat began to walk and then
the People began to walk too beside the steamboat, watching the young men for a while then Ikkemotubbe and David
Hogganbeck for a while as the steamboat walked out of the
Plantation where hardly seven suns ago Ikkemotubbe and

David Hogganbeck would sit all day long and half the night too until Herman Basket's aunt would come out with Herman Basket's dead uncle's gun, on the gallery of Herman Basket's house while Log-in-the-Creek lay on the floor with his harmonica cupped to his mouth and Log-in-the-Creek's wife shelled corn or peas into old Dave Colbert's wife's grand-niece's second cousin by marriage's wine pitcher. Presently Ikkemotubbe was gone completely away, to be gone a long time before he came back named Doom, with his new white friend whom no man wished to love either and the eight more slaves which we had no use for either because at times someone would have to get up and walk somewhere to find something for the ones we already owned to do, and the fine gold-trimmed clothes and the little gold box of salt which caused the other four puppies to become dead too one after another, and then anything else which happened to stand between Doom and what he wanted. But he was not quite gone yet. He was just Ikkemotubbe yet, one of the young men, another of the young men who loved and was not loved in return and could hear the words and see the fact, yet who, like the young men who had been before him and the ones who would come after him, still could not understand it.

"But not for her!" Ikkemotubbe said. "And not even because it was Log-in-the-Creek. Perhaps they are for myself: that such a son as Log-in-the-Creek could cause them to wish to flow."

"Don't think about her," David Hogganbeck said.

"I don't. I have already stopped. See?" Ikkemotubbe said while the sunset ran down his face as if it had already been rain instead of light when it entered the window. "There was a wise man of ours who said once how a woman's fancy is like a butterfly which, hovering from flower to flower, pauses at the last as like as not where a horse has stood."

"There was a wise man of ours named Solomon who often

said something of that nature too," David Hogganbeck said. "Perhaps there is just one wisdom for all men, no matter who speaks it."

"Aihee. At least, for all men one same heart-break," Ikkemotubbe said. Then he drew the crying-rope, because the boat was now passing the house where Log-in-the-Creek and his wife lived, and now the steamboat sounded like it did the first night while Captain Studenmare still thought David Hogganbeck would come and show it the way back to Natchez, until David Hogganbeck made Ikkemotubbe stop. Because they would need the steam because the steamboat did not always walk. Sometimes it crawled, and each time its feet came up there was mud on them, and sometimes it did not even crawl until David Hogganbeck drew the crying-rope as the rider speaks to the recalcitrant horse to remind it with his voice just who is up. Then it crawled again and then it walked again, until at last the People could no longer keep up, and it cried once more beyond the last bend and then there was no longer either the black shapes of the young men leaping to hurl wood into its red stomach or even the sound of its voice in the Plantation or the night. That's how it was in the old days.

Lo!

THE PRESIDENT STOOD motionless at the door of the Dressing Room, fully dressed save for his boots. It was half-past six in the morning and it was snowing; already he had stood for an hour at the window, watching the snow. Now he stood just inside the door to the corridor, utterly motionless in his stockings, stooped a little from his lean height as though listening, on his face an expression of humorless concern, since humor had departed from his situation and his view of it almost three weeks before. Hanging from his hand, low against his flank, was a hand mirror of elegant French design, such as should have been lying upon a lady's dressing table: certainly at this hour of a February day.

At last he put his hand on the knob and opened the door infinitesimally; beneath his hand the door crept by inches and without any sound; still with that infinitesimal silence he put his eye to the crack and saw, lying upon the deep, rich pile of the corridor carpet, a bone. It was a cooked bone, a rib; to it still adhered close shreds of flesh holding in mute and overlapping halfmoons the marks of human teeth. Now that the door was open he could hear the voices too. Still without any sound, with that infinite care, he raised and advanced the mirror. For an instant he caught his own reflection in it and he paused for a time and with a kind of cold unbelief he examined his own face—the face of the shrewd and coura-

geous fighter, of that wellnigh infallible expert in the antici-
pation of and controlling of man and his doings, overlaid
now with the baffled helplessness of a child. Then he slanted
the glass a little further until he could see the corridor reflected in it. Squatting and facing one another across the
carpet as across a stream of water were two men. He did not
know the faces, though he knew the Face, since he had
looked upon it by day and dreamed upon it by night for
three weeks now. It was a squat face, dark, a little flat, a little
Mongol; secret, decorous, impenetrable, and grave. He had
seen it repeated until he had given up trying to count it or
even estimate it; even now, though he could see the two men
squatting before him and could hear the two quiet voices, it
seemed to him that in some idiotic moment out of attenuated
sleeplessness and strain he looked upon a single man facing
himself in a mirror.

They wore beaver hats and new frock coats; save for the
minor detail of collars and waistcoats they were impeccably
dressed—though a little early—for the forenoon of the time,
down to the waist. But from here down credulity, all sense
of fitness and decorum, was outraged. At a glance one would
have said that they had come intact out of Pickwickian England, save that the tight, light-colored smallclothes ended not
in Hessian boots nor in any boots at all, but in dark, naked
feet. On the floor beside each one lay a neatly rolled bundle
of dark cloth; beside each bundle in turn, mute toe and toe
and heel and heel, as though occupied by invisible sentries
facing one another across the corridor, sat two pairs of new
boots. From a basket woven of whiteoak withes beside one
of the squatting men there shot suddenly the snake-like head
and neck of a game cock, which glared at the faint flash of
the mirror with a round, yellow, outraged eye. It was from
these that the voices came, pleasant, decorous, quiet:

"That rooster hasn't done you much good up here."

"That's true. Still, who knows? Besides, I certainly couldn't have left him at home, with those damned lazy Indians. I wouldn't find a feather left. You know that. But it is a nuisance, having to lug this cage around with me day and night."

"This whole business is a nuisance, if you ask me."

"You said it. Squatting here outside this door all night long. without a gun or anything. Suppose bad men tried to get in during the night: what could we do? If anyone would want to get in. I don't."

"Nobody does. It's for honor."

"Whose honor? Yours? Mine? Frank Weddel's?"

"White man's honor. You don't understand white people. They are like children: you have to handle them careful because you never know what they are going to do next. So if it's the rule for guests to squat all night long in the cold outside this man's door, we'll just have to do it. Besides, hadn't you rather be in here than out yonder in the snow in one of those damn tents?"

"You said it. What a climate. What a country. I wouldn't have this town if they gave it to me."

"Of course you wouldn't. But that's white men: no accounting for taste. So as long as we are here, we'll have to try to act like these people believe that Indians ought to act. Because you never know until afterward just what you have done to insult or scare them. Like this having to talk white talk all the time. . . ."

The President withdrew the mirror and closed the door quietly. Once more he stood silent and motionless in the middle of the room, his head bent, musing, baffled yet indomitable: indomitable since this was not the first time that he had faced odds; baffled since he faced not an enemy in the open field, but was besieged within his very high and lonely office by them to whom he was, by legal if not divine appointment. father. In the iron silence of the winter dawn he seemed, clairvoyant of walls, to be ubiquitous and one with the waking of the stately House. Invisible and in a kind of musing horror he seemed to be of each group of his Southern guests—that one squatting without the door, that larger one like so many figures carved of stone in the very rotunda itself of this concrete and visible apotheosis of the youthful Nation's pride—in their new beavers and frock coats and woolen drawers. With their neatly rolled pantaloons under their arms and their virgin shoes in the other hand; dark, timeless, decorous and serene beneath the astonished faces and golden braid, the swords and ribbons and stars, of European diplomats.

The President said quietly, "Damn. Damn. Damn." He moved and crossed the room, pausing to take up his boots from where they sat beside a chair, and approached the opposite door. Again he paused and opened this door too quietly and carefully, out of the three weeks' habit of expectant fatalism, though there was only his wife beyond it, sleeping peacefully in bed. He crossed this room in turn, carrying his boots, pausing to replace the hand glass on the dressing table, among its companion pieces of the set which the new French Republic had presented to a predecessor, and tiptoed on and into the anteroom, where a man in a long cloak looked up and then rose, also in his stockings. They looked at one another soberly.. "All clear?" the President said in a low tone.

"Yes, General."

"Good. Did you . . ." The other produced a second long, plain cloak. "Good, good," the President said. He swung the cloak about him before the other could move. "Now the . . ." This time the other anticipated him; the President drew the hat well down over his face. They left the room on tiptoe, carrying their boots in their hands.

The back stairway was cold: their stockinged toes curled

away from the treads, their vaporized breath wisped about their heads. They descended quietly and sat on the bottom step and put on their boots.

Outside it still snowed; invisible against snow-colored sky and snow-colored earth, the flakes seemed to materialize with violent and silent abruptness against the dark orifice of the stables. Each bush and shrub resembled a white balloon whose dark shroud lines descended, light and immobile, to the white earth. Interspersed among these in turn and with a certain regularity were a dozen vaguely tent-shaped mounds, from the ridge of each of which a small column of smoke rose into the windless snow, as if the snow itself were in a state of peaceful combustion. The President looked at these, once, grimly. "Get along," he said. The other, his head lowered and his cloak held closely about his face, scuttled on and ducked into the stable. Perish the day when these two words were applied to the soldier chief of a party and a nation, yet the President was so close behind him that their breaths made one cloud. And perish the day when the word *flight* were so applied, yet they had hardly vanished into the stable when they emerged, mounted now and already at a canter, and so across the lawn and past the snow-hidden tents and toward the gates which gave upon that Avenue in embryo yet but which in time would be the stage upon which each four years would parade the proud panoply of the young Nation's lusty man's estate for the admiration and envy and astonishment of the weary world. At the moment, though, the gates were occupied by those more immediate than splendid augurs of the future.

"Look out," the other man said, reining back. They reined aside—the President drew the cloak about his face—and allowed the party to enter: the squat, broad, dark men dark against the snow, the beaver hats, the formal coats, the solid legs clad from thigh to ankle in woolen drawers. Among them moved three horses on whose backs were lashed the carcasses of six deer. They passed on, passing the two horsemen without a glance.

"Damn, damn, damn," the President said; then aloud: "You found good hunting."

One of the group glanced at him, briefly. He said courteously, pleasantly, without inflection, going on: "So so."

The horses moved again. "I didn't see any guns," the other man said.

"Yes," the President said grimly. "I must look into this, too. I gave strict orders. . . ." He said fretfully, "Damn. Damn. Do they carry their pantaloons when they go hunting too, do you know?"

The Secretary was at breakfast, though he was not eating. Surrounded by untasted dishes he sat, in his dressing gown and unshaven; his expression too was harried as he perused the paper which lay upon his empty plate. Before the fire were two men—one a horseman with unmelted snow still upon his cloak, seated on a wooden settle, the other standing, obviously the secretary to the Secretary. The horseman rose as the President and his companion entered. "Sit down, sit down," the President said. He approached the table, slipping off the cloak, which the secretary came forward and took. "Give us some breakfast," the President said. "We don't dare go home." He sat down; the Secretary served him in person. "What is it now?" the President said.

"Do you ask?" the Secretary said. He took up the paper again and glared at it. "From Pennsylvania, this time." He struck the paper. "Maryland, New York, and now Pennsylvania; apparently the only thing that can stop them is the temperature of the water in the Potomac River." He spoke in a harsh, irascible voice. "Complaint, complaint, complaint: here is a farmer near Gettysburg. His Negro slave was in the barn, milking by lantern light after dark, when—the Negro doubtless thought about two hundred, since the farmer estimated them at ten or twelve—springing suddenly out of the darkness in plug hats and carrying knives and naked from the waist down. Result, item: One barn and loft of hay and cow destroyed when the lantern was kicked over; item: one able-bodied slave last seen departing from the scene at a high rate of speed, headed for the forest, and doubtless now dead of fear or by the agency of wild beasts. Debit the Government of the United States: for barn and hay, one hundred dollars; for cow, fifteen dollars; for Negro slave, two hundred dollars. He demands it in gold."

"Is that so?" the President said, eating swiftly. "I suppose the Negro and the cow took them to be ghosts of Hessian soldiers."

"I wonder if they thought the cow was a deer," the horseman said.

"Yes," the President said. "That's something else I want. . . ."

"Who wouldn't take them for anything on earth or under it?" the Secretary said. "The entire Atlantic seaboard north of the Potomac River overrun by creatures in beaver hats and frock coats and woolen drawers, frightening women and children, setting fire to barns and running off slaves, killing deer. . . ."

"Yes," the President said. "I want to say a word about that, myself. I met a party of them returning as I came out. They had six deer. I thought I gave strict orders that they were not to be permitted guns."

Again it was the horseman who spoke. "They don't use guns."

"What?" the President said. "But I saw myself . . ."

"No, sir. They use knives. They track the deer down and slip up on them and cut their throats."

"What?" the President said.

"All right, sir. I seen one of the deer. It never had a mark on it except its throat cut up to the neckbone with one lick."

Again the President said, "Damn. Damn. Damn." Then the President ceased and the Soldier cursed steadily for a while. The others listened, gravely, their faces carefully averted, save the Secretary, who had taken up another paper. "If you could just persuade them to keep their pantaloons on," the President said. "At least about the House. . . ."

The Secretary started back, his hair upcrested like an outraged, iron-gray cockatoo. "I, sir? *I* persuade them?"

"Why not? Aren't they subject to your Department? I'm just the President. Confound it, it's got to where my wife no longer dares leave her bedroom, let alone receive lady guests. How am I to explain to the French Ambassador, for instance, why his wife no longer dares call upon my wife because the corridors and the very entrance to the House are blocked by half-naked Chickasaw Indians asleep on the floor or gnawing at half-raw ribs of meat? And I, myself, having to hide away from my own table and beg breakfast, while the official representative of the Government has nothing to do but . . ."

". . . but explain again each morning to the Treasury," the Secretary said in shrill rage, "why another Dutch farmer in Pennsylvania or New York must have three hundred dollars in gold in payment for the destruction of his farm and livestock, and explain to the State Department that the capital is not being besieged by demons from hell itself, and explain to the War Department why twelve brand-new army tents must be ventilated at the top with butcher knives. . . ."

"I noticed that, too," the President said mildly. "I had forgot it."

"Ha. Your Excellency noted it," the Secretary said fiercely. "Your Excellency saw it and then forgot it. I have neither seen it nor been permitted to forget it. And now

Your Excellency wonders why *I* do not persuade them to wear their pantaloons."

"It does seem like they would," the President said fretfully. "The other garments seem to please them well enough. But there's no accounting for taste." He ate again. The Secretary looked at him, about to speak. Then he did not. As he watched the oblivious President a curious, secret expression came into his face; his gray and irate crest settled slowly, as if it were deflating itself. When he spoke now his tone was bland, smooth; now the other three men were watching the President with curious, covert expressions.

"Yes," the Secretary said, "there's no accounting for taste. Though it does seem that when one has been presented with a costume as a mark of both honor and esteem, let alone decorum, and by the chief of a well, tribe . . ."

"That's what I thought," the President said innocently. Then he ceased chewing and said "Eh?" sharply, looking up. The three lesser men looked quickly away, but the Secretary continued to watch the President with that bland, secret expression. "What the devil do you mean?" the President said. He knew what the Secretary meant, just as the other three knew. A day or two after his guest had arrived without warning, and after the original shock had somewhat abated, the President had decreed the new clothing for them. He commanded, out of his own pocket, merchants and hatters as he would have commanded gunsmiths and bulletmakers in war emergency; incidentally he was thus able to estimate the number of them, the men at least, and within forty-eight hours he had transformed his guest's grave and motley train into the outward aspect of decorum at least. Then, two mornings after that, the guest—the half Chickasaw, half Frenchman, the squat, obese man with the face of a Gascon brigand and the mannerisms of a spoiled eunuch and dingy lace at throat and wrist, who for three weeks now had dogged his

waking hours and his sleeping dreams with bland inescapa-
bility—called formally upon him while he and his wife were
still in bed at five o'clock in the morning, with two of his
retainers carrying a bundle and what seemed to the President
at least a hundred others, men, women and children, throng-
ing quietly into the bedroom, apparently to watch him array
himself in it. For it was a costume—even in the shocked
horror of the moment, the President found time to wonder
wildly where in the capital Weddel (or Vidal) had found it
—a mass, a network, of gold braid—frogs, epaulets, sash and
sword—held loosely together by bright green cloth and presented to him in return. This is what the Secretary meant,
while the President glared at him and while behind them both
the three other men stood looking at the fire with immobile
gravity. "Have your joke," the President said. "Have it
quickly. Are you done laughing now?"

"I laugh?" the Secretary said. "At what?"

"Good," the President said. He thrust the dishes from him.
"Then we can get down to business. Have you any docu-
ments you will need to refer to?"

The Secretary's secretary approached. "Shall I get the
other papers, sir?"

"Papers?" the Secretary said; once more his crest began to
rise. "What the devil do I need with papers? What else have
I thought about night and day for three weeks?"

"Good; good," the President said. "Suppose you review
the matter briefly, in case I have forgot anything else."

"Your Excellency is indeed a fortunate man, if you have
been able to forget," the Secretary said. From the pocket of
his dressing gown he took a pair of steel-bowed spectacles.
But he used them merely to glare again at the President in
cockatoo-crested outrage. "This man, Weddel, Vidal—whatever his name is—he and his family or clan or whatever they
are—claim to own the entire part of Mississippi which lies

on the west side of this river in question. Oh, the grant is in order: that French father of his from New Orleans saw to that.—Well, it so happens that facing his home or plantation is the only ford in about three hundred miles."

"I know all this," the President said impatiently. "Naturally I regret now that there was any way of crossing the river at all. But otherwise I don't see . . ."

"Neither did they," the Secretary said. "Until the white man came."

"Ah," the President said. "The man who was mur . . ."

The Secretary raised his hand. "Wait. He stayed about a month with them, ostensibly hunting, since he would be absent all day long, though obviously what he was doing was assuring himself that there was no other ford close by. He never brought any game in; I imagine they laughed at that a good deal, in their pleasant way."

"Yes," the President said. "Weddel must have found that very amusing."

". . . or Vidal—whatever his name is," the Secretary said fretfully. "He don't even seem to know or even to care what his own name is."

"Get on," the President said. "About the ford."

"Yes. Then one day, after a month, the white man offered to buy some of Weddel's land—Weddel, Vidal—Damn, da . . ."

"Call him Weddel," the President said.

". . . from Weddel. Not much; a piece about the size of this room, for which Weddel or V—— charged him about ten prices. Not out of any desire for usufruct, you understand; doubtless Weddel would have given the man the land or anyway wagered it on a game of mumble peg, it not having yet occurred to any of them apparently that the small plot which the man wanted contained the only available entrance to or exit from the ford. Doubtless the trading protracted it-

self over several days or perhaps weeks, as a kind of game to
while away otherwise idle afternoons or evenings, with the
bystanders laughing heartily and pleasantly at the happy
scene. They must have laughed a great deal, especially when
the man paid Weddel's price; they must have laughed hugely
indeed later when they watched the white man out in the
sun, building a fence around his property, it doubtless not
even then occurring to them that what the white man had
done was to fence off the only entrance to the ford."

"Yes," the President said impatiently. "But I still don't
see . . ."

Again the Secretary lifted his hand, pontifical, admonitory.
"Neither did they; not until the first traveler came along and
crossed at the ford. The white man had built himself a tollgate."

"Oh," the President said.

"Yes. And now it must have been, indeed, amusing for
them to watch the white man sitting now in the shade—he
had a deerskin pouch fastened to a post for the travelers to
drop their coins in, and the gate itself arranged so he could
operate it by a rope from the veranda of his one-room domi-
cile without having to even leave his seat; and to begin to
acquire property—among which was the horse."

"Ah," the President said. "Now we are getting at it."

"Yes. They got at it swiftly from then on. It seems that
the match was between the white man's horse and this nephew's horse, the wager the ford and tollgate against a thousand
or so acres of land. The nephew's horse lost. And that
night . . ."

"Ah," the President said. "I see. And that night the white
man was mur . . ."

"Let us say, died," the Secretary said primly, "since it is so
phrased in the agent's report. Though he did add in a private

communication that the white man's disease seemed to be a split skull. But that is neither here nor there."

"No," the President said. "It's up yonder at the House." Where they had been for three weeks now, men, women, children and Negro slaves, coming for fifteen hundred miles in slow wagons since that day in late autumn when the Chickasaw agent had appeared to inquire into the white man's death. For fifteen hundred miles, across winter swamps and rivers, across the trackless eastern backbone of the continent, led by the bland, obese mongrel despot and patriarch in a carriage, dozing, his nephew beside him and one fat, ringed hand beneath its fall of soiled lace lying upon the nephew's knee to hold him in charge. "Why didn't the agent stop him?" the President said.

"Stop him?" the Secretary cried. "He finally compromised to the extent of offering to allow the nephew to be tried on the spot, by the Indians themselves, he reserving only the intention of abolishing the tollgate, since no one knew the white man anyway. But no. The nephew must come to you, to be absolved or convicted in person."

"But couldn't the agent stop the rest of them? Keep the rest of them from . . ."

"Stop them?" the Secretary cried again. "Listen. He moved in there and lived—Weddel, Vi—Damn! damn!! Where was—Yes. Weddel told him that the house was his; soon it was. Because how could he tell there were fewer faces present each morning than the night before? Could you have? Could you now?"

"I wouldn't try," the President said. "I would just declare a national thanksgiving. So they slipped away at night."

"Yes. Weddel and the carriage and a few forage wagons went first; they had been gone about a month before the agent realized that each morning the number which remained had diminished somewhat. They would load the wagons and go at night, by families—grandparents, parents, children; slaves, chattels and dogs—everything. And why not? Why should they deny themselves this holiday at the expense of the Government? Why should they miss, at the mere price of a fifteen-hundred-mile journey through unknown country in the dead of winter, the privilege and pleasure of spending a few weeks or months in new beavers and broadcloth coats and underdrawers, in the home of the beneficent White Father?"

"Yes," the President said. He said: "And you have told him that there is no charge here against this nephew?"

"Yes. And that if they will go back home, the agent himself will declare the nephew innocent publicly, in whatever ceremony they think fit. And he said—how was it he put it?" The Secretary now spoke in a pleasant, almost lilting tone, in almost exact imitation of the man whom he repeated: "All we desire is justice. If this foolish boy has murdered a white man, I think that we should know it."

"Damn, damn, damn," the President said. "All right. We'll hold the investigation. Get them down here and let's have it over with."

"Here?" The Secretary started back. "In my house?"

"Why not? I've had them for three weeks; at least you can have them for an hour." He turned to the companion. "Hurry. Tell them we are waiting here to hold his nephew's trial."

And now the President and the Secretary sat behind the cleared table and looked at the man who stood as though framed by the opened doors through which he had entered, holding his nephew by the hand like an uncle conducting for the first time a youthful provincial kinsman into a metropolitan museum of wax figures. Immobile, they contemplated the soft, paunchy man facing them with his soft, bland,

inscrutable face—the long, monk-like nose, the slumbrous
lids, the flabby, *café-au-lait*-colored jowls above a froth of
soiled lace of an elegance fifty years outmoded and vanished;
the mouth was full, small, and very red. Yet somewhere behind the face's expression of flaccid and weary disillusion, as
behind the bland voice and the almost feminine mannerisms,
there lurked something else: something willful, shrewd, unpredictable and despotic. Behind him clotted, quiet and
gravely decorous, his dark retinue in beavers and broadcloth
and woolen drawers, each with his neatly rolled pantaloons
beneath his arm.

For a moment longer he stood, looking from face to face
until he found the President. He said, in a voice of soft reproach: "This is not your house."

"No," the President said. "This is the house of this chief
whom I have appointed myself to be the holder of justice
between me and my Indian people. He will deal justice to
you."

The uncle bowed slightly. "That is all that we desire."

"Good," the President said. On the table before him sat
inkstand, quill, and sandbox, and many papers with ribbons
and golden seals much in evidence, though none could have
said if the heavy gaze had remarked them or not. The President looked at the nephew. Young, lean, the nephew stood,
his right wrist clasped by his uncle's fat, lace-foamed hand,
and contemplated the President quietly, with grave and alert
repose. The President dipped the quill into the ink. "Is this
the man who . . ."

"Who performed this murder?" the uncle said pleasantly.
"That is what we made this long winter's journey to discover. If he did, if this white man really did not fall from that
swift horse of his perhaps and strike his head upon a sharp
stone, then this nephew of mine should be punished. We do
not think that it is right to slay white men like a confounded

Cherokee or Creek." Perfectly inscrutable, perfectly decorous, he looked at the two exalted personages playing behind
the table their clumsy deception with dummy papers; for an
instant the President himself met the slumbrous eyes and
looked down. The Secretary though, upthrust, his crest
roached violently upward, glared at the uncle.

"You should have held this horse-race across the ford itself," he said. "Water wouldn't have left that gash in the
white man's skull."

The President, glancing quickly up, saw the heavy, secret
face musing upon the Secretary with dark speculation. But
almost immediately the uncle spoke. "So it would. But this
white man would have doubtless required a coin of money
from my nephew for passing through his gate." Then he
laughed, mirthful, pleasant, decorous. "Perhaps it would have
been better for that white man if he had allowed my nephew
to pass through free. But that is neither here nor there now."

"No," the President said, almost sharply, so that they
looked at him again. He held the quill above the paper.
"What is the correct name? Weddel or Vidal?"

Again the pleasant, inflectionless voice came: "Weddel or
Vidal. What does it matter by what name the White Chief
calls us? We are but Indians: remembered yesterday and forgotten tomorrow."

The President wrote upon the paper. The quill scratched
steadily in the silence in which there was but one other
sound: a faint, steady, minor sound which seemed to emerge
from the dark and motionless group behind the uncle and
nephew. He sanded what he had written and folded it and
rose and stood for a moment so while they watched him
quietly—the soldier who had commanded men well on more
occasions than this. "Your nephew is not guilty of this murder. My chief whom I have appointed to hold justice be-

tween us says for him to return home and never do this again,
because next time he will be displeased."

His voice died into a shocked silence; even for that instant
the heavy lids fluttered, while from the dark throng behind
him that faint, unceasing sound of quiet scratching by heat
and wool engendered, like a faint, constant motion of the
sea, also ceased for an instant. The uncle spoke in a tone of
shocked unbelief: "My nephew is free?"

"He is free," the President said. The uncle's shocked gaze
traveled about the room.

"This quick? And in here? In this house? I had thought.
. . . But no matter." They watched him; again the face was
smooth, enigmatic, blank. "We are only Indians; doubtless
these busy white men have but little time for our small affairs.
Perhaps we have already incommoded them too much."

"No, no," the President said quickly. "To me, my Indian
and my white people are the same." But again the uncle's
gaze was traveling quietly about the room; standing side by
side, the President and the Secretary could feel from one to
another the same dawning alarm. After a while the President
said: "Where had you expected this council to be held?"

The uncle looked at him. "You will be amused. In my ig-
norance I had thought that even our little affair would have
been concluded in . . . But no matter."

"In what?" the President said.

The bland, heavy face mused again upon him for a moment. "You will laugh; nevertheless, I will obey you. In the
big white council house beneath the golden eagle."

"What?" the Secretary cried, starting again. "In the . . ."

The uncle looked away. "I said that you would be amused.
But no matter. We will have to wait, anyway."

"Have to wait?" the President said. "For what?"

"This is really amusing," the uncle said. He laughed again,
in his tone of mirthful detachment. "More of my people are

about to arrive. We can wait for them, since they will wish to see and hear also." No one exclaimed at all now, not even the Secretary. They merely stared at him while the bland voice went on: "It seems that some of them mistook the town. They had heard the name of the White Chief's capital spoken, but it so happens that there is also a town in our country with the same name, so that when some of the People inquired on the road, they became misdirected and went there instead, poor ignorant Indians." He laughed, with fond and mirthful tolerance behind his enigmatic and sleepy face. "But a messenger has arrived; they will arrive themselves within the week. Then we will see about punishing this headstrong boy." He shook the nephew's arm lightly. Except for this the nephew did not move, watching the President with his grave and unwinking regard.

For a long moment there was no sound save the faint, steady scratching of the Indians. Then the Secretary began to speak, patiently, as though addressing a child: "Look. Your nephew is free. This paper says that he did not slay the white man and that no man shall so accuse him again, else both I and the great chief beside me will be angered. He can return home now, at once. Let all of you return home at once. For is it not well said that the graves of a man's fathers are never quiet in his absence?"

Again there was silence. Then the President said, "Besides, the white council house beneath the golden eagle is being used now by a council of chiefs who are more powerful there than I am."

The uncle's hand lifted; foamed with soiled lace, his forefinger waggled in reproachful deprecation. "Do not ask even an ignorant Indian to believe that," he said. Then he said, with no change of inflection whatever; the Secretary did not know until the President told him later, that the uncle was now addressing him: "And these chiefs will doubtless be occupying the white council hut for some time yet, I suppose."

"Yes," the Secretary said. "Until the last snow of winter has melted among the flowers and the green grass."

"Good," the uncle said. "We will wait, then. Then the rest of the People will have time to arrive."

And so it was that up that Avenue with a high destiny the cavalcade moved in the still falling snow, led by the carriage containing the President and the uncle and nephew, the fat, ringed hand lying again upon the nephew's knee, and followed by a second carriage containing the Secretary and his secretary, and this followed in turn by two files of soldiers between which walked the dark and decorous cloud of men, women and children on foot and in arms; so it was that behind the Speaker's desk of that chamber which was to womb and contemplate the high dream of a destiny superior to the injustice of events and the folly of mankind, the President and the Secretary stood, while below them, ringed about by the living manipulators of, and interspersed by the august and watching ghosts of the dreamers of, the destiny, the uncle and nephew stood, with behind them the dark throng of kin and friends and acquaintances from among which came steadily and unabated that faint sound of wool and flesh in friction. The President leaned to the Secretary.

"Are they ready with the cannon?" he whispered. "Are you sure they can see my arm from the door? And suppose those damned guns explode: they have not been fired since Washington shot them last at Cornwallis: will they impeach me?"

"Yes," the Secretary hissed.

"Then God help us. Give me the book." The Secretary passed it to him: it was Petrarch's Sonnets, which the Secretary had snatched from his table in passing. "Let us hope that I remember enough law Latin to keep it from sounding like either English or Chickasaw," the President said. He opened

the book, and then again the President, the conqueror of
men, the winner of battles diplomatic, legal and martial, drew
himself erect and looked down upon the dark, still, intent,
waiting faces; when he spoke his voice was the voice which
before this had caused men to pause and attend and then
obey: "Francis Weddel, chief in the Chickasaw Nation, and
you, nephew of Francis Weddel and some day to be a chief,
hear my words." Then he began to read. His voice was full,
sonorous, above the dark faces, echoing about the august
dome in profound and solemn syllables. He read ten sonnets.
Then, with his arm lifted, he perorated; his voice died profoundly away and he dropped his arm. A moment later, from
outside the building, came a ragged crash of artillery. And
now for the first time the dark throng stirred; from among
them came a sound, a murmur, of pleased astonishment. The
President spoke again: "Nephew of Francis Weddel, you are
free. Return to your home."

And now the uncle spoke; again his finger waggled from
out its froth of lace. "Heedless boy," he said. "Consider the
trouble which you have caused these busy men." He turned
to the Secretary, almost briskly; again his voice was bland,
pleasant, almost mirthful: "And now, about the little matter
of this cursed ford. . . ."

With the autumn sun falling warmly and pleasantly across
his shoulders, the President said, "That is all," quietly and
turned to his desk as the secretary departed. While he took
up the letter and opened it the sun fell upon his hands and
upon the page, with its inference of the splendid dying of
the year, of approaching harvests and of columns of quiet
wood smoke—serene pennons of peace—above peaceful
chimneys about the land.

Suddenly the President started; he sprang up, the letter in
his hand, glaring at it in shocked and alarmed consternation

while the bland words seemed to explode one by one in his comprehension like musketry:

Dear sir and friend:

This is really amusing. Again this hot-headed nephew—he must have taken his character from his father's people, since it is none of mine—has come to trouble you and me. It is this cursed ford again. Another white man came among us, to hunt in peace we thought, since God's forest and the deer which He put in it belong to all. But he too became obsessed with the idea of owning this ford, having heard tales of his own kind who, after the curious and restless fashion of white men, find one side of a stream of water superior enough to the other to pay coins of money for the privilege of reaching it. So the affair was arranged as this white man desired it. Perhaps I did wrong, you will say. But—do I need to tell you?—I am a simple man and some day I shall be old, I trust, and the continuous interruption of these white men who wish to cross and the collecting and care of the coins of money is only a nuisance. For what can money be to me, whose destiny it apparently is to spend my declining years beneath the shade of familiar trees from whose peaceful shade my great white friend and chief has removed the face of every enemy save death? That was my thought, but when you read further you will see that it was not to be.

Once more it is this rash and heedless boy. It seems that he challenged this new white man of ours (or the white man challenged him: the truth I will leave to your unerring wisdom to unravel) to a swimming race in the river, the stakes to be this cursed ford against a few miles of land, which (this will amuse you) this wild nephew of mine did not even own. The race took place, but unfortunately our white man failed to emerge from the river until after he was dead. And now your agent has arrived, and he seems to feel that perhaps

*this swimming race should not have taken place at all. And
so now there is nothing for me to do save to bestir old bones
and bring this rash boy to you for you to reprimand him. We
will arrive in about . . .*

The President sprang to the bell and pulled it violently.
When his secretary entered, he grasped the man by the
shoulders and whirled him toward the door again. "Get me
the Secretary of War, and maps of all the country between
here and New Orleans!" he cried. "Hurry."

And so again we see him; the President is absent now and
it is the Soldier alone who sits with the Secretary of War
behind the map-strewn table, while there face them the
officers of a regiment of cavalry. At the table his secretary is
writing furiously while the President looks over his shoulder.
"Write it big," he says, "so that even an Indian cannot mistake it. *Know all men by these presents,*" he quotes. "*Francis
Weddel his heirs, descendants and assigns from now on in
perpetuity . . . provided*—Have you got provided? Good—
*provided that neither he nor his do ever again cross to the
eastern side of the above described River. . . .* And now to
that damned agent," he said. "The sign must be in duplicate,
at both ends of the ford: *The United States accepts no responsibility for any man, woman or child, black, white, yellow or red, who crosses this ford, and no white man shall buy,
lease or accept it as a gift save under the severest penalty of
the law.* Can I do that?"

"I'm afraid not, Your Excellency," the Secretary said.

The President mused swiftly. "Damn," he said. "Strike out
The United States, then." The Secretary did so. The President folded the two papers and handed them to the cavalry
colonel. "Ride," he said. "Your orders are, Stop them."

"Suppose they refuse to stop," the colonel said. "Shall I
fire then?"

"Yes," the President said, "Shoot every horse, mule, and ox. I know they won't walk. Off with you, now." The officers withdrew. The President turned back to the maps—the Soldier still: eager, happy, as though he rode himself with the regiment, or as if in spirit already he deployed it with that shrewd cunning which could discern and choose the place most disadvantageous to the enemy, and get there first. "It will be here," he said. He put his finger on the map. "A horse, General, that I may meet him here and turn his flank and drive him."

"Done, General," the Secretary said.

IV · THE WASTELAND

Ad Astra

I DONT KNOW what we were. With the exception of Comyn, we had started out Americans, but after three years, in our British tunics and British wings and here and there a ribbon, I dont suppose we had even bothered in three years to wonder what we were, to think or to remember.

And on that day, that evening, we were even less than that, or more than that: either beneath or beyond the knowledge that we had not even wondered in three years. The subadar—after a while he was there, in his turban and his trick major's pips—said that we were like men trying to move in water. "But soon it will clear away," he said. "The effluvium of hatred and of words. We are like men trying to move in water, with held breath watching our terrific and infinitesimal limbs, watching one another's terrific stasis without touch, without contact, robbed of all save the impotence and the need."

We were in the car then, going to Amiens, Sartoris driving and Comyn sitting half a head above him in the front seat like a tackling dummy, the subadar, Bland and I in back, each with a bottle or two in his pockets. Except the subadar, that is. He was squat, small and thick, yet his sobriety was colossal. In that maelstrom of alcohol where the rest of us had fled our inescapable selves he was like a rock, talking quietly in a grave bass four sizes too big for him: "In my country I was prince. But all men are brothers."

But after twelve years I think of us as bugs in the surface of the water, isolant and aimless and unflagging. Not on the surface; in it, within that line of demarcation not air and not water, sometimes submerged, sometimes not. You have watched an unbreaking groundswell in a cove, the water shallow, the cove quiet, a little sinister with satiate familiarity, while beyond the darkling horizon the dying storm has raged on. That was the water, we the flotsam. Even after twelve years it is no clearer than that. It had no beginning and no ending. Out of nothing we howled, unwitting the storm which we had escaped and the foreign strand which we could not escape; that in the interval between two surges of the swell we died who had been too young to have ever lived.

We stopped in the middle of the road to drink again. The land was dark and empty. And quiet: that was what you noticed, remarked. You could hear the earth breathe, like coming out of ether, like it did not yet know, believe, that it was awake. "But now it is peace," the subadar said. "All men are brothers."

"You spoke before the Union once," Bland said. He was blond and tall. When he passed through a room where women were he left a sighing wake like a ferry boat entering the slip. He was a Southerner, too, like Sartoris; but unlike Sartoris, in the five months he had been out, no one had ever found a bullet hole in his machine. But he had transferred out of an Oxford battalion—he was a Rhodes scholar —with a barnacle and a wound-stripe. When he was tight he would talk about his wife, though we all knew that he was not married.

He took the bottle from Sartoris and drank. "I've got the sweetest little wife," he said. "Let me tell you about her."

"Dont tell us," Sartoris said. "Give her to Comyn. He wants a girl."

"All right," Bland said. "You can have her, Comyn."

"Is she blonde?" Comyn said.

"I dont know," Bland said. He turned back to the subadar. "You spoke before the Union once. I remember you."

"Ah," the subadar said. "Oxford. Yes."

"He can attend their schools among the gentleborn, the bleach-skinned," Bland said. "But he cannot hold their commission, because gentility is a matter of color and not lineage or behavior."

"Fighting is more important than truth," the subadar said. "So we must restrict the prestige and privileges of it to the few so that it will not lose popularity with the many who have to die."

"Why more important?" I said. "I thought this one was being fought to end war forevermore."

The subadar made a brief gesture, dark, deprecatory, tranquil. "I was a white man also for that moment. It is more important for the Caucasian because he is only what he can do; it is the sum of him."

"So you see further than we see?"

"A man sees further looking out of the dark upon the light than a man does in the light and looking out upon the light. That is the principle of the spyglass. The lens is only to tease him with that which the sense that suffers and desires can never affirm."

"What do you see, then?" Bland said.

"I see girls," Comyn said. "I see acres and acres of the yellow hair of them like wheat and me among the wheat. Have ye ever watched a hidden dog quartering a wheat field, any of yez?"

"Not hunting bitches," Bland said.

Comyn turned in the seat, thick and huge. He was big as

all outdoors. To watch two mechanics shoehorning him into
the cockpit of a Dolphin like two chambermaids putting an
emergency bolster into a case too small for it, was a sight to
see. "I will beat the head off ye for a shilling," he said.

"So you believe in the rightness of man?" I said.

"I will beat the heads off yez all for a shilling," Comyn
said.

"I believe in the pitiableness of man," the subadar said.
"That is better."

"I will give yez a shilling, then," Comyn said.

"All right," Sartoris said. "Did you ever try a little whisky
for the night air, any of you all?"

Comyn took the bottle and drank. "Acres and acres of
them," he said, "with their little round white woman parts
gleaming among the moiling wheat."

So we drank again, on the lonely road between two beet
fields, in the dark quiet, and the turn of the inebriation
began to make. It came back from wherever it had gone,
rolling down upon us and upon the grave sober rock of the
subadar until his voice sounded remote and tranquil and
dreamlike, saying that we were brothers. Monaghan was
there then, standing beside our car in the full glare of the
headlights of his car, in an R.F.C. cap and an American tunic
with both shoulder straps flapping loose, drinking from
Comyn's bottle. Beside him stood a second man, also in a
tunic shorter and trimmer than ours, with a bandage about
his head.

"I'll fight you," Comyn told Monaghan. "I'll give you
the shilling."

"All right," Monaghan said. He drank again.

"We are all brothers," the subadar said. "Sometimes we
pause at the wrong inn. We think it is night and we stop,
when it is not night. That is all."

"I'll give you a sovereign," Comyn told Monaghan.

"All right," Monaghan said. He extended the bottle to the other man, the one with the bandaged head.

"I thangk you," the man said. "I haf plenty yet."

"I'll fight him," Comyn said.

"It is because we can do only within the heart," the subadar said. "While we see beyond the heart."

"I'll be damned if you will," Monaghan said. "He's mine." He turned to the man with the bandaged head. "Aren't you mine? Here; drink."

"I haf plenty, I thangk you, gentlemen," the other said. But I dont think any of us paid much attention to him until we were inside the Cloche-Clos. It was crowded, full of noise and smoke. When we entered all the noise ceased, like a string cut in two, the end raveling back into a sort of shocked consternation of pivoting faces, and the waiter—an old man in a dirty apron—falling back before us, slack-jawed, with an expression of outraged unbelief, like an atheist confronted with either Christ or the devil. We crossed the room, the waiter retreating before us, paced by the turning outraged faces, to a table adjacent to one where three French officers sat watching us with that same expression of astonishment and then outrage and then anger. As one they rose; the whole room, the silence, became staccato with voices, like machine guns. That was when I turned and looked at Monaghan's companion for the first time, in his green tunic and his black snug breeks and his black boots and his bandage. He had cut himself recently shaving, and with his bandaged head and his face polite and dazed and bloodless and sick, he looked like Monaghan had been using him pretty hard. Roundfaced, not old, with his immaculately turned bandage which served only to emphasize the generations of difference between him and the turbaned subadar, flanked by Monaghan with his wild face and wild tunic and surrounded by the French people's shocked and outraged faces, he appeared to contemplate with a polite and alert concern his own struggle against the inebriation which Monaghan was forcing upon him. There was something Anthony-like about him: rigid, soldierly, with every button in place, with his unblemished bandage and his fresh razor cuts, he appeared to muse furiously upon a clear flame of a certain conviction of individual behavior above a violent and inexplicable chaos. Then I remarked Monaghan's second companion: an American military policeman. He was not drinking. He sat beside the German, rolling cigarettes from a cloth sack.

On the German's other side Monaghan was filling his glass. "I brought him down this morning," he said. "I'm going to take him home with me."

"Why?" Bland said. "What do you want with him?"

"Because he belongs to me," Monaghan said. He set the full glass before the German. "Here; drink."

"I once thought about taking one home to my wife," Bland said. "So I could prove to her that I have only been to a war. But I never could find a good one. A whole one, I mean."

"Come on," Monaghan said. "Drink."

"I haf plenty," the German said. "All day I haf plenty."

"Do you want to go to America with him?" Bland said: "Yes. I would ligk it. Thanks."

"Sure you'll like it," Monaghan said. "I'll make a man of you. Drink."

The German raised the glass, but he merely held it in his hand. His face was strained, deprecatory, yet with a kind of sereneness, like that of a man who has conquered himself. I imagine some of the old martyrs must have looked at the lions with that expression. He was sick, too. Not from the liquor: from his head. "I haf in Beyreuth a wife and a little wohn. Mine son. I haf not him yet seen."

"Ah," the subadar said. "Beyreuth. I was there one spring."

"Ah," the German said. He looked quickly at the subadar. "So? The music?"

"Yes," the subadar said. "In your music a few of you have felt, tasted, lived, the true brotherhood. The rest of us can only look beyond the heart. But we can follow them for a little while in the music."

"And then we must return," the German said. "That iss not good. Why must we yet return always?"

"It is not the time for that yet," the subadar said. "But soon . . . It is not as far as it once was. Not now."

"Yes," the German said. "Defeat will be good for us. Defeat iss good for art; victory, it iss not good."

"So you admit you were whipped," Comyn said. He was sweating again, and Sartoris' nostrils were quite white. I thought of what the subadar had said about men in water. Only our water was drunkenness: that isolation of alcoholism which drives men to shout and laugh and fight, not with one another but with their unbearable selves which, drunk, they are even more fain and still less fell to escape. Loud and overloud, unwitting the black thunderhead of outraged France (steadily the other tables were being emptied; the other customers were now clotted about the high desk where the patronne, an old woman in steel spectacles, sat, a wad of knitting on the ledge before her) we shouted at one another, speaking in foreign tongues out of our inescapable isolations, reiterant, unlistened to by one another; while submerged by us and more foreign still, the German and the subadar talked quietly of music, art, the victory born of defeat. And outside in the chill November darkness was the suspension, the not-quite-believing, not-quite-awakened nightmare, the breathing spell of the old verbiaged lusts and the buntinged and panoplied greeds.

"By God, I'm shanty Irish," Monaghan said. "That's what I am."

"What about it?" Sartoris said, his nostrils like chalk against his high-colored face. His twin brother had been killed in July. He was in a Camel squadron below us, and Sartoris was down there when it happened. For a week after that, as soon as he came in from patrol he would fill his tanks and drums and go out again, alone. One day somebody saw him, roosting about five thousand feet above an old Ak.W. I suppose the other guy who was with his brother that morning had seen the markings on the Hun patrol leader's crate; anyway, that's what Sartoris was doing, using the Ak.W. for bait. Where he got it and who he got to fly it, we didn't know. But he got three Huns that week, catching them dead when they dived on the Ak.W., and on the eighth day he didn't go out again. "He must have got him," Hume said. But we didn't know. He never told us. But after that, he was all right again. He never did talk much; just did his patrols and maybe once a week he'd sit and drink his nostrils white in a quiet sort of way.

Bland was filling his glass, a drop at a time almost, with a catlike indolence. I could see why men didn't like him and why women did. Comyn, his arms crossed on the table, his cuff in a pool of spilt liquor, was staring at the German. His eyes were bloodshot, a little protuberant. Beneath his downcrushed monkey cap the American M.P. smoked his meager cigarettes, his face quite blank. The steel chain of his whistle looped into his breast pocket, his pistol was hunched forward onto his lap. Beyond, the French people, the soldiers, the waiter, the patronne, clotted at the desk. I could hear their voices like from a distance, like crickets in September grass, the shadows of their hands jerking up the wall and flicking away.

"I'm not a soldier," Monaghan said. "I'm not a gentleman.

I'm not anything." At the base of each flapping shoulder strap there was a small rip; there were two longer ones parallel above his left pocket where his wings and ribbon had been. "I dont know what I am. I have been in this damn war for three years and all I know is, I'm not dead. I—"

"How do you know you're not dead?" Bland said.

Monaghan looked at Bland, his mouth open upon his uncompleted word.

"I'll kill you for a shilling," Comyn said. "I dont like your bloody face, Lootenant. Bloody lootenant."

"I'm shanty Irish," Monaghan said. "That's what I am. My father was shanty Irish, by God. And I dont know what my grandfather was. I dont know if I had one. My father dont remember one. Likely it could have been one of several. So he didn't even have to be a gentleman. He never had to be. That's why he could make a million dollars digging sewers in the ground. So he could look up at the tall glittering windows and say—I've heard him, and him smoking the pipe would gas the puking guts out of you damn, niggling, puny—"

"Are you bragging about your father's money or about his sewers?" Bland said.

"—would look up at them and he'd say to me, he'd say, 'When you're with your fine friends, the fathers and mothers and sisters of them you met at Yale, ye might just remind them that every man is the slave of his own refuse and so your old dad they would be sending around to the forty-story back doors of their kitchens is the king of them all—' What did you say?" He looked at Bland.

"Look here, buddy," the M.P. said. "This is about enough of this. I've got to report this prisoner."

"Wait," Monaghan said. He did not cease to look at Bland. "What did you say?"

"Are you bragging about your father's money or about his sewers?" Bland said.

"No," Monaghan said. "Why should I? Any more than I would brag about the thirteen Huns I got, or the two ribbons, one of which his damned king—" he jerked his head at Comyn—"gave me."

"Dont call him my damned king," Comyn said, his cuff soaking slowly in the spilt liquor.

"Look," Monaghan said. He jerked his hand at the rips on his flapping shoulder straps, at the two parallel rips on his breast. "That's what I think of it. Of all your goddamn twaddle about glory and gentlemen. I was young; I thought you had to be. Then I was in it and there wasn't time to stop even when I found it didn't count. But now it's over; finished now. Now I can be what I am. Shanty Irish; son of an immigrant that knew naught but shovel and pick until youth and the time for pleasuring was wore out of him before his time. Out of a peat bog he came, and his son went to their gentlemen's school and returned across the water to swank it with any of them that owned the peat bogs and the bitter sweat of them that mired it, and the king said him well."

"I will give yez the shilling and I will beat the head off yez," Comyn said.

"But why do you want to take him back with you?" Bland said. Monaghan just looked at Bland. There was something of the crucified about Monaghan, too: furious, inarticulate not with stupidity but at it, like into him more than any of us had distilled the ceased drums of the old lust and greed waking at last aghast at their own impotence and accrued despair. Bland sat on his spine, legs extended, his hands in his slacks, his handsome face calmly insufferable. "What stringed pick would he bow? maybe a shovel strung with the gut of an alley-cat? he will create perhaps in music the flushed toilets of Manhattan to play for your father after supper of an evening?" Monaghan just looked at Bland with that wild, rapt expression. Bland turned his lazy face a little to the German.

"Look here," the M.P. said.

"You have a wife, Herr Leutnant?" Bland said.

The German looked up. He glanced swiftly from face to face. "Yes, thank you," he said. He still had not touched his full glass save to hold it in his hand. But he was no nearer sober than before, the liquor become the hurting of his head, his head the pulse and beat of alcohol in him. "My people are of Prussia little barons. There are four brothers: the second for the Army, the third who did nothing in Berlin, the little one a cadet of dragoons; I, the eldest, in the University. There I learned. There wass a time then. It was as though we, young from the quiet land, were brought together, chosen and worthy to witness a period quick like a woman with a high destiny of the earth and of man. It iss as though the old trash, the old litter of man's blundering, iss to be swept away for a new race that will in the heroic simplicity of olden time walk the new earth. You knew that time, not? When the eye sparkled, the blut ran quick?" He looked about at our faces. "No? Well, in America perhaps not. America iss new; in a new house it is not the litter so much as in old." He looked at his glass for a moment, his face tranquil. "I return home; I say to my father, in the University I haf learned it iss not good; baron I will not be. He cannot believe. He talks of Germany, the fatherland; I say to him, It iss there; so. You say fatherland; I, brotherland, I say, the word *father* iss that barbarism which will be first swept away; it iss the symbol of that hierarchy which hass stained the history of man with injustice of arbitrary instead of moral; force instead of love.

"From Berlin they send for that one; from the Army that

one comes. I still say baron I will not be, for it iss not good. We are in the little hall where my ancestors on the walls hang; I stand before them like court-martial; I say that Franz must be baron, for I will not be. My father says you can; you will; it iss for Germany. Then I say, For Germany then will my wife be baroness? And like a court-martial I tell them I haf married the daughter of a musician who wass peasant.

"So it iss that. That one of Berlin iss to be baron. He and Franz are twin, but Franz iss captain already, and the most humble of the Army may eat meat with our kaiser; he does not need to be baron. So I am in Beyreuth with my wife and my music. It iss as though I am dead. I do not get letter until to say my father iss dead and I haf killed him, and that one iss now home from Berlin to be baron. But he does not stay at home. In 1912 he iss in Berlin newspaper dead of a lady's husband and so Franz iss baron after all.

"Then it iss war. But I am in Beyreuth with my wife and my music, because we think that it will not be long, since it was not long before. The fatherland in its pride needed us of the schools, but when it needed us it did not know it. And when it did realize that it needed us it wass too late and any peasant who would be hard to die would do. And so—"

"Why did you go, then?" Bland said. "Did the women make you? throw eggs at you, maybe?"

The German looked at Bland. "I am German; that iss beyond the I, the I am. Not for baron and kaiser." Then he quit looking at Bland without moving his eyes. "There wass a Germany before there wass barons," he said. "And after, there will be."

"Even after this?"

"More so. Then it was pride, a word in the mouth. Now it is a—how you call it? . . ."

"A nation vanquishes its banners," the subadar said. "A man conquers himself."

"Or a woman a child bears," the German said.

"Out of the lust, the travail," the subadar said; "out of the travail, the affirmation, the godhead; truth."

The M.P. was rolling another cigarette. He watched the subadar, upon his face an expression savage, restrained, and cold. He licked the cigarette and looked at me.

"When I came to this goddamn country," he said, "I thought niggers were niggers. But now I'll be damned if I know what they are. What's he? snake-charmer?"

"Yes," I said. "Snake-charmer."

"Then he better get his snake out and beat it. I've got to report this prisoner. Look at those frogs yonder." As I turned and looked three of the Frenchmen were leaving the room, insult and outrage in the shapes of their backs. The German was talking again.

"I hear by the newspapers how Franz is colonel and then general, and how the cadet, who wass still the round-headed boy part of a gun always when I last saw him, iss now ace with iron cross by the kaiser's own hand. Then it iss 1916. I see by the paper how the cadet iss killed by your Bishop—" he bowed slightly to Comyn—"that good man. So now I am cadet myself. It iss as though I know. It iss as though I see what iss to be. So I transfer to be aviator, and yet though I know now that Franz iss general of staff and though to myself each night I say, 'You have again returned,' I know that it iss no good.

"That, until our kaiser fled. Then I learn that Franz iss now in Berlin; I believe that there iss a truth, that we haf not forfeited all in pride, because we know it will not be much longer now, and Franz in Berlin safe, the fighting away from.

"Then it iss this morning. Then comes the letter in my

mother's hand that I haf not seen in seven years, addressed
to me as baron. Franz iss shot from his horse by German
soldier in Berlin street. It iss as though all had been forgotten,
because women can forget all that quick, since to them
nothing iss real—truth, justice, all—nothing that cannot be
held in the hands or cannot die. So I burn all my papers, the
picture of my wife and my son that I haf not yet seen,
destroy my identity disk and remove all insignia from my
tunic—" he gestured toward his collar.

"You mean," Bland said, "that you had no intention of
coming back? Why didn't you take a pistol to yourself and
save your government an aeroplane?"

"Suicide iss just for the body," the German said. "The
body settles nothing. It iss of no importance. It iss just to
be kept clean when possible."

"It is merely a room in the inn," the subadar said. "It is
just where we hide for a little while."

"The lavatory," Bland said; "the toilet."

The M.P. rose. He tapped the German on the shoulder.
Comyn was staring at the German.

"So you admit you were whipped," he said.

"Yes," the German said. "It wass our time first, because
we were the sickest. It will be your England's next. Then
she too will be well."

"Dont say my England," Comyn said. "I am of the Irish
nation." He turned to Monaghan. "You said, my damned
king. Dont say my damned king. Ireland has had no king
since the Ur Neill, God bless the red-haired stern of him."

Rigid, controlled, the German made a faint gesture. "You
see?" he said to no one at all.

"The victorious lose that which the vanquished gain," the
subadar said.

"And what will you do now?" Bland said.

The German did not answer. He sat bolt upright with his sick face and his immaculate bandage.

"What will you do?" the subadar said to Bland. "What will any of us do? All this generation which fought in the war are dead tonight. But we do not yet know it."

We looked at the subadar: Comyn with his bloodshot pig's eyes, Sartoris with his white nostrils, Bland slumped in his chair, indolent, insufferable, with his air of a spoiled woman. Above the German the M.P. stood.

"It seems to worry you a hell of a lot," Bland said.

"You do not believe?" the subadar said. "Wait. You will see."

"Wait?" Bland said. "I dont think I've done anything in the last three years to have acquired that habit. In the last twenty-six years. Before that I dont remember. I may have."

"Then you will see sooner than waiting," the subadar said. "You will see." He looked about at us, gravely serene. "Those who have been four years rotting out yonder—" he waved his short thick arm—"are not more dead than we."

Again the M.P. touched the German's shoulder. "Hell," he said. "Come along, buddy." Then he turned his head and we all looked up at the two Frenchmen, an officer and a sergeant, standing beside the table. For a while we just remained so. It was like all the little bugs had suddenly found that their orbits had coincided and they wouldn't even have to be aimless any more or even to keep on moving. Beneath the alcohol I could feel that hard, hot ball beginning in my stomach, like in combat, like when you know something is about to happen; that instant when you think Now. Now I can dump everything overboard and just be. Now. Now. It is quite pleasant.

"Why is that here, monsieur?" the officer said. Monaghan looked up at him, thrust backward and sideways in his chair, poised on the balls of his thighs as though they were feet,

his arm lying upon the table. "Why do you make desagre-
able for France, monsieur, eh?" the officer said.

Someone grasped Monaghan as he rose; it was the M.P.
behind him, holding him half risen. "Wa-a-a-i-daminute,"
the M.P. said; "wa-a-a-i-daminute." The cigarette bobbed
on his lower lip as he talked, his hands on Monaghan's shoulders, the brassard on his arm lifted into bold relief. "What's
it to you, Frog?" he said. Behind the officer and the sergeant
the other French people stood, and the old woman. She was
trying to push through the circle. "This is my prisoner," the
M.P. said. "I'll take him anywhere I please and keep him
there as long as I like. What do you think about that?"

"By which authority, monsieur?" the officer said. He was
tall, with a gaunt, tragic face. I saw then that one of his eyes
was glass. It was motionless, rigid in a face that looked even
deader than the spurious eye.

The M.P. glanced toward his brassard, then instead he
looked at the officer again and tapped the pistol swinging
low now against his flank. "I'll take him all over your goddamn lousy country. I'll take him into your goddamn senate
and kick your president up for a chair for him and you can
suck your chin until I come back to wipe the latrine off
your feet again."

"Ah," the officer said, "a devil-dog, I see." He said "dehvil-
dahg" between his teeth, with no motion of his dead face,
in itself insult. Behind him the patronne began to shriek in
French:

"Boche! Boche! Broken! Broken! Every cup, every saucer,
glass, plate—all, all! I will show you! I have kept them for this
day. Eight months since the obus I have kept them in a box
against this day: plates, cups, saucers, glasses, all that I have
had since thirty years, all gone, broken at one time! And it
costing me fifty centimes the glass for such that I shame
myself to have my patrons—"

There is an unbearable point, a climax, in weariness. Even alcohol cannot approach it. Mobs are motivated by it, by a sheer attenuation of sameness become unbearable. As Monaghan rose, the M.P. flung him back. Then it was as though we all flung everything overboard at once, facing unbashed and without shame the specter which for four years we had been decking out in high words, leaping forward with concerted and orderly promptitude each time the bunting slipped. I saw the M.P. spring at the officer, then Comyn rose and met him. I saw the M.P. hit Comyn three times on the point of the jaw with his fist before Comyn picked him up bodily and threw him clean over the crowd, where he vanished, horizontal in midair, tugging at his pistol. I saw three poilus on Monaghan's back and the officer trying to hit him with a bottle, and Sartoris leaping upon the officer from behind. Comyn was gone; through the gap which he had made the patronne emerged, shrieking. Two men caught at her and she strove forward, trying to spit on the German. "Boche! Boche!" she shrieked, spitting and slobbering, her gray hair broken loose about her face; she turned and spat full at me. "Thou, too!" she shrieked, "it was not England that was devastated! Thou, too, come to pick the bones of France. Jackal! Vulture! Animal! Broken, broken! All! All! All!" And beneath it all, unmoved, unmoving, alert, watchful and contained, the German and the subadar sat, the German with his high, sick face, the subadar tranquil as a squat idol, the both of them turbaned like prophets in the Old Testament.

It didn't take long. There was no time in it. Or rather, we were outside of time; within, not on, that surface, that demarcation between the old where we knew we had not died and the new where the subadar said that we were dead. Beyond the brandished bottles, the blue sleeves and the grimed hands, the faces like masks grimaced into rigid and

soundless shouts to frighten children, I saw Comyn again.
He came plowing up like a laden ship in a chop sea; beneath
his arm was the ancient waiter, to his lips he held the M.P.'s
whistle. Then Sartoris swung a chair at the single light.

It was cold in the street, a cold that penetrated the clothing, the alcohol-distended pores, and murmured to the skeleton itself. The plaza was empty, the lights infrequent and
remote. So quiet it was that I could hear the faint water in
the fountain. From some distance away came sound, remote
too under the thick low sky—shouting, far-heard, on a thin
female note like all shouting, even a mob of men, broken now
and then by the sound of a band. In the shadow of the wall
Monaghan and Comyn held the German on his feet. He was
unconscious; the three of them invisible save for the faint
blur of the bandage, inaudible save for the steady monotone
of Monaghan's cursing.

"There should never have been an alliance between
Frenchmen and Englishmen," the subadar said. He spoke
without effort; invisible, his effortless voice had an organ
quality, out of all proportion to his size. "Different nations
should never join forces to fight for the same object. Let each
fight for something different; ends that do not conflict, each
in his own way." Sartoris passed us, returning from the fountain, carrying his bulging cap carefully before him, bottom-
up. We could hear the water dripping from it between his
footsteps. He became one of the blob of thicker shadow
where the bandage gleamed and where Monaghan cursed
steadily and quietly. "And each after his own tradition," the
subadar said. "My people. The English gave them rifles. They
looked at them and came to me: 'This spear is too short and
too heavy: how can a man slay a swift enemy with a spear
of this size and weight?' They gave them tunics with buttons
to be kept buttoned; I have passed a whole trench of them
squatting, motionless, buried to the ears in blankets, straw,

empty sand bags, their faces gray with cold; I have lifted the blankets away from patient torsos clad only in a shirt.

"The English officers would say to them, 'Go there and do thus'; they would not stir. Then one day at full noon the whole battalion, catching movement beyond a crater, sprang from the trench, carrying me and an officer with it. We carried the trench without firing a shot; what was left of us—the officer, I, and seventeen others—lived three days in a traverse of the enemy's front line; it required a whole brigade to extricate us. 'Why didn't you shoot?' the officer said. 'You let them pick you off like driven pheasant.' They did not look at him. Like children they stood, murmurous, alert, without shame. I said to the headman, 'Were the rifles loaded, O Das?' Like children they stood, diffident, without shame. 'O Son of many kings,' Das said. 'Speak the truth of thy knowing to the sahib,' I said. 'They were not loaded, sahib,' Das said."

Again the band came, remote, thudding in the thick air. They were giving the German drink from a bottle. Monaghan said: "Now. Feel better now?"

"It iss mine head," the German said. They spoke quietly, like they were discussing wall-paper.

Monaghan cursed again. "I'm going back. By God, I—"

"No, no," the German said. "I will not permit. You haf already obligated—"

We stood in the shadow beneath the wall and drank. We had one bottle left. Comyn crashed it, empty, against the wall.

"Now what?" Bland said.

"Girls," Comyn said. "Would ye watch Comyn of the Irish nation among the yellow hair of them like a dog among the wheat?"

We stood there, hearing the far band, the far shouting. "You sure you feel all right?" Monaghan said.

"Thanks," the German said. "I feel goot."

"Come on, then," Comyn said.

"You going to take him with you?" Bland said.

"Yes," Monaghan said. "What of it?"

"Why not take him on to the A.P.M.? He's sick."

"Do you want me to bash your bloody face in?" Monaghan said.

"All right," Bland said.

"Come on," Comyn said. "What fool would rather fight than fush? All men are brothers, and all their wives are sisters. So come along, yez midnight fusileers."

"Look here," Bland said to the German, "do you want to go with them?" With his bandaged head, he and the subadar alone were visible, like two injured men among five spirits.

"Hold him up a minute," Monaghan told Comyn. Monaghan approached Bland. He cursed Bland. "I like fighting," he said, in that same monotone. "I even like being whipped."

"Wait," the German said. "Again I will not permit." Monaghan halted, he and Bland not a foot apart. "I haf wife and son in Beyreuth," the German said. He was speaking to me. He gave me the address, twice, carefully.

"I'll write to her," I said. "What shall I tell her?"

"Tell her it iss nothing. You will know."

"Yes. I'll tell her you are all right."

"Tell her this life iss nothing."

Comyn and Monaghan took his arms again, one on either side. They turned and went on, almost carrying him. Comyn looked back once. "Peace be with you," he said.

"And with you, peace," the subadar said. They went on. We watched them come into silhouette in the mouth of an alley where a light was. There was an arch there, and the faint cold pale light on the arch and on the walls so that it was like a gate and they entering the gate, holding the German up between them.

"What will they do with him?" Bland said. "Prop him in

the corner and turn the light off? Or do French brothels have he-beds too?"

"Who the hell's business is that?" I said.

The sound of the band came, thudding; it was cold. Each time my flesh jerked with alcohol and cold I believed that I could hear it rasp on the bones.

"Since seven years now I have been in this climate," the subadar said. "But still I do not like the cold." His voice was deep, quiet, like he might be six feet tall. It was like when they made him they said among themselves, "We'll give him something to carry his message around with." "Why? Who'll listen to his message?" "He will. So we'll give him something to hear it with."

"Why dont you go back to India then?" Bland said.

"Ah," the subadar said. "I am like him; I too will not be baron."

"So you clear out and let foreigners who will treat the people like oxen or rabbits come in and take it."

"By removing myself I undid in one day what it took two thousand years to do. Is not that something?"

We shook with the cold. Now the cold was the band, the shouting, murmuring with cold hands to the skeleton, not the ears.

"Well," Bland said, "I suppose the English government is doing more to free your people than you could."

The subadar touched Bland on the chest, lightly. "You are wise, my friend. Let England be glad that all Englishmen are not so wise."

"So you will be an exile for the rest of your days, eh?"

The subadar jerked his short, thick arm toward the empty arch where Comyn and the German and Monaghan had disappeared. "Did you not hear what he said? This life is nothing."

"You can think so," Bland said. "But, by God, I'd hate to

think that what I saved out of the last three years is nothing."

"You saved a dead man," the subadar said serenely. "You will see."

"I saved my destiny," Bland said. "You nor nobody else knows what that will be."

"What is your destiny except to be dead? It is unfortunate that your generation had to be the one. It is unfortunate that for the better part of your days you will walk the earth a spirit. But that was your destiny." From far away came the shouting, on that sustained note, feminine and childlike all at once, and then the band again, brassy, thudding, like the voices, forlornly gay, hysteric, but most of all forlorn. The arch in the cold glow of the light yawned empty, profound, silent, like the gate to another city, another world. Suddenly Sartoris left us. He walked steadily to the wall and leaned against it on his propped arms, vomiting.

"Hell," Bland said. "I want a drink." He turned to me. "Where's your bottle?"

"It's gone."

"Gone where? You had two."

"I haven't got one now, though. Drink water."

"Water?" he said. "Who the hell drinks water?"

Then the hot hard ball came into my stomach again, pleasant, unbearable, real; again that instant when you say Now. Now I can dump everything. "You will, you goddamn son," I said.

Bland was not looking at me. "Twice," he said in a quiet, detached tone. "Twice in an hour. How's that for high?" He turned and went toward the fountain. Sartoris came back, walking steadily erect. The band blent with the cold along the bones.

"What time is it?" I said.

Sartoris peered at his wrist. "Twelfth."

"It's later than midnight," I said. "It must be."

"I said it was the twelfth," Sartoris said.

Bland was stooping at the fountain. There was a little light there. As we reached him he stood up, mopping at his face. The light was on his face and I thought for some time that he must have had his whole head under to be mopping that high up his face before I saw that he was crying. He stood there, mopping at his face, crying hard but quiet.

"My poor little wife," he said. "My poor little wife."

Victory

I

THOSE WHO SAW HIM descend from the Marseilles express in
the Gare de Lyon on that damp morning saw a tall man, a
little stiff, with a bronze face and spike-ended moustaches
and almost white hair. "A milord," they said, remarking his
sober, correct suit, his correct stick correctly carried, his
sparse baggage; "a milord military. But there is something
the matter with his eyes." But there was something the matter with the eyes of so many people, men and women too,
in Europe since four years now. So they watched him go on,
a half head above the French people, with his gaunt, strained
eyes, his air strained, purposeful, and at the same time assured, and vanish into a cab, thinking, if they thought about
him any more at all: "You will see him in the Legation
offices or at a table on the Boulevards, or in a carriage with
the fine English ladies in the Bois." That was all.

And those who saw him descend from the same cab at the
Gare du Nord, they thought: "This milord returns home by
haste"; the porter who took his bag wished him good morning in fair English and told him that he was going to England, receiving for reply the English glare which the porter
perhaps expected, and put him into a first-class carriage of
the boat train. And that was all, too. That was all right, too,
even when he got down at Amiens. English milords even did

that. It was only at Rozières that they began to look at him
and after him when he had passed.

In a hired car he jounced through a gutted street between
gutted walls rising undoored and unwindowed in jagged
shards in the dusk. The street was partially blocked now and
then by toppled walls, with masses of masonry in the cracks
of which a thin grass sprouted, passing empty and ruined
courtyards, in one of which a tank, mute and tilted, rusted
among rank weeds. This was Rozières, but he didn't stop
there because no one lived there and there was no place to
stop.

So the car jounced and crept on out of the ruin. The
muddy and unpaved street entered a village of harsh new
brick and sheet iron and tarred paper roofs made in America,
and halted before the tallest house. It was flush with the
street: a brick wall with a door and one window of American glass bearing the word RESTAURANT. "Here you are, sir,"
the driver said.

The passenger descended, with his bag, his ulster, his correct stick. He entered a biggish, bare room chill with new
plaster. It contained a billiard table at which three men
played. One of the men looked over his shoulder and said,
"Bonjour, monsieur."

The newcomer did not reply at all. He crossed the room,
passing the new zinc bar, and approached an open door beyond which a woman of any age around forty looked at
him above the sewing on her lap.

"Bong jour, madame," he said. "Dormie, madame?"

The woman gave him a single glance, brief, still. "C'est ça,
monsieur," she said, rising.

"Dormie, madame?" he said, raising his voice a little, his
spiked moustache beaded a little with rain, dampness beneath his strained yet assured eyes. "Dormie, madame?"

"Bon, monsieur," the woman said. "Bon. Bon."

"Dor—" the newcomer essayed again. Someone touched his arm. It was the man who had spoken from the billiard table when he entered.

"Regardez, Monsieur l'Anglais," the man said. He took the bag from the newcomer and swept his other arm toward the ceiling. "La chambre." He touched the traveler again; he laid his face upon his palm and closed his eyes; he gestured again toward the ceiling and went on across the room toward a wooden stair without balustrade. As he passed the bar he took a candle stub from it and lit the candle (the big room and the room beyond the door where the woman sat were lighted by single bulbs hanging naked on cords from the ceiling) at the foot of the stair.

They mounted, thrusting their fitful shadows before them, into a corridor narrow, chill, and damp as a tomb. The walls were of rough plaster not yet dried. The floor was of pine, without carpet or paint. Cheap metal doorknobs glinted symmetrically. The sluggish air lay like a hand upon the very candle. They entered a room, smelling too of wet plaster, and even colder than the corridor; a sluggish chill almost substantial, as though the atmosphere between the dead and recent walls were congealing, like a patent three-minute dessert. The room contained a bed, a dresser, a chair, a washstand; the bowl, pitcher, and slop basin were of American enamel. When the traveler touched the bed the linen was soundless under his hand, coarse as sacking, clinging damply to the hand in the dead air in which their two breathings vaporized in the faint candle.

The host set the candle on the dresser. "Dîner, monsieur?" he said. The traveler stared down at the host, incongruous in his correct clothes, with that strained air. His waxed moustaches gleamed like faint bayonets above a cravat striped with what the host could not have known was the patterned coloring of a Scottish regiment. "Manger?" the host shouted.

He chewed violently in pantomime. "Manger?" he roared, his shadow aping his gesture as he pointed toward the floor.

"Yes," the traveler shouted in reply, their faces not a yard apart. "Yes. Yes."

The host nodded violently, pointed toward the floor and then at the door, nodded again, went out.

He returned below stairs. He found the woman now in the kitchen, at the stove. "He will eat," the host said.

"I knew that," the woman said.

"You would think that they would stay at home," the host said. "I'm glad I was not born of a race doomed to a place too small to hold all of us at one time."

"Perhaps he has come to look at the war," the woman said.

"Of course he has," the host said. "But he should have come four years ago. That was when we needed Englishmen to look at the war."

"He was too old to come then," the woman said. "Didn't you see his hair?"

"Then let him stay at home now," the host said. "He is no younger."

"He may have come to look at the grave of his son," the woman said.

"Him?" the host said. "That one? He is too cold to ever have had a son."

"Perhaps you are right," the woman said. "After all, that is his affair. It is our affair only that he has money."

"That's right," the host said. "A man in this business, he cannot pick and choose."

"He can pick, though," the woman said.

"Good!" the host said. "Very good! Pick! That is worth telling to the English himself."

"Why not let him find it out when he leaves?"

"Good!" the host said. "Better still. Good! Oh, good!"

"Attention," the woman said. "Here he comes."

They listened to the traveler's steady tramp, then he appeared in the door. Against the lesser light of the bigger room, his dark face and his white hair looked like a kodak negative.

The table was set for two, a carafe of red wine at each place. As the traveller seated himself, the other guest entered and took the other place—a small, rat-faced man who appeared at first glance to have no eyelashes at all. He tucked his napkin into the top of his vest and took up the soup ladle (the tureen sat between them in the center of the table) and offered it to the other. "Faites-moi l'honneur, monsieur," he said. The other bowed stiffly, accepting the ladle. The small man lifted the cover from the tureen. "Vous venez examiner ce scène de nos victoires, monsieur?" he said, helping himself in turn. The other looked at him. "Monsieur l'Anglais a peut-être beaucoup des amis qui sont tombés en voisinage."

"A speak no French," the other said, eating.

The little man did not eat. He held his yet unwetted spoon above his bowl. "What agreeable for me. I speak the Engleesh. I am Suisse, me. I speak all langue." The other did not reply. He ate steadily, not fast. "You ave return to see the grave of your galant countreemans, eh? You ave son here, perhaps, eh?"

"No," the other said. He did not cease to eat.

"No?" The other finished his soup and set the bowl aside. He drank some wine. "What deplorable, that man who ave," the Swiss said. "But it is finish now. Not?" Again the other said nothing. He was not looking at the Swiss. He did not seem to be looking at anything, with his gaunt eyes, his rigid moustaches upon his rigid face. "Me, I suffer too. All suffer. But I tell myself, What would you? It is war."

Still the other did not answer. He ate steadily, deliberately, and finished his meal and rose and left the room. He lit his

candle at the bar, where the host, leaning beside a second
man in a corduroy coat, lifted a glass slightly to him. "Au
bon dormir, monsieur," the host said.

The traveler looked at the host, his face gaunt in the
candle, his waxed moustaches rigid, his eyes in shadow.
"What?" he said. "Yes. Yes." He turned and went toward
the stairs. The two men at the bar watched him, his stiff,
deliberate back.

Ever since the train left Arras, the two women had been
watching the other occupant of the carriage. It was a third-
class carriage because no first-class trains ran on this line, and
they sat with their shawled heads and the thick, still hands of
peasants folded upon closed baskets on their laps, watching
the man sitting opposite them—the white distinction of the
hair against the bronze, gaunt face, the needles of the moustaches, the foreign-made suit and the stick—on a worn and
greasy wooden seat, looking out the window. At first they
had just looked, ready to avert their gaze, but as the man did
not seem to be aware of them, they began to whisper quietly
to one another behind their hands. But the man did not seem
to notice this, so they soon were talking in undertone, watching with bright, alert, curious eyes the stiff, incongruous
figure leaning a little forward on the stick, looking out a foul
window beyond which there was nothing to see save an
occasional shattered road and man-high stump of shattered
tree breaking small patches of tilled land whorled with apparent unreason about islands of earth indicated by low
signboards painted red, the islands inscrutable, desolate above
the destruction which they wombed. Then the train, slowing, ran suddenly among tumbled brick, out of which rose
a small house of corrugated iron bearing a name in big letters;
they watched the man lean forward.

"See!" one of the women said. "His mouth. He is reading

the name. What did I tell you? It is as I said. His son fell
here."

"Then he had lots of sons," the other woman said. "He has
read the name each time since we left Arras. Eh! Eh! Him a
son? That cold?"

"They do get children, though."

"That is why they drink whisky. Otherwise . . ."

"That's so. They think of nothing save money and eating,
the English."

Presently they got out; the train went on. Then others
entered the carriage, other peasants with muddy boots,
carrying baskets or live or dead beasts; they in turn watched
the rigid, motionless figure leaning at the window while the
train ran across the ruined land and past the brick or iron
stations among the tumbled ruins, watching his lips move as
he read the names. "Let him look at the war, about which he
has apparently heard at last," they told one another. "Then
he can go home. It was not in his barnyard that it was
fought."

"Nor in his house," a woman said.

II

THE BATTALION stands at ease in the rain. It has been in rest
billets two days, equipment has been replaced and cleaned,
vacancies have been filled and the ranks closed up, and it now
stands at ease with the stupid docility of sheep in the ceaseless
rain, facing the streaming shape of the sergeant-major.

Presently the colonel emerges from a door across the
square. He stands in the door a moment, fastening his trench
coat, then, followed by two A.D.C.'s, he steps gingerly into
the mud in polished boots and approaches.

"Para-a-a-de— 'Shun!" the sergeant-major shouts. The
battalion clashes, a single muffled, sullen sound. The sergeant-

major turns, takes a pace toward the officers, and salutes, his stick beneath his armpit. The colonel jerks his stick toward his cap peak.

"Stand at ease, men," he says. Again the battalion clashes, a single sluggish, trickling sound. The officers approach the guide file of the first platoon, the sergeant-major falling in behind the last officer. The sergeant of the first platoon takes a pace forward and salutes. The colonel does not respond at all. The sergeant falls in behind the sergeant-major, and the five of them pass down the company front, staring in turn at each rigid, forward-staring face as they pass it. First Company.

The sergeant salutes the colonel's back and returns to his original position and comes to attention. The sergeant of the second company has stepped forward, saluted, is ignored, and falls in behind the sergeant-major, and they pass down the second company front. The colonel's trench coat sheathes water onto his polished boots. Mud from the earth creeps up his boots and meets the water and is channelled by the water as the mud creeps up the polished boots again.

Third Company. The colonel stops before a soldier, his trench coat hunched about his shoulders where the rain trickles from the back of his cap, so that he looks somehow like a choleric and outraged bird. The other two officers, the sergeant-major and the sergeant halt in turn, and the five of them glare at the five soldiers whom they are facing. The five soldiers stare rigid and unwinking straight before them, their faces like wooden faces, their eyes like wooden eyes.

"Sergeant," the colonel says in his pettish voice, "has this man shaved today?"

"Sir!" the sergeant says in a ringing voice; the sergeant-major says:

"Did this man shave today, Sergeant?" and all five of them glare now at the soldier, whose rigid gaze seems to pass through and beyond them, as if they were not there. "Take a pace forward when you speak in ranks!" the sergeant-major says.

The soldier, who has not spoken, steps out of ranks, splashing a jet of mud yet higher up the colonel's boots.

"What is your name?" the colonel says.

"024186 Gray," the soldier raps out glibly. The company, the battalion, stares straight ahead.

"Sir!" the sergeant-major thunders.

"Sir-r," the soldier says.

"Did you shave this morning?" the colonel says.

"Nae, sir-r."

"Why not?"

"A dinna shave, sir-r."

"You dont shave?"

"A am nae auld enough tae shave."

"Sir!" the sergeant-major thunders.

"Sir-r," the soldier says.

"You are not . . ." The colonel's voice dies somewhere behind his choleric glare, the trickling water from his cap peak. "Take his name, Sergeant-major," he says, passing on.

The battalion stares rigidly ahead. Presently it sees the colonel, the two officers and the sergeant-major reappear in single file. At the proper place the sergeant-major halts and salutes the colonel's back. The colonel jerks his stick hand again and goes on, followed by the two officers, at a trot toward the door from which he had emerged.

The sergeant-major faces the battalion again. "Para-a-a-de—" he shouts. An indistinguishable movement passes from rank to rank, an indistinguishable precursor of that damp and sullen clash which dies borning. The sergeant-major's stick has come down from his armpit; he now leans on it, as officers do. For a time his eye roves along the battalion front.

"Sergeant Cunninghame!" he says at last.

"Sir!"

"Did you take that man's name?"

There is silence for a moment—a little more than a short moment, a little less than a long one. Then the sergeant says: "What man, sir?"

"You, soldier!" the sergeant-major says.

The battalion stands rigid. The rain lances quietly into the mud between it and the sergeant-major as though it were too spent to either hurry or cease.

"You soldier that dont shave!" the sergeant-major says.

"Gray, sir!" the sergeant says.

"Gray. Double out 'ere."

The man Gray appears without haste and tramps stolidly before the battalion, his kilts dark and damp and heavy as a wet horse-blanket. He halts, facing the sergeant-major.

"Why didn't you shave this morning?" the sergeant-major says.

"A am nae auld enough tae shave," Gray says.

"Sir!" the sergeant-major says.

Gray stares rigidly beyond the sergeant-major's shoulder.

"Say *sir* when addressing a first-class warrant officer!" the sergeant-major says. Gray stares doggedly past his shoulder, his face beneath his vizorless bonnet as oblivious of the cold lances of rain as though it were granite. The sergeant-major raises his voice:

"Sergeant Cunninghame!"

"Sir!"

"Take this man's name for insubordination also."

"Very good, sir!"

The sergeant-major looks at Gray again. "And I'll see that you get the penal battalion, my man. Fall in!"

Gray turns without haste and returns to his place in ranks, the sergeant-major watching him. The sergeant-major raises his voice again:

"Sergeant Cunninghame!"

"Sir!"

"You did not take that man's name when ordered. Let that happen again and you'll be for it yourself."

"Very good, sir!"

"Carry on!" the sergeant-major says.

"But why did ye no shave?" the corporal asked him. They were back in billets: a stone barn with leprous walls, where no light entered, squatting in the ammoniac air on wet straw about a reeking brazier. "Ye kenned we were for inspection thae mor-rn."

"A am nae auld enough tae shave," Gray said.

"But ye kenned thae colonel would mar-rk ye on parade."

"A am nae auld enough tae shave," Gray repeated doggedly and without heat.

III

"FOR TWO HUNDRED YEARS," Matthew Gray said, "there's never a day, except Sunday, has passed but there is a hull rising on Clyde or a hull going out of Clydemouth with a Gray-driven nail in it." He looked at young Alec across his steel spectacles, his neck bowed. "And not excepting their godless Sabbath hammering and sawing either. Because if a hull could be built in a day, Grays could build it," he added with dour pride. "And now, when you are big enough to go down to the yards with your grandadder and me and take a man's place among men, to be trusted manlike with hammer and saw yersel."

"Whisht, Matthew," old Alec said. "The lad can saw as straight a line and drive as mony a nail a day as yersel or even me."

Matthew paid his father no attention. He continued to speak his slow, considered words, watching his oldest son across the spectacles. "And with John Wesley not old enough by two years, and wee Matthew by ten, and your grandfather an auld man will soon be—"

"Whisht," old Alec said. "I'm no but sixty-eight. Will you be telling the lad he'll make his bit journey to London and come back to find me in the parish house, mayhap? 'Twill be over by Christmastide."

"Christmastide or no," Matthew said, "a Gray, a shipwright, has no business at an English war."

"Whisht ye," old Alec said. He rose and went to the chimney cupboard and returned, carrying a box. It was of wood, dark and polished with age, the corners bound with iron, and fitted with an enormous iron lock which any child with a hairpin could have solved. From his pocket he took an iron key almost as big as the lock. He opened the box and lifted carefully out a small velvet-covered jeweler's box and opened it in turn. On the satin lining lay a medal, a bit of bronze on a crimson ribbon: a Victoria Cross. "I kept the hulls going out of Clydemouth while your uncle Simon was getting this bit of brass from the Queen," old Alec said. "I heard naught of complaint. And if need be, I'll keep them going out while Alec serves the Queen a bit himsel. Let the lad go," he said. He put the medal back into the wooden box and locked it "A bit fighting winna hurt the lad. If I were his age, or yours either, for that matter, I'd gang mysel. Alec, lad, hark ye. Ye'll see if they'll no take a hale lad of sixty-eight and I'll gang wi ye and leave the auld folk like Matthew to do the best they can. Nay, Matthew; dinna ye thwart the lad; have no the Grays ever served the Queen in her need?"

So young Alec went to enlist, descending the hill on a weekday in his Sunday clothes, with a New Testament and a loaf of homebaked bread tied in a handkerchief. And this was the last day's work which old Alec ever did, for soon after that, one morning Matthew descended the hill to the shipyard alone, leaving old Alec at home. And after that, on the sunny days (and sometimes on the bad days too, until his daughter-in-law found him and drove him back into the house) he would sit shawled in a chair on the porch, gazing south and eastward, calling now and then to his son's wife within the house: "Hark now. Do you hear them? The guns."

"I hear nothing," the daughter-in-law would say. "It's only the sea at Kinkeadbight. Come into the house, now. Matthew will be displeased."

"Whisht, woman. Do you think there is a Gray in the world could let off a gun and me not know the sound of it?"

They had a letter from him shortly after he enlisted, from England, in which he said that being a soldier, England, was different from being a shipwright, Clydeside, and that he would write again later. Which he did, each month or so, writing that soldiering was different from building ships and that it was still raining. Then they did not hear from him for seven months. But his mother and father continued to write him a joint letter on the first Monday of each month, letters almost identical with the previous one, the previous dozen:

We are well. Ships are going out of Clyde faster than they can sink them. You still have the Book?

This would be in his father's slow, indomitable hand. Then, in his mother's:

Are you well? Do you need anything? Jessie and I are knitting the stockings and will send them. Alec, Alec.

He received this one during the seven months, during his term in the penal battalion, forwarded to him by his old corporal, since he had not told his people of his changed life. He answered it, huddled among his fellow felons, squatting

in the mud with newspapers buttoned inside his tunic and
his head and feet wrapped in strips of torn blanket:

I am well. Yes I still have the Book (not telling them that his
platoon was using it to light tobacco with and that they were
now well beyond Lamentations). *It still rains. Love to Grandadder and Jessie and Matthew and John Wesley.*

Then his time in the penal battalion was up. He returned
to his old company, his old platoon, finding some new faces,
and a letter:

*We are well. Ships are going out of Clyde yet. You have a
new sister. Your Mother is well.*

He folded the letter and put it away. "A see mony new
faces in thae battalion," he said to the corporal. "We ha a
new sair-rgeant-major too, A doot not?"

"Naw," the corporal said. " 'Tis the same one." He was
looking at Gray, his gaze intent, speculative; his face cleared.
"Ye ha shaved thae mor-rn," he said.

"Ay," Gray said. "Am auld enough tae shave noo."

That was the night on which the battalion was to go up to
Arras. It was to move at midnight, so he answered the letter
at once:

*I am well. Love to Grandadder and Jessie and Matthew and
John Wesley and the baby.*

"Morning! Morning!" The General, lap-robed and
hooded, leans from his motor and waves his gloved hand and
shouts cheerily to them as they slog past the car on the
Bapaume road, taking the ditch to pass.

"A's a cheery auld card," a voice says.

"Awfficers," a second drawls; he falls to cursing as he slips
in the greaselike mud, trying to cling to the crest of the
kneedeep ditch.

"Aweel," a third says, "thae awfficers wud gang tae thae war-r too, A doot not."

"Why dinna they gang then?" a fourth says. "Thae war-r is no back that way."

Platoon by platoon they slip and plunge into the ditch and drag their heavy feet out of the clinging mud and pass the halted car and crawl terrifically onto the crown of the road again: "A says tae me, a says: 'Fritz has a new gun that will carry to Par-ris,' a says, and A says tae him: ' 'Tis nawthin: a has one that will hit our Cor-rps Headquar-rters.' "

"Morning! Morning!" The General continues to wave his glove and shout cheerily as the battalion detours into the ditch and heaves itself back onto the road again.

They are in the trench. Until the first rifle explodes in their faces, not a shot has been fired. Gray is the third man. During all the while that they crept between flares from shell-hole to shellhole, he has been working himself nearer to the sergeant-major and the Officer; in the glare of that first rifle he can see the gap in the wire toward which the Officer was leading them, the moiled rigid glints of the wire where bullets have nicked the mud and rust from it, and against the glare the tall, leaping shape of the sergeant-major. Then Gray, too, springs bayonet first into the trench full of grunting shouts and thudding blows.

Flares go up by dozens now; in the corpse glare Gray sees the sergeant-major methodically tossing grenades into the next traverse. He runs toward him, passing the Officer leaning, bent double, against the fire step. The sergeant-major has vanished beyond the traverse. Gray follows and comes upon the sergeant-major. Holding the burlap curtain aside with one hand, the sergeant-major is in the act of tossing a grenade into a dugout as if he might be tossing an orange hull into a cellar.

The sergeant-major turns in the rocket glare. " 'Tis you, Gray," he says. The earth-muffled bomb thuds; the sergeant-major is in the act of catching another bomb from the sack about his neck as Gray's bayonet goes into his throat. The sergeant-major is a big man. He falls backward, holding the rifle barrel with both hands against his throat, his teeth glaring, pulling Gray with him. Gray clings to the rifle. He tries to shake the speared body on the bayonet as he would shake a rat on an umbrella rib.

He frees the bayonet. The sergeant-major falls. Gray reverses the rifle and hammers its butt into the sergeant-major's face, but the trench floor is too soft to supply any resistance. He glares about. His gaze falls upon a duckboard upended in the mud. He drags it free and slips it beneath the sergeant-major's head and hammers the face with his rifle-butt. Behind him in the first traverse the Officer is shouting: "Blow your whistle, Sergeant-major!"

IV

IN THE CITATION it told how Private Gray, on a night raid, one of four survivors, following the disablement of the Officer and the death of all the N.C.O.'s, took command of the situation and (the purpose of the expedition was a quick raid for prisoners); held a foothold in the enemy's front line until a supporting attack arrived and consolidated the position. The Officer told how he ordered the men back out, ordering them to leave him and save themselves, and how Gray appeared with a German machine gun from somewhere and, while his three companions built a barricade, overcame the Officer and took from him his Very pistol and fired the colored signal which called for the attack; all so quickly that support arrived before the enemy could counterattack or put down a barrage.

It is doubtful if his people ever saw the citation at all. Anyway, the letters which he received from them during his sojourn in hospital, the tenor of them, were unchanged: "We are well. Ships are still going out."

His next letter home was once more months late. He wrote it when he was sitting up again, in London:

I have been sick but I am better now. I have a ribbon like in the box but not all red. The Queen was there. Love to Grandadder and Jessie and Matthew and John Wesley and the baby.

The reply was written on Friday:

Your mother is glad that you are better. Your grandfather is dead. The baby's name is Elizabeth. We are well. Your mother sends her love.

His next letter was three months later, in winter again:

My hurt is well. I am going to a school for officers. Love to Jessie and Matthew and John Wesley and Elizabeth.

Matthew Gray pondered over this letter for a long while; so long that the reply was a week late, written on the second Monday instead of the first. He wrote it carefully, waiting until his family was in bed. It was such a long letter, or he had been at it so long, that after a time his wife came into the room in her nightdress.

"Go back to bed," he told her. "I'll be coming soon. 'Tis something to be said to the lad."

When at last he laid the pen down and sat back to reread the letter, it was a long one, written out slowly and deliberately and without retraction or blot:

... your bit ribbon ... for that way lies vainglory and pride. The pride and vainglory of going for an officer. Never mis-

call your birth, Alec. You are not a gentleman. You are a
Scottish shipwright. If your grandfather were here he would
not be last to tell you so. . . . We are glad your hurt is well.
Your mother sends her love.

He sent home the medal, and his photograph in the new
tunic with the pips and ribbon and the barred cuffs. But he
did not go home himself. He returned to Flanders in the
spring, with poppies blowing in the churned beet- and cab-
bage-fields. When his leaves came, he spent them in London,
in the haunts of officers, not telling his people that he had
any leave.

He still had the Book. Occasionally he came upon it among
his effects and opened it at the jagged page where his life
had changed: *. . . and a voice said, Peter, raise thyself; kill—*
Often his batman would watch him as, unawares and oblivious, he turned the Book and mused upon the jagged page
—the ranker, the gaunt, lonely man with a face that belied
his years or lack of them: a sobriety, a profound and mature
calm, a grave and deliberate conviction of expression and
gesture ("like a mout be Haig hissel," the batman said)—
watching him at his clean table, writing steadily and slowly,
his tongue in his cheek as a child writes:

I am well. It has not rained in a fortnight. Love to Jessie and
Matthew and John Wesley and Elizabeth.

Four days ago the battalion came down from the lines. It
has lost its major and two captains and most of the subalterns,
so that now the remaining captain is major, and two subalterns and a sergeant have the companies. Meanwhile, re-
placements have come up, the ranks are filled, and the
battalion is going in again tomorrow. So today K Company
stands with ranks open for inspection while the subaltern-
captain (his name is Gray) moves slowly along each platoon
front.

He passes from man to man, slowly, thoroughly, the sergeant behind him. He stops.

"Where is your trenching tool?" he says.

"Blawn—" the soldier begins. Then he ceases, staring rigidly before him.

"Blawn out of your pack, eh?" the captain finishes for him. "Since when? What battles have ye taken par-rt in since four days?"

The soldier stares rigidly across the drowsy street. The captain moves on. "Take his name, Sergeant."

He moves on to the second platoon, to the third. He halts again. He looks the soldier up and down.

"What is your name?"

"010801 McLan, sir-r."

"Replacement?"

"Replacement, sir-r."

The captain moves on. "Take his name, Sergeant. Rifle's filthy."

The sun is setting. The village rises in black silhouette against the sunset; the river gleams in mirrored fire. The bridge across the river is a black arch upon which slowly and like figures cut from black paper, men are moving.

The party crouches in the roadside ditch while the captain and the sergeant peer cautiously across the parapet of the road. "Do ye make them out?" the captain says in a low voice.

"Huns, sir-r," the sergeant whispers. "A ken their-r helmets."

Presently the column has crossed the bridge. The captain and the sergeant crawl back into the ditch, where the party crouches, among them a wounded man with a bandaged head. "Keep yon man quiet, now," the captain says.

He leads the way along the ditch until they reach the outskirts of the village. Here they are out of the sun, and here they sit quietly beneath a wall, surrounding the wounded man, while the captain and the sergeant again crawl away. They return in five minutes. "Fix bayonets," the sergeant says in a low voice. "Quiet, now."

"Wull A stay wi thae hur-rt lad, Sair-rgent?" one whispers.

"Nay," the sergeant says. "A'll tak's chance wi us. For-rard."

They steal quietly along the wall, behind the captain. The wall approaches at right angles to the street, the road which crosses the bridge. The captain raises his hand. They halt and watch him as he peers around the corner. They are opposite the bridgehead. It and the road are deserted; the village dreams quietly in the setting sun. Against the sky beyond the village the dust of the retreating column hangs, turning to rose and gold.

Then they hear a sound, a short, guttural word. Not ten yards away and behind a ruined wall leveled breast-high and facing the bridge, four men squat about a machine gun. The captain raises his hand again. They grasp their rifles: a rush of hobnails on cobblestones, a cry of astonishment cut sharply off; blows, short, hard breaths, curses; not a shot.

The man with the bandaged head begins to laugh, shrilly, until someone hushes him with a hand that tastes like brass. Under the captain's direction they bash in the door of the house and drag the gun and the four bodies into it. They hoist the gun upstairs and set it up in a window looking down upon the bridgehead. The sun sinks further, the shadows fall long and quiet across village and river. The man with the bandaged head babbles to himself.

Another column swings up the road, dogged and orderly beneath coalhod helmets. It crosses the bridge and passes on through the village. A party detaches itself from the rear of the column and splits into three squads. Two of them have machine guns, which they set up on opposite sides of the street, the near one utilizing the barricade behind which the other gun had been captured. The third squad returns to the bridge, carrying sappers' tools and explosive. The sergeant tells off six of the nineteen men, who descend the stairs silently. The captain remains with the gun in the window.

Again there is a brief rush, a scuffle, blows. From the window the captain sees the heads of the machine-gun crew across the street turn, then the muzzle of the gun swings, firing. The captain rakes them once with his gun, then he sweeps with it the party on the bridge, watching it break like a covey of quail for the nearest wall. The captain holds the gun on them. They wilt running and dot the white road and become motionless. Then he swings the gun back to the gun across the street. It ceases.

He gives another order. The remaining men, except the man with the bandage, run down the stairs. Half of them stop at the gun beneath the window and drag it around. The others dash on across the street, toward the second gun. They are halfway across when the other gun rattles. The running men plunge as one in midstep. Their kilts whip forward and bare their pale thighs. The gun rakes across the doorway where the others are freeing the first gun of bodies. As the captain sweeps his gun down again, dust puffs from the left side of the window, his gun rings metallically, something sears along his arm and across his ribs, dust puffs from the right side of the window. He rakes the other gun again. It ceases. He continues to fire into the huddled clump about it long after the gun has ceased.

The dark earth bites into the sun's rim. The street is now all in shadow; a final level ray comes into the room, and fades. Behind him in the twilight the wounded man laughs, then his laughter sinks into a quiet contented gibberish.

Just before dark another column crosses the bridge. There

is still enough light for it to be seen that these troops wear khaki and that their helmets are flat. But likely there is no one to see, because when a party mounted to the second story and found the captain propped in the window beside the cold gun, they thought that he was dead.

This time Matthew Gray saw the citation. Someone clipped it from the *Gazette* and sent it to him, and he sent it in turn to his son in the hospital, with a letter:

. . . Since you must go to a war we are glad that you are doing well in it. Your mother thinks that you have done your part and that you should come home. But women do not understand such things. But I myself think that it is time they stopped fighting. What is the good in the high wages when food is so high that there is profit for none save the profiteers. When a war gets to where the battles do not even prosper the people who win them, it is time to stop.

V

IN THE BED NEXT HIS, and later in the chair next his on the long glassed veranda, there was a subaltern. They used to talk. Or rather, the subaltern talked while Gray listened. He talked of peace, of what he would do when it was over, talking as if it were about finished, as if it would not last past Christmas.

"We'll be back out there by Christmas," Gray said.

"Gas cases? They don't send gas cases out again. They have to be cured."

"We will be cured."

"But not in time. It will be over by Christmas. It can't last another year. You don't believe me, do you? Sometimes I believe you want to go back. But it will be. It will be finished by Christmas, and then I'm off. Canada. Nothing at home for us now." He looked at the other, at the gaunt, wasted figure with almost white hair, lying with closed eyes in the fall sunlight. "You'd better come with me."

"I'll meet you in Givenchy on Christmas Day," Gray said.

But he didn't. He was in the hospital on the eleventh of November, hearing the bells, and he was still there on Christmas Day, where he received a letter from home:

You can come on home now. It will not be too soon now. They will need ships worse than ever now, now that the pride and the vainglory have worn themselves out.

The medical officer greeted him cheerfully. "Dammit, stuck here, when I know a place in Devon where I could hear a nightingale, by jove." He thumped Gray's chest. "Not much: just a bit of a murmur. Give you no trouble, if you'll stop away from wars from now on. Might keep you from getting in again, though." He waited for Gray to laugh, but Gray didn't laugh. "Well, it's all finished now, damn them. Sign here, will you." Gray signed. "Forget it as quickly as it began, I hope. Well—" He extended his hand, smiling his antiseptic smile. "Cheer-O, Captain. And good luck."

Matthew Gray, descending the hill at seven oclock in the morning, saw the man, the tall, hospital-colored man in city clothing and carrying a stick, and stopped.

"Alec?" he said. "Alec." They shook hands. "I could not— I did not . . ." He looked at his son, at the white hair, the waxed moustaches. "You have two ribbons now for the box, you have written." Then Matthew turned back up the hill at seven oclock in the morning. "We'll go to your mother."

Then Alec Gray reverted for an instant. Perhaps he had not progressed as far as he thought, or perhaps he had been climbing a hill, and the return was not a reversion so much

as something like an avalanche waiting the pebble, momentary though it was to be. "The shipyard, Father."

His father strode firmly on, carrying his lunchpail. " 'Twill
wait," he said. "We'll go to your mother."

His mother met him at the door. Behind her he saw young
Matthew, a man now, and John Wesley, and Elizabeth whom
he had never seen. "You did not wear your uniform home,"
young Matthew said.

"No, he said. "No, I—"

"Your mother had wanted to see you in your regimentals
and all," his father said.

"No," his mother said. "No! Never! Never!"

"Hush, Annie, his father said. "Being a captain now, with
two ribbons now for the box. This is false modesty. Ye hae
shown courage; ye should have— But 'tis of no moment: the
proper unifor for a Gray is an overall and a hammer."

"Ay, sir," Alec said, who had long since found out that
no man has courage but that any man may blunder blindly
into valor as one stumbles into an open manhole in the street.

He did not tell his father until that night, after his mother
and the children had gone to bed. "I am going back to England. I have work promised there."

"Ah," his father said. "At Bristol, perhaps? They build
ships there."

The lamp glowed, touching with faint gleams the black
and polished surface of the box on the mantel-shelf. There
was a wind getting up, hollowing out the sky like a dark
bowl, carving house and hill and headland out of dark space.
" 'Twill be blowing out yon the night," his father said.

"There are other things," Alec said. "I have made friends,
you see."

His father removed the iron-rimmed spectacles. "You have
made friends. Officers and such, I doubt not?"

"Yes, sir."

"And friends are good to have, to sit about the hearth of nights and talk with. But beyond that, only them that love you will bear your faults. You must love a man well to put up with all his trying ways, Alec."

"But they are not that sort of friends, sir. They are . . ." He ceased. He did not look at his father. Matthew sat, slowly polishing the spectacles with his thumb. They could hear the wind. "If this fails, I'll come back to the shipyard."

His father watched him gravely, polishing the spectacles slowly. "Shipwrights are not made like that, Alec. To fear God, to do your work like it was your own hull you were putting the ribs in . . ." He moved. "We'll see what the Book will say." He replaced the glasses. On the table was a heavy, brass-bound Bible. He opened it; the words seemed to him to rise to meet him from the page. Yet he read them, aloud: ". . . *and the captains of thousands and the captains of ten thousands* . . . A paragraph of pride. He faced his son, bowing his neck to see across the glasses. "You will go to London, then?"

"Yes, sir," Alec said.

VI

His position was waiting. It was in an office. He had already had cards made: Captain A. Gray, M.C., D.S.M., and on his return to London he joined the Officers' Association, donating to the support of the widows and orphans.

He had rooms in the proper quarter, and he would walk to and from the office, with his cards and his waxed moustaches, his sober correct clothes and his stick carried in a manner inimitable, at once jaunty and unobtrusive, giving his coppers to blind and maimed in Piccadilly, asking of them the names of their regiments. Once a month he wrote home:

*I am well. Love to Jessie and Matthew and John Wesley and
Elizabeth.*

During that first year Jessie was married. He sent her a
gift of plate, stinting himself a little to do so, drawings from
his savings. He was saving, not against old age; he believed
too firmly in the Empire to do that, who had surrendered
completely to the Empire like a woman, a bride. He was
saving against the time when he would recross the Channel
among the dead scenes of his lost and found life.

That was three years later. He was already planning to
ask for leave, when one day the manager broached the subject himself. With one correct bag he went to France. But
he did not bear eastward at once. He went to the Riviera;
for a week he lived like a gentleman, spending his money
like a gentleman, lonely, alone in that bright aviary of the
svelte kept women of all Europe.

That was why those who saw him descend from the Medi-
terranean Express that morning in Paris said, "Here is a
rich milord," and why they continued to say it in the hard-
benched third-class trains, as he sat leaning forward on his
stick, lip-moving the names on sheet-iron stations about the
battered and waking land lying now three years quiet beneath the senseless and unbroken battalions of days.

He reached London and found what he should have known
before he left. His position was gone. Conditions, the manager told him, addressing him punctiliously by his rank.

What savings he had left melted slowly; he spent the last
of them on a black silk dress for his mother, with the letter:

I am well. Love to Matthew and John Wesley and Elizabeth.

He called upon his friends, upon the officers whom he had
known. One, the man he knew best, gave him whisky in a
comfortable room with a fire: "You aren't working now?

Rotten luck. By the way, you remember Whiteby? He had a company in the —th. Nice chap: no people, though. He killed himself last week. Conditions."

"Oh. Did he? Yes. I remember him. Rotten luck."

"Yes. Rotten luck. Nice chap."

He no longer gave his pennies to the blind and the maimed in Piccadilly. He needed them for papers:

Artisans needed
Become stonemason
Men to drive motorcars. War record not necessary
Shop-assistants (must be under twenty-one)
Shipwrights needed

and at last:

Gentleman with social address and connections to meet out-of-town clients. Temporary

He got the place, and with his waxed moustaches and his correct clothes he revealed the fleshpots of the West End to Birmingham and Leeds. It was temporary.

Artisans
Carpenters
Housepainters

Winter was temporary, too. In the spring he took his waxed moustaches and his ironed clothes into Surrey, with a set of books, an encyclopedia, on commission. He sold all his things save what he stood in, and gave up his rooms in town.

He still had his stick, his waxed moustaches, his cards. Surrey, gentle, green, mild. A tight little house in a tight little garden. An oldish man in a smoking jacket puttering in a flower bed: "Good day, sir. Might I—"

The man in the smoking jacket looks up. "Go to the side, can't you? Don't come this way."

He goes to the side entrance. A slatted gate, freshly white, bearing an enameled plate:

NO   HAWKERS
        BEGGARS

He passes through and knocks at a tidy door smug beneath a vine. "Good day, miss. May I see the—"

"Go away. Didn't you see the sign on the gate?"

"But I—"

"Go away, or I'll call the master."

In the fall he returned to London. Perhaps he could not have said why himself. Perhaps it was beyond any saying, instinct perhaps bringing him back to be present at the instant out of all time of the manifestation, apotheosis, of his life which had died again. Anyway, he was there, still with his waxed moustaches, erect, his stick clasped beneath his left armpit, among the Household troops in brass cuirasses, on dappled geldings, and Guards in scarlet tunics, and the Church militant in stole and surplice and Prince defenders of God in humble mufti, all at attention for two minutes, listening to despair. He still had thirty shillings, and he replenished his cards: Captain A. Gray, M.C., D.S.M.

It is one of those spurious, pale days like a sickly and premature child of spring while spring itself is still weeks away. In the thin sunlight buildings fade upward into misty pinks and golds. Women wear violets pinned to their furs, appearing to bloom themselves like flowers in the languorous, treacherous air.

It is the women who look twice at the man standing against the wall at a corner: a gaunt man with white hair, and moustaches twisted into frayed points, with a bleached and frayed regimental scarf in a celluloid collar, a once-good suit now threadbare yet apparently pressed within twenty-four hours, standing against the wall with closed eyes, a dilapidated hat held bottom-up before him.

He stood there for a long time, until someone touched his arm. It was a constable. "Move along, sir. Against orders." In his hat were seven pennies and three halfpence. He bought a cake of soap and a little food.

Another anniversary came and passed; he stood again, his stick at his armpit, among the bright, silent uniforms, the quiet throng in either frank or stubborn cast-offs, with patient, bewildered faces. In his eyes now is not that hopeful resignation of a beggar, but rather that bitterness, that echo as of bitter and unheard laugher of a hunchback.

A meager fire burns on the sloping cobbles. In the fitful light the damp, fungus-grown wall of the embankment and the stone arch of the bridge loom. At the foot of the cobbled slope the invisible river clucks and gurgles with the tide.

Five figures lie about the fire, some with heads covered as though in slumber, others smoking and talking. One man sits upright, his back to the wall, his hands lying beside him; he is blind: he sleeps that way. He says that he is afraid to lie down.

"Cant you tell you are lying down, without seeing you are?" another says.

"Something might happen," the blind man says.

"What? Do you think they would give you a shell, even if it would bring back your sight?"

"They'd give him the shell, all right," a third said.

"Ow. Why dont they line us all up and put down a bloody barrage on us?"

"Was that how he lost his sight?" a fourth says. "A shell?"

"Ow. He was at Mons. A dispatch rider, on a motorbike. Tell them about it, mate."

The blind man lifts his face a little. Otherwise he does not move. He speaks in a flat voice. "She had the bit of scar on her wrist. That was how I could tell. It was me put the scar on her wrist, you might say. We was working in the shop one day. I had picked up an old engine and we was fitting it onto a bike so we could—"

"What?" the fourth says. "What's he talking about?"

"Shhhh," the first says. "Not so loud. He's talking about his girl. He had a bit of a bike shop on the Brighton Road and they were going to marry." He speaks in a low tone, his voice just under the weary, monotonous voice of the blind man. "Had their picture taken and all the day he enlisted and got his uniform. He had it with him for a while, until one day he lost it. He was fair wild. So at last we got a bit of a card about the same size of the picture. 'Here's your picture, mate,' we says. 'Hold onto it this time.' So he's still got the card. Likely he'll show it to you before he's done. So dont you let on."

"No," the other says. "I shant let on."

The blind man talks. "—got them at the hospital to write her a letter, and sure enough, here she come. I could tell her by the bit of scar on her wrist. Her voice sounded different, but then everything sounded different since. But I could tell by the scar. We would sit and hold hands, and I could touch the bit of scar inside her left wrist. In the cinema too. I would touch the scar and it would be like I—"

"The cinema?" the fourth says. "Him?"

"Yes," the other says. "She would take him to the cinema, the comedies, so he could hear them laughing."

The blind man talks. "—told me how the pictures hurt her eyes, and that she would leave me at the cinema and when it was over she would come and fetch me. So I said it was all right. And the next night it was again. And I said it was all right. And the next night I told her I wouldn't go either. I said we would stop at home, at the hospital. And then she didn't say anything for a long while. I could hear her breathing. Then she said it was all right. So after that we didn't go to the cinema. We would just sit, holding hands, and me feeling the scar now and then. We couldn't talk loud in the hospital, so we would whisper. But mostly we didn't talk. We just held hands. And that was for eight nights. I counted. Then it was the eighth night. We were sitting there, with the other hand in my hand, and me touching the scar now and then. Then on a sudden the hand jerked away. I could hear her standing up. 'Listen,' she says. 'This cant go on any longer. You will have to know sometime,' she says. And I says, 'I dont want to know but one thing. What is your name?' I says. She told me her name; one of the nurses. And she says—"

"What?" the fourth says. "What is this?"

"He told you," the first said. "It was one of the nurses in the hospital. The girl had been buggering off with another fellow and left the nurse for him to hold her hand, thinking he was fooled."

"But how did he know?" the fourth says.

"Listen," the first says.

"—'and you knew all the time,' she says, 'since the first time?' 'It was the scar,' I says. 'You've got it on the wrong wrist. You've got it on your right wrist,' I says. 'And two nights ago, I lifted up the edge of it a bit. What is it,' I says. 'Courtplaster?' " The blind man sits against the wall, his face lifted a little, his hands motionless beside him. "That's how I knew, by the scar. Thinking they could fool me, when it was me put the scar on her, you might say—"

The prone figure farthest from the fire lifts its head. "Hup," he says; "'ere e comes."

The others turn as one and look toward the entrance.

"Here who comes?" the blind man says. "Is it the bobbies?"

They do not answer. They watch the man who enters: a tall man with a stick. They cease to talk, save the blind man, watching the tall man come among them. "Here who comes, mates?" the blind man says. "Mates!"

The newcomer passes them, and the fire; he does not look at them. He goes on. "Watch, now," the second says. The blind man is now leaning a little forward; his hands fumble at the ground beside him as though he were preparing to rise.

"Watch who?" he says. "What do you see?"

They do not answer. They are watching the newcomer covertly, attentively, as he disrobes and then, a white shadow, a ghostly gleam in the darkness, goes down to the water and washes himself, slapping his body hard with icy and filthy handfuls of river water. He returns to the fire; they turn their faces quickly aside, save the blind man (he still sits forward, his arms propped beside him as though on the point of rising, his wan face turned toward the sound, the movement) and one other. "Yer stones is ot, sir," this one says. "I've ad them right in the blaze."

"Thanks," the newcomer says. He still appears to be utterly oblivious of them, so they watch him again, quietly, as he spreads his sorry garments on one stone and takes a second stone from the fire and irons them. While he is dressing, the man who spoke to him goes down to the water and returns with the cake of soap which he had used. Still watching, they see the newcomer rub his fingers on the cake of soap and twist his moustaches into points.

"A bit more on the left one, sir," the man holding the soap says. The newcomer soaps his fingers and twists his left moustache again, the other man watching him, his head bent and tilted a little back, in shape and attitude and dress like a caricatured scarecrow.

"Right. now?" the newcomer says.

"Right, sir," the scarecrow says. He retreats into the darkness and returns without the cake of soap, and carrying instead the hat and the stick. The newcomer takes them. From his pocket he takes a coin and puts it into the scarecrow's hand. The scarecrow touches his cap; the newcomer is gone. They watch him, the tall shape, the erect back, the stick, until he disappears.

"What do you see, mates?" the blind man says. "Tell a man what you see."

VII

AMONG THE DEMOBILIZED officers who emigrated from England after the Armistice was a subaltern named Walkley. He went out to Canada, where he raised wheat and prospered, both in pocket and in health. So much so that, had he been walking out of the Gare de Lyon in Paris instead of in Piccadilly Circus on this first evening (it is Christmas eve) of his first visit home, they would have said, "Here is not only a rich milord; it is a well one."

He had been in London just long enough to outfit himself with the beginning of a wardrobe, and in his new clothes (bought of a tailor which in the old days he could not have afforded) he was enjoying himself too much to even go anywhere. So he just walked the streets, among the cheerful throngs, until suddenly he stopped dead still, staring at a face. The man had almost white hair, moustaches waxed to needle points. He wore a frayed scarf in which could be barely distinguished the colors and pattern of a regiment. His threadbare clothes were freshly ironed and he carried a stick. He was standing at the curb, and he appeared to be saying something to the people who passed, and Walkley moved suddenly forward, his hand extended. But the other man only stared at him with eyes that were perfectly dead.

"Gray," Walkley said, "don't you remember me?" The other stared at him with that dead intensity. "We were in hospital together. I went out to Canada. Don't you remember?"

"Yes," the other said. "I remember you. You are Walkley." Then he quit looking at Walkley. He moved a little aside, turning to the crowd again, his hand extended; it was only then that Walkley saw that the hand contained three or four boxes of the matches which may be bought from any tobacconist for a penny a box. "Matches? Matches, sir?" he said. "Matches? Matches?"

Walkley moved also, getting again in front of the other. "Gray—" he said.

The other looked at Walkley again, this time with a kind of restrained yet raging impatience. "Let me alone, you son of a bitch!" he said, turning immediately toward the crowd again, his hand extended. "Matches! Matches, sir!" he chanted.

Walkley moved on. He paused again, half turning, looking back at the gaunt face above the waxed moustaches. Again the other looked him full in the face, but the glance passed on, as though without recognition. Walkley went on. He walked swiftly. "My God," he said. "I think I am going to vomit."

Crevasse

THE PARTY GOES ON, skirting the edge of the barrage weaving down into shell craters old and new, crawling out again. Two men half drag, half carry between them a third, while two others carry the three rifles. The third man's head is bound in a bloody rag; he stumbles his aimless legs along, his head lolling, sweat channeling slowly down his mud-crusted face.

The barrage stretches on and on across the plain, distant, impenetrable. Occasionally a small wind comes up from nowhere and thins the dun smoke momentarily upon clumps of bitten poplars. The party enters and crosses a field which a month ago was sown to wheat and where yet wheatspears thrust and cling stubbornly in the churned soil, among scraps of metal and seething hunks of cloth.

It crosses the field and comes to a canal bordered with tree stumps sheared roughly at a symmetrical five-foot level. The men flop and drink of the contaminated water and fill their water bottles. The two bearers let the wounded man slip to earth; he hangs lax on the canal bank with both arms in the water and his head too, had not the others held him up. One of them raises water in his helmet, but the wounded man cannot swallow. So they set him upright and the other holds the helmet brim to his lips and refills the helmet and pours the water on the wounded man's head, sopping the bandage. Then he takes a filthy rag from his pocket and dries the wounded man's face with clumsy gentleness.

The captain, the subaltern and the sergeant, still standing, are poring over a soiled map. Beyond the canal the ground rises gradually; the canal cutting reveals the chalk formation of the land in pallid strata. The captain puts the map away and the sergeant speaks the men to their feet, not loud. The two bearers raise the wounded man and they follow the canal bank, coming after a while to a bridge formed by a water-logged barge hull lashed bow and stern to either bank, and so pass over. Here they halt again while once more the captain and the subaltern consult the map.

Gunfire comes across the pale spring noon like a prolonged clashing of hail on an endless metal roof. As they go on the chalky soil rises gradually underfoot. The ground is dryly rough, shaling, and the going is harder still for the two who carry the wounded man. But when they would stop the wounded man struggles and wrenches free and staggers on alone, his hands at his head, and stumbles, falling. The bearers catch and raise him and hold him muttering between them and wrenching his arms. He is muttering ". . . bonnet . . ." and he frees his hands and tugs again at his bandage. The commotion passes forward. The captain looks back and stops; the party halts also, unbidden, and lowers rifles.

"A's pickin at's bandage, sir-r," one of the bearers tells the captain. They let the man sit down between them; the captain kneels beside him.

". . . bonnet . . . bonnet," the man mutters. The captain loosens the bandage. The sergeant extends a water bottle and the captain wets the bandage and lays his hand on the man's brow. The others stand about, looking on with a kind of sober, detached interest. The captain rises. The bearers raise the wounded man again. The sergeant speaks them into motion.

They gain the crest of the ridge. The ridge slopes westward into a plateau slightly rolling. Southward, beneath its dun pall, the barrage still rages; westward and northward about the shining empty plain smoke rises lazily here and there above clumps of trees. But this is the smoke of burning things, burning wood and not powder, and the two officers gaze from beneath their hands, the men halting again without order and lowering arms.

"Gad, sir," the subaltern says suddenly in a high, thin voice; "it's houses burning! They're retreating! Beasts! Beasts!"

" 'Tis possible," the captain says, gazing beneath his hand. "We can get around that barrage now. Should be a road just yonder." He strides on again.

"For-rard," the sergeant says, in that tone not loud. The men slope arms once more with unquestioning docility.

The ridge is covered with a tough, gorselike grass. Insects buzz in it, zip from beneath their feet and fall to slatting again beneath the shimmering noon. The wounded man is babbling again. At intervals they pause and give him water and wet the bandage again, then two others exchange with the bearers and they hurry the man on and close up again.

The head of the line stops; the men jolt prodding into one another like a train of freight cars stopping. At the captain's feet lies a broad shallow depression in which grows a sparse, dead-looking grass like clumps of bayonets thrust up out of the earth. It is too big to have been made by a small shell, and too shallow to have been made by a big one. It bears no traces of having been made by anything at all, and they look quietly down into it. "Queer," the subaltern says. "What do you fancy could have made it?"

The captain does not answer. He turns. They circle the depression, looking down into it quietly as they pass it. But they have no more than passed it when they come upon another one, perhaps not quite so large. "I didn't know they had anything that could make that," the subaltern says. Again the captain does not answer. They circle this one also and keep on along the crest of the ridge. On the other hand the ridge sheers sharply downward stratum by stratum of pallid eroded chalk.

A shallow ravine gashes its crumbling yawn abruptly across their path. The captain changes direction again, paralleling the ravine, until shortly afterward the ravine turns at right angles and goes on in the direction of their march. The floor of the ravine is in shadow; the captain leads the way down the shelving wall, into the shade. They lower the wounded man carefully and go on.

After a time the ravine opens. They find that they have debouched into another of those shallow depressions. This one is not so clearly defined, though, and the opposite wall of it is nicked by what is apparently another depression, like two overlapping disks. They cross the first depression, while more of the dead-looking grass bayonets saber their legs dryly, and pass through the gap into the next depression.

This one is like a miniature valley between miniature cliffs. Overhead they can see only the drowsy and empty bowl of the sky, with a few faint smoke smudges to the northwest. The sound of the barrage is now remote and far away: a vibration in earth felt rather than heard. There are no recent shell craters or marks here at all. It is as though they had strayed suddenly into a region, a world where the war had not reached, where nothing had reached, where no life is, and silence itself is dead. They give the wounded man water and go on.

The valley, the depression, strays vaguely before them. They can see that it is a series of overlapping, vaguely circular basins formed by no apparent or deducible agency. Pallid grass bayonets saber at their legs, and after a time they

are again among old healed scars of trees to which there
cling sparse leaves neither green nor dead, as if they too had
been overtaken and caught by a hiatus in time, gossiping
dryly among themselves though there is no wind. The floor
of the valley is not level. It in itself descends into vague
depressions, rises again as vaguely between its shelving walls.
In the center of these smaller depressions whitish knobs of
chalk thrust up through the thin topsoil. The ground has a
resilient quality, like walking on cork; feet make no sound.
"Jolly walking," the subaltern says. Though his voice is not
raised, it fills the small valley with the abruptness of a thunderclap, filling the silence, the words seeming to hang about
them as though silence here had been so long undisturbed
that it had forgot its purpose; as one they look quietly and
soberly about, at the shelving walls, the stubborn ghosts of
trees, the bland, hushed sky. "Topping hole-up for embusqué
birds and such," the subaltern says.

"Ay," the captain says. His word in turn hangs sluggishly
and fades. The men at the rear close up, the movement passing forward, the men looking quietly and soberly about.

"But no birds here," the subaltern says. "No insects even."

"Ay," the captain says. The word fades, the silence comes
down again, sunny, profoundly still. The subaltern pauses
and stirs something with his foot. The men halt also, and
the subaltern and the captain, without touching it, examine
the half-buried and moldering rifle. The wounded man is
babbling again.

"What is it, sir?" the subaltern says. "Looks like one of
those things the Canadians had. A Ross. Right?"

"French," the captain says; "1914."

"Oh," the subaltern says. He turns the rifle aside with his
toe. The bayonet is still attached to the barrel, but the stock
has long since rotted away. They go on, across the uneven
ground, among the chalky knobs thrusting up through the

soil. Light, the wan and drowsy sunlight, is laked in the valley, stagnant, bodiless, without heat. The saberlike grass thrusts sparsely and rigidly upward. They look about again at the shaling walls, then the ones at the head of the party watch the subaltern pause and prod with his stick at one of the chalky knobs and turn presently upward its earth-stained eyesockets and its unbottomed grin.

"Forward," the captain says sharply. The party moves; the men look quietly and curiously at the skull as they pass. They go on, among the other whitish knobs like marbles studded at random in the shallow soil.

"All in the same position, do you notice, sir?" the subaltern says, his voice chattily cheerful; "all upright. Queer way to bury chaps: sitting down. Shallow, too."

"Ay," the captain says. The wounded man babbles steadily. The two bearers stop with him, but the others crowd on after the officers, passing the two bearers and the wounded man. "Dinna stop to gi's sup water," one of the bearers says. "A'll drink walkin." They take up the wounded man again and hurry him on while one of them tries to hold the neck of a water bottle to the wounded man's mouth, clattering it against his teeth and spilling the water down the front of his tunic. The captain looks back.

"What's this?" he says sharply. The men crowd up. Their eyes are wide, sober; he looks about at the quiet, intent faces. "What's the matter back there, Sergeant?"

"Wind-up," the subaltern says. He looks about at the eroded walls, the whitish knobs thrusting quietly out of the earth. "Feel it myself," he says. He laughs, his laughter a little thin, ceasing. "Let's get out of here, sir," he says. "Let's get into the sun again."

"You are in the sun here," the captain says. "Ease off there, men. Stop crowding. We'll be out soon. We'll find the road and get past the barrage and make contact again." He turns and goes on. The party gets into motion again.

Then they all stop as one, in the attitudes of walking, in an utter suspension, and stare at one another. Again the earth moves under their feet. A man screams, high, like a woman or a horse; as the firm earth shifts for a third time beneath them the officers whirl and see beyond the down-plunging man a gaping hole with dry dust still crumbling about the edges before the orifice crumbles again beneath a second man. Then a crack springs like a sword slash beneath them all; the earth breaks under their feet and tilts like jagged squares of pale fudge, framing a black yawn out of which, like a silent explosion, bursts the unmistakable smell of rotted flesh. While they scramble and leap (in silence now; there has been no sound since the first man screamed) from one cake to another, the cakes tilt and slide until the whole floor of the valley rushes slowly under them and plunges them downward into darkness. A grave rumbling rises into the sunlight on a blast of decay and of faint dust which hangs and drifts in the faint air about the black orifice.

The captain feels himself plunging down a sheer and shifting wall of moving earth, of sounds of terror and of struggling in the ink dark. Someone else screams. The scream ceases; he hears the voice of the wounded man coming thin and reiterant out of the plunging bowels of decay: "A'm no dead! A'm no dead!" and ceasing abruptly, as if a hand had been laid on his mouth.

Then the moving cliff down which the captain plunges slopes gradually off and shoots him, uninjured, onto a hard floor, where he lies for a time on his back while across his face the lightward- and airward-seeking blast of death and dissolution rushes. He has fetched up against something; it tumbles down upon him lightly, with a muffled clatter as if it had come to pieces.

Then he begins to see the light, the jagged shape of the cavern mouth high overhead, and then the sergeant is bend-

ing over him with a pocket torch. "McKie?" the captain
says. For reply the sergeant turns the flash upon his own
face. "Where's Mr. McKie?" the captain says.

"A's gone, sir-r," the sergeant says in a husky whisper.
The captain sits up.

"How many are left?"

"Fourteen, sir-r," the sergeant whispers.

"Fourteen. Twelve missing. We'll have to dig fast." He
gets to his feet. The faint light from above falls coldly upon
the heaped avalanche, upon the thirteen helmets and the
white bandage of the wounded man huddled about the foot
of the cliff. "Where are we?"

For answer the sergeant moves the torch. It streaks later-
ally into the darkness, along a wall, a tunnel, into yawning
blackness, the walls faceted with pale glints of chalk. About
the tunnel, sitting or leaning upright against the walls, are
skeletons in dark tunics and bagging Zouave trousers, their
moldering arms beside them; the captain recognizes them as
Senegalese troops of the May fighting of 1915, surprised
and killed by gas probably in the attitudes in which they
had taken refuge in the chalk caverns. He takes the torch
from the sergeant.

"We'll see if there's anyone else," he says. "Have out the
trenching tools." He flashes the light upon the precipice. It
rises into gloom, darkness, then into the faint rumor of daylight overhead. With the sergeant behind him he climbs the
shifting heap, the earth sighing beneath him and shaling
downward. The injured man begins to wail again, "A'm no
dead! A'm no dead!" until his voice goes into a high sustained
screaming. Someone lays a hand over his mouth. His voice
is muffled, then it becomes laughter on a rising note, becomes
screaming again, is choked again.

The captain and the sergeant mount as high as they dare,
prodding at the earth while the earth shifts beneath them in

long hushed sighs. At the foot of the precipice the men huddle, their faces lifted faint, white, and patient into the light. The captain sweeps the torch up and down the cliff. There is nothing, no arm, no hand, in sight. The air is clearing slowly. "We'll get on," the captain says.

"Ay, sir-r," the sergeant says.

In both directions the cavern fades into darkness, plumbless and profound, filled with the quiet skeletons sitting and leaning against the walls, their arms beside them.

"The cave-in threw us forward," the captain says.

"Ay, sir-r," the sergeant whispers.

"Speak out," the captain says. "It's but a bit of a cave. If men got into it, we can get out."

"Ay, sir-r," the sergeant whispers.

"If it threw us forward, the entrance will be yonder."

"Ay, sir-r," the sergeant whispers.

The captain flashes the torch ahead. The men rise and huddle quietly behind him, the wounded man among them. He whimpers. The cavern goes on, unrolling its glinted walls out of the darkness; the sitting shapes grin quietly into the light as they pass. The air grows heavier; soon they are trotting, gasping, then the air grows lighter and the torch sweeps up another slope of earth, closing the tunnel. The men halt and huddle. The captain mounts the slope. He snaps off the light and crawls slowly along the crest of the slide, where it joins the ceiling of the cavern, sniffing. The light flashes on again. "Two men with trenching tools," he says.

Two men mount to him. He shows them the fissure through which air seeps in small, steady breaths. They begin to dig, furiously, hurling the dirt back. Presently they are relieved by two others; presently the fissure becomes a tunnel and four men can work at once. The air becomes fresher. They burrow furiously, with whimpering cries like dogs. The wounded man, hearing them perhaps, catching the excitement perhaps, begins to laugh again, meaningless and high. Then the man at the head of the tunnel bursts through. Light rushes in around him like water; he burrows madly; in silhouette they see his wallowing buttocks lunge from sight and a burst of daylight surges in.

The others leave the wounded man and surge up the slope, fighting and snarling at the opening. The sergeant springs after them and beats them away from the opening with a trenching spade, cursing in his hoarse whisper.

"Let them go, Sergeant," the captain says. The sergeant desists. He stands aside and watches the men scramble into the tunnel. Then he descends, and he and the captain help the wounded man up the slope. At the mouth of the tunnel the wounded man rebels.

"A'm no dead! A'm no dead!" he wails, struggling. By cajolery and force they thrust him, still wailing and struggling, into the tunnel, where he becomes docile again and scuttles through.

"Out with you, Sergeant," the captain says.

"After you, sir-r," the sergeant whispers.

"Out wi ye, man!" the captain says. The sergeant enters the tunnel. The captain follows. He emerges onto the outer slope of the avalanche which had closed the cave, at the foot of which the fourteen men are kneeling in a group. On his hands and knees like a beast, the captain breathes, his breath making a hoarse sound. "Soon it will be summer," he thinks, dragging the air into his lungs faster than he can empty them to respire again. "Soon it will be summer, and the long days." At the foot of the slope the fourteen men kneel. The one in the center has a Bible in his hand, from which he is intoning monotonously. Above his voice the wounded man's gibberish rises, meaningless and unemphatic and sustained.

Turnabout

THE AMERICAN—the older one—wore no pink Bedfords. His breeches were of plain whipcord, like the tunic. And the tunic had no long London-cut skirts, so that below the Sam Browne the tail of it stuck straight out like the tunic of a military policeman beneath his holster belt. And he wore simple puttees and the easy shoes of a man of middle age, instead of Savile Row boots, and the shoes and the puttees did not match in shade, and the ordnance belt did not match either of them, and the pilot's wings on his breast were just wings. But the ribbon beneath them was a good ribbon, and the insigne on his shoulders were the twin bars of a captain. He was not tall. His face was thin, a little aquiline; the eyes intelligent and a little tired. He was past twenty-five; looking at him, one thought, not Phi Beta Kappa exactly, but Skull and Bones perhaps, or possibly a Rhodes scholarship.

One of the men who faced him probably could not see him at all. He was being held on his feet by an American military policeman. He was quite drunk, and in contrast with the heavy-jawed policeman who held him erect on his long, slim, boneless legs, he looked like a masquerading girl. He was possibly eighteen, tall, with a pink-and-white face and blue eyes, and a mouth like a girl's mouth. He wore a pea-coat, buttoned awry and stained with recent mud, and upon his blond head, at that unmistakable and rakish swagger which no other people can ever approach or imitate, the cap of a Royal Naval Officer.

"What's this, corporal?" the American captain said. "What's the trouble? He's an Englishman. You'd better let their M. P.'s take care of him."

"I know he is," the policeman said. He spoke heavily, breathing heavily, in the voice of a man under physical strain; for all his girlish delicacy of limb, the English boy was heavier—or more helpless—than he looked. "Stand up!" the policeman said. "They're officers!"

The English boy made an effort then. He pulled himself together, focusing his eyes. He swayed, throwing his arms about the policeman's neck, and with the other hand he saluted, his hand flicking, fingers curled a little, to his right ear, already swaying again and catching himself again. "Cheer-o, sir," he said. "Name's not Beatty, I hope."

"No," the captain said.

"Ah," the English boy said. "Hoped not. My mistake. No offense, what?"

"No offense," the captain said quietly. But he was looking at the policeman. The second American spoke. He was a lieutenant, also a pilot. But he was not twenty-five and he wore the pink breeches, the London boots, and his tunic might have been a British tunic save for the collar.

"It's one of those navy eggs," he said. "They pick them out of the gutters here all night long. You don't come to town often enough."

"Oh," the captain said. "I've heard about them. I remember now." He also remarked now that, though the street was a busy one—it was just outside a popular café—and there were many passers, soldier, civilian, women, yet none of them so much as paused, as though it were a familiar sight. He was looking at the policeman. "Can't you take him to his ship?"

"I thought of that before the captain did," the policeman said. "He says he can't go aboard his ship after dark because he puts the ship away at sundown."

"Puts it away?"

"Stand up, sailor!" the policeman said savagely, jerking at his lax burden. "Maybe the captain can make sense out of it. Damned if I can. He says they keep the boat under the wharf. Run it under the wharf at night, and that they can't get it out again until the tide goes out tomorrow."

"Under the wharf? A boat? What is this?" He was now speaking to the lieutenant. "Do they operate some kind of aquatic motorcycles?"

"Something like that," the lieutenant said. "You've seen them—the boats. Launches, camouflaged and all. Dashing up and down the harbor. You've seen them. They do that all day and sleep in the gutters here all night."

"Oh," the captain said. "I thought those boats were ship commanders' launches. You mean to tell me they use officers just to—"

"I don't know," the lieutenant said. "Maybe they use them to fetch hot water from one ship to another. Or buns. Or maybe to go back and forth fast when they forget napkins or something."

"Nonsense," the captain said. He looked at the English boy again.

"That's what they do," the lieutenant said. "Town's lousy with them all night long. Gutters full, and their M. P.'s carting them away in batches, like nursemaids in a park. Maybe the French give them the launches to get them out of the gutters during the day."

"Oh," the captain said, "I see." But it was clear that he didn't see, wasn't listening, didn't believe what he did hear. He looked at the English boy. "Well, you can't leave him here in that shape," he said.

Again the English boy tried to pull himself together. "Quite all right, 'sure you," he said glassily, his voice pleasant, cheerful almost, quite courteous. "Used to it. Confounded rough *pavé*, though. Should force French do something about it. Visiting lads jolly well deserve decent field to play on, what?"

"And he was jolly well using all of it too," the policeman said savagely. "He must think he's a one-man team, maybe."

At that moment a fifth man came up. He was a British military policeman. "Nah then," he said. "What's this? What's this?" Then he saw the Americans' shoulder bars. He saluted. At the sound of his voice the English boy turned, swaying, peering.

"Oh, hullo, Albert," he said.

"Nah then, Mr. Hope," the British policeman said. He said to the American policeman, over his shoulder: "What is it this time?"

"Likely nothing," the American said. "The way you guys run a war. But I'm a stranger here. Here. Take him."

"What is this, corporal?" the captain said. "What was he doing?"

"He won't call it nothing," the American policeman said, jerking his head at the British policeman. "He'll just call it a thrush or a robin or something. I turn into this street about three blocks back a while ago, and I find it blocked with a line of trucks going up from the docks, and the drivers all hollering ahead what the hell the trouble is. So I come on, and I find it is about three blocks of them, blocking the cross streets too; and I come on to the head of it where the trouble is, and I find about a dozen of the drivers out in front, holding a caucus or something in the middle of the street, and I come up and I say, 'What's going on here?' and they leave me through and I find this egg here laying—"

"Yer talking about one of His Majesty's officers, my man," the British policeman said.

"Watch yourself, corporal," the captain said. "And you found this officer—"

"He had done gone to bed in the middle of the street, with an empty basket for a pillow. Laying there with his hands under his head and his knees crossed, arguing with them about whether he ought to get up and move or not. He said that the trucks could turn back and go around by another street, but that he couldn't use any other street, because this street was his."

"His street?"

The English boy had listened, interested, pleasant. "Billet, you see," he said. "Must have order, even in war emergency. Billet by lot. This street mine; no poaching, eh? Next street Jamie Wutherspoon's. But trucks can go by that street because Jamie not using it yet. Not in bed yet. Insomnia. Knew so. Told them. Trucks go that way. See now?"

"Was that it, corporal?" the captain said.

"He told you. He wouldn't get up. He just laid there, arguing with them. He was telling one of them to go somewhere and bring back a copy of their articles of war—"

"King's Regulations; yes," the captain said.

"—and see if the book said whether he had the right of way, or the trucks. And then I got him up, and then the captain come along. And that's all. And with the captain's permission I'll now hand him over to His Majesty's wet nur—"

"That'll do, corporal," the captain said. "You can go. I'll see to this." The policeman saluted and went on. The British policeman was now supporting the English boy. "Can't you take him?" the captain said. "Where are their quarters?"

"I don't rightly know, sir, if they have quarters or not.

We—I usually see them about the pubs until daylight. They don't seem to use quarters."

"You mean, they really aren't off of ships?"

"Well, sir, they might be ships, in a manner of speaking. But a man would have to be a bit sleepier than him to sleep in one of them."

"I see," the captain said. He looked at the policeman. "What kind of boats are they?"

This time the policeman's voice was immediate, final and completely inflectionless. It was like a closed door. "I don't rightly know, sir."

"Oh," the captain said. "Quite. Well, he's in no shape to stay about pubs until daylight this time."

"Perhaps I can find him a bit of a pub with a back table, where he can sleep," the policeman said. But the captain was not listening. He was looking across the street, where the lights of another café fell across the pavement. The English boy yawned terrifically, like a child does, his mouth pink and frankly gaped as a child's.

The captain turned to the policeman:

"Would you mind stepping across there and asking for Captain Bogard's driver? I'll take care of Mr. Hope."

The policeman departed. The captain now supported the English boy, his hand beneath the other's arm. Again the boy yawned like a weary child. "Steady," the captain said. "The car will be here in a minute."

"Right," the English boy said through the yawn.

II

ONCE IN THE CAR, he went to sleep immediately with the peaceful suddenness of babies, sitting between the two Americans. But though the aerodrome was only thirty minutes away, he was awake when they arrived, apparently quite fresh, and asking for whisky. When they entered the mess he appeared quite sober, only blinking a little in the lighted room, in his raked cap and his awry-buttoned pea-jacket and a soiled silk muffler, embroidered with a club insignia which Bogard recognized to have come from a famous preparatory school, twisted about his throat.

"Ah," he said, his voice fresh, clear now, not blurred, quite cheerful, quite loud, so that the others in the room turned and looked at him. "Jolly. Whisky, what?" He went straight as a bird dog to the bar in the corner, the lieutenant following. Bogard had turned and gone on to the other end of the room, where five men sat about a card table.

"What's he admiral of?" one said.

"Of the whole Scotch navy, when I found him," Bogard said.

Another looked up. "Oh, I thought I'd seen him in town." He looked at the guest. "Maybe it's because he was on his feet that I didn't recognize him when he came in. You usually see them lying down in the gutter."

"Oh," the first said. He, too, looked around. "Is he one of those guys?"

"Sure. You've seen them. Sitting on the curb, you know, with a couple of limey M. P.'s hauling at their arms."

"Yes. I've seen them," the other said. They all looked at the English boy. He stood at the bar, talking, his voice loud, cheerful. "They all look like him too," the speaker said. "About seventeen or eighteen. They run those little boats that are always dashing in and out."

"Is that what they do?" a third said. "You mean, there's a male marine auxiliary to the Waacs? Good Lord, I sure made a mistake when I enlisted. But this war never was advertised right."

"I don't know," Bogard said. "I guess they do more than just ride around."

But they were not listening to him. They were looking
at the guest. "They run by clock," the first said. "You can
see the condition of one of them after sunset and almost tell
what time it is. But what I don't see is, how a man that's
in that shape at one o'clock every morning can even see a
battleship the next day."

"Maybe when they have a message to send out to a ship,"
another said, "they just make duplicates and line the launches
up and point them toward the ship and give each one a duplicate of the message and let them go. And the ones that miss
the ship just cruise around the harbor until they hit a dock
somewhere."

"It must be more than that," Bogard said.

He was about to say something else, but at that moment
the guest turned from the bar and approached, carrying a
glass. He walked steadily enough, but his color was high
and his eyes were bright, and he was talking, loud, cheerful,
as he came up.

"I say. Won't you chaps join—" He ceased. He seemed to
remark something; he was looking at their breasts. "Oh, I say.
You fly. All of you. Oh, good gad! Find it jolly, eh?"

"Yes," somebody said. "Jolly."

"But dangerous, what?"

"A little faster than tennis," another said. The guest
looked at him, bright, affable, intent.

Another said quickly, "Bogard says you command a vessel."

"Hardly a vessel. Thanks, though. And not command.
Ronnie does that. Ranks me a bit. Age."

"Ronnie?"

"Yes. Nice. Good egg. Old, though. Stickler."

"Stickler?"

"Frightful. You'd not believe it. Whenever we sight
smoke and I have the glass, he sheers away. Keeps the ship

hull down all the while. No beaver then. Had me two down a fortnight yesterday."

The Americans glanced at one another. "No beaver?"

"We play it. With basket masts, you see. See a basket mast. Beaver! One up. The Ergenstrasse doesn't count any more, though."

The men about the table looked at one another. Bogard spoke. "I see. When you or Ronnie see a ship with basket masts, you get a beaver on the other. I see. What is the Ergenstrasse?"

"She's German. Interned. Tramp steamer. Foremast rigged so it looks something like a basket mast. Booms, cables, I dare say. I didn't think it looked very much like a basket mast, myself. But Ronnie said yes. Called it one day. Then one day they shifted her across the basin and I called her on Ronnie. So we decided to not count her any more. See now, eh?"

"Oh," the one who had made the tennis remark said, "I see. You and Ronnie run about in the launch, playing beaver. H'm'm. That's nice. Did you ever pl—"

"Jerry," Bogard said. The guest had not moved. He looked down at the speaker, still smiling, his eyes quite wide.

The speaker still looked at the guest. "Has yours and Ronnie's boat got a yellow stern?"

"A yellow stern?" the English boy said. He had quit smiling, but his face was still pleasant.

"I thought that maybe when the boats had two captains, they might paint the sterns yellow or something."

"Oh," the guest said. "Burt and Reeves aren't officers."

"Burt and Reeves," the other said, in a musing tone. "So they go, too. Do they play beaver too?"

"Jerry," Bogard said. The other looked at him. Bogard jerked his head a little. "Come over here." The other rose. They went aside. "Lay off of him," Bogard said. "I mean it, now. He's just a kid. When you were that age, how much sense did you have? Just about enough to get to chapel on time."

"My country hadn't been at war going on four years, though," Jerry said. "Here we are, spending our money and getting shot at by the clock, and it's not even our fight, and these limeys that would have been goose-stepping twelve months now if it hadn't been—"

"Shut it," Bogard said. "You sound like a Liberty Loan."

"—taking it like it was a fair or something. 'Jolly.'" His voice was now falsetto, lilting. "'But dangerous, what?'"

"Sh-h-h-h," Bogard said.

"I'd like to catch him and his Ronnie out in the harbor, just once. Any harbor. London's. I wouldn't want anything but a Jenny, either. Jenny? Hell, I'd take a bicycle and a pair of water wings! I'll show him some war."

"Well, you lay off him now. He'll be gone soon."

"What are you going to do with him?"

"I'm going to take him along this morning. Let him have Harper's place out front. He says he can handle a Lewis. Says they have one on the boat. Something he was telling me—about how he once shot out a channel-marker light at seven hundred yards."

"Well, that's your business. Maybe he can beat you."

"Beat me?"

"Playing beaver. And then you can take on Ronnie."

"I'll show him some war, anyway," Bogard said. He looked at the guest. "His people have been in it three years now, and he seems to take it like a sophomore in town for the big game." He looked at Jerry again. "But you lay off him now."

As they approached the table, the guest's voice was loud and cheerful: ". . . if he got the glasses first, he would go in close and look, but when I got them first, he'd sheer off where I couldn't see anything but the smoke. Frightful stickler. Frightful. But Ergenstrasse not counting any more. And if you make a mistake and call her, you lose two beaver from your score. If Ronnie were only to forget and call her we'd be even."

III

AT TWO O'CLOCK the English boy was still talking, his voice bright, innocent and cheerful. He was telling them how Switzerland had been spoiled by 1914, and instead of the vacation which his father had promised him for his sixteenth birthday, when that birthday came he and his tutor had had to do with Wales. But that he and the tutor had got pretty high and that he dared to say—with all due respect to any present who might have had the advantage of Switzerland, of course—that one could see probably as far from Wales as from Switzerland. "Perspire as much and breathe as hard, anyway," he added. And about him the Americans sat, a little hard-bitten, a little sober, somewhat older, listening to him with a kind of cold astonishment. They had been getting up for some time now and going out and returning in flying clothes, carrying helmets and goggles. An orderly entered with a tray of coffee cups, and the guest realized that for some time now he had been hearing engines in the darkness outside.

At last Bogard rose. "Come along," he said. "We'll get your togs." When they emerged from the mess, the sound of the engines was quite loud—an idling thunder. In alignment along the invisible tarmac was a vague rank of short banks of flickering blue-green fire suspended apparently in mid-air. They crossed the aerodrome to Bogard's quarters, where the lieutenant, McGinnis, sat on a cot fastening his flying boots. Bogard reached down a Sidcott suit and threw it across the cot. "Put this on," he said.

"Will I need all this?" the guest said. "Shall we be gone that long?"

"Probably," Bogard said. "Better use it. Cold upstairs."

The guest picked up the suit. "I say," he said. "I say, Ronnie and I have a do ourselves, tomor—today. Do you think Ronnie won't mind if I am a bit late? Might not wait for me."

"We'll be back before teatime," McGinnis said. He seemed quite busy with his boot. "Promise you." The English boy looked at him.

"What time should you be back?" Bogard said.

"Oh, well," the English boy said, "I dare say it will be all right. They let Ronnie say when to go, anyway. He'll wait for me if I should be a bit late."

"He'll wait," Bogard said. "Get your suit on."

"Right," the other said. They helped him into the suit. "Never been up before," he said, chattily, pleasantly. "Dare say you can see farther than from mountains, eh?"

"See more, anyway," McGinnis said. "You'll like it."

"Oh, rather. If Ronnie only waits for me. Lark. But dangerous, isn't it?"

"Go on," McGinnis said. "You're kidding me."

"Shut your trap, Mac," Bogard said. "Come along. Want some more coffee?" He looked at the guest, but McGinnis answered:

"No. Got something better than coffee. Coffee makes such a confounded stain on the wings."

"On the wings?" the English boy said. "Why coffee on the wings."

"Stow it, I said, Mac," Bogard said. "Come along."

They recrossed the aerodrome, approaching the muttering banks of flame. When they drew near, the guest began to discern the shape, the outlines, of the Handley-Page. It looked like a Pullman coach run upslanted aground into the skeleton of the first floor of an incomplete skyscraper. The guest looked at it quietly.

"It's larger than a cruiser," he said in his bright, interested voice. "I say, you know. This doesn't fly in one lump. You can't pull my leg. Seen them before. It comes in two parts: Captain Bogard and me in one; Mac and 'nother chap in other. What?"

"No," McGinnis said. Bogard had vanished. "It all goes up in one lump. Big lark, eh? Buzzard, what?"

"Buzzard?" the guest murmured. "Oh, I say. A cruiser. Flying. I say, now."

"And listen," McGinnis said. His hand came forth; something cold fumbled against the hand of the English boy— a bottle. "When you feel yourself getting sick, see? Take a pull at it."

"Oh, shall I get sick?"

"Sure. We all do. Part of flying. This will stop it. But if it doesn't. See?"

"What? Quite. What?"

"Not overside. Don't spew it overside."

"Not overside?"

"It'll blow back in Bogy's and my face. Can't see. Bingo. Finished. See?"

"Oh, quite. What shall I do with it?" Their voices were quiet, brief, grave as conspirators.

"Just duck your head and let her go."

"Oh, quite."

Bogard returned. "Show him how to get into the front pit, will you?" he said. McGinnis led the way through the trap. Forward, rising to the slant of the fuselage, the passage narrowed; a man would need to crawl.

"Crawl in there and keep going," McGinnis said.

"It looks like a dog kennel," the guest said.

"Doesn't it, though?" McGinnis agreed cheerfully. "Cut

along with you." Stooping, he could hear the other scuttling forward. "You'll find a Lewis gun up there, like as not," he said into the tunnel.

The voice of the guest came back: "Found it."

"The gunnery sergeant will be along in a minute and show you if it is loaded."

"It's loaded," the guest said; almost on the heels of his words the gun fired, a brief staccato burst. There were shouts, the loudest from the ground beneath the nose of the aeroplane. "It's quite all right," the English boy's voice said. "I pointed it west before I let it off. Nothing back there but Marine office and your brigade headquarters. Ronnie and I always do this before we go anywhere. Sorry if I was too soon. Oh, by the way," he added, "my name's Claude. Don't think I mentioned it."

On the ground, Bogard and two other officers stood. They had come up running. "Fired it west," one said. "How in hell does he know which way is west?"

"He's a sailor," the other said. "You forgot that."

"He seems to be a machine gunner too," Bogard said.

"Let's hope he doesn't forget that," the first said.

IV

NEVERTHELESS, Bogard kept an eye on the silhouetted head rising from the round gunpit in the nose ten feet ahead of him. "He did work that gun, though," he said to McGinnis beside him. "He even put the drum on himself, didn't he?"

"Yes," McGinnis said. "If he just doesn't forget and think that that gun is him and his tutor looking around from a Welsh alp."

"Maybe I should not have brought him," Bogard said. McGinnis didn't answer. Bogard jockeyed the wheel a little. Ahead, in the gunner's pit, the guest's head moved this way and that continuously, looking. "We'll get there and unload and haul air for home," Bogard said. "Maybe in the dark— Confound it, it would be a shame for his country to be in this mess for four years and him not even to see a gun pointed in his direction."

"He'll see one tonight if he don't keep his head in," McGinnis said.

But the boy did not do that. Not even when they had reached the objective and McGinnis had crawled down to the bomb toggles. And even when the searchlights found them and Bogard signaled to the other machines and dived, the two engines snarling full speed into and through the bursting shells, he could see the boy's face in the searchlight's glare, leaned far overside, coming sharply out as a spotlighted face on a stage, with an expression upon it of child-like interest and delight. "But he's firing that Lewis," Bogard thought. "Straight too"; nosing the machine farther down, watching the pinpoint swing into the sights, his right hand lifted, waiting to drop into McGinnis' sight. He dropped his hand; above the noise of the engines he seemed to hear the click and whistle of the released bombs as the machine, freed of the weight, shot zooming in a long upward bounce that carried it for an instant out of the light. Then he was pretty busy for a time, coming into and through the shells again, shooting athwart another beam that caught and held long enough for him to see the English boy leaning far over the side, looking back and down past the right wing, the undercarriage. "Maybe he's read about it somewhere," Bogard thought, turning, looking back to pick up the rest of the flight.

Then it was all over, the darkness cool and empty and peaceful and almost quiet, with only the steady sound of the engines. McGinnis climbed back into the office, and standing up in his seat, he fired the colored pistol this time and stood for a moment longer, looking backward toward where the searchlights still probed and sabered. He sat down again.

"O.K.," he said. "I counted all four of them. Let's haul air." Then he looked forward. "What's become of the King's Own? You didn't hang him onto a bomb release, did you?" Bogard looked. The forward pit was empty. It was in dim silhouette again now, against the stars, but there was nothing there now save the gun. "No," McGinnis said: "there he is. See? Leaning overside. Dammit, I told him not to spew it! There he comes back." The guest's head came into view again. But again it sank out of sight.

"He's coming back," Bogard said. "Stop him. Tell him we're going to have every squadron in the Hun Channel group on top of us in thirty minutes."

McGinnis swung himself down and stooped at the entrance to the passage. "Get back!" he shouted. The other was almost out; they squatted so, face to face like two dogs, shouting at one another above the noise of the still-unthrottled engines on either side of the fabric walls. The English boy's voice was thin and high.

"Bomb!" he shrieked.

"Yes," McGinnis shouted, "they were bombs! We gave them hell! Get back, I tell you! Have every Hun in France on us in ten minutes! Get back to your gun!"

Again the boy's voice came, high, faint above the noise: "Bomb! All right?"

"Yes! Yes! All right. Back to your gun, damn you!"

McGinnis climbed back into the office. "He went back. Want me to take her awhile?"

"All right," Bogard said. He passed McGinnis the wheel. "Ease her back some. I'd just as soon it was daylight when they come down on us."

"Right," McGinnis said. He moved the wheel suddenly. "What's the matter with that right wing?" he said. "Watch it. . . . See? I'm flying on the right aileron and a little rudder. Feel it."

Bogard took the wheel a moment. "I didn't notice that. Wire somewhere, I guess. I didn't think any of those shells were that close. Watch her, though."

"Right," McGinnis said. "And so you are going with him on his boat tomorrow—today."

"Yes. I promised him. Confound it, you can't hurt a kid, you know."

"Why don't you take Collier along, with his mandolin? Then you could sail around and sing."

"I promised him," Bogard said. "Get that wing up a little."

"Right," McGinnis said.

Thirty minutes later it was beginning to be dawn; the sky was gray. Presently McGinnis said: "Well, here they come. Look at them! They look like mosquitoes in September. I hope he don't get worked up now and think he's playing beaver. If he does he'll just be one down to Ronnie, provided the devil has a beard. . . . Want the wheel?"

V

AT EIGHT O'CLOCK the beach, the Channel, was beneath them. Throttled back, the machine drifted down as Bogard ruddered it gently into the Channel wind. His face was strained, a little tired.

McGinnis looked tired, too, and he needed a shave.

"What do you guess he is looking at now?" he said. For again the English boy was leaning over the right side of the cockpit, looking backward and downward past the right wing.

"I don't know," Bogard said. "Maybe bullet holes." He blasted the port engine. "Must have the riggers—"

"He could see some closer than that," McGinnis said. "I'll

swear I saw tracer going into his back at one time. Or maybe it's the ocean he's looking at. But he must have seen that when he came over from England." Then Bogard leveled off; the nose rose sharply, the sand, the curling tide edge fled alongside. Yet still the English boy hung far overside, looking backward and downward at something beneath the right wing, his face rapt, with utter and childlike interest. Until the machine was completely stopped he continued to do so. Then he ducked down, and in the abrupt silence of the engines they could hear him crawling in the passage. He emerged just as the two pilots climbed stiffly down from the office, his face bright, eager; his voice high, excited.

"Oh, I say! Oh, good gad! What a chap. What a judge of distance! If Ronnie could only have seen! Oh, good gad! Or maybe they aren't like ours—don't load themselves as soon as the air strikes them."

The Americans looked at him. "What don't what?" McGinnis said. "The bomb. It was magnificent; I say, I shan't forget it. Oh, I say, you know! It was splendid!"

After a while McGinnis said, "The bomb?" in a fainting voice. Then the two pilots glared at each other; they said in unison: "That right wing!" Then as one they clawed down through the trap and, with the guest at their heels, they ran around the machine and looked beneath the right wing. The bomb, suspended by its tail, hung straight down like a plumb bob beside the right wheel, its tip just touching the sand. And parallel with the wheel track was the long delicate line in the sand where its ultimate tip had dragged. Behind them the English boy's voice was high, clear, childlike:

"Frightened, myself. Tried to tell you. But realized you knew your business better than I. Skill. Marveloas. Oh, I say, I shan't forget it."

VI

A MARINE with a bayoneted rifle passed Bogard onto the wharf and directed him to the boat. The wharf was empty, and he didn't even see the boat until he approached the edge of the wharf and looked directly down into it and upon the backs of two stooping men in greasy dungarees, who rose and glanced briefly at him and stooped again.

It was about thirty feet long and about three feet wide. It was painted with gray-green camouflage. It was quarter-decked forward, with two blunt, raked exhaust stacks. "Good Lord," Bogard thought, "if all that deck is engine—" Just aft the deck was the control seat; he saw a big wheel, an instrument panel. Rising to a height of about a foot above the free-board, and running from the stern forward to where the deck began, and continuing on across the after edge of the deck and thence back down the other gunwale to the stern, was a solid screen, also camouflaged, which inclosed the boat save for the width of the stern, which was open. Facing the steersman's seat like an eye was a hole in the screen about eight inches in diameter. And looking down into the long, narrow, still, vicious shape, he saw a machine gun swiveled at the stern, and he looked at the low screen —including which the whole vessel did not sit much more than a yard above water level—with its single empty forward-staring eye, and he thought quietly: "It's steel. It's made of steel." And his face was quite sober, quite thoughtful, and he drew his trench coat about him and buttoned it, as though he were getting cold.

He heard steps behind him and turned. But it was only an orderly from the aerodrome, accompanied by the marine with the rifle. The orderly was carrying a largish bundle wrapped in paper.

"From Lieutenant McGinnis to the captain," the orderly said.

Bogard took the bundle. The orderly and the marine retreated. He opened the bundle. It contained some objects and a scrawled note. The objects were a new yellow silk sofa cushion and a Japanese parasol, obviously borrowed, and a comb and a roll of toilet paper. The note said:

Couldn't find a camera anywhere and Collier wouldn't let me have his mandolin. But maybe Ronnie can play on the comb.

MAC.

Bogard looked at the objects. But his face was still quite thoughtful, quite grave. He rewrapped the things and carried the bundle on up the wharf and dropped it quietly into the water.

As he returned toward the invisible boat he saw two men approaching. He recognized the boy at once—tall, slender, already talking, voluble, his head bent a little toward his shorter companion, who plodded along beside him, hands in pockets, smoking a pipe. The boy still wore the pea-coat beneath a flapping oilskin, but in place of the rakish and casual cap he now wore an infantryman's soiled Balaclava helmet, with, floating behind him as though upon the sound of his voice, a curtainlike piece of cloth almost as long as a burnous.

"Hullo, there!" he cried, still a hundred yards away.

But it was the second man that Bogard was watching, thinking to himself that he had never in his life seen a more curious figure. There was something stolid about the very shape of his hunched shoulders, his slightly down-looking face. He was a head shorter than the other. His face was ruddy, too, but its mold was of a profound gravity that was almost dour. It was the face of a man of twenty who has been for a year trying, even while asleep, to look twenty-one. He wore a high-necked sweater and dungaree slacks; above this a leather jacket; and above this a soiled naval officer's warmer that reached almost to his heels and which had one shoulder strap missing and not one remaining button at all. On his head was a plaid fore-and-aft deer stalker's cap, tied on by a narrow scarf brought across and down, hiding his ears, and then wrapped once about his throat and knotted with a hangman's noose beneath his left ear. It was unbelievably soiled, and with his hands elbow-deep in his pockets and his hunched shoulders and his bent head, he looked like someone's grandmother hung, say, for a witch. Clamped upside down between his teeth was a short brier pipe.

"Here he is!" the boy cried. "This is Ronnie. Captain Bogard."

"How are you?" Bogard said. He extended his hand. The other said no word, but his hand came forth, limp. It was quite cold, but it was hard, calloused. But he said no word; he just glanced briefly at Bogard and then away. But in that instant Bogard caught something in the look, something strange—a flicker; a kind of covert and curious respect, something like a boy of fifteen looking at a circus trapezist.

But he said no word. He ducked on; Bogard watched him drop from sight over the wharf edge as though he had jumped feet first into the sea. He remarked now that the engines in the invisible boat were running.

"We might get aboard too," the boy said. He started toward the boat, then he stopped. He touched Bogard's arm. "Yonder!" he hissed. "See?" His voice was thin with excitement.

"What?" Bogard also whispered; automatically he looked backward and upward, after old habit. The other was gripping his arm and pointing across the harbor.

"There! Over there. The Ergenstrasse. They have shifted

her again." Across the harbor lay an ancient, rusting, sway-backed hulk. It was small and nondescript, and, remembering, Bogard saw that the foremast was a strange mess of cables and booms, resembling—allowing for a great deal of license or looseness of imagery—a basket mast. Beside him the boy was almost chortling. "Do you think that Ronnie noticed?" he hissed. "Do you?"

"I don't know," Bogard said.

"Oh, good gad! If he should glance up and call her before he notices, we'll be even. Oh, good gad! But come along." He went on; he was still chortling. "Careful," he said. "Frightful ladder."

He descended first, the two men in the boat rising and saluting. Ronnie had disappeared, save for his backside, which now filled a small hatch leading forward beneath the deck. Bogard descended gingerly.

"Good Lord," he said. "Do you have to climb up and down this every day?"

"Frightful, isn't it?" the other said, in his happy voice. "But you know yourself. Try to run a war with makeshifts, then wonder why it takes so long." The narrow hull slid and surged, even with Bogard's added weight. "Sits right on top, you see," the boy said. "Would float on a lawn, in a heavy dew. Goes right over them like a bit of paper."

"It does?" Bogard said.

"Oh, absolutely. That's why, you see." Bogard didn't see, but he was too busy letting himself gingerly down to a sitting posture. There were no thwarts; no seats save a long, thick, cylindrical ridge which ran along the bottom of the boat from the driver's seat to the stern. Ronnie had backed into sight. He now sat behind the wheel, bent over the instrument panel. But when he glanced back over his shoulder he did not speak. His face was merely interrogatory. Across his face there was now a long smudge of grease. The boy's face was empty, too, now.

"Right," he said. He looked forward, where one of the seamen had gone. "Ready forward?" he said.

"Aye, sir," the seaman said.

The other seaman was at the stern line. "Ready aft?"

"Aye, sir."

"Cast off." The boat sheered away, purring, a boiling of water under the stern. The boy looked down at Bogard. "Silly business. Do it shipshape, though. Can't tell when silly fourstriper—" His face changed again, immediate, solicitous. "I say. Will you be warm? I never thought to fetch—"

"I'll be all right," Bogard said. But the other was already taking off his oilskin. "No, no," Bogard said. "I won't take it."

"You'll tell me if you get cold?"

"Yes. Sure." He was looking down at the cylinder on which he sat. It was a half cylinder—that is, like the hot-water tank to some Gargantuan stove, sliced down the middle and bolted, open side down, to the floor plates. It was twenty feet long and more than two feet thick. Its top rose as high as the gunwales and between it and the hull on either side was just room enough for a man to place his feet to walk.

"That's Muriel," the boy said.

"Muriel?"

"Yes. The one before that was Agatha. After my aunt. The first one Ronnie and I had was Alice in Wonderland. Ronnie and I were the White Rabbit. Jolly, eh?"

"Oh, you and Ronnie have had three, have you?"

"Oh, yes," the boy said. He leaned down. "He didn't notice," he whispered. His face was again bright, gleeful. "When we come back," he said. "You watch."

"Oh," Bogard said. "The Ergenstrasse." He looked astern, and then he thought: "Good Lord! We must be going— traveling." He looked out now, broadside, and saw the harbor line fleeing past, and he thought to himself that the boat was well-nigh moving at the speed at which the Handley-

Page flew, left the ground. They were beginning to bound now, even in the sheltered water, from one wave crest to the next with a distinct shock. His hand still rested on the cylinder on which he sat. He looked down at it again, following it from where it seemed to emerge beneath Ronnie's seat, to where it beveled into the stern. "It's the air in her, I suppose," he said.

"The what?" the boy said.

"The air. Stored up in her. That makes the boat ride high."

"Oh, yes. I dare say. Very likely. I hadn't thought about it." He came forward, his burnous whipping in the wind, and sat down beside Bogard. Their heads were below the top of the screen.

Astern the harbor fled, diminishing, sinking into the sea. The boat had begun to lift now, swooping forward and down, shocking almost stationary for a moment, then lifting and swooping again; a gout of spray came aboard over the bows like a flung shovelful of shot. "I wish you'd take this coat," the boy said.

Bogard didn't answer. He looked around at the bright face. "We're outside, aren't we?" he said quietly.

"Yes. . . . Do take it, won't you?"

"Thanks, no. I'll be all right. We won't be long, anyway, I guess."

"No. We'll turn soon. It won't be so bad then."

"Yes. I'll be all right when we turn." Then they did turn. The motion became easier. That is, the boat didn't bang head-on, shuddering, into the swells. They came up beneath now, and the boat fled with increased speed, with a long, sickening, yawing motion, first to one side and then the other. But it fled on, and Bogard looked astern with that same soberness with which he had first looked down into the boat. "We're going east now," he said.

"With just a spot of north," the boy said. "Makes her ride a bit better, what?"

"Yes," Bogard said. Astern there was nothing now save empty sea and the delicate needlelike cant of the machine gun against the boiling and slewing wake, and the two seamen crouching quietly in the stern. "Yes. It's easier." Then he said: "How far do we go?"

The boy leaned closer. He moved closer. His voice was happy, confidential, proud, though lowered a little: "It's Ronnie's show. He thought of it. Not that I wouldn't have, in time. Gratitude and all that. But he's the older, you see. Thinks fast. Courtesy, *noblesse oblige*—all that. Thought of it soon as I told him this morning. I said, 'Oh, I say. I've been there. I've seen it'; and he said, 'Not flying'; and I said, 'Strewth'; and he said 'How far? No lying now'; and I said, 'Oh, far. Tremendous. Gone all night'; and he said, 'Flying all night. That must have been to Berlin'; and I said, 'I don't know. I dare say'; and he thought. I could see him thinking. Because he is the older, you see. More experience in courtesy, right thing. And he said, 'Berlin. No fun to that chap, dashing out and back with us.' And he thought and I waited, and I said, 'But we can't take him to Berlin. Too far. Don't know the way, either'; and he said—fast, like a shot—said, 'But there's Kiel'; and I knew—"

"What?" Bogard said. Without moving, his whole body sprang. "Kiel? In this?"

"Absolutely. Ronnie thought of it. Smart, even if he is a stickler. Said at once, 'Zeebrugge no show at all for that chap. Must do best we can for him. Berlin,' Ronnie said. 'My Gad! Berlin.'"

"Listen," Bogard said. He had turned now, facing the other, his face quite grave. "What is this boat for?"

"For?"

"What does it do?" Then, knowing beforehand the

answer to his own question, he said, putting his hand on the
cylinder: "What is this in here? A torpedo, isn't it?"

"I thought you knew," the boy said.

"No," Bogard said. "I didn't know." His voice seemed to
reach him from a distance, dry, cricketlike: "How do you
fire it?"

"Fire it?"

"How do you get it out of the boat? When that hatch
was open a while ago I could see the engines. They were
right in front of the end of this tube."

"Oh," the boy said. "You pull a gadget there and the torpedo drops out astern. As soon as the screw touches the
water it begins to turn, and then the torpedo is ready, loaded.
Then all you have to do is turn the boat quickly and the
torpedo goes on."

"You mean—" Bogard said. After a moment his voice
obeyed him again. "You mean you aim the torpedo with
the boat and release it and it starts moving, and you turn
the boat out of the way and the torpedo passes through the
same water that the boat just vacated?"

"Knew you'd catch on," the boy said. "Told Ronnie so.
Airman. Tamer than yours, though. But can't be helped.
Best we can do, just on water. But knew you'd catch on."

"Listen,' Bogard said. His voice sounded to him quite
calm. The boat fled on, yawing over the swells. He sat quite
motionless. It seemed to him that he could hear himself talking to himself: "Go on. Ask him. Ask him what? Ask him
how close to the ship do you have to be before you fire. . . .
Listen," he said, in that calm voice. "Now, you tell Ronnie,
you see. You just tell him—just say—" He could feel his
voice ratting off on him again, so he stopped it. He sat quite
motionless, waiting for it to come back; the boy leaning
now, looking at his face. Again the boy's voice was solicitous:

"I say. You're not feeling well. These confounded shallow boats."

"It's not that," Bogard said. "I just— Do your orders say Kiel?"

"Oh, no. They let Ronnie say. Just so we bring the boat back. This is for you. Gratitude. Ronnie's idea. Tame, after flying. But if you'd rather, eh?"

"Yes, some place closer. You see, I—"

"Quite. I see. No vacations in wartime. I'll tell Ronnie." He went forward. Bogard did not move. The boat fled in long, slewing swoops. Bogard looked quietly astern, at the scudding sea, the sky.

"My God!" he thought. "Can you beat it? Can you beat it?"

The boy came back; Bogard turned to him a face the color of dirty paper. "All right now," the boy said. "Not Kiel. Nearer place, hunting probably just as good. Ronnie says he knows you will understand." He was tugging at his pocket. He brought out a bottle. "Here. Haven't forgot last night. Do the same for you. Good for the stomach, eh?"

Bogard drank, gulping—a big one. He extended the bottle, but the boy refused. "Never touch it on duty," he said. "Not like you chaps. Tame here."

The boat fled on. The sun was already down the west. But Bogard had lost all count of time, of distance. Ahead he could see white seas through the round eye opposite Ronnie's face, and Ronnie's hand on the wheel and the granitelike jut of his profiled jaw and the dead upside-down pipe. The boat fled on.

Then the boy leaned and touched his shoulder. He half rose. The boy was pointing. The sun was reddish; against it, outside them and about two miles away, a vessel—a trawler, it looked like—at anchor swung a tall mast.

"Lightship!" the boy shouted. "Theirs." Ahead Bogard

could see a low, flat mole—the entrance to a harbor. "Channel!" the boy shouted. He swept his arm in both directions. "Mines!" His voice swept back on the wind. "Place filthy with them. All sides. Beneath us too. Lark, eh?"

VIi

AGAINST THE MOLE a fair surf was beating. Running before the seas now, the boat seemed to leap from one roller to the next; in the intervals while the screw was in the air the engine seemed to be trying to tear itself out by the roots. But it did not slow; when it passed the end of the mole the boat seemed to be standing almost erect on its rudder, like a sailfish. The mole was a mile away. From the end of it little faint lights began to flicker like fireflies. The boy leaned. "Down," he said. "Machine guns. Might stop a stray."

"What do I do?" Bogard shouted. "What can I do?"

"Stout fellow! Give them hell, what? Knew you'd like it!"

Crouching, Bogard looked up at the boy, his face wild. "I can handle the machine gun!"

"No need," the boy shouted back. "Give them first innings. Sporting. Visitors, eh?" He was looking forward. "There she is. See?" They were in the harbor now, the basin opening before them. Anchored in the channel was a big freighter. Painted midships of the hull was a huge Argentine flag. "Must get back to stations!" the boy shouted down to him. Then at that moment Ronnie spoke for the first time. The boat was hurtling along now in smoother water. Its speed did not slacken and Ronnie did not turn his head when he spoke. He just swung his jutting jaw and the clamped cold pipe a little, and said from the side of his mouth a single word:

"Beaver."

The boy, stooped over what he had called his gadget,

jerked up, his expression astonished and outraged. Bogard also looked forward and saw Ronnie's arm pointing to starboard. It was a light cruiser at anchor a mile away. She had basket masts, and as he looked a gun flashed from her after turret. "Oh, damn!" the boy cried. "Oh, you putt! Oh, confound you, Ronnie! Now I'm three down!" But he had already stooped again over his gadget, his face bright and empty and alert again; not sober; just calm, waiting. Again Bogard looked forward and felt the boat pivot on its rudder and head directly for the freighter at terrific speed, Ronnie now with one hand on the wheel and the other lifted and extended at the height of his head.

But it seemed to Bogard that the hand would never drop. He crouched, not sitting, watching with a kind of quiet horror the painted flag increase like a moving picture of a locomotive taken from between the rails. Again the gun crashed from the cruiser behind them, and the freighter fired point-blank at them from its poop. Bogard heard neither shot.

"Man, man!" he shouted. "For God's sake!"

Ronnie's hand dropped. Again the boat spun on its rudder. Bogard saw the bow rise, pivoting; he expected the hull to slam broadside on into the ship. But it didn't. It shot off on a long tangent. He was waiting for it to make a wide sweep, heading seaward, putting the freighter astern, and he thought of the cruiser again. "Get a broadside, this time, once we clear the freighter," he thought. Then he remembered the freighter, the torpedo, and he looked back toward the freighter to watch the torpedo strike, and saw to his horror that the boat was now bearing down on the freighter again, in a skidding turn. Like a man in a dream, he watched himself rush down upon the ship and shoot past under her counter, still skidding, close enough to see the faces on her decks. "They missed and they are going to run down the

torpedo and catch it and shoot it again," he thought idioti-
cally.

So the boy had to touch his shoulder before he knew he
was behind him. The boy's voice was quite calm: "Under
Ronnie's seat there. A bit of a crank handle. If you'll just
hand it to me—"

He found the crank. He passed it back; he was thinking
dreamily: "Mac would say they had a telephone on board."
But he didn't look at once to see what the boy was doing
with it, for in that still and peaceful horror he was watching
Ronnie, the cold pipe rigid in his jaw, hurling the boat at
top speed round and round the freighter, so near that he
could see the rivets in the plates. Then he looked aft, his face
wild, importunate, and he saw what the boy was doing with
the crank. He had fitted it into what was obviously a small
windlass low on one flank of the tube near the head. He
glanced up and saw Bogard's face. "Didn't go that time!"
he shouted cheerfully.

"Go?" Bogard shouted. "It didn't— The torpedo—"

The boy and one of the seamen were quite busy, stooping
over the windlass and the tube. "No. Clumsy. Always happening. Should think clever chaps like engineers— Happens,
though. Draw her in and try her again."

"But the nose, the cap!" Bogard shouted. "It's still in the
tube, isn't it? It's all right, isn't it?"

"Absolutely. But it's working now. Loaded. Screw's
started turning. Get it back and drop it clear. If we should
stop or slow up it would overtake us. Drive back into the
tube. Bingo! What?"

Bogard was on his feet now, turned, braced to the terrific
merry-go-round of the boat. High above them the freighter
seemed to be spinning on her heel like a trick picture in the
movies. "Let me have that winch!" he cried.

"Steady!" the boy said. "Mustn't draw her back too fast.

Jam her into the head of the tube ourselves. Same bingo! Best let us. Every cobbler to his last, what?"

"Oh, quite," Bogard said. "Oh, absolutely." It was like someone else was using his mouth. He leaned, braced, his hands on the cold tube, beside the others. He was hot inside, but his outside was cold. He could feel all his flesh jerking with cold as he watched the blunt, grained hand of the seaman turning the windlass in short, easy, inch-long arcs, while at the head of the tube the boy bent, tapping the cylinder with a spanner, lightly, his head turned with listening delicate and deliberate as a watchmaker. The boat rushed on in those furious, slewing turns. Bogard saw a long, drooping thread loop down from somebody's mouth, between his hands, and he found that the thread came from his own mouth.

He didn't hear the boy speak, nor notice when he stood up. He just felt the boat straighten out, flinging him to his knees beside the tube. The seaman had gone back to the stern and the boy stooped again over his gadget. Bogard knelt now, quite sick. He did not feel the boat when it swung again, nor hear the gun from the cruiser which had not dared to fire and the freighter which had not been able to fire, firing again. He did not feel anything at all when he saw the huge, painted flag directly ahead and increasing with locomotive speed, and Ronnie's lifted hand drop. But this time he knew that the torpedo was gone; in pivoting and spinning this time the whole boat seemed to leave the water; he saw the bow of the boat shoot skyward like the nose of a pursuit ship going into a wingover. Then his outraged stomach denied him. He saw neither the geyser nor heard the detonation as he sprawled over the tube. He felt only a hand grasp him by the slack of his coat, and the voice of one of the seamen: "Steady all, sir. I've got you."

VIII

A VOICE ROUSED HIM, a hand. He was half sitting in the narrow starboard runway, half lying across the tube. He had been there for quite a while; quite a while ago he had felt someone spread a garment over him. But he had not raised his head. "I'm all right," he had said. "You keep it."

"Don't need it," the boy said. "Going home now."

"I'm sorry I—" Bogard said.

"Quite. Confounded shallow boats. Turn any stomach until you get used to them. Ronnie and I both, at first. Each time. You wouldn't believe it. Believe human stomach hold so much. Here." It was the bottle. "Good drink. Take enormous one. Good for stomach."

Bogard drank. Soon he did feel better, warmer. When the hand touched him later, he found that he had been asleep.

It was the boy again. The pea-coat was too small for him; shrunken, perhaps. Below the cuffs his long, slender, girl's wrists were blue with cold. Then Bogard realized what the garment was that had been laid over him. But before Bogard could speak, the boy leaned down, whispering; his face was gleeful: "He didn't notice!"

"What?"

"Ergenstrasse! He didn't notice that they had shifted her. Gad, I'd be just one down, then." He watched Bogard's face with bright, eager eyes. "Beaver, you know. I say. Feeling better, eh?"

"Yes," Bogard said, "I am."

"He didn't notice at all. Oh, gad! Oh, Jove!"

Bogard rose and sat on the tube. The entrance to the harbor was just ahead; the boat had slowed a little. It was just dusk. He said quietly: "Does this often happen?" The boy looked at him. Bogard touched the tube. "This. Failing to go out."

"Oh, yes. Why they put the windlass on them. That was later. Made first boat; whole thing blew up one day. So put on windlass."

"But it happens sometimes, even now? I mean, sometimes they blow up, even with the windlass?"

"Well, can't say, of course. Boats go out. Not come back. Possible. Not ever know, of course. Not heard of one captured yet, though. Possible. Not to us, though. Not yet."

"Yes," Bogard said. "Yes." They entered the harbor, the boat moving still fast, but throttled now and smooth, across the dusk-filled basin. Again the boy leaned down, his voice gleeful.

"Not a word, now!" he hissed. "Steady all!" He stood up; he raised his voice: "I say, Ronnie." Ronnie did not turn his head, but Bogard could tell that he was listening. "That Argentine ship was amusing, eh? In there. How do you suppose it got past us here? Might have stopped here as well. French would buy the wheat." He paused, diabolical— Machiavelli with the face of a strayed angel. "I say. How long has it been since we had a strange ship in here? Been months, eh?" Again he leaned, hissing. "Watch, now!" But Bogard could not see Ronnie's head move at all. "He's looking, though!" the boy whispered, breathed. And Ronnie was looking, though his head had not moved at all. Then there came into view, in silhouette against the dusk-filled sky, the vague, basket-like shape of the interned vessel's foremast. At once Ronnie's arm rose, pointing; again he spoke without turning his head, out of the side of his mouth, past the cold, clamped pipe, a single word:

"Beaver."

The boy moved like a released spring, like a heeled dog freed. "Oh, damn you!" he cried. "Oh, you putt! It's the Ergenstrasse! Oh, confound you! I'm just one down now!" He had stepped in one stride completely over Bogard, and he now leaned down over Ronnie. "What?" The boat was slowing in toward the wharf, the engine idle. "Aren't I, Ronnie? Just one down now?"

The boat drifted in; the seaman had again crawled forward onto the deck. Ronnie spoke for the third and last time. "Right," he said.

IX

"I WANT," Bogard said, "a case of Scotch. The best we've got. And fix it up good. It's to go to town. And I want a responsible man to deliver it." The responsible man came. "This is for a child," Bogard said, indicating the package. "You'll find him in the Street of the Twelve Hours, somewhere near the Café Twelve Hours. He'll be in the gutter. You'll know him. A child about six feet long. Any English M. P. will show him to you. If he is asleep, don't wake him. Just sit there and wait until he wakes up. Then give him this. Tell him it is from Captain Bogard."

X

ABOUT A MONTH LATER a copy of the English Gazette which had strayed onto an American aerodrome carried the following item in the casualty lists:

MISSING: Torpedo Boat XOOI. Midshipmen R. Boyce Smith and L. C. W. Hope, R. N. R., Boatswain's Mate Burt and Able Seaman Reeves. Channel Fleet, Light Torpedo Division. Failed to return from coast patrol duty.

Shortly after that the American Air Service headquarters also issued a bulletin:

For extraordinary valor over and beyond the routine of

duty, Captain H. S. Bogard, with his crew, composed of
Second Lieutenant Darrel McGinnis and Aviation Gunners
Watts and Harper, on a daylight raid and without scout protection, destroyed with bombs an ammunition depot several
miles behind the enemy's lines. From here, beset by enemy
aircraft in superior numbers, these men proceeded with what
bombs remained to the enemy's corps headquarters at Blank
and partially demolished this château, and then returned
safely without loss of a man.

And regarding which exploit, it might have added, had it
failed and had Captain Bogard come out of it alive, he would
have been immediately and thoroughly court-martialed.

Carrying his remaining two bombs, he had dived the
Handley-Page at the château where the generals sat at
lunch, until McGinnis, at the toggles below him, began to
shout at him, before he ever signaled. He didn't signal until
he could discern separately the slate tiles of the roof. Then
his hand dropped and he zoomed, and he held the aeroplane
so, in its wild snarl, his lips parted, his breath hissing, thinking: "God! God! If they were all there—all the generals,
the admirals, the presidents and the kings—theirs, ours—all
of them."

All the Dead Pilots

IN THE PICTURES, the snapshots hurriedly made, a little faded, a little dog-eared with the thirteen years, they swagger a little. Lean, hard, in their brass-and-leather martial harness, posed standing beside or leaning upon the esoteric shapes of wire and wood and canvas in which they flew without parachutes, they too have an esoteric look; a look not exactly human, like that of some dim and threatful apotheosis of the race seen for an instant in the glare of a thunderclap and then forever gone.

Because they are dead, all the old pilots, dead on the eleventh of November, 1918. When you see modern photographs of them, the recent pictures made beside the recent shapes of steel and canvas with the new cowlings and engines and slotted wings, they look a little outlandish: the lean young men who once swaggered. They look lost, baffled. In this saxophone age of flying they look as out of place as, a little thick about the waist, in the sober business suits of thirty and thirty-five and perhaps more than that, they would look among the saxophones and miniature brass bowlers of a night club orchestra. Because they are dead too, who had learned to respect that whose respect in turn their hardness had commanded before there were welded center sections and parachutes and ships that would not spin. That's why they watch the saxophone girls and boys with slipstream-proof lipstick and aeronautical flasks piling up the saxophone crates in private driveways and on golf greens, with the quick sympathy and the bafflement too. "My gad," one of them—ack emma, warrant officer pilot, captain and M.C. in turn—said to me once; "if you can treat a crate that way, why do you want to fly at all?"

But they are all dead now. They are thick men now, a little thick about the waist from sitting behind desks, and maybe not so good at it, with wives and children in suburban homes almost paid out, with gardens in which they putter in the long evenings after the 5:15 is in, and perhaps not so good at that either: the hard, lean men who swaggered hard and drank hard because they had found that being dead was not as quiet as they had heard it would be. That's why this story is composite: a series of brief glares in which, instantaneous and without depth or perspective, there stood into sight the portent and the threat of what the race could bear and become, in an instant between dark and dark.

II

IN 1918 I was at Wing Headquarters, trying to get used to a mechanical leg, where, among other things, I had the censoring of mail from all squadrons in the Wing. The job itself wasn't bad, since it gave me spare time to experiment with a synchronized camera on which I was working. But the opening and reading of the letters, the scrawled, brief pages of transparent and honorable lies to mothers and sweethearts, in the script and spelling of schoolboys. But a war is such a big thing, and it takes so long. I suppose they who run them (I dont mean the staffs, but whoever or whatever it is that controls events) do get bored now and then. And it's when you get bored that you turn petty, play horse.

So now and then I would go up to a Camel squadron behind Amiens and talk with the gunnery sergeant about the
synchronization of the machine guns. This was Spoomer's
squadron. His uncle was the corps commander, the K.G., and
so Spoomer, with his Guards' Captaincy, had also got in turn
a Mons Star, a D.S.O., and now a pursuit squadron of single
seaters, though the third barnacle on his tunic was still the
single wing of an observer.

In 1914 he was in Sandhurst: a big, ruddy-colored chap
with china eyes, and I like to think of his uncle sending for
him when the news got out, the good news. Probably at the
uncle's club (the uncle was a brigadier then, just recalled
hurriedly from Indian service) and the two of them opposite
one another across the mahogany, with the newsboys crying
in the street, and the general saying, "By gad, it will be the
making of the Army. Pass the wine, sir."

I daresay the general was put out, not to say outraged,
when he finally realized that neither the Hun nor the Home
Office intended running this war like the Army wanted it
run. Anyway, Spoomer had already gone out to Mons and
come back with his Star (though Ffollansbye said that the
general sent Spoomer out to get the Star, since it was going
to be one decoration you had to be on hand to get) before the
uncle got him transferred to his staff, where Spoomer could
get his D.S.O. Then perhaps the uncle sent him out again to
tap the stream where it came to surface. Or maybe Spoomer
went on his own this time. I like to think so. I like to think
that he did it through pro patria, even though I know that
no man deserves praise for courage or opprobrium for cow-
ardice, since there are situations in which any man will show
either of them. But he went out, and came back a year later
with his observer's wing and a dog almost as large as a calf.

That was in 1917, when he and Sartoris first came together,
collided. Sartoris was an American. from a plantation at

Mississippi, where they grew grain and Negroes, or the Negroes grew the grain—something. Sartoris had a working
vocabulary of perhaps two hundred words, and I daresay to
tell where and how and why he lived was beyond him, save
that he lived in the plantation with his great-aunt and his
grandfather. He came through Canada in 1916, and he was at
Pool. Ffollansbye told me about it. It seems that Sartoris had
a girl in London, one of those three-day wives and three-year
widows. That's the bad thing about war. They—the Sartor-
ises and such—didn't die until 1918, some of them. But the
girls, the women, they died on the fourth of August, 1914.

So Sartoris had a girl. Ffollansbye said they called her
Kitchener, "because she had such a mob of soldiers." He said
they didn't know if Sartoris knew this or not, but that anyway for a while Kitchener—Kit—appeared to have ditched
them all for Sartoris. They would be seen anywhere and any
time together, then Ffollansbye told me how he found Sartoris alone and quite drunk one evening in a restaurant. Ffollansbye told how he had already heard that Kit and Spoomer
had gone off somewhere together about two days ago. He
said that Sartoris was sitting there, drinking himself blind,
waiting for Spoomer to come in. He said he finally got Sartoris into a cab and sent him to the aerodrome. It was about
dawn then, and Sartoris got a captain's tunic from someone's
kit, and a woman's garter from someone else's kit, perhaps his
own, and pinned the garter on the tunic like a barnacle ribbon. Then he went and waked a corporal who was an ex-pro-
fessional boxer and with whom Sartoris would put on the
gloves now and then, and made the corporal put on the tunic
over his underclothes. "Namesh Spoomer," Sartoris told the
corporal. "Cap'm Spoomer"; swaying and prodding at the
garter with his finger. "Dishtinguish Sheries Thighs," Sartoris
said. Then he and the corporal in the borrowed tunic, with

his woolen underwear showing beneath, stood there in the dawn, swinging at one another with their naked fists.

III

You'd think that when a war had got you into it, it would let you be. That it wouldn't play horse with you. But maybe it wasn't that. Maybe it was because the three of them, Spoomer and Sartoris and the dog, were so humorless about it. Maybe a humorless person is an unflagging challenge to them above the thunder and the alarms. Anyway, one afternoon—it was in the spring, just before Cambrai fell—I went up to the Camel aerodrome to see the gunnery sergeant, and I saw Sartoris for the first time. They had given the squadron to Spoomer and the dog the year before, and the first thing they did was to send Sartoris out to it.

The afternoon patrol was out, and the rest of the people were gone too, to Amiens I suppose, and the aerodrome was deserted. The sergeant and I were sitting on two empty petrol tins in the hangar door when I saw a man thrust his head out the door of the officers' mess and look both ways along the line, his air a little furtive and very alert. It was Sartoris, and he was looking for the dog.

"The dog?" I said. Then the sergeant told me, this too composite, out of his own observation and the observation of the entire enlisted personnel exchanged and compared over the mess tables or over pipes at night: that terrible and omniscient inquisition of those in an inferior station.

When Spoomer left the aerodrome, he would lock the dog up somewhere. He would have to lock it up in a different place each time, because Sartoris would hunt until he found it, and let it out. It appeared to be a dog of intelligence, because if Spoomer had only gone down to Wing or somewhere on business, the dog would stay at home, spending the

interval grubbing in the refuse bin behind the men's mess, to
which it was addicted in preference to that of the officers.
But if Spoomer had gone to Amiens, the dog would depart up
the Amiens road immediately on being freed, to return later
with Spoomer in the squadron car.

"Why does Mr. Sartoris let it out?" I said. "Do you mean
that Captain Spoomer objects to the dog eating kitchen
refuse?"

But the sergeant was not listening. His head was craned
around the door, and we watched Sartoris. He had emerged
from the mess and he now approached the hangar at the end
of the line, his air still alert, still purposeful. He entered the
hangar. "That seems a rather childish business for a grown
man," I said.

The sergeant looked at me. Then he quit looking at me.
"He wants to know if Captain Spoomer went to Amiens or
not."

After a while I said, "Oh. A young lady. Is that it?"

He didn't look at me. "You might call her a young lady. I
suppose they have young ladies in this country."

I thought about that for a while. Sartoris emerged from
the first hangar and entered the second one. "I wonder if
there are any young ladies any more anywhere," I said.

"Perhaps you are right, sir. War is hard on women."

"What about this one?" I said. "Who is she?"

He told me. They ran an estaminet, a "bit of a pub" he
called it—an old harridan of a woman, and the girl. A little
place on a back street, where officers did not go. Perhaps that
was why Sartoris and Spoomer created such a furore in that
circle. I gathered from the sergeant that the contest between
the squadron commander and one of his greenest cubs was
the object of general interest and the subject of the warmest
conversation and even betting among the enlisted element of
the whole sector of French and British troops. "Being officers
and all," he said.

"They frightened the soldiers off, did they?" I said. "Is that it?" The sergeant did not look at me. "Were there many soldiers to frighten off?"

"I suppose you know these young women," the sergeant said. "This war and all."

And that's who the girl was. What the girl was. The sergeant said that the girl and the old woman were not even related. He told me how Sartoris bought her things—clothes, and jewelry; the sort of jewelry you might buy in Amiens, probably. Or maybe in a canteen, because Sartoris was not much more than twenty. I saw some of the letters which he wrote to his great-aunt back home, letters that a third-form lad in Harrow could have written, perhaps bettered. It seemed that Spoomer did not make the girl any presents. "Maybe because he is a captain," the sergeant said. "Or maybe because of them ribbons he dont have to."

"Maybe so," I said.

And that was the girl, the girl who, in the centime jewelry which Sartoris gave her, dispensed beer and wine to British and French privates in an Amiens back street, and because of whom Spoomer used his rank to betray Sartoris with her by keeping Sartoris at the aerodrome on special duties, locking up the dog to hide from Sartoris what he had done. And Sartoris taking what revenge he could by letting out the dog in order that it might grub in the refuse of plebeian food.

He entered the hangar in which the sergeant and I were: a tall lad with pale eyes in a face that could be either merry or surly, and quite humorless. He looked at me. "Hello," he said.

"Hello," I said. The sergeant made to get up.

"Carry on," Sartoris said. "I dont want anything." He went on to the rear of the hangar. It was cluttered with petrol drums and empty packing cases and such. He was utterly without self-consciousness, utterly without shame of his childish business.

The dog was in one of the packing cases. It emerged, huge, of a napped, tawny color; Ffollansbye had told me that, save for Spoomer's wing and his Mons Star and his D.S.O., he and the dog looked alike. It quitted the hangar without haste, giving me a brief, sidelong glance. We watched it go on and disappear around the corner of the men's mess. Then Sartoris turned and went back to the officers' mess and also disappeared.

Shortly afterward, the afternoon patrol came in. While the machines were coming up to the line, the squadron car turned onto the aerodrome and stopped at the officers' mess and Spoomer got out. "Watch him," the sergeant said. "He'll try to do it like he wasn't watching himself, noticing himself."

He came along the hangars, big, hulking, in green golf stockings. He did not see me until he was turning into the hangar. He paused; it was almost imperceptible, then he entered, giving me a brief, sidelong glance. "How do," he said in a high, fretful, level voice. The sergeant had risen. I had never seen Spoomer even glance toward the rear, toward the overturned packing case, yet he had stopped. "Sergeant," he said.

"Sir," the sergeant said.

"Sergeant," Spoomer said. "Have those timers come up yet?"

"Yes, sir. They came up two weeks ago. They're all in use now, sir."

"Quite so. Quite so." He turned; again he gave me a brief, sidelong glance, and went on down the hangar line, not fast. He disappeared. "Watch him, now," the sergeant said. "He wont go over there until he thinks we have quit watching him."

We watched. Then he came into sight again, crossing toward the men's mess, walking briskly now. He disappeared beyond the corner. A moment later he emerged, dragging the huge, inert beast by the scruff of its neck. "You mustn't eat that stuff," he said. "That's for soldiers."

IV

I DIDN'T KNOW at the time what happened next. Sartoris didn't tell me until later, afterward. Perhaps up to that time he had not anything more than instinct and circumstantial evidence to tell him that he was being betrayed: evidence such as being given by Spoomer some duty not in his province at all and which would keep him on the aerodrome for the afternoon, then finding and freeing the hidden dog and watching it vanish up the Amiens road at its clumsy hand gallop.

But something happened. All I could learn at the time was, that one afternoon Sartoris found the dog and watched it depart for Amiens. Then he violated his orders, borrowed a motor bike and went to Amiens too. Two hours later the dog returned and repaired to the kitchen door of the men's mess, and a short time after that, Sartoris himself returned on a lorry (they were already evacuating Amiens) laden with household effects and driven by a French soldier in a peasant's smock. The motor bike was on the lorry too, pretty well beyond repair. The soldier told how Sartoris had driven the bike full speed into a ditch, trying to run down the dog.

But nobody knew just what had happened, at the time. But I had imagined the scene, before he told me. I imagined him there, in that bit of a room full of French soldiers, and the old woman (she could read pips, no doubt; ribbons, anyway) barring him from the door to the living quarters. I can imagine him, furious, baffled, inarticulate (he knew no French) standing head and shoulders above the French people whom he could not understand and that he believed were laughing at him. "That was it," he told me. "Laughing at me behind their faces, about a woman. Me knowing that he was up there, and them knowing I knew that if I busted in and dragged him out and bashed his head off, I'd not only be cashiered, I'd be clinked for life for having infringed the articles of alliance by invading foreign property without warrant or something."

Then he returned to the aerodrome and met the dog on the road and tried to run it down. The dog came on home, and Spoomer returned, and he was just dragging it by the scruff of the neck from the refuse bin behind the men's mess, when the afternoon patrol came in. They had gone out six and come back five, and the leader jumped down from his machine before it had stopped rolling. He had a bloody rag about his right hand and he ran toward Spoomer stooped above the passive and stiff-legged dog. "By gad," he said, "they have got Cambrai!"

Spoomer did not look up. "Who have?"

"Jerry has, by gad!"

"Well, by gad," Spoomer said. "Come along, now. I have told you about that muck."

A man like that is invulnerable. When Sartoris and I talked for the first time, I started to tell him that. But then I learned that Sartoris was invincible too. We talked, that first time. "I tried to get him to let me teach him to fly a Camel," Sartoris said. "I will teach him for nothing. I will tear out the cockpit and rig the duals myself, for nothing."

"Why?" I said. "What for?"

"Or anything. I will let him choose it. He can take an S.E. if he wants to, and I will take an Ak.W. or even a Fee and I will run him clean out of the sky in four minutes. I will run him so far into the ground he will have to stand on his head to swallow."

We talked twice: that first time, and the last time. "Well, you did better than that," I said the last time we talked.

He had hardly any teeth left then, and he couldn't talk

very well, who had never been able to talk much, who lived and died with maybe two hundred words. "Better than what?" he said.

"You said before that you would run him clean out of the sky. You didn't do that; you did better: you have run him clean off the continent of Europe."

V

I think I said that he was invulnerable too. November 11, 1918, couldn't kill him, couldn't leave him growing a little thicker each year behind an office desk, with what had once been hard and lean and immediate grown a little dim, a little baffled, and betrayed, because by that day he had been dead almost six months.

He was killed in July, but we talked that second time, that other time before that. This last time was a week after the patrol had come in and told that Cambrai had fallen, a week after we heard the shells falling in Amiens. He told me about it himself, through his missing teeth. The whole squadron went out together. He left his flight as soon as they reached the broken front, and flew back to Amiens with a bottle of brandy in his overall leg. Amiens was being evacuated, the roads full of lorries and carts of household goods, and ambulances from the Base hospital, and the city and its immediate territory was now interdict.

He landed in a short meadow. He said there was an old woman working in a field beyond the canal (he said she was still there when he returned an hour later, stooping stubbornly among the green rows, beneath the moist spring air shaken at slow and monstrous intervals by the sound of shells falling in the city) and a light ambulance stopped halfway in the roadside ditch.

He went to the ambulance. The engine was still running.

The driver was a young man in spectacles. He looked like a student, and he was dead drunk, half sprawled out of the cab. Sartoris had a drink from his own bottle and tried to rouse the driver, in vain. Then he had another drink (I imagine that he was pretty well along himself by then; he told me how only that morning, when Spoomer had gone off in the car and he had found the dog and watched it take the Amiens road, how he had tried to get the operations officer to let him off patrol and how the operations officer had told him that La Fayette awaited him on the Santerre plateau) and tumbled the driver back into the ambulance and drove on to Amiens himself.

He said the French corporal was drinking from a bottle in a doorway when he passed and stopped the ambulance before the estaminet. The door was locked. He finished his brandy bottle and he broke the estaminet door in by diving at it as they do in American football. Then he was inside. The place was empty, the benches and tables overturned and the shelves empty of bottles, and he said that at first he could not remember what it was he had come for, so he thought it must be a drink. He found a bottle of wine under the bar and broke the neck off against the edge of the bar, and he told how he stood there, looking at himself in the mirror be-hind the bar, trying to think what it was he had come to do. "I looked pretty wild," he said.

Then the first shell fell. I can imagine it: he standing there in that quiet, peaceful, redolent, devastated room, with the bashed-in door and the musing and waiting city beyond it, and then that slow, unhurried, reverberant sound coming down upon the thick air of spring like a hand laid without haste on the damp silence; he told how dust or sand or plaster, something, sifted somewhere, whispering down in a faint hiss, and how a big, lean cat came up over the bar without a sound and flowed down to the floor and vanished like dirty quick-silver.

Then he saw the closed door behind the bar and he remembered what he had come for. He went around the bar. He expected this door to be locked too, and he grasped the knob and heaved back with all his might. It wasn't locked. He said it came back into the shelves with a sound like a pistol, jerking him off his feet. "My head hit the bar," he said. "Maybe I was a little groggy after that."

Anyway, he was holding himself up in the door, looking down at the old woman. She was sitting on the bottom stair, her apron over her head, rocking back and forth. He said that the apron was quite clean, moving back and forth like a piston, and he standing in the door, drooling a little at the mouth. "Madame," he said. The old woman rocked back and forth. He propped himself carefully and leaned and touched her shoulder. " 'Toinette," he said. "Où est-elle, 'Toinette?" That was probably all the French he knew; that, with *vin* added to his 196 English words, composed his vocabulary.

Again the old woman did not answer. She rocked back and forth like a wound-up toy. He stepped carefully over her and mounted the stair. There was a second door at the head of the stair. He stopped before it, listening. His throat filled with a hot, salty liquid. He spat it, drooling; his throat filled again. This door was unlocked also. He entered the room quietly. It contained a table, on which lay a khaki cap with the bronze crest of the Flying Corps, and as he stood drooling in the door, the dog heaved up from the corner furthest from the window, and while he and the dog looked at one another above the cap, the sound of the second shell came dull and monstrous into the room, stirring the limp curtains before the window.

As he circled the table the dog moved too, keeping the table between them, watching him. He was trying to move quietly, yet he struck the table in passing (perhaps while watching the dog) and he told how, when he reached the opposite door and stood beside it, holding his breath, drooling, he could hear the silence in the next room. Then a voice said:

"Maman?"

He kicked the locked door, then he dived at it, again like the American football, and through it, door and all. The girl screamed. But he said he never saw her, never saw anyone. He just heard her scream as he went into the room on all-fours. It was a bedroom; one corner was filled by a huge wardrobe with double doors. The wardrobe was closed, and the room appeared to be empty. He didn't go to the wardrobe. He said he just stood there on his hands and knees, drooling, like a cow, listening to the dying reverberation of the third shell, watching the curtains on the window blow once into the room as though to a breath.

He got up. "I was still groggy," he said. "And I guess that brandy and the wine had kind of got joggled up inside me." I daresay they had. There was a chair. Upon it lay a pair of slacks, neatly folded, a tunic with an observer's wing and two ribbons, an ordnance belt. While he stood looking down at the chair, the fourth shell came.

He gathered up the garments. The chair toppled over and he kicked it aside and lurched along the wall to the broken door and entered the first room, taking the cap from the table as he passed. The dog was gone.

He entered the passage. The old woman still sat on the bottom step, her apron over her head, rocking back and forth. He stood at the top of the stair, holding himself up, waiting to spit. Then beneath him a voice said: "Que faites-vous en haut?"

He looked down upon the raised moustached face of the French corporal whom he had passed in the street drinking from the bottle. For a time they looked at one another. Then the corporal said, "Descendez," making a peremptory gesture with his arm. Clasping the garments in one hand, Sartoris put the other hand on the stair rail and vaulted over it.

The corporal jumped aside. Sartoris plunged past him and into the wall, banging his head hollowly again. As he got to his feet and turned, the corporal kicked at him, striking for his pelvis. The corporal kicked him again. Sartoris knocked the corporal down, where he lay on his back in his clumsy overcoat, tugging at his pocket and snapping his boot at Sartoris' groin. Then the corporal freed his hand and shot point-blank at Sartoris with a short-barreled pistol.

Sartoris sprang upon him before he could shoot again, trampling the pistol hand. He said he could feel the man's bones through his boot, and that the corporal began to scream like a woman behind his brigand's moustaches. That was what made it funny, Sartoris said: that noise coming out of a pair of moustaches like a Gilbert and Sullivan pirate. So he said he stopped it by holding the corporal up with one hand and hitting him on the chin with the other until the noise stopped. He said that the old woman had not ceased to rock back and forth under her starched apron. "Like she might have dressed up to get ready to be sacked and ravaged," he said.

He gathered up the garments. In the bar he had another pull at the bottle, looking at himself in the mirror. Then he saw that he was bleeding at the mouth. He said he didn't know if he had bitten his tongue when he jumped over the stair rail or if he had cut his mouth with the broken bottle neck. He emptied the bottle and flung it to the floor.

He said he didn't know then what he intended to do. He said he didn't realize it even when he had dragged the unconscious driver out of the ambulance and was dressing him in Captain Spoomer's slacks and cap and ribboned tunic, and tumbled him back into the ambulance.

He remembered seeing a dusty inkstand behind the bar. He sought and found in his overalls a bit of paper, a bill rendered him eight months ago by a London tailor, and, leaning on the bar, drooling and spitting, he printed on the back of the bill Captain Spoomer's name and squadron number and aerodrome, and put the paper into the tunic pocket beneath the ribbons and the wing, and drove back to where he had left his aeroplane.

There was an Anzac battalion resting in the ditch beside the road. He left the ambulance and the sleeping passenger with them, and four of them helped him to start his engine, and held the wings for his tight take-off.

Then he was back at the front. He said he did not remember getting there at all; he said the last thing he remembered was the old woman in the field beneath him, then suddenly he was in a barrage, low enough to feel the concussed air between the ground and his wings, and to distinguish the faces of troops. He said he didn't know what troops they were, theirs or ours, but that he strafed them anyway. "Because I never heard of a man on the ground getting hurt by an aeroplane," he said. "Yes, I did; I'll take that back. There was a farmer back in Canada plowing in the middle of a thousand-acre field, and a cadet crashed on top of him."

Then he returned home. They told at the aerodrome that he flew between two hangars in a slow roll, so that they could see the valve stems in both wheels, and that he ran his wheels across the aerodrome and took off again. The gunnery sergeant told me that he climbed vertically until he stalled, and that he held the Camel mushing on its back. "He was watching the dog," the sergeant said. "It had been home about an hour and it was behind the men's mess, grubbing in the refuse bin." He said that Sartoris dived at the dog and then looped, making two turns of an upward spin, coming off on one wing and still upside down. Then the sergeant said that he probably did not set back the air valve, because at a hundred feet the engine conked, and upside down Sartoris cut the tops out of the only two poplar trees they had left.

The sergeant said they ran then, toward the gout of dust and the mess of wire and wood. Before they reached it, he said the dog came trotting out from behind the men's mess. He said the dog got there first and that they saw Sartoris on his hands and knees, vomiting, while the dog watched him. Then the dog approached and sniffed tentatively at the vomit and Sartoris got up and balanced himself and kicked it, weakly but with savage and earnest purpose.

VI

THE AMBULANCE DRIVER, in Spoomer's uniform, was sent back to the aerodrome by the Anzac major. They put him to bed, where he was still sleeping when the brigadier and the Wing Commander came up that afternoon. They were still there when an ox cart turned onto the aerodrome and stopped, with, sitting on a wire cage containing chickens, Spoomer in a woman's skirt and a knitted shawl. The next day Spoomer returned to England. We learned that he was to be a temporary colonel at ground school.

"The dog will like that, anyway," I said.

"The dog?" Sartoris said.

"The food will be better there," I said.

"Oh," Sartoris said. They had reduced him to second lieutenant, for dereliction of duty by entering a forbidden zone with government property and leaving it unguarded, and he had been transferred to another squadron, to the one which even the B.E. people called the Laundry.

This was the day before he left. He had no front teeth at all now, and he apologized for the way he talked, who had never really talked with an intact mouth. "The joke is," he said, "it's another Camel squadron. I have to laugh."

"Laugh?" I said.

"Oh, I can ride them. I can sit there with the gun out and keep the wings level now and then. But I can't fly Camels. You have to land a Camel by setting the air valve and flying it into the ground. Then you count ten, and if you have not crashed, you level off. And if you can get up and walk away, you have made a good landing. And if they can use the crate again, you are an ace. But that's not the joke."

"What's not?"

"The Camels. The joke is, this is a night-flying squadron. I suppose they are all in town and they dont get back until after dark to fly them. They're sending me to a night-flying squadron. That's why I have to laugh."

"I would laugh," I said. "Isn't there something you can do about it?"

"Sure. Just keep that air valve set right and not crash. Not wash out and have those wing flares explode. I've got that beat. I'll just stay up all night, pop the flares and sit down after sunrise. That's why I have to laugh, see. I cant fly Camels in the daytime, even. And they dont know it."

"Well, anyway, you did better than you promised," I said. "You have run him off the continent of Europe."

"Yes," he said. "I sure have to laugh. He's got to go back to England, where all the men are gone. All those women, and not a man between fourteen and eighty to help him. I have to laugh."

VII

WHEN JULY CAME, I was still in the Wing office, still trying to get used to my mechanical leg by sitting at a table equipped with a paper cutter, a pot of glue and one of red ink, and laden with the meager, thin, here soiled and here clean envelopes that came down in periodical batches—envelopes addressed to cities and hamlets and sometimes less than hamlets, about England—when one day I came upon two addressed to the same person in America: a letter and a parcel. I took the letter first. It had neither location nor date:

Dear Aunt Jenny

Yes I got the socks Elnora knitted. They fit all right because I gave them to my batman he said they fit all right. Yes I like it here better than where I was these are good guys here except these damn Camels. I am all right about going to church we dont always have church. Sometimes they have it for the ak emmas because I reckon a ak emma needs it but usually I am pretty busy Sunday but I go enough I reckon. Tell Elnora much oblige for the socks they fit all right but maybe you better not tell her I gave them away. Tell Isom and the other niggers hello and Grandfather tell him I got the money all right but war is expensive as hell.

Johnny.

But then, the Malbroucks dont make the wars, anyway. I suppose it takes too many words to make a war. Maybe that's why.

The package was addressed like the letter, to Mrs Virginia Sartoris, Jefferson, Mississippi, U.S.A., and I thought, What in the world would it ever occur to him to send to her? I could not imagine him choosing a gift for a woman in a foreign country; choosing one of those trifles which some men can choose with a kind of infallible tact. His would be, if he thought to send anything at all, a section of crank shaft or maybe a handful of wrist pins salvaged from a Hun crash. So I opened the package. Then I sat there, looking at the contents.

It contained an addressed envelope, a few dog-eared papers, a wrist watch whose strap was stiff with some dark dried liquid, a pair of goggles without any glass in one lens, a silver belt buckle with a monogram. That was all.

So I didn't need to read the letter. I didn't have to look at the contents of the package, but I wanted to. I didn't want to read the letter, but I had to.

—*Squadron, R.A.F., France.*
5th July, 1918.

Dear Madam,
I have to tell you that your son was killed on yesterday morning. He was shot down while in pursuit of duty over the enemy lines. Not due to carelessness or lack of skill. He was a good man. The E.A. outnumbered your son and had more height and speed which is our misfortune but no fault of the Government which would give us better machines if they had them which is no satisfaction to you. Another of ours, Mr R. Kyerling 1000 feet below could not get up there since your son spent much time in the hangar and had a new engine in his machine last week. Your son took fire in ten seconds Mr Kyerling said and jumped from your son's machine since he was side slipping safely until the E.A. shot away his stabiliser and controls and he began to spin. I am very sad to send you these sad tidings though it may be a comfort to you that he was buried by a minister. His other effects sent you later.

I am, madam, and etc.
C. Kaye Major

He was buried in the cemetary just north of Saint Vaast since we hope it will not be shelled again since we hope it will be over soon by our padre since there were just two Camels and seven E.A. and so it was on our side by that time.
C. K. Mjr.

The other papers were letters, from his great-aunt, not many and not long. I dont know why he had kept them. But he had. Maybe he just forgot them, like he had the bill from the London tailor he had found in his overalls in Amiens that day in the spring.

. . . let those foreign women alone. I lived through a war myself and I know how women act in war, even with Yankees. And a good-for-nothing hellion like you . . .

And this:

. . . we think it's about time you came home. Your grandfather is getting old, and it don't look like they will ever get done fighting over there. So you come on home. The Yankees are in it now. Let them fight if they want to. It's their war. It's not ours.

And that's all. That's it. The courage, the recklessness, call it what you will, is the flash, the instant of sublimation; then flick! the old darkness again. That's why. It's too strong for steady diet. And if it were a steady diet, it would not be a flash, a glare. And so, being momentary, it can be preserved and prolonged only on paper: a picture, a few written words that any match, a minute and harmless flame that any child can engender, can obliterate in an instant. A one-inch sliver of sulphur-tipped wood is longer than memory or grief; a flame no larger than a sixpence is fiercer than courage or despair.

V · THE MIDDLE GROUND

Wash

SUTPEN STOOD ABOVE the pallet bed on which the mother and child lay. Between the shrunken planking of the wall the early sunlight fell in long pencil strokes, breaking upon his straddled legs and upon the riding whip in his hand, and lay across the still shape of the mother, who lay looking up at him from still, inscrutable, sullen eyes, the child at her side wrapped in a piece of dingy though clean cloth. Behind them an old Negro woman squatted beside the rough hearth where a meager fire smoldered.

"Well, Milly," Sutpen said, "too bad you're not a mare. Then I could give you a decent stall in the stable."

Still the girl on the pallet did not move. She merely continued to look up at him without expression, with a young, sullen, inscrutable face still pale from recent travail. Sutpen moved, bringing into the splintered pencils of sunlight the face of a man of sixty. He said quietly to the squatting Negress, "Griselda foaled this morning."

"Horse or mare?" the Negress said.

"A horse. A damned fine colt. . . . What's this?" He indicated the pallet with the hand which held the whip.

"That un's a mare, I reckon."

"Hah," Sutpen said. "A damned fine colt. Going to be the spit and image of old Rob Roy when I rode him North in '61. Do you remember?"

"Yes, Marster."

"Hah." He glanced back towards the pallet. None could have said if the girl still watched him or not. Again his whip hand indicated the pallet. "Do whatever they need with whatever we've got to do it with." He went out, passing out the crazy doorway and stepping down into the rank weeds (there yet leaned rusting against the corner of the porch the scythe which Wash had borrowed from him three months ago to cut them with) where his horse waited, where Wash stood holding the reins.

When Colonel Sutpen rode away to fight the Yankees, Wash did not go. "I'm looking after the Kernel's place and niggers," he would tell all who asked him and some who had not asked—a gaunt, malaria-ridden man with pale, questioning eyes, who looked about thirty-five, though it was known that he had not only a daughter but an eight-year-old granddaughter as well. This was a lie, as most of them—the few remaining men between eighteen and fifty—to whom he told it, knew, though there were some who believed that he himself really believed it, though even these believed that he had better sense than to put it to the test with Mrs. Sutpen or the Sutpen slaves. Knew better or was just too lazy and shiftless to try it, they said, knowing that his sole connection with the Sutpen plantation lay in the fact that for years now Colonel Sutpen had allowed him to squat in a crazy shack on a slough in the river bottom on the Sutpen place, which Sutpen had built for a fishing lodge in his bachelor days and which had since fallen in dilapidation from disuse, so that now it looked like an aged or sick wild beast crawled terrifically there to drink in the act of dying.

The Sutpen slaves themselves heard of his statement. They laughed. It was not the first time they had laughed at him, calling him white trash behind his back. They began to ask him themselves, in groups, meeting him in the faint road which led up from the slough and the old fish camp, "Why ain't you at de war, white man?"

Pausing, he would look about the ring of black faces and white eyes and teeth behind which derision lurked. "Because I got a daughter and family to keep," he said. "Git out of my road, niggers."

"Niggers?" they repeated; "niggers?" laughing now. "Who him, calling us niggers?"

"Yes," he said. "I ain't got no niggers to look after my folks if I was gone."

"Nor nothing else but dat shack down yon dat Cunnel wouldn't *let* none of us live in."

Now he cursed them; sometimes he rushed at them, snatching up a stick from the ground while they scattered before him, yet seeming to surround him still with that black laughing, derisive, evasive, inescapable, leaving him panting and impotent and raging. Once it happened in the very back yard of the big house itself. This was after bitter news had come down from the Tennessee mountains and from Vicksburg, and Sherman had passed through the plantation, and most of the Negroes had followed him. Almost everything else had gone with the Federal troops, and Mrs. Sutpen had sent word to Wash that he could have the scuppernongs ripening in the arbor in the back yard. This time it was a house servant, one of the few Negroes who remained; this time the Negress had to retreat up the kitchen steps, where she turned. "Stop right dar, white man. Stop right whar you is. You ain't never crossed dese steps whilst Cunnel here, and you ain't ghy' do hit now."

This was true. But there was this of a kind of pride: he had never tried to enter the big house, even though he believed that if he had, Sutpen would have received him, permitted him. "But I ain't going to give no black nigger the

chance to tell me I can't go nowhere," he said to himself.
"I ain't even going to give Kernel the chance to have to
cuss a nigger on my account." This, though he and Sutpen
had spent more than one afternoon together on those rare
Sundays when there would be no company in the house.
Perhaps his mind knew that it was because Sutpen had nothing else to do, being a man who could not bear his own
company. Yet the fact remained that the two of them would
spend whole afternoons in the scuppernong arbor, Sutpen
in the hammock and Wash squatting against a post, a pail of
cistern water between them, taking drink for drink from
the same demijohn. Meanwhile on weekdays he would see
the fine figure of the man—they were the same age almost
to a day, though neither of them (perhaps because Wash
had a grandchild while Sutpen's son was a youth in school)
ever thought of himself as being so—on the fine figure of
the black stallion, galloping about the plantation. For that
moment his heart would be quiet and proud. It would seem
to him that that world in which Negroes, whom the Bible
told him had been created and cursed by God to be brute
and vassal to all men of white skin, were better found and
housed and even clothed than he and his; that world in which
he sensed always about him mocking echoes of black laughter was but a dream and an illusion, and that the actual
world was this one across which his own lonely apotheosis
seemed to gallop on the black thoroughbred, thinking how
the Book said also that all men were created in the image of
God and hence all men made the same image in God's eyes
at least; so that he could say, as though speaking of himself,
"A fine proud man. If God Himself was to come down and
ride the natural earth, that's what He would aim to look
like."

Sutpen returned in 1865, on the black stallion. He seemed
to have aged ten years. His son had been killed in action the

same winter in which his wife had died. He returned with his citation for gallantry from the hand of General Lee to a ruined plantation, where for a year now his daughter had subsisted partially on the meager bounty of the man to whom fifteen years ago he had granted permission to live in that tumbledown fishing camp whose very existence he had at the time forgotten. Wash was there to meet him, unchanged: still gaunt, still ageless, with his pale, questioning gaze, his air diffident, a little servile, a little familiar. "Well, Kernel," Wash said, "they kilt us but they ain't whupped us yit, air they?"

That was the tenor of their conversation for the next five years. It was inferior whisky which they drank now together from a stoneware jug, and it was not in the scuppernong arbor. It was in the rear of the little store which Sutpen managed to set up on the highroad: a frame shelved room where, with Wash for clerk and porter, he dispensed kerosene and staple foodstuffs and stale gaudy candy and cheap beads and ribbons to Negroes or poor whites of Wash's own kind, who came afoot or on gaunt mules to haggle tediously for dimes and quarters with a man who at one time could gallop (the black stallion was still alive; the stable in which his jealous get lived was in better repair than the house where the master himself lived) for ten miles across his own fertile land and who had led troops gallantly in battle; until Sutpen in fury would empty the store, close and lock the doors from the inside. Then he and Wash would repair to the rear and the jug. But the talk would not be quiet now, as when Sutpen lay in the hammock, delivering an arrogant monologue while Wash squatted guffawing against his post. They both sat now, though Sutpen had the single chair while Wash used whatever box or keg was handy, and even this for just a little while, because soon Sutpen would reach that stage of impotent and furious un-defeat in which he would rise, swaying and plunging, and declare again that he would take his pistol and the black stallion and ride single-handed into Washington and kill Lincoln, dead now, and Sherman, now a private citizen. "Kill them!" he would shout. "Shoot them down like the dogs they are—"

"Sho, Kernel; sho, Kernel," Wash would say, catching Sutpen as he fell. Then he would commandeer the first passing wagon or, lacking that, he would walk the mile to the nearest neighbor and borrow one and return and carry Sutpen home. He entered the house now. He had been doing so for a long time, taking Sutpen home in whatever borrowed wagon might be, talking him into locomotion with cajoling murmurs as though he were a horse, a stallion himself. The daughter would meet them and hold open the door without a word. He would carry his burden through the once white formal entrance, surmounted by a fanlight imported piece by piece from Europe and with a board now nailed over a missing pane, across a velvet carpet from which all nap was now gone, and up a formal stairs, now but a fading ghost of bare boards between two strips of fading paint, and into the bedroom. It would be dusk by now, and he would let his burden sprawl onto the bed and undress it and then he would sit quietly in a chair beside. After a time the daughter would come to the door. "We're all right now," he would tell her. "Don't you worry none, Miss Judith."

Then it would become dark, and after a while he would lie down on the floor beside the bed, though not to sleep, because after a time—sometimes before midnight—the man on the bed would stir and groan and then speak. "Wash?"

"Hyer I am, Kernel. You go back to sleep. We ain't whupped yit, air we? Me and you kin do hit."

Even then he had already seen the ribbon about his granddaughter's waist. She was now fifteen, already mature, after the early way of her kind. He knew where the ribbon came from; he had been seeing it and its kind daily for three years, even if she had lied about where she got it, which she did not, at once bold, sullen, and fearful. "Sho now," he said. "Ef Kernel wants to give hit to you, I hope you minded to thank him."

His heart was quiet, even when he saw the dress, watching her secret, defiant, frightened face when she told him that Miss Judith, the daughter, had helped her to make it. But he was quite grave when he approached Sutpen after they closed the store that afternoon, following the other to the rear.

"Get the jug," Sutpen directed.

"Wait," Wash said. "Not yit for a minute."

Neither did Sutpen deny the dress. "What about it?" he said.

But Wash met his arrogant stare; he spoke quietly. "I've knowed you for going on twenty years. I ain't never yit denied to do what you told me to do. And I'm a man nigh sixty. And she ain't nothing but a fifteen-year-old gal."

"Meaning that I'd harm a girl? I, a man as old as you are?"

"If you was ara other man, I'd say you was as old as me. And old or no old, I wouldn't let her keep that dress nor nothing else that come from your hand. But you are different."

"How different?" But Wash merely looked at him with his pale, questioning, sober eyes. "So that's why you are afraid of me?"

Now Wash's gaze no longer questioned. It was tranquil, serene. "I ain't afraid. Because you air brave. It ain't that you were a brave man at one minute or day of your life and got a paper to show hit from General Lee. But you air brave, the same as you air alive and breathing. That's where hit's different. Hit don't need no ticket from nobody to tell me that. And I know that whatever you handle or tech, whether hit's a regiment of men or a ignorant gal or just a hound dog, that you will make hit right."

Now it was Sutpen who looked away, turning suddenly, brusquely. "Get the jug," he said sharply.

"Sho, Kernel," Wash said.

So on that Sunday dawn two years later, having watched the Negro midwife, which he had walked three miles to fetch, enter the crazy door beyond which his granddaughter lay wailing, his heart was still quiet though concerned. He knew what they had been saying—the Negroes in cabins about the land, the white men who loafed all day long about the store, watching quietly the three of them: Sutpen, himself, his granddaughter with her air of brazen and shrinking defiance as her condition became daily more and more obvious, like three actors that came and went upon a stage. "I know what they say to one another," he thought. "I can almost hyear them: *Wash Jones has fixed old Sutpen at last. Hit taken him twenty years, but he has done hit at last.*"

It would be dawn after a while, though not yet. From the house, where the lamp shone dim beyond the warped doorframe, his granddaughter's voice came steadily as though run by a clock, while thinking went slowly and terrifically, fumbling, involved somehow with a sound of galloping hooves, until there broke suddenly free in mid-gallop the fine proud figure of the man on the fine proud stallion, galloping; and then that at which thinking fumbled, broke free too and quite clear, not in justification nor even explanation, but as the apotheosis, lonely, explicable, beyond all fouling by human touch: "He is bigger than all them Yankees that kilt his son and his wife and taken his niggers and ruined his land, bigger than this hyer durn country that he fit for and that has denied him into keeping a little country store; bigger than the denial which hit helt to his lips like the bitter cup in the Book. And how could I have lived this nigh to him for twenty years without being teched and changed by him? Maybe I ain't as big as him and maybe I ain't done none of the galloping. But at least I done been drug along. Me and him kin do hit, if so be he will show me what he aims for me to do."

Then it was dawn. Suddenly he could see the house, and the old Negress in the door looking at him. Then he realized that his granddaughter's voice had ceased. "It's a girl," the Negress said. "You can go tell him if you want to." She re-entered the house.

"A girl," he repeated; "a girl"; in astonishment, hearing the galloping hooves, seeing the proud galloping figure emerge again. He seemed to watch it pass, galloping through avatars which marked the accumulation of years, time, to the climax where it galloped beneath a brandished saber and a shot-torn flag rushing down a sky in color like thunderous sulphur, thinking for the first time in his life that perhaps Sutpen was an old man like himself. "Gittin a gal," he thought in that astonishment; then he thought with the pleased surprise of a child: "Yes, sir. Be dawg if I ain't lived to be a great-grandpaw after all."

He entered the house. He moved clumsily, on tiptoe, as if he no longer lived there, as if the infant which had just drawn breath and cried in light had dispossessed him, be it of his own blood too though it might. But even above the pallet he could see little save the blur of his granddaughter's exhausted face. Then the Negress squatting at the hearth spoke, "You better gawn tell him if you going to. Hit's daylight now."

But this was not necessary. He had no more than turned the corner of the porch where the scythe leaned which he had borrowed three months ago to clear away the weeds through which he walked, when Sutpen himself rode up on the old stallion. He did not wonder how Sutpen had got the word. He took it for granted that this was what had brought the other out at this hour on Sunday morning, and he stood while the other dismounted, and he took the reins from Sutpen's hand, an expression on his gaunt face almost imbecile with a kind of weary triumph, saying, "Hit's a gal, Kernel. I be dawg if you ain't as old as I am—" until Sutpen passed him and entered the house. He stood there with the reins in his hand and heard Sutpen cross the floor to the pallet. He heard what Sutpen said, and something seemed to stop dead in him before going on.

The sun was now up, the swift sun of Mississippi latitudes, and it seemed to him that he stood beneath a strange sky, in a strange scene, familiar only as things are familiar in dreams, like the dreams of falling to one who has never climbed. "I kain't have heard what I thought I heard," he thought quietly. "I know I kain't." Yet the voice, the familiar voice which had said the words was still speaking, talking now to the old Negress about a colt foaled that morning. "That's why he was up so early," he thought. "That was hit. Hit ain't me and mine. Hit ain't even hisn that got him outen bed."

Sutpen emerged. He descended into the weeds, moving with that heavy deliberation which would have been haste when he was younger. He had not yet looked full at Wash. He said, "Dicey will stay and tend to her. You better—" Then he seemed to see Wash facing him and paused. "What?" he said.

"You said—" To his own ears Wash's voice sounded flat and ducklike, like a deaf man's. "You said if she was a mare, you could give her a good stall in the stable."

"Well?" Sutpen said. His eyes widened and narrowed,

almost like a man's fists flexing and shutting, as Wash began to advance towards him, stooping a little. Very astonishment kept Sutpen still for the moment, watching that man whom in twenty years he had no more known to make any motion save at command than he had the horse which he rode. Again his eyes narrowed and widened; without moving he seemed to rear suddenly upright. "Stand back," he said suddenly and sharply. "Don't you touch me."

"I'm going to tech you, Kernel," Wash said in that flat, quiet, almost soft voice, advancing.

Sutpen raised the hand which held the riding whip; the old Negress peered around the crazy door with her black gargoyle face of a worn gnome. "Stand back, Wash," Sutpen said. Then he struck. The old Negress leaped down into the weeds with the agility of a goat and fled. Sutpen slashed Wash again across the face with the whip, striking him to his knees. When Wash rose and advanced once more he held in his hands the scythe which he had borrowed from Sutpen three months ago and which Sutpen would never need again.

When he reëntered the house his granddaughter stirred on the pallet bed and called his name fretfully. "What was that?" she said.

"What was what, honey?"

"That ere racket out there."

" 'Twarn't nothing," he said gently. He knelt and touched her hot forehead clumsily. "Do you want ara thing?"

"I want a sup of water," she said querulously. "I been laying here wanting a sup of water a long time, but don't nobody care enough to pay me no mind."

"Sho now," he said soothingly. He rose stiffly and fetched the dipper of water and raised her head to drink and laid her back and watched her turn to the child with an absolutely stonelike face. But a moment later he saw that she was crying quietly. "Now, now," he said, "I wouldn't do that. Old Dicey says hit's a right fine gal. Hit's all right now. Hit's all over now. Hit ain't no need to cry now."

But she continued to cry quietly, almost sullenly, and he rose again and stood uncomfortably above the pallet for a time, thinking as he had thought when his own wife lay so and then his daughter in turn: "Women. Hit's a mystry to me. They seem to want em, and yit when they git em they cry about hit. Hit's a mystry to me. To ara man." Then he moved away and drew a chair up to the window and sat down.

Through all that long, bright, sunny forenoon he sat at the window, waiting. Now and then he rose and tiptoed to the pallet. But his granddaughter slept now, her face sullen and calm and weary, the child in the crook of her arm. Then he returned to the chair and sat again, waiting, wondering why it took them so long, until he remembered that it was Sunday. He was sitting there at mid-afternoon when a half-grown white boy came around the corner of the house upon the body and gave a choked cry and looked up and glared for a mesmerized instant at Wash in the window before he turned and fled. Then Wash rose and tiptoed again to the pallet.

The granddaughter was awake now, wakened perhaps by the boy's cry without hearing it. "Milly," he said, "air you hungry?" She didn't answer, turning her face away. He built up the fire on the hearth and cooked the food which he had brought home the day before: fatback it was, and cold corn pone; he poured water into the stale coffee pot and heated it. But she would not eat when he carried the plate to her, so he ate himself, quietly, alone, and left the dishes as they were and returned to the window.

Now he seemed to sense, feel, the men who would be gathering with horses and guns and dogs—the curious, and

the vengeful: men of Sutpen's own kind, who had made
the company about Sutpen's table in the time when Wash
himself had yet to approach nearer to the house than the
scuppernong arbor—men who had also shown the lesser
ones how to fight in battle, who maybe also had signed
papers from the generals saying that they were among the
first of the brave; who had also galloped in the old days
arrogant and proud on the fine horses across the fine plantations—symbols also of admiration and hope; instruments too
of despair and grief.

That was whom they would expect him to run from. It
seemed to him that he had no more to run from than he had
to run to. If he ran, he would merely be fleeing one set of
bragging and evil shadows for another just like them, since
they were all of a kind throughout all the earth which he
knew, and he was old, too old to flee far even if he were to
flee. He could never escape them, no matter how much or
how far he ran: a man going on sixty could not run that
far. Not far enough to escape beyond the boundaries of
earth where such men lived, set the order and the rule of
living. It seemed to him that he now saw for the first time,
after five years, how it was that Yankees or any other living
armies had managed to whip them: the gallant, the proud,
the brave; the acknowledged and chosen best among them
all to carry courage and honor and pride. Maybe if he had
gone to the war with them he would have discovered them
sooner. But if he had discovered them sooner, what would
he have done with his life since? How could he have borne
to remember for five years what his life had been before?

Now it was getting toward sunset. The child had been
crying; when he went to the pallet he saw his granddaughter
nursing it, her face still bemused, sullen, inscrutable. "Air
you hungry yit?" he said.

"I don't want nothing."

"You ought to eat."

This time she did not answer at all, looking down at the child. He returned to his chair and found that the sun had set. "Hit kain't be much longer," he thought. He could feel them quite near now, the curious and the vengeful. He could even seem to hear what they were saying about him, the undercurrent of believing beyond the immediate fury: *Old Wash Jones he come a tumble at last. He thought he had Sutpen, but Sutpen fooled him. He thought he had Kernel where he would have to marry the gal or pay up. And Kernel refused.* "But I never expected that, Kernel!" he cried aloud, catching himself at the sound of his own voice, glancing quickly back to find his granddaughter watching him.

"Who you talking to now?" she said.

"Hit ain't nothing. I was just thinking and talked out before I knowed hit."

Her face was becoming indistinct again, again a sullen blur in the twilight. "I reckon so. I reckon you'll have to holler louder than that before he'll hear you, up yonder at that house. And I reckon you'll need to do more than holler before you get him down here too."

"Sho now," he said. "Don't you worry none." But already thinking was going smoothly on: "You know I never. You know how I ain't never expected or asked nothing from ara living man but what I expected from you. And I never asked that. I didn't think hit would need. I said, *I don't need to. What need has a fellow like Wash Jones to question or doubt the man that General Lee himself says in a handwrote ticket that he was brave?* Brave," he thought. "Better if nara one of them had never rid back home in '65"; thinking *Better if his kind and mine too had never drawn the breath of life on this earth. Better that all who remain of us be blasted from the face of earth than that another Wash Jones*

*should see his whole life shredded from him and shrivel
away like a dried shuck thrown onto the fire.*

He ceased, became still. He heard the horses, suddenly
and plainly; presently he saw the lantern and the movement
of men, the glint of gun barrels, in its moving light. Yet
he did not stir. It was quite dark now, and he listened to
the voices and the sounds of underbrush as they surrounded
the house. The lantern itself came on; its light fell upon the
quiet body in the weeds and stopped, the horses tall and
shadowy. A man descended and stooped in the lantern light,
above the body. He held a pistol; he rose and faced the
house. "Jones," he said.

"I'm here," Wash said quietly from the window. "That
you, Major?"

"Come out."

"Sho," he said quietly. "I just want to see to my granddaughter."

"We'll see to her. Come on out."

"Sho, Major. Just a minute."

"Show a light. Light your lamp."

"Sho. In just a minute." They could hear his voice retreat
into the house, though they could not see him as he went
swiftly to the crack in the chimney where he kept the
butcher knife: the one thing in his slovenly life and house
in which he took pride, since it was razor sharp. He approached the pallet, his granddaughter's voice:

"Who is it? Light the lamp, grandpaw."

"Hit won't need no light, honey. Hit won't take but a
minute," he said, kneeling, fumbling toward her voice,
whispering now. "Where air you?"

"Right here," she said fretfully. "Where would I be?
What is . . ." His hand touched her face. "What is . . .
Grandpaw! Grand. . . ."

"Jones!" the sheriff said. "Come out of there!"

"In just a minute, Major," he said. Now he rose and moved swiftly. He knew where in the dark the can of kerosene was, just as he knew that it was full, since it was not two days ago that he had filled it at the store and held it there until he got a ride home with it, since the five gallons were heavy. There were still coals on the hearth; besides, the crazy building itself was like tinder: the coals, the hearth, the walls exploding in a single blue glare. Against it the waiting men saw him in a wild instant springing toward them with the lifted scythe before the horses reared and whirled. They checked the horses and turned them back toward the glare, yet still in wild relief against it the gaunt figure ran toward them with the lifted scythe.

"Jones!" the sheriff shouted; "stop! Stop, or I'll shoot. Jones! *Jones!*" Yet still the gaunt, furious figure came on against the glare and roar of the flames. With the scythe lifted, it bore down upon them, upon the wild glaring eyes of the horses and the swinging glints of gun barrels, without any cry, any sound.

Honor

I WALKED right through the anteroom without stopping. Miss West says, "He's in conference now," but I didn't stop. I didn't knock, either. They were talking and he quit and looked up across the desk at me.

"How much notice do you want to write me off?" I said.

"Write you off?" he said.

"I'm quitting," I said. "Will one day be notice enough?"

He looked at me, frog-eyed. "Isn't our car good enough for you to demonstrate?" he said. His hand lay on the desk, holding the cigar. He's got a ruby ring the size of a tail-light. "You've been with us three weeks," he says. "Not long enough to learn what that word on the door means."

He don't know it, but three weeks is pretty good; it's within two days of the record. And if three weeks is a record with him, he could have shaken hands with the new champion without moving.

The trouble is, I had never learned to do anything. You know how it was in those days, with even the college campuses full of British and French uniforms, and us all scared to death it would be over before we could get in and swank a pair of pilot's wings ourselves. And then to get in and find something that suited you right down to the ground, you see.

So after the Armistice I stayed in for a couple of years as

a test pilot. That was when I took up wing-walking, to relieve the monotony. A fellow named Waldrip and I used to hide out at about three thousand on a Nine while I muscled around on top of it. Because Army life is pretty dull in peacetime: nothing to do but lay around and lie your head off all day and play poker all night. And isolation is bad for poker. You lose on tick, and on tick you always plunge.

There was a fellow named White lost a thousand one night. He kept on losing and I wanted to quit but I was winner and he wanted to play on, plunging and losing every pot. He gave me a check and I told him it wasn't any rush, to forget it, because he had a wife out in California. Then the next night he wanted to play again. I tried to talk him out of it, but he got mad. Called me yellow. So he lost fifteen hundred more that night.

Then I said I'd cut him, double or quit, one time. He cut a queen. So I said, "Well, that beats me. I won't even cut." And I flipped his cut over and riffled them and we saw a gob of face cards and three of the aces. But he insisted, and I said, "What's the use? The percentage would be against me, even with a full deck." But he insisted. I cut the case ace. I would have paid to lose. I offered again to tear up the checks, but he sat there and cursed me. I left him sitting at the table, in his shirt sleeves and his collar open, looking at the ace.

The next day we had the job, the speed ship. I had done everything I could. I couldn't offer him the checks again. I will let a man who is worked up curse me once. But I won't let him twice. So we had the job, the speed ship. I wouldn't touch it. He took it up five thousand feet and dived the wings off at two thousand with a full gun.

So I was out again after four years, a civ again. And while I was still drifting around—that was when I first tried selling automobiles—I met Jack, and he told me about a bird that wanted a wing-walker for his barn-storming circus. And that was how I met her.

II

JACK—he gave me a note to Rogers—told me about what a good pilot Rogers was, and about her, how they said she was unhappy with him.

"So is your old man," I said.

"That's what they say," Jack said. So when I saw Rogers and handed him the note—he was one of these lean, quiet-looking birds—I said to myself he was just the kind that would marry one of these flighty, passionate, good-looking women they used to catch during the war with a set of wings, and have her run out on him the first chance. So I felt safe. I knew she'd not have had to wait any three years for one like me.

So I expected to find one of these long, dark, snake-like women surrounded by ostrich plumes and Woolworth incense, smoking cigarettes on the divan while Rogers ran out to the corner delicatessen for sliced ham and potato salad on paper plates. But I was wrong. She came in with an apron on over one of these little pale squashy dresses, with flour or something on her arms, without apologizing or flurrying around or anything. She said Howard—that was Rogers—had told her about me and I said, "What did he tell you?" But she just said:

"I expect you'll find this pretty dull for spending the evening, having to help cook your own dinner. I imagine you'd rather go out to dance with a couple of bottles of gin."

"Why do you think that?" I said. "Don't I look like I could do anything else?"

"Oh, don't you?" she said.

We had washed the dishes then and we were sitting in the

firelight, with the lights off, with her on a cushion on the floor, her back against Rogers' knees, smoking and talking, and she said, "I know you had a dull time. Howard suggested that we go out for dinner and to dance somewhere. But I told him you'd just have to take us as we are, first as well as later. Are you sorry?"

She could look about sixteen, especially in the apron. By that time she had bought one for me to wear, and the three of us would all go back to the kitchen and cook dinner. "We don't expect you to enjoy doing this any more than we do," she said. "It's because we are so poor. We're just an aviator."

"Well, Howard can fly well enough for two people," I said. "So that's all right, too."

"When he told me you were just a flyer too, I said, 'My Lord, a wing-walker? When you were choosing a family friend,' I said, 'why didn't you choose a man we could invite to dinner a week ahead and not only count on his being there, but on his taking us out and spending his money on us?' But he had to choose one that is as poor as we are." And once she said to Rogers: "We'll have to find Buck a girl, too. He's going to get tired of just us some day." You know how they say things like that: things that sound like they meant something until you look at them and find their eyes perfectly blank, until you wonder if they were even thinking about you, let alone talking about you.

Or maybe I'd have them out to dinner and a show. "Only I didn't mean that like it sounded," she said. "That wasn't a hint to take us out."

"Did you mean that about getting me a girl too?" I said.

Then she looked at me with that wide, blank, innocent look. That was when I would take them by my place for a cocktail—Rogers didn't drink, himself—and when I would come in that night I'd find traces of powder on my dresser or maybe her handkerchief or something, and I'd go to bed with the room smelling like she was still there. She said: "Do you want us to find you one?" But nothing more was ever said about it, and after a while, when there was a high step or any of those little things which men do for women that means touching them, she'd turn to me like it was me was her husband and not him; and one night a storm caught us downtown and we went to my place and she and Rogers slept in my bed and I slept in a chair in the sitting-room.

One evening I was dressing to go out there when the 'phone rang. It was Rogers. "I am—" he said, then something cut him off. It was like somebody had put a hand on his mouth, and I could hear them talking, murmuring: her, rather. "Well, what—" Rogers says. Then I could hear her breathing into the mouth-piece, and she said my name.

"Don't forget you're to come out to-night," she said.

"I hadn't," I said. "Or did I get the date wrong? If this is not the night—"

"You come on out," she said. "Goodbye."

When I got there he met me. His face looked like it always did, but I didn't go in. "Come on in," he said.

"Maybe I got the date wrong," I said. "So if you'll just—"

He swung the door back. "Come on in," he said.

She was lying on the divan, crying. I don't know what; something about money. "I just can't stick it," she said. "I've tried and I've tried, but I just can't stand it."

"You know what my insurance rates are," he said. "If something happened, where would you be?"

"Where am I, anyway? What tenement woman hasn't got more than I have?" She hadn't looked up, lying there on her face, with the apron twisted under her. "Why don't you quit and do something that you can get a decent insurance rate, like other men?"

"I must be getting along," I said. I didn't belong there. I just got out. He came down to the door with me, and then we were both looking back up the stairs toward the door where she was lying on her face on the couch.

"I've got a little stake," I said. "I guess because I've eaten so much of your grub I haven't had time to spend it. So if it's anything urgent. . . ." We stood there, he holding the door open. "Of course, I wouldn't try to muscle in where I don't . . ."

"I wouldn't, if I were you," he said. He opened the door. "See you at the field tomorrow."

"Sure," I said. "See you at the field."

I didn't see her for almost a week, didn't hear from her. I saw him every day, and at last I said, "How's Mildred these days?"

"She's on a visit," he said. "At her mother's."

For the next two weeks I was with him every day. When I was out on top I'd look back at his face behind the goggles. But we never mentioned her name, until one day he told me she was home again and that I was invited out to dinner that night.

It was in the afternoon. He was busy all that day hopping passengers, so I was doing nothing, just killing time waiting for evening and thinking about her, wondering some, but mostly just thinking about her being home again, breathing the same smoke and soot I was breathing, when all of a sudden I decided to go out there. It was plain as a voice saying, "Go out there. Now, at once." So I went. I didn't even wait to change. She was alone, reading before the fire. It was like gasoline from a broken line blazing up around you.

III

IT WAS FUNNY. When I'd be out on top I'd look back at his face behind the windscreen, wondering what he knew. He must have known almost at once. Why, say, she didn't have any discretion at all. She'd say and do things, you know: insist on sitting close to me; touching me in that different way from when you hold an umbrella or a raincoat over them, and such that any man can tell at one look, when she thought he might not see: not when she knew he couldn't, but when she thought *maybe* he wouldn't. And when I'd unfasten my belt and crawl out I'd look back at his face and wonder what he was thinking, how much he knew or suspected.

I'd go out there in the afternoon when he was busy. I'd stall around until I saw that he would be lined up for the rest of the day, then I'd give some excuse and beat it. One afternoon I was all ready to go, waiting for him to take off, when he cut the gun and leaned out and beckoned me. "Don't go off," he said. "I want to see you."

So I knew he knew then, and I waited until he made the last hop and was taking off his monkey suit in the office. He looked at me and I looked at him. "Come out to dinner," he said.

When I came in they were waiting. She had on one of those little squashy dresses and she came and put her arms around me and kissed me with him watching.

"I'm going with you," she said. "We've talked it over and have both agreed that we couldn't love one another any more after this and that this is the only sensible thing to do. Then he can find a woman he can love, a woman that's not bad like I am."

He was looking at me, and she running her hands over my face and making a little moaning sound against my neck, and me like a stone or something. Do you know what I was thinking? I wasn't thinking about her at all. I was thinking that he and I were upstairs and me out on top and I had just found that he had thrown the stick away and was flying her on the rudder alone and that he knew that I knew the stick was gone and so it was all right now, whatever happened. So it was like a piece of wood with another piece of wood leaning against it, and she held back and looked at my face.

"Don't you love me any more?" she said, watching my face. "If you love me, say so. I have told him everything."

I wanted to be out of there. I wanted to run. I wasn't scared. It was because it was all kind of hot and dirty. I wanted to be away from her a little while, for Rogers and me to be out where it was cold and hard and quiet, to settle things.

"What do you want to do?" I said. "Will you give her a divorce?"

She was watching my face very closely. Then she let me go and she ran to the mantel and put her face into the bend of her arm, crying.

"You were lying to me," she said. "You didn't mean what you said. Oh God, what have I done?"

You know how it is. Like there is a right time for everything. Like nobody is anything in himself: like a woman, even when you love her, is a woman to you just a part of the time and the rest of the time she is just a person that don't look at things the same way a man has learned to. Don't have the same ideas about what is decent and what is not. So I went over and stood with my arms about her, thinking, "God damn it, if you'll just keep out of this for a little while! We're both trying our best to take care of you, so it won't hurt you."

Because I loved her, you see. Nothing can marry two people closer than a mutual sin in the world's eyes. And he had had his chance. If it had been me that knew her first and married her and he had been me, I would have had my chance. But it was him that had had it, so when she said, "Then say what you tell me when we are alone. I tell you I have told him everything," I said.

"Everything? Have you told him everything?" He was watching us. "Has she told you everything?" I said.

"It doesn't matter," he said. "Do you want her?" Then before I could speak, he said: "Do you love her? Will you be good to her?"

His face was gray-looking, like when you see a man again after a long time and you say, "Good God, is that Rogers?" When I finally got away the divorce was all settled.

IV

So THE NEXT MORNING when I reached the field, Harris, the man who owned the flying circus, told me about the special job; I had forgotten it, I suppose. Anyway, he said he had told me about it. Finally I said I wouldn't fly with Rogers.

"Why not?" Harris said.

"Ask him," I said.

"If he agrees to fly you, will you go up?"

So I said yes. And then Rogers came out; he said that he would fly me. And so I believed that he had known about the job all the time and had laid for me, sucked me in. We waited until Harris went out. "So this is why you were so mealy-mouthed last night," I said. I cursed him. "You've got me now, haven't you?"

"Take the stick yourself," he said. "I'll do your trick."

"Have you ever done any work like this before?"

"No. But I can, as long as you fly her properly."

I cursed him. "You feel good," I said. "You've got me. Come on; grin on the outside of your face. Come on!"

He turned and went to the crate and began to get into the front seat. I went and caught his shoulder and jerked him back. We looked at one another.

"I won't hit you now," he said, "if that's what you want. Wait till we get down again."

"No," I said. "Because I want to hit back once."

We looked at one another; Harris was watching us from the office.

"All right," Rogers said. "Let me have your shoes, will you? I haven't got any rubber soles out here."

"Take your seat," I said. "What the hell does it matter? I guess I'd do the same thing in your place."

The job was over an amusement park, a carnival. There must have been twenty-five thousand of them down there, like colored ants. I took chances that day that I had never taken, chances you can't see from the ground. But every time the ship was right under me, balancing me against side pressure and all, like he and I were using the same mind. I thought he was playing with me, you see. I'd look back at his face, yelling at him: "Come on; now you've got me. Where are your guts?"

I was a little crazy, I guess. Anyway, when I think of the two of us up there, yelling back and forth at one another, and all the little bugs watching and waiting for the big show, the loop. He could hear me, but I couldn't hear him; I could just see his lips moving. "Come on," I'd yell; "shake the wing a little; I'll go off easy, see?"

I was a little crazy. You know how it is, how you want to rush into something you know is going to happen, no matter what it is. I guess lovers and suicides both know that feeling. I'd yell back at him: "You want it to look all right, eh? And to lose me off the level ship wouldn't look so good, would it? All right," I yelled, "let's go." I went back to the center section and cast the rope loose where it loops around the forward jury struts and I got set against it and looked back at him and gave him the signal. I was a little crazy. I was still yelling at him; I don't know what I was yelling. I thought maybe I had already fallen off and was dead and didn't know it. The wires began to whine and I was looking straight down at the ground and the little colored dots. Then the wires were whistling proper and he gunned her and the ground began to slide back under the nose. I waited until it was gone and the horizon had slid back under too and I couldn't see anything but sky. Then I let go one end of the rope and jerked it out and threw it back at his head and held my arms out as she zoomed into the loop.

I wasn't trying to kill myself. I wasn't thinking about myself. I was thinking about him. Trying to show him up like he had shown me up. Give him something he must fail at like he had given me something I failed at. I was trying to break him.

We were over the loop before he lost me. The ground had come back, with the little colored dots, and then the pressure went off my soles and I was falling. I made a half somersault and was just going into the first turn of a flat spin, with my face to the sky, when something banged me in the back. It knocked the wind out of me, and for a second I must have been completely out. Then I opened my eyes and I was lying on my back on the top wing, with my head hanging over the back edge.

I was too far down the slope of the camber to bend my knees over the leading edge, and I could feel the wing creeping under me. I didn't dare move. I knew that if I tried to sit up against the slip stream, I would go off backward. I could see by the tail and the horizon that we were upside now, in a shallow dive, and I could see Rogers standing up in his cockpit, unfastening his belt, and I could turn my head a little more and see that when I went off I would miss the fuselage altogether, or maybe hit it with my shoulder.

So I lay there with the wing creeping under me, feeling my shoulders beginning to hang over space, counting my backbones as they crept over the edge, watching Rogers crawl forward along the fuselage toward the front seat. I watched him for a long time, inching himself along against the pressure, his trouser-legs whipping. After a while I saw his legs slide into the front cockpit and then I felt his hands on me.

There was a fellow in my squadron. I didn't like him and he hated my guts. All right. One day he got me out of a tight jam when I was caught ten miles over the lines with a blowing valve. When we were down he said, "Don't think I was just digging you out. I was getting a Hun, and I got him." He cursed me, with his goggles cocked up and his hands on his hips, cursing me like he was smiling. But that's all right. You're each on a Camel; if you go out, that's too bad; if he goes out, it's just too bad. Not like when you're on the center section and he's at the stick, and just by stalling her for a second or ruddering her a little at the top of the loop.

But I was young, then. Good Lord, I used to be young! I remember Armistice night in '18, and me chasing all over Amiens with a lousy prisoner we had brought down that morning on an Albatross, trying to keep the frog M.P.'s from getting him. He was a good guy, and those damned infantrymen wanting to stick him in a pen full of S. O. S. and ginned-up cooks and such. I felt sorry for the bastard, being so far from home and licked and all. I was sure young.

We were all young. I remember an Indian, a prince, an Oxford man, with his turban and his trick major's pips, that said we were all dead that fought in the war. "You will not know it," he said, "but you are all dead. With this difference: those out there"—jerking his arm toward where the front was—"do not care, and you do not know it." And something else he said, about breathing for a long time yet, some kind of walking funerals; catafalques and tombs and epitaphs of men that died on the fourth of August, 1914, without knowing that they had died, he said. He was a card, queer. A good little guy, too.

But I wasn't quite dead while I was lying on the top wing of that Standard and counting my backbones as they crawled over the edge like a string of ants, until Rogers grabbed me. And when he came to the station that night to say goodbye, he brought me a letter from her, the first I ever had. The handwriting looked exactly like her; I could almost smell the scent she used and feel her hands touching me. I tore it in two without opening it and threw the pieces down. But he picked them up and gave them back to me. "Don't be a fool," he said.

And that's all. They've got a kid now, a boy of six. Rogers wrote me; about six months afterward the letter caught up with me. I'm his godfather. Funny to have a godfather that's never seen you and that you'll never see, isn't it?

V

So I said to Reinhardt: "Will one day be enough notice?"

"One minute will be enough," he said. He pressed the buzzer. Miss West came in. She is a good kid. Now and then, when I'd just have to blow off some steam, she and I would have lunch at the dairy place across the street, and I could tell her about them, about the women. They are the worst. You know; you get a call for a demonstration, and there'll be a whole car full of them waiting on the porch and we'd pile in and all go shopping. Me dodging around in the traffic, hunting a place to park, and her saying, "John insisted that I try this car. But what I tell him, it's foolish to buy a car that is as difficult to find parking space for as this one appears to be."

And them watching the back of my head with that bright, hard, suspicious way. God knows what they thought we had; maybe one that would fold up like a deck chair and lean against a fire plug. But hell, I couldn't sell hair straightener to the widow of a nigger railroad accident.

So Miss West comes in; she is a good kid, only somebody told her I had had three or four other jobs in a year without sticking, and that I used to be a war pilot, and she'd keep on after me about why I quit flying and why I didn't go back to it, now that crates were more general, since I wasn't much good at selling automobiles or at anything else, like women will. You know: urgent and sympathetic, and you can't shut them up like you could a man; she came in and Reinhardt says, "We are letting Mr. Monaghan go. Send him to the cashier."

"Don't bother," I said. "Keep it to buy yourself a hoop with."

Dr. Martino

HUBERT JARROD met Louise King at a Christmas house party in Saint Louis. He had stopped there on his way home to Oklahoma to oblige, with his aura of oil wells and Yale, the sister of a classmate. Or so he told himself, or so he perhaps believed. He had planned to stop off at Saint Louis two days and he stayed out the full week, going on to Tulsa overnight to spend Christmas Day with his mother and then returning, "to play around a little more with my swamp angel," he told himself. He thought about her quite a lot on the return train—a thin, tense, dark girl. "That to come out of Mississippi," he thought. "Because she's got it: a kid born and bred in a Mississippi swamp." He did not mean sex appeal. He could not have been fooled by that alone, who had been three years now at New Haven, belonging to the right clubs and all and with money to spend. And besides, Louise was a little on the epicene. What he meant was a quality of which he was not yet consciously aware: a beyond-looking, a passionate sense for and belief in immanent change to which the rhinoceroslike sufficiency of his Yale and oil-well veneer was a little impervious at first. All he remarked at first was the expectation, the seeking, which he immediately took to himself.

Apparently he was not wrong. He saw her first across the dinner-table. They had not yet been introduced, yet ten minutes after they left the table she had spoken to him, and ten minutes after that they had slipped out of the house and were in a taxi, and she had supplied the address.

He could not have told himself how it happened, for all his practice, his experience in surreptitiousness. Perhaps he was too busy looking at her; perhaps he was just beginning to be aware that the beyond-looking, the tense expectation, was also beyond him—his youth, his looks, the oil wells and Yale. Because the address she had given was not toward any lights or music apparently, and she sitting beside him, furred and shapeless, her breath vaporizing faster than if she had been trying to bring to life a dead cigarette. He watched the dark houses, the dark, mean streets. "Where are we going?" he said.

She didn't answer, didn't look at him, sitting a little forward on the seat. "Mamma didn't want to come," she said.

"Your mother?"

"She's with me. Back there at the party. You haven't met her yet."

"Oh. So that's what you are slipping away from. I flattered myself. I thought I was the reason." She was sitting forward, small, tense, watching the dark houses: a district half dwellings and half small shops. "Your mother won't let him come to call on you?"

She didn't answer, but leaned forward. Suddenly she tapped on the glass. "Here, driver!" she said. "Right here." The cab stopped. She turned to face Jarrod, who sat back in his corner, muffled, his face cold. "I'm sorry. I know it's a rotten trick. But I had to."

"Not at all," Jarrod said. "Don't mention it."

"I know it's rotten. But I just had to. If you just understood."

"Sure," Jarrod said. "Do you want me to come back and get you? I'd better not go back to the party alone."

"You come in with me."

"Come in?"

"Yes. It'll be all right. I know you can't understand. But it'll be all right. You come in too."

He looked at her face. "I believe you really mean it," he said. "I guess not. But I won't let you down. You set a time, and I'll come back."

"Don't you trust me?"

"Why should I? It's no business of mine. I never saw you before to-night. I'm glad to oblige you. Too bad I am leaving to-morrow. But I guess you can find somebody else to use. You go on in; I'll come back for you."

He left her there and returned in two hours. She must have been waiting just inside the door, because the cab had hardly stopped before the door opened and she ran down the steps and sprang into the cab before he could dismount. "Thank you," she said. "Thank you. You were kind. You were so kind."

When the cab stopped beneath the porte-cochère of the house from which music now came, neither of them moved at once. Neither of them made the first move at all, yet a moment later they kissed. Her mouth was still, cold. "I like you," she said. "I do like you."

Before the week was out Jarrod offered to serve her again so, but she refused, quietly. "Why?" he said. "Don't you want to see him again?" But she wouldn't say, and he had met Mrs. King by that time and he said to himself, "The old girl is after me, anyway." He saw that at once; he took that also as the meed due his oil wells and his Yale nimbus, since three years at New Haven, leading no classes and winning no football games, had done nothing to dispossess him of the belief that he was the natural prey of all mothers of daughters. But he didn't flee, not even after he found, a few evenings later, Louise again unaccountably absent, and knew that she had gone, using someone else for the stalking horse, to that quiet house in the dingy street. "Well, I'm done," he said to himself. "I'm through now." But still he didn't flee, perhaps because she had used someone else this time. "She cares that much, anyway," he said to himself.

When he returned to New Haven he had Louise's promise to come to the spring prom. He knew now that Mrs. King would come too. He didn't mind that; one day he suddenly realized that he was glad. Then he knew that it was because he too knew, believed, that Louise needed looking after; that he had already surrendered unconditionally to one woman of them, he who had never once mentioned love to himself, to any woman. He remembered that quality of beyond-looking and that dark, dingy house in Saint Louis, and he thought, "Well, we have her. We have the old woman." And one day he believed that he had found the reason if not the answer. It was in class, in psychology, and he found himself sitting bolt upright, looking at the instructor. The instructor was talking about women, about young girls in particular, about that strange, mysterious phase in which they live for a while. "A blind spot, like that which racing aviators enter when making a fast turn. When what they see is neither good nor evil, and so what they do is likely to be either one. Probably more likely to be evil, since the very evilness of evil stems from its own fact, while good is an absence of fact. A time, an hour, in which they themselves are victims of that by means of which they victimize."

That night he sat before his fire for some time, not study-ing, not doing anything. "We've got to be married soon," he said. "Soon."

Mrs. King and Louise arrived for the prom. Mrs. King was a gray woman, with a cold, severe face, not harsh, but watchful, alert. It was as though Jarrod saw Louise, too, for the first time. Until then he had not been aware that he was conscious of the beyond-looking quality. It was only now that he saw it by realizing how it had become tenser, as though it were now both dread and desire; as though with the approach of summer she were approaching a climax, a crisis. So he thought that she was ill.

"Maybe we ought to be married right away," he said to Mrs. King. "I don't want a degree, anyway." They were allies now, not yet antagonists, though he had not told her of the two Saint Louis expeditions, the one he knew of and the one he suspected. It was as though he did not need to tell her. It was as though he knew that she knew; that she knew he knew she knew.

"Yes," she said. "At once."

But that was as far as it got, though when Louise and Mrs. King left New Haven, Louise had his ring. But it was not on her hand, and on her face was that strained, secret, beyond-looking expression which he now knew was beyond him too, and the effigy and shape which the oil wells and Yale had made. "Till July, then," he said.

"Yes," she said. "I'll write. I'll write you when to come."

And that was all. He went back to his clubs, his classes; in psychology especially he listened. "It seems I'm going to need psychology," he thought, thinking of the dark, small house in Saint Louis, the blank, dark door through which, running, she had disappeared. That was it: a man he had never seen, never heard of, shut up in a little dingy house on a back street on Christmas eve. He thought, fretfully, "And me young, with money, a Yale man. And I don't even know his name."

Once a week he wrote to Louise; perhaps twice a month he received replies—brief, cold notes mailed always at a different place—resorts and hotels—until mid-June, within a week of Commencement and his degree. Then he received a wire. It was from Mrs. King. It said *Come at once* and the location was Cranston's Wells, Mississippi. It was a town he had never heard of.

That was Friday; thirty minutes later his roommate came in and found him packing. "Going to town?" the roommate said.

"Yes," Jarrod said.

"I'll go with you. I need a little relaxation myself, before facing the cheering throngs at the Dean's altar."

"No," Jarrod said. "This is business."

"Sure," the roommate said. "I know a business woman in New York, myself. There's more than one in that town."

"No," Jarrod said. "Not this time."

"Beano," the roommate said.

The place was a resort owned by a neat, small, gray spinster who had inherited it, and some of the guests as well, from her father thirty years ago—a rambling frame hotel and a housed spring where old men with pouched eyes and parchment skin and old women dropsical with good living gathered from the neighboring Alabama and Mississippi towns to drink the iron-impregnated waters. This was the place where Louise had been spending her summers since she was born; and from the veranda of the hotel where the idle old women with their idle magazines and embroidery and their bright shawls had been watching each summer the comedy of which he was just learning, he could see the tips of the crepe myrtle copse hiding the bench on which the man whom he had come to fear, and whose face he had not even seen, had been sitting all day long for three months each summer for more than fifteen years.

So he stood beside the neat, gray proprietress on the top step in the early sunlight, while the old women went to and fro between house and spring, watching him with covert, secret, bright, curious looks. "Watching Louise's young man compete with a dead man and a horse," Jarrod thought.

But his face did not show this. It showed nothing at all, not even a great deal of intelligence as, tall, erect, in flannels and a tweed jacket in the Mississippi June, where the other men wore linen when they wore coats at all, he talked with the proprietress about the man whose face he had not seen and whose name he had just learned.

"It's his heart," the proprietress said to Jarrod. "He has to be careful. He had to give up his practice and everything. He hasn't any people and he has just enough money to come down here every summer and spend the summer sitting on his bench; we call it Doctor Martino's bench. Each summer I think it will be the last time; that we shan't see him again. But each May I get the message from him, the reservation. And do you know what I think? I think that it is Louise King that keeps him alive. And that Alvina King is a fool."

"How a fool?" Jarrod said.

The proprietress was watching him—this was the morning after his arrival; looking down at her he thought at first, "She is wondering how much I have heard, how much they have told me." Then he thought, "No. It's because she stays busy. Not like them, those others with their magazines. She has to stay too busy keeping them fed to have learned who I am, or to have been thinking all this time what the others have been thinking."

She was watching him. "How long have you known Louise?"

"Not long. I met her at a dance at school."

"Oh. Well, I think that the Lord has taken pity on Doctor Martino and He is letting him use Louise's heart, somehow. That's what I think. And you can laugh if you want to."

"I'm not laughing," Jarrod said. "Tell me about him."

She told him, watching his face, her air bright, birdlike, telling him about how the man had appeared one June, in his crumpled linen and panama hat, and about his eyes. ("They looked like shoe-buttons. And when he moved it was as slow as if he had to keep on telling himself, even after he had started moving, 'Go on, now; keep on moving, now.' ") And about how he signed the book in script almost too small to read: Jules Martino, Saint Louis, Missouri. And how after that year he came back each June, to sit all day long on the bench in the crepe myrtle copse, where the old Negro porter would fetch him his mail: the two medical journals, the Saint Louis paper, and the two letters from Louise King—the one in June saying that she would arrive next week, and the one in late August saying that she had reached home. But the proprietress didn't tell how she would walk a little way down the path three or four times a day to see if he were all right, and he not aware of it; and watching her while she talked, Jarrod thought, "What rivers has he made *you* swim, I wonder?"

"He had been coming here for three years," the proprietress said, "without knowing anybody, without seeming to want to know anybody, before even I found out about his heart. But he kept on coming (I forgot to say that Alvina King was already spending the summer here, right after Louise was born) and then I noticed how he would always be sitting where he could watch Louise playing, and so I thought that maybe he had lost his child. That was before he told me that he had never married and he didn't have any family at all. I thought that was what attracted him to Louise. And so I would watch him while he watched Louise growing up. I would see them talking, and him watching her year after year, and so after a while I said to myself. 'He wants to be married. He's waiting for Louise to grow up.' That's what I thought then." The proprietress was not looking at Jarrod now. She laughed a little. "My Lord, I've thought a lot of foolishness in my time."

"I don't know that that was so foolish," Jarrod said.

"Maybe not. Louise would make anybody a wife to be proud of. And him being all alone, without anybody to look after him when he got old." The proprietress was beyond fifty herself. "I reckon I've passed the time when I believe it's important whether women get married or not. I reckon, running this place single-handed this way, I've come to believe it ain't very important what anybody does, as long as they are fed good and have a comfortable bed." She ceased. For a time she seemed to muse upon the shade-dappled park, the old women clotting within the marquee above the spring.

"Did he make her do things, then?" Jarrod said.

"You've been listening to Alvina King," the proprietress said. "He never made her do anything. How could he? He never left that bench. He never leaves it. He would just sit there and watch her playing, until she began to get too old to play in the dirt. Then they would talk, sitting on the bench there. How could he make her do things, even if he had wanted to?"

"I think you are right," Jarrod said. "Tell me about when she swam the river."

"Oh, yes. She was always afraid of water. But one summer she learned to swim, learned by herself, in the pool. He wasn't even there. Nor at the river either. He didn't know about that until we knew it. He just told her not to be afraid, ever. And what's the harm in that, will you tell me?"

"None," Jarrod said.

"No," the proprietress said, as though she were not listening, had not heard him. "So she came in and told me, and I said, 'With the snakes and all, weren't you afraid?' And she said:

" 'Yes. I was afraid. That's why I did it.'

" 'Why you did it?' I said. And she said:

" 'When you are afraid to do something you know that you are alive. But when you are afraid to do what you are afraid of you are dead.'

" 'I know where you got that,' I said. 'I'll be bound he didn't swim the river too.' And she said:

" 'He didn't have to. Every time he wakes up in the morning he does what I had to swim the river to do. This is what I got for doing it: see?' And she took something on a string out of the front of her dress and showed it to me. It was a rabbit made out of metal or something, about an inch tall, like you buy in the ten-cent stores. He had given it to her.

" 'What does that mean?' I said.

" 'That's my being afraid,' she said. 'A rabbit: don't you see? But it's brass now; the shape of being afraid, in brass that nothing can hurt. As long as I keep it I am not even afraid of being afraid.'

" 'And if you are afraid,' I said, 'then what?'

" 'Then I'll give it back to him,' she said. And what's the harm in that, pray tell me? even though Alvina King always has been a fool. Because Louise came back in about an hour. She had been crying. She had the rabbit in her hand. 'Will you keep this for me?' she said. 'Don't let anybody have it except me. Not anybody. Will you promise?'

"And I promised, and I put the rabbit away for her. She asked me for it just before they left. That was when Alvina said they were not coming back the next summer. 'This foolishness is going to end,' she said. 'He will get her killed; he is a menace.'

"And, sure enough, next summer they didn't come. I heard that Louise was sick, and I knew why. I knew that Alvina had driven her into sickness, into bed. But Doctor Jules came in June. 'Louise has been right sick,' I told him.

" 'Yes,' he said; 'I know.' So I thought he had heard, that she had written to him. But then I thought how she must have been too sick to write, and that that fool mother of hers anyway . . ." The proprietress was watching Jarrod. "Because she wouldn't have to write him."

"Wouldn't have to?"

"He knew she was sick. He knew it. She didn't have to write him. Now you'll laugh."

"I'm not laughing. How did he know?"

"He knew. Because I knew he knew; and so when he didn't go on back to Saint Louis, I knew that she would come. And so in August they did come. Louise had grown a lot taller, thinner, and that afternoon I saw them standing together for the first time. She was almost as tall as he was. That was when I first saw that Louise was a woman. And now Alvina worrying about that horse that Louise says she's going to ride."

"It's already killed one man," Jarrod said.

"Automobiles have killed more than that. But you ride in an automobile, yourself. You came in one. It never hurt her when she swam that river, did it?"

"But this is different. How do you know it won't hurt her?"

"I just know."

"How know?"

"You go out there where you can see that bench. Don't bother him; just go and look at him. Then you'll know too."

"Well, I'd want a little more assurance than that," Jarrod said.

He had returned to Mrs. King. With Louise he had had one interview, brief, violent, bitter. That was the night before; to-day she had disappeared. "Yet he is still sitting there on that bench," Jarrod thought. "She's not even with him. They don't even seem to have to be together: he can tell all the way from Mississippi to Saint Louis when she is sick. Well, I know who's in the blind spot now."

Mrs. King was in her room. "It seems that my worst competitor is that horse," Jarrod said.

"Can't you see he is making her ride it for the same reason he made her swim that snake-filled river? To show that he can, to humiliate me?"

"What can I do?" Jarrod said. "I tried to talk to her last night. But you saw where I got."

"If I were a man, I shouldn't have to ask what to do. If I saw the girl I was engaged to being ruined, ruined by a man, any man, and a man I never saw before and don't even know who he is—old or not old; heart or no heart . . ."

"I'll talk to her again."

"Talk?" Mrs. King said. "Talk? Do you think I sent you that message to hurry down here just to talk to her?"

"You wait, now," Jarrod said. "It'll be all right. I'll attend to this."

He had to do a good bit of waiting, himself. It was nearly noon when Louise entered the empty lobby where he sat. He rose. "Well?"

They looked at each other. "Well?"

"Are you still going to ride that horse this afternoon?" Jarrod asked.

"I thought we settled this last night. But you're still meddling. I didn't send for you to come down here."

"But I'm here. I never thought, though, that I was being sent for to compete with a horse." She watched him, her eyes hard. "With worse than a horse. With a damned dead man. A man that's been dead for twenty years; he says so himself, they tell me. And he ought to know, being a doctor, a heart specialist. I suppose you keep him alive by scaring him—like strychnine, Florence Nightingale." She watched him, her face quite still, quite cold. "I'm not jealous," he went on. "Not of that bird. But when I see him making you ride that horse that has already killed . . ." He looked down at her cold face. "Don't you want to marry me, Louise?"

She ceased to look at him. "It's because we are young yet. We have so much time, all the rest of time. And maybe next year even, this very day next year, with everything pretty and warm and green, and he will be . . . You don't understand. I didn't at first, when he first told me how it was to live day after day with a match box full of dynamite caps in your breast pocket. Then he told me one day, when I was big enough to understand, how there is nothing in the world but living, being alive, knowing you are alive. And to be afraid is to know you are alive, but to do what you are afraid of, then you *live*. He says it's better even to be afraid than to be dead. He told me all that while he was still afraid, before he gave up the being afraid and he knew he was alive without living. And now he has even given that up, and now he is just afraid. So what can I do?"

"Yes. And I can wait, because I haven't got a match box of dynamite caps in my shirt. Or a box of conjuring powder, either."

"I don't expect you to see. I didn't send for you. I didn't want to get you mixed up in it."

"You never thought of that when you took my ring. Besides, you had already got me mixed up in it, the first night I ever saw you. You never minded then. So now I know a lot I didn't know before. And what does he think about that ring, by the way?" She didn't answer. She was not looking at him; neither was her face averted. After a time he said, "I see. He doesn't know about the ring. You never showed it to him." Still she didn't answer, looking neither at him nor away. "All right," he said "I'll give you one more chance."

She looked at him. "One more chance for what?" Then she said, "Oh. The ring. You want it back." He watched her, erect, expressionless, while she drew from inside her dress a slender cord on which was suspended the ring and a second object which he recognized in the flicking movement which broke the cord, to be the tiny metal rabbit of which the proprietress had told him. Then it was gone, and her hand flicked again, and something struck him a hard, stinging blow on the cheek. She was already running toward the stairs. After a time he stooped and picked up the ring from the floor. He looked about the lobby. "They're all down at the spring," he thought, holding the ring on his palm. "That's what people come here for: to drink water."

They were there, clotting in the marquee above the well, with their bright shawls and magazines. As he approached, Mrs. King came quickly out of the group, carrying one of the stained tumblers in her hand. "Yes?" she said. "Yes?" Jarrod extended his hand on which the ring lay. Mrs. King looked down at the ring, her face cold, quiet, outraged. "Sometimes I wonder if she can be my daughter. What will you do now?"

Jarrod, too, looked down at the ring, his face also cold, still. "At first I thought I just had to compete with a horse," he said. "But it seems there is more going on here than I knew of, than I was told of."

"Fiddlesticks," Mrs. King said. "Have you been listening to that fool Lily Cranston, to these other old fools here?"

"Not to learn any more than everybody else seems to have known all the time. But then, I'm only the man she was engaged to marry." He looked down at the ring. "What do you think I had better do now?"

"If you're a man that has to stop to ask advice from a woman in a case like this, then you'd better take the advice and take your ring and go on back to Nebraska or Kansas or wherever it is."

"Oklahoma," Jarrod said sullenly. He closed his hand on the ring. "He'll be on that bench," he said.

"Why shouldn't he?" Mrs. King said. "He has no one to fear here."

But Jarrod was already moving away. "You go on to Louise," he said. "I'll attend to this."

Mrs. King watched him go on down the path. Then she turned herself and flung the stained tumbler into an oleander bush and went to the hotel, walking fast, and mounted the stairs. Louise was in her room, dressing. "So you gave Hubert back his ring," Mrs. King said. "That man will be pleased now. You will have no secret from him now, if the ring ever was a secret. Since you don't seem to have any private affairs where he is concerned; don't appear to desire any—"

"Stop," Louise said. "You can't talk to me like that."

"Ah. He would be proud of that, too, to have heard that from his pupil."

"He wouldn't let me down. But you let me down. He wouldn't let me down." She stood thin and taut, her hands clenched at her sides. Suddenly she began to cry, her face lifted, the tears rolling down her cheeks. "I worry and I worry and I don't know what to do. And now you let me down, my own mother."

Mrs. King sat on the bed. Louise stood in her underthings, the garments she had removed scattered here and there, on the bed and on the chairs. On the table beside the bed lay the little metal rabbit; Mrs. King looked at it for a moment. "Don't you want to marry Hubert?" she said.

"Didn't I promise him, you and him both? Didn't I take his ring? But you won't let me alone. He won't give me time, a chance. And now you let me down, too. Everybody lets me down except Doctor Jules."

Mrs. King watched her, cold, immobile. "I believe that fool Lily Cranston is right. I believe that man has some criminal power over you. I just thank God he has not used

it for anything except to try to make you kill yourself, make
a fool of yourself. Not yet, that is—"

"Stop," Louise said; "stop!" She continued to say "Stop.
Stop," even when Mrs. King walked up and touched her.
"But you let me down! And now Hubert has let me down.
He told you about that horse after he had promised me he
wouldn't."

"I knew that already. That's why I sent for him. I could
do nothing with you. Besides, it's anybody's business to keep
you from riding it."

"You can't keep me. You may keep me locked up in this
room to-day, but you can't always. Because you are older
than I am. You'll have to die first, even if it takes a hundred
years. And I'll come back and ride that horse if it takes a
thousand years."

"Maybe I won't be here then," Mrs. King said. "But
neither will he. I can outlive him. And I can keep you locked
up in this room for one day, anyway."

Fifteen minutes later the ancient porter knocked at the
locked door. Mrs. King went and opened it. "Mr. Jarrod
wants to see you downstairs," the porter said.

She locked the door behind her. Jarrod was in the lobby.
It was empty. "Yes?" Mrs. King said. "Yes?"

"He said that if Louise would tell him herself she wants
to marry me. Send him a sign."

"A sign?" They both spoke quietly, a little tensely, though
quite calm, quite grave.

"Yes. I showed him the ring, and him sitting there on
that bench, in that suit looking like he had been sleeping
in it all summer, and his eyes watching me like he didn't
believe she had ever seen the ring. Then he said, 'Ah. You
have the ring. Your proof seems to be in the hands of the
wrong party. If you and Louise are engaged, she should
have the ring. Or am I just old fashioned?' And me standing

there like a fool and him looking at the ring like it might have come from Woolworth's. He never even offered to touch it."

"You showed him the ring? The *ring*? You fool. What—"

"Yes. I don't know. It was just the way he sat there, the way he makes her do things, I guess. It was like he was laughing at me, like he knew all the time there was nothing I could do, nothing I could think of doing about it he had not already thought about; that he knew he could always get between us before—in time. . . ."

"Then what? What kind of a sign did he say?"

"He didn't say. He just said a sign, from her hand to his. That he could believe, since my having the ring had exploded my proof. And then I caught my hand just before it hit him—and him sitting there. He didn't move; he just sat there with his eyes closed and the sweat popping out on his face. And then he opened his eyes and said, 'Now, strike me.' "

"Wait," Mrs. King said. Jarrod had not moved. Mrs. King gazed across the empty lobby, tapping her teeth with her fingernail. "Proof," she said. "A sign." She moved. "You wait here." She went back up the stairs; a heavy woman, moving with that indomitable, locomotivelike celerity. She was not gone long. "Louise is asleep," she said, for no reason that Jarrod could have discerned, even if he had been listening. She held her closed hand out. "Can you have your car ready in twenty minutes?"

"Yes. But what—?"

"And your bags packed. I'll see to everything else."

"And Louise— You mean—"

"You can be married in Meridian; you will be there in an hour."

"Married? Has Louise—?"

"I have a sign from her that he will believe. You get your

things all ready and don't you tell anyone where you are going, do you hear?"

"Yes. Yes. And Louise has——?"

"Not a soul. Here"—she put something into his hand. "Get your things ready, then take this and give it to him. He may insist on seeing her. But I'll attend to that. You just be ready. Maybe he'll just write a note, anyway. You do what I told you." She turned back toward the stairs, fast, with that controlled swiftness, and disappeared. Then Jarrod opened his hand and looked at the object which she had given him. It was the metal rabbit. It had been gilded once, but that was years ago, and it now lay on his palm in mute and tarnished oxidation. When he left the room he was not exactly running either. But he was going fast.

But when he re-entered the lobby fifteen minutes later, he was running. Mrs. King was waiting for him.

"He wrote the note," Jarrod said. "One to Louise, and one to leave here for Miss Cranston. He told me I could read the one to Louise." But Mrs. King had already taken it from his hand and opened it. "He said I could read it," Jarrod said. He was breathing hard, fast. "He watched me do it, sitting there on that bench; he hadn't moved even his hands since I was there before, and then he said, 'Young Mr. Jarrod, you have been conquered by a woman, as I have been. But with this difference: it will be a long time yet before you will realize that you have been slain.' And I said, 'If Louise is to do the slaying, I intend to die every day for the rest of my life or hers.' And he said, 'Ah; Louise. Were you speaking of Louise?' And I said, 'Dead.' I said, 'Dead.' I said, 'Dead.'"

But Mrs. King was not there. She was already half way up the stairs. She entered the room. Louise turned on the bed, her face swollen, with tears or with sleep. Mrs. King handed her the note. "There, honey. What did I tell you? He was

just making a fool of you. Just using you to pass the time
with."

The car was going fast when it turned into the highroad.
"Hurry," Louise said. The car increased speed; she looked
back once toward the hotel, the park massed with oleander
and crepe myrtle, then she crouched still lower in the seat
beside Jarrod. "Faster," she said.

"I say faster, too," Jarrod said. He glanced down at her;
then he looked down at her again. She was crying. "Are
you that glad?" he said.

"I've lost something," she said, crying quietly. "Something
I've had a long time, given to me when I was a child. And
now I've lost it. I had it just this morning, and now I can't
find it."

"Lost it?" he said. "Given to you . . ." His foot lifted;
the car began to slow. "Why, you sent . . ."

"No, no!" Louise said. "Don't stop! Don't turn back!
Go on!"

The car was coasting now, slowing, the brakes not yet on.
"Why, you . . . She said you were asleep." He put his foot
on the brakes.

"No, no!" Louise cried. She had been sitting forward;
she did not seem to have heard him at all. "Don't turn back!
Go on! Go on!"

"And he knew," Jarrod thought. "Sitting there on the
bench, he knew. When he said what he said that I would
not know that I had been slain."

The car was almost stopped. "Go on!" Louise cried. "Go
on!" He was looking down at her. Her eyes looked as if
they were blind; her face was pale, white, her mouth open,
shaped to an agony of despair and a surrender in particular
which, had he been older, he would have realized that he
would never see again on any face. Then he watched his
hand set the lever back into gear, and his foot come down

again on the throttle. "He said it himself," Jarrod thought: "to be afraid, and yet to do. He said it himself: there's nothing in the world but being alive, knowing you are alive."

"Faster!" Louise cried. "Faster!" The car rushed on; the house, the broad veranda where the bright shawls were now sibilant, fell behind.

In that gathering of wide summer dresses, of sucked old breaths and gabbling females staccato, the proprietress stood on the veranda with the second note in her hand. "Married?" she said. "Married?" As if she were someone else, she watched herself open the note and read it again. It did not take long:

> Lily:
> Don't worry about me for a while longer. I'll sit here until supper time. Don't worry about me.
>
> J. M.

"Don't worry *about* me," she said. "*About* me." She went into the lobby, where the old Negro was pottering with a broom. "And Mr. Jarrod gave you this?"

"Yessum. Give it to me runnin' and tole me to git his bags into de cyar, and next I know, here Miss Louise and him whoosh! outen de drive and up de big road like a patter-roller."

"And they went toward Meridian?"

"Yessum. Right past de bench whar Doctor Jules settin'."

"Married," the proprietress said. "Married." Still carrying the note, she left the house and followed the path until she came in sight of the bench on which sat a motionless figure in white. She stopped again and re-read the note; again she looked up the path toward the bench which faced the road. Then she returned to the house. The women had now dispersed into chairs, though their voices still filled the veranda, sibilant, inextricable one from another; they ceased suddenly as the proprietress approached and entered the house again. She entered the house, walking fast. That was about an hour to sundown.

Dusk was beginning to fall when she entered the kitchen. The porter was now sitting on a chair beside the stove, talking to the cook. The proprietress stopped in the door. "Uncle Charley," she said, "Go and tell Doctor Jules supper will be ready soon."

The porter rose and left the kitchen by the side door. When he passed the veranda, the proprietress stood on the top step. She watched him go on and disappear up the path toward the bench. A woman passed and spoke to her, but she made no reply; it was as though she had not heard, watching the shubbery beyond which the Negro had disappeared. And when he reappeared, the guests on the veranda saw her already in motion, descending the steps before they were even aware that the Negro was running, and they sat suddenly hushed and forward and watched her pass the Negro without stopping, her skirts lifted from her trim, school-mistress ankles and feet, and disappear up the path herself, running too. They were still sitting forward, hushed, when she too reappeared; they watched her come through the dusk and mount the porch, with on her face also a look of having seen something which she knew to be true but which she was not quite yet ready to believe. Perhaps that was why her voice was quite quiet when she addressed one of the guests by name, calling her "honey":

"Doctor Martino has just died. Will you telephone to town for me?"

Fox Hunt

An hour before daylight three Negro stable-boys approached the stable, carrying a lantern. While one of them unlocked and slid back the door, the bearer of the lantern lifted it and turned the beam into the darkness where a clump of pines shouldered into the paddock fence. Out of this darkness three sets of big, spaced eyes glared mildly for a moment, then vanished. "Heyo," the Negro called. "Yawl cole?" No reply, no sound came from the darkness; the mule-eyes did not show again. The Negroes entered the barn, murmuring among themselves; a burst of laughter floated back out of the stable, mellow and meaningless and idiotic.

"How many of um you see?" the second Negro said.

"Just three mules," the lantern-bearer said. "It's more than that, though. Unc Mose he come in about two o'clock, where he been up with that Jup'ter horse; he say it was already two of um waiting there then. Clay-eaters. Hoo."

Inside the stalls horses began to whinny and stamp; over the white-washed doors the high, long muzzles moved with tossing, eager shadows; the atmosphere was rich, warm, ammoniac, and clean. The Negroes began to put feed into the patent troughs, moving from stall to stall with the clever agility of monkeys, with short, mellow, meaningless cries, "Hoo. Stand over dar. Ghy ketch dat fox to-day."

In the darkness where the clump of pines shouldered the paddock fence, eleven men squatted, surrounded by eleven tethered mules. It was November, and the morning was chill, and the men squatted shapeless and motionless, not talking. From the stable came the sound of the eating horses; just before day broke a twelfth man came up on a mule and dismounted and squatted among the others without a word. When day came and the first saddled horse was led out of the stable, the grass was rimed with frost, and the roof of the stable looked like silver in the silver light.

It could be seen then that the squatting men were all white men and all in overalls, and that all of the mules save two were saddleless. They had gathered from one-room, clay-floored cabins about the pine land, and they squatted, decorous, grave, and patient among their gaunt and mud-caked and burr-starred mules, watching the saddled horses, the fine horses with pedigrees longer than Harrison Blair's, who owned them, being led one by one from a steam-heated stable and up the gravel path to the house, before which a pack of hounds already moiled and yapped, and on the veranda of which men and women in boots and red coats were beginning to gather.

Sloven, unhurried, outwardly scarcely attentive, the men in overalls watched Harrison Blair, who owned the house and the dogs and some of the guests too, perhaps, mount a big, vicious-looking black horse, and they watched another man lift Harrison Blair's wife onto a chestnut mare and then mount a bay horse in his turn.

One of the men in overalls was chewing tobacco slowly. Beside him stood a youth, in overalls too, gangling, with a soft stubble of beard. They spoke without moving their heads, hardly moving their lips.

"That the one?" the youth said.

The older man spat deliberately, without moving. "The one what?"

"His wife's one."

"Whose wife's one?"

"Blair's wife's one."

The other contemplated the group before the house. He appeared to, that is. His gaze was inscrutable, blank, without haste; none could have said if he were watching the man and woman or not. "Don't believe anything you hear, and not more than half you see," he said.

"What do you think about it?" the youth said.

The other spat deliberately and carefully. "Nothing," he said. "It ain't none of my wife." Then he said, without raising his voice and without any change in inflection, though he was now speaking to the head groom who had come up beside him. "That fellow don't own no horse."

"Which fellow don't?" the groom said. The white man indicated the man who was holding the bay horse against the chestnut mare's flank. "Oh," the groom said. "Mr. Gawtrey. Pity the horse, if he did."

"Pity the horse that *he* owns, too," the white man said. "Pity anything he owns."

"You mean Mr. Harrison?" the groom said. "Does these here horses look like they needs your pity?"

"Sho," the white man said. "That's right. I reckon that black horse does like to be rode like he rides it."

"Don't you be pitying no Blair horses," the groom said.

"Sho," the white man said. He appeared to contemplate the blooded horses that lived in a steam-heated house, the people in boots and pink coats, and Blair himself sitting the plunging black. "He's been trying to catch that vixen for three years now," he said. "Whyn't he let one of you boys shoot it or pizen it?"

"Shoot it or pizen it?" the groom said. "Don't you know that ain't no way to catch a fox?"

"Why ain't it?"

"It ain't spo'tin," the groom said. "You ought to been

hanging around um long enough by now to know how gempmuns hunts."

"Sho," the white man said. He was not looking at the groom. "Wonder how a man rich as folks says he is"—again he spat, in the action something meager but without intended insult, as if he might have been indicating Blair with a jerked finger—"is got time to hate one little old fox bitch like that. Don't even want the dogs to catch it. Trying to outride the dogs so he can kill it with a stick like it was a snake. Coming all the way down here every year, bringing all them folks and boarding and sleeping them, to run one little old mangy fox that I could catch in one night with a axe and a possum dog."

"That's something else about gempmuns you won't never know," the groom said.

"Sho," the white man said.

The ridge was a long shoal of pine and sand, broken along one flank into gaps through which could be seen a fallow rice field almost a mile wide which ended against a brier-choked dyke. The two men in overalls, the older man and the youth, sat their mules in one of these gaps, looking down into the field. Farther on down the ridge, about a half mile away, the dogs were at fault; the yapping cries came back up the ridge, baffled, ringing, profoundly urgent.

"You'd think he would learn in three years that he ain't going to catch ere Cal-lina fox with them Yankee city dogs," the youth said.

"He knows it," the other said. "He don't want them dogs to catch it. He can't even bear for a blooded dog to go in front of him."

"They're in front of him now though."

"You think so?"

"Where is he, then?"

"I don't know. But I know that he ain't no closer to them

fool dogs right now than that fox is. Wherever that fox is squatting right now, laughing at them dogs, that's where he is heading for."

"You mean to tell me that ere a man in the world can smell out a fox where even a city dog can't untangle it?"

"Them dogs yonder can't smell out a straight track because they don't hate that fox. A good fox- or coon- or possum-dog is a good dog because he hates a fox or a coon or a possum, not because he's got a extra good nose. It ain't his nose that leads him; it's his hating. And that's why when I see which-a-way that fellow's riding, I'll tell you which-a-way that fox has run."

The youth made a sound in his throat and nostrils. "A growed-up man. Hating a durn little old mangy fox. I be durn if it don't take a lot of trouble to be rich. I be durn if it don't."

They looked down into the field. From farther on down the ridge the eager, baffled yapping of the dogs came. The last rider in boots and pink had ridden up and passed them and gone on, and the two men sat their mules in the profound and winy and sunny silence, listening, with expressions identical and bleak and sardonic on their gaunt, yellow faces. Then the youth turned on his mule and looked back up the ridge in the direction from which the race had come. At that moment the older man turned also and, motionless, making no sound, they watched two more riders come up and pass. They were the woman on the chestnut mare and the man on the bay horse. They passed like one beast, like a double or hermaphroditic centaur with two heads and eight legs. The woman carried her hat in her hand; in the slanting sun the fine, soft cloud of her unbobbed hair gleamed like the chestnut's flank, like soft fire, the mass of it appearing to be too heavy for her slender neck. She was sitting the mare with a kind of delicate awkwardness, leaning forward as though she were trying to outpace it, with a quality about her of flight within flight, separate and distinct from the speed of the mare.

The man was holding the bay horse against the mare's flank at full gallop. His hand lay on the woman's hand which held the reins, and he was slowly but steadily drawing both horses back, slowing them. He was leaning toward the woman; the two men on the mules could see his profile stoop past with a cold and ruthless quality like that of a stooping hawk; they could see that he was talking to the woman. They passed so, with that semblance of a thrush and a hawk in terrific immobility in mid-air, with an apparitionlike suddenness: a soft rush of hooves in the sere needles, and were gone, the man stooping, the woman leaning forward like a tableau of flight and pursuit on a lightning bolt.

Then they were gone. After a while the youth said, "That one don't seem to need no dogs neither." His head was still turned after the vanished riders. The other man said nothing. "Yes, sir," the youth said. "Just like a fox. I be durn if I see how that skinny neck of hern . . . Like you look at a fox and you wonder how a durn little critter like it can tote all that brush. And once I heard him say"—he in turn indicated, with less means than even spitting, that it was the rider of the black horse and not the bay, of whom he spoke—"something to her that a man don't say to a woman in comp'ny, and her eyes turned red like a fox's and then brown again like a fox." The other did not answer. The youth looked at him.

The older man was leaning a little forward on his mule, looking down into the field. "What's that down there?" he said. The youth looked also. From the edge of the woods beneath them came a mold-muffled rush of hooves and then a crash of undergrowth; then they saw, emerging from the woods at full gallop, Blair on the black horse. He entered the rice field at a dead run and began to cross it with the unfaltering and undeviating speed of a crow's flight, following a course as straight as a surveyor's line toward the dyke which bounded the field at its other side. "What did I tell you?" the older man said. "That fox is hid yonder on that ditchbank. Well, it ain't the first time they ever seen one another eye to eye. He got close enough to it once two years ago to throw that ere leather riding-switch at it."

"Sho," the youth said. "These folks don't need no dogs."

In the faint, sandy road which followed the crest of the ridge, and opposite another gap in the trees through which could be seen a pie-shaped segment of the rice field, and some distance in the rear of the hunt, stood a Ford car with a light truck body. Beneath the wheel sat a uniformed chauffeur; beside him, hunched into a black overcoat, was a man in a derby hat. He had a smooth, flaccid, indoors face and he was smoking a cigarette: a face sardonic and composed, yet at the moment a little wearily savage, like that of an indoors-bred and -inclined man subject to and helpless before some natural inclemency like cold or wet. He was talking.

"Sure. This all belongs to her, house and all. His old man owned it before they moved to New York and got rich, and Blair was born here. He bought it back and gave it to her for a wedding present. All he kept was this what-ever-it-is he's trying to catch."

"And he can't catch that," the chauffeur said.

"Sure. Coming down here every year and staying two months, without nothing to see and nowheres to go except these clay-eaters and Nigras. If he wants to live in a herd of nigras for two months every year, why don't he go and spend a while on Lenox Avenue? You don't have to drink the gin. But he's got to buy this place and give it to her for a present because she is one of these Southerns and she might get homesick or something. Well, that's all right, I guess. But Fourteenth Street is far enough south for me. But still, if it ain't this, it might be Europe or somewheres. I don't know which is worse."

"Why did he marry her, anyways?" the chauffeur said.

"You want to know why he married her? It wasn't the jack, even if they did have a pot full of it, of this Oklahoma Indian oil. . . ."

"Indian oil?"

"Sure. The government give this Oklahoma to the Indians because nobody else would have it, and when the first Indian got there and seen it and dropped dead and they tried to bury him, when they stuck the shovel into the ground the oil blowed the shovel out of the fellow's hand, and so the white folks come. They would come up with a new Ford with a man from the garage driving it and they would go to an Indian and say, 'Well, John, how much rotten-water you catchum your front yard?' and the Indian would say three wells or thirteen wells or whatever it is and the white man would say, 'That's too bad. The way the White Father put the bee on you boys, it's too bad. Well, never mind. You see this fine new car here? Well, I'm going to give it to you so you can load up your folks and go on to where the water don't come out of the ground rotten and where the White Father can't put the bee on you no more.' So the Indian would load his family into the car, and the garage man would head the car west, I guess, and show the Indian where the gasoline lever was and hop off and snag the first car back to town. See?"

"Oh," the chauffeur said.

"Sure. So here we was in England one time, minding our own business, when here this old dame and her red-headed gal come piling over from Europe or somewheres where the gal was going to the high school, and here it ain't a week before Blair says, 'Well, Ernie, we're going to get married.

What the hell do you think of that?' And him a fellow that
hadn't done nothing all his life but dodge skirts so he could
drink all night and try to ride a horse to death all day, getting
married in less than a week. But soon as I see this old dame,
I know which one of her and her husband it was that had
took them oil wells off the Indians."

"She must have been good, to put it on Blair at all, let
alone that quick," the chauffeur said. "Tough on her, though.
I'd hate for my daughter to belong to him. Not saying nothing against him, of course."

"I'd hate for my dog to belong to him. I see him kill a dog
once because it wouldn't mind him. Killed it with a walking
stick, with one lick. He says, 'Here. Send Andrews here to
haul this away.' "

"I don't see how you put up with him," the chauffeur said.
"Driving his cars, that's one thing. But you, in the house
with him day and night. . . ."

"We settled that. He used to ride me when he was drinking. One day he put his hand on me and I told him I would
kill him. 'When?' he says. 'When you get back from the
hospital?' 'Maybe before I go there,' I says. I had my hand
in my pocket. 'I believe you would,' he says. So we get along
now. I put the rod away and he don't ride me any more and
we get along."

"Why didn't you quit?"

"I don't know. It's a good job, even if we do stay all over
the place all the time. Jees! half the time I don't know if the
next train goes to Ty. Juana or Italy; I don't know half the
time where I'm at or if I can read the newspaper next morning even. And I like him and he likes me."

"Maybe he quit riding you because he had something else
to ride," the chauffeur said.

"Maybe so. Anyways, when they married, she hadn't
never been on a horse before in all her life until he bought

this chestnut horse for her to match her hair. We went all
the way to Kentucky for it, and he come back in the same
car with it. I wouldn't do it; I says I would do anything in
reason for him but I wasn't going to ride in no horse Pullman
with it empty, let alone with a horse already in it. So I come
back in a lower.

"He didn't tell her about the horse until it was in the
stable. 'But I don't want to ride,' she says.

" 'My wife will be expected to ride,' he says. 'You are
not in Oklahoma now.'

" 'But I can't ride,' she says.

" 'You can at least sit on top of the horse so they will think
you can ride on it,' he says.

"So she goes to Callaghan, riding them practice plugs of
his with the children and the chorines that have took up horse
riding to get ready to get drafted from the bushes out in
Brooklyn or New Jersey to the Drive or Central Park. And
her hating a horse like it was a snake ever since one day when
she was a kid and gets sick on a merry-go-round."

"How did you know all this?" the chauffeur said.

"I was there. We used to stop there now and then in the
afternoon to see how she was coming on the horse. Sometimes she wouldn't even know we was there, or maybe she
did. Anyways, here she would go, round and round among
the children and one or two head of Zigfield's prize stock,
passing us and not looking at us, and Blair standing there
with that black face of his like a subway tunnel, like he knew
all the time she couldn't ride no horse even on a merry-go-
round and like he didn't care if she learned or not, just so he
could watch her trying and not doing it. So at last even
Callaghan come to him and told him it wasn't no use. 'Very
well,' Blair says. 'Callaghan says you may be able to sit on
the top of a painted horse, so I will buy you a horse out of a

dump cart and nail him to the front porch, and you can at least be sitting on top of it when we come up.'

" 'I'll go back to momma's,' she says.

" 'I wish you would,' Blair says. 'My old man tried all his life to make a banker out of me, but your old woman done it in two months.' "

"I thought you said they had jack of their own," the chauffeur said. "Why didn't she spend some of that?"

"I don't know. Maybe there wasn't no exchange for Indian money in New York. Anyways, you would have thought she was a conductor on a Broadway surface car. Sometimes she wouldn't even wait until I could get Blair under a shower and a jolt into him before breakfast, to make the touch. So the gal goes to the old dame (she lives on Park Avenue) and the gal . . ."

"Was you there too?" the chauffeur said.

"Cried . . . What? Oh. This was a maid, a little Irish kid named Burke; me and her used to go out now and then. She was the one told me about this fellow, this Yale college boy, this Indian sweetheart."

"Indian sweetheart?"

"They went to the same ward school out at Oklahoma or something. Swapped Masonic rings or something before the gal's old man found three oil wells in the henhouse and dropped dead and the old dame took the gal off to Europe to go to the school there. So this boy goes to Yale College and last year what does he do but marry a gal out of a tank show that happened to be in town. Well, when she finds that Callaghan has give her up, she goes to her old woman in Park Avenue. She cries. 'I begin to think that maybe I won't look funny to his friends, and then he comes there and watches me. He don't say nothing,' she says, 'he just stands there and watches me.'

" 'After all I've done for you,' the old dame says. 'Got you a husband that any gal in New York would have snapped up. When all he asks is that you learn to sit on top of a horse and not shame him before his swell friends. After all I done for you,' the old dame says.

"'I didn't,' she says. 'I didn't want to marry him.'

"'Who did you want to marry?' the old dame says.

"'I didn't want to marry nobody,' the gal says.

"So now the old dame digs up about this boy, this Allen boy that the gal . . ."

"I thought you said his name was Yale," the chauffeur said.

"No. Allen. Yale is where he went to this college."

"You mean Columbia."

"No. Yale. It's another college."

"I thought the other one was named Cornell or something," the chauffeur said.

"No. It's another one. Where these college boys all come from when these hotchachacha deadfalls get raided and they give them all a ride downtown in the wagon. Don't you read no papers?"

"Not often," the chauffeur said. "I don't care nothing about politics."

"All right. So this Yale boy's poppa had found a oil well too and he was lousy with it too, and besides the old dame was mad because Blair wouldn't leave her live in the house with them and wouldn't take her nowheres when we went. So the old dame give them all three—her and Blair and this college boy—the devil until the gal jumps up and says she will ride on a horse or bust, and Blair told her to go on and bust if she aimed to ride on this chestnut horse we brought all the way back from Kentucky. 'I don't aim for you to ruin this good horse,' Blair says. 'You'll ride on the horse I tell you to ride on.'

"So then she would slip out the back way and go off and try to ride this horse, this good one, this Kentucky plug, to

learn how first and then surprise him. The first time didn't
hurt her, but the second time it broke her collar bone, and
she was scared how Blair would find it out until she found
out how he had knew it all the time that she was riding on
it. So when we come down here for the first time that year
and Blair started chasing this lyron or whatever it—"

"Fox," the chauffeur said.

"All right. That's what I said. So when—"

"You said lyron," the chauffeur said.

"All right. Leave it be a lyron. Anyways, she would ride
on this chestnut horse, trying to keep up, and Blair already
outrun the dogs and all, like this time two years ago when
he run off from the dogs and got close enough to this lyron
to hit it with his riding whip—"

"You mean fox," the chauffeur said. "A fox, not a lyron.
Say . . ." The other man, the valet, secretary, whatever he
might have been, was lighting another cigarette, crouched
into his upturned collar, the derby slanted down upon his
face.

"Say what?" he said.

"I was wondering," the chauffeur said.

"Wondering what?"

"If it's as hard for him to ride off and leave her as he
thinks it is. To not see her ruining this good Kentucky
horse. If he has to ride as fast to do it as he thinks he does."

"What about that?"

"Maybe he don't have to ride as fast this year as he did last
year, to run off from her. What do you think about it?"

"Think about what?"

"I was wondering."

"What wondering?"

"If he knowed he don't have to ride as fast this year or
not."

"Oh. You mean Gawtrey."

"That his name? Gawtrey?"

"That's it. Steve Gawtrey."

"What about him?"

"He's all right. He'll eat your grub and drink your liquor and fool your women and let you say when."

"Well, what about that?"

"Nothing. I said he was all right. He's fine by me."

"How by you?"

"Just fine, see? I done him a little favor once, and he done me a little favor, see?"

"Oh," the chauffeur said. He did not look at the other. "How long has she known him?"

"Six months and maybe a week. We was up in Connecticut and he was there. He hates a horse about as much as she does, but me and Callaghan are all right too; I done Callaghan a little favor once too, so about a week after we come back from Connecticut, I have Callaghan come in and tell Blair about this other swell dog, without telling Blair who owned it. So that night I says to Blair, 'I hear Mr. Van Dyming wants to buy this horse from Mr. Gawtrey too.' 'Buy what horse?' Blair says. 'I don't know,' I says. 'One horse looks just like another to me as long as it stays out doors where it belongs,' I says. 'So do they to Gawtrey,' Blair says. 'What horse are you talking about?' 'This horse Callaghan was telling you about,' I says. Then he begun to curse Callaghan. 'He told me he would get that horse for me,' he says. 'It don't belong to Callaghan,' I says, 'it's Mr. Gawtrey's horse.' So here it's two nights later when he brings Gawtrey home to dinner with him. That night I says, 'I guess you bought that horse.' He had been drinking and he cursed Gawtrey and Callaghan too. 'He won't sell it,' he says. 'You want to keep after him,' I says. 'A man will sell anything.' 'How keep after him, when he won't listen to a price?' he says. 'Leave your wife do the talking,' I says. 'He'll listen to her.' That was when he hit me. . . ."

"I thought you said he just put his hand on you," the chauffeur said.

"I mean he just kind of flung out his hand when he was talking, and I happened to kind of turn my face toward him at the same time. He never aimed to hit me because he knowed I would have took him. I told him so. I had the rod in my hand, inside my coat, all the while.

"So after that Gawtrey would come back maybe once a week because I told him I had a good job and I didn't aim to have to shoot myself out of it for no man except myself maybe. He come once a week. The first time she wouldn't leave him in. Then one day I am reading the paper (you ought to read a paper now and then. You ought to keep up with the day of the week, at least) and I read where this Yale Allen boy has run off with a show gal and they had fired him off the college for losing his amateur's standing, I guess. I guess that made him mad, after he had done jumped the college anyways. So I cut it out, and this Burke kid (me and her was all right, too) she puts it on the breakfast tray that A.M. And that afternoon, when Gawtrey happens to come back, she leaves him in, and this Burke kid happens to walk into the room sudden with something—I don't know what it was—and here is Gawtrey and her like a fade-out in the pitchers."

"So Blair got his horse," the chauffeur said.

"What horse?"

"The horse Gawtrey wouldn't sell him."

"How could he, when Gawtrey never owned no horse no more than I do, unless it's maybe some dog still finishing last year's Selling Plate at Pimlico? Besides, Gawtrey don't owe Blair no horse yet."

"Not yet?"

"She don't like him, see. The first time he come to the house alone she wouldn't leave him into the front door. And the next time, too, if this Burke kid hadn't happened to left that piece out of the papers about this college boy on the breakfast tray. And the time after that when he come, she wouldn't leave him in again; it was like he might have been a horse maybe, or even a dog, because she hated a dog worse than she did a horse even, even if she didn't have to try to ride on no dog. If it had have been a dog, Blair wouldn't have never got her to even try to ride on it. So I'd have to go out and steam Callaghan up again until it got to where I wasn't no more than one of these Russian droshkies or something."

"A Russian what?"

"One of these fellows that can't call their own soul. Every time I would leave the house I would have to meet Gawtrey in a dump somewheres and then go to see Callaghan and soap him down, because he is one of these boys with ideas, see?"

"What kind of ideas?"

"Just ideas. Out of the Sunday school paper. About how this wasn't right because he liked her and felt sorry for her and so he wanted to tell Blair he had been lying and that Gawtrey hadn't never owned no horse. Because a fellow that won't take a nickel when it's throwed right in his face, he ain't never as big a fool to nobody as he is to the man that can have some sense about religion and keep all these golden rules in the Sunday school paper where they come from. If the Lord didn't want a man to cut his own grass, why did He put Sunday on Sunday like he did? Tell me that."

"I guess you're right," the chauffeur said.

"Sure I'm right. Jees! I told Callaghan Blair would cut his throat and mine both for a Rockefeller quarter, same as any sensible man, and I ast him if he thought gals had done all give out with Blair's wife; if she was going to be the last one they made."

"So he don't . . ." the chauffeur said. He ceased; then he said, "Look there."

The other man looked. Through the gap in the trees, in the center of the segment of visible rice field, they could see a tiny pink-and-black dot. It was almost a mile away; it did not appear to be moving fast.

"What's that?" the other said. "The fox?"

"It's Blair," the chauffeur said. "He's going fast. I wonder where the others are." They watched the pink-and-black dot go on and disappear.

"They've went back home if they had any sense," the other said. "So we might as well go back too."

"I guess so," the chauffeur said. "So Gawtrey don't owe Blair no horse yet."

"Not yet. She don't like him. She wouldn't leave him in the house again after that day, and this Burke kid says she come back from a party one night because Gawtrey was there. And if it hadn't been for me, Gawtrey wouldn't a got invited down here, because she told Blair that if he come, she wouldn't come. So I'd have to work on Callaghan again so he would come in once a day and steam Blair up again about the horse to get Gawtrey invited, because Blair was going to make her come." The chauffeur got out of the car and went around to the crank. The other man lighted a cigarette. "But Blair ain't got his horse yet. You take a woman with long hair like she's got, long as she keeps her hair up, it's all right. But once you catch her with her hair down, it's just been too bad."

The chauffeur engaged the crank. Then he paused, stooped, his head turned. "Listen," he said.

"What?"

"That horn." The silver sound came again, faint, distant, prolonged.

"What's that?" the other said. "Do they have to keep soldiers here?"

"It's the horn they blow," the chauffeur said. "It means they have caught that fox."

"Jees!" the other said. "Maybe we will go back to town to-morrow."

The two men on the mules recrossed the rice field and mounted the ridge into the pines.

"Well," the youth said, "I reckon he's satisfied now."

"You reckon he is?" the other said. He rode a little in front of the youth. He did not turn his head when he spoke.

"He's run that fox three years," the youth said. "And now he's killed it. How come he ain't satisfied?"

The older man did not look back. He slouched on his gaunt, shabby mule, his overalled legs dangling. He spoke in a tone of lazy and ironical contempt. "I reckon that's something about gentle-men you won't never know."

"Fox is fox, to me," the youth said. "Can't eat it. Might as well pizen it and save them horses."

"Sho," the other said. "That's something else about them you won't never know."

"About who?"

"Gentle-men." They mounted the ridge and turned into the faint, sandy road. "Well," the older man said, "gentle-man or not, I reckon that's the only fox in Cal-lina that ever got itself killed that-a-way. Maybe that's the way they kills a fox up north."

"Then I be durn if I ain't glad I don't live up there," the youth said.

"I reckon so," the other said. "I done got along pretty well here for some time, myself."

"I'd like to see it once though," the youth said.

"I don't reckon I would," the other said, "if living there makes a man go to all this trouble to kill a fox."

They were riding up the ridge, among the pines, the holly

bushes, the huckleberries and briers. Suddenly the older man checked his mule, extending his hand backward.

"What?" the youth said. "What is it?"

The pause was hardly a pause; again the older man rode on, though he began to whistle, the tone carrying and clear though not loud, the tune lugubrious and hymnlike; from beyond the bushes which bordered the path just ahead of them there came the snort of a horse. "Who is it?" the youth said. The other said nothing. The two mules went on in single file. Then the youth said quietly, "She's got her hair down. It looks like the sun on a spring branch." The mules paced on in the light, whispering soil, their ears bobbing, the two men sitting loose, with dangling, stirrupless feet.

The woman sat the mare, her hair a bright cloud, a copper cascade in the sun, about her shoulders, her arms lifted and her hands busy in it. The man sat the bay horse a short distance away. He was lighting a cigarette. The two mules came up, tireless, shambling, with drooping heads and nodding ears. The youth looked at the woman with a stare at once bold and covert; the older man did not cease his mellow, slow, tuneless whistling; he did not appear to look at them at all. He appeared to be about to ride past without a sign when the man on the bay spoke to him.

"They caught it, did they?" he said. "We heard the horn."

"Yaas," the man in overalls said, in a dry, drawling tone. "Yaas. It got caught. 'Twarn't nothing else it could do but get caught."

The youth watched the woman looking at the older man, her hands arrested for an instant in her hair.

"What do you mean?" the man on the bay said.

"He rode it down on that black horse," the man in overalls said.

"You mean, there were no dogs there?"

"I reckon not," the other said. "Them dogs never had no

black horses to ride." The two mules had halted; the older
man faced the man on the bay a little, his face hidden beneath his shapeless hat. "It crossed the old field and dropped
over that ditch-bank and hid, allowing for him to jump the
ditch, and then it aimed to double back, I reckon. I reckon
it wasn't scared of the dogs. I reckon it had fooled them so
much it wasn't worried about them. I reckon he was what
worried it. I reckon him and it knowed one another after
these three years same as you maybe knowed your maw or
your wife maybe, only you ain't never been married none
to speak of. Anyway it was on the ditch-bank, and he
knowed it was there and he cut straight across the field without giving it no spell to breathe in. I reckon maybe yawl
seen him, riding straight across that field like he could see
like a hawk and smell like a dog. And the fox was there,
where it had done fooled the dogs. But it never had no spell
to breathe in, and when it had to run again and dropped over
the ditch-bank, it dropped into the briers, I reckon, and it
was too tired to get out and run. And he come up and jumped
that ditch, just like that fox aimed for him to. Only the fox
was still in the briers, and while he was going through the air
he looked down and seen the fox and he clumb off the horse
while it was jumping and dropped feet first into the briers
like the fox done. Maybe it dodged some then; I don't
know. He says it just swirled and jumped at his face and he
knocked it down with his fist and trompled it dead with his
boot-heels. The dogs hadn't got there then. But it so happened he never needed them." He ceased talking and sat for
a moment longer, sloven and inert upon the shabby, patient
mule, his face shadowed beneath his hat. "Well," he said, "I
reckon I'll get on. I ain't had ne'er a bite of breakfast yet.
I'll bid yawl good morning." He put his mule into motion,
the second mule following. He did not look back.

But the youth did. He looked back at the man on the bay

horse, the cigarette burning in his hand, the plume of smoke faint and windless in the sunny silence, and at the woman on the chestnut, her arms lifted and her hands busy in her bright, cloudy hair; projecting, trying to project, himself, after the way of the young, toward that remote and inaccessible she, trying to encompass the vain and inarticulate instant of division and despair which, being young, was very like rage: rage at the lost woman, despair of the man in whose shape there walked the tragic and inescapable earth her ruin. "She was crying," he said, then he began to curse, savagely, without point or subject.

"Come on," the older man said. He did not look back. "I reckon them hunt breakfast hoe-cakes will be about ready time we get home."

Pennsylvania Station

THEY SEEMED to bring with them the smell of the snow falling in Seventh Avenue. Or perhaps the other people who had entered before them had done it, bringing it with them in their lungs and exhaling it, filling the arcade with a stale chill like that which might lie unwinded and spent upon the cold plains of infinity itself. In it the bright and serried shop-windows had a fixed and insomniac glare like the eyes of people drugged with coffee, sitting up with a strange corpse.

In the rotunda, where the people appeared as small and intent as ants, the smell and sense of snow still lingered, though high now among the steel girders, spent and vitiated too and filled here with a weary and ceaseless murmuring, like the voices of pilgrims upon the infinite plain, like the voices of all the travelers who had ever passed through it quiring and ceaseless as lost children.

They went on toward the smoking room. It was the old man who looked in the door. "All right," he said. He looked sixty, though he was probably some age like forty-eight or fifty-two or fifty-eight. He wore a long overcoat with a collar which had once been fur, and a cap with earflaps like the caricature of an up-State farmer. His shoes were not mates. "There ain't many here yet. It will be some time now." While they stood there three other men came and looked into the smoking room with that same air not quite diffident and not quite furtive, with faces and garments that seemed to give off that same effluvium of soup kitchens and Salvation Army homes. They entered; the old man led the way toward the rear of the room, among the heavy, solid benches on which still more men of all ages sat in attitudes of thought or repose and looking as transient as scarecrows blown by a departed wind upon a series of rock ledges. The old man chose a bench and sat down, making room for the young man beside him. "I used to think that if you sat somewhere about the middle, he might skip you. But I found out that it don't make much difference where you sit."

"Nor where you lie, either," the young man said. He wore an army overcoat, new, and a pair of yellow army brogans of the sort that can be bought from so-called army stores for a dollar or so. He had not shaved in some time. "And it don't make a hell of a lot of difference whether you are breathing or not while you are lying there. I wish I had a cigarette. I have got used to not eating but be damned if I don't hate to get used to not smoking."

"Sure now," the old man said. "I wish I had a cigarette to give you. I ain't used tobacco myself since I went to Florida. That was funny: I hadn't smoked in ten years, yet as soon as I got back to New York, that was the first thing I thought about. Isn't that funny?"

"Yes," the young man said. "Especially if you never had any tobacco when you thought about wanting it again."

"Wanting it and not having it couldn't have worried me then," the old man said. "I was all right then. Until I—" He settled himself. Into his face came that rapt expression of the talkative old, without heat or bewilderment or rancor. "What confused me was I thought all the time that the burying money was all right. As soon as I found out about Danny's trouble I come right back to New York ——"

II

"Who is this Danny, anyway?" the young man said.

"Didn't I tell you? He's Sister's boy. There wasn't any of us left but Sister and Danny and me. Yet I was the weakly one. The one they all thought wouldn't live. I was give up to die twice before I was fifteen, yet I outlived them all. Outlived all eight of them when Sister died three years ago. That was why I went to Florida to live. Because I thought I couldn't stand the winters here. Yet I have stood three of them now since Sister died. But sometimes it looks like a man can stand just about anything if he don't believe he can stand it. Don't you think so?"

"I don't know," the young man said. "Which trouble was this?"

"Which?"

"Which trouble was Danny in now?"

"Don't get me wrong about Danny. He wasn't bad; just wild, like any young fellow. But not bad."

"All right," the young man said. "It wasn't any trouble then."

"No. He's a good boy. He's in Chicago now. Got a good job now. The lawyer in Jacksonville got it for him right after I come back to New York. I didn't know he had it until I tried to wire him that Sister was dead. Then I found that he was in Chicago, with a good job. He sent Sister a wreath of flowers that must have cost two hundred dollars. Sent it by air; that cost something, too. He couldn't come himself because he had just got the job and his boss was out of town and he couldn't get away. He was a good boy. That was why when that trouble come up about that woman on the floor below that accused him of stealing the clothes off her clothes-line, that I told Sister I would send him the railroad fare to Jacksonville, where I could look after him. Get

him clean away from them low-life boys around the saloons
and such. I come all the way from Florida to see about him.
That was how I happened to go with Sister to see Mr. Pinckski, before she ever begun to pay on the coffin. She wanted
me to go with her. Because you know how an old woman
is. Only she wasn't old, even if her and me had outlived all
the other seven. But you know how an old woman seems
to get comfort out of knowing she will be buried right in
case there isn't any of her kin there to 'tend to it. I guess
maybe that keeps a lot of them going."

"And especially with Danny already too busy to see if
she was buried at all, himself."

The old man, his mouth already shaped for further speech,
paused and looked at the young man. "What?"

"I say, if getting into the ground at last don't keep some
of them going, I don't know what it is that does."

"Oh. Maybe so. That ain't never worried me. I guess
because I was already give up to die twice before I was
fifteen. Like now every time a winter gets through, I just
say to myself, 'Well, I'll declare. Here I am again.' That was
why I went to Florida: because of the winters here. I hadn't
been back until I got Sister's letter about Danny, and I didn't
stay long then. And if I hadn't got the letter about Danny,
maybe I wouldn't ever have come back. But I come back,
and that was when she took me with her to see Mr. Pinckski
before she begun to pay on the coffin, for me to see if it was
all right like Mr. Pinckski said. He told her how the insurance companies would charge her interest all the time. He
showed us with the pencil and paper how if she paid her
money to the insurance companies it would be the same as
if she worked six minutes longer every night and give the
money for the extra six minutes to the insurance company.
But Sister said she wouldn't mind that, just six minutes,

because at three or four o'clock in the morning six minutes wouldn't ——"

"Three or four o'clock in the morning?"

"She scrubbed in them tall buildings down about Wall Street somewhere. Her and some other ladies. They would help one another night about, so they could get done at the same time and come home on the subway together. So Mr. Pinckski showed us with the pencil and paper how if she lived fifteen years longer say for instance Mr. Pinckski said, it would be the same as if she worked three years and eighty-five days without getting any pay for it. Like for three years and eighty-five days she would be working for the insurance companies for nothing. Like instead of living fifteen years, she would actually live only eleven years and two hundred and eight days. Sister stood there for a while, holding her purse under her shawl. Then she said, 'If I was paying the insurance companies to bury me instead of you, I would have to live three years and eighty-five days more before I could afford to die?'

" 'Well,' Mr. Pinckski said, like he didn't know what to say. 'Why, yes. Put it that way, then. You would work for the insurance companies three years and eighty-five days and not get any pay for it.'

" 'It ain't the work I mind,' Sister said. 'It ain't the working.' Then she took the first half a dollar out of her purse and put it down on Mr. Pinckski's desk."

III

Now AND THEN, with a long and fading reverberation, a subway train passed under their feet. Perhaps they thought momentarily of two green eyes tunneling violently through the earth without apparent propulsion or guidance, as though of their own unparalleled violence creating, like

spaced beads on a string, lighted niches in whose wan and
fleeting glare human figures like corpses set momentarily on
end in a violated grave yard leaned in one streaming and
rigid direction and flicked away.

"Because I was a weak child. They give me up to die
twice before I was fifteen. There was an insurance agent
sold me a policy once, worried at me until I said all right,
I would take it. Then they examined me and the only policy
they would give me was a thousand dollars at the rate of
fifty years old. And me just twenty-seven then. I was the
third one of eight, yet when Sister died three years ago I
had outlived them all. So when we got that trouble of
Danny's about the woman that said he stole the clothes
fixed up, Sister could ——"

"How did you get it fixed up?"

"We paid the money to the man that his job was to look
after the boys that Danny run with. The alderman knew
Danny and the other boys. It was all right then. So Sister
could go on paying the fifty cents to Mr. Pinckski every
week. Because we fixed it up for me to send the railroad
fare for Danny as soon as I could, so he could be in Florida
where I could look out for him. And I went back to Jacksonville and Sister could pay Mr. Pinckski the fifty cents without worrying. Each Sunday morning when her and the
other ladies got through, they would go home by Mr.
Pinckski's and wake him up and Sister would give him the
fifty cents.

"He never minded what time it was because Sister was a
good customer. He told her it would be all right, whatever
time she got there, to wake him up and pay him. So sometimes it would be as late as four o'clock, especially if they
had had a parade or something and the buildings messed up
with confetti and maybe flags. Maybe four times a year the
lady that lived next door to Sister would write me a letter

telling me how much Sister had paid to Mr. Pinckski and that Danny was getting along fine, behaving and not running around with them tough boys any more. So when I could I sent Danny the railroad fare to Florida. I never expected to hear about the money.

"That was what confused me. Sister could read some. She could read the church weekly fine that the priest gave her, but she never was much for writing. She said if she could just happen to find a pencil the size of a broom handle that she could use both hands on, that she could write fine. But regular pencils were too small for her. She said she couldn't feel like she had anything in her hand. So I never expected to hear about the money. I just sent it and then I fixed up with the landlady where I was living for a place for Danny, just thinking that some day soon Danny would just come walking in with his suit-case. The landlady kept the room a week for me, and then a man come in to rent it, so there wasn't anything she could do but give me the refusal of it.

"That wasn't no more than fair, after she had already kept it open a week for me. So I begun to pay for the room and when Danny didn't come I thought maybe something had come up, with the hard winter and all, and Sister needed the money worse than to send Danny to Florida on it, or maybe she thought he was too young yet. So after three months I let the room go. Every three or four months I would get the letter from the lady next door to Sister, about how every Sunday morning Sister and the other ladies would go to Mr. Pinckski and pay him the fifty cents. After fifty-two weeks, Mr. Pinckski set the coffin aside, with her name cut on a steel plate and nailed onto the coffin, her full name: Mrs. Margaret Noonan Gihon.

"It was a cheap coffin at first, just a wooden box, but after she had paid the second fifty-two half a dollars he took the name plate off of it and nailed it onto a better coffin, letting her pick it out herself in case she died that year. And after the third fifty-two half a dollars he let her pick out a still finer one, and the next year one with gold handles on it. He would let her come in and look at it whenever she wanted and bring whoever she wanted with her, to see the coffin and her name cut in the steel plate and nailed onto it. Even at four o'clock in the morning he would come down in his night-shirt and unlock the door and turn the light on for Sister and the other ladies to go back and look at the coffin.

"Each year it got to be a better coffin, with Mr. Pinckski showing the other ladies with the pencil and paper how Sister would have the coffin paid out soon and then she would just be paying on the gold handles and the lining. He let her pick out the lining too that she wanted and when the lady next door wrote me the next letter, Sister sent me a sample of the lining and a picture of the handles. Sister drew the picture, but she never could use a pencil because she always said the handle was too small for her to hold, though she could read the church weekly the priest gave her, because she said the Lord illuminated it for her."

"Is that so?" the young man said. "Jesus, I wish I either had a smoke or I would quit thinking about it."

"Yes. And a sample of the lining. But I couldn't tell much about it except that it suited Sister and that she liked it how Mr. Pinckski would let her bring in the other ladies to look at the trimmings and help her make up her mind. Because Mr. Pinckski said he would trust her because he didn't believe she would go and die on him to hurt his business like some did, and him not charging her a cent of interest like the insurance companies would charge. All she had to do was just to stop there every Sunday morning and pay him the half a dollar."

"Is that so?" the young man said. "He must be in the poor-house now."

"What?" The old man looked at the young man, his expression fixed. "Who in the poor-house now?"

IV

"Where was Danny all this time? Still doing his settlement work?"

"Yes. He worked whenever he could get a job. But a high-spirited young fellow, without nobody but a widow woman mother, without no father to learn him how you have to give and take in this world. That was why I wanted him down in Florida with me."

Now his arrested expression faded; he went easily into narration again with a kind of physical and unlistening joy, like a checked and long-broken horse slacked off again.

"That was what got me confused. I had already sent the money for him to come to Jacksonville on and when I never heard about it I just thought maybe Sister needed it with the hard winter and all or maybe she thought Danny was too young, like women will. And then about eight months after I let the room go I had a funny letter from the lady that lived next door to Sister. It said how Mr. Pinckski had moved the plate onto the next coffin and it said how glad Sister was that Danny was doing so well and she knew I would take good care of him because he was a good boy, besides being all Sister had. Like Danny was already in Florida, all the time.

"But I never knew he was there until I got the wire from him. It come from Augustine, not any piece away; I never found out until Sister died how Mrs. Zilich, that's the lady next door to her, that wrote the letters for Sister, had written me that Danny was coming to Florida the day he left, the day after the money come. Mrs. Zilich told how she had written the letter for Sister and give it to Danny himself to mail the night before he left. I never got it. I reckon Danny never mailed it. I reckon, being a young, high-spirited boy, he decided he wanted to strike out himself and show us what he could do without any help from us, like I did when I come to Florida.

"Mrs. Zilich said she thought of course Danny was with me and that she thought at the time it was funny that when I would write to Sister I never mentioned Danny. So when she would read the letters to Sister she would put in something about Danny was all right and doing fine. So when I got the wire from Danny in Augustine I telephoned Mrs. Zilich in New York. It cost eleven dollars. I told her that Danny was in a little trouble, not serious, and for her to not tell Sister it was serious trouble, to just tell her that we would need some money. Because I had sent money for Danny to come to Florida on and I had paid the three months for the room and I had just paid the premium on my insurance, and so the lawyer looked at Danny and Danny sitting there on the cot in the cell without no collar on and Danny said, 'Where would I get any money,' only it was jack he called it.

"And the lawyer said, 'Where would you get it?' and Danny said, 'Just set me down back home for ten minutes. I'll show you.' 'Seventy-five bucks,' he says, telling me that was all of it. Then the lawyer says that was neither here nor there and so I telephoned to Mrs. Zilich and told her to tell Sister to go to Mr. Pinckski and ask him to let her take back some of the coffin money; he could put the name plate back on the coffin she had last year or maybe the year before, and as soon as I could get some money on my insurance policy I would pay Mr. Pinckski back and some interest too. I telephoned from the jail, but I didn't say where I was telephoning from; I just said we would need some money quick."

"What was he in for this time?" the young man said.

"He wasn't in jail the other time, about them clothes off that line. That woman was lying about him. After we paid the money, she admitted she was probably mistaken."

"All right," the young man said. "What was he in for?"

"They called it grand larceny and killing a policeman. They framed him, them others did that didn't like him. He was just wild. That was all. He was a good boy. When Sister died he couldn't come to the funeral. But he sent a wreath that must have cost $200 if it cost a cent. By air mail, with the high postage in the . . ."

His voice died away; he looked at the young man with a kind of pleased astonishment. "I'll declare I made a joke. But I didn't mean ——"

"Sure. I know you didn't mean to make a joke. What about the jail?"

"The lawyer was already there when I got there. Some friends had sent the lawyer to help him. And he swore to me on his mother's name that he wasn't even there when the cop got shot. He was in Orlando at the time. He showed me a ticket from Orlando to Waycross that he had bought and missed the train; that was how he happened to have it with him. It had the date punched in it, the same night the policeman got killed, showing that Danny wasn't even there and that them other boys had framed him. He was mad. The lawyer said how he would see the friends that had sent him to help Danny and get them to help. 'By God, they better,' Danny said. 'If they think I'm going to take this laying down they better ——'

"Then the lawyer got him quiet again, like he did when Danny was talking about that money the man he worked for or something had held out on him back in New York. And

so I telephoned Mrs. Zilich, so as not to worry Sister, and
told her to go to Mr. Pinckski. Two days later I got the
telegram from Mrs. Zilich. I guess Mrs. Zilich hadn't never
sent a telegram before and so she didn't know she had ten
words without counting the address because it just said
You and Danny come home quick Mrs. Sophie Zilich New
York.

"I couldn't make nothing out of it and we talked it over
and the lawyer said I better go and see, that he would take
care of Danny till I got back. So we fixed up a letter from
Danny to Sister, for Mrs. Zilich to read to her, about how
Danny was all right and getting along fine ———"

V

AT THAT moment there entered the room a man in the uniform of the railway company. As he entered, from about
him somewhere—behind, above—a voice came. Though it
spoke human speech it did not sound like a human voice,
since it was too big to have emerged from known man
and it had a quality at once booming, cold, and forlorn, as
though it were not interested in nor listening to what it said.

"There," the old man said.

He and the young man turned and looked back across
the benches, as most of the other heads had done, as though
they were all dummies moved by a single wire. The man in
uniform advanced slowly into the room, moving along the
first bench. As he did so the men on that bench and on the
others began to rise and depart, passing the man in uniform
as though he were not there; he too moving on into the
room as if it were empty. "I guess we'll have to move."

"Hell," the young man said. "Let him come in and ask
for them. They pay him to do it."

"He caught me the other night. The second time, too."

"What about that? This time won't make but three. What did you do then?"

"Oh, yes," the old man said. "I knew that was the only thing to do, after that telegram. Mrs. Zilich wouldn't have spent the money to telegraph without good reason. I didn't know what she had told Sister. I just knew that Mrs. Zilich thought there wasn't time to write a letter and that she was trying to save money on the telegram, not knowing she had ten words and the man at the telegraph office not telling her better. So I didn't know what was wrong. I never suspicioned it at all. That was what confused me, you see."

He turned and looked back again toward the man in uniform moving from bench to bench while just before him the men in mismated garments, with that identical neatness of indigence, with that identical air of patient and indomitable forlornness, rose and moved toward the exit in a monstrous and outrageous analogy to flying fish before the advancing prow of a ship.

"What confused you?" the young man said.

"Mrs. Zilich told me. I left Danny in the jail. (Them friends that sent him the lawyer got him out the next day. When I heard from him again, he was already in Chicago, with a good job; he sent that wreath. I didn't know he was even gone from the jail until I tried to get word to him about Sister), and I come on to New York. I had just enough money for that, and Mrs. Zilich met me at the station and told me. At this station right here. It was snowing that night, too. She was waiting at the top of the steps.

" 'Where's Sister?' I said. 'She didn't come with you?'

" 'What is it now?' Mrs. Zilich said. 'You don't need to tell me he is just sick.'

" 'Did you tell Sister he ain't just sick?' I said. 'I didn't have to,' Mrs. Zilich said. 'I didn't have time to, even if I would have.' She told about how it was cold that night and

so she waited up for Sister, keeping the fire going and a pot
of coffee ready, and how she waited till Sister had took off
her coat and shawl and was beginning to get warm, setting
there with a cup of coffee; then Mrs. Zilich said, 'Your
brother telephoned from Florida.' That's all she had time to
say. She never even had to tell Sister how I said for her to
go to Mr. Pinckski, because Sister said right off, 'He will
want that money.' Just what I had said, you see.

"Mrs. Zilich noticed it too. 'Maybe it's because you are
kin, both kin to that—' Then she stopped and said, 'Oh, I
ain't going to say anything about him. Don't worry. The
time to do that is past now.' Then she told me how she said
to Sister, 'You can stop there on the way down this afternoon and see Mr. Pinckski.' But Sister was already putting
on her coat and shawl again and her not an hour home from
work and it snowing. She wouldn't wait."

"She had to take back the coffin money, did she?" the
young man said.

"Yes. Mrs. Zilich said that her and Sister went to Mr.
Pinckski and woke him up. And he told them that Sister had
already taken the money back."

"What?" the young man said. "Already?"

"Yes. He said how Danny had come to him about a year
back, with a note from Sister saying to give Danny the
money that she had paid in to Mr. Pinckski and that Mr.
Pinckski did it. And Sister standing there with her hands
inside her shawl, not looking at anything until Mrs. Zilich
said, 'A note? Mrs. Gihon never sent you a note because she
can't write,' and Mr. Pinckski said, 'Should I know if she
can't write or not when her own son brings me a note signed
with her name?' and Mrs. Zilich says, 'Let's see it.'

"Sister hadn't said anything at all, like she wasn't even
there, and Mr. Pinckski showed them the note. I saw it too.
It said, 'Received of Mr. Pinckski a hundred and thirty

dollars being the full amount deposited with him less interest. Mrs. Margaret N. Gihon.' And Mrs. Zilich said how she thought about that hundred and thirty dollars and she thought how Sister had paid twenty-six dollars a year for five years and seven months, and she said, 'Interest? What interest?' and Mr. Pinckski said, 'For taking the name off the coffin,' because that made the coffin second-handed. And Mrs. Zilich said that Sister turned and went toward the door. 'Wait,' Mrs. Zilich said. 'We're going to stay right here until you get that money. There's something funny about this because you can't write to sign a note.' But Sister just went on toward the door until Mrs. Zilich said, 'Wait, Margaret.' And then Sister said, 'I signed it.' "

VI

THE VOICE of the man in uniform could be heard now as he worked slowly toward them: "Tickets. Tickets. Show your tickets."

"I guess it's hard enough to know what a single woman will do," the old man said. "But a widow woman with just one child. I didn't know she could write, either. I guess she picked it up cleaning up them offices every night. Anyway, Mr. Pinckski showed me the note, how she admitted she signed it, and he explained to me how the difference was; that he had to charge to protect himself in case the coffins ever were refused and become second-hand; that some folks was mighty particular about having a brand new coffin.

"He had put the plate with Sister's name on it back onto the cheap coffin that she started off with, so she was still all right for a coffin, even if it never had any handles and lining. I never said anything about that; that twenty-six dollars she had paid in since she give the money to Danny wouldn't have helped any; I had already spent that much getting back to see about the money, and anyway, Sister still had a coffin ——"

The voice of the man in uniform was quite near now, with a quality methodical, monotonous, and implacable: "Tickets. Tickets. Show your tickets. All without railroad tickets."

The young man rose. "I'll be seeing you," he said. The old man rose too. Beyond the man in uniform the room was almost empty.

"I guess it's about time," the old man said. He followed the young man into the rotunda. There was an airplane in it, motionless, squatting, with a still, beetling look like a huge bug preserved in alcohol. There was a placard beside it. about how it had flown over mountains and vast wastes of snow.

"They might have tried it over New York," the young man said. "It would have been closer."

"Yes," the old man said. "It costs more, though. But I guess that's fair, since it is faster. When Sister died, Danny sent a wreath of flowers by air. It must have cost two hundred dollars. The wreath did, I mean. I don't know what it cost to send it by air."

Then they both looked up the ramp and through the arcade, toward the doors on Seventh Avenue. Beyond the doors lay a thick, moribund light that seemed to fill the arcade with the smell of snow and of cold, so that for a while longer they seemed to stand in the grip of a dreadful reluctance and inertia.

"So they went on back home," the old man said. "Mrs. Zilich said how Sister was already shaking and she got Sister to bed. And that night Sister had a fever and Mrs. Zilich sent for the doctor and the doctor looked at Sister and told Mrs. Zilich she had better telegraph if there was anybody to telegraph to. When I got home Sister didn't know me. The priest was already there, and we never could tell if she knew anything or not, not even when we read the letter from Danny that we had fixed up in the jail, about how he was all right. The priest read it to her, but we couldn't tell if she heard him or not. That night she died."

"Is that so?" The young man said, looking up the ramp. He moved. "I'm going to the Grand Central."

Again the old man moved, with that same unwearying alacrity. "I guess that's the best thing to do. We might have a good while there." He looked up at the clock; he said with pleased surprise: "Half past one already. And a half an hour to get there. And if we're lucky, we'll have two hours before he comes along. Maybe three. That'll be five o'clock. Then it will be only two hours more till daylight."

Artist at Home

Roger Howes was a fattish, mild, nondescript man of forty, who came to New York from the Mississippi Valley somewhere as an advertisement writer and married and turned novelist and sold a book and bought a house in the Valley of Virginia and never went back to New York again, even on a visit. For five years he had lived in the old brick house with his wife Anne and their two children, where old ladies came to tea in horsedrawn carriages or sent the empty carriages for him or sent by Negro servants in the otherwise empty carriages shoots and cuttings of flowering shrubs and jars of pickle or preserves and copies of his books for autographs.

He didn't go back to New York any more, but now and then New York came to visit him: the ones he used to know, the artists and poets and such he knew before he began to earn enough food to need a cupboard to put it in. The painters, the writers, that hadn't sold a book or a picture—men with beards sometimes in place of collars, who came and wore his shirts and socks and left them under the bureau when they departed, and women in smocks but sometimes not: those gaunt and eager and carnivorous tymbesteres of Art.

At first it had been just hard to refuse them, but now it was harder to tell his wife that they were coming. Sometimes he did not know himself they were coming. They usually wired him, on the day on which they would arrive, usually collect. He lived four miles from the village and the book hadn't sold quite enough to own a car too, and he was a little fat, a little overweight, so sometimes it would be two or three days before he would get his mail. Maybe he would just wait for the next batch of company to bring the mail up with them. After the first year the man at the station (he was the telegraph agent and the station agent and Roger's kind of town agent all in one) got to where he could recognize them on sight. They would be standing on the little platform, with that blank air, with nothing to look at except a little yellow station and the back end of a moving train and some mountains already beginning to get dark, and the agent would come out of his little den with a handful of mail and a package or so, and the telegram. "He lives about four miles up the Valley. You can't miss it."

"Who lives about four miles up the valley?"

"Howes does. If you all are going up there, I thought maybe you wouldn't mind taking these letters to him. One of them is a telegram."

"A telegram?"

"It come this a.m. But he ain't been to town in two-three days. I thought maybe you'd take it to him."

"Telegram? Hell. Give it here."

"It's forty-eight cents to pay on it."

"Keep it, then. Hell."

So they would take everything except the telegram and they would walk the four miles to Howes', getting there after supper. Which would be all right, because the women would all be too mad to eat anyway, including Mrs. Howes, Anne. So a couple of days later, someone would send a carriage for Roger and he would stop at the village and pay out the wire telling him how his guests would arrive two days ago.

So when this poet in the sky-blue coat gets off the train,

the agent comes right out of his little den, with the telegram. "It's about four miles up the Valley," he says. "You can't miss it. I thought maybe you'd take this telegram up to him. It come this a.m., but he ain't been to town for two-three days. You can take it. It's paid."

"I know it is," the poet says. "Hell. You say it is four miles up there?"

"Right straight up the road. You can't miss it."

So the poet took the telegram and the agent watched him go on out of sight up the Valley Road, with a couple or three other folks coming to the doors to look at the blue coat maybe. The agent grunted. "Four miles," he said. "That don't mean no more to that fellow than if I had said four switch frogs. But maybe with that dressing-sacque he can turn bird and fly it."

Roger hadn't told his wife, Anne, about this poet at all, maybe because he didn't know himself. Anyway, she didn't know anything about it until the poet came limping into the garden where she was cutting flowers for the supper table, and told her she owed him forty-eight cents.

"Forty-eight cents?" Anne said.

He gave her the telegram. "You don't have to open it now, you see," the poet said. "You can just pay me back the forty-eight cents and you won't have to even open it." She stared at him, with a handful of flowers and the scissors in the other hand, so finally maybe it occurred to him to tell her who he was. "I'm John Blair," he said. "I sent this telegram this morning to tell you I was coming. It cost me forty-eight cents. But now I'm here, so you don't need the telegram."

So Anne stands there, holding the flowers and the scissors, saying "Damn, Damn, Damn" while the poet tells her how she ought to get her mail oftener. "You want to keep up with what's going on," he tells her, and her saying "Damn, Damn.

Damn," until at last he says he'll just stay to supper and then walk back to the village, if it's going to put her out that much.

"Walk?" she said, looking him up and down. "You walk? Up here from the village? I don't believe it. Where is your baggage?"

"I've got it on. Two shirts, and I have an extra pair of socks in my pocket. Your cook can wash, can't she?"

She looks at him, holding the flowers and the scissors. Then she tells him to come on into the house and live there forever. Except she didn't say exactly that. She said: "You walk? Nonsense. I think you're sick. You come in and sit down and rest." Then she went to find Roger and tell him to bring down the pram from the attic. Of course she didn't say exactly that, either.

Roger hadn't told her about this poet; he hadn't got the telegram himself yet. Maybe that was why she hauled him over the coals so that night: because he hadn't got the telegram.

They were in their bedroom. Anne was combing out her hair. The children were spending the summer up in Connecticut, with Anne's folks. He was a minister, her father was. "You told me that the last time would be the last. Not a month ago. Less than that, because when that last batch left I had to paint the furniture in the guest room again to hide where they put their cigarettes on the dressing table and the window ledges. And I found in a drawer a broken comb I would not have asked Pinkie (Pinkie was the Negro cook) to pick up, and two socks that were not even mates that I bought for you myself last winter, and a single stocking that I couldn't even recognize any more as mine. You tell me that Poverty looks after its own: well, let it. But why must we be instruments of Poverty?"

"This is a poet. That last batch were not poets. We haven't

had a poet in the house in some time. Place losing all its mel-
lifluous overtones and subtleties."

"How about that woman that wouldn't bathe in the bathroom? who insisted on going down to the creek every morning without even a bathing suit, until Amos Crain's (he was
a farmer that lived across the creek from them) wife had to
send me word that Amos was afraid to try to plow his lower
field? What do people like that think that out-doors, the
country, is? I cannot understand it, any more than I can understand why you feel that you should feed and lodge ———"

"Ah, that was just a touch of panic fear that probably did
Amos good. Jolted him out of himself, out of his rut."

"The rut where he made his wife's and children's daily
bread, for six days. And worse than that. Amos is young. He
probably had illusions about women until he saw that creature down there without a stitch on."

"Well, you are in the majority, you and Mrs. Crain." He
looked at the back of her head, her hands combing out her
hair, and her probably watching him in the mirror and him
not knowing it, what with being an artist and all. "This is a
man poet."

"Then I suppose he will refuse to leave the bathroom at all.
I suppose you'll have to carry a tray to him in the tub three
times a day. Why do you feel compelled to lodge and feed
these people? Can't you see they consider you an easy mark?
that they eat your food and wear your clothes and consider
us hopelessly bourgeois for having enough food for other
people to eat, and a little soft-brained for giving it away?
And now this one, in a sky-blue dressing-sacque."

"There's a lot of wear and tear to just being a poet. I don't
think you realize that."

"Oh, I don't mind. Let him wear a lamp shade or a sauce
pan too. What does he want of you? advice, or just food and
lodging?"

"Not advice. You must have gathered at supper what his opinion of my mentality is."

"He revealed pretty clearly what his own mentality is. The only thing in the house that really pleased him was Pinkie's colored head-rag."

"Not advice," Roger said. "I don't know why he shows me his stuff. He does it like you'd give caviar to an elephant."

"And of course you accept his dictum about the elephant. And I suppose you are going to get them to publish his book, too."

"Well, there's some good stuff in it. And maybe if he sees it in print, he'll really get busy. Work. Or maybe someone will make him mad enough to really write something. Something with an entrail in it. He's got it in him. It may not be but one poem. But it's there. Maybe if he can just stop talking long enough to get it out. And I thought if he came down here, where he will have to walk four miles to find somebody to talk to, once Amos comes to recognize that blue coat."

"Ah," Anne said. "So you wrote him to come. I knew you had, but I'm glad to hear you admit it of your own free will. Go on to bed," she said. "You haven't done a stroke of work today, and Lord only knows now when you will."

Thus life went along in its old pleasant way. Because poets are all different from one another, it seemed; this one, anyway. Because it soon developed that Anne doesn't see this poet at all, hardly. It seems that she can't even know he is in the house unless she hears him snoring at night. So it took her two weeks to get steamed up again. And this time she is not even combing her hair. "Is it two weeks he's been here, or just two years?" She is sitting at the dressing table, but she is not doing anything, which any husband, even an artist, should know is a bad sign. When you see a woman sitting half dressed before a dressing table with a mirror and not even watching herself talk in the mirror, it's time to smell smoke in the wind.

"He has been here two weeks, but unless I happen to go to the kitchen, I never see him, since he prefers Pinkie's company to ours. And when he was missing that first Wednesday night, on Pinkie's evening off, I said at first, 'What tact.' That was before I learned that he had taken supper with Pinkie's family at her house and had gone with them to prayer meeting. And he went again Sunday night and again last Wednesday night, and now tonight (and though he tells me I have neither intelligence nor imagination) he would be surprised to know that I am imagining right now that sky-blue dressing-sacque in a wooden church full of sweating niggers without any incongruity at all."

"Yes. It's quite a picture, isn't it?"

"But apart from such minor embarrassments like not knowing where our guest is, and bearing upon our patient brows a certain amount of reflected ridiculousness, he is a very pleasant companion. Instructing, edifying, and self-effacing. I never know he is even in the house unless I hear your typewriter, because I know it is not you because you have not written a line in—is it two weeks, or just two years? He enters the room which the children are absolutely forbidden and puts his one finger on that typewriter which Pinkie is not even permitted to touch with a dust-cloth, and writes a poem about freedom and flings it at you to commend and applaud. What is it he says?"

"You tell. This is fine."

"He flings it at you like—like . . . Wait; I've got it: like flinging caviar at an elephant, and he says, 'Will this sell?' Not, Is this good? or Do you like it? Will this sell? and you ——"

"Go on. I couldn't hope to even compete."

"You read it, carefully. Maybe the same poem, I don't

know; I've learned recently on the best authority that I am
not intelligent enough to get my poetry at first hand. You
read it, carefully, and then you say, 'It ought to. Stamps in
the drawer there.' " She went to the window. "No, I haven't
evolved far enough yet to take my poetry straight; I won't
understand it. It has to be fed to me by hand, when he has
time, on the terrace after supper on the nights when there is
no prayer meeting at Pinkie's church. Freedom. Equality. In
words of one syllable, because it seems that, being a woman,
I don't want freedom and don't know what equality means,
until you take him up and show him in professional words
how he is not so wise, except he is wise enough to shut up
then and let you show both of us how you are not so wise
either." The window was above the garden. There were curtains in it. She stood between the curtains, looking out. "So
Young Shelley has not crashed through yet."

"Not yet. But it's there. Give him time."

"I'm glad to hear that. He's been here two weeks now. I'm
glad his racket is poetry, something you can perpetrate in
two lines. Otherwise, at this rate . . ." She stood between the
curtains. They were blowing, slow, in and out. "Damn.
Damn. Damn. He doesn't eat enough."

So Roger went and put another cushion in the pram. Only
she didn't say exactly that and he didn't do exactly that.

Now get this. This is where it starts. On the days when
there wasn't any prayer meeting at the nigger church, the
poet has taken to doping along behind her in the garden while
she cut the flowers for the supper table, talking to her about
poetry or freedom or maybe about the flowers. Talking
about something, anyway; maybe when he quit talking all of
a sudden that night when he and she were walking in the
garden after supper, it should have tipped her off. But it
didn't. Or at least, when they came to the end of the path

and turned, the next thing she seemed to know was his mug all set for the haymaker. Anyway, she didn't move until the clinch was over. Then she flung back, her hand lifted. "You damned idiot!" she says.

He doesn't move either, like he is giving her a fair shot. "What satisfaction will it be to slap this mug?" he says.

"I know that," she says. She hits him on the chest with her fist, light, full, yet restrained all at the same time: mad and careful too. "Why did you do such a clumsy thing?"

But she doesn't get anything out of him. He just stands there, offering her a clean shot; maybe he is not even looking at her, with his hair all over the place and this sky-blue coat that fits him like a short horse-blanket. You take a rooster, an old rooster. An old bull is different. See him where the herd has run him out, blind and spavined or whatever, yet he still looks married. Like he was saying, "Well, boys, you can look at me now. But I was a husband and father in my day." But an old rooster. He just looks unmarried, a born bachelor. Born a bachelor in a world without hens and he found it out so long ago he don't even remember there are not any hens. "Come along," she says, turning fast, stiff-backed, and the poet doping along behind her. Maybe that's what gave him away. Anyway, she looks back, slowing. She stops. "So you think you are the hot shot, do you?" she says. "You think I'm going to tell Roger, do you?"

"I don't know," he says. "I hadn't thought about it."

"You mean, you don't care whether I tell him or not?"

"Yes," he says.

"Yes what?"

It seems she can't tell whether he's looking at her or not, whether he ever looked at her. He just stands there, doping, about twice as tall as she is. "When I was a little boy, we would have sherbet on Sunday," he says. "Just a breath of lemon in it. Like narcissus smells, I remember. I think I re-

member. I was ... four ... three. Mother died and we moved
to a city. Boarding-house. A brick wall. There was one window, like a one-eyed man with sore eyes. And a dead cat.
But before that we had lots of trees, like you have. I would
sit on the kitchen steps in the late afternoon, watching the
Sunday light in the trees, eating sherbet."

She is watching him. Then she turns, walking fast. He follows, doping along a little behind her, so that when she stops
in the shadow of a clump of bushes, with her face all fixed, he
stands there like this dope until she touches him. And even
then he doesn't get it. She has to tell him to hurry. So he gets
it, then. A poet is human, it seems, just like a man.

But that's not it. That can be seen in any movie. This is
what it is, what is good.

About this time, coincident with this second clinch, Roger
happens to come out from behind this bush. He comes out
kind of happen-so; pleasant and quiet from taking a little
stroll in the moonlight to settle his supper. They all three
stroll back to the house, Roger in the middle. They get there
so quick that nobody thinks to say goodnight when Anne
goes on in the house and up the stairs. Or maybe it is because
Roger is doing all the talking himself at that moment, poetry
having gone into a slump, you might say. "Moonlight,"
Roger is saying, looking at the moon like he owned it too; "I
can't stand it any more. I run to walls, an electric light. That
is, moonlight used to make me feel sad and old and I would
do that. But now I'm afraid it don't even make me feel lonely
any more. So I guess I am old."

"That's a fact," the poet says. "Where can we talk?"

"Talk?" Roger says. He looked like a head-waiter, anyway: a little bald, flourishing, that comes to the table and lifts
off a cover and looks at it like he is saying, "Well, you can
eat this muck, if you want to pay to do it." "Right this way."

he says. They go to the office, the room where he writes his books, where he doesn't even let the children come at all. He sits behind the typewriter and fills his pipe. Then he sees that the poet hasn't sat down. "Sit down," he says.

"No," the poet says. "Listen," he says. "Tonight I kissed your wife. I'm going to again, if I can."

"Ah," Roger says. He is too busy filling the pipe right to look at the poet, it seems. "Sit down."

"No," the poet says.

Roger lights the pipe. "Well," he says, "I'm afraid I can't advise you about that. I have written a little poetry, but I never could seduce women." He looks at the poet now. "Look here," he says, "you are not well. You go on to bed. We'll talk about this tomorrow."

"No," the poet says, "I cannot sleep under your roof."

"Anne keeps on saying you are not well," Roger says. "Do you know of anything that's wrong with you?"

"I don't know," the poet says.

Roger sucks at the pipe. He seems to be having a little trouble making it burn right. Maybe that is why he slams the pipe down on the desk, or maybe he is human too, like a poet. Anyway, he slams the pipe down on the desk so that the tobacco pops out burning among the papers. And there they are: the bald husband with next week's flour and meat actually in sight, and the home-wrecker that needs a haircut, in one of these light blue jackets that ladies used to wear with lace boudoir caps when they would be sick and eat in bed. "What in hell do you mean," Roger says, "coming in my house and eating my food and bothering Anne with your damned . . ." But that was all. But even that was pretty good for a writer, an artist; maybe that's all that should be expected from them. Or maybe it was because the poet wasn't even listening to him. "He's not even here," Roger says to himself; like he had told the poet, he used to write poetry himself, and so he knew them. "He's up there at Anne's door now, kneeling outside her door." And outside that door was as close to Anne as Roger got too, for some time. But that was later, and he and the poet are now in the office, with him trying to make the poet shut his yap and go up to bed, and the poet refusing.

"I cannot lie under your roof," the poet says. "May I see Anne?"

"You can see her in the morning. Any time. All day, if you want to. Don't talk drivel."

"May I speak to Anne?" the poet says, like he might have been speaking to a one-syllable feeb.

So Roger goes up and tells Anne and comes back and sits behind the typewriter again and then Anne comes down and Roger hears her and the poet goes out the front door. After awhile Anne comes back alone. "He's gone," she says.

"Is he?" Roger says, like he is not listening. Then he jumps up. "Gone? He can't—this late. Call him back."

"He won't come back," Anne says. "Let him alone." She goes on upstairs. When Roger went up a little later, the door was locked.

Now get this. This is it. He came back down to the office and put some paper into the typewriter and began to write. He didn't go very fast at first, but by daylight he was sounding like forty hens in a sheet-iron corn-crib, and the written sheets on the desk were piling up. . . .

He didn't see or hear of the poet for two days. But the poet was still in town. Amos Crain saw him and came and told Roger. It seems that Amos happened to come to the house for something, because that was the only way anybody could have got to Roger to tell him anything for two days and nights. "I heard that typewriter before I crossed the creek," Amos says. "I see that blue dressing-sacque at the hotel yesterday," he says.

That night, while Roger was at work, Anne came down the stairs. She looked in the office door. "I'm going to meet him," she said.

"Will you tell him to come back?" Roger said. "Will you tell him I sent the message?"

"No," Anne said.

And the last thing she heard when she went out and when she came back an hour later and went upstairs and locked her door (Roger was sleeping on the sleeping-porch now, on an army cot) was the typewriter.

And so life went on in its old, pleasant, happy way. They saw one another often, sometimes twice a day after Anne quit coming down to breakfast. Only, a day or so after that, she missed the sound of the typewriter; maybe she missed being kept awake by it. "Have you finished it?" she said. "The story?"

"Oh. No. No, it's not finished yet. Just resting for a day or so." Bull market in typewriting, you might say.

It stayed bullish for several days. He had got into the habit of going to bed early, of being in his cot on the sleeping-porch when Anne came back into the house. One night she came out onto the sleeping-porch, where he was reading in bed. "I'm not going back again," she said. "I'm afraid to."

"Afraid of what? Aren't two children enough for you? Three, counting me."

"I don't know." It was a reading lamp and her face was in the shadow. "I don't know." He turned the light, to shine it on her face, but before it got to her face she turned, running. He got there just in time to have the door banged in his face. "Blind! Blind!" she said beyond the door. "Go away! Go away!"

He went away, but he couldn't get to sleep. So after a while he took the metal shade off the reading lamp and jimmied the window into the room where the children slept. The door from here into Anne's room wasn't locked. Anne was asleep. The moon was getting down then, and he could see her face. He hadn't made any noise, but she waked anyway, looking up at him, not moving. "He's had nothing, nothing. The only thing he remembers of his mother is the taste of sherbet on Sunday afternoon. He says my mouth tastes like that. He says my mouth is his mother." She began to cry. She didn't move, face-up on the pillow, her arms under the sheet, crying. Roger sat on the edge of the bed and touched her and she flopped over then, with her face down against his knee, crying.

They talked until about daylight. "I don't know what to do. Adultery wouldn't get me—anybody—into that place where he lives. Lives? He's never lived. He's ——" She was breathing quiet, her face turned down, but still against his knee—him stroking her shoulder. "Would you take me back?"

"I don't know." He stroked her shoulder. "Yes. Yes. I'd take you back."

And so the typewriting market picked up again. It took a spurt that night, as soon as Anne got herself cried off to sleep, and the market held steady for three or four days, without closing at night, even after Pinkie told him how the telephone was out of fix and he found where the wires were cut and knows where he can find the scissors that did it when he wants to. He doesn't go to the village at all, even when he had a free ride. He would spend half a morning sitting by the road, waiting for somebody to pass that would bring him back a package of tobacco or sugar or something. "If I went to the village, he might have left town," he said.

On the fifth day, Amos Crain brought him his mail. That was the day the rain came up. There was a letter for Anne.

"He evidently doesn't want my advice on this," he said to himself. "Maybe he has already sold it." He gave the letter to Anne. She read it, once.

"Will you read it?" she said.

"I wouldn't care to," he said.

But the typing market is still steady, so that when the rain came up this afternoon, he had to turn on the light. The rain was so hard on the house that he could watch his fingers (he used two or three of them) hitting the keys without hearing a sound. Pinkie didn't come, so after a while he quit and fixed a tray and took it up and left it on a chair outside Anne's door. He didn't stop to eat, himself.

It was after dark when she came down the first time. It was still raining. He saw her cross the door, going fast, in a raincoat and a rubber hat. He caught her as she opened the front door, with the rain blowing in. "Where are you going?" he said.

She tried to jerk her arm loose. "Let me alone."

"You can't go out in this. What is it?"

"Let me alone. Please." She jerked her arm, pulling at the door which he was holding.

"You can't. What is it? I'll do it. What is it?"

But she just looked at him, jerking at her arm and at the door knob. "I must go to the village. Please, Roger."

"You can't do that. At night, and in all this rain."

"Please. Please." He held her. "Please. Please." But he held her, and she let the door go and went back up stairs. And he went back to the typewriter, to this market still going great guns.

He is still at it at midnight. This time Anne has on a bathrobe. She stands in the door, holding to the door. Her hair is down. "Roger," she says. "Roger."

He goes to her, fast for a fat man; maybe he thinks she is sick. "What? What is it?"

She goes to the front door and opens it; the rain comes in again. "There," she says. "Out there."

"What?"

"He is. Blair."

He draws her back. He makes her go to the office, then he puts on his raincoat and takes the umbrella and goes out. "Blair!" he calls. "John!" Then the shade on the office window goes up, where Anne has raised it and carried the desk lamp to the window and turned the light out-doors, and then he sees Blair, standing in the rain, without any hat, with his blue coat like it was put on him by a paper-hanger, with his face lifted toward Anne's window.

And here we are again: the bald husband, the rural plute, and this dashing blade, this home-wrecking poet. Both gentlemen, being artists: the one that doesn't want the other to get wet; the other whose conscience won't let him wreck the house from inside. Here we are, with Roger trying to hold one of these green silk, female umbrellas over himself and the poet too, jerking at the poet's arm.

"You damned fool! Come in the house!"

"No." His arm gives a little as Roger jerks at it, but the poet himself doesn't move.

"Do you want to drown? Come on, man!"

"No."

Roger jerks at the poet's arm, like jerking at the arm of a wet saw-dust doll. Then he begins to yell at the house: "Anne! Anne!"

"Did she say for me to come in?" the poet says.

"I—Yes. Yes. Come in the house. Are you mad?"

"You're lying," the poet says. "Let me alone."

"What are you trying to do?" Roger says. "You can't stand here like this."

"Yes, I can. You go on in. You'll take cold."

Roger runs back to the house; they have an argument first

because Roger wants the poet to keep the umbrella and the poet won't do it. So Roger runs back to the house. Anne is at the door. "The fool," Roger says. "I can't ——"

"Come in!" Anne calls. "John! Please!" But the poet has stepped out of the light and vanished. "John!" Anne calls. Then she began to laugh, staring at Roger from between her hair brushing at her hair with her hands. "He—he looked so f—funny. He l—looked so ——" Then she was not laughing and Roger had to hold her up. He carried her upstairs and put her to bed and sat with her until she could stop crying. Then he went back to the office. The lamp was still at the window, and when he moved it the light went across the lawn and he saw Blair again. He was sitting on the ground, with his back against a tree, his face raised in the rain toward Anne's window. Roger rushed out again, but when he got there, Blair was gone. Roger stood under the umbrella and called him for a while, but he never got any answer. Maybe he was going to try again to make the poet take the umbrella. So maybe he didn't know as much about poets as he thought he did. Or maybe he was thinking about Pope. Pope might have had an umbrella.

They never saw the poet again. This one, that is. Because this happened almost six months ago, and they still live there. But they never saw this one. Three days later, Anne gets the second letter, mailed from the village. It is a menu card from the Elite Café, or maybe they call it the Palace. It was already autographed by the flies that eat there, and the poet had written on the back of it. Anne left it on Roger's desk and went out, and then Roger read it.

It seems that this was the shot. The one that Roger had always claimed to be waiting for. Anyway, the magazines that don't have any pictures took the poem, stealing it from one another while the interest or whatever it was ate up the money that the poet never got for it. But that was all right, too, because by that time Blair was dead.

Amos Crain's wife told them how the poet had left town. And a week later Anne left too. She went up to Connecticut to spend the rest of the summer with her mother and father, where the children were. The last thing she heard when she left the house was the typewriter.

But it was two weeks after Anne left before Roger finished it, wrote the last word. At first he wanted to put the poem in too, this poem on the menu card that wasn't about freedom, either, but he didn't. Conscience, maybe he called it, put over the old haymaker, and Roger took it standing, like a little man, and sent off the poem for the magazines to jaw over, and tied up the papers he had written and sent them off too. And what was it he had been writing? Him, and Anne, and the poet. Word for word, between the waiting spells to find out what to write down next, with a few changes here and there, of course, because live people do not make good copy, the most interesting copy being gossip, since it mostly is not true.

So he bundled the pages up and sent them off and they sent him the money. It came just in time, because the winter was coming and he still owed a balance on Blair's hospital and funeral. So he paid that, and with the rest of the money he bought Anne a fur coat and himself and the children some winter underwear.

Blair died in September. Anne and the children were still away when he got the wire, three or four days late, since the next batch of them had not arrived yet. So here he is, sitting at his desk, in the empty house, with the typewriting all finished, holding the wire in his hand. "Shelley," he says. "His whole life was a not very successful imitation of itself. Even to the amount of water it took."

He didn't tell Anne about the poet until after the fur coat came. "Did you see that he . . . ." Anne said.

"Yes. He had a nice room, in the sun. A good nurse. The doctor didn't want him to have a special nurse at first. Damn butcher."

Sometimes when a man thinks about them making poets and artists and such pay these taxes which they say indicates that a man is free, twenty-one, and capable of taking care of himself in this close competition, it seems like they are obtaining money under false pretenses. Anyway, here's the rest of it, what they did next.

He reads the book, the story, to her, and her not saying anything until he had finished. "So that's what you were doing," she said.

He doesn't look at her, either; he is busy evening the pages, getting them smooth again. "It's your fur coat," he said.

"Oh," she says. "Yes. My fur coat."

So the fur coat comes. And what does she do then? She gave it away. Yes. Gave it to Mrs. Crain. Gave it to her, and her in the kitchen, churning, with her hair in her face, brushing her hair back with a wrist that looked like a lean ham. "Why, Miz Howes," she says. "I caint. I reely caint."

"You'll have to take it," Anne says. "We—I got it under false pretenses. I don't deserve it. You put bread into the ground and reap it; I don't. So I can't wear a coat like this."

And they leave it there with Mrs. Crain and they go back home, walking. Only they stop in broad daylight, with Mrs. Crain watching them from the window, and go into a clinch on their own account. "I feel better," Anne says.

"So do I," Roger says. "Because Blair wasn't there to see Mrs. Crain's face when you gave her that coat. No freedom there, or equality either."

But Anne is not listening. "Not to think," she says, "that he . . . to dress me in the skins of little slain beasts. . . . You put him in a book, but you didn't finish it. You didn't know about that coat, did you? God beat you, that time, Roger."

"Ay," Roger says. "God beats me lots of times. But there's one thing about it. Their children are bigger than ours, and even Mrs. Crain can't wear my underclothes. So that's all right."

Sure. That was all right. Because it was Christmas soon, and then spring; and then summer, the long summer, the long days.

The Brooch

THE TELEPHONE waked him. He waked already hurrying, fumbling in the dark for robe and slippers, because he knew before waking that the bed beside his own was still empty, and the instrument was downstairs just opposite the door beyond which his mother had lain propped upright in bed for five years, and he knew on waking that he would be too late because she would already have heard it, just as she heard everything that happened at any hour in the house.

She was a widow, he the only child. When he went away to college she went with him; she kept a house in Charlottesville, Virginia, for four years while he graduated. She was the daughter of a well-to-do merchant. Her husband had been a travelling man who came one summer to the town with letters of introduction: one to a minister, the other to her father. Three months later the travelling man and the daughter were married. His name was Boyd. He resigned his position within the year and moved into his wife's house and spent his days sitting in front of the hotel with the lawyers and the cotton-planters—a dark man with a gallant swaggering way of removing his hat to ladies. In the second year, the son was born. Six months later, Boyd departed. He just went away, leaving a note to his wife in which he told her that he could no longer bear to lie in bed at night and watch her rolling onto empty spools the string saved from parcels from the stores. His wife never heard of him again, though she refused to let her father have the marriage annulled and change the son's name.

Then the merchant died, leaving all his property to the daughter and the grandson who, though he had been out of Fauntleroy suits since he was seven or eight, at twelve wore even on weekdays clothes which made him look not like a child but like a midget; he probably could not have long associated with other children even if his mother had let him. In due time the mother found a boys' school where the boy could wear a round jacket and a man's hard hat with impunity, though by the time the two of them removed to Charlottesville for these next four years, the son did not look like a midget. He looked now like a character out of Dante—a man a little slighter than his father but with something of his father's dark handsomeness, who hurried with averted head, even when his mother was not with him, past the young girls on the streets not only of Charlottesville but of the little lost Mississippi hamlet to which they presently returned, with an expression of face like the young monks or angels in fifteenth-century allegories. Then his mother had her stroke, and presently the mother's friends brought to her bed reports of almost exactly the sort of girl which perhaps even the mother might have expected the son to become not only involved with but to marry.

Her name was Amy, daughter of a railroad conductor who had been killed in a wreck. She lived now with an aunt who kept a boarding-house—a vivid, daring girl whose later reputation was due more to folly and the caste handicap of the little Southern town than to badness and which at the last was doubtless more smoke than fire; whose name, though she always had invitations to the more public dances, was a light word, especially among the older women, daughters

of decaying old houses like this in which her future husband
had been born.

So presently the son had acquired some skill in entering
the house and passing the door beyond which his mother lay
propped in bed, and mounting the stairs in the dark to his
own room. But one night he failed to do so. When he
entered the house the transom above his mother's door was
dark, as usual, and even if it had not been he could not have
known that this was the afternoon on which the mother's
friends had called and told her about Amy, and that his
mother had lain for five hours, propped bolt upright, in the
darkness, watching the invisible door. He entered quietly
as usual, his shoes in his hand, yet he had not even closed
the front door when she called his name. Her voice was not
raised. She called his name once:

"Howard."

He opened the door. As he did so the lamp beside her bed
came on. It sat on a table beside the bed; beside it sat a clock
with a dead face; to stop it had been the first act of his
mother when she could move her hands two years ago. He
approached the bed from which she watched him—a thick
woman with a face the color of tallow and dark eyes apparently both pupil-less and iris-less beneath perfectly white
hair. "What?" he said. "Are you sick?"

"Come closer," she said. He came nearer. They looked at
one another. Then he seemed to know; perhaps he had been
expecting it.

"I know who's been talking to you," he said. "Those
damned old buzzards."

"I'm glad to hear it's carrion," she said. "Now I can rest
easy that you won't bring it into our house."

"Go on. Say, your house."

"Not necessary. Any house where a lady lives." They
looked at one another in the steady lamp which possessed

that stale glow of sickroom lights. "You are a man. I don't reproach you. I am not even surprised. I just want to warn you before you make yourself ridiculous. Don't confuse the house with the stable."

"With the—Hah!" he said. He stepped back and jerked the door open with something of his father's swaggering theatricalism. "With your permission," he said. He did not close the door. She lay bolt upright on the pillows and looked into the dark hall and listened to him go to the telephone, call the girl, and ask her to marry him tomorrow. Then he reappeared at the door. "With your permission," he said again, with that swaggering reminiscence of his father, closing the door. After a while the mother turned the light off. It was daylight in the room then.

They were not married the next day, however. "I'm scared to," Amy said. "I'm scared of your mother. What does she say about me?"

"I don't know. I never talk to her about you."

"You don't even tell her you love me?"

"What does it matter? Let's get married."

"And live there with her?" They looked at one another. "Will you go to work, get us a house of our own?"

"What for? I have enough money. And it's a big house."

"Her house. Her money."

"It'll be mine—ours some day. Please."

"Come on. Let's try to dance again." This was in the parlor of the boarding-house, where she was trying to teach him to dance, but without success. The music meant nothing to him; the noise of it or perhaps the touch of her body destroyed what little co-ordination he could have had. But he took her to the Country Club dances; they were known to be engaged. Yet she still staid out dances with other men, in the parked cars about the dark lawn. He tried to argue with her about it, and about drinking.

"Sit out and drink with me, then," he said.

"We're engaged. It's no fun with you."

"Yes," he said, with the docility with which he accepted each refusal; then he stopped suddenly and faced her. "What's no fun with me?" She fell back a little as he gripped her shoulder. "What's no fun with me?"

"Oh," she said. "You're hurting me!"

"I know it. What's no fun with me?"

Then another couple came up and he let her go. Then an hour later, during an intermission, he dragged her, screaming and struggling, out of a dark car and across the dance floor, empty now and lined with chaperones like a theater audience, and drew out a chair and took her across his lap and spanked her. By daylight they had driven twenty miles to another town and were married.

That morning Amy called Mrs. Boyd "Mother" for the first and (except one, and that perhaps shocked out of her by surprise or perhaps by exultation) last time, though the same day Mrs. Boyd formally presented Amy with the brooch: an ancient, clumsy thing, yet valuable. Amy carried it back to their room, and he watched her stand looking at it, perfectly cold, perfectly inscrutable. Then she put it into a drawer. She held it over the open drawer with two fingers and released it and then drew the two fingers across her thigh.

"You will have to wear it sometimes," Howard said.

"Oh, I will. I'll show my gratitude. Don't worry." Presently it seemed to him that she took pleasure in wearing it. That is, she began to wear it quite often. Then he realized that it was not pleasure but vindictive incongruity; she wore it for an entire week once on the bosom of a gingham house dress, an apron. But she always wore it where Mrs. Boyd would see it, always when she and Howard had dressed to

go out and would stop in the mother's room to say good
night.

They lived upstairs, where, a year later, their child was
born. They took the child down for Mrs. Boyd to see it.
She turned her head on the pillows and looked at the child
once. "Ah," she said. "I never saw Amy's father, that I
know of. But then, I never travelled on a train a great deal."

"The old—the old—" Amy cried, shuddering and clinging to Howard. "Why does she hate me so? What have I
ever done to her? Let's move. You can work."

"No. She won't live always."

"Yes, she will. She'll live forever, just to hate me."

"No," Howard said. In the next year the child died. Again
Amy tried to get him to move.

"Anywhere. I won't care how we have to live."

"No. I can't leave her helpless on her back. You will have
to start going out again. Dance. Then it won't be so bad."

"Yes," she said, quieter. "I'll have to. I can't stand this."

One said "you," the other, "I." Neither of them said
"we." So, on Saturday nights Amy would dress and Howard
would put on scarf and overcoat, sometimes over his shirt-
sleeves, and they would descend the stairs and stop at Mrs.
Boyd's door and then Howard would put Amy into the
car and watch her drive away. Then he would re-enter the
house and with his shoes in his hand return up the stairs, as he
had used to do before they married, slipping past the lighted
transom. Just before midnight, in the overcoat and scarf
again, he would slip back down the stairs and past the still
lighted transom and be waiting on the porch when Amy
drove up. Then they would enter the house and look into
Mrs. Boyd's room and say good night.

One night it was one o'clock before she returned. He had
been waiting for an hour in slippers and pajamas on the

porch; it was November. The transom above Mrs. Boyd's door was dark and they did not stop.

"Some jelly beans set the clock back," she said. She did not look at him, dragging her clothes off, flinging the brooch along with her other jewelry onto the dressing table. "I had hoped you wouldn't be fool enough to stand out there and wait for me."

"Maybe next time they set the clock back I won't."

She stopped, suddenly and perfectly still, looking at him over her shoulder. "Do you mean that?" she said. He was not looking at her; he heard, felt, her approach and stand beside him. Then she touched his shoulder. "Howard?" she said. He didn't move. Then she was clinging to him, flung onto his lap, crying wildly: "What's happening to us?" striking herself against him with a wild abandon: "What is it? What is it?" He held her quiet, though after they were each in their beds (they already had two of them) he heard and then felt her cross the intervening gap and fling herself against him again with that wild terrified abandon not of a woman but of a child in the dark, enveloping him, whispering: "You don't *have* to trust me, Howard! You can! You can! You don't *have* to!"

"Yes," he said. "I know. It's all right. It's all right." So after that, just before twelve, he would put on the overcoat and scarf, creep down the stairs and past the lighted transom, open and close the front door noisily, and then open his mother's door where the mother would be propped high on the pillows, the book open and face down on her knees.

"Back already?" Mrs. Boyd would say.

"Yes. Amy's gone on up. Do you want anything?"

"No. Good night."

"Good night."

Then he would go up and go to bed, and after a time (sometimes) to sleep. But before this sometimes, taking it

sometimes into sleep with him, he would think, tell himself
with that quiet and fatalistic pessimism of the impotent intelligent: *But this cannot go on forever. Some night something is going to happen; she is going to catch Amy. And I
know what she is going to do. But what am I going to do?*
He believed that he did know. That is, the top of his mind
assured him that it knew, but he discounted this; the intelligence again: not to bury it, flee from it: just discounting it,
the intelligence speaking out of the impotence: *Because no
man ever knows what he will do in any given situation, set
of circumstances: the wise, others perhaps, drawing conclu-
sions, but never himself.* The next morning Amy would be
in the other bed, and then, in the light of day, it would be
gone. But now and then, even by daylight, it returned and
he from the detachment of his cerebration contemplating his
life, that faulty whole whose third the two of them had produced yet whose lack the two of them could not fill, telling
himself, *Yes. I know what she will do and I know what
Amy will ask me to do and I know that I will not do that.
But what will I do?* but not for long, telling himself now
that it had not happened so far, and that anyway it was six
long days until Saturday: the impotence now, not even the
intellect.

II

So it was that when he waked to the bell's shrilling he
already knew that the bed beside his own was still empty,
just as he knew that, no matter how quickly he reached the
telephone, it would already be too late. He did not even
wait for his slippers; he ran down the now icy stairs, seeing
the transom above his mother's door come alight as he passed
it and went to the phone and took the receiver down: "Oh,
Howard, I'm so sorry—this is Martha Ross—so sorry to dis-

turb you, but I knew that Amy would be anxious about it.
I found it in the car, tell her, when we got back home."

"Yes," he said. "In the car."

"In our car. After she lost her switch key and we brought
her home, to the corner. We tried to get her to come on
home with us and have some ham and eggs, but she—"
Then the voice died away. He held the cold receiver to his
ear and heard the other end of the wire, the silence, fill with
a sort of consternation like an indrawn breath: something
instinctive and feminine and self-protective. But the pause
itself was hardly a pause; almost immediately the voice went
on, though completely changed now, blank, smooth, reserved: "Amy's in bed, I suppose."

"Yes. She's in bed."

"Oh. So sorry I bothered you, got you up. But I knew
she would be anxious about it, since it was your mother's,
the family piece. But of course, if she hasn't missed it yet,
you won't need to bother her." The wire hummed, tense.
"That I called or anything." The wire hummed. "Hello.
Howard?"

"No," he said. "I won't bother her tonight. You can call
her in the morning."

"Yes, I will. So sorry I bothered you. I hope I didn't
wake your mother."

He put the receiver back. He was cold. He could feel his
bare toes curling back from the icelike floor as he stood
looking at the blank door beyond which his mother would
be sitting, high-propped on the pillows, with her tallow face
and dark inscrutable eyes and the hair which Amy said resembled weathered cotton, beside the clock whose hands
she had stopped herself at ten minutes to four on the afternoon five years ago when she first moved again. When he
opened the door his picture had been exact, almost to the
position of the hands even.

"She is not in this house," Mrs. Boyd said.

"Yes. She's in bed. You know when we came in. She just left one of her rings with Martha Ross tonight and Martha telephoned."

But apparently she had not even listened to him. "So you swear she is in this house this minute."

"Yes. Of course she is. She's asleep, I tell you."

"Then send her down here to say good night to me."

"Nonsense. Of course I won't."

They looked at one another across the bed's footboard. "You refuse?"

"Yes."

They looked at one another a moment longer. Then he began to turn away; he could feel her watching him. "Then tell me something else. It was the brooch she lost."

He did not answer this either. He just looked at her again as he closed the door: the two of them curiously similar, mortal and implacable foes in the fierce close antipathy of blood. He went out.

He returned to the bedroom and turned on the light and found his slippers and went to the fire and put some coal on the embers and punched and prodded it into flame. The clock on the mantel said twenty minutes to one. Presently he had a fair blaze; he had quit shivering. He went back to bed and turned off the light, leaving only the firelight pulsing and gleaming on the furniture and among the phials and mirrors of the dressing table, and in the smaller mirror above his own chest of drawers, upon which sat the three silver photograph frames, the two larger ones containing himself and Amy, the smaller one between them empty. He just lay. He was not thinking at all. He had just thought once, quietly, *So that's that. So now I suppose I will know, find out what I am going to do* and then no more, not even thinking that again.

The house seemed still to be filled with the shrill sound of the telephone like a stubborn echo. Then he began to hear the clock on the mantel, reiterant, cold, not loud. He turned on the light and took up the book face down and open from the table beside his pillow, but he found that he could not keep his mind on the words for the sound which the clock made, so he rose and went to the mantel. The hands were now at half past two. He stopped the clock and turned its face to the wall and brought his book to the fire and found that he could now keep his mind on the words, the sense, reading on now untroubled by time. So he could not have said just when it was that he found he had ceased to read, had jerked his head up. He had heard no sound, yet he knew that Amy was in the house. He did not know how he knew: he just sat holding his breath, immobile, the peaceful book raised and motionless, waiting. Then he heard Amy say, "It's me, Mother."

She said "Mother," he thought, not moving yet. *She called her "Mother" again.* He moved now, putting the book carefully down, his place marked, but as he crossed the room he walked naturally, not trying to deaden his footsteps, to the door and opened it and saw Amy just emerging from Mrs. Boyd's room. She began to mount the stairs, walking naturally too, her hard heels sharp and unnaturally loud in the nightbound house. She must have stooped when Mother called her and put her slippers on again, he thought. She had not seen him yet, mounting steadily, her face in the dim hall light vague and petal-like against the collar of her fur coat, projecting already ahead of her to where he waited a sort of rosy and crystal fragrance of the frozen night out of which she had just emerged. Then she saw him at the head of the stairs. For just a second, an instant, she stopped dead still, though she was moving again before it could have been called pause, already speaking as she passed him where he

stood aside, and entered the bedroom: "Is it very late? I was
with the Rosses. They just let me out at the corner; I lost
my car key out at the club. Maybe it was the car that
waked her."

"No. She was already awake. It was the telephone."

She went on to the fire and spread her hands to it, still in
her coat; she did not seem to have heard him, her face rosy
in the firelight, her presence emanating that smell of cold,
that frosty fragrance which had preceded her up the stairs:
"I suppose so. Her light was already on. I knew as soon as
I opened the front door that we were sunk. I hadn't even
got in the house good when she said 'Amy' and I said 'It's
me, Mother' and she said, 'Come in here, please,' and there
she was with those eyes that haven't got any edges to them
and that hair that looks like somebody pulled it out of the
middle of a last year's cotton bale, and she said, 'Of course
you understand that you will have to leave this house at
once. Good night.'"

"Yes," he said. "She has been awake since about half past
twelve. But there wasn't anything to do but insist that you
were already in bed asleep and trust to luck."

"You mean, she hasn't been asleep at all?"

"No. It was the telephone, like I told you. About half
past twelve."

With her hands still spread to the fire she glanced at him
over her furred shoulder, her face rosy, her eyes at once
bright and heavy, like a woman's eyes after pleasure, with
a kind of inattentive conspiratorial commiseration. "Telephone? Here? At half past twelve? What absolutely putrid
—But no matter." She turned now, facing him, as if she
had only been waiting until she became warm, the rich coat
open upon the fragile glitter of her dress; there was a quality
actually beautiful about her now—not of the face whose
impeccable replica looks out from the covers of a thousand

magazines each month, nor of the figure, the shape of deliberately epicene provocation into which the miles of celluloid film have constricted the female body of an entire race; but a quality completely female in the old eternal fashion, primitive assured and ruthless as she approached him, already raising her arms. "Yes! I say luck too!" she said, putting her arms around him, her upper body leaned back to look into his face, her own face triumphant, the smell now warm woman-odor where the frosty fragrance had thawed. "She said at once, now. So we can go. You see? Do you understand? We can leave now. Give her the money, let her have it all. We won't care. You can find work; I won't care how and where we will have to live. You don't have to stay here now, with her now. She has— what do you call it? absolved you herself. Only I have lost the car key. But no matter: we can walk. Yes, walk; with nothing, taking nothing of hers, like we came here."

"Now?" he said. "Tonight?"

"Yes! She said at once. So it will have to be tonight."

"No," he said. That was all, no indication of which question he had answered, which denied. But then, he did not need to because she still held him; it was only the expression of her face that changed. It did not die yet nor even become terrified yet: it just became unbelieving, like a child's incredulity. "You mean, you still won't go? You still won't leave her? That you would just take me to the hotel for tonight and that you will come back here tomorrow? Or do you mean you won't even stay at the hotel with me tonight? That you will take me there and leave me and then you—" She held him, staring at him; she began to say, "Wait, wait. There must be some reason, something— Wait," she cried; "wait! You said, telephone. At half past twelve." She still stared at him, her hands hard, her pupils like pinpoints, her face ferocious. "That's it. That's the

reason. Who was it that telephoned here about me? Tell me!
I defy you to! I will explain it. Tell me!"

"It was Martha Ross. She said she had just let you out at
the corner."

"She lied!" she cried at once, immediately, scarce waiting
to hear the name. "She lied! They did bring me home then
but it was still early and so I decided to go on with them to
their house and have some ham and eggs. So I called to
Frank before he got turned around and I went with them.
Frank will prove it! She lied! They just this minute put me
out at the corner!"

She looked at him. They stared at one another for a full
immobile moment. Then he said, "Then where is the
brooch?"

"The brooch?" she said. "What brooch?" But already he
had seen her hand move upward beneath the coat; besides,
he could see her face and watch it gape like that of a child
which has lost its breath before she began to cry with a wild
yet immobile abandon, so that she spoke through the weeping in the choked gasping of a child, with complete and
despairing surrender: "Oh, Howard! I wouldn't have done
that to you! I wouldn't have! I wouldn't have!"

"All right," he said. "Hush, now. Hush, Amy. She will
hear you."

"All right. I'm trying to." But she still faced him with
that wrung and curiously rigid face beneath its incredible
flow of moisture, as though not the eyes but all the pores had
sprung at once; now she too spoke directly out of thinking,
without mention of subject or circumstance, nothing more
of defiance or denial: "Would you have gone with me if
you hadn't found out?"

"No. Not even then. I won't leave her. I will not, until
she is dead. Or this house. I won't. I can't. I—" They looked
at one another, she staring at him as if she saw reflected in

his pupils not herself but the parchment-colored face below stairs—the piled dirty white hair, the fierce implacable eyes —her own image blanked out by something beyond mere blindness: by a quality determined, invincible, and crucified.

"Yes," she said. From somewhere she produced a scrap of chiffon and began to dab at her eyes, delicately, even now by instinct careful of the streaked mascara. "She beat us. She lay there in that bed and beat us." She turned and went to the closet and drew out an overnight bag and put the crystal objects from the dressing-table into it and opened a drawer. "I can't take everything tonight. I will have to ——"

He moved also; from the chest of drawers where the small empty photograph frame sat he took his wallet and removed the bills from it and returned and put the money into her hand. "I don't think there is very much here. But you won't need money until tomorrow."

"Yes," she said. "You can send the rest of my things then, too."

"Yes," he said. She folded and smoothed the notes in her fingers; she was not looking at him. He did not know what she was looking at except it was not at the money. "Haven't you got a purse or something to carry it in?"

"Yes," she said. But she did not stop folding and smoothing the bills, still not looking at them, apparently not aware of them, as if they had no value and she had merely picked them idly up without being aware of it. "Yes," she said. "She beat us. She lay there in that bed she will never move from until they come in and carry her out some day, and took that brooch and beat us both." Then she began to cry. It was as quiet now as the way she had spoken. "My little baby," she said. "My dear little baby."

He didn't even say Hush now. He just waited until she dried her eyes again, almost briskly, rousing, looking at him with an expression almost like smiling, her face, the make-up, the careful evening face haggard and streaked and filled with the weary and peaceful aftermath of tears. "Well," she said. "It's late." She stooped, but he anticipated her and took the bag; they descended the stairs together; they could see the lighted transom above Mrs. Boyd's door.

"It's too bad you haven't got the car," he said.

"Yes. I lost the key at the club. But I telephoned the garage. They will bring it in in the morning."

They stopped in the hall while he telephoned for a cab. Then they waited, talking quietly now and then. "You had better go straight to bed."

"Yes. I'm tired. I danced a good deal."

"What was the music? Was it good?"

"Yes. I don't know. I suppose so. When you are dancing yourself, you don't usually notice whether the music is or isn't."

"Yes, I guess that's so." Then the car came. They went out to it, he in pajamas and robe; the earth was frozen and iron-hard, the sky bitter and brilliant. He helped her in.

"Now you run back into the house," she said. "You didn't even put on your overcoat."

"Yes. I'll get your things to the hotel early."

"Not too early. Run, now." She had already sat back, the coat close about her. He had already remarked how sometime, at some moment back in the bedroom, the warm woman-odor had congealed again and that she now emanated once more that faint frosty fragrance, fragile, impermanent and forlorn; the car moved away, he did not look back. As he was closing the front door his mother called his name. But he did not pause or even glance toward the door. He just mounted the stairs, out of the dead, level, unsleeping, peremptory voice. The fire had burned down: a strong rosy glow, peaceful and quiet and warmly reflected from mirror and polished wood. The book still lay, face down and open, in the chair. He took it up and went to the table between the two beds and sought and found the cellophane envelope which had once contained pipe cleaners, which he used for a bookmark, and marked his place and put the book down. It was the coat-pocket size, Modern Library *Green Mansions*. He had discovered the book during adolescence; he had read it ever since. During that period he read only the part about the journey of the three people in search of the Riolama which did not exist, seeking this part out and reading it in secret as the normal boy would have normal and conventional erotica or obscenity, mounting the barren mountain with Rima toward the cave, not knowing then that it was the cave-symbol which he sought, escaping it at last through the same desire and need to flee and escape which Rima had, following her on past the cave to where she poised, not even waiting for him, impermanent as a match flame and as weak, in the cold and ungrieving moon. In his innocence then he believed, with a sort of urgent and despairing joy, that the mystery about her was not mystery since it was physical: that she was corporeally impenetrable, incomplete; with peaceful despair justifying, vindicating, what he was through (so he believed) no fault of his own, with what he read in books, as the young do. But after his marriage he did not read the book again until the child died and the Saturday nights began. And then he avoided the journey to Riolama as he had used to seek it out. Now he read only where Abel (the one man on earth who knew that he was alone) wandered in the impervious and interdict forest filled with the sound of birds. Then he went to the chest and opened again the drawer where he kept the wallet and stood for a moment, his hand still lying on the edge of the drawer. "Yes," he said quietly, aloud: "it seems to have been right all the time about what I will do."

The bathroom was at the end of the hall, built onto the house later, warm too where he had left the electric heater on for Amy and they had forgot it. It was here that he kept his whiskey also. He had begun to drink after his mother's stroke, in the beginning of what he had believed to be his freedom, and since the death of the child he had begun to keep a two-gallon keg of corn whiskey in the bathroom. Although it was detached from the house proper and the whole depth of it from his mother's room, he nevertheless stuffed towels carefully about and beneath the door, and then removed them and returned to the bedroom and took the down coverlet from Amy's bed and returned and stuffed the door again and then hung the coverlet before it. But even then he was not satisfied. He stood there, thoughtful, musing, a little pudgy (he had never taken any exercise since he gave up trying to learn to dance, and now what with the steady drinking, there was little of the young Italian novice about his figure any more), the pistol hanging from his hand. He began to look about. His glance fell upon the bath mat folded over the edge of the tub. He wrapped his hand, pistol and all, in the mat and pointed it toward the rear wall and fired it, the report muffled and jarring though not loud. Yet even now he stood and listened as if he expected to hear from this distance. But he heard nothing; even when, the door freed again, he moved quietly down the hall and then down the steps to where he could see clearly the dark transom above his mother's door. But again he did not pause. He returned up the stairs, quietly, hearing the cold and impotent ratiocination without listening to it: *Like your father, you cannot seem to live with either of them, but unlike your father you cannot seem to live without them;* telling himself quietly, "Yes, it seems that it was right. It seems to have known us better than I did," and he shut the bathroom door again and stuffed the towels carefully about and beneath it. But he did not hang the coverlet this time. He drew it over himself, squatting, huddling into it, the muzzle of the pistol between his teeth like a pipe, wadding the thick soft coverlet about his head, hurrying, moving swiftly now because he was already beginning to suffocate.

My Grandmother Millard and General Bedford Forrest and The Battle of Harrykin Creek

I

IT WOULD BE right after supper, before we had left the table. At first, beginning with the day the news came that the Yankees had taken Memphis, we did it three nights in succession. But after that, as we got better and better and faster and faster, once a week suited Granny. Then after Cousin Melisandre finally got out of Memphis and came to live with us, it would be just once a month, and when the regiment in Virginia voted Father out of the colonelcy and he came home and stayed three months while he made a crop and got over his mad and organized his cavalry troop for General Forrest's command, we quit doing it at all. That is, we did it one time with Father there too, watching, and that night Ringo and I heard him laughing in the library, the first time he had laughed since he came home, until in about a half a minute Granny came out already holding her skirts up and went sailing up the stairs. So we didn't do it any more until Father had organized his troop and was gone again.

Granny would fold her napkin beside her plate. She would speak to Ringo standing behind her chair without even turning her head:

"Go call Joby and Lucius."

And Ringo would go back through the kitchen without stopping. He would just say, "All right. Look out," at Louvinia's back and go to the cabin and come back with not only Joby and Lucius and the lighted lantern but Philadelphia too, even though Philadelphia wasn't going to do anything but stand and watch and then follow to the orchard and back to the house until Granny said we were done for that time and she and Lucius could go back home to bed. And we would bring down from the attic the big trunk (we had done it so many times by now that we didn't even need the lantern any more to go to the attic and get the trunk) whose lock it was my job to oil every Monday morning with a feather dipped in chicken fat, and Louvinia would come in from the kitchen with the unwashed silver from supper in a dishpan under one arm and the kitchen clock under the other and set the clock and the dishpan on the table and take from her apron pocket a pair of Granny's rolled-up stockings and hand them to Granny and Granny would unroll the stockings and take from the toe of one of them a wadded rag and open the rag and take out the key to the trunk and unpin her watch from her bosom and fold it into the rag and put the rag back into the stocking and roll the stockings back into a ball and put the ball into the trunk. Then with Cousin Melisandre and Philadelphia watching, and Father too on that one time when he was there, Granny would stand facing the clock, her hands raised and about eight inches apart and her neck bowed so she could watch the clock-face over her spectacles, until the big hand reached the nearest hour-mark.

The rest of us watched her hands. She wouldn't speak again. She didn't need to. There would be just the single light loud pop of her palms when the hand came to the nearest hour-mark; sometimes we would be already moving, even before her hands came together, all of us that is except Philadelphia. Granny wouldn't let her help at all, because of Lucius, even though Lucius had done nearly all the digging of the pit and did most of the carrying of the trunk each time.

But Philadelphia had to be there. Granny didn't have to tell her but once. "I want the wives of all the free men here too," Granny said. "I want all of you free folks to watch what the rest of us that aint free have to do to keep that way."

That began about eight months ago. One day even I realized that something had happened to Lucius. Then I knew that Ringo had already seen it and that he knew what it was, so that when at last Louvinia came and told Granny, it was not as if Lucius had dared his mother to tell her but as if he had actually forced somebody, he didn't care who, to tell her. He had said it more than once, in the cabin one night probably for the first time, then after that in other places and to other people, to Negroes from other plantations even. Memphis was already gone then, and New Orleans, and all we had left of the River was Vicksburg and although we didn't believe it then, we wouldn't have that long. Then one morning Louvinia came in where Granny was cutting down the worn-out uniform pants Father had worn home from Virginia so they would fit me, and told Granny how Lucius was saying that soon the Yankees would have all of Mississippi and Yoknapatawpha County too and all the niggers would be free and that when that happened, he was going to be long gone. Lucius was working in the garden that morning. Granny went out to the back gallery, still carrying the pants and the needle. She didn't even push her spectacles up. She said, "You, Lucius," just once, and Lucius came out of the garden with the hoe and Granny stood looking down at him over the spectacles as she looked over them at everything she did, from reading or sewing to watching the clock-face until the instant came to start burying the silver.

"You can go now," she said. "You needn't wait on the Yankees."

"Go?" Lucius said. "I aint free."

"You've been free for almost three minutes," Granny said. "Go on."

Lucius blinked his eyes while you could have counted about ten. "Go where?" he said.

"I can't tell you," Granny said. "I aint free. I would imagine you will have all Yankeedom to move around in."

Lucius blinked his eyes. He didn't look at Granny now. "Was that all you wanted?" he said.

"Yes," Granny said. So he went back to the garden. And that was the last we heard about being free from him. That is, it quit showing in the way he acted, and if he talked any more of it, even Louvinia never thought it was worth bothering Granny with. It was Granny who would do the reminding of it, especially to Philadelphia, especially on the nights when we would stand like race-horses at the barrier, watching Granny's hands until they clapped together.

Each one of us knew exactly what he was to do. I would go upstairs for Granny's gold hatpin and her silver-headed umbrella and her plumed Sunday hat because she had already sent her ear-rings and brooch to Richmond a long time ago, and to Father's room for his silver-backed brushes and to Cousin Melisandre's room after she came to live with us for her things because the one time Granny let Cousin Melisandre try to help too, Cousin Melisandre brought all her dresses down. Ringo would go to the parlor for the candlesticks and Granny's dulcimer and the medallion of Father's mother back in Carolina. And we would run back to the dining-room where Louvinia and Lucius would have the sideboard almost cleared, and Granny still standing there and watching the clock-face and the trunk both now with her hands ready to pop again and they would pop and Ringo and I would stop at the cellar door just long enough to snatch up the shovels and run on to the orchard and snatch the brush and grass and the criss-crossed sticks away and have the pit

open and ready by the time we saw them coming: first Louvinia with the lantern, then Joby and Lucius with the trunk
and Granny walking beside it and Cousin Melisandre and
Philadelphia (and on that one time Father, walking along and
laughing) following behind. And on that first night, the
kitchen clock wasn't in the trunk. Granny was carrying it,
while Louvinia held the lantern so that Granny could watch
the hand, Granny made us put the trunk into the pit and
shovel the dirt back and smooth it off and lay the brush and
grass back over it again and then dig up the trunk and carry
it back to the house. And one night, it seemed like we had
been bringing the trunk down from the attic and putting the
silver into it and carrying it out to the pit and uncovering the
pit and then covering the pit again and turning around and
carrying the trunk back to the house and taking the silver
out and putting it back where we got it from all winter and
all summer too;—that night, and I don't know who thought
of it first, maybe it was all of us at once. But anyway the
clock-hand had passed four hour-marks before Granny's
hands even popped for Ringo and me to run and open the
pit. And they came with the trunk and Ringo and I hadn't
even put down the last armful of brush and sticks, to save
having to stoop to pick it up again, and Lucius hadn't even
put down his end of the trunk for the same reason and I
reckon Louvinia was the only one that knew what was coming next because Ringo and I didn't know that the kitchen
clock was still sitting on the dining-room table. Then Granny
spoke. It was the first time we had ever heard her speak between when she would tell Ringo, "Go call Joby and Lucius," and then tell us both about thirty minutes later: "Wash
your feet and go to bed." It was not loud and not long, just
two words: "Bury it." And we lowered the trunk into the
pit and Joby and Lucius threw the dirt back in and even then
Ringo and I didn't move with the brush until Granny spoke

again, not loud this time either: "Go on. Hide the pit." And
we put the brush back and Granny said, "Dig it up." And we
dug up the trunk and carried it back into the house and put
the things back where we got them from and that was when
I saw the kitchen clock still sitting on the dining-room table.
And we all stood there watching Granny's hands until they
popped together and that time we filled the trunk and carried it out to the orchard and lowered it into the pit quicker
than we had ever done before.

II

AND THEN when the time came to really bury the silver, it
was too late. After it was all over and Cousin Melisandre and
Cousin Philip were finally married and Father had got done
laughing, Father said that always happened when a hetero-
geneous collection of people who were cohered simply by an
uncomplex will for freedom engaged with a tyrannous machine. He said they would always lose the first battles, and if
they were outnumbered and outweighed enough, it would
seem to an outsider that they were going to lose them all. But
they would not. They could not be defeated; if they just
willed that freedom strongly and completely enough to
sacrifice all else for it—ease and comfort and fatness of spirit
and all, until whatever it was they had left would be enough,
no matter how little it was—that very freedom itself would
finally conquer the machine as a negative force like drouth
or flood could strangle it. And later still, after two more years
and we knew we were going to lose the war, he was still
saying that. He said, "I won't see it but you will. You will
see it in the next war, and in all the wars Americans will have
to fight from then on. There will be men from the South in
the forefront of all the battles, even leading some of them,
helping those who conquered us defend that same freedom

which they believed they had taken from us." And that happened: thirty years later, and General Wheeler, whom Father would have called apostate, commanding in Cuba, and whom old General Early did call apostate and matricide too in the office of the Richmond editor when he said: "I would like to have lived so that when my time comes, I will see Robert Lee again. But since I haven't, I'm certainly going to enjoy watching the devil burn that blue coat off Joe Wheeler."

We didn't have time. We didn't even know there were any Yankees in Jefferson, let alone within a mile of Sartoris. There never had been many. There was no railroad then and no river big enough for big boats and nothing in Jefferson they would have wanted even if they had come, since this was before Father had had time to worry them enough for General Grant to issue a general order with a reward for his capture. So we had got used to the war. We thought of it as being definitely fixed and established as a railroad or a river is, moving east along the railroad from Memphis and south along the River toward Vicksburg. We had heard tales of Yankee pillage and most of the people around Jefferson stayed ready to bury their silver fast too, though I don't reckon any of them practiced doing it like we did. But nobody we knew was even kin to anyone who had been pillaged, and so I don't think that even Lucius really expected any Yankees until that morning.

It was about eleven o'clock. The table was already set for dinner and everybody was beginning to kind of ease up so we would be sure to hear when Louvinia went out to the back gallery and rang the bell, when Ab Snopes came in at a dead run, on a strange horse as usual. He was a member of Father's troop. Not a fighting member; he called himself father's horse-captain, whatever he meant by it, though we had a pretty good idea, and none of us at least knew what he

was doing in Jefferson when the troop was supposed to be
up in Tennessee with General Bragg, and probably nobody
anywhere knew the actual truth about how he got the horse,
galloping across the yard and right through one of Granny's
flower beds because I reckon he figured that carrying a message he could risk it, and on around to the back because he
knew that, message or no message, he better not come to
Granny's front door hollering that way, sitting that strange
blown horse with a U.S. army brand on it you could read
three hundred yards and yelling up at Granny that General
Forrest was in Jefferson but there was a whole regiment of
Yankee cavalry not a half a mile down the road.

So we never had time. Afterward Father admitted that
Granny's error was not in strategy nor tactics either, even
though she had copied from someone else. Because he said it
had been a long time now since originality had been a com-
ponent of military success. It just happened too fast. I went
for Joby and Lucius and Philadelphia because Granny had
already sent Ringo down to the road with a cup towel to
wave when they came in sight. Then she sent me to the front
window where I could watch Ringo. When Ab Snopes came
back from hiding his new Yankee horse, he offered to go upstairs to get the things there. Granny had told us a long time
ago never to let Ab Snopes go anywhere about the house
unless somebody was with him. She said she would rather
have Yankees in the house any day because at least Yankees
would have more delicacy, even if it wasn't anything but
good sense, than to steal a spoon or candlestick and then try
to sell it to one of her own neighbors, as Ab Snopes would
probably do. She didn't even answer him. She just said,
"Stand over there by that door and be quiet." So Cousin Melisandre went upstairs after all and Granny and Philadelphia
went to the parlor for the candlesticks and the medallion and
the dulcimer, Philadelphia not only helping this time, free or
not, but Granny wasn't even using the clock.

It just all happened at once. One second Ringo was sitting on the gate-post, looking up the road. The next second he was standing on it and waving the cup towel and then I was running and hollering, back to the dining-room, and I remember the whites of Joby's and Lucius's and Philadelphia's eyes and I remembered Cousin Melisandre's eyes where she leaned against the sideboard with the back of her hand against her mouth, and Granny and Louvinia and Ab Snopes glaring at one another across the trunk and I could hear Louvinia's voice even louder than mine:

"Miz Cawmpson! Miz Cawmpson!"

"What?" Granny cried. "What? Mrs. Compson?" Then we all remembered. It was when the first Yankee scouting patrol entered Jefferson over a year ago. The war was new then and I suppose General Compson was the only Jefferson soldier they had heard of yet. Anyway, the officer asked someone in the Square where General Compson lived and old Doctor Holston sent his Negro boy by back alleys and across lots to warn Mrs. Compson in time, and the story was how the Yankee officer sent some of his men through the empty house and himself rode around to the back where old Aunt Roxanne was standing in front of the outhouse behind the closed door of which Mrs. Compson was sitting, fully dressed even to her hat and parasol, on the wicker hamper containing her plate and silver. "Miss in dar," Roxanne said. "Stop where you is." And the story told how the Yankee officer said, "Excuse me," and raised his hat and even backed the horse a few steps before he turned and called his men and rode away. "The privy!" Granny cried.

"Hell fire, Miz Millard!" Ab Snopes said. And Granny never said anything. It wasn't like she didn't hear, because she was looking right at him. It was like she didn't care; that she might have even said it herself. And that shows how things were then: we just never had time for anything. "Hell fire," Ab Snopes said, "all north Missippi has done heard about that! There aint a white lady between here and Memphis that aint setting in the back house on a grip full of silver right this minute."

"Then we're already late," Granny said. "Hurry."

"Wait!" Ab Snopes said. "Wait! Even them Yankees have done caught onto that by now!"

"Then let's hope these are different Yankees," Granny said. "Hurry."

"But Miz Millard!" Ab Snopes cried. "Wait! Wait!"

But then we could hear Ringo yelling down at the gate and I remember Joby and Lucius and Philadelphia and Louvinia and the balloon-like swaying of Cousin Melisandre's skirts as they ran across the back yard, the trunk somewhere among them; I remember how Joby and Lucius tumbled the trunk into the little tall narrow flimsy sentry-box and Louvinia thrust Cousin Melisandre in and slammed the door and we could hear Ringo yelling good now, almost to the house, and then I was back at the front window and I saw them just as they swept around the house in a kind of straggling-clump —six men in blue, riding fast yet with something curious in the action of the horses, as if they were not only yoked together in spans but were hitched to a single wagon-tongue, then Ringo on foot running and not yelling now, and last of all the seventh rider, bareheaded and standing in his stirrups and with a sabre over his head. Then I was on the back gallery again, standing beside Granny above that moil of horses and men in the yard, and she was wrong. It was as if these were not only the same ones who had been at Mrs. Compson's last year, but somebody had even told them exactly where our outhouse was. The horses were yoked in pairs, but it was not a wagon-tongue, it was a pole, almost a log, twenty feet long, slung from saddle to saddle between the three span; and I remember the faces, unshaven and wan and not so much peering as frantically gleeful, glaring up at us for an instant before the men leaped down and unslung the pole and jerked the horses aside and picked up the pole, three to a side, and began to run across the yard with it as the last rider came around the house, in gray (an officer: it was Cousin Philip, though of course we didn't know that then, and there was going to be a considerable more uproar and confusion before he finally became Cousin Philip and of course we didn't know that either), the sabre still lifted and not only standing in the stirrups but almost lying down along the horse's neck. The six Yankees never saw him. And we used to watch Father drilling his troop in the pasture, changing them from column to troop front at full gallop, and you could hear his voice even above the sound of the galloping hooves but it wasn't a bit louder than Granny's. "There's a lady in there!" she said. But the Yankees never heard her any more than they had seen Cousin Philip yet, the whole mass of them, the six men running with the pole and Cousin Philip on the horse, leaning out above them with a lifted sabre, rushing on across the yard until the end of the pole struck the outhouse door. It didn't just overturn, it exploded. One second it stood there, tall and narrow and flimsy; the next second it was gone and there was a boil of yelling men in blue coats darting and dodging around under Cousin Philip's horse and the flashing sabre until they could find a chance to turn and run. Then there was a scatter of planks and shingles and Cousin Melisandre sitting beside the trunk in the middle of it, in the spread of her hoops, her eyes shut and her mouth open, still screaming, and after a while a feeble popping of pistol-shots from down along the creek that didn't sound any more like war than a boy with firecrackers.

"I tried to tell you to wait!" Ab Snopes said behind us, "I tried to tell you them Yankees had done caught on!"

After Joby and Lucius and Ringo and I finished burying the trunk in the pit and hiding the shovel-marks, I found

Cousin Philip in the summer house. His sabre and belt were propped against the wall but I don't reckon even he knew what had become of his hat. He had his coat off too and was wiping it with his handkerchief and watching the house with one eye around the edge of the door. When I came in he straightened up and I thought at first he was looking at me. Then I don't know what he was looking at. "That beautiful girl," he said. "Fetch me a comb."

"They're waiting for you in the house," I said. "Granny wants to know what's the matter." Cousin Melisandre was all right now. It took Louvinia and Philadelphia both and finally Granny to get her into the house but Louvinia brought the elder-flower wine before Granny had time to send her after it and now Cousin Melisandre and Granny were waiting in the parlor.

"Your sister," Cousin Philip said. "And a hand-mirror."

"No, Sir," I said. "She's just our cousin. From Memphis. Granny says—" Because he didn't know Granny. It was pretty good for her to wait any time for anybody. But he didn't even let me finish.

"That beautiful, tender girl," he said. "And send a nigger with a basin of water and a towel." I went back toward the house. This time when I looked back I couldn't see his eye around the door-edge. "And a clothes brush," he said.

Granny wasn't waiting very much. She was at the front door. "Now what?" she said. I told her. "Does the man think we are giving a ball here in the middle of the day? Tell him I said to come on in and wash on the back gallery like we do. Louvinia's putting dinner on, and we're already late." But Granny didn't know Cousin Philip either. I told her again. She looked at me. "What did he say?" she said.

"He didn't say anything," I said. "Just that beautiful girl."

"That's all he said to me too," Ringo said. I hadn't heard

him come in. " 'Sides the soap and water. Just that beautiful girl."

"Was he looking at you either when he said it?" I said.

"No," Ringo said. "I just thought for a minute he was."

Now Granny looked at Ringo and me both. "Hah," she said, and afterward when I was older I found out that Granny already knew Cousin Philip too, that she could look at one of them and know all the other Cousin Melisandres and Cousin Philips both without having to see them. "I sometimes think that bullets are just about the least fatal things that fly, especially in war.—All right," she said. "Take him his soap and water. But hurry."

We did. This time he didn't say "that beautiful girl." He said it twice. He took off his coat and handed it to Ringo. "Brush it good," he said. "Your sister, I heard you say."

"No, you didn't," I said.

"No matter," he said. "I want a nosegay. To carry in my hand."

"Those flowers are Granny's," I said.

"No matter," he said. He rolled up his sleeves and began to wash. "A small one. About a dozen blooms. Get something pink."

I went and got the flowers. I don't know whether Granny was still at the front door or not. Maybe she wasn't. At least she never said anything. So I picked the ones Ab Snope's new Yankee horse had already trampled down and wiped the dirt off of them and straightened them out and went back to the summer house where Ringo was holding the hand-glass while Cousin Philip combed his hair. Then he put on his coat and buckled on his sabre again and held his feet out one at a time for Ringo to wipe his boots off with the towel, and Ringo saw it. I wouldn't have spoken at all because we were already later for dinner than ever now, even if there hadn't never been a Yankee on the place. "You tore your britches on them Yankees," Ringo said.

So I went back to the house. Granny was standing in the hall. This time she just said, "Yes?" It was almost quiet.

"He tore his britches," I said. And she knew more about Cousin Philip than even Ringo could find out by looking at him. She had the needle already threaded in the bosom of her dress. And I went back to the summer house and then we came back to the house and up to the front door and I waited for him to go into the hall but he didn't, he just stood there holding the nosegay in one hand and his hat in the other, not very old, looking at that moment anyway not very much older than Ringo and me for all his braid and sash and sabre and boots and spurs, and even after just two years looking like all our soldiers and most of the other people too did: as if it had been so long now since he had had all he wanted to eat at one time that even his memory and palate had forgotten it and only his body remembered, standing there with his nosegay and that beautiful-girl look in his face like he couldn't have seen anything even if he had been looking at it.

"No," he said. "Announce me. It should be your nigger. But no matter." He said his full name, all three of them, twice, as if he thought I might forget them before I could reach the parlor.

"Go on in," I said. "They're waiting for you. They had already been waiting for you even before you found your pants were torn."

"Announce me," he said. He said his name again. "Of Tennessee. Lieutenant, Savage's Battalion, Forrest's Command, Provisional Army, Department of the West."

So I did. We crossed the hall to the parlor, where Granny stood between Cousin Melisandre's chair and the table where the decanter of elder-flower wine and three fresh glasses and even a plate of the tea cakes Louvinia had learned to make from cornmeal and molasses were sitting, and he stopped again at that door too and I know he couldn't even see Cousin Melisandre for a minute, even though he never had looked at anything else but her. "Lieutenant Philip St-Just Backhouse," I said. I said it loud, because he had repeated it to me three times so I would be sure to get it right and I wanted to say it to suit him too since even if he had made us a good hour late for dinner, at least he had saved the silver. "Of Tennessee," I said. "Savage's Battalion, Forrest's Command, Provisional Army, Department of the West."

While you could count maybe five, there wasn't anything at all. Then Cousin Melisandre screamed. She sat bolt upright on the chair like she had sat beside the trunk in the litter of planks and shingles in the back yard this morning, with her eyes shut and her mouth open again, screaming.

III

So WE were still another half an hour late for dinner. Though this time it never needed anybody but Cousin Philip to get Cousin Melisandre upstairs. All he needed to do was to try to speak to her again. Then Granny came back down and said, "Well, if we don't want to just quit and start calling it supper, we'd better walk in and eat it within the next hour and a half at least." So we walked in. Ab Snopes was already waiting in the dining-room. I reckon he had been waiting longer than anybody, because after all Cousin Melisandre wasn't any kin to him. Ringo drew Granny's chair and we sat down. Some of it was cold. The rest of it had been on the stove so long now that when you ate it it didn't matter whether it was cold or not. But Cousin Philip didn't seem to mind. And maybe it didn't take his memory very long to remember again what it was like to have all he wanted to eat, but I don't think his palate ever tasted any of it. He would

sit there eating like he hadn't seen any food of any kind in at
least a week, and like he was expecting what was even already on his fork to vanish before he could get it into his
mouth. Then he would stop with the fork halfway to his
mouth and sit there looking at Cousin Melisandre's empty
place, laughing. That is, I don't know what else to call it but
laughing. Until at last I said,

"Why don't you change your name?"

Then Granny quit eating too. She looked at me over her
spectacles. Then she took both hands and lifted the spectacles
up her nose until she could look at me through them. Then
she even pushed the spectacles up into her front hair and
looked at me. "That's the first sensible thing I've heard said
on this place since eleven o'clock this morning," she said.
"It's so sensible and simple that I reckon only a child could
have thought of it." She looked at him. "Why don't you?"

He laughed some more. That is, his face did the same way
and he made the same sound again. "My grandfather was at
King's Mountain, with Marion all through Carolina. My
uncle was defeated for Governor of Tennessee by a corrupt
and traitorous cabal of tavern-keepers and Republican Aboli-
tionists, and my father died at Chapultepec. After that, the
name they bore is not mine to change. Even my life is not
mine so long as my country lies bleeding and ravished beneath an invader's iron heel." Then he stopped laughing, or
whatever it was. Then his face looked surprised. Then it quit
looking surprised, the surprise fading out of it steady at first
and gradually faster but not very much faster like the heat
fades out of a piece of iron on a blacksmith's anvil until his
face just looked amazed and quiet and almost peaceful. "Unless I lose it in battle," he said.

"You can't very well do that sitting here," Granny said.

"No," he said. But I don't think he even heard her except
with his ears. He stood up. Even Ab Snopes was watching

him now, his knife stopped halfway to his mouth with a wad
of greens on the end of the blade. "Yes," Cousin Philip said.
His face even had the beautiful-girl look on it again. "Yes,"
he said. He thanked Granny for his dinner. That is, I reckon
that's what he had told his mouth to say. It didn't make much
sense to us, but I don't think he was paying any attention to
it at all. He bowed. He wasn't looking at Granny nor at anything else. He said "Yes" again. Then he went out. Ringo and
I followed to the front door and watched him mount his
horse and sit there for a minute, bareheaded, looking up at
the upstairs windows. It was Granny's room he was looking
at, with mine and Ringo's room next to it. But Cousin Melisandre couldn't have seen him even if she had been in either
one of them, since she was in bed on the other side of the
house with Philadelphia probably still wringing the cloths out
in cold water to lay on her head. He sat the horse well. He
rode it well too: light and easy and back in the saddle and
toes in and perpendicular from ankle to knee as Father had
taught me. It was a good horse too.

"It's a damn good horse," I said.

"Git the soap," Ringo said.

But even then I looked quick back down the hall, even if
I could hear Granny talking to Ab Snopes in the dining-
room. "She's still in there," I said.

"Hah," Ringo said. "I done tasted soap in my mouth for a
cuss I thought was a heap further off than that."

Then Cousin Philip spurred the horse and was gone. Or so
Ringo and I thought. Two hours ago none of us had ever
even heard of him; Cousin Melisandre had seen him twice
and sat with her eyes shut screaming both times. But after we
were older, Ringo and I realized that Cousin Philip was probably the only one in the whole lot of us that really believed
even for one moment that he had said goodbye forever, that
not only Granny and Louvinia knew better but Cousin Meli-

sandre did too, no matter what his last name had the bad
luck to be.

We went back to the dining-room. Then I realized that Ab
Snopes had been waiting for us to come back. Then we both
knew he was going to ask Granny something because nobody
wanted to be alone when they had to ask Granny something
even when they didn't know they were going to have trouble
with it. We had known Ab for over a year now. I should
have known what it was like Granny already did. He stood
up. "Well, Miz Millard," he said. "I figger you'll be safe all
right from now on, with Bed Forrest and his boys right there
in Jefferson. But until things quiet down a mite more, I'll just
leave the horses in your lot for a day or two."

"What horses?" Granny said. She and Ab didn't just look
at one another. They watched one another.

"Them fresh-captured horses from this morning," Ab said.

"What horses?" Granny said. Then Ab said it.

"My horses." Ab watched her.

"Why?" Granny said. But Ab knew what she meant.

"I'm the only grown man here," he said. Then he said, "I
seen them first. They were chasing me before ——" Then
he said, talking fast now; his eyes had gone kind of glazed for
a second but now they were bright again, looking in the stub-
bly dirt-colored fuzz on his face like two chips of broken
plate in a worn-out door-mat: "Spoils of war! I brought them
here! I tolled them in here: a military and-bush! And as the
only and ranking Confedrit military soldier present ——"

"You ain't a soldier," Granny said. "You stipulated that to
Colonel Sartoris yourself while I was listening. You told him
yourself you would be his independent horse-captain but
nothing more."

"Ain't that just exactly what I am trying to be?" he said.
"Didn't I bring all six of them horses in here in my own
possession, the same as if I was leading them on a rope?"

"Hah," Granny said. "A spoil of war or any other kind of spoil don't belong to a man or a woman either until they can take it home and put it down and turn their back on it. You never had time to get home with even the one you were riding. You ran in the first open gate you came to, no matter whose gate it was."

"Except it was the wrong one," he said. His eyes quit looking like china. They didn't look like anything. But I reckon his face would still look like an old door-mat even after he had turned all the way white. "So I reckon I got to even walk back to town," he said. "The woman that would . . ." His voice stopped. He and Granny looked at one another.

"Don't you say it," Granny said.

"Nome," he said. He didn't say it. ". . . a man of seven horses ain't likely to lend him a mule."

"No," Granny said. "But you won't have to walk."

We all went out to the lot. I don't reckon that even Ab knew until then that Granny had already found where he thought he had hidden the first horse and had it brought up to the lot with the other six. But at least he already had his saddle and bridle with him. But it was too late. Six of the horses moved about loose in the lot. The seventh one was tied just inside the gate with a piece of plow-line. It wasn't the horse Ab had come on because that horse had a blaze. Ab had known Granny long enough too. He should have known. Maybe he did. But at least he tried. He opened the gate.

"Well," he said, "it ain't getting no earlier. I reckon I better ——"

"Wait," Granny said. Then we looked at the horse which was tied to the fence. At first glance it looked the best one of the seven. You had to see it just right to tell its near leg was sprung a little, maybe from being worked too hard too young under too much weight. "Take that one," Granny said.

"That ain't mine," Ab said. "That's one of yourn. I'll just —— "

"Take that one," Granny said. Ab looked at her. You could have counted at least ten.

"Hell fire, Miz Millard," he said.

"I've told you before about cursing on this place," Granny said.

"Yessum," Ab said. Then he said it again: "Hell fire." He went into the lot and rammed the bit into the tied horse's mouth and clapped the saddle on and snatched the piece of plow-line off and threw it over the fence and got up and Granny stood there until he had ridden out of the lot and Ringo closed the gate and that was the first time I noticed the chain and padlock from the smokehouse door and Ringo locked it and handed Granny the key and Ab sat for a minute, looking down at her. "Well, good-day," he said. "I just hope for the sake of the Confedricy that Bed Forrest don't never tangle with you with all the horses he's got." Then he said it again, maybe worse this time because now he was already on a horse pointed toward the gate: "Or you'll damn shore leave him just one more passel of infantry before he can spit twice."

Then he was gone too. Except for hearing Cousin Melisandre now and then, and those six horses with U.S. branded on their hips standing in the lot, it might never have happened. At least Ringo and I thought that was all of it. Every now and then Philadelphia would come downstairs with the pitcher and draw some more cold water for Cousin Melisandre's cloths but we thought that after a while even that would just wear out and quit. Then Philadelphia came down again and came in to where Granny was cutting down a pair of Yankee pants that Father had worn home last time so they would fit Ringo. She didn't say anything. She just stood in the door until Granny said. "All right. What now?"

"She want the banjo," Philadelphia said.

"What?" Granny said. "My dulcimer? She can't play it. Go back upstairs."

But Philadelphia didn't move. "Could I ax Mammy to come help me?"

"No," Granny said. "Louvinia's resting. She's had about as much of this as I want her to stand. Go back upstairs. Give her some more wine if you can't think of anything else." And she told Ringo and me to go somewhere else, anywhere else, but even in the yard you could still hear Cousin Melisandre talking to Philadelphia. And once we even heard Granny though it was still mostly Cousin Melisandre telling Granny that she had already forgiven her, that nothing whatever had happened and that all she wanted now was peace. And after a while Louvinia came up from the cabin without even being sent for and went upstairs and then it began to look like we were going to be late for supper too. But Philadelphia finally came down and cooked it and carried Cousin Melisandre's tray up and then we quit eating; we could hear Louvinia overhead, in Granny's room now, and she came down and set the untasted tray on the table and stood beside Granny's chair with the key to the trunk in her hand.

"All right," Granny said. "Go call Joby and Lucius." We got the lantern and the shovels. We went to the orchard and removed the brush and dug up the trunk and got the dulcimer and buried the trunk and put the brush back and brought the key in to Granny. And Ringo and I could hear her from our room and Granny was right. We heard her for a long time and Granny was surely right; she just never said but half of it. The moon came up after a while and we could look down from our window into the garden, at Cousin Melisandre sitting on the bench with the moonlight glinting on the pearl inlay of the dulcimer, and Philadelphia squatting on the sill of the gate with her apron over her head. Maybe she was asleep. It was already late. But I don't see how.

So we didn't hear Granny until she was already in the room, her shawl over her nightgown and carrying a candle. "In a minute I'm going to have about all of this I aim to stand too," she said. "Go wake Lucius and tell him to saddle the mule," she told Ringo. "Bring me the pen and ink and a sheet of paper." I fetched them. She didn't sit down. She stood at the bureau while I held the candle, writing even and steady and not very much, and signed her name and let the paper lie open to dry until Lucius came in. "Ab Snopes said that Mr. Forrest is in Jefferson," she told Lucius. "Find him. Tell him I will expect him here for breakfast in the morning and to bring that boy." She used to know General Forrest in Memphis before he got to be a general. He used to trade with Grandfather Millard's supply house and sometimes he would come out to sit with Grandfather on the front gallery and sometimes he would eat with them. "You can tell him I have six captured horses for him," she said. "And never mind patter-rollers or soldiers either. Haven't you got my signature on that paper?"

"I ain't worrying about them," Lucius said. "But suppose them Yankees——"

"I see," Granny said. "Hah. I forgot. You've been waiting for Yankees, haven't you? But those this morning seemed to be too busy trying to stay free to have much time to talk about it, didn't they?—Get along," she said. "Do you think any Yankee is going to dare ignore what a Southern soldier or even a patter-roller wouldn't?—And you go to bed," she said.

We lay down, both of us on Ringo's pallet. We heard the mule when Lucius left. Then we heard the mule and at first we didn't know we had been asleep, the mule coming back now and the moon had started down the west and Cousin

Melisandre and Philadelphia were gone from the garden, to where Philadelphia at least could sleep better than sitting on a square sill with an apron over her head, or at least where it was quieter. And we heard Lucius fumbling up the stairs but we never heard Granny at all because she was already at the top of the stairs, talking down at the noise Lucius was trying not to make. "Speak up," she said. "I ain't asleep but I ain't a lip-reader either. Not in the dark."

"Genl Fawhrest say he respectful compliments," Lucius said, "and he can't come to breakfast this morning because he gonter to be whuppin Genl Smith at Tallahatchie Crossing about that time. But providin he ain't too fur away in the wrong direction when him and Genl Smith git done, he be proud to accept your invitation next time he in the neighborhood. And he say 'whut boy'."

While you could count about five, Granny didn't say anything. Then she said, "What?"

"He say 'whut boy'," Lucius said.

Then you could have counted ten. All we could hear was Lucius breathing. Then Granny said: "Did you wipe the mule down?"

"Yessum," Lucius said.

"Did you turn her back into the pasture?"

"Yessum," Lucius said.

"Then go to bed," Granny said. "And you too," she said.

General Forrest found out what boy. This time we didn't know we had been asleep either, and it was no one mule now. The sun was just rising. When we heard Granny and scrambled to the window, yesterday wasn't a patch on it. There were at least fifty of them now, in gray; the whole outdoors was full of men on horses, with Cousin Philip out in front of them, sitting his horse in almost exactly the same spot where he had been yesterday, looking up at Granny's window and not seeing it or anything else this time either. He had a hat now. He was holding it clamped over his heart and he hadn't shaved and yesterday he had looked younger than Ringo because Ringo always had looked about ten years older than me. But now, with the first sun-ray making a little soft fuzz in the gold-colored stubble on his face, he looked even younger than I did, and gaunt and worn in the face like he hadn't slept any last night and something else in his face too: like he not only hadn't slept last night but by godfrey he wasn't going to sleep tonight either as long as he had anything to do with it. "Goodbye," he said. "Goodbye," and whirled his horse, spurring, and raised the new hat over his head like he had carried the sabre yesterday and the whole mass of them went piling back across flower beds and lawns and all and back down the drive toward the gate while Granny still stood at her window in her nightgown, her voice louder than any man's anywhere, I don't care who he is or what he would be doing: "Backhouse! Backhouse! You, Backhouse!"

So we ate breakfast early. Granny sent Ringo in his nightshirt to wake Louvinia and Lucius both. So Lucius had the mule saddled before Louvinia even got the fire lit. This time Granny didn't write a note. "Go to Tallahatchie Crossing," she told Lucius. "Sit there and wait for him if necessary."

"Suppose they done already started the battle?" Lucius said.

"Suppose they have?" Granny said. "What business is that of yours or mine either? You find Bedford Forrest. Tell him this is important; it won't take long. But don't you show your face here again without him."

Lucius rode away. He was gone four days. He didn't even get back in time for the wedding, coming back up the drive about sundown on the fourth day with two soldiers in one of General Forrest's forage wagons with the mule tied to the tailgate. He didn't know where he had been and he never

did catch up with the battle. "I never even heard it," he told
Joby and Lucius and Louvinia and Philadelphia and Ringo
and me. "If wars always moves that far and that fast, I don't
see how they ever have time to fight."

But it was all over then. It was the second day, the day
after Lucius left. It was just after dinner this time and by
now we were used to soldiers. But these were different, just
five of them, and we never had seen just that few of them
before and we had come to think of soldiers as either jumping
on and off horses in the yard or going back and forth through
Granny's flower beds at full gallop. These were all officers
and I reckon maybe I hadn't seen so many soldiers after all
because I never saw this much braid before. They came up
the drive at a trot, like people just taking a ride, and stopped
without trompling even one flower bed and General Forrest
got down and came up the walk toward where Granny
waited on the front gallery—a big, dusty man with a big
beard so black it looked almost blue and eyes like a sleepy
owl, already taking off his hat. "Well, Miss Rosie," he said.

"Don't call me Rosie," Granny said. "Come in. Ask your
gentlemen to alight and come in."

"They'll wait there," General Forrest said. "We are a little
rushed. My plans have. . . ." Then we were in the library. He
wouldn't sit down. He looked tired all right, but there was
something else a good deal livelier than just tired. "Well,
Miss Rosie," he said. "I ——"

"Don't call me Rosie," Granny said. "Can't you even say
Rosa?"

"Yessum," he said. But he couldn't. At least, he never did.
"I reckon we both have had about enough of this. That
boy ——"

"Hah," Granny said. "Night before last you were saying
what boy. Where is he? I sent you word to bring him with
you."

"Under arrest," General Forrest said. It was a considerable more than just tired. "I spent four days getting Smith just where I wanted him. After that, this boy here could have fought the battle." He said 'fit' for fought just as he said 'druv' for drove and 'drug' for dragged. But maybe when you fought battles like he did, even Granny didn't mind how you talked. "I won't bother you with details. He didn't know them either. All he had to do was exactly what I told him. I did everything but draw a diagram on his coat-tail of exactly what he was to do, no more and no less, from the time he left me until he saw me again: which was to make contact and then fall back. I gave him just exactly the right number of men so that he couldn't do anything else but that. I told him exactly how fast to fall back and how much racket to make doing it and even how to make the racket. But what do you think he did?"

"I can tell you," Granny said. "He sat on his horse at five o'clock yesterday morning, with my whole yard full of men behind him, yelling goodbye at my window."

"He divided his men and sent half of them into the bushes to make a noise and took the other half who were the nearest to complete fools and led a sabre charge on that outpost. He didn't fire a shot. He drove it clean back with sabres onto Smith's main body and scared Smith so that he threw out all his cavalry and pulled out behind it and now I don't know whether I'm about to catch him or he's about to catch me. My provost finally caught the boy last night. He had come back and got the other thirty men of his company and was twenty miles ahead again, trying to find something to lead another charge against. 'Do you want to be killed?' I said. 'Not especially,' he said. 'That is, I don't especially care one way or the other.' 'Then neither do I,' I said. 'But you risked a whole company of my men.' 'Ain't that what they enlisted for?' he said. 'They enlisted into a military establishment the purpose of which is to expend each man only at a profit. Or maybe you don't consider me a shrewd enough trader in human meat?' 'I can't say,' he said. 'Since day before yesterday I ain't thought very much about how you or anybody else runs this war.' 'And just what were you doing day before yesterday that changed your ideas and habits?' I said. 'Fighting some of it,' he said. 'Dispersing the enemy.' 'Where?' I said. 'At a lady's house a few miles from Jefferson,' he said. 'One of the niggers called her Granny like the white boy did. The others called her Miss Rosie.' " This time Granny didn't say anything. She just waited.

"Go on," she said.

" 'I'm still trying to win battles, even if since day before yesterday you ain't,' I said. 'I'll send you down to Johnston at Jackson,' I said. 'He'll put you inside Vicksburg, where you can lead private charges day and night too if you want.' 'Like hell you will,' he said. And I said—excuse me—'Like hell I won't.' " And Granny didn't say anything. It was like day before yesterday with Ab Snopes: not like she hadn't heard but as if right now it didn't matter, that this was no time either to bother with such.

"And did you?" she said.

"I can't. He knows it. You can't punish a man for routing an enemy four times his weight. What would I say back there in Tennessee, where we both live, let alone that uncle of his, the one they licked for Governor six years ago, on Bragg's personal staff now, with his face over Bragg's shoulder every time Bragg opens a dispatch or picks up a pen. And I'm still trying to win battles. But I can't. Because of a girl, one single lone young female girl that ain't got anything under the sun against him except that, since it was his misfortune to save her from a passel of raiding enemy in a situation that everybody but her is trying to forget, she can't seem to bear to hear his last name. Yet because of that, every battle

I plan from now on will be at the mercy of a twenty-two-year-old shavetail—excuse me again—who might decide to lead a private charge any time he can holler at least two men in gray coats into moving in the same direction." He stopped. He looked at Granny. "Well?" he said.

"So now you've got to it," Granny said. "Well what, Mr. Forrest?"

"Why, just have done with this foolishness. I told you I've got that boy, in close arrest, with a guard with a bayonet. But there won't be any trouble there. I figured even yesterday morning that he had already lost his mind. But I reckon he's recovered enough of it since the Provost took him last night to comprehend that I still consider myself his commander even if he don't. So all necessary now is for you to put your foot down. Put it down hard. Now. You're her grandma. She lives in your home. And it looks like she is going to live in it a good while yet before she gets back to Memphis to that uncle or whoever it is that calls himself her guardian. So just put your foot down. Make her. Mr. Millard would have already done that if he had been here. And I know when. It would have been two days ago by now."

Granny waited until he got done. She stood with her arms crossed, holding each elbow in the other. "Is that all I'm to do?" she said.

"Yes," General Forrest said. "If she don't want to listen to you right at first, maybe as his commander ——"

Granny didn't even say "Hah." She didn't even send me. She didn't even stop in the hall and call. She went upstairs herself and we stood there and I thought maybe she was going to bring the dulcimer too and I thought how if I was General Forrest I would go back and get Cousin Philip and make him sit in the library until about supper-time while Cousin Melisandre played the dulcimer and sang. Then he could take Cousin Philip on back and then he could finish the war without worrying.

She didn't have the dulcimer. She just had Cousin Melisandre. They came in and Granny stood to one side again with her arms crossed, holding her elbows. "Here she is," she said. "Say it—This is Mr. Bedford Forrest," she told Cousin Melisandre. "Say it," she told General Forrest.

He didn't have time. When Cousin Melisandre first came, she tried to read aloud to Ringo and me. It wasn't much. That is, what she insisted on reading to us wasn't so bad, even if it was mostly about ladies looking out windows and playing on something (maybe they were dulcimers too) while somebody else was off somewhere fighting. It was the way she read it. When Granny said this is Mister Forrest, Cousin Melisandre's face looked exactly like her voice would sound when she read to us. She took two steps into the library and curtsied, spreading her hoops back, and stood up. "General Forrest," she said. "I am acquainted with an associate of his. Will the General please give him the sincerest wishes for triumph in war and success in love, from one who will never see him again?" Then she curtsied again and spread her hoops backward and stood up and took two steps backward and turned and went out.

After a while Granny said, "Well, Mr. Forrest?"

General Forrest began to cough. He lifted his coattail with one hand and reached the other into his hip pocket like he was going to pull at least a musket out of it and got his handkerchief and coughed into it a while. It wasn't very clean. It looked about like the one Cousin Philip was trying to wipe his coat off with in the summer house day before yesterday. Then he put the handkerchief back. He didn't say "Hah" either. "Can I reach the Holly Branch road without having to go through Jefferson?" he said.

Then Granny moved. "Open the desk," she said. "Lay out

a sheet of note-paper." I did. And I remember how I stood at one side of the desk and General Forrest at the other, and watched Granny's hand move the pen steady and not very slow and not very long across the paper because it never did take her very long to say anything, no matter what it was, whether she was talking it or writing it. Though I didn't see it then, but only later, when it hung framed under glass above Cousin Melisandre's and Cousin Philip's mantel: the fine steady slant of Granny's hand and General Forrest's sprawling signatures below it that looked itself a good deal like a charge of massed cavalry:

Lieutenant P. S. Backhouse, Company D, Tennessee Cavalry, was this day raised to the honorary rank of Brevet Major General & killed while engaging the enemy. Vice whom Philip St-Just Backus is hereby appointed Lieutenant, Company D, Tennessee Cavalry.

N. B. Forrest Genl

I didn't see it then. General Forrest picked it up. "Now I've got to have a battle," he said. "Another sheet, son." I laid that one out on the desk.

"A battle?" Granny said.

"To give Johnston," he said. "Confound it, Miss Rosie, can't you understand either that I'm just a fallible mortal man trying to run a military command according to certain fixed and inviolable rules, no matter how foolish the business looks to superior outside folks?"

"All right," Granny said. "You had one. I was looking at it."

"So I did," General Forrest said. "Hah," he said. "The battle of Sartoris."

"No," Granny said. "Not at my house."

"They did all the shooting down at the creek," I said.

"What creek?" he said.

So I told him. It ran through the pasture. Its name was Hurricane Creek but not even the white people called it hurricane except Granny. General Forrest didn't either when he sat down at the desk and wrote the report to General Johnston at Jackson:

A unit of my command on detached duty engaged a body of the enemy & drove him from the field & dispersed him this day 28th ult. April 1862 at Harrykin Creek. With loss of one man.

N. B. Forrest Genl

I saw that. I watched him write it. Then he got up and folded the sheets into his pocket and was already going toward the table where his hat was.

"Wait," Granny said. "Lay out another sheet," she said. "Come back here."

General Forrest stopped and turned. "Another one?"

"Yes!" Granny said. "A furlough, pass—whatever you busy military establishments call them! So John Sartoris can come home long enough to ——" and she said it herself, she looked straight at me and even backed up and said some of it over as though to make sure there wouldn't be any mistake: "—— can come back home and give away that damn bride!"

IV

AND THAT was all. The day came and Granny waked Ringo and me before sunup and we ate what breakfast we had from two plates on the back steps. And we dug up the trunk and brought it into the house and polished the silver and Ringo and I brought dogwood and redbud branches from the pasture and Granny cut the flowers, all of them, cutting them herself with Cousin Melisandre and Philadelphia just carrying the baskets; so many of them until the house was so full that

Ringo and I would believe we smelled them even across the pasture each time we came up. Though of course we could, it was just the food—the last ham from the smokehouse and the chickens and the flour which Granny had been saving and the last of the sugar which she had been saving along with the bottle of champagne for the day when the North surrendered—which Louvinia had been cooking for two days now, to remind us each time we approached the house of what was going on and that the flowers were there. As if we could have forgotten about the food. And they dressed Cousin Melisandre and, Ringo in his new blue pants and I in my gray ones which were not so new, we stood in the late afternoon on the gallery—Granny and Cousin Melisandre and Louvinia and Philadelphia and Ringo and I—and watched them enter the gate. General Forrest was not one. Ringo and I had thought maybe he might be, if only to bring Cousin Philip. Then we thought that maybe, since Father was coming anyway, General Forrest would let Father bring him, with Cousin Philip maybe handcuffed to Father and the soldier with the bayonet following, or maybe still just handcuffed to the soldier until he and Cousin Melisandre were married and Father unlocked him.

But General Forrest wasn't one, and Cousin Philip wasn't handcuffed to anybody and there was no bayonet and not even a soldier because these were all officers too. And we stood in the parlor while the home-made candles burnt in the last of sunset in the bright candlesticks which Philadelphia and Ringo and I had polished with the rest of the silver because Granny and Louvinia were both busy cooking and even Cousin Melisandre polished a little of it although Louvinia could pick out the ones she polished without hardly looking and hand them to Philadelphia to polish again:— Cousin Melisandre in the dress which hadn't needed to be altered for her at all because Mother wasn't much older than

Cousin Melisandre even when she died, and which would still button on Granny too just like it did the day she married in it, and the chaplain and Father and Cousin Philip and the four others in their gray and braid and sabres and Cousin Melisandre's face was all right now and Cousin Philip's was too because it just had the beautiful-girl look on it and none of us had ever seen him look any other way. Then we ate, and Ringo and I anyway had been waiting on that for three days and then we did it and then it was over too, fading just a little each day until the palate no longer remembered and only our mouths would run a little water as we would name the dishes aloud to one another, until even the water would run less and less and less and it would take something we just hoped to eat some day if they ever got done fighting, to make it run at all.

And that was all. The last sound of wheel and hoof died away, Philadelphia came in from the parlor carrying the candlesticks and blowing out the candles as she came, and Louvinia set the kitchen clock on the table and gathered the last of soiled silver from supper into the dishpan and it might never have even been. "Well," Granny said. She didn't move, leaning her forearms on the table a little and we had never seen that before. She spoke to Ringo without turning her head: "Go call Joby and Lucius." And even when we brought the trunk in and set it against the wall and opened back the lid, she didn't move. She didn't even look at Louvinia either. "Put the clock in too," she said. "I don't think we'll bother to time ourselves tonight."

Golden Land

IF HE had been thirty, he would not have needed the two aspirin tablets and the half glass of raw gin before he could bear the shower's needling on his body and steady his hands to shave. But then when he had been thirty neither could he have afforded to drink as much each evening as he now drank; certainly he would not have done it in the company of the men and the women in which, at forty-eight, he did each evening, even though knowing during the very final hours filled with the breaking of glass and the shrill cries of drunken women above the drums and saxophones—the hours during which he carried a little better than his weight both in the amount of liquor consumed and in the number and sum of checks paid—that six or eight hours later he would rouse from what had not been sleep at all but instead that dreamless stupefaction of alcohol out of which last night's turgid and licensed uproar would die, as though without any interval for rest or recuperation, into the familiar shape of his bedroom—the bed's foot silhouetted by the morning light which entered the bougainvillaea-bound windows beyond which his painful and almost unbearable eyes could see the view which might be called the monument to almost twenty-five years of industry and desire, of shrewdness and luck and even fortitude—the opposite canyonflank dotted with the white villas halfhidden in imported

701

olive groves or friezed by the sombre spaced columns of cypress like the façades of eastern temples, whose owners' names and faces and even voices were glib and familiar in back corners of the United States and of America and of the world where those of Einstein and Rousseau and Esculapius had never sounded.

He didn't waken sick. He never wakened ill nor became ill from drinking, not only because he had drunk too long and too steadily for that, but because he was too tough even after the thirty soft years; he came from too tough stock on that day thirty-four years ago when at fourteen he had fled, on the brakebeam of a westbound freight, the little lost Nebraska town named for, permeated with, his father's history and existence—a town to be sure, but only in the sense that any shadow is larger than the object which casts it. It was still frontier even as he remembered it at five and six—the projected and increased shadow of a small outpost of sodroofed dugouts on the immense desolation of the plains where his father, Ira Ewing too, had been first to essay to wring wheat during the six days between those when, outdoors in spring and summer and in the fetid halfdark of a snowbound dugout in the winter and fall, he preached. The second Ira Ewing had come a long way since then, from that barren and treeless village which he had fled by a night freight to where he now lay in a hundred-thousand-dollar house, waiting until he knew that he could rise and go to the bath and put the two aspirin tablets into his mouth. They—his mother and father—had tried to explain it to him —something about fortitude, the will to endure. At fourteen he could neither answer them with logic and reason nor explain what he wanted: he could only flee. Nor was he fleeing his father's harshness and wrath. He was fleeing the scene itself—the treeless immensity in the lost center of which he seemed to see the sum of his father's and mother's dead youth and bartered lives as a tiny forlorn spot which nature permitted to green into brief and niggard wheat for a season's moment before blotting it all with the primal and invincible snow as though (not even promise, not even threat) in grim and almost playful augury of the final doom of all life. And it was not even this that he was fleeing because he was not fleeing: it was only that absence, removal, was the only argument which fourteen knew how to employ against adults with any hope of success. He spent the next ten years half tramp half casual laborer as he drifted down the Pacific Coast to Los Angeles; at thirty he was married, to a Los Angeles girl, daughter of a carpenter, and father of a son and a daughter and with a foothold in real estate; at forty-eight he spent fifty thousand dollars a year, owning a business which he had built up unaided and preserved intact through nineteen-twenty-nine; he had given to his children luxuries and advantages which his own father not only could not have conceived in fact but would have condemned completely in theory—as it proved, as the paper which the Filipino chauffeur, who each morning carried him into the house and undressed him and put him to bed, had removed from the pocket of his topcoat and laid on the reading table proved, with reason. On the death of his father twenty years ago he had returned to Nebraska, for the first time, and fetched his mother back with him, and she was now established in a home of her own only the less sumptuous because she refused (with a kind of abashed and thoughtful unshakability which he did not remark) anything finer or more elaborate. It was the house in which they had all lived at first, though he and his wife and children had moved within the year. Three years ago they had moved again, into the house where he now waked in a select residential section of Beverley Hills, but not once in the nineteen years had he failed to stop (not even during the last five, when to move at all in the mornings required a terrific drain on that character or strength which the elder Ira had bequeathed him, which had enabled the other Ira to pause on the Nebraska plain and dig a hole for his wife to bear children in while he planted wheat) on his way to the office (twenty miles out of his way to the office) and spend ten minutes with her. She lived in as complete physical ease and peace as he could devise. He had arranged her affairs so that she did not even need to bother with money, cash, in order to live; he had arranged credit for her with a neighboring market and butcher so that the Japanese gardener who came each day to water and tend the flowers could do her shopping for her; she never even saw the bills. And the only reason she had no servant was that even at seventy she apparently clung stubbornly to the old habit of doing her own cooking and housework. So it would seem that he had been right. Perhaps there were times when, lying in bed like this and waiting for the will to rise and take the aspirin and the gin (mornings perhaps following evenings when he had drunk more than ordinarily and when even the six or seven hours of oblivion had not been sufficient to enable him to distinguish between reality and illusion) something of the old strong harsh Campbellite blood which the elder Ira must have bequeathed him might have caused him to see or feel or imagine his father looking down from somewhere upon him, the prodigal, and what he had accomplished. If this were so, then surely the elder Ira, looking down for the last two mornings upon the two tabloid papers which the Filipino removed from his master's topcoat and laid on the reading table, might have taken advantage of that old blood and taken his revenge, not just for that afternoon thirty-four years ago but for the entire thirty-four years.

When he gathered himself, his will, his body, at last and rose from the bed he struck the paper so that it fell to the floor and lay open at his feet, but he did not look at it. He just stood so, tall, in silk pajamas, thin where his father had been gaunt with the years of hard work and unceasing struggle with the unpredictable and implacable earth (even now, despite the life which he had led, he had very little paunch) looking at nothing while at his feet the black headline flared above the row of five or six tabloid photographs from which his daughter alternately stared back or flaunted long pale shins: APRIL LALEAR BARES ORGY SECRETS. When he moved at last he stepped on the paper, walking on his bare feet into the bath; now it was his trembling and jerking hands that he watched as he shook the two tablets onto the glass shelf and set the tumbler into the rack and unstoppered the gin bottle and braced his knuckles against the wall in order to pour into the tumbler. But he did not look at the paper, not even when, shaved, he re-entered the bedroom and went to the bed beside which his slippers sat and shoved the paper aside with his foot in order to step into them. Perhaps, doubtless, he did not need to. The trial was but entering its third tabloidal day now, and so for two days his daughter's face had sprung out at him, hard, blonde and inscrutable, from every paper he opened; doubtless he had never forgot her while he slept even, that he had waked into thinking about remembering her as he had waked into the dying drunken uproar of the evening eight hours behind him without any interval between for rest or forgetting.

Nevertheless as, dressed, in a burnt orange turtleneck sweater beneath his gray flannels, he descended the Spanish staircase, he was outwardly calm and possessed. The delicate iron balustrade and the marble steps coiled down to the tile-floored and barnlike living room beyond which he could hear his wife and son talking on the breakfast terrace. The son's name was Voyd. He and his wife had named the two children by what might have been called mutual contemptu-

ous armistice—his wife called the boy Voyd, for what
reason he never knew; he in his turn named the girl (the
child whose woman's face had met him from every paper
he touched for two days now beneath or above the name,
April Lalear) Samantha, after his own mother. He could
hear them talking—the wife between whom and himself
there had been nothing save civility, and not always a great
deal of that, for ten years now; and the son who one afternoon two years ago had been delivered at the door drunk
and insensible by a car whose occupants he did not see and,
it devolving upon him to undress the son and put him to bed,
whom he discovered to be wearing, in place of underclothes,
a woman's brassière and step-ins. A few minutes later, hearing the blows perhaps, Voyd's mother ran in and found her
husband beating the still unconscious son with a series of
towels which a servant was steeping in rotation in a basin of
ice-water. He was beating the son hard, with grim and deliberate fury. Whether he was trying to sober the son up or
was merely beating him, possibly he himself did not know.
His wife though jumped to the latter conclusion. In his
raging disillusionment he tried to tell her about the woman's
garments but she refused to listen; she assailed him in turn
with virago fury. Since that day the son had contrived to see
his father only in his mother's presence (which neither the
son nor the mother found very difficult, by the way) and at
which times the son treated his father with a blend of cringing spite and vindictive insolence half a cat's and half a
woman's.

    He emerged onto the terrace; the voices ceased. The sun,
strained by the vague high soft almost nebulous California
haze, fell upon the terrace with a kind of treacherous un-
brightness. The terrace, the sundrenched terra cotta tiles,
butted into a rough and savage shear of canyonwall bare yet
without dust, on or against which a solid mat of flowers

bloomed in fierce lush myriad-colored paradox as though in place of being rooted into and drawing from the soil they lived upon air alone and had been merely leaned intact against the sustenanceless lavawall by someone who would later return and take them away. The son, Voyd, apparently naked save for a pair of straw-colored shorts, his body brown with sun and scented faintly by the depilatory which he used on arms, chest and legs, lay in a wicker chair, his feet in straw beach shoes, an open newspaper across his brown legs. The paper was the highest class one of the city, yet there was a black headline across half of it too, and even without pausing, without even being aware that he had looked, Ira saw there too the name which he recognized. He went on to his place; the Filipino who put him to bed each night, in a white service jacket now, drew his chair. Beside the glass of orange juice and the waiting cup lay a neat pile of mail topped by a telegram. He sat down and took up the telegram; he had not glanced at his wife until she spoke:

"Mrs. Ewing telephoned. She says for you to stop in there on your way to town."

He stopped; his hands opening the telegram stopped. Still blinking a little against the sun he looked at the face opposite him across the table—the smooth dead makeup, the thin lips and the thin nostrils and the pale blue unforgiving eyes, the meticulous platinum hair which looked as though it had been transferred to her skull with a brush from a book of silver leaf such as window painters use. "What?" he said. "Telephoned? Here?"

"Why not? Have I ever objected to any of your women telephoning you here?"

The unopened telegram crumpled suddenly in his hand. "You know what I mean," he said harshly. "She never telephoned me in her life. She don't have to. Not that message.

When have I ever failed to go by there on my way to town?"

"How do I know?" she said. "Or are you the same model son you have been a husband and seem to be a father?" Her voice was not shrill yet, nor even very loud, and none could have told how fast her breathing was because she sat so still, rigid beneath the impeccable and unbelievable hair, looking at him with that pale and outraged unforgiveness. They both looked at each other across the luxurious table—the two people who at one time twenty years ago would have turned as immediately and naturally and unthinkingly to one another in trouble, who even ten years ago might have done so.

"You know what I mean," he said, harshly again, holding himself too against the trembling which he doubtless believed was from last night's drinking, from the spent alcohol. "She don't read papers. She never even sees one. Did you send it to her?"

"I?" she said. "Send what?"

"Damnation!" he cried. "A paper! Did you send it to her? Don't lie to me."

"What if I did?" she cried. "Who is she, that she must not know about it? Who is she, that you should shield her from knowing it? Did you make any effort to keep me from knowing it? Did you make any effort to keep it from happening? Why didn't you think about that all those years while you were too drunk, too besotted with drink, to know or notice or care what Samantha was—"

"Miss April Lalear of the cinema, if you please," Voyd said. They paid no attention to him; they glared at one another across the table.

"Ah," he said, quiet and rigid, his lips scarcely moving. "So I am to blame for this too, am I? I made my daughter a bitch, did I? Maybe you will tell me next that I made my son a f—"

"Stop!" she cried. She was panting now; they glared at one another across the suave table, across the five feet of irrevocable division.

"Now, now," Voyd said. "Don't interfere with the girl's career. After all these years, when at last she seems to have found a part that she can—" He ceased; his father had turned and was looking at him. Voyd lay in his chair, looking at his father with that veiled insolence that was almost feminine. Suddenly it became completely feminine; with a muffled halfscream he swung his legs out to spring up and flee but it was too late; Ira stood above him, gripping him not by the throat but by the face with one hand, so that Voyd's mouth puckered and slobbered in his father's hard, shaking hand. Then the mother sprang forward and tried to break Ira's grip but he flung her away and then caught and held her, struggling too, with the other hand when she sprang in again.

"Go on," he said. "Say it." But Voyd could say nothing because of his father's hand gripping his jaws open, or more than likely because of terror. His body was free of the chair now, writhing and thrashing while he made his slobbering, moaning sound of terror while his father held him with one hand and held his screaming mother with the other one. Then Ira flung Voyd free, onto the terrace; Voyd rolled once and came onto his feet, crouching, retreating toward the French windows with one arm flung up before his face while he cursed his father. Then he was gone. Ira faced his wife, holding her quiet too at last, panting too, the skillful map of makeup standing into relief now like a paper mask trimmed smoothly and pasted onto her skull. He released her.

"You sot," she said. "You drunken sot. And yet you wonder why your children—"

"Yes," he said quietly. "All right. That's not the question. That's all done. The question is, what to do about it. My

father would have known. He did it once." He spoke in a
dry light pleasant voice: so much so that she stood, panting
still but quiet, watching him. "I remember. I was about ten.
We had rats in the barn. We tried everything. Terriers.
Poison. Then one day father said, 'Come.' We went to the
barn and stopped all the cracks, the holes. Then we set fire
to it. What do you think of that?" Then she was gone too.
He stood for a moment, blinking a little, his eyeballs beating
faintly and steadily in his skull with the impact of the soft
unchanging sunlight, the fierce innocent mass of the flowers.
"Philip!" he called. The Filipino appeared, brownfaced, impassive, with a pot of hot coffee, and set it beside the empty
cup and the icebedded glass of orange juice. "Get me a
drink," Ira said. The Filipino glanced at him, then he became busy at the table, shifting the cup and setting the pot
down and shifting the cup again while Ira watched him.
"Did you hear me?" Ira said. The Filipino stood erect and
looked at him.

"You told me not to give it to you until you had your
orange juice and coffee."

"Will you or won't you get me a drink?" Ira shouted.

"Very good, sir," the Filipino said. He went out. Ira
looked after him; this had happened before: he knew well
that the brandy would not appear until he had finished the
orange juice and the coffee, though just where the Filipino
lurked to watch him he never knew. He sat again and opened
the crumpled telegram and read it, the glass of orange juice
in the other hand. It was from his secretary: MADE SETUP
BEFORE I BROKE STORY LAST NIGHT STOP
THIRTY PERCENT FRONT PAGE STOP MADE
APPOINTMENT FOR YOU COURTHOUSE THIS
P.M. STOP WILL YOU COME TO OFFICE OR CALL
ME. He read the telegram again, the glass of orange juice
still poised. Then he put both down and rose and went and

lifted the paper from the terrace where Voyd had flung it, and read the half headline: LALEAR WOMAN DAUGH-TER OF PROMINENT LOCAL FAMILY. Admits Real Name Is Samantha Ewing, Daughter of Ira Ewing, Local Realtor. He read it quietly; he said quietly, aloud:

"It was that Jap that showed her the paper. It was that damned gardener." He returned to the table. After a while the Filipino came, with the brandy-and-soda, and wearing now a jacket of bright imitation tweed, telling him that the car was ready.

II

HIS MOTHER lived in Glendale; it was the house which he had taken when he married and later bought, in which his son and daughter had been born—a bungalow in a cul-de-sac of pepper trees and flowering shrubs and vines which the Japanese tended, backed into a barren foothill combed and curried into a cypress-and-marble cemetery dramatic as a stage set and topped by an electric sign in red bulbs which, in the San Fernando valley fog, glared in broad sourceless ruby as though just beyond the crest lay not heaven but hell. The length of his sports model car in which the Filipino sat reading a paper dwarfed it. But she would have no other, just as she would have neither servant, car, nor telephone—a gaunt spare slightly stooped woman upon whom even California and ease had put no flesh, sitting in one of the chairs which she had insisted on bringing all the way from Nebraska. At first she had been content to allow the Nebraska furniture to remain in storage, since it had not been needed (when Ira moved his wife and family out of the house and into the second one, the intermediate one, they had bought new furniture too, leaving the first house furnished complete for his mother) but one day, he could not recall just when, he discovered that she had taken the one chair out of storage and was using it in the house. Later, after he began to sense that quality of unrest in her, he had suggested that she let him clear the house of its present furniture and take all of hers out of storage but she declined, apparently preferring or desiring to leave the Nebraska furniture where it was. Sitting so, a knitted shawl about her shoulders, she looked less like she lived in or belonged to the house, the room, than the son with his beach burn and his faintly theatrical gray temples and his bright expensive suavely antiphonal garments did. She had changed hardly at all in the thirty-four years; she and the older Ira Ewing too, as the son remembered him, who, dead, had suffered as little of alteration as while he had been alive. As the sod Nebraska outpost had grown into a village and then into a town, his father's aura alone had increased, growing into the proportions of a giant who at some irrevocable yet recent time had engaged barehanded in some titanic struggle with the pitiless earth and endured and in a sense conquered —it too, like the town, a shadow out of all proportion to the gaunt gnarled figure of the actual man. And the actual woman too as the son remembered them back in that time. Two people who drank air and who required to eat and sleep as he did and who had brought him into the world, yet were strangers as though of another race, who stood side by side in an irrevocable loneliness as though strayed from another planet, not as husband and wife but as blood brother and sister, even twins, of the same travail because they had gained a strange peace through fortitude and the will and strength to endure.

"Tell me again what it is," she said. "I'll try to understand."

"So it was Kazimura that showed you the damned paper," he said. She didn't answer this; she was not looking at him.

"You tell me she has been in the pictures before, for two years. That that was why she had to change her name, that they all have to change their names."

"Yes. They call them extra parts. For about two years, God knows why."

"And then you tell me that this—that all this was so she could get into the pictures—"

He started to speak, then he caught himself back out of some quick impatience, some impatience perhaps of grief or despair or at least rage, holding his voice, his tone, quiet: "I said that that was one possible reason. All I know is that the man has something to do with pictures, giving out the parts. And that the police caught him and Samantha and the other girl in an apartment with the doors all locked and that Samantha and the other woman were naked. They say that he was naked too and he says he was not. He says in the trial that he was framed—tricked; that they were trying to blackmail him into giving them parts in a picture; that they fooled him into coming there and arranged for the police to break in just after they had taken off their clothes; that one of them made a signal from the window. Maybe so. Or maybe they were all just having a good time and were innocently caught." Unmoving, rigid, his face broke, wrung with faint bitter smiling as though with indomitable and impassive suffering, or maybe just smiling, just rage. Still his mother did not look at him.

"But you told me she was already in the pictures. That that was why she had to change her—"

"I said, extra parts," he said. He had to catch himself again, out of his jangled and outraged nerves, back from the fierce fury of the impatience. "Can't you understand that you don't get into the pictures just by changing your name? and that you don't even stay there when you get in? that you can't even stay there by being female? that they come here in droves on every train—girls younger and prettier than Samantha and who will do anything to get into the pictures? So will she, apparently; but who know or are willing to learn to do more things than even she seems to have thought of? But let's don't talk about it. She has made her bed; all I can do is to help her up: I can't wash the sheets. Nobody can. I must go, anyway; I'm late." He rose, looking down at her. "They said you telephoned me this morning. Is this what it was?"

"No," she said. Now she looked up at him; now her gnarled hands began to pick faintly at one another. "You offered me a servant once."

"Yes. I thought fifteen years ago that you ought to have one. Have you changed your mind? Do you want me to—"

Now she stopped looking at him again, though her hands did not cease. "That was fifteen years ago. It would have cost at least five hundred dollars a year. That would be—"

He laughed, short and harsh. "I'd like to see the Los Angeles servant you could get for five hundred dollars a year. But what—" He stopped laughing, looking down at her.

"That would be at least five thousand dollars," she said.

He looked down at her. After a while he said, "Are you asking me again for money?" She didn't answer nor move, her hands picking slowly and quietly at one another. "Ah," he said. "You want to go away. You want to run from it. So do I!" he cried, before he could catch himself this time; "so do I! But you did not choose me when you elected a child; neither did I choose my two. But I shall have to bear them and you will have to bear all of us. There is no help for it." He caught himself now, panting, quieting himself by will as when he would rise from bed, though his voice was still harsh: "Where would you go? Where would you hide from it?"

"Home," she said.

"Home?" he repeated; he repeated in a kind of amazement: "home?" before he understood. "You would go back there? with those winters, that snow and all? Why, you wouldn't live to see the first Christmas: don't you know that?" She didn't move nor look up at him. "Nonsense," he said. "This will blow over. In a month there will be two others and nobody except us will even remember it. And you don't need money. You have been asking me for money for years, but you don't need it. I had to worry about money so much at one time myself that I swore that the least I could do was to arrange your affairs so you would never even have to look at the stuff. I must go; there is something at the office today. I'll see you tomorrow."

It was already one o'clock. "Courthouse," he told the Filipino, settling back into the car. "My God, I want a drink." He rode with his eyes closed against the sun; the secretary had already sprung onto the runningboard before he realized that they had reached the courthouse. The secretary, bareheaded too, wore a jacket of authentic tweed; his turtleneck sweater was dead black, his hair was black too, varnished smooth to his skull; he spread before Ira a dummy newspaper page laid out to embrace the blank space for the photograph beneath the caption: APRIL LALEAR'S FATHER. Beneath the space was the legend: IRA EWING, PRESIDENT OF THE EWING REALTY CO.,—WILSHIRE BOULEVARD, BEVERLY HILLS.

"Is thirty percent all you could get?" Ira said. The secretary was young; he glared at Ira for an instant in vague impatient fury.

"Jesus, thirty percent is thirty percent. They are going to print a thousand extra copies and use our mailing list. It will be spread all up and down the Coast and as far East as Reno. What do you want? We can't expect them to put under your picture, 'Turn to page fourteen for halfpage ad,' can we?" Ira sat again with his eyes closed, waiting for his head to stop.

"All right," he said. "Are they ready now?"

"All set. You will have to go inside. They insisted it be inside, so everybody that sees it will know it is the courthouse."

"All right," Ira said. He got out; with his eyes half closed and the secretary at his elbow he mounted the steps and entered the courthouse. The reporter and the photographer were waiting but he did not see them yet; he was aware only of being enclosed in a gaping crowd which he knew would be mostly women, hearing the secretary and a policeman clearing the way in the corridor outside the courtroom door.

"This is O.K.," the secretary said. Ira stopped; the darkness was easier on his eyes though he did not open them yet; he just stood, hearing the secretary and the policeman herding the women, the faces, back; someone took him by the arm and turned him; he stood obediently; the magnesium flashed and glared, striking against his painful eyeballs like blows; he had a vision of wan faces craned to look at him from either side of a narrow human lane; with his eyes shut tight now he turned, blundering until the reporter in charge spoke to him:

"Just a minute, chief. We better get another one just in case." This time his eyes were tightly closed; the magnesium flashed, washed over them; in the thin acrid smell of it he turned and with the secretary again at his elbow he moved blindly back and into the sunlight and into his car. He gave no order this time, he just said, "Get me a drink." He rode with his eyes closed again while the car cleared the downtown traffic and then began to move quiet, powerful and fast under him; he rode so for a long while before he felt the car swing into the palmbordered drive, slowing. It stopped; the doorman opened the door for him, speaking to him by name. The elevator boy called him by name too, stopping at the right floor without direction; he followed the corridor and knocked at a door and was fumbling for the key when the door opened upon a woman in a bathing suit beneath a loose beach cloak—a woman with treated hair also and brown eyes, who swung the door back for him to enter and then to behind him, looking at him with the quick bright faint serene smiling which only a woman nearing forty can give to a man to whom she is not married and from whom she has had no secrets physical and few mental over a long time of pleasant and absolute intimacy. She had been married though and divorced; she had a child, a daughter of fourteen, whom he was now keeping in boarding school. He looked at her, blinking, as she closed the door.

"You saw the papers," he said. She kissed him, not suddenly, without heat, in a continuation of the movement which closed the door, with a sort of warm envelopment; suddenly he cried, "I can't understand it! After all the advantages that . . . after all I tried to do for them—"

"Hush," she said. "Hush, now. Get into your trunks; I'll have a drink ready for you when you have changed. Will you eat some lunch if I have it sent up?"

"No. I don't want any lunch. —after all I have tried to give—"

"Hush, now. Get into your trunks while I fix you a drink. It's going to be swell at the beach." In the bedroom his bathing trunks and robe were laid out on the bed. He changed, hanging his suit in the closet where her clothes hung, where there hung already another suit of his and clothes for the evening. When he returned to the sitting room she had fixed the drink for him; she held the match to his cigarette and watched him sit down and take up the glass, watching him still with that serene impersonal smiling. Now he watched her slip off the cape and kneel at the cellarette, filling a silver flask, in the bathing costume of the moment, such as ten thousand wax female dummies wore in ten thousand shop windows that summer, such as a hundred thousand young girls wore on California beaches; he looked at her, kneeling—back, buttocks and flanks trim enough, even firm enough (so firm in fact as to be a little on the muscular side, what with unremitting and perhaps even rigorous care) but still those of forty. But I don't want a young girl, he thought. Would to God that all young girls, all young female flesh, were removed, blasted even, from the earth. He finished the drink before she had filled the flask.

"I want another one," he said.

"All right," she said. "As soon as we get to the beach."

"No. Now."

"Let's go on to the beach first. It's almost three o'clock. Won't that be better?"

"Just so you are not trying to tell me I can't have another drink now."

"Of course not," she said, slipping the flask into the cape's pocket and looking at him again with that warm, faint, inscrutable smiling. "I just want to have a dip before the water gets too cold." They went down to the car; the Filipino knew this too: he held the door for her to slip under the wheel, then he got himself into the back. The car moved on; she drove well. "Why not lean back and shut your eyes," she told Ira, "and rest until we get to the beach? Then we will have a dip and a drink."

"I don't want to rest," he said. "I'm all right." But he did close his eyes again and again the car ran powerful, smooth, and fast beneath him, performing its afternoon's jaunt over the incredible distances of which the city was composed;

from time to time, had he looked, he could have seen the city in the bright soft vague hazy sunlight, random, scattered about the arid earth like so many gay scraps of paper blown without order, with its curious air of being rootless— of houses bright beautiful and gay, without basements or foundations, lightly attached to a few inches of light penetrable earth, lighter even than dust and laid lightly in turn upon the profound and primeval lava, which one good hard rain would wash forever from the sight and memory of man as a firehose flushes down a gutter—that city of almost incalculable wealth whose queerly appropriate fate it is to be erected upon a few spools of a substance whose value is computed in billions and which may be completely destroyed in that second's instant of a careless match between the moment of striking and the moment when the striker might have sprung and stamped it out.

"You saw your mother today," she said. "Has she—"

"Yes." He didn't open his eyes. "That damned Jap gave it to her. She asked me for money again. I found out what she wants with it. She wants to run, to go back to Nebraska. I told her, so did I. . . . If she went back there, she would not live until Christmas. The first month of winter would kill her. Maybe it wouldn't even take winter to do it."

She still drove, she still watched the road, yet somehow she had contrived to become completely immobile. "So that's what it is," she said.

He did not open his eyes. "What what is?"

"The reason she has been after you all this time to give her money, cash. Why, even when you won't do it, every now and then she asks you again."

"What what . . ." He opened his eyes, looking at her profile; he sat up suddenly. "You mean, she's been wanting to go back there all the time? That all these years she has been asking me for money, that that was what she wanted with it?"

She glanced at him swiftly, then back to the road. "What else can it be? What else could she use money for?"

"Back there?" he said. "To those winters, that town, that way of living, where she's bound to know that the first winter would . . . You'd almost think she wanted to die, wouldn't you?"

"Hush," she said quickly. "Shhhhh. Don't say that. Don't say that about anybody." Already they could smell the sea; now they swung down toward it; the bright salt wind blew upon them, with the long-spaced sound of the rollers; now they could see it—the dark blue of water creaming into the blanched curve of beach dotted with bathers. "We won't go through the club," she said. "I'll park in here and we can go straight to the water." They left the Filipino in the car and descended to the beach. It was already crowded, bright and gay with movement. She chose a vacant space and spread her cape.

"Now that drink," he said.

"Have your dip first," she said. He looked at her. Then he slipped his robe off slowly; she took it and spread it beside her own; he looked down at her.

"Which is it? Will you always be too clever for me, or is it that every time I will always believe you again?"

She looked at him, bright, warm, fond and inscrutable. "Maybe both. Maybe neither. Have your dip; I will have the flask and a cigarette ready when you come out." When he came back from the water, wet, panting, his heart a little too hard and fast, she had the towel ready, and she lit the cigarette and uncapped the flask as he lay on the spread robes. She lay too, lifted to one elbow, smiling down at him, smoothing the water from his hair with the towel while he panted, waiting for his heart to slow and quiet. Steadily between them and the water, and as far up and down the beach as they could see, the bathers passed—young people, young men in trunks, and young girls in little more, with bronzed, unselfconscious bodies. Lying so, they seemed to him to walk along the rim of the world as though they and their kind alone inhabited it, and he with his forty-eight years were the forgotten last survivor of another race and kind, and they in turn precursors of a new race not yet seen on the earth: of men and women without age, beautiful as gods and goddesses, and with the minds of infants. He turned quickly and looked at the woman beside him—at the quiet face, the wise, smiling eyes, the grained skin and temples, the hairroots showing where the dye had grown out, the legs veined faint and blue and myriad beneath the skin. "You look better than any of them!" he cried. "You look better to me than any of them!"

III

THE JAPANESE GARDENER, with his hat on, stood tapping on the glass and beckoning and grimacing until old Mrs. Ewing went out to him. He had the afternoon's paper with its black headline: LALEAR WOMAN CREATES SCENE IN COURTROOM. "You take," the Japanese said. "Read while I catch water." But she declined; she just stood in the soft halcyon sunlight, surrounded by the myriad and almost fierce blooming of flowers, and looked quietly at the head- line without even taking the paper, and that was all.

"I guess I won't look at the paper today," she said. "Thank you just the same." She returned to the living room. Save for the chair, it was exactly as it had been when she first saw it that day when her son brought her into it and told her that it was now her home and that her daughter-in-law and her grandchildren were now her family. It had changed very little, and that which had altered was the part which her son knew nothing about, and that too had changed not at all in so long that she could not even remember now when she had added the last coin to the hoard. This was in a china vase on the mantel. She knew what was in it to the penny; nevertheless, she took it down and sat in the chair which she had brought all the way from Nebraska and emptied the coins and the worn timetable into her lap. The timetable was folded back at the page on which she had folded it the day she walked downtown to the ticket office and got it fifteen years ago, though that was so long ago now that the pencil circle about the name of the nearest junction point to Ewing, Nebraska, had faded away. But she did not need that either; she knew the distance to the exact halfmile, just as she knew the fare to the penny, and back in the early twenties when the railroads began to become worried and passenger fares began to drop, no broker ever watched the grain and utilities market any closer than she watched the railroad advertisements and quotations. Then at last the fares became stabilized with the fare back to Ewing thirteen dollars more than she had been able to save, and at a time when her source of income had ceased. This was the two grandchildren. When she entered the house that day twenty years ago and looked at the two babies for the first time, it was with diffidence and eagerness both. She would be dependent for the rest of her life, but she would give something in return for it. It was not that she would attempt to make another Ira and Samantha Ewing of them; she had made that mistake with her own son and had driven him from home. She was wiser now; she saw now that it was not the repetition of hardship: she would merely take what had been of value in hers and her husband's hard lives—that which they had learned through hardship and endurance of honor and courage and pride—

and transmit it to the children without their having to suffer the hardship at all, the travail and the despairs. She had expected that there would be some friction between her and the young daughter-in-law, but she had believed that her son, the actual Ewing, would be her ally; she had even reconciled herself after a year to waiting, since the children were still but babies; she was not alarmed, since they were Ewings too: after she had looked that first searching time at the two puttysoft little faces feature by feature, she had said it was because they were babies yet and so looked like no one. So she was content to bide and wait; she did not even know that her son was planning to move until he told her that the other house was bought and that the present one was to be hers until she died. She watched them go; she said nothing; it was not to begin then. It did not begin for five years, during which she watched her son making money faster and faster and easier and easier, gaining with apparent contemptible and contemptuous ease that substance for which in niggard amounts her husband had striven while still clinging with undeviating incorruptibility to honor and dignity and pride, and spending it, squandering it, in the same way. By that time she had given up the son and she had long since learned that she and her daughter-in-law were irrevocable and implacable moral enemies. It was in the fifth year. One day in her son's home she saw the two children take money from their mother's purse lying on a table. The mother did not even know how much she had in the purse; when the grandmother told her about it she became angry and dared the older woman to put it to the test. The grandmother accused the children, who denied the whole affair with perfectly straight faces. That was the actual break between herself and her son's family; after that she saw the two children only when the son would bring them with him occasionally on his unfailing daily visits. She

had a few broken dollars which she had brought from Nebraska and had kept intact for five years, since she had no
need for money here; one day she planted one of the coins
while the children were there, and when she went back to
look, it was gone too. The next morning she tried to talk
to her son about the children, remembering her experience
with the daughter-in-law and approaching the matter in-
directly, speaking generally of money. "Yes," the son said.
"I'm making money. I'm making it fast while I can. I'm
going to make a lot of it. I'm going to give my children
luxuries and advantages that my father never dreamed a
child might have."

"That's it," she said. "You make money too easy. This
whole country is too easy for us Ewings. It may be all right
for them that have been born here for generations; I don't
know about that. But not for us."

"But these children were born here."

"Just one generation. The generation before that they
were born in a sodroofed dugout on the Nebraska wheat
frontier. And the one before that in a log house in Missouri.
And the one before that in a Kentucky blockhouse with
Indians around it. This world has never been easy for
Ewings. Maybe the Lord never intended it to be."

"But it is from now on," he said; he spoke with a kind
of triumph. "For you and me too. But mostly for them."

And that was all. When he was gone she sat quietly in
the single Nebraska chair which she had taken out of storage—the first chair which the older Ira Ewing had bought
for her after he built a house and in which she had rocked
the younger Ira to sleep before he could walk, while the
older Ira himself sat in the chair which he had made out of
a flour barrel, grim, quiet and incorruptible, taking his
earned twilight ease between a day and a day—telling herself quietly that that was all. Her next move was curiously

direct; there was something in it of the actual pioneer's opportunism, of taking immediate and cold advantage of Spartan circumstance; it was as though for the first time in her life she was able to use something, anything, which she had gained by bartering her youth and strong maturity against the Nebraska immensity, and this not in order to live further but in order to die; apparently she saw neither paradox in it nor dishonesty. She began to make candy and cake of the materials which her son bought for her on credit, and to sell them to the two grandchildren for the coins which their father gave them or which they perhaps purloined also from their mother's purse, hiding the coins in the vase with the timetable, watching the niggard hoard grow. But after a few years the children outgrew candy and cake, and then she had watched railroad fares go down and down and then stop thirteen dollars away. But she did not give up, even then. Her son had tried to give her a servant years ago and she had refused; she believed that when the time came, the right moment, he would not refuse to give her at least thirteen dollars of the money which she had saved him. Then this had failed. "Maybe it wasn't the right time," she thought. "Maybe I tried it too quick. I was surprised into it," she told herself, looking down at the heap of small coins in her lap. "Or maybe he was surprised into saying No. Maybe when he has had time . . ." She roused; she put the coins back into the vase and set it on the mantel again, looking at the clock as she did so. It was just four, two hours yet until time to start supper. The sun was high; she could see the water from the sprinkler flashing and glinting in it as she went to the window. It was still high, still afternoon; the mountains stood serene and drab against it; the city, the land, lay sprawled and myriad beneath it—the land, the earth which spawned a thousand new faiths, nostrums and cures each year but no disease to even disprove them on—

beneath the golden days unmarred by rain or weather, the changeless monotonous beautiful days without end countless out of the halcyon past and endless into the halcyon future.

"I will stay here and live forever," she said to herself.

There Was a Queen

ELNORA entered the back yard, coming up from her cabin. In the long afternoon the huge, square house, the premises, lay somnolent, peaceful, as they had lain for almost a hundred years, since John Sartoris had come from Carolina and built it. And he had died in it and his son Bayard had died in it, and Bayard's son John and John's son Bayard in turn had been buried from it even though the last Bayard didn't die there.

` So the quiet was now the quiet of womenfolks. As Elnora crossed the back yard toward the kitchen door she remembered how ten years ago at this hour old Bayard, who was her half-brother (though possibly but not probably neither of them knew it, including Bayard's father), would be tramping up and down the back porch, shouting stableward for the Negro men and for his saddle mare. But he was dead now, and his grandson Bayard was also dead at twenty-six years old, and the Negro men were gone: Simon, Elnora's mother's husband, in the graveyard too, and Caspey, Elnora's husband, in the penitentiary for stealing, and Joby, her son, gone to Memphis to wear fine clothes on Beale Street. So there were left in the house only the first John Sartoris' sister, Virginia, who was ninety years old and who lived in a wheel chair beside a window above the flower garden, and Narcissa, young Bayard's widow, and her son. Virginia Du Pre had come out to Mississippi in '69, the last of the Carolina family, bringing with her the clothes in which she stood and a basket containing a few panes of colored glass from a Carolina window and a few flower cuttings and two bottles of port. She had seen her brother die and then her nephew and then her great-nephew and then her two great-great-nephews, and now she lived in the unmanned house with her great-great-nephew's wife and his son, Benbow, whom she persisted in calling Johnny after his uncle, who was killed in France. And for Negroes there were Elnora who cooked, and her son Isom who tended the grounds, and her daughter Saddie who slept on a cot beside Virginia Du Pre's bed and tended her as though she were a baby.

But that was all right. "I can take care of her," Elnora thought, crossing the back yard. "I don't need no help," she said aloud, to no one—a tall, coffee-colored woman with a small, high, fine head. "Because it's a Sartoris job. Cunnel knowed that when he died and tole me to take care of her. Tole me. Not no outsiders from town." She was thinking of what had caused her to come up to the house an hour before it was necessary. This was that, while busy in her cabin, she had seen Narcissa, young Bayard's wife, and the ten-year-old boy going down across the pasture in the middle of the afternoon. She had come to her door and watched them—the boy and the big young woman in white going through the hot afternoon, down across the pasture toward the creek. She had not wondered where they were going, nor why, as a white woman would have wondered. But she was half black, and she just watched the white woman with that expression of quiet and grave contempt with which she contemplated or listened to the orders of the wife of the house's heir even while he was alive. Just as she had listened two days ago when Narcissa had informed her that she was going to Memphis for a day or so and that Elnora would have to take care of the old aunt alone. "Like I ain't always done it," Elnora thought. "It's little you done for anybody since you come out here. We never needed you. Don't you never think it." But she didn't say this. She just thought it, and she helped Narcissa prepare for the trip and watched the carriage roll away toward town and the station without comment. "And you needn't to come back," she thought, watching the carriage disappear. But this morning Narcissa had returned, without offering to explain the sudden journey or the sudden return, and in the early afternoon Elnora from her cabin door had watched the woman and the boy go down across the pasture in the hot June sunlight.

"Well, it's her business where she going," Elnora said aloud, mounting the kitchen steps. "Same as it her business how come she went off to Memphis, leaving Miss Jenny setting yonder in her chair without nobody but niggers to look after her," she added, aloud still, with brooding inconsistency. "I ain't surprised she went. I just surprised she come back. No. I ain't even that. She ain't going to leave this place, now she done got in here." Then she said quietly, aloud, without rancor, without heat: "Trash. Town trash."

She entered the kitchen. Her daughter Saddie sat at the table, eating from a dish of cold turnip greens and looking at a thumbed and soiled fashion magazine. "What you doing back here?" she said. "Why ain't you up yonder where you can hear Miss Jenny if she call you?"

"Miss Jenny ain't need nothing," Saddie said. "She setting there by the window."

"Where did Miss Narcissa go?"

"I don't know'm," Saddie said. "Her and Bory went off somewhere. Ain't come back yet."

Elnora grunted. Her shoes were not laced, and she stepped out of them in two motions and left the kitchen and went up the quiet, high-ceiled hall filled with scent from the garden and with the drowsing and myriad sounds of the June afternoon, to the open library door. Beside the window (the sash was raised now, with its narrow border of colored Carolina glass which in the winter framed her head and bust like a hung portrait) an old woman sat in a wheel chair. She sat erect; a thin, upright woman with a delicate nose and hair the color of a whitewashed wall. About her shoulders lay a shawl of white wool, no whiter than her hair against her black dress. She was looking out the window; in profile her face was high-arched, motionless. When Elnora entered she turned her head and looked at the Negress with an expression immediate and interrogative.

"They ain't come in the back way, have they?" she said.

"Nome," Elnora said. She approached the chair.

The old woman looked out the window again. "I must say I don't understand this at all. Miss Narcissa's doing a mighty lot of traipsing around all of a sudden. Picking up and—"

Elnora came to the chair. "A right smart," she said in her cold, quiet voice, "for a woman lazy as her."

"Picking up—" the old woman said. She ceased. "You stop talking that way about her."

"I ain't said nothing but the truth," Elnora said.

"Then you keep it to yourself. She's Bayard's wife. A Sartoris woman, now."

"She won't never be a Sartoris woman," Elnora said.

The other was looking out the window. "Picking up all of a sudden two days ago and going to Memphis to spend two nights, that hadn't spent a night away from that boy since he was born. Leaving him for two whole nights, mind you, without giving any reason, and then coming home and taking him off to walk in the woods in the middle of the day. Not that he missed her. Do you think he missed her at all while she was gone?"

"Nome," Elnora said. "Ain't no Sartoris man never missed nobody."

"Of course he didn't." The old woman looked out the window. Elnora stood a little behind the chair. "Did they go on across the pasture?"

"I don't know. They went out of sight, still going. Toward the creek."

"Toward the creek? What in the world for?"

Elnora didn't answer. She stood a little behind the chair, erect, still as an Indian. The afternoon was drawing on. The sun was now falling level across the garden below the window, and soon the jasmine in the garden began to smell with evening, coming into the room in slow waves almost palpable; thick, sweet, oversweet. The two women were motionless in the window: the one leaning a little forward in the wheel chair, the Negress a little behind the chair, motionless too and erect as a caryatid.

The light in the garden was beginning to turn copper-colored when the woman and the boy entered the garden and approached the house. The old woman in the chair leaned suddenly forward. To Elnora it seemed as if the old woman in the wheel chair had in that motion escaped her helpless body like a bird and crossed the garden to meet the child; moving forward a little herself Elnora could see on the other's face an expression fond, immediate, and oblivious. So the two people had crossed the garden and were almost to the house when the old woman sat suddenly and sharply back. "Why, they're wet!" she said. "Look at their clothes. They have been in the creek with their clothes on!"

"I reckon I better go and get supper started," Elnora said.

II

IN THE kitchen Elnora prepared the lettuce and the tomatoes, and sliced the bread (not honest cornbread, not even biscuit) which the woman whose very name she did not speak unless it was absolutely necessary, had taught her to bake. Isom and

Saddie sat in two chairs against the wall. "I got nothing against her," Elnora said. "I nigger and she white. But my black children got more blood than she got. More behavior."

"You and Miss Jenny both think ain't nobody been born since Miss Jenny," Isom said.

"Who is been?" Elnora said.

"Miss Jenny get along all right with Miss Narcissa," Isom said. "Seem to me like she the one to say. I ain't heard her say nothing about it."

"Because Miss Jenny quality," Elnora said. "That's why. And that's something you don't know nothing about, because you born too late to see any of it except her."

"Look to me like Miss Narcissa good quality as anybody else," Isom said. "I don't see no difference."

Elnora moved suddenly from the table. Isom as suddenly sprang up and moved his chair out of his mother's path. But she only went to the cupboard and took a platter from it and returned to the table, to the tomatoes. "Born Sartoris or born quality of any kind ain't *is*, it's *does*." She talked in a level, inflectionless voice above her limber, brown, deft hands. When she spoke of the two women she used "she" indiscriminately, putting the least inflection on the one which referred to Miss Jenny. "Come all the way here by Herself, and the country still full of Yankees. All the way from Cal-lina, with Her folks all killed and dead except old Marse John, and him two hundred miles away in Missippi—"

"It's moren two hundred miles from here to Cal-lina," Isom said. "Learnt that in school. It's nigher two thousand."

Elnora's hands did not cease. She did not seem to have heard him. "With the Yankees done killed Her paw and Her husband and burned the Cal-lina house over Her and Her mammy's head, and She come all the way to Missippi by Herself, to the only kin She had left. Getting here in the dead of winter without nothing in this world of God's but

a basket with some flower seeds and two bottles of wine and
them colored window panes old Marse John put in the library window so She could look through it like it was Cal-
lina. She got here at dusk-dark on Christmas Day and old
Marse John and the chillen and my mammy waiting on the
porch, and Her setting high-headed in the wagon for old
Marse John to lift Her down. They never even kissed
then, out where folks could see them. Old Marse John just
said, 'Well, Jenny,' and she just said, 'Well, Johnny,' and
they walked into the house, him leading Her by the hand,
until they was inside the house where the commonalty
couldn't spy on them. Then She begun to cry, and old Marse
John holding Her, after all them four thousand miles—"

"It ain't four thousand miles from here to Cal-lina," Isom
said. "Ain't but two thousand. What the book say in school."

Elnora paid no attention to him at all; her hands did not
cease. "It took Her hard, the crying did. 'It's because I ain't
used to crying,' she said. 'I got out of the habit of it. I never
had the time. Them goddamn Yankees,' she said. 'Them goddamn Yankees.' " Elnora moved again, to the cupboard. It
was as though she walked out of the sound of her voice on
her silent, naked feet, leaving it to fill the quiet kitchen
though the voice itself had ceased. She took another platter
down and returned to the table, her hands busy again among
the tomatoes and lettuce, the food which she herself could
not eat. "And that's how it is that she" (she was now speaking of Narcissa; the two Negroes knew it) "thinks she can
pick up and go to Memphis and frolic, and leave Her alone
in this house for two nights without nobody but niggers to
look after Her. Move out here under a Sartoris roof and eat
Sartoris food for ten years, and then pick up and go to
Memphis same as a nigger on a excursion, without even telling
why she was going."

"I thought you said Miss Jenny never needed nobody but

you to take care of her," Isom said. "I thought you said yesterday you never cared if she come back or not."

Elnora made a sound, harsh, disparaging, not loud. "Her not come back? When she worked for five years to get herself married to Bayard? Working on Miss Jenny all the time Bayard was off to that war? I watched her. Coming out here two or three times a week, with Miss Jenny thinking she was just coming out to visit like quality. But I knowed. I knowed what she was up to all the time. Because I knows trash. I knows the way trash goes about working in with quality. Quality can't see that, because it quality. But I can."

"Then Bory must be trash, too," Isom said.

Elnora turned now. But Isom was already out of his chair before she spoke. "You shut your mouth and get yourself ready to serve supper." She watched him go to the sink and prepare to wash his hands. Then she turned back to the table, her long hands brown and deft among the red tomatoes and the pale absinth-green of the lettuce. "Needings," she said. "It ain't Bory's needings and it ain't Her needings. It's dead folks' needings. Old Marse John's and Cunnel's and Mister John's and Bayard's that's dead and can't do nothing about it. That's where the needings is. That's what I'm talking about. And not nobody to see to it except Her yonder in that chair, and me, a nigger, back here in this kitchen. I ain't got nothing against her. I just say to let quality consort with quality, and unquality do the same thing. You get that coat on, now. This here is all ready."

III

It was the boy who told her. She leaned forward in the wheel chair and watched through the window as the woman and the child crossed the garden and passed out of sight beyond the angle of the house. Still leaning forward and looking down into the garden, she heard them enter the house and pass the library door and mount the stairs. She did not move, nor look toward the door. She continued to look down into the garden, at the now stout shrubs which she had fetched from Carolina as shoots not much bigger than matches. It was in the garden that she and the younger woman who was to marry her nephew and bear a son, had become acquainted. That was back in 1918, and young Bayard and his brother John were still in France. It was before John was killed, and two or three times a week Narcissa would come out from town to visit her while she worked among the flowers. "And she engaged to Bayard all the time and not telling me," the old woman thought. "But it was little she ever told me about anything," she thought, looking down into the garden which was beginning to fill with twilight and which she had not entered in five years. "Little enough about anything. Sometimes I wonder how she ever got herself engaged to Bayard, talking so little. Maybe she did it by just being, filling some space, like she got that letter." That was one day shortly before Bayard returned home. Narcissa came out and stayed for two hours, then just before she left she showed the letter. It was anonymous and obscene; it sounded mad, and at the time she had tried to get Narcissa to let her show the letter to Bayard's grandfather and have him make some effort to find the man and punish him, but Narcissa refused. "I'll just burn it and forget about it," Narcissa said. "Well, that's your business," the older woman said. "But that should not be permitted. A lady should not be at the mercy of a man like that, even by mail. Any gentleman will believe that, act upon it. Besides, if you don't do something about it, he'll write you again." "Then I'll show it to Colonel Sartoris," Narcissa said. She was an orphan, her brother also in France. "But can't you see I just can't have any man know that anybody thought such things about me."

"Well, I'd rather have the whole world know that somebody thought that way about me once and got horsewhipped for it, than to have him keep on thinking that way about me, unpunished. But it's your affair." "I'll just burn it and forget about it," Narcissa said. Then Bayard returned, and shortly afterward he and Narcissa were married and Narcissa came out to the house to live. Then she was pregnant, and before the child was born Bayard was killed in an airplane, and his grandfather, old Bayard, was dead and the child came, and it was two years before she thought to ask her niece if any more letters had come; and Narcissa told her no.

So they had lived quietly then, their women's life in the big house without men. Now and then she had urged Narcissa to marry again. But the other had refused, quietly, and they had gone on so for years, the two of them and the child whom she persisted in calling after his dead uncle. Then one evening a week ago, Narcissa had a guest for supper; when she learned that the guest was to be a man, she sat quite still in her chair for a time. "Ah," she thought, quietly. "It's come. Well. But it had to; she is young. And to live out here alone with a bedridden old woman. Well. But I wouldn't have her do as I did. Would not expect it of her. After all, she is not a Sartoris. She is no kin to them, to a lot of fool proud ghosts." The guest came. She did not see him until she was wheeled in to the supper table. Then she saw a bald, youngish man with a clever face and a Phi Beta Kappa key on his watch chain. The key she did not recognize, but she knew at once that he was a Jew, and when he spoke to her her outrage became fury and she jerked back in the chair like a striking snake, the motion strong-enough to thrust the chair back from the table. "Narcissa," she said, "what is this Yankee doing here?"

There they were, about the candle-lit table, the three rigid people. Then the man spoke: "Madam," he said, "there'd be no Yankees left if your sex had ever taken the field against us."

"You don't have to tell me that, young man," she said. "You can thank your stars it was just men your grandfather fought." Then she had called Isom and had herself wheeled from the table, taking no supper. And even in her bedroom she would not let them turn on the light, and she refused the tray which Narcissa sent up. She sat beside her dark window until the stranger was gone.

Then three days later Narcissa made her sudden and mysterious trip to Memphis and stayed two nights, who had never before been separated overnight from her son since he was born. She had gone without explanation and returned without explanation, and now the old woman had just watched her and the boy cross the garden, their garments still damp upon them, as though they had been in the creek.

It was the boy who told her. He came into the room in fresh clothes, his hair still damp, though neatly combed now. She said no word as he entered and came to her chair. "We been in the creek," he said. "Not swimming, though. Just sitting in the water. She wanted me to show her the swimming hole. But we didn't swim. I don't reckon she can. We just sat in the water with our clothes on. All evening. She wanted to do it."

"Ah," the old woman said. "Oh. Well. That must have been fun. Is she coming down soon?"

"Yessum. When she gets dressed."

"Well. . . . You'll have time to go outdoors a while before supper, if you want to."

"I just as soon stay in here with you, if you want me to."

"No. You go outdoors. I'll be all right until Saddie comes."

"All right." He left the room.

The window faded slowly as the sunset died. The old woman's silver head faded too, like something motionless on a sideboard. The sparse colored panes which framed the window dreamed, rich and hushed. She sat there and presently she heard her nephew's wife descending the stairs. She sat quietly, watching the door, until the young woman entered.

She wore white: a large woman in her thirties, within the twilight something about her of that heroic quality of statuary. "Do you want the light?" she said.

"No," the old woman said. "No. Not yet." She sat erect in the wheel chair, motionless, watching the young woman cross the room, her white dress flowing slowly, heroic, like a caryatid from a temple façade come to life. She sat down.

"It was those let—" she said.

"Wait," the old woman said. "Before you begin. The jasmine. Do you smell it?"

"Yes. It was those—"

"Wait. Always about this time of day it begins. It has begun about this time of day in June for fifty-seven years this summer. I brought them from Carolina, in a basket. I remember how that first March I sat up all one night, burning newspapers about the roots. Do you smell it?"

"Yes."

"If it's marriage, I told you. I told you five years ago that I wouldn't blame you. A young woman, a widow. Even though you have a child, I told you that a child would not be enough. I told you I would not blame you for not doing as I had done. Didn't I?"

"Yes. But it's not that bad."

"Not? Not how bad?" The old woman sat erect, her head back a little, her thin face fading into the twilight with a profound quality. "I won't blame you. I told you that. You are not to consider me. My life is done; I need little; nothing the Negroes can't do. Don't you mind me, do you hear?" The other said nothing, motionless too, serene; their voices seemed to materialize in the dusk between them, unsourced of either mouth, either still and fading face. "You'll have to tell me, then," the old woman said.

"It was those letters. Thirteen years ago: don't you remember? Before Bayard came back from France, before you even knew that we were engaged. I showed you one of them and you wanted to give it to Colonel Sartoris and let him find out who sent it and I wouldn't do it and you said that no lady would permit herself to receive anonymous love letters, no matter how badly she wanted to."

"Yes. I said it was better for the world to know that a lady had received a letter like that, than to have one man in secret thinking such things about her, unpunished. You told me you burned it."

"I lied. I kept it. And I got ten more of them. I didn't tell you because of what you said about a lady."

"Ah," the old woman said.

"Yes. I kept them all. I thought I had them hidden where nobody could ever find them."

"And you read them again. You would take them out now and then and read them again."

"I thought I had them hidden. Then you remember that night after Bayard and I were married when somebody broke into our house in town; the same night that book-keeper in Colonel Sartoris' bank stole that money and ran away? The next morning the letters were gone, and then I knew who had sent them."

"Yes," the old woman said. She had not moved, her fading head like something inanimate in silver.

"So they were out in the world. They were somewhere. I was crazy for a while. I thought of people, men, reading them, seeing not only my name on them, but the marks of my eyes where I had read them again and again. I was wild. When Bayard and I were on our honeymoon, I was wild.

I couldn't even think about him alone. It was like I was having to sleep with all the men in the world at the same time.

"Then it was almost twelve years ago, and I had Bory, and I supposed I had got over it. Got used to having them out in the world. Maybe I had begun to think that they were gone, destroyed, and I was safe. Now and then I would remember them, but it was like somehow that Bory was protecting me, that they couldn't pass him to reach me. As though if I just stayed out here and was good to Bory and you— And then, one afternoon, after twelve years, that man came out to see me, that Jew. The one who stayed to supper that night."

"Ah," the old woman said. "Yes."

"He was a Federal agent. They were still trying to catch the man who had robbed the bank, and the agent had got hold of my letters. Found them where the book-keeper had lost them or thrown them away that night while he was running away, and the agent had had them twelve years, working on the case. At last he came out to see me, trying to find out where the man had gone, thinking I must know, since the man had written me letters like that. You remember him: how you looked at him and you said, 'Narcissa, who is this Yankee?' "

"Yes. I remember."

"That man had my letters. He had had them for twelve years. He—"

"*Had* had?" the old woman said. "*Had* had?"

"Yes. I have them now. He hadn't sent them to Washington yet, so nobody had read them except him. And now nobody will ever read them." She ceased; she breathed quietly, tranquil. "You don't understand yet, do you? He had all the information the letters could give him, but he would have to turn them in to the Department anyway and I asked him for them but he said he would have to turn them in and I asked him if he would make his final decision in Memphis and he said why Memphis and I told him why. I knew I couldn't buy them from him with money, you see. That's why I had to go to Memphis. I had that much regard for Bory and you, to go somewhere else. And that's all. Men are all about the same, with their ideas of good and bad. Fools." She breathed quietly. Then she yawned, deep, with utter relaxation. Then she stopped yawning. She looked again at the rigid, fading silver head opposite her. "Don't you understand yet?" she said. "I had to do it. They were mine; I had to get them back. That was the only way I could do it. But I would have done more than that. So I got them. And now they are burned up. Nobody will ever see them. Because he can't tell, you see. It would ruin him to ever tell that they even existed. They might even put him in the penitentiary. And now they are burned up."

"Yes," the old woman said. "And so you came back home and you took Johnny so you and he could sit together in the creek, the running water. In Jordan. Yes, Jordan at the back of a country pasture in Missippi."

"I had to get them back. Don't you see that?"

"Yes," the old woman said. "Yes." She sat bolt upright in the wheel chair. "Well, my Lord. Us poor, fool women —Johnny!" Her voice was sharp, peremptory.

"What?" the young woman said. "Do you want something?"

"No," the other said. "Call Johnny. I want my hat." The young woman rose. "I'll get it."

"No. I want Johnny to do it."

The young woman stood looking down at the other, the old woman erect in the wheel chair beneath the fading silver crown of her hair. Then she left the room. The old woman did not move. She sat there in the dusk until the boy

entered, carrying a small black bonnet of an ancient shape.
Now and then, when the old woman became upset, they
would fetch her the hat and she would place it on the exact
top of her head and sit there by the window. He brought
the bonnet to her. His mother was with him. It was full
dusk now; the old woman was invisible save for her hair.
"Do you want the light now?" the young woman said.

"No," the old woman said. She set the bonnet on the top
of her head. "You all go on to supper and let me rest awhile.
Go on, all of you." They obeyed, leaving her sitting there:
a slender, erect figure indicated only by the single gleam of
her hair, in the wheel chair beside the window framed by
the sparse and defunctive Carolina glass.

IV

SINCE THE BOY's eighth birthday, he had had his dead grandfather's place at the end of the table. Tonight however his
mother rearranged things. "With just the two of us," she
said. "You come and sit by me." The boy hesitated. "Please.
Won't you? I got so lonesome for you last night in Memphis.
Weren't you lonesome for me?"

"I slept with Aunt Jenny," the boy said. "We had a good
time."

"Please."

"All right," he said. He took the chair beside hers.

"Closer," she said. She drew the chair closer. "But we
won't ever again, ever. Will we?" She leaned toward him,
taking his hand.

"What? Sit in the creek?"

"Not ever leave one another again."

"I didn't get lonesome. We had a good time."

"Promise. Promise, Bory." His name was Benbow, her
family name.

"All right."

Isom, in a duck jacket, served them and returned to the kitchen.

"She ain't coming to supper?" Elnora said.

"Nome," Isom said. "Setting yonder by the window, in the dark. She say she don't want no supper."

Elnora looked at Saddie. "What was they doing last time you went to the library?"

"Her and Miss Narcissa talking."

"They was still talking when I went to 'nounce supper," Isom said. "I tole you that."

"I know," Elnora said. Her voice was not sharp. Neither was it gentle. It was just peremptory, soft, cold. "What were they talking about?"

"I don't know'm," Isom said. "You the one taught me not to listen to white folks."

"What were they talking about, Isom?" Elnora said. She was looking at him, grave, intent, commanding.

" 'Bout somebody getting married. Miss Jenny say 'I tole you long time ago I ain't blame you. A young woman like you. I want you to marry. Not do like I done,' what she say."

"I bet she fixing to marry, too," Saddie said.

"Who marry?" Elnora said. "Her marry? What for? Give up what she got here? That ain't what it is. I wished I knowed what been going on here this last week. . . ." Her voice ceased; she turned her head toward the door as though she were listening for something. From the dining-room came the sound of the young woman's voice. But Elnora appeared to listen to something beyond this. Then she left the room. She did not go hurriedly, yet her long silent stride carried her from sight with an abruptness like that of an inanimate figure drawn on wheels, off a stage.

She went quietly up the dark hall, passing the dining-room

door unremarked by the two people at the table. They sat close. The woman was talking, leaning toward the boy. Elnora went on without a sound: a converging of shadows upon which her lighter face seemed to float without body, her eyeballs faintly white. Then she stopped suddenly. She had not reached the library door, yet she stopped, invisible, soundless, her eyes suddenly quite luminous in her almost-vanished face, and she began to chant in faint sing-song: "Oh, Lawd; oh, Lawd," not loud. Then she moved, went swiftly on to the library door and looked into the room where beside the dead window the old woman sat motion-less, indicated only by that faint single gleam of white hair, as though for ninety years life had died slowly up her spare, erect frame, to linger for a twilit instant about her head be-fore going out, though life itself had ceased. Elnora looked for only an instant into the room. Then she turned and retraced her swift and silent steps to the dining-room door. The woman still leaned toward the boy, talking. They did not remark Elnora at once. She stood in the doorway, tall, not touching the jamb on either side. Her face was blank; she did not appear to be looking at, speaking to, any one.

"You better come quick, I reckon," she said in that soft, cold, peremptory voice.

Mountain Victory

THROUGH THE CABIN WINDOW the five people watched the cavalcade toil up the muddy trail and halt at the gate. First came a man on foot, leading a horse. He wore a broad hat low on his face, his body shapeless in a weathered gray cloak from which his left hand emerged, holding the reins. The bridle was silvermounted, the horse a gaunt, mudsplashed, thoroughbred bay, wearing in place of saddle a navy blue army blanket bound on it by a piece of rope. The second horse was a shortbodied, bigheaded, scrub sorrel, also mudsplashed. It wore a bridle contrived of rope and wire, and an army saddle in which, perched high above the dangling stirrups. crouched a shapeless something larger than a child, which at that distance appeared to wear no garment or garments known to man.

One of the three men at the cabin window left it quickly. The others, without turning, heard him cross the room swiftly and then return, carrying a long rifle.

"No, you don't," the older man said.

"Don't you see that cloak?" the younger said. "That rebel cloak?"

"I wont have it," the other said. "They have surrendered. They have said they are whipped."

Through the window they watched the horses stop at the gate. The gate was of sagging hickory, in a rock fence which straggled down a gaunt slope sharp in relief against the valley and a still further range of mountains dissolving into the low, dissolving sky.

They watched the creature on the second horse descend and hand his reins also into the same left hand of the man in gray that held the reins of the thoroughbred. They watched the creature enter the gate and mount the path and disappear beyond the angle of the window. Then they heard it cross the porch and knock at the door. They stood there and heard it knock again.

After a while the older man said, without turning his head, "Go and see."

One of the women, the older one, turned from the window, her feet making no sound on the floor, since they were bare. She went to the front door and opened it. The chill, wet light of the dying April afternoon fell in upon her— upon a small woman with a gnarled expressionless face, in a gray shapeless garment. Facing her across the sill was a creature a little larger than a large monkey, dressed in a voluminous blue overcoat of a private in the Federal army, with, tied tentlike over his head and falling about his shoulders, a piece of oilcloth which might have been cut square from the hood of a sutler's wagon; within the orifice the woman could see nothing whatever save the whites of two eyes, momentary and phantomlike, as with a single glance the Negro examined the woman standing barefoot in her faded calico garment, and took in the bleak and barren interior of the cabin hall.

"Marster Major Soshay Weddel send he compliments en say he wishful fo sleeping room fo heself en boy en two hawses," he said in a pompous, parrot-like voice. The woman looked at him. Her face was like a spent mask. "We been up yonder a ways, fighting dem Yankees," the Negro said. "Done quit now. Gwine back home."

The woman seemed to speak from somewhere behind her face, as though behind an effigy or a painted screen: "I'll ask him."

"We ghy pay you," the Negro said.

"Pay?" Pausing, she seemed to muse upon him. "Hit aint near a ho-tel on the mou-tin."

The Negro made a large gesture. "Don't make no diffunce. We done stayed de night in worse places den whut dis is. You just tell um it Marse Soshay Weddel." Then he saw that the woman was looking past him. He turned and saw the man in the worn gray cloak already halfway up the path from the gate. He came on and mounted the porch, removing with his left hand the broad slouched hat bearing the tarnished wreath of a Confederate field officer. He had a dark face, with dark eyes and black hair, his face at once thick yet gaunt, and arrogant. He was not tall, yet he topped the Negro by five or six inches. The cloak was weathered, faded about the shoulders where the light fell strongest. The skirts were bedraggled, frayed, mudsplashed: the garment had been patched again and again, and brushed again and again; the nap was completely gone.

"Goodday, madam," he said. "Have you stableroom for my horses and shelter for myself and my boy for the night?"

The woman looked at him with a static, musing quality, as though she had seen without alarm an apparition.

"I'll have to see," she said.

"I shall pay," the man said. "I know the times."

"I'll have to ask him," the woman said. She turned, then stopped. The older man entered the hall behind her. He was big, in jean clothes, with a shock of iron-gray hair and pale eyes.

"I am Saucier Weddel," the man in gray said. "I am on my way home to Mississippi from Virginia. I am in Tennessee now?"

"You are in Tennessee," the other said. "Come in."

Weddel turned to the Negro. "Take the horses on to the stable," he said.

The Negro returned to the gate, shapeless in the oilcloth cape and the big overcoat, with that swaggering arrogance which he had assumed as soon as he saw the woman's bare feet and the meagre, barren interior of the cabin. He took up the two bridle reins and began to shout at the horses with needless and officious vociferation, to which the two horses paid no heed, as though they were long accustomed to him. It was as if the Negro himself paid no attention to his cries, as though the shouting were merely concomitant to the action of leading the horses out of sight of the door, like an effluvium by both horses and Negro accepted and relegated in the same instant.

II

THROUGH THE KITCHEN WALL the girl could hear the voices of the men in the room from which her father had driven her when the stranger approached the house. She was about twenty: a big girl with smooth, simple hair and big, smooth hands, standing barefoot in a single garment made out of flour sacks. She stood close to the wall, motionless, her head bent a little, her eyes wide and still and empty like a sleepwalker's, listening to her father and the guest enter the room beyond it.

The kitchen was a plank leanto built against the log wall of the cabin proper. From between the logs beside her the clay chinking, dried to chalk by the heat of the stove, had fallen away in places. Stooping, the movement slow and lush and soundless as the whispering of her bare feet on the floor, she leaned her eye to one of these cracks. She could see a bare table on which sat an earthenware jug and a box of musket cartridges stenciled *U. S. Army*. At the table her two brothers sat in splint chairs, though it was only the younger one, the boy, who looked toward the door, though she knew, could hear now, that the stranger was in the room. The older brother was taking the cartridges one by one from the box and crimping them and setting them upright at his hand like a mimic parade of troops, his back to the door where she knew the stranger was now standing. She breathed quietly. "Vatch would have shot him," she said, breathed, to herself, stooping. "I reckon he will yet."

Then she heard feet again and her mother came toward the door to the kitchen, crossing and for a moment blotting the orifice. Yet she did not move, not even when her mother entered the kitchen. She stooped to the crack, her breathing regular and placid, hearing her mother clattering the stove-lids behind her. Then she saw the stranger for the first time and then she was holding her breath quietly, not even aware that she had ceased to breathe. She saw him standing beside the table in his shabby cloak, with his hat in his left hand. Vatch did not look up.

"My name is Saucier Weddel," the stranger said.

"Soshay Weddel," the girl breathed into the dry chinking, the crumbled and powdery wall. She could see him at full length, in his stained and patched and brushed cloak, with his head lifted a little and his face worn, almost gaunt, stamped with a kind of indomitable weariness and yet arrogant too, like a creature from another world with other air to breathe and another kind of blood to warm the veins. "Soshay Weddel," she breathed.

"Take some whiskey," Vatch said without moving.

Then suddenly, as it had been with the suspended breath-ing, she was not listening to the words at all, as though it were no longer necessary for her to hear, as though curiosity too had no place in the atmosphere in which the stranger dwelled and in which she too dwelled for the moment as she watched the stranger standing beside the table, looking at Vatch, and Vatch now turned in his chair, a cartridge in his hand, looking up at the stranger. She breathed quietly into the crack through which the voices came now without heat or significance out of that dark and smoldering and violent and childlike vanity of men:

"I reckon you know these when you see them, then?"

"Why not? We used them too. We never always had the time nor the powder to stop and make our own. So we had to use yours now and then. Especially during the last."

"Maybe you would know them better if one exploded in your face."

"Vatch." She now looked at her father, because he had spoken. Her younger brother was raised a little in his chair, leaning a little forward, his mouth open a little. He was seventeen. Yet still the stranger stood looking quietly down at Vatch, his hat clutched against his worn cloak, with on his face that expression arrogant and weary and a little quizzical.

"You can show your other hand too," Vatch said. "Don't be afraid to leave your pistol go."

"No," the stranger said. "I am not afraid to show it."

"Take some whiskey, then," Vatch said, pushing the jug forward with a motion slighting and contemptuous.

"I am obliged infinitely," the stranger said. "It's my stomach. For three years of war I have had to apologize to my stomach; now, with peace, I must apologize for it. But if I might have a glass for my boy? Even after four years, he cannot stand cold."

"Soshay Weddel," the girl breathed into the crumbled dust beyond which the voices came, not yet raised yet forever irreconcilable and already doomed, the one blind victim, the other blind executioner:

"Or maybe behind your back you would know it better."

"You, Vatch."

"Stop, sir. If he was in the army for as long as one year, he has run too, once. Perhaps oftener, if he faced the Army of Northern Virginia."

"Soshay Weddel," the girl breathed, stooping. Now she saw Weddel, walking apparently straight toward her, a thick tumbler in his left hand and his hat crumpled beneath the same arm.

"Not that way," Vatch said. The stranger paused and looked back at Vatch. "Where are you aiming to go?"

"To take this out to my boy," the stranger said. "Out to the stable. I thought perhaps this door—" His face was in profile now, worn, haughty, wasted, the eyebrows lifted with quizzical and arrogant interrogation. Without rising Vatch jerked his head back and aside. "Come away from that door." But the stranger did not stir. Only his head moved a little, as though he had merely changed the direction of his eyes.

"He's looking at paw," the girl breathed. "He's waiting for paw to tell him. He aint skeered of Vatch. I knowed it."

"Come away from that door," Vatch said. "You damn nigra."

"So it's my face and not my uniform," the stranger said. "And you fought four years to free us, I understand."

Then she heard her father speak again. "Go out the front way and around the house, stranger," he said.

"Soshay Weddel," the girl said. Behind her her mother clattered at the stove. "Soshay Weddel," she said. She did not say it aloud. She breathed again, deep and quiet and without haste. "It's like a music. It's like a singing."

III

The Negro was squatting in the hallway of the barn, the sagging and broken stalls of which were empty save for the two horses. Beside him was a worn rucksack, open. He was engaged in polishing a pair of thin dancing slippers with a cloth and a tin of paste, empty save for a thin rim of polish about the circumference of the tin. Beside him on a piece of plank sat one finished shoe. The upper was cracked; it had a crude sole nailed recently and crudely on by a clumsy hand.

"Thank de Lawd folks cant see de bottoms of yo feets," the Negro said. "Thank de Lawd it's just dese hyer mountain trash. I'd even hate fo Yankees to see yo feets in dese things." He rubbed the shoe, squinted at it, breathed upon it, rubbed it again upon his squatting flank.

"Here," Weddel said, extending the tumbler. It contained a liquid as colorless as water.

The Negro stopped, the shoe and the cloth suspended. "Which?" he said. He looked at the glass. "Whut's dat?"

"Drink it," Weddel said.

"Dat's water. Whut you bringing me water fer?"

"Take it," Weddel said. "It's not water."

The Negro took the glass gingerly. He held it as if it contained nitroglycerin. He looked at it, blinking, bringing the glass slowly under his nose. He blinked. "Where'd you git dis hyer?" Weddel didn't answer. He had taken up the finished slipper, looking at it. The Negro held the glass under his nose. "It smell kind of like it ought to," he said. "But I be dawg ef it look like anything. Dese folks fixing to pizen you." He tipped the glass and sipped gingerly, and lowered the glass, blinking.

"I didn't drink any of it," Weddel said. He set the slipper down.

"You better hadn't," the Negro said. "When here I done been fo years trying to take care of you en git you back home like whut Mistis tole me to do, and here you sleeping in folks' barns at night like a tramp, like a pater-roller nigger—" He put the glass to his lips, tilting it and his head in a single jerk. He lowered the glass, empty; his eyes were closed; he said, "Whuf!" shaking his head with a violent, shuddering motion. "It smells right, and it act right. But I be dawg ef it look right. I reckon you better let it alone, like you started out. When dey try to make you drink it you send um to me. I done already stood so much I reckon I can stand a little mo fer Mistis' sake."

He took up the shoe and the cloth again. Weddel stooped above the rucksack. "I want my pistol," he said.

Again the Negro ceased, the shoe and the cloth poised. "Whut fer?" He leaned and looked up the muddy slope toward the cabin. "Is dese folks Yankees?" he said in a whisper.

"No," Weddel said, digging in the rucksack with his left hand. The Negro did not seem to hear him.

"In Tennessee? You tole me we was in Tennessee, where Memphis is, even if you never tole me it was all disyer up-and-down land in de Memphis country. I know I never seed none of um when I went to Memphis wid yo paw dat time. But you says so. And now you telling me dem Memphis folks is Yankees?"

"Where is the pistol?" Weddel said.

"I done tole you," the Negro said. "Acting like you does. Letting dese folks see you come walking up de road, leading Caesar caze you think he tired; making me ride whilst you walks when I can outwalk you any day you ever lived and you knows it, even if I is fawty en you twenty-eight. I ghy tell yo maw. I ghy tell um."

Weddel rose, in his hand a heavy cap-and-ball revolver. He chuckled it in his single hand, drawing the hammer back, letting it down again. The Negro watched him, crouched like an ape in the blue Union army overcoat. "You put dat thing back," he said. "De war done wid now. Dey tole us back dar at Ferginny it was done wid. You dont need no pistol now. You put it back, you hear me?"

"I'm going to bathe," Weddel said. "Is my shirt—"

"Bathe where? In whut? Dese folks aint never seed a bathtub."

"Bathe at the well. Is my shirt ready?"

"Whut dey is of it. . . . You put dat pistol back, Marse Soshay. I ghy tell yo maw on you. I ghy tell um. I just wish Marster was here."

"Go to the kitchen," Weddel said. "Tell them I wish to bathe in the well house. Ask them to draw the curtain on that window there." The pistol had vanished beneath the grey cloak. He went to the stall where the thoroughbred was. The horse nuzzled at him, its eyes rolling soft and wild. He patted its nose with his left hand. It whickered, not loud, its breath sweet and warm.

IV

THE NEGRO entered the kitchen from the rear. He had removed the oilcloth tent and he now wore a blue forage cap which, like the overcoat, was much too large for him, resting upon the top of his head in such a way that the unsupported brim oscillated faintly when he moved as though with a life of its own. He was completely invisible save for his face between cap and collar like a dried Dyak trophy and almost as small and dusted lightly over as with a thin pallor of wood ashes by the cold. The older woman was at the stove on which frying food now hissed and sputtered; she did not look up when the Negro entered. The girl was standing in the middle of the room, doing nothing at all. She looked at the Negro, watching him with a slow, grave, secret, unwinking gaze as he crossed the kitchen with that air of swaggering caricatured assurance, and upended a block of wood beside the stove and sat upon it.

"If disyer is de kind of weather yawl has up here all de

time," he said, "I dont care ef de Yankees does has dis coun-try." He opened the overcoat, revealing his legs and feet as being wrapped, shapeless and huge, in some muddy and anonymous substance resembling fur, giving them the ap-pearance of two muddy beasts the size of halfgrown dogs lying on the floor; moving a little nearer the girl, the girl thought quietly *Hit's fur. He taken and cut up a fur coat to wrap his feet in* "Yes, suh," the Negro said. "Just yawl let me git home again, en de Yankees kin have all de rest of it."

"Where do you-uns live?" the girl said.

The Negro looked at her. "In Miss'ippi. On de Domain. Aint you never hyeard tell of Countymaison?"

"Countymaison?"

"Dat's it. His grandpappy named it Countymaison caze it's bigger den a county to ride over. You cant ride across it on a mule betwixt sunup and sundown. Dat's how come." He rubbed his hands slowly on his thighs. His face was now turned toward the stove; he snuffed loudly. Already the ashy overlay on his skin had disappeared, leaving his face dead black, wizened, his mouth a little loose, as though the muscles had become slack with usage, like rubber bands—not the eating muscles, the talking ones. "I reckon we is gittin nigh home, after all. Leastways dat hawg meat smell like it do down whar folks lives."

"Countymaison," the girl said in a rapt, bemused tone, looking at the Negro with her grave, unwinking regard. Then she turned her head and looked at the wall, her face perfectly serene, perfectly inscrutable, without haste, with a profound and absorbed deliberation.

"Dat's it," the Negro said. "Even Yankees is heard tell of Weddel's Countymaison en erbout Marster Francis Weddel. Maybe yawl seed um pass in de carriage dat time he went to Washn'ton to tell yawl's president how he aint like de way yawl's president wuz treating de people. He rid all de way

to Washn'ton in de carriage, wid two niggers to drive en to
heat de bricks to kept he foots warm, en de man done gone
on ahead wid de wagon en de fresh hawses. He carried yawl's
president two whole dressed bears en eight sides of smoked
deer venison. He must a passed right out dar in front yawl's
house. I reckon yo pappy or maybe his pappy seed um pass."
He talked on, voluble, in soporific singsong, his face beginning to glisten, to shine a little with the rich warmth, while
the mother bent over the stove and the girl, motionless, static,
her bare feet cupped smooth and close to the rough pun-
cheons, her big, smooth, young body cupped soft and richly
mammalian to the rough garment, watching the Negro
with her ineffable and unwinking gaze, her mouth open a
little.

The Negro talked on, his eyes closed, his voice interminable, boastful, his air lazily intolerant, as if he were still at
home and there had been no war and no harsh rumors of
freedom and of change, and he (a stableman, in the domestic
hierarchy a man of horses) were spending the evening in the
quarters among field hands, until the older woman dished the
food and left the room, closing the door behind her. He
opened his eyes at the sound and looked toward the door and
then back to the girl. She was looking at the wall, at the
closed door through which her mother had vanished. "Dont
dey lets you eat at de table wid um?" he said.

The girl looked at the Negro, unwinking. "Countymaison," she said. "Vatch says he is a nigra too."

"Who? Him? A nigger? Marse Soshay Weddel? Which
un is Vatch?" The girl looked at him. "It's caze yawl aint
never been nowhere. Ain't never seed nothing. Living up
here on a nekkid hill whar you cant even see smoke. Him a
nigger? I wish his maw could hear you say dat." He looked
about the kitchen, wizened, his eyeballs rolling white, ceaseless, this way and that. The girl watched him.

"Do the girls there wear shoes all the time?" she said.

The Negro looked about the kitchen, "Where does yawl keep dat ere Tennessee spring water? Back here somewhere?"

"Spring water?"

The Negro blinked slowly. "Dat ere light-drinking kahysene."

"Kahysene?"

"Dat ere light colored lamp oil whut yawl drinks. Aint you got a little of it hid back here somewhere?"

"Oh," the girl said. "You mean corn." She went to a corner and lifted a loose plank in the floor, the Negro watching her, and drew forth another earthen jug. She filled another thick tumbler and gave it to the Negro and watched him jerk it down his throat, his eyes closed. Again he said, "Whuf!" and drew his back hand across his mouth.

"Whut wuz dat you axed me?" he said.

"Do the girls down there at Countymaison wear shoes?"

"De ladies does. If dey didn't have none, Marse Soshay could sell a hun'ed niggers en buy um some . . . Which un is it say Marse Soshay a nigger?"

The girl watched him. "Is he married?"

"Who married? Marse Soshay?" The girl watched him. "How he have time to git married, wid us fighting de Yankees for fo years? Aint been home in fo years now where no ladies to marry is." He looked at the girl, his eyewhites a little bloodshot, his skin shining in faint and steady highlights. Thawing, he seemed to have increased in size a little too. "Whut's it ter you, if he married or no?"

They looked at each other. The Negro could hear her breathing. Then she was not looking at him at all, though she had not yet even blinked nor turned her head. "I dont reckon he'd have any time for a girl that didn't have any shoes." she said. She went to the wall and stooped again to the

crack. The Negro watched her. The older woman entered
and took another dish from the stove and departed without
having looked at either of them.

V

THE FOUR MEN, the three men and the boy, sat about the supper table. The broken meal lay on thick plates. The knives
and forks were iron. On the table the jug still sat. Weddel
was now cloakless. He was shaven, his still damp hair combed
back. Upon his bosom the ruffles of the shirt frothed in the
lamplight, the right sleeve, empty, pinned across his breast
with a thin gold pin. Under the table the frail and mended
dancing slippers rested among the brogans of the two men
and the bare splayed feet of the boy.

"Vatch says you are a nigra," the father said.

Weddel was leaning a little back in his chair. "So that ex-
plains it," he said. "I was thinking that he was just congenitally illtempered. And having to be a victor, too."

"Are you a nigra?" the father said.

"No," Weddel said. He was looking at the boy, his weathered and wasted face a little quizzical. Across the back of his
neck his hair, long, had been cut roughly as though with a
knife or perhaps a bayonet. The boy watched him in complete and rapt immobility. *As if I might be an apparition* he
thought. *A hant. Maybe I am.* "No," he said. "I am not a
Negro."

"Who are you?" the father said.

Weddel sat a little sideways in his chair, his hand lying on
the table. "Do you ask guests who they are in Tennessee?"
he said. Vatch was filling a tumbler from the jug. His face
was lowered, his hands big and hard. His face was hard.
Weddel looked at him. "I think I know how you feel," he
said. "I expect I felt that way once. But it's hard to keep on
feeling any way for four years. Even feeling at all."

Vatch said something, sudden and harsh. He clapped the tumbler on to the table, splashing some of the liquor out. It looked like water, with a violent, dynamic odor. It seemed to possess an inherent volatility which carried a splash of it across the table and on to the foam of frayed yet immaculate linen on Weddel's breast, striking sudden and chill through the cloth against his flesh.

"Vatch!" the father said.

Weddel did not move; his expression arrogant, quizzical, and weary, did not change. "He did not mean to do that," he said.

"When I do," Vatch said, "it will not look like an accident."

Weddel was looking at Vatch. "I think I told you once," he said. "My name is Saucier Weddel. I am a Mississippian. I live at a place named Contalmaison. My father built it and named it. He was a Choctaw chief named Francis Weddel, of whom you have probably not heard. He was the son of a Choctaw woman and a French émigré of New Orleans, a general of Napoleon's and a knight of the Legion of Honor. His name was François Vidal. My father drove to Washington once in his carriage to remonstrate with President Jackson about the Government's treatment of his people, sending on ahead a wagon of provender and gifts and also fresh horses for the carriage, in charge of the man, the native overseer, who was a full blood Choctaw and my father's cousin. In the old days The Man was the hereditary title of the head of our clan; but after we became Europeanised like the white people, we lost the title to the branch which refused to become polluted, though we kept the slaves and the land. The Man now lives in a house a little larger than the cabins of the Negroes—an upper servant. It was in Washington that my father met and married my mother. He was killed in the Mexican War. My mother died two years ago, in '63, of a complication of pneumonia acquired while superintending the burying of some silver on a wet night when Federal troops entered the county, and of unsuitable food; though my boy refuses to believe that she is dead. He refuses to believe that the country would have permitted the North to deprive her of the imported Martinique coffee and the beaten biscuit which she had each Sunday noon and Wednesday night. He believes that the country would have risen in arms first. But then, he is only a Negro, member of an oppressed race burdened with freedom. He has a daily list of my misdoings which he is going to tell her on me when we reach home. I went to school in France, but not very hard. Until two weeks ago I was a major of Mississippi infantry in the corps of a man named Longstreet, of whom you may have heard."

"So you were a major," Vatch said.

"That appears to be my indictment; yes."

"I have seen a rebel major before," Vatch said. "Do you want me to tell you where I saw him?"

"Tell me," Weddel said.

"He was lying by a tree. We had to stop there and lie down, and he was lying by the tree, asking for water. 'Have you any water, friend?' he said. 'Yes. I have water,' I said. 'I have plenty of water.' I had to crawl; I couldn't stand up. I crawled over to him and I lifted him so that his head would be propped against the tree. I fixed his face to the front."

"Didn't you have a bayonet?" Weddel said. "But I forgot; you couldn't stand up."

"Then I crawled back. I had to crawl back a hundred yards, where—"

"Back?"

"It was too close. Who can do decent shooting that close? I had to crawl back, and then the damned musket—"

"Damn musket?" Weddel sat a little sideways in his chair, his hand on the table, his face quizzical and sardonic, contained.

"I missed, the first shot. I had his face propped up and turned, and his eyes open watching me, and then I missed. I hit him in the throat and I had to shoot again because of the damned musket."

"Vatch," the father said.

Vatch's hands were on the table. His head, his face, were like his father's, though without the father's deliberation. His face was furious, still, unpredictable. "It was that damn musket. I had to shoot three times. Then he had three eyes, in a row across his face propped against the tree, all three of them open, like he was watching me with three eyes. I gave him another eye, to see better with. But I had to shoot twice because of the damn musket."

"You, Vatch," the father said. He stood now, his hands on the table, propping his gaunt body. "Dont you mind Vatch, stranger. The war is over now."

"I dont mind him," Weddel said. His hands went to his bosom, disappearing into the foam of linen while he watched Vatch steadily with his alert, quizzical, sardonic gaze. "I have seen too many of him for too long a time to mind one of him any more."

"Take some whiskey," Vatch said.

"Are you just making a point?"

"Damn the pistol," Vatch said. "Take some whiskey."

Weddel laid his hand again on the table. But instead of pouring, Vatch held the jug poised over the tumbler. He was looking past Weddel's shoulder. Weddel turned. The girl was in the room, standing in the doorway with her mother just behind her. The mother said as if she were speaking to the floor under her feet: "I tried to keep her back, like you said. I tried to. But she is strong as a man; hardheaded like a man."

"You go back," the father said.

"Me to go back?" the mother said to the floor.

The father spoke a name; Weddel did not catch it; he did not even know that he had missed it. "You go back."

The girl moved. She was not looking at any of them. She came to the chair on which lay Weddel's worn and mended cloak and opened it, revealing the four ragged slashes where the sable lining had been cut out as though with a knife. She was looking at the cloak when Vatch grasped her by the shoulder, but it was at Weddel that she looked. "You cut hit out and gave hit to that nigra to wrap his feet in," she said. Then the father grasped Vatch in turn. Weddel had not stirred, his face turned over his shoulder; beside him the boy was upraised out of his chair by his arms, his young, slacked face leaned forward into the lamp. But save for the breathing of Vatch and the father there was no sound in the room.

"I am stronger than you are, still," the father said. "I am a better man still, or as good."

"You wont be always," Vatch said.

The father looked back over his shoulder at the girl. "Go back," he said. She turned and went back toward the hall, her feet silent as rubber feet. Again the father called that name which Weddel had not caught; again he did not catch it and was not aware again that he had not. She went out the door. The father looked at Weddel. Weddel's attitude was unchanged, save that once more his hand was hidden inside his bosom. They looked at one another—the cold, Nordic face and the half Gallic half Mongol face thin and worn like a bronze casting, with eyes like those of the dead, in which only vision has ceased and not sight. "Take your horses, and go," the father said.

VI

IT WAS dark in the hall, and cold, with the black chill of the mountain April coming up through the floor about her bare legs and her body in the single coarse garment. "He cut the lining outen his cloak to wrap that nigra's feet in," she said. "He done hit for a nigra." The door behind her opened. Against the lamplight a man loomed, then the door shut behind him. "Is it Vatch or paw?" she said. Then something struck her across the back—a leather strap. "I was afeared it would be Vatch," she said. The blow fell again.

"Go to bed," the father said.

"You can whip me, but you cant whip him," she said.

The blow fell again: a thick, flat, soft sound upon her immediate flesh beneath the coarse sacking.

VII

IN THE deserted kitchen the Negro sat for a moment longer on the upturned block beside the stove, looking at the door. Then he rose carefully, one hand on the wall

"Whuf!" he said. "Wish us had a spring on de Domain whut run dat. Stock would git trompled to death, sho mon." He blinked at the door, listening, then he moved, letting himself carefully along the wall, stopping now and then to look toward the door and listen, his air cunning, unsteady, and alert. He reached the corner and lifted the loose plank, stooping carefully, bracing himself against the wall. He lifted the jug out, whereupon he lost his balance and sprawled on his face, his face ludicrous and earnest with astonishment. He got up and sat flat on the floor, carefully, the jug between his knees, and lifted the jug and drank. He drank a long time.

"Whuf!" he said. "On de Domain we'd give disyer stuff to de hawgs. But deseyer ign'unt mountain trash—" He drank again; then with the jug poised there came into his face an expression of concern and then consternation. He set the jug down and tried to get up, sprawling above the jug, gaining his feet at last, stooped, swaying, drooling, with that expression of outraged consternation on his face. Then he fell headlong to the floor, overturning the jug.

VIII

THEY STOOPED above the Negro, talking quietly to one another—Weddel in his frothed shirt, the father and the boy.

"We'll have to tote him," the father said.

They lifted the Negro. With his single hand Weddel jerked the Negro's head up, shaking him. "Jubal," he said.

The Negro struck out, clumsily, with one arm. "Le'm be," he muttered. "Le'm go."

"Jubal!" Weddel said.

The Negro thrashed, sudden and violent. "You le'm be," he said. "I ghy tell de Man. I ghy tell um." He ceased, muttering: "Field hands. Field niggers."

"We'll have to tote him," the father said.

"Yes," Weddel said. "I'm sorry for this. I should have warned you. But I didn't think there was another jug he could have gained access to." He stooped, getting his single hand under the Negro's shoulders.

"Get away," the father said. "Me and Hule can do it." He and the boy picked the Negro up. Weddel opened the door. They emerged into the high black cold. Below them the barn loomed. They carried the Negro down the slope. "Get them horses out, Hule," the father said.

"Horses?" Weddel said. "He cant ride now. He cant stay on a horse."

They looked at one another, each toward the other voice, in the cold, the icy silence.

"You wont go now?" the father said.

"I am sorry. You see I cannot depart now. I will have to stay until daylight, until he is sober. We will go then."

"Leave him here. Leave him one horse, and you ride on. He is nothing but a nigra."

"I am sorry. Not after four years." His voice was quizzical, whimsical almost, yet with that quality of indomitable weariness. "I've worried with him this far; I reckon I will get him on home."

"I have warned you," the father said.

"I am obliged. We will move at daylight. If Hule will be kind enough to help me get him into the loft."

The father had stepped back. "Put that nigra down, Hule," he said.

"He will freeze here," Weddel said. "I must get him into the loft." He hauled the Negro up and propped him against the wall and stooped to hunch the Negro's lax body onto his shoulder. The weight rose easily, though he did not understand why until the father spoke again:

"Hule. Come away from there."

"Yes; go," Weddel said quietly. "I can get him up the ladder." He could hear the boy's breathing, fast, young, swift with excitement perhaps. Weddel did not pause to speculate, nor at the faintly hysterical tone of the boy's voice:

"I'll help you."

Weddel didn't object again. He slapped the Negro awake and they set his feet on the ladder rungs, pushing him upward. Halfway up he stopped; again he thrashed out at them. "I ghy tell um. I ghy tell de Man. I ghy tell Mistis. Field hands. Field niggers."

IX

THEY LAY side by side in the loft, beneath the cloak and the two saddle blankets. There was no hay. The Negro snored, his breath reeking and harsh, thick. Below, in its stall, the Thoroughbred stamped now and then. Weddel lay on his back, his arm across his chest, the hand clutching the stub of the other arm. Overhead, through the cracks in the roof the sky showed—the thick chill, black sky which would rain again tomorrow and on every tomorrow until they left the mountains. "If I leave the mountains," he said quietly, motionless on his back beside the snoring Negro, staring upward. "I was concerned. I had thought that it was exhausted; that I had lost the privilege of being afraid. But I have not. And so I am happy. Quite happy." He lay rigid on his back in the cold darkness, thinking of home. "Contalmaison. Our lives are summed up in sounds and made significant. Victory. Defeat. Peace. Home. That's why we must do so much to invent meanings for the sounds, so damned much. Especially if you are unfortunate enough to be victorious: so damned much. It's nice to be whipped; quiet to be whipped. To be whipped and to lie under a broken roof, thinking of home." The Negro snored. "So damned much"; seeming to watch the words shape quietly in the darkness above his mouth. "What would happen, say, a man in the lobby of the Gayoso, in Memphis, laughing suddenly aloud. But I am quite happy—" Then he heard the sound. He lay utterly still then, his hand clutching the butt of the pistol warm beneath the stub of his right arm, hearing the quiet, almost infinitesimal sound as it mounted the ladder. But he made no move until he saw the dim orifice of the trap door blotted out. "Stop where you are," he said.

"It's me," the voice said; the voice of the boy, again with that swift, breathless quality which even now Weddel did not pause to designate as excitement or even to remark at all. The boy came on his hands and knees across the dry, sibilant chaff which dusted the floor. "Go ahead and shoot," he said. On his hands and knees he loomed above Weddel with his panting breath. "I wish I was dead. I so wish hit. I wish we was both dead. I could wish like Vatch wishes. Why did you uns have to stop here?"

Weddel had not moved. "Why does Vatch wish I was dead?"

"Because he can still hear you uns yelling. I used to sleep with him and he wakes up at night and once paw had to keep him from choking me to death before he waked up and him sweating, hearing you uns yelling still. Without nothing but unloaded guns, yelling, Vatch said, like scarecrows across a cornpatch, running." He was crying now, not aloud. "Damn you! Damn you to hell!"

"Yes," Weddel said. "I have heard them, myself. But why do you wish you were dead?"

"Because she was trying to come, herself. Only she had to—"

"Who? She? Your sister?"

"—had to go through the room to get out. Paw was awake. He said, 'If you go out that door, dont you never come back.' And she said, 'I dont aim to.' And Vatch was awake too and he said, 'Make him marry you quick because you are going to be a widow at daylight.' And she come back and told me. But I was awake too. She told me to tell you."

"Tell me what?" Weddel said. The boy cried quietly, with a kind of patient and utter despair.

"I told her if you was a nigra, and if she done that—I told her that I—"

"What? If she did what? What does she want you to tell me?"

"About the window into the attic where her and me sleep. There is a foot ladder I made to come back from hunting at night for you to get in. But I told her if you was a nigra and if she done that I would—"

"Now then," Weddel said sharply; "pull yourself together now. Dont you remember? I never even saw her but that one time when she came in the room and your father sent her out."

"But you saw her then. And she saw you."

"No," Weddel said.

The boy ceased to cry. He was quite still above Weddel. "No what?"

"I wont do it. Climb up your ladder."

For a while the boy seemed to muse above him, motionless, breathing slow and quiet now; he spoke now in a musing, almost dreamy tone: "I could kill you easy. You aint got but one arm, even if you are older. . . ." Suddenly he moved, with almost unbelievable quickness; Weddel's first intimation was when the boy's hard, overlarge hands took him by the throat. Weddel did not move. "I could kill you easy. And wouldn't none mind."

"Shhhhhh," Weddel said. "Not so loud."

"Wouldn't none care." He held Weddel's throat with hard, awkward restraint. Weddel could feel the choking and the shaking expend itself somewhere about the boy's forearms before it reached his hands, as though the connection between brain and hands was incomplete. "Wouldn't none care. Except Vatch would be mad."

"I have a pistol," Weddel said.

"Then shoot me with it. Go on."

"No."

"No what?"

"I told you before."

"You swear you wont do it? Do you swear?"

"Listen a moment," Weddel said; he spoke now with a sort of soothing patience, as though he spoke one-syllable words to a child: "I just want to go home. That's all. I have been away from home for four years. All I want is to go home. Dont you see? I want to see what I have left there, after four years."

"What do you do there?" The boy's hands were loose and hard about Weddel's throat, his arms still, rigid. "Do you hunt all day, and all night too if you want, with a horse to

ride and nigras to wait on you, to shine your boots and saddle the horse, and you setting on the gallery, eating, until
time to go hunting again?"

"I hope so. I haven't been home in four years, you see. So
I dont know any more."

"Take me with you."

"I dont know what's there, you see. There may not be
anything there: no horses to ride and nothing to hunt. The
Yankees were there, and my mother died right afterward,
and I dont know what we would find there, until I can go and
see."

"I'll work. We'll both work. You can get married in
Mayesfield. It's not far."

"Married? Oh. Your . . . I see. How do you know I am
not already married?" Now the boy's hands shut on his
throat, shaking him. "Stop it!" he said.

"If you say you have got a wife, I will kill you," the boy
said.

"No," Weddel said. "I am not married."

"And you dont aim to climb up that foot ladder?"

"No. I never saw her but once. I might not even know her
if I saw her again."

"She says different. I dont believe you. You are lying."

"No," Weddel said.

"Is it because you are afraid to?"

"Yes. That's it."

"Of Vatch?"

"Not Vatch. I'm just afraid. I think my luck has given out.
I know that it has lasted too long; I am afraid that I shall find
that I have forgot how to be afraid. So I cant risk it. I cant
risk finding that I have lost touch with truth. Not like Jubal
here. He believes that I still belong to him; he will not believe that I have been freed. He wont even let me tell him so.
He does not need to bother about truth, you see."

"We would work. She might not look like the Miss'ippi women that wear shoes all the time. But we would learn. We would not shame you before them."

"No," Weddel said. "I cannot."

"Then you go away. Now."

"How can I? You see that he cannot ride, cannot stay on a horse." The boy did not answer at once; an instant later Weddel could almost feel the tenseness, the utter immobility, though he himself had heard no sound; he knew that the boy, crouching, not breathing, was looking toward the ladder. "Which one is it?" Weddel whispered.

"It's paw."

"I'll go down. You stay here. You keep my pistol for me."

X

THE DARK AIR was high, chill, cold. In the vast invisible darkness the valley lay, the opposite cold and invisible range black on the black sky. Clutching the stub of his missing arm across his chest, he shivered slowly and steadily.

"Go," the father said.

"The war is over," Weddel said. "Vatch's victory is not my trouble."

"Take your horses and nigra, and ride on."

"If you mean your daughter, I never saw her but once and I never expect to see her again."

"Ride on," the father said. "Take what is yours, and ride on."

"I cannot." They faced one another in the darkness. "After four years I have bought immunity from running."

"You have till daylight."

"I have had less than that in Virginia for four years. And this is just Tennessee." But the other had turned; he dissolved into the black slope. Weddel entered the stable and mounted the ladder. Motionless above the snoring Negro the boy squatted.

"Leave him here," the boy said. "He aint nothing but a nigra. Leave him, and go."

"No," Weddel said.

The boy squatted above the snoring Negro. He was not looking at Weddel, yet there was between them, quiet and soundless, the copse, the sharp dry report, the abrupt wild thunder of upreared horse, the wisping smoke. "I can show you a short cut down to the valley. You will be out of the mountains in two hours. By daybreak you will be ten miles away."

"I cant. He wants to go home too. I must get him home too." He stooped; with his single hand he spread the cloak awkwardly, covering the Negro closer with it. He heard the boy creep away, but he did not look. After a while he shook the Negro. "Jubal," he said. The Negro groaned; he turned heavily, sleeping again. Weddel squatted above him as the boy had done. "I thought that I had lost it for good," he said. "—The peace and the quiet; the power to be afraid again."

XI

THE CABIN was gaunt and bleak in the thick cold dawn when the two horses passed out the sagging gate and into the churned road, the Negro on the Thoroughbred, Weddel on the sorrel. The Negro was shivering. He sat hunched and high, with updrawn knees, his face almost invisible in the oilcloth hood.

"I tole you dey wuz fixing to pizen us wid dat stuff," he said. "I tole you. Hillbilly rednecks. En you not only let um pizen me, you fotch me de pizen wid yo own hand. O Lawd, O Lawd! If we ever does git home."

Weddel looked back at the cabin, at the weathered, blank

house where there was no sign of any life, not even smoke. "She has a young man, I suppose—a beau." He spoke aloud, musing, quizzical. "And that boy. Hule. He said to come within sight of a laurel copse where the road disappears, and take a path to the left. He said we must not pass that copse."

"Who says which?" the Negro said. "I aint going nowhere. I going back to dat loft en lay down."

"All right," Weddel said. "Get down."

"Git down?"

"I'll need both horses. You can walk on when you are through sleeping."

"I ghy tell yo maw," the Negro said. "I ghy tell um. Ghy tell how after four years you aint got no more sense than to not know a Yankee when you seed um. To stay de night wid Yankees en let um pizen one of Mistis' niggers. I ghy tell um."

"I thought you were going to stay here," Weddel said. He was shivering too. "Yet I am not cold," he said. "I am not cold."

"Stay here? Me? How in de world you ever git home widout me? Whut I tell Mistis when I come in widout you en she ax me whar you is?"

"Come," Weddel said. He lifted the sorrel into motion. He looked quietly back at the house, then rode on. Behind him on the Thoroughbred the Negro muttered and mumbled to himself in woebegone singsong. The road, the long hill which yesterday they had toiled up, descended now. It was muddy, rockchurned, scarred across the barren and rocky land beneath the dissolving sky, jolting downward to where the pines and laurel began. After a while the cabin had disappeared.

"And so I am running away," Weddel said. "When I get home I shall not be very proud of this. Yes, I will. It means that I am still alive. Still alive, since I still know fear and desire. Since life is an affirmation of the past and a promise to the future. So I am still alive—Ah." It was the laurel copse. About three hundred yards ahead it seemed to have sprung motionless and darkly secret in the air which of itself was mostly water. He drew rein sharply, the Negro, hunched, moaning, his face completely hidden, overriding him unawares until the Thoroughbred stopped of its own accord. "But I dont see any path—" Weddel said; then a figure emerged from the copse, running toward them. Weddel thrust the reins beneath his groin and withdrew his hand inside his cloak. Then he saw that it was the boy. He came up trotting. His face was white, strained, his eyes quite grave.

"It's right yonder," he said.

"Thank you," Weddel said. "It was kind of you to come and show us, though we could have found it, I imagine."

"Yes," the boy said as though he had not heard. He had already taken the sorrel's bridle. "Right tother of the brush. You cant see hit until you are in hit."

"In whut?" the Negro said. "I ghy tell um. After four years you aint got no more sense. . . ."

"Hush," Weddel said. He said to the boy, "I am obliged to you. You'll have to take that in lieu of anything better. And now you get on back home. We can find the path. We will be all right now."

"They know the path too," the boy said. He drew the sorrel forward. "Come on."

"Wait," Weddel said, drawing the sorrel up. The boy still tugged at the bridle, looking on ahead toward the copse. "So we have one guess and they have one guess. Is that it?"

"Damn you to hell, come on!" the boy said, in a kind of thin frenzy. "I am sick of hit. Sick of hit."

"Well," Weddel said. He looked about, quizzical, sardonic, with his gaunt, weary, wasted face. "But I must move. I cant stay here, not even if I had a house, a roof to live under. So I have to choose between three things. That's what throws a

man off—that extra alternative. Just when he has come to
realize that living consists in choosing wrongly between two
alternatives, to have to choose among three. You go back
home."

The boy turned and looked up at him. "We'd work. We
could go back to the house now, since paw and Vatch are
. . . We could ride down the mou-tin, two on one horse and
two on tother. We could go back to the valley and get married at Mayesfield. We would not shame you."

"But she has a young man, hasn't she? Somebody that
waits for her at church on Sunday and walks home and takes
Sunday dinner, and maybe fights the other young men because of her?"

"You wont take us, then?"

"No. You go back home."

For a while the boy stood, holding the bridle, his face lowered. Then he turned; he said quietly: "Come on, then. We
got to hurry."

"Wait," Weddel said; "what are you going to do?"

"I'm going a piece with you. Come on." He dragged the
sorrel forward, toward the roadside.

"Here," Weddel said, "you go on back home. The war is
over now. Vatch knows that."

The boy did not answer. He led the sorrel into the underbrush. The Thoroughbred hung back. "Whoa, you Caesar!"
the Negro said. "Wait, Marse Soshay. I aint gwine ride down
no. . . ."

The boy looked over his shoulder without stopping. "You
keep back there," he said. "You keep where you are."

The path was a faint scar, doubling and twisting among
the brush. "I see it now," Weddel said. "You go back."

"I'll go a piece with you," the boy said; so quietly that
Weddel discovered that he had been holding his breath, in
a taut, strained alertness. He breathed again, while the sorrel

jolted stiffly downward beneath him. "Nonsense," he thought. "He will have me playing Indian also in five minutes more. I had wanted to recover the power to be afraid, but I seem to have outdone myself." The path widened; the Thoroughbred came alongside, the boy walking between them; again he looked at the Negro.

"You keep back, I tell you," he said.

"Why back?" Weddel said. He looked at the boy's wan, strained face; he thought swiftly, "I dont know whether I am playing Indian or not." He said aloud: "Why must he keep back?"

The boy looked at Weddel; he stopped, pulling the sorrel up. "We'd work," he said. "We wouldn't shame you."

Weddel's face was now as sober as the boy's. They looked at one another. "Do you think we have guessed wrong? We had to guess. We had to guess one out of three."

Again it was as if the boy had not heard him. "You wont think hit is me? You swear hit?"

"Yes. I swear it." He spoke quietly, watching the boy; they spoke now as two men or two children. "What do you think we ought to do?"

"Turn back. They will be gone now. We could . . ." He drew back on the bridle; again the Thoroughbred came abreast and forged ahead.

"You mean, it could be along here?" Weddel said. Suddenly he spurred the sorrel, jerking the clinging boy forward. "Let go," he said. The boy held onto the bridle, swept forward until the two horses were again abreast. On the Thoroughbred the Negro perched, highkneed, his mouth still talking, flobbed down with ready speech, easy and worn with talk like an old shoe with walking.

"I done tole him en tole him," the Negro said.

"Let go!" Weddel said, spurring the sorrel, forcing its shoulder into the boy. "Let go!"

"You wont turn back?" the boy said. "You wont?"

"Let go!" Weddel said. His teeth showed a little beneath his mustache; he lifted the sorrel bodily with the spurs. The boy let go of the bridle and ducked beneath the Thoroughbred's neck; Weddel, glancing back as the sorrel leaped, saw the boy surge upward and on to the Thoroughbred's back, shoving the Negro back along its spine until he vanished.

"They think you will be riding the good horse," the boy said in a thin, panting voice; "I told them you would be riding . . . Down the mou-tin!" he cried as the Thoroughbred swept past; "the horse can make hit! Git outen the path! Git outen the. . . ." Weddel spurred the sorrel; almost abreast the two horses reached the bend where the path doubled back upon itself and into a matted shoulder of laurel and rhododendron. The boy looked back over his shoulder. "Keep back!" he cried. "Git outen the path!" Weddel rowelled the sorrel. On his face was a thin grimace of exasperation and anger almost like smiling.

It was still on his dead face when he struck the earth, his foot still fast in the stirrup. The sorrel leaped at the sound and dragged Weddel to the path side and halted and whirled and snorted once, and began to graze. The Thoroughbred however rushed on past the curve and whirled and rushed back, the blanket twisted under its belly and its eyes rolling, springing over the boy's body where it lay in the path, the face wrenched sideways against a stone, the arms back-sprawled, openpalmed, like a woman with lifted skirts springing across a puddle. Then it whirled and stood above Weddel's body, whinnying, with tossing head, watching the laurel copse and the fading gout of black powder smoke as it faded away.

The Negro was on his hands and knees when the two men emerged from the copse. One of them was running. The Negro watched him run forward, crying monotonously,

"The durned fool! The durned fool! The durned fool!" and then stop suddenly and drop the gun; squatting, the Negro saw him become stone still above the fallen gun, looking dawn at the boy's body with an expression of shock and amazement like he was waking from a dream. Then the Negro saw the other man. In the act of stopping, the second man swung the rifle up and began to reload it. The Negro did not move. On his hands and knees he watched the two white men, his irises rushing and wild in the bloodshot whites. Then he too moved and, still on hands and knees, he turned and scuttled to where Weddel lay beneath the sorrel and crouched over Weddel and looked again and watched the second man backing slowly away up the path, loading the rifle. He watched the man stop; he did not close his eyes nor look away. He watched the rifle elongate and then rise and diminish slowly and become a round spot against the white shape of Vatch's face like a period on a page. Crouching, the Negro's eyes rushed wild and steady and red, like those of a cornered animal.

VI · BEYOND

Beyond

THE HARD ROUND ear of the stethoscope was cold and unpleasant upon his naked chest; the room, big and square,
furnished with clumsy walnut—the bed where he had first
slept alone, which had been his marriage bed, in which his
son had been conceived and been born and lain dressed for
the coffin—the room familiar for sixty-five years, by ordinary peaceful and lonely and so peculiarly his own as to
have the same odor which he had, seemed to be cluttered
with people, though there were but three of them and all
of them he knew: Lucius Peabody who should have been
down town attending to his medical practice, and the two
Negroes, the one who should be in the kitchen and the
other with the lawn mower on the lawn, making some pre-
tence toward earning the money which on Saturday night
they would expect.

But worst of all was the hard cold little ear of the stethoscope, worse even than the outrage of his bared chest with
its fine delicate matting of gray hair. In fact, about the
whole business there was just one alleviating circumstance.
"At least," he thought with fretted and sardonic humor, "I
am spared that uproar of female connections which might
have been my lot, which is the ordinary concomitant of occasions of marriage or divorcement. And if he will just move

his damned little toy telephone and let my niggers go back
to work—"

And then, before he had finished the thought, Peabody
did remove the stethoscope. And then, just as he was settling
himself back into the pillow with a sigh of fretted relief, one
of the Negroes, the woman, set up such a pandemonium ot
wailing as to fetch him bolt upright in the bed, his hands to
his ears. The Negress stood at the foot of the bed, her long
limber black hands motionless on the footboard, her eyes
whitely backrolled into her skull and her mouth wide open,
while from it rolled slow billows of soprano sound as mellow
as high-register organ tones and wall-shattering as a steamer
siren.

"Chlory!" he shouted. "Stop that!" She didn't stop. Apparently she could neither see nor hear. "You, Jake!" he
shouted to the Negro man who stood beside her, his hands
too on the footboard, his face brooding upon the bed with
an expression darkly and profoundly enigmatic; "get her out
of here! At once!" But Jake too did not move, and he then
turned to Peabody in angry outrage. "Here! Loosh! Get
these damn niggers out of here!" But Peabody also did not
seem to hear him. The Judge watched him methodically
folding the stethoscope into its case; glared at him for a
moment longer while the woman's shattering noise billowed
through the room. Then he flung the covers back and rose
from the bed and hurried furiously from the room and from
the house.

At once he realized that he was still in his pajamas, so he
buttoned his overcoat. It was of broadcloth, black, brushed,
of an outmoded elegance, with a sable collar. "At least they
didn't have time to hide this from me," he thought in fretted
rage. "Now, if I just had my. . . ." He looked down at his
feet. "Ah. I seem to have. . . ." He looked at his shoes.
"That's fortunate, too." Then the momentary surprise faded

too, now that outrage had space in which to disseminate itself. He touched his hat, then he put his hand to his lapel. The jasmine was there. Say what he would, curse Jake as he often had to do, the Negro never forgot whatever flower in its season. Always it would be there, fresh and recent and unblemished, on the morning coffee tray. The flower and the. . . . He clasped his ebony stick beneath his arm and opened the briefcase. The two fresh handkerchiefs were there, beside the book. He thrust one of them into his breast pocket and went on. After a while the noise of Chlory's wailing died away.

Then for a little while it was definitely unpleasant. He detested crowds: the milling and aimless and patient stupidity; the concussion of life-quick flesh with his own. But presently, if not soon, he was free, and standing so, still a little ruffled, a little annoyed, he looked back with fading outrage and distaste at the throng as it clotted quietly through the entrance. With fading distaste until the distaste was gone, leaving his face quiet and quite intelligent, with a faint and long constant overtone of quizzical bemusement not yet tinctured with surprised speculation, not yet puzzled, not yet wary. That was to come later. Hence it did not show in his voice, which was now merely light, quizzical, contained, "There seems to be quite a crowd of them."

"Yes," the other said. The Judge looked at him and saw a young man in conventional morning dress with some subtle effluvium of weddings, watching the entrance with a strained, patient air.

"You are expecting someone?" the Judge said.

Now the other looked at him. "Yes. You didn't see— But you don't know her."

"Know whom?"

"My wife. That is, she is not my wife yet. But the wedding was to be at noon."

"Something happened, did it?"

"I had to do it." The young man looked at him, strained, anxious. "I was late. That's why I was driving fast. A child ran into the road. I was going too fast to stop. So I had to turn."

"But you missed the child?"

"Yes." The other looked at him. "You don't know her?"

"And are you waiting here to. . . ." The judge stared at the other. His eyes were narrowed, his gaze was piercing, hard. He said suddenly, sharply, "Nonsense."

"What? What did you say?" the other asked with his vague, strained, almost beseeching air. The Judge looked away. His frowning concentration, his reflex of angry astonishment, was gone. He seemed to have wiped it from his face by a sudden deliberate action. He was like a man who, not a swordsman, has practiced with a blade a little against a certain improbable crisis, and who suddenly finds himself, blade in hand, face to face with the event. He looked at the entrance, his face alert, musing swiftly: he seemed to muse upon the entering faces with a still and furious concentration, and quietly; quietly he looked about, then at the other again. The young man still watched him.

"You're looking for your wife too, I suppose," he said. "I hope you find her. I hope you do." He spoke with a sort of quiet despair. "I suppose she is old, as you are. It must be hell on the one who has to watch and wait for the other one he or she has grown old in marriage with, because it is so terrible to wait and watch like me, for a girl who is a maiden to you. Of course I think mine is the most unbearable. You see if it had only been the next day—anything. But then if it had, I guess I could not have turned out for that kid. I guess I just think mine is so terrible. It can't be as bad as I think it is. It just can't be. I hope you find her."

The Judge's lip lifted. "I came here to escape someone;

not to find anyone." He looked at the other. His face was still broken with that grimace which might have been smiling. But his eyes were not smiling. "If I were looking for anybody, it would probably be my son."

, "Oh. A son. I see."

"Yes. He would be about your age. He was ten when he died."

"Look for him here."

Now the Judge laughed outright, save for his eyes. The other watched him with that grave anxiety leavened now with quiet interested curiosity. "You mean you don't believe?" The Judge laughed aloud. Still laughing, he produced a cloth sack of tobacco and rolled a slender cigarette. When he looked up, the other was watching the entrance again. The Judge ceased to laugh.

"Have you a match?" he said. The other looked at him. The Judge raised the cigarette. "A match."

The other sought in his pockets. "No." He looked at the Judge. "Look for him here," he said.

"Thank you," the Judge answered. "I may avail myself of your advice later." He turned away. Then he paused and looked back. The young man was watching the entrance. The Judge watched him, bemused, his lip lifted. He turned on, then he stopped still. His face was now completely shocked, into complete immobility like a mask; the sensitive, worn mouth, the delicate nostrils, the eyes all pupil or pupilless. He could not seem to move at all. Then Mothershed turned and saw him. For an instant Mothershed's pale eyes flickered, his truncated jaw, collapsing steadily with a savage, toothless motion, ceased.

"Well?" Mothershed said.

"Yes," the Judge said; "it's me." Now it was that, as the mesmerism left him, the shadow bewildered and wary and complete, touched his face. Even to himself his words

sounded idiotic. "I thought that you were dea. . . ." Then he
made a supreme and gallant effort, his voice light, quizzical,
contained again, "Well?"

Mothershed looked at him—a squat man in a soiled and
mismatched suit stained with grease and dirt, his soiled collar innocent of tie—with a pale, lightly slumbering glare
filled with savage outrage. "So they got you here, too, did
they?"

"That depends on who you mean by 'they' and what you
mean by 'here.' "

Mothershed made a savage, sweeping gesture with one
arm. "Here, by God! The preachers. The Jesus shouters."

"Ah," the Judge said. "Well, if I am where I am beginning to think I am, I don't know whether I am here or not.
But you are not here at all, are you?" Mothershed cursed
violently. "Yes," the Judge said, "we never thought, sitting
in my office on those afternoons, discussing Voltaire and
Ingersoll, that we should ever be brought to this, did we?
You, the atheist whom the mere sight of a church spire on
the sky could enrage; and I who have never been able to
divorce myself from reason enough to accept even your
pleasant and labor-saving theory of nihilism."

"Labor-saving!" Mothershed cried. "By God, I. . . ." He
cursed with impotent fury. The Judge might have been
smiling save for his eyes. He sealed the cigarette again.

"Have you a match?"

"What?" Mothershed said. He glared at the Judge, his
mouth open. He sought through his clothes. From out the
savage movement, strapped beneath his armpit, there peeped
fleetly the butt of a heavy pistol. "No," he said. "I ain't."

"Yes," the Judge said. He twisted the cigarette, his gaze
light, quizzical. "But you still haven't told me what you
are doing here. I heard that you had. . . ."

Again Mothershed cursed, prompt, outraged. "I ain't. I

just committed suicide." He glared at the Judge. "God damn it, I remember raising the pistol; I remember the little cold ring it made against my ear; I remember when I told my finger on the trigger. . . ." He glared at the Judge. "I thought that that would be one way I could escape the preachers, since by the church's own token. . . ." He glared at the Judge, his pale gaze apoplectic and outraged. "Well, I know why you are here. You come here looking for that boy."

The Judge looked down, his lip lifted, the movement pouched upward about his eyes. He said quietly, "No."

Mothershed watched him, glared at him. "Looking for that boy. Agnosticism." He snarled it. "Won't say 'Yes' and won't say 'No' until you see which way the cat will jump. Ready to sell out to the highest bidder. By God, I'd rather have give up and died in sanctity, with every heaven-yelping fool in ten miles around. . . ."

"No," the Judge said quietly behind the still, dead gleam of his teeth. Then his teeth vanished quietly, though he did not look up. He sealed the cigarette carefully again. "There seem to be a lot of people here." Mothershed now began to watch him with speculation, tasting his savage gums, his pale furious glare arrested. "You have seen other familiar faces besides my own here, I suppose. Even those of men whom you know only by name, perhaps?"

"Oh," Mothershed said. "I see. I get you now." The Judge seemed to be engrossed in the cigarette. "You want to take a whirl at them too, do you? Go ahead. I hope you will get a little more out of them that will stick to your guts than I did. Maybe you will, since you don't seem to want to know as much as you want something new to be uncertain about. Well, you can get plenty of that from any of them."

"You mean you have. . . ."

Again Mothershed cursed, harsh, savage. "Sure. Ingersoll. Paine. Every bastard one of them that I used to waste my time reading when I had better been sitting on the sunny side of a log."

"Ah," the Judge said. "Ingersoll. Is he. . . ."

"Sure. On a bench just inside the park yonder. And maybe on the same bench you'll find the one that wrote the little women books. If he ain't there, he ought to be."

So the Judge sat forward, elbows on knees, the unlighted cigarette in his fingers. "So you too are reconciled," he said. The man who Mothershed said was Ingersoll looked at his profile quietly. "To this place."

"Ah," the other said. He made a brief, short gesture. "Reconciled."

The Judge did not look up. "You accept it? You acquiesce?" He seemed to be absorbed in the cigarette. "If I could just see Him, talk to Him." The cigarette turned slowly in his fingers. "Perhaps I was seeking Him. Perhaps I was seeking Him all the time I was reading your books, and Voltaire and Montesquieu. Perhaps I was." The cigarette turned slowly. "I have believed in you. In your sincerity. I said, if Truth is to be found by man, this man will be among those who find it. At one time—I was in the throes of that suffering from a still green hurt which causes even an intelligent man to cast about for anything, any straw—I had a foolish conceit: you will be the first to laugh at it as I myself did later. I thought, perhaps there is a hereafter, a way station into nothingness perhaps, where for an instant lesser men might speak face to face with men like you whom they could believe; could hear from such a man's own lips the words: 'There is hope,' or: 'There is nothing.' I said to myself, in such case it will not be Him whom I shall seek; it will be Ingersoll or Paine or Voltaire." He watched the cigarette. "Give me your word now. Say either of these to me. I will believe."

The other looked at the Judge for a time. Then he said, "Why? Believe why?"

The paper about the cigarette had come loose. The Judge twisted it carefully back, handling the cigarette carefully. "You see, I had a son. He was the last of my name and race. After my wife died we lived alone, two men in the house. It had been a good name, you see. I wanted him to be manly, worthy of it. He had a pony which he rode all the time. I have a photograph of them which I use as a bookmark. Often, looking at the picture or watching them unbeknownst as they passed the library window, I would think *What hopes ride yonder;* of the pony I would think *What burden do you blindly bear, dumb brute.* One day they telephoned me at my office. He had been found dragging from the stirrup. Whether the pony had kicked him or he had struck his head in falling, I never knew."

He laid the cigarette carefully on the bench beside him and opened the briefcase. He took out a book. "Voltaire's *Philosophical Dictionary*," he said. "I always carry a book with me. I am a great reader. It happens that my life is a solitary one, owing to the fact that I am the last of my family, and perhaps to the fact that I am a Republican office-holder in a Democratic stronghold. I am a Federal judge, from a Mississippi district. My wife's father was a Republican." He added quickly, "I believe the tenets of the Republican Party to be best for the country. You will not believe it, but for the last fifteen years my one intellectual companion has been a rabid atheist, almost an illiterate, who not only scorns all logic and science, but who has a distinct body odor as well. Sometimes I have thought, sitting with him in my office on a summer afternoon—a damp one—that if a restoration of faith could remove his prejudice against bathing, I should be justified in going to that length myself even." He took a photograph from the book and extended it. "This was my son."

The other looked at the picture without moving, without offering to take it. From the brown and fading cardboard a boy of ten, erect upon the pony, looked back at them with a grave and tranquil hauteur. "He rode practically all the time. Even to church (I attended church regularly then. I still do, at times, even now). We had to take an extra groom along in the carriage to. . . ." He looked at the picture, musing. "After his mother died I never married again. My own mother was sickly, an invalid. I could cajole her. In the absence of my aunts I could browbeat her into letting me go barefoot in the garden, with two house servants on watch to signal the approach of my aunts. I would return to the house, my manhood triumphant, vindicated, until I entered the room where she waited for me. Then I would know that for every grain of dust which pleasured my feet, she would pay with a second of her life. And we would sit in the dusk like two children, she holding my hand and crying quietly, until my aunts entered with the lamp. 'Now, Sophia. Crying again. What have you let him bulldoze you into doing this time?' She died when I was fourteen; I was twenty-eight before I asserted myself and took the wife of my choice; I was thirty-seven when my son was born." He looked at the photograph, his eyes pouched, netted by two delicate hammocks of myriad lines as fine as etching. "He rode all the time. Hence the picture of the two of them, since they were inseparable. I have used this picture as a bookmark in the printed volumes where his and my ancestry can be followed for ten generations in our American annals, so that as the pages progressed it would be as though with my own eyes I watched him ride in the flesh down the long road which his blood and bone had traveled before it became his." He held the picture With his other hand he took up the cigarette. The paper had come loose: he held it raised a little and then arrested so, as if he did not dare raise it farther. "And you can give me your word. I will believe."

"Go seek your son," the other said. "Go seek him."

Now the Judge did not move at all. Holding the picture and the dissolving cigarette, he sat in a complete immobility. He seemed to sit in a kind of terrible and unbreathing suspension. "And find him? And find him?" The other did not answer. Then the Judge turned and looked at him, and then the cigarette dropped quietly into dissolution as the tobacco rained down upon his neat, gleaming shoe. "Is that your word? I will believe, I tell you." The other sat, shapeless, gray, sedentary, almost nondescript, looking down. "Come. You cannot stop with that. You cannot."

Along the path before them people passed constantly. A woman passed, carrying a child and a basket, a young woman in a plain, worn, brushed cape. She turned upon the man who Mothershed had said was Ingersoll a plain, bright, pleasant face and spoke to him in a pleasant, tranquil voice. Then she looked at the Judge, pleasantly, a full look without boldness or diffidence, and went on. "Come. You cannot. You cannot." Then his face went completely blank. In the midst of speaking his face emptied; he repeated "cannot. *Cannot*" in a tone of musing consternation. "Cannot," he said. "You mean, you *can*not give me any word? That you do not know? That you, yourself, do not *know*? You, Robert Ingersoll? Robert *Ingersoll*?" The other did not move. "Is Robert Ingersoll telling me that for twenty years I have leaned upon a reed no stronger than myself?"

Still the other did not look up. "You saw that young woman who just passed, carrying a child. Follow her. Look into her face."

"A young woman. With a. . . ." The Judge looked at the other. "Ah. I see. Yes. I will look at the child and I shall

see scars. Then I am to look into the woman's face. Is that
it?" The other didn't answer. "That is your answer? your
final word?" The other did not move. The Judge's lip lifted.
The movement pouched upward about his eyes as though
despair, grief, had flared up for a final instant like a dying
flame, leaving upon his face its ultimate and fading gleam
in a faint grimace of dead teeth. He rose and put the photograph back into the briefcase. "And this is the man who
says that he was once Robert Ingersoll." Above his teeth his
face mused in that expression which could have been smiling
save for the eyes. "It is not proof that I sought. I, of all men,
know that proof is but a fallacy invented by man to justify
to himself and his fellows his own crass lust and folly. It
was not proof that I sought." With the stick and the briefcase clasped beneath his arm he rolled another slender cigarette. "I don't know who you are, but I don't believe you
are Robert Ingersoll. Perhaps I could not know it even if
you were. Anyway, there is a certain integral consistency
which, whether it be right or wrong, a man must cherish
because it alone will ever permit him to die. So what I have
been, I am; what I am, I shall be until that instant comes
when I am not. And then I shall have never been. How does
it go? *Non fui. Sum. Fui. Non sum.*"

With the unlighted cigarette in his fingers he thought at
first that he would pass on. But instead he paused and looked
down at the child. It sat in the path at the woman's feet,
surrounded by tiny leaden effigies of men, some erect and
some prone. The overturned and now empty basket lay at
one side. Then the Judge saw that the effigies were Roman
soldiers in various stages of dismemberment—some headless,
some armless and legless—scattered about, lying profoundly
on their faces or staring up with martial and battered in-
scrutability from the mild and inscrutable dust. On the exact
center of each of the child's insteps was a small scar. There

was a third scar in the palm of its exposed hand, and as the Judge looked down with quiet and quizzical bemusement, the child swept flat the few remaining figures and he saw the fourth scar. The child began to cry.

"Shhhhhhhhh," the woman said. She glanced up at the Judge, then she knelt and set the soldiers up. The child cried steadily, with a streaked and dirty face, strong, unhurried, passionless, without tears. "Look!" the woman said, "See? Here! Here's Pilate too! Look!" The child ceased. Tearless, it sat in the dust, looking at the soldiers with an expression as inscrutable as theirs, suspended, aldermanic, and reserved. She swept the soldiers flat. "There!" she cried in a fond, bright voice, "see?" For a moment longer the child sat. Then it began to cry. She took it up and sat on the bench, rocking it back and forth, glancing up at the Judge. "Now, now," she said. "Now, now."

"Is he sick?" the Judge said.

"Oh, no. He's just tired of his toys, as children will get." She rocked the child with an air fond and unconcerned. "Now, now. The gentleman is watching you."

The child cried steadily. "Hasn't he other toys?" the Judge said.

"Oh, yes. So many that I don't dare walk about the house in the dark. But he likes his soldiers the best. An old gentleman who has lived here a long time, they say, and is quite wealthy, gave them to him. An old gentleman with a white mustache and that kind of popping eyes that old people have who eat too much; I tell him so. He has a footman to carry his umbrella and overcoat and steamer rug, and he sits here with us for more than an hour, sometimes, talking and breathing hard. He always has candy or something." She looked down at the child, her face brooding and serene. It cried steadily. Quizzical, bemused, the Judge stood, looking quietly down at the child's scarred, dirty feet. The woman

glanced up and followed his look. "You are looking at his
scars and wondering how he got them, aren't you? The
other children did it one day when they were playing. Of
course they didn't know they were going to hurt him. I
imagine they were as surprised as he was. You know how
children are when they get too quiet."

"Yes," the Judge said. "I had a son too."

"You have? Why don't you bring him here? I'm sure we
would be glad to have him play with our soldiers too."

The Judge's teeth glinted quietly. "I'm afraid he's a little
too big for toys." He took the photograph from the briefcase. "This was my son."

The woman took the picture. The child cried steady and
strong. "Why, it's Howard. Why, we see him every day. He
rides past here every day. Sometimes he stops and lets us
ride too. I walk beside to hold him on," she added, glancing
up. She showed the picture to the child. "Look! See Howard
on his pony? See?" Without ceasing to cry, the child contemplated the picture, its face streaked with tears and dirt,
its expression detached, suspended, as though it were living
two distinct and separate lives at one time. She returned the
picture. "I suppose you are looking for him."

"Ah," the Judge said behind his momentary teeth. He
replaced the picture carefully in the briefcase, the unlighted
cigarette in his fingers.

The woman moved on the bench, gathering her skirts in
with invitation. "Won't you sit down? You will be sure to
see him pass here."

"Ah," the Judge said again. He looked at her, quizzical,
with the blurred eyes of the old. "It's like this, you see. He
always rides the same pony, you say?"

"Why, yes." She looked at him with grave and tranquil
surprise.

"And how old would you say the pony is?"

"Why, I. . . . It looks just the right size for him."

"A young pony, you would say then?"

"Why . . . yes. Yes." She watched him, her eyes wide.

"Ah," the Judge said again behind his faint still teeth. He closed the briefcase carefully. From his pocket he took a half dollar. "Perhaps he is tired of the soldiers too. Perhaps with this. . . ."

"Thank you," she said. She did not look again at the coin. "Your face is so sad. There: when you think you are smiling it is sadder than ever. Aren't you well?" She glanced down at his extended hand. She did not offer to take the coin. "He'd just lose it, you see. And it's so pretty and bright. When he is older, and can take care of small playthings. . . . He's so little now, you see."

"I see," the Judge said. He put the coin back into his pocket. "Well, I think I shall—"

"You wait here with us. He always passes here. You'll find him quicker that way."

"Ah," the Judge said. "On the pony, the same pony. You see, by that token, the pony would have to be thirty years old. That pony died at eighteen, six years unridden, in my lot. That was twelve years ago. So I had better get on."

And again it was quite unpleasant. It should have been doubly so, what with the narrow entrance and the fact that, while the other time he was moving with the crowd, this time he must fight his way inch by inch against it. "But at least I know where I am going," he thought, beneath his crushed hat, his stick and briefcase dragging at his arms; "which I did not seem to know before." But he was free at last, and looking up at the clock on the courthouse, as he never failed to do on descending his office stairs, he saw that he had a full hour before supper would be ready, before the neighbors would be ready to mark his clocklike passing.

"I shall have time to go the cemetery," he thought, and

looking down at the raw and recent excavation, he swore
with fretful annoyance, for some of the savage clods had
fallen or been thrown upon the marble slab beside it. "Damn
that Pettigrew," he said. "He should have seen to this. I
told him I wanted the two of them as close as possible, but
at least I thought that he. . . ." Kneeling, he tried to remove
the earth which had fallen upon the slab. But it was beyond
his strength to do more than clear away that which partially
obscured the lettering: *Howard Allison II. April 3, 1903.
August 22, 1913,* and the quietly cryptic Gothic lettering at
the foot: *Auf Wiedersehen, Little Boy.* He continued to
smooth, to stroke the letters after the earth was gone, his
face bemused, quiet, as he spoke to the man who Mothershed had said was Ingersoll, "You see, if I could believe that
I shall see and touch him again, I shall not have lost him.
And if I have not lost him, I shall never have had a son.
Because I am I through bereavement and because of it. I do
not know what I was nor what I shall be. But because of
death, I know that I am. And that is all the immortality of
which intellect is capable and flesh should desire. Anything
else is for peasants, clods, who could never have loved a son
well enough to have lost him." His face broke, myriad,
quizzical, while his hand moved lightly upon the quiet lettering. "No. I do not require that. To lie beside him will be
sufficient for me. There will be a wall of dust between us:
that is true, and he is already dust these twenty years. But
some day I shall be dust too. And—" he spoke now firmly,
quietly, with a kind of triumph: "who is he who will affirm
that there must be a web of flesh and bone to hold the shape
of love?"

Now it was late. "Probably they are setting their clocks
back at this very moment," he thought, pacing along the
street toward his home. Already he should have been hearing
the lawn mower. and then in the instant of exasperation at

Jake, he remarked the line of motor cars before his gate and a sudden haste came upon him. But not so much but what, looking at the vehicle at the head of the line, he cursed again. "Damn that Pettigrew! I told him, in the presence of witnesses when I signed my will, that I would not be hauled feet first through Jefferson at forty miles an hour. That if he couldn't find me a decent pair of horses. . . . I am a good mind to come back and haunt him, as Jake would have me do."

But the haste, the urgency, was upon him. He hurried round to the back door (he remarked that the lawn was freshly and neatly trimmed, as though done that day) and entered. Then he could smell the flowers faintly and hear the voice; he had just time to slip out of his overcoat and pajamas and leave them hanging neatly in the closet, and cross the hall into the odor of cut flowers and the drone of the voice, and slip into his clothes. They had been recently pressed, and his face had been shaved too. Nevertheless they were his own, and he fitted himself to the olden and familiar embrace which no iron could change, with the same lascivious eagerness with which he shaped his limbs to the bedclothes on a winter night.

"Ah," he said to the man who Mothershed had said was Ingersoll, "this is best, after all. An old man is never at home save in his own garments: his own old thinking and beliefs; old hands and feet, elbow, knee, shoulder which he knows will fit."

Now the light vanished with a mute, faint, decorous hollow sound which drove for a fading instant down upon him the dreadful, macabre smell of slain flowers; at the same time he became aware that the droning voice had ceased. "In my own house too," he thought, waiting for the smell of the flowers to fade; "yet I did not once think to notice who was speaking, nor when he ceased." Then he heard or felt the decorous scuffing of feet about him, and he lay in the close

dark, his hands folded upon his breast as he slept, as the old
sleep, waiting for the moment. It came. He said quietly
aloud, quizzical, humorous, peaceful, as he did each night
in his bed in his lonely and peaceful room when a last full
exhalation had emptied his body of waking and he seemed
for less than an instant to look about him from the portal of
sleep, "Gentlemen of the Jury, you may proceed."

Black Music

THIS IS about Wilfred Midgleston, fortune's favorite, chosen of the gods. For fifty-six years, a clotting of the old gutful compulsions and circumscriptions of clocks and bells, he met walking the walking image of a small, snuffy, nondescript man whom neither man nor woman had ever turned to look at twice, in the monotonous shopwindows of monotonous hard streets. Then his apotheosis soared glaring, and to him at least not brief, across the unfathomed sky above his lost earth like that of Elijah of old.

I found him in Rincon, which is not large; less large even than one swaybacked tanker looming above the steel docks of the Universal Oil Company and longer than the palm- and abode-lined street paved with dust marked by splayed naked feet where the violent shade lies by day and the violent big stars by night.

"He came from the States," they told me. "Been here twenty-five years. He hasn't changed at all since the day he arrived, except that the clothes he came in have wore out and he hasn't learned more than ten words of Spanish." That was the only way you could tell that he was an old man, that he was getting along: he hadn't learned to speak hardly a word of the language of the people with whom he had lived twenty-five years and among whom it appeared that he intended to die and be buried. Appeared: he had no job: a

mild, hopelessly mild man who looked like a book-keeper
in a George Ade fable dressed as a tramp for a Presbyterian
social charade in 1890, and quite happy.

Quite happy and quite poor. "He's either poor, or he's
putting up an awful front. But they can't touch him now.
We told him that a long time ago, when he first come here.
We said, 'Why don't you go on and spend it, enjoy it?
They've probably forgot all about it by now.' Because if I
went to the trouble and risk of stealing and then the hard-
ship of having to live the rest of my life in a hole like this,
I'd sure enjoy what I went to the trouble to get."

"Enjoy what?" I said.

"The money. The money he stole and had to come down
here. What else do you reckon he would come down here
and stay twenty-five years for? just to look at the country?"

"He doesn't act and look very rich," I said.

"That's a fact. But a fellow like that. His face. I don't
guess he'd have judgment enough to steal good. And not
judgment enough to keep it, after he got it stole. I guess
you are right. I guess all he got out of it was the running
away and the blame. While somebody back there where he
run from is spending the money and singing loud in the choir
twice a week."

"Is that what happens?" I said.

"You're damned right it is. Some damn fellow that's too
rich to afford to be caught stealing sets back and leaves a
durn fool that never saw twenty-five hundred dollars before
in his life at one time, pull his chestnuts for him. Twenty-
five hundred seems a hell of a lot when somebody else owns
it. But when you have got to pick up overnight and run a
thousand miles, paying all your expenses, how long do you
think twenty-five hundred will last?"

"How long did it last?" I said.

"Just about two years, by God. And then there I—" He

stopped. He glared at me, who had paid for the coffee and the bread which rested upon the table between us. He glared at me. "Who do you think you are, anyway? Wm. J. Burns?"

"I don't think so. I meant no offense. I just was curious to know how long his twenty-five hundred dollars lasted him."

"Who said he had twenty-five hundred dollars? I was just citing an example. He never had nothing, not even twenty-five hundred cents. Or if he did, he hid it and it's stayed hid ever since. He come here sponging on us white men, and when we got tired of it he took to sponging on these Spigs. And a white man has got pretty low when he's got so stingy with his stealings that he will live with Spiggotties before he'll dig up his own money and live like a white man."

"Maybe he never stole any money," I said.

"What's he doing down here, then?"

"I'm down here."

"I don't know you ain't run, either."

"That's so," I said. "You don't know."

"Sure I don't. Because that's your business. Every man has got his own private affairs, and no man respects them quicker than I do. But I know that a man, a white man, has got to have durn good reason. . . . Maybe he ain't got it now. But you can't tell me a white man would come down here to live and die without no reason."

"And you consider that stealing money is the only reason?"

He looked at me, with disgust and a little contempt. "Did you bring a nurse with you? Because you ought to have, until you learn enough about human nature to travel alone. Because human nature, I don't care who he is nor how loud he sings in church, will steal whenever he thinks he can get away with it. If you ain't learned that yet, you better go back home and stay there where your folks can take care of you."

But I was watching Midgleston across the street. He was standing beside a clump of naked children playing in the shady dust: a small, snuffy man in a pair of dirty drill trousers which had not been made for him. "Whatever it is," I said, "it doesn't seem to worry him."

"Oh. Him. He ain't got sense enough to know he needs to worry about nothing."

Quite poor and quite happy. His turn to have coffee and bread with me came at last. No: that's wrong. I at last succeeded in evading his other down-at-heel compatriots like my first informant; men a little soiled and usually unshaven, who were unavoidable in the cantinas and coffee shops, loud, violent, maintaining the superiority of the white race and their own sense of injustice and of outrage among the grave white teeth, the dark, courteous, fatal, speculative alien faces, and had Midgleston to breakfast with me. I had to invite him and then insist. He was on hand at the appointed hour, in the same dirty trousers, but his shirt was now white and whole and ironed, and he had shaved. He accepted the meal without servility, without diffidence, without eagerness. Yet when he raised the handleless bowl I watched his hands tremble so that for a time he could not make junction with his lips. He saw me watching his hands and he looked at my face for the first time and I saw that his eyes were the eyes of an old man. He said, with just a trace of apology for his clumsiness: "I ain't et nothing to speak of in a day or so."

"Haven't eaten in two days?" I said.

"This hot climate. A fellow don't need so much. Feels better for not eating so much. That was the hardest trouble I had when I first come here. I was always a right hearty eater back home."

"Oh," I said. I had meat brought then, he protesting. But he ate the meat, ate all of it. "Just look at me," he said. "I ain't et this much breakfast in twenty-five years. But when a fellow gets along, old habits are hard to break. No, sir. Not since I left home have I et this much for breakfast."

"Do you plan to go back home?" I said.

"I guess not; no. This suits me here. I can live simple here. Not all cluttered up with things. My own boss (I used to be an architect's draughtsman) all day long. No. I don't guess I'll go back." He looked at me. His face was intent, watchful, like that of a child about to tell something, divulge itself. "You wouldn't guess where I sleep in a hundred years."

"No. I don't expect I could. Where do you sleep?"

"I sleep in that attic over that cantina yonder. The house belongs to the Company, and Mrs. Widrington, Mr. Widrington's wife, the manager's wife, she lets me sleep in the attic. It's high and quiet, except for a few rats. But when in Rome, you got to act like a Roman, I say. Only I wouldn't name this country Rome; I'd name it Ratville. But that ain't it." He watched me. "You'd never guess it in the world."

"No," I said. "I'd never guess it."

He watched me. "It's my bed."

"Your bed?"

"I told you you'd never guess it."

"No," I said. "I give up now."

"My bed is a roll of tarred roofing paper."

"A roll of what?"

"Tarred roofing paper." His face was bright, peaceful; his voice quiet, full of gleeful quiet. "At night I just unroll it and go to bed and the next a. m. I just roll it back up and lean it in the corner. And then my room is all cleaned up for the day. Ain't that fine? No sheets, no laundry, no noth-

ing. Just roll up my whole bed like an umbrella and carry
it under my arm when I want to move."

"Oh," I said. "You have no family, then."

"Not with me. No."

"You have a family back home, then?"

He was quite quiet. He did not feign to be occupied with
something on the table. Neither did his eyes go blank,
though he mused peacefully for a moment. "Yes. I have a
wife back home. Likely this climate wouldn't suit her. She
wouldn't like it here. But she is all right. I always kept my
insurance paid up; I carried a right smart more than you
would figure a architect's draughtsman on a seventy-five-
dollar salary would keep up. If I told you the amount, you
would be surprised. She helped me to save; she is a good
woman. So she's got that. She earned it. And besides, I don't
need money."

"So you don't plan to go back home."

"No," he said. He watched me; again his expression was
that of a child about to tell on itself. "You see, I done something."

"Oh. I see."

He talked quietly: "It ain't what you think. Not what
them others—" he jerked his head, a brief embracing gesture
—"think. I never stole any money. Like I always told Martha—she is my wife; Mrs. Midgleston—money is too easy
to earn to risk the bother of trying to steal it. All you got
to do is work. 'Have we ever suffered for it?' I said to her.
'Of course, we don't live like some. But some is born for one
thing and some is born for another thing. And the fellow
that is born a tadpole, when he tries to be a salmon all he is
going to be is a sucker.' That's what I would tell her. And
she done her part and we got along right well; if I told you
how much life insurance I carried, you would be surprised.
No; she ain't suffered any. Don't you think that."

"No," I said.

"But then I done something. Yes, sir."

"Did what? Can you tell?"

"Something. Something that ain't in the lot and plan for mortal human man to do."

"What was it you did?"

He looked at me. "I ain't afraid to tell. I ain't never been afraid to tell. It was just that these folks—" again he jerked his head slightly—"wouldn't have understood. Wouldn't have knowed what I was talking about. But you will. You'll know." He watched my face. "At one time in my life I was a farn."

"A farn?"

"Farn. Don't you remember in the old books where they would drink the red grape wine, how now and then them rich Roman and Greek senators would up and decide to tear up a old grape vineyard or a wood away off somewheres the gods used, and build a summer house to hold their frolics in where the police wouldn't hear them, and how the gods wouldn't hear them, and how the gods wouldn't like it about them married women running around nekkid, and so the woods god named—named—"

"Pan," I said.

"That's it. Pan. And he would send them little fellows that was half a goat to scare them out—"

"Oh," I said. "A faun."

"That's it. A farn. That's what I was once. I was raised religious; I have never used tobacco or liquor; and I don't think now that I am going to hell. But the Bible says that them little men were myths. But I know they ain't, and so I have been something outside the lot and plan for mortal human man to be. Because for one day in my life I was a farn."

II

IN THE OFFICE where Midgleston was a draughtsman they
would discuss the place and Mrs. Van Dyming's unique
designs upon it while they were manufacturing the plans,
the blue prints. The tract consisted of a meadow, a southern
hillside where grapes grew, and a woodland. "Good land,
they said. But wouldn't anybody live on it."

"Why not?" I said.

"Because things happened on it. They told how a long
time ago a New England fellow settled on it and cleaned up
the grape vines to market the grapes. Going to make jelly
or something. He made a good crop, but when time came
to gather them, he couldn't gather them."

"Why couldn't he gather them?"

"Because his leg was broke. He had some goats, and a old
ram that he couldn't keep out of the grape lot. He tried
every way he knew, but he couldn't keep the ram out. And
when the man went in to gather the grapes to make jelly,
the ram ran over him and knocked him down and broke
his leg. So the next spring the New England fellow moved
away.

"And they told about another man, a I-talian lived the
other side of the woods. He would gather the grapes and
make wine out of them, and he built up a good wine trade.
After a while his trade got so good that he had more trade
than he did wine. So he began to doctor the wine up with
water and alcohol, and he was getting rich. At first he used
a horse and wagon to bring the grapes home on his private
road through the woods, but he got rich and he bought a
truck, and he doctored the wine a little more and he got
richer and he bought a bigger truck. And one night a storm
come up while he was away from home, gathering the
grapes, and he didn't get home that night. The next a. m.

his wife found him. That big truck had skidded off the road and turned over and he was dead under it."

"I don't see how that reflected on the place," I said.

"All right. I'm just telling it. The neighbor folks thought different, anyway. But maybe that was because they were not anything but country folks. Anyway, none of them would live on it, and so Mr. Van Dyming bought it cheap. For Mrs. Van Dyming. To play with. Even before we had the plans finished, she would take a special trainload of them down there to look at it, and not even a cabin on the place then, not nothing but the woods and that meadow growed up in grass tall as a man, and that hillside where them grapes grew tangled. But she would stand there, with them other rich Park Avenue folks, showing them how here would be the community house built to look like the Coliseum and the community garage yonder made to look like it was a Acropolis, and how the grape vine would be grubbed up entire and the hillside terraced to make a outdoors theatre where they could act in one another's plays; and how the meadow would be a lake with one of them Roman barges towed back and forth on it by a gas engine, with mattresses and things for them to lay down on while they et."

"What did Mr. Van Dyming say about all this?"

"I don't reckon he said anything. He was married to her, you know. He just says, one time, 'Now, Mattie—' and she turns on him, right there in the office, before us all, and says, 'Don't you call me Mattie.'" He was quiet for a time. Then he said: "She wasn't born on Park Avenue. Nor Westchester neither. She was born in Poughkeepsie. Her name was Lumpkin.

"But you wouldn't know it, now. When her picture would be in the paper with all them Van Dyming diamonds, it wouldn't say how Mrs. Carleton Van Dyming used to be Miss Mathilda Lumpkin of Poughkeepsie. No, sir. Even a newspaper wouldn't dared say that to her. And I reckon Mr. Van Dyming never either, unless he forgot like the day in the office. So she says, 'Don't you call me Mattie' and he hushed and he just stood there—a little man; he looked kind of like me, they said—tapping one of them little highprice cigars on his glove, with his face looking like he had thought about smiling a little and then he decided it wasn't even any use in that.

"They built the house first. It was right nice; Mr. Van Dyming planned it. I guess maybe he said more than just Mattie that time. And I guess that maybe Mrs. Van Dyming never said, 'Don't you call me Mattie' that time. Maybe he promised her he wouldn't interfere with the rest of it. Anyway, the house was right nice. It was on the hill, kind of in the edge of the woods. It was logs. But it wasn't too much logs. It belonged there, fitted. Logs where logs ought to be, and good city bricks and planks where logs ought not to be. It was there. Belonged there. It was all right. Not to make anybody mad. Can you see what I mean?"

"Yes. I think I can see what you mean."

"But the rest of it he never interfered with; her and her Acropolises and all." He looked at me quite intently. "Sometimes I thought. . . ."

"What? Thought what?"

"I told you him and me were the same size, looked kind of alike." He watched me. "Like we could have talked, for all of him and his Park Avenue clothes and his banks and his railroads, and me a seventy-five a week draughtsman living in Brooklyn, and not young neither. Like I could have said to him what was in my mind at any time, and he could have said to me what was in his mind at any time, and we would have understood one another. That's why sometimes I thought. . . ." He looked at me, intently, not groping exactly. "Sometimes men have more sense than women. They know

what to leave be, and women don't always know that. He
don't need to be religious in the right sense or religious in
the wrong sense. Nor religious at all." He looked at me,
intently. After a while he said, in a decisive tone, a tone of
decisive irrevocation: "This will seem silly to you."

"No. Of course not. Of course it won't."

He looked at me. Then he looked away. "No. It will just
sound silly. Just take up your time."

"No. I swear it won't. I want to hear it. I am not a man
who believes that people have learned everything." He
watched me. "It has taken a million years to make what is,
they tell us," I said. "And a man can be made and worn out
and buried in threescore and ten. So how can a man be
expected to know even enough to doubt?"

"That's right," he said. "That's sure right."

"What was it you sometimes thought?"

"Sometimes I thought that, if it hadn't been me, they
would have used him. Used Mr. Van Dyming like they
used me."

"They?" We looked at one another, quite sober, quite
quiet.

"Yes. The ones that used that ram on that New England
fellow, and that storm on that I-talian."

"Oh. Would have used Mr. Van Dyming in your place,
if you had not been there at the time. How did they use
you?"

"That's what I am going to tell. How I was chosen and
used. I did not know that I had been chosen. But I was
chosen to do something beyond the lot and plan for mortal
human man. It was the day that Mr. Carter (he was the boss,
the architect) got the hurryup message from Mrs. Van
Dyming. I think I told you the house was already built, and
there was a big party of them down there where they could
watch the workmen building the Coliseums and the Acropo-

lises. So the hurryup call came. She wanted the plans for the theatre, the one that was to be on the hillside where the grapes grew. She was going to build it first, so the company could set and watch them building the Acropolises and Coliseums. She had already begun to grub up the grape vines, and Mr. Carter put the theatre prints in a portfolio and give me the weekend off to take them down there to her."

"Where was the place?"

"I don't know. It was in the mountains, the quiet mountains where never many lived. It was a kind of green air, chilly too, and a wind. When it blew through them pines it sounded kind of like a organ, only it didn't sound tame like a organ. Not tame; that's how it sounded. But I don't know where it was. Mr. Carter had the ticket all ready and he said it would be somebody to meet me when the train stopped.

"So I telephoned Martha and I went home to get ready. When I got home, she had my Sunday suit all pressed and my shoes shined. I didn't see any use in that, since I was just going to take the plans and come back. But Martha said how I had told her it was company there. 'And you are going to look as nice as any of them,' she says. 'For all they are rich and get into the papers. You're just as good as they are.' That was the last thing she said when I got on the train, in my Sunday suit, with the portfolio: 'You're just as good as they are, even if they do get into the papers.' And then it started."

"What started? The train?"

"No. It. The train had been running already a good while; we were out in the country now. I didn't know then that I had been chosen. I was just setting there in the train, with the portfolio on my knees where I could take care of it. Even when I went back to the ice water I didn't know that I had been chosen. I carried the portfolio with me and I was standing there, looking out the window and drinking out of the little paper cup. There was a bank running along by the train then, with a white fence on it, and I could see animals inside the fence, but the train was going too fast to tell what kind of animals they were.

"So I had filled the cup again and I was drinking, looking out at the bank and the fence and the animals inside the fence, when all of a sudden it felt like I had been thrown off the earth. I could see the bank and the fence go whirling away. And then I saw it. And just as I saw it, it was like it had kind of exploded inside my head. Do you know what it was I saw?"

"What was it you saw?"

He watched me. "I saw a face. In the air, looking at me across that white fence on top of the bank. It was not a man's face, because it had horns, and it was not a goat's face because it had a beard and it was looking at me with eyes like a man and its mouth was open like it was saying something to me when it exploded inside my head."

"Yes. And then what? What did you do next?"

"You are saying 'He saw a goat inside that fence.' I know. But I didn't ask you to believe. Remember that. Because I am twenty-five years past bothering if folks believe me or not. That's enough for me. And I guess that's all anything amounts to."

"Yes," I said. "What did you do then?"

"Then I was laying down, with my face all wet and my mouth and throat feeling like it was on fire. The man was just taking the bottle away from my mouth (there were two men there, and the porter and the conductor) and I tried to sit up. 'That's whiskey in that bottle,' I said.

" 'Why, sure not, doc,' the man said. 'You know I wouldn't be giving whiskey to a man like you. Anybody could tell by looking at you that you never took a drink in your life. Did you?' I told him I hadn't. 'Sure you haven't,' he said. 'A man could tell by the way it took that curve to throw you down that you belonged to the ladies' temperance. You sure took a bust on the head, though. How do you feel now? Here, take another little shot of this tonic.'

" 'I think that's whiskey,' I said.

"And was it whiskey?"

"I dont know. I have forgotten. Maybe I knew then. Maybe I knew what it was when I took another dose of it. But that didn't matter, because it had already started then."

"The whiskey had already started?"

"No. It. It was stronger than whiskey. Like it was drinking out of the bottle and not me. Because the men held the bottle up and looked at it and said, 'You sure drink it like it ain't whiskey, anyway. You'll sure know soon if it is or not, won't you?'

"When the train stopped where the ticket said, it was all green, the light was, and the mountains. The wagon was there, and the two men when they helped me down from the train and handed me the portfolio, and I stood there and I said, 'Let her rip.' That's what I said: 'Let her rip'; and the two men looking at me like you are looking at me."

"How looking at you?"

"Yes. But you dont have to believe. And I told them to wait while I got the whistle—"

"Whistle?"

"There was a store there, too. The store and the depot, and then the mountains and the green cold without any sun, and the dust kind of pale looking where the wagon was standing. Then we—"

"But the whistle," I said.

"I bought it in the store. It was a tin one, with holes in it. I couldn't seem to get the hang of it. So I threw the portfolio into the wagon and I said, 'Let her rip.' That was what I said. One of them took the portfolio out of the wagon

and gave it back to me and said, 'Say, doc, ain't this valuable?'
and I took it and threw it back into the wagon and I said,
'Let her rip.'

"We all rode on the seat together, me in the middle. We
sung. It was cold, and we went along the river, singing, and
came to the mill and stopped. While one of them went inside
the mill I began to take off my clothes—"

"Take off your clothes?"

"Yes. My Sunday suit. Taking them off and throwing
them right down in the dust, by gummy."

"Wasn't it cold?"

"Yes It was cold. Yes. When I took off my clothes I
could feel the cold on me. Then the one came back from the
mill with a jug and we drank out of the jug—"

"What was in the jug?"

"I dont know. I dont remember. It wasn't whiskey. I
could tell by the way it looked. It was clear like water."

"Couldn't you tell by the smell?"

"I dont smell, you see. I dont know what they call it. But
ever since I was a child, I couldn't smell some things. They
say that's why I have stayed down here for twenty-five
years.

"So we drank and I went to the bridge rail. And just as I
jumped I could see myself in the water. And I knew that it
had happened then. Because my body was a human man's
body. But my face was the same face that had gone off
inside my head back there on the train, the face that had
horns and a beard.

"When I got back into the wagon we drank again out of
the jug and we sung, only after a while I put on my underclothes and my pants like they wanted me to, and then we
went on, singing.

"When we came in sight of the house I got out of the
wagon. 'You dont want to get out here,' they said. 'We are

in the pasture where they keep that bull chained up.' But I
got out of the wagon, with my Sunday coat and vest and the
portfolio, and the tin flute."

III

HE CEASED. He looked at me, quite grave, quite quiet.

"Yes," I said. "Yes. Then what?"

He watched me. "I never asked you to believe nothing, did
I? I will have to say that for you." His hand was inside his
bosom. "Well, you had some pretty hard going, so far. But
now I will take the strain off of you."

From his bosom he drew out a canvas wallet. It was
roughly sewn by a clumsy hand and soiled with much usage.
He opened it. But before he drew out the contents he looked
at me again. "Do you ever make allowances?"

"Allowances?"

"For folks. For what folks think they see. Because nothing
ever looks the same to two different people. Never looks the
same to one person, depending on which side of it he looks
at it from."

"Oh," I said. "Allowances. Yes. Yes."

From the wallet he drew a folded sheet of newspaper.
The page was yellow with age, the broken seams glued carefully with strips of soiled cloth. He opened it carefully,
gingerly, and turned it and laid it on the table before me.
"Dont try to pick it up," he said. "It's kind of old now, and
it's the only copy I have. Read it."

I looked at it: the fading ink, the blurred page dated
twenty-five years ago:

MANIAC AT LARGE IN VIRGINIA
MOUNTAINS

PROMINENT NEW YORK SOCIETY WOMAN
ATTACKED IN OWN GARDEN

Mrs. Carleton Van Dyming Of New York And
Newport Attacked By Half Nude Madman And
Maddened Bull In Garden Of Her Summer Lodge.
Maniac Escapes. Mrs. Van Dyming Prostrate

It went on from there, with pictures and diagrams, to tell
how Mrs. Van Dyming, who was expecting a man from the
office of her New York architect, was called from the dinner
table to meet, as she supposed, the architect's man. The story
continued in Mrs. Van Dyming's own words:

> I went to the library, where I had directed that the
> architect's man be brought, but there was no one there.
> I was about to ring for the footman when it occurred
> to me to go to the front door, since it is a local custom
> among these country people to come to the front and
> refuse to advance further or to retreat until the master
> or the mistress of the house appears. I went to the door.
> There was no one there.
>
> I stepped out onto the porch. The light was on, but
> at first I could see no one. I started to re-enter the
> house but the footman had told me distinctly that the
> wagon had returned from the village, and I thought that
> the man had perhaps gone on to the edge of the lawn
> where he could see the theatre site, where the workmen
> had that day begun to prepare the ground by digging
> up the old grape vines. So I went in that direction. I had
> almost reached the end of the lawn when something
> caused me to turn. I saw, in relief between me and the
> lighted porch, a man bent over and hopping on one leg,
> who to my horror I realised to be in the act of removing
> his trousers.
>
> I screamed for my husband. When I did so, the man
> freed his other leg and turned and came toward me run-
> ning, clutching a knife (I could see the light from the
> porch gleaming on the long blade) in one hand, and a
> flat, square object in the other. I turned then and ran
> screaming toward the woods.

I had lost all sense of direction. I simply ran for my life. I found that I was inside the old vineyard, among the grape vines, running directly away from the house. I could hear the man running behind me and suddenly I heard him begin to make a strange noise. It sounded like a child trying to blow upon a penny whistle, then I realised that it was the sound of his breath whistling past the knifeblade clinched between his teeth.

Suddenly something overtook and passed me, making a tremendous uproar in the shrubbery. It rushed so near me that I could see its glaring eyes and the shape of a huge beast with horns, which I recognised a moment later as Carleton's—Mr. Van Dyming's—prize Durham bull; an animal so dangerous that Mr. Dyming is forced to keep it locked up. It was now free and it rushed past and on ahead, cutting off my advance, while the madman with the knife cut off my retreat. I was at bay; I stopped with my back to a tree, screaming for help.

"How did the bull get out?" I said.

He was watching my face while I read, like I might have been a teacher grading his school paper. "When I was a boy, I used to take subscriptions to the *Police Gazette*, for premiums. One of the premiums was a little machine guaranteed to open any lock. I dont use it anymore, but I still carry it in my pocket, like a charm or something, I guess. Anyway, I had it that night." He looked down at the paper on the table. "I guess folks tell what they believe they saw. So you have to believe what they think they believe. But that paper dont tell how she kicked off her slippers (I nigh broke my neck over one of them) so she could run better, and how I could hear her going wump-wump-wump inside like a dray horse, and how when she would begin to slow up a little I would let out another toot on the whistle and off she would go again.

"I couldn't even keep up with her, carrying that portfolio

and trying to blow on that whistle too; seemed like I never would get the hang of it, somehow. But maybe that was because I had to start trying so quick, before I had time to kind of practice up, and running all the time too. So I threw the portfolio away and then I caught up with her where she was standing with her back against the tree, and that bull running round and round the tree, not bothering her, just running around the tree, making a right smart of fuss, and her leaning there whispering 'Carleton. Carleton' like she was afraid she would wake him up."

The account continued:

> I stood against the tree, believing that each circle which the bull made, it would discover my presence. That was why I ceased to scream. Then the man came up where I could see him plainly for the first time. He stopped before me; for one both horrid and joyful moment I thought he was Mr. Van Dyming. "Carleton!" I said.
>
> He didn't answer. He was stooped over again; then I saw that he was engaged with the knife in his hand. "Carleton!" I cried.
>
> " 'Dang if I can get the hang of it, somehow,' he kind of muttered, busy with the murderous knife.
>
> "Carleton!" I cried. "Are you mad?"
>
> He looked up then. I saw that it was not my husband, that I was at the mercy of a madman, a maniac, and a maddened bull. I saw the man raise the knife to his lips and blow again upon it that fearful shriek. Then I fainted.

IV

AND THAT WAS ALL. The account merely went on to say how the madman had vanished, leaving no trace, and that Mrs. Van Dyming was under the care of her physician, with a special train waiting to transport her and her household,

lock, stock, and barrel, back to New York; and that Mr. Van
Dyming in a brief interview had informed the press that his
plans about the improvement of the place had been definitely
rescinded and that the place was now for sale.

I folded the paper as carefully as he would have. "Oh," I
said. "And so that's all."

"Yes. I waked up about daylight the next morning, in the
woods. I didn't know when I went to sleep nor where I was
at first. I couldn't remember at first what I had done. But
that aint strange. I guess a man couldn't lose a day out of his
life and not know it. Do you think so?"

"Yes," I said. "That's what I think too."

"Because I know I aint as evil to God as I guess I look to
a lot of folks. And I guess that demons and such and even the
devil himself aint quite as evil to God as lots of folks that
claim to know a right smart about His business would make
you believe. Dont you think that's right?" The wallet lay on
the table, open. But he did not at once return the newspaper
to it.

Then he quit looking at me; at once his face became diffident, childlike again. He put his hand into the wallet; again
he did not withdraw it at once.

"That aint exactly all," he said, his hand inside the wallet,
his eyes downcast, and his face: that mild, peaceful, nondescript face across which a mild moustache straggled. "I
was a powerful reader, when I was a boy. Do you read
much?"

"Yes. A good deal."

But he was not listening. "I would read about pirates and
cowboys, and I would be the head pirate or cowboy—me, a
durn little tyke that never saw the ocean except at Coney
Island or a tree except in Washington Square day in and out.
But I read them, believing like every boy, that some day . . .
that living wouldn't play a trick on him like getting him
alive and then. . . . When I went home that morning to get

ready to take the train, Martha says, 'You're just as good as
any of them Van Dymings, for all they get into the papers.
If all the folks that deserved it got into the papers, Park
Avenue wouldn't hold them, or even Brooklyn,' she says."
He drew his hand from the wallet. This time it was only a
clipping, one column wide, which he handed me, yellow and
faded too, and not long:

MYSTERIOUS DISAPPEARANCE

FOUL PLAY SUSPECTED

Wilfred Middleton, New York Architect, Disap-
pears From Millionaire's Country House

POSSE SEEKS BODY OF ARCHITECT BELIEVED SLAIN BY
MADMAN IN VIRGINIA MOUNTAINS

May Be Coupled With Mysterious Attack
On Mrs. Van Dyming

Mountain Neighborhood In State Of Terror

.........., Va. April 8, ... Wilfred Middleton, 56,
architect, of New York City, mysteriously disappeared
sometime on April 6th, while en route to the country
house of Mr. Carleton Van Dyming near here. He had
in his possession some valuable drawings which were
found this morning near the Van Dyming estate, thus
furnishing the first clue. Chief of Police Elmer Harris
has taken charge of the case, and is now awaiting the
arrival of a squad of New York detectives, when he
promises a speedy solution if it is in the power of skilled
criminologists to do so.

MOST BAFFLING IN ALL HIS EXPERIENCE

"When I solve this disappearance," Chief Harris is
quoted, "I will also solve the attack on Mrs. Van Dyming on the same date."

Middleton leaves a wife, Mrs. Martha Middleton,
..............st., Brooklyn.

He was watching my face. "Only it's one mistake in it,"
he said.

"Yes," I said. "They got your name wrong."

"I was wondering if you'd see that. But that's not the mistake. . . ." He had in his hand a second clipping which he
now extended. It was like the other two; yellow, faint. I
looked at it, the fading, peaceful print through which, like a
thin, rotting net, the old violence had somehow escaped,
leaving less than the dead gesture fallen to quiet dust. "Read
this one. Only that's not the mistake I was thinking about.
But then, they couldn't have known at that time. . . ."

I was reading, not listening to him. This was a reprinted
letter, an 'agony column' letter:

> *New Orleans, La.*
> *April 10, ...*

> *To the Editor, New York Times*
> *New York, N. Y.*
> *Dear Sir*
> *In your issue of April 8, this year you got the name of
> the party wrong. The name is Midgleston not Middle-
> ton. Would thank you to correct this error in local and
> metropolitan columns as the press a weapon of good &
> evil into every American home. And a power of that
> weight cannot afford mistakes even about people as
> good as any man or woman even if they dont get into
> the papers every day.*
> > *Thanking you again, beg to remain*
> > > *A Friend*

"Oh," I said. "I see. You corrected it."

"Yes. But that's not the mistake. I just did that for her.

You know how women are. Like as not she would rather not see it in the papers at all than to see it spelled wrong."

"She?"

"My wife. Martha. The mistake was, if she got them or not."

"I dont—Maybe you'd better tell me."

"That's what I am doing. I got two of the first one, the one about the disappearance, but I waited until the letter come out. Then I put them both into a piece of paper with *A Friend* on it, and put them into a envelope and mailed them to her. But I dont know if she got them or not. That was the mistake."

"The mistake?"

"Yes. She moved. She moved to Park Avenue when the insurance was paid. I saw that in a paper after I come down here. It told about how Mrs. Martha Midgleston of Park Avenue was married to a young fellow he used to be associated with the Maison Payot on Fifth Avenue. It didn't say when she moved, so I dont know if she got them or not."

"Oh," I said. He was putting the clippings carefully back into the canvas wallet.

"Yes, sir. Women are like that. It dont cost a man much to humor them now and then. Because they deserve it; they have a hard time. But it wasn't me. I didn't mind how they spelled it. What's a name to a man that's done and been something outside the lot and plan for mortal human man to do and be?"

The Leg

THE BOAT—it was a yawl boat with a patched weathered sail—made two reaches below us while I sat with the sculls poised, watching her over my shoulder, and George clung to the pile, spouting Milton at Everbe Corinthia. When it made the final tack I looked back at George. But he was now but well into Comus' second speech, his crooked face raised, and the afternoon bright on his close ruddy head.

"Give way, George," I said. But he held us stationary at the pile, his glazed hat lifted, spouting his fine and cadenced folly as though the lock, the Thames, time and all, belonged to him, while Sabrina (or Hebe or Chloe or whatever name he happened to be calling Corinthia at the time) with her dairy-maid's complexion and her hair like mead poured in sunlight stood above us in one of her endless succession of neat print dresses, her hand on the lever and one eye on George and the other on the yawl, saying "Yes, milord" dutifully whenever George paused for breath.

The yawl luffed and stood away; the helmsman shouted for the lock.

"Let go, George," I said. But he clung to the pile in his fine and incongruous oblivion. Everbe Corinthia stood above us, her hand on the lever, bridling a little and beginning to reveal a certain concern, and looking from her to the yawl and back again I thought how much time she and I had both spent thus since that day three years ago when, cow-eyed and bridling, she had opened the lock for us for the first time, with George holding us stationary while he apostrophised her in the metaphor of Keats and Spenser.

Again the yawl's crew shouted at us, the yawl aback and in stays. "Let go, you fool!" I said, digging the sculls. "Lock, Corinthia!"

George looked at me. Corinthia was now watching the yawl with both eyes. "What, Davy?" George said. "Must even thou help Circe's droves into the sea? Pull, then, O Super-Gadarene!"

And he shoved us off. I had not meant to pull away. And even if I had, I could still have counteracted the movement if Everbe Corinthia hadn't opened the lock. But open it she did, and looked once back to us and sat flat on the earth, crisp fresh dress and all. The skiff shot away under me; I had a fleeting picture of George still clinging with one arm around the pile, his knees drawn up to his chin and the hat in his lifted hand and of a long running shadow carrying the shadow of a boat-hook falling across the lock. Then I was too busy steering. I shot through the gates, carrying with me that picture of George, the glazed hat still gallantly aloft like the mastheaded pennant of a man-of-war, vanishing beneath the surface. Then I was floating quietly in slack water while the round eyes of two men stared quietly down at me from the yawl.

"Yer've lost yer mate, sir," one of them said in a civil voice. Then they had drawn me alongside with a boat-hook and standing up in the skiff, I saw George. He was standing in the towpath now, and Simon, Everbe Corinthia's father, and another man—he was the one with the boat-hook, whose shadow I had seen across the lock—were there too. But I saw only George with his ugly crooked face and his round head now dark in the sunlight. One of the watermen was still talking. "Steady, sir. Lend 'im a 'and, Sam'l. There. 'E'll do now. Give 'im a turn, seeing 'is mate. . . ."

"You fool, you damned fool!" I said. George stooped beside me, wringing his sopping flannels, while Simon and the second man—Simon with his iron-gray face and his iron-gray whisker that made him look like nothing so much as an aged bull peering surlily and stupidly across a winter hedgerow, and the second man, younger, with a ruddy capable face, in a hard, boardlike, town-made suit—watched us. Corinthia sat on the ground, weeping hopelessly and quietly. "You damned fool. Oh, you damned fool."

"Oxford young gentlemen," Simon said in a harsh disgusted voice. "Oxford young gentlemen."

"Eh, well," George said, "I daresay I haven't damaged your lock over a farthing's worth." He rose, and saw Corinthia. "What, Circe!" he said, "tears over the accomplishment of your appointed destiny?" He went to her, trailing a thread of water across the packed earth, and took her arm. It moved willing enough, but she herself sat flat on the ground, looking up at him with streaming hopeless eyes. Her mouth was open a little and she sat in an attitude of patient despair, weeping tears of crystal purity. Simon watched them, the boat-hook—he had taken it from the second man, who was now busy at the lock mechanism, and I knew that he was the brother who worked in London, of whom Corinthia had once told us—clutched in his big knotty fist. The yawl was now in the lock, the two faces watching us across the parapet like two severed heads in a quiet row upon the footway. "Come, now," George said. "You'll soil your dress sitting there."

"Up, lass," Simon said, in that harsh voice of his which at the same time was without ill-nature, as though harshness were merely the medium through which he spoke. Corinthia

rose obediently, still weeping, and went on toward the neat
little dove-cote of a house in which they lived. The sunlight
was slanting level across it and upon George's ridiculous
figure. He was watching me.

"Well, Davy," he said, "if I didn't know better, I'd say
from your expression that you are envying me."

"Am I?" I said. "You fool. You ghastly lunatic."

Simon had gone to the lock. The two quiet heads rose
slowly, as though they were being thrust gradually upward
from out the earth, and Simon now stooped with the boat-
hook over the lock. He rose, with the limp anonymity of
George's once gallant hat on the end of the boat-hook, and
extended it. George took it as gravely. "Thanks," he said.
He dug into his pocket and gave Simon a coin. "For wear
and tear on the boat-hook," he said. "And perhaps a bit of
balm for your justifiable disappointment, eh, Simon?"
Simon grunted and turned back to the lock. The brother
was still watching us. "And I am obliged to you," George
said. "Hope I'll never have to return the favor in kind." The
brother said something, short and grave, in a slow pleasant
voice. George looked at me again. "Well, Davy."

"Come on. Let's go."

"Right you are. Where's the skiff?" Then I was staring
at him again, and for a moment he stared at me. Then he
shouted, a long ringing laugh, while the two heads in the
yawl watched us from beyond Simon's granite-like and
contemptuous back. I could almost hear Simon thinking
Oxford young gentlemen. "Davy, have you lost the skiff?"

"She's tied up below a bit, sir," the civil voice in the yawl
said. "The gentleman walked out of 'er like she were a keb,
without looking back."

The June afternoon slanted across my shoulder, full
upon George's face. He would not take my jacket. "I'll pull

down and keep warm," he said. The once-glazed hat lay between his feet.

"Why don't you throw that thing out?" I said. He pulled steadily, looking at me. The sun was full in his eyes, striking the yellow flecks in them into fleeting, mica-like sparks. "That hat," I said. "What do you want with it?"

"Oh; that. Cast away the symbol of my soul?" He unshipped one scull and picked up the hat and turned and cocked it on the stem, where it hung with a kind of gallant and dissolute jauntiness. "The symbol of my soul rescued from the deep by—"

"Hauled out of a place it had no business being whatever, by a public servant who did not want his public charge cluttered up."

"At least you admit the symbology," he said. "And that the empire rescued it. So it is worth something to the empire. Too much for me to throw it away. That which you have saved from death or disaster will be forever dear to you, Davy; you cannot ignore it. Besides, it will not let you. What is it you Americans say?"

"We say, bunk. Why not use the river for a while? It's paid for."

He looked at me. "Ah. That is . . . Well, anyway, it's American, isn't it. That's something."

But he got out into the current again. A barge was coming up, in tow. We got outside her and watched her pass, empty of any sign of life, with a solemn implacability like a huge barren catafalque, the broad-rumped horses, followed by a boy in a patched coat and carrying a peeled goad, plodding stolidly along the path. We dropped slowly astern. Over her freeboard a motionless face with a dead pipe in its teeth contemplated us with eyes empty of any thought.

"If I could have chosen," George said, "I'd like to have been pulled out by that chap yonder. Can't you see him

picking up a boat-hook without haste and fishing you out
without even shifting the pipe?"

"You should have chosen your place better, then. But it
seems to me you're in no position to complain."

"But Simon showed annoyance. Not surprise nor concern: just annoyance. I don't like to be hauled back into
life by an annoyed man with a boat-hook."

"You could have said so at the time. Simon didn't have
to save you. He could have shut the gates until he got
another head of water, and flushed you right out of his
bailiwick without touching you, and saved himself trouble
and ingratitude. Besides Corinthia's tears."

"Ay; tears. Corinthia will at least cherish a tenderness for
me from now on."

"Yes; but if you'd only not got out at all. Or having not
got in at all. Falling into that filthy lock just to complete a
gesture. I think——"

"Do not think, my good David. When I had the choice
of holding on to the skiff and being haled safely and meekly
away, or of giving the lie to the stupid small gods at the
small price of being temporarily submerged in this——" he
let go one oar and dipped his hand in the water, then he
flung it outward in dripping, burlesque magniloquence. "O
Thames!" he said. "Thou mighty sewer of an empire!"

"Steer the boat," I said. "I lived in America long enough to
have learned something of England's pride."

"And so you consider a bath in this filthy old sewer that
has flushed this land since long before He who made it had
any need to invent God . . . a rock about which man and
all his bawling clamor seethes away to sluttishness. . . ."

We were twenty-one then; we talked like that, tramping
about that peaceful land where in green petrification the old
splendid bloody deeds, the spirits of the blundering coura-
geous men, slumbered in every stone and tree. For that was

1914, and in the parks bands played Valse Septembre, and girls and young men drifted in punts on the moonlit river and sang Mister Moon and There's a Bit of Heaven, and George and I sat in a window in Christ Church while the curtains whispered in the twilight, and talked of courage and honor and Napier and love and Ben Jonson and death. The next year was 1915, and the bands played God Save the King, and the rest of the young men—and some not so young—sang Mademoiselle of Armentieres in the mud, and George was dead.

He had gone out in October, a subaltern in the regiment of which his people were hereditary colonels. Ten months later I saw him sitting with an orderly behind a ruined chimney on the edge of Givenchy. He had a telephone strapped to his ears and he was eating something which he waved at me as we ran past and ducked into the cellar which we sought.

II

I TOLD HIM to wait until they got done giving me the ether; there were so many of them moving back and forth that I was afraid someone would brush against him and find him there. "And then you'll have to go back," I said.

"I'll be careful," George said.

"Because you'll have to do something for me," I said. "You'll have to."

"All right. I will. What is it?"

"Wait until they go away, then I can tell you. You'll have to do it, because I can't. Promise you will."

"All right. I promise." So we waited until they got done and had moved down to my leg. Then George came nearer. "What is it?" he said.

"It's my leg," I said. "I want you to be sure it's dead. They may cut it off in a hurry and forget about it."

"All right. I'll see about it."

"I couldn't have that, you know. That wouldn't do at all. They might bury it and it couldn't lie quiet. And then it would be lost and we couldn't find it to do anything."

"All right. I'll watch." He looked at me. "Only I don't have to go back."

"You don't? You don't have to go back at all?"

"I'm out of it. You aren't out of it yet. You'll have to go back."

"I'm not?" I said. . . . "Then it will be harder to find it than ever. So you see about it. . . . And you don't have to go back. You're lucky, aren't you?"

"Yes. I'm lucky. I always was lucky. Give the lie to the stupid small gods at the mere price of being temporarily submerged in—"

"There were tears," I said. "She sat flat on the earth to weep them."

"Ay; tears," he said. "The flowing of all men's tears under the sky. Horror and scorn and hate and fear and indignation, and the world seething away to sluttishness while you look on."

"No; she sat flat in a green afternoon and wept for the symbol of your soul."

"Not for the symbol, but because the empire saved it, hoarded it. She wept for wisdom."

"But there were tears. . . . And you'll see to it? You'll not go away?"

"Ay," George said; "tears."

In the hospital it was better. It was a long room full of constant movement, and I didn't have to be afraid all the time that they would find him and send him away, though now and then it did happen—a sister or an orderly coming into the middle of our talk, with ubiquitous hands and cheerful aseptic voices: "Now, now. He's not going. Yes, yes; he'll come back. Lie still, now."

So I would have to lie there, surrounding, enclosing that gaping sensation below my thigh where the nerve- and muscle-ends twitched and jerked, until he returned.

"Can't you find it?" I said. "Have you looked good?"

"Yes. I've looked everywhere. I went back out there and looked, and I looked here. It must be all right. They must have killed it."

"But they didn't. I told you they were going to forget it."

"How do you know they forgot it?"

"I know. I can feel it. It jeers at me. It's not dead."

"But if it just jeers at you."

"I know. But that won't do. Don't you see that won't do?"

"All right. I'll look again."

"You must. You must find it. I don't like this."

So he looked again. He came back and sat down and he looked at me. His eyes were bright and intent.

"It's nothing to feel bad about," I said. "You'll find it some day. It's all right; just a leg. It hasn't even another leg to walk with." Still he didn't say anything, just looking at me. "Where are you living now?"

"Up there," he said.

I looked at him for a while. "Oh," I said. "At Oxford?"

"Yes."

"Oh," I said. . . . "Why didn't you go home?"

"I don't know."

He still looked at me. "Is it nice there now? It must be. Are there still punts on the river? Do they still sing in the punts like they did that summer, the men and girls, I mean?" He looked at me, wide, intent, a little soberly.

"You left me last night," he said.

"Did I?"

"You jumped into the skiff and pulled away. So I came back here."

"Did I? Where was I going?"

"I don't know. You hurried away, up-river. You could have told me, if you wanted to be alone. You didn't need to run."

"I shan't again." We looked at one another. We spoke quietly now. "So you must find it now."

"Yes. Can you tell what it is doing?"

"I don't know. That's it."

"Does it feel like it's doing something you don't want it to?"

"I don't know. So you find it. You find it quick. Find it and fix it so it can get dead."

But he couldn't find it. We talked about it quietly, between silences, watching one another. "Can't you tell anything about where it is?" he said. I was sitting up now, practicing accustoming myself to the wood-and-leather one. The gap was still there, but we had now established a sort of sullen armistice. "Maybe that's what it was waiting for," he said. "Maybe now . . ."

"Maybe so. I hope so. But they shouldn't have forgot to —Have I run away any more since that night?"

"I don't know."

"You don't know?" He was watching me with his bright, intent, fading eyes. "George," I said. "Wait, George!" But he was gone.

I didn't see him again for a long time. I was at the Observers' School—it doesn't require two legs to operate a machine gun and a wireless key and to orient maps from the gunner's piano stool of an R.E. or an F.E.—then, and I had almost finished the course. So my days were pretty well filled, what with work and with that certitude of the young which so arbitrarily distinguishes between verities and illusions, establishing with such assurance that line between truth and delirium which sages knit their brows over. And my nights were filled too, with the nerve- and muscle-ends chafed now by an immediate cause: the wood-and-leather leg. But the gap was still there, and sometimes at night, isolated by invisibility, it would become filled with the immensity of darkness and silence despite me. Then, on the poised brink of sleep, I would believe that he had found it at last and seen that it was dead, and that some day he would return and tell me about it. Then I had the dream.

Suddenly I knew that I was about to come upon it. I could feel in the darkness the dark walls of the corridor and the invisible corner, and I knew that it was just around the corner. I could smell a rank, animal odor. It was an odor which I had never smelled before, but I knew it at once, blown suddenly down the corridor from the old fetid caves where experience began. I felt dread and disgust and determination, as when you sense suddenly a snake beside a garden path. And then I was awake, rigid, sweating; the darkness flowed with a long rushing sigh. I lay with the fading odor in my nostrils while my sweat cooled, staring up into the darkness, not daring to close my eyes. I lay on my back, curled about the gaping hole like a doughnut, while the odor faded. At last it was gone, and George was looking at me.

"What is it, Davy?" he said. "Can't you say what it is?"

"It's nothing." I could taste sweat on my lips. "It isn't anything. I won't again. I swear I shan't any more."

He was looking at me. "You said you had to come back to town. And then I saw you on the river. You saw me and hid, Davy. Pulled up under the bank, in the shadow. There was a girl with you." He watched me, his eyes bright and grave.

"Was there a moon?" I said.

"Yes. There was a moon."

"Oh God, oh God," I said. "I won't again, George! You must find it. You must!"

"Ah, Davy," he said. His face began to fade.

"I won't! I won't again!" I said. "George! George!"

A match flared; a face sprang out of the darkness above me. "Wake up," it said. I lay staring at it, sweating. The match burned down, the face fell back into darkness, from which the voice came bodiless: "All right now?"

"Yes, thanks. Dreaming. Sorry I waked you."

For the next few nights I didn't dare let go into sleep again. But I was young, my body was getting strong again and I was out of doors all day; one night sleep overtook me unawares, and I waked next morning to find that I had eluded it, whatever it was. I found a sort of peace. The days passed; I had learned the guns and the wireless and the maps, and most of all, to not observe what should not be observed. My thigh was almost reconciled to the new member, and, freed now of the outcast's doings, I could give all my time to seeking George. But I did not find him; somewhere in the mazy corridor where the mother of dreams dwells I had lost them both.

So I did not remark him at first even when he stood beside me in the corridor just beyond the corner of which It waited. The sulphur reek was all about me; I felt horror and dread and something unspeakable: delight. I believe I felt what women in labor feel. And then George was there, looking steadily down at me. He had always sat beside my head, so we could talk, but now he stood beyond the foot of the bed, looking down at me and I knew that this was farewell.

"Don't go, George!" I said. "I shan't again. I shan't any more, George!" But his steady, grave gaze faded slowly,

implacable, sorrowful, but without reproach. "Go, then!"
I said. My teeth felt dry against my lip like sandpaper. "Go,
then!"

And that was the last of it. He never came back, nor the
dream. I knew it would not, as a sick man who wakes with
his body spent and peaceful and weak knows that the illness
will not return. I knew it was gone; I knew that when I
realized that I thought of it only with pity. Poor devil, I
would think. Poor devil.

But it took George with it. Sometimes, when dark and
isolation had robbed me of myself, I would think that perhaps in killing it he had lost his own life: the dead dying
in order to slay the dead. I sought him now and then in the
corridors of sleep, but without success; I spent a week with
his people in Devon, in a rambling house where his crooked
ugly face and his round ruddy head and his belief that
Marlowe was a better lyric poet than Shakespeare and
Thomas Campion than either, and that breath was not a
bauble given a man for his own pleasuring, eluded me behind
every stick and stone. But I never saw him again.

III

THE PADRE had driven up from Poperinghe in the dark, in
the side car of a motorcycle. He sat beyond the table, talking of Jotham Rust, Everbe Corinthia's brother and Simon's
son, whom I had seen three times in my life. Yesterday I
saw Jotham for the third and last time, arraigned before
a court martial for desertion: the scarecrow of that
once sturdy figure with its ruddy, capable face, who had
pulled George out of the lock with a boat-hook that afternoon three years ago, charged now for his life, offering
no extenuation nor explanation, expecting and asking no
clemency.

"He does not want clemency," the padre said. The padre was a fine, honest man, incumbent of a modest living in the Midlands somewhere, who had brought the kind and honest stupidity of his convictions into the last place on earth where there was room for them. "He does not want to live." His face was musing and dejected, shocked and bewildered. "There comes a time in the life of every man when the world turns its dark side to him and every man's shadow is his mortal enemy. Then he must turn to God, or perish. Yet he . . . I cannot seem . . . " His eyes held that burly bewilderment of oxen; above his stock his shaven chin dejected, but not vanquished yet. "And you say you know of no reason why he should have attacked you?"

"I never saw the man but twice before," I said. "One time was night before last, the other was . . . two—three years ago, when I passed through his father's lock in a skiff while I was at Oxford. He was there when his sister let us through. And if you hadn't told me his sister's name, I wouldn't have remembered him then."

He brooded. "The father is dead, too."

"What? Dead? Old Simon dead?"

"Yes. He died shortly after the—the other. Rust says he left his father after the sister's funeral, talking with the sexton in Abingdon churchyard, and a week later he was notified in London that his father was dead. He says the sexton told him his father had been giving directions about his own funeral. The sexton said that every day Simon would come up to see him about it, made all the arrangements, and that the sexton joked him a little about it, because he was such a hale old chap, thinking that he was just off balance for the time with the freshness of his grief. And then, a week later, he was dead."

"Old Simon dead," I said. "Corinthia, then Simon, and

now Jotham." The candle flame stood steady and unwavering on the table.

"Was that her name?" he said. "Everbe Corinthia?" He sat in the lone chair, puzzlement, bewilderment in the very shape of his shadow on the wall behind him. The light fell on one side of his face, the major's crown on that shoulder glinting dully. I rose from the cot, the harness of the leg creaking with explosive loudness, and leaned over his shoulder and took a cigarette from my magneto case tobacco-box, and fumbled a match in my single hand. He glanced up.

"Permit me," he said. He took the box and struck a match. "You're fortunate to have escaped with just that." He indicated my sling.

"Yes, sir. If it hadn't been for my leg, I'd have got the knife in my ribs instead of my arm."

"Your leg?"

"I keep it propped on a chair beside the bed, so I can reach it easily. He stumbled over it and waked me. Otherwise he'd have stuck me like a pig."

"Oh," he said. He dropped the match and brooded again with his stubborn bewilderment. "And yet, his is not the face of an assassin in the dark. There is a forthrightness in it, a—a—what shall I say? a sense of social responsibility, integrity, that . . . And you say that you—I beg your pardon; I do not doubt your word; it is only that—Yet the girl is indubitably dead; it was he who discovered her and was with her until she died and saw her buried. He heard the man laugh once, in the dark."

"But you cannot slash a stranger's arm simply because you heard a laugh in the dark, sir. The poor devil is crazy with his own misfortunes."

"Perhaps so," the padre said. "He told me that he has other proof, something incontrovertible; what, he would not tell me."

"Then let him produce it. If I were in his place now . . ."

He brooded, his hands clasped on the table. "There is a justice in the natural course of events. . . . My dear sir, are you accusing Providence of a horrible and meaningless practical joke? No, no; to him who has sinned, that sin will come home to him. Otherwise . . . God is at least a gentleman. Forgive me: I am not—You understand how this comes home to me, in this unfortunate time when we already have so much to reproach ourselves with. We are responsible for this." He touched the small metal cross on his tunic, then he swept his arm in a circular gesture that shaped in the quiet room between us the still and sinister darkness in which the fine and resounding words men mouthed so glibly were the vampire's teeth with which the vampire fed. "The voice of God waking His servants from the sloth into which they have sunk. . . ."

"What, padre?" I said. "Is the damn thing making a dissenter of you too?"

He mused again, his face heavy in the candle light. "That the face of a willful shedder of blood, of an assassin in the dark? No, no; you cannot tell me that."

I didn't try. I didn't tell him either my belief that only necessity, the need for expedition and silence, had reduced Jotham to employing a knife, an instrument of any kind; that what he wanted was my throat under his hands.

He had gone home on his leave, to that neat little dovecote beside the lock, and at once he found something strained in its atmosphere and out of tune. That was last summer, about the time I was completing my course at the Observers' School.

Simon appeared to be oblivious of the undercurrent, but Jotham had not been home long before he discovered that every evening about dusk Corinthia quitted the house for an hour or so, and something in her manner, or maybe in the taut atmosphere of the house itself, caused him to question her. She was evasive, blazed suddenly out at him in anger which was completely unlike her at all, then became passive and docile. Then he realized that the passiveness was secretive, the docility dissimulation; one evening he surprised her slipping away. He drove her back to the house, where she took refuge in her room and locked the door, and from a window he thought he caught a glimpse of the man disappearing beyond a field. He pursued, but found no one. For an hour after dusk he lay in a nearby coppice, watching the house, then he returned. Corinthia's door was still locked and old Simon filled the house with his peaceful snoring.

Later something waked him. He sat up in bed, then sprang to the floor and went to the window. There was a moon and by its light he saw something white flitting along the towpath. He pursued and overtook Corinthia, who turned like a vicious small animal at the edge of the coppice where he had lain in hiding. Beyond the towpath a punt lay at the bank. It was empty. He grasped Corinthia's arm. She raged at him; it could not have been very pretty. Then she collapsed as suddenly and from the tangled darkness of the coppice behind them a man's laugh came, a jeering sound that echoed once across the moonlit river and ceased. Corinthia now crouched on the ground, watching him, her face like a mask in the moonlight. He rushed into the coppice and beat it thoroughly, finding nothing. When he emerged the punt was gone. He ran down to the water, looking this way and that. While he stood there the laugh came again, from the shadows beneath the other shore.

He returned to Corinthia. She sat as he had left her, her loosened hair about her face, looking out across the river. He spoke to her, but she did not reply. He lifted her to her feet. She came docilely and they returned to the cottage. He tried to talk to her again, but she moved stonily beside

him, her loosened hair about her cold face. He saw her to
her room and locked the door himself and took the key
back to bed with him. Simon had not awakened. The next
morning she was gone, the door still locked.

He told Simon then and all that day they sought her,
assisted by the neighbors. Neither of them wished to notify
the police, but at dusk that day a constable appeared with
his notebook, and they dragged the lock, without finding
anything. The next morning, just after dawn, Jotham found
her lying in the towpath before the door. She was unconscious, but showed no physical injury. They brought her
into the house and applied their spartan, homely remedies,
and after a time she revived, screaming. She screamed all
that day until sunset. She lay on her back screaming, her
eyes wide open and perfectly empty, until her voice left
her and her screaming was only a ghost of screaming, making no sound. At sunset she died.

He had now been absent from his battalion for a hundred
and twelve days. God knows how he did it; he must have
lived like a beast, hidden, eating when he could, lurking in
the shadow with every man's hand against him, as he sought
through the entire B.E.F. for a man whose laugh he had
heard one time, knowing that the one thing he could surely
count on finding would be his own death, and to be foiled
on the verge of success by an artificial leg propped on a
chair in the dark.

How much later it was I don't know. The candle was
lighted again, but the man who had awakened me was bending over the cot, between me and the light. But despite the
light, it was a little too much like that night before last; I
came out of sleep upstanding this time, with my automatic.
"As you were," I said. "You'll not—" Then he moved back
and I recognized the padre. He stood beside the table, the
light falling on one side of his face and chest. I sat up and

put the pistol down. "What is it, padre? Do they want me again?"

"He wants nothing," the padre said. "Man cannot injure him further now." He stood there, a portly figure that should have been pacing benignantly in a shovel hat in green lanes between summer fields. Then he thrust his hand into his tunic and produced a flat object and laid it on the table. "I found this among Jotham Rust's effects which he gave me to destroy, an hour ago," he said. He looked at me, then he turned and went to the door, and turned again and looked at me.

"Is he—I thought it was to be at dawn."

"Yes," he said. "I must hurry back." He was either looking at me or not. The flame stood steady above the candle. Then he opened the door. "May God have mercy on your soul," he said, and went out.

I sat in the covers and heard him blunder on in the darkness, then I heard the motorcycle splutter into life and die away. I swung my foot to the floor and rose, holding on to the chair on which the artificial leg rested. It was chilly; it was as though I could feel the toes even of the absent leg curling away from the floor, so I braced my hip on the chair and reached the flat object from the table and returned to bed and drew the blanket about my shoulders. My wrist watch said three o'clock.

It was a photograph, a cheap thing such as itinerant photographers turn out at fairs. It was dated at Abingdon in June of the summer just past. At that time I was lying in the hospital talking to George, and I sat quite still in the blankets, looking at the photograph, because it was my own face that looked back at me. It had a quality that was not mine: a quality vicious and outrageous and unappalled, and beneath it was written in a bold sprawling hand like that of a child: "To Everbe Corinthia" followed by an unprintable phrase, yet it was my own face, and I sat holding the picture quietly in my hand while the candle flame stood high and steady above the wick and on the wall my huddled shadow held the motionless photograph. In slow and gradual diminishment of cold tears the candle appeared to sink, as though burying itself in its own grief. But even before this came about, it began to pale and fade until only the tranquil husk of the small flame stood unwinded as a feather above the wax, leaving upon the wall the motionless husk of my shadow. Then I saw that the window was gray, and that was all. It would be dawn at Pop too, but it must have been some time, and the padre must have got back in time.

I told him to find it and kill it. The dawn was cold; on these mornings the butt of the leg felt as though it were made of ice. I told him to. I told him.

Mistral

IT WAS THE LAST of the Milanese brandy. I drank, and passed
the bottle to Don, who lifted the flask until the liquor
slanted yellowly in the narrow slot in the leather jacket,
and while he held it so the soldier came up the path, his
tunic open at the throat, pushing the bicycle. He was a
young man, with a bold lean face. He gave us a surly good
day and looked at the flask a moment as he passed. We
watched him disappear beyond the crest, mounting the bicycle as he went out of sight.

Don took a mouthful, then he poured the rest out. It
splattered on the parched earth, pocking it for a fading moment. He shook the flask to the ultimate drop. "Salut," he
said, returning the flask. "Thanks, O gods. My Lord, if I
thought I'd have to go to bed with any more of that in my
stomach."

"It's too bad, the way you have to drink it," I said. "Just
have to drink it." I stowed the flask away and we went on,
crossing the crest. The path began to descend, still in
shadow. The air was vivid, filled with sun which held a
quality beyond that of mere light and heat, and a sourceless
goat bell somewhere beyond the next turn of the path, distant and unimpeded.

"I hate to see you lugging the stuff along day after day," Don said. "That's the reason I do. You couldn't drink it, and you wouldn't throw it away."

"Throw it away? It cost ten lire. What did I buy it for?"

"God knows," Don said. Against the sun-filled valley the trees were like the bars of a grate, the path a gap in the bars, the valley blue and sunny. The goat bell was somewhere ahead. A fainter path turned off at right angles, steeper than the broad one which we were following. "He went that way," Don said.

"Who did?" I said. Don was pointing to the faint mark of bicycle tires where they had turned into the fainter path.

"See."

"This one must not have been steep enough for him," I said.

"He must have been in a hurry."

"He sure was, after he made that turn."

"Maybe there's a haystack at the bottom."

"Or he could run on across the valley and up the other mountain and then run back down that one and up this one again until his momentum gave out."

"Or until he starved to death," Don said.

"That's right," I said. "Did you ever hear of a man starving to death on a bicycle?"

"No," Don said. "Did you?"

"No," I said. We descended. The path turned, and then we came upon the goat bell. It was on a laden mule cropping with delicate tinkling jerks at the pathside near a stone shrine. Beside the shrine sat a man in corduroy and a woman in a bright shawl, a covered basket beside her. They watched us as we approached.

"Good day, signor," Don said. "Is it far?"

"Good day, signori," the woman said. The man looked at us. He had blue eyes with dissolving irises, as if they had been soaked in water for a long time. The woman touched his arm, then she made swift play with her fingers before his face. He said, in a dry metallic voice like a cicada's:

"Good day, signori."

"He doesn't hear any more," the woman said. "No, it is not far. From yonder you will see the roofs."

"Good," Don said. "We are fatigued. Might one rest here, signora?"

"Rest, signori," the woman said. We slipped our packs and sat down. The sun slanted upon the shrine, upon the serene, weathered figure in the niche and upon two bunches of dried mountain asters lying there. The woman was making play with her fingers before the man's face. Her other hand in repose upon the basket beside her was gnarled and rough. Motionless, it had that rigid quality of unaccustomed idleness, not restful so much as quite spent, dead. It looked like an artificial hand attached to the edge of the shawl, as if she had donned it with the shawl for conventional complement. The other hand, the one with which she talked to the man, was swift and supple as a prestidigitator's.

The man looked at us. "You walk, signori," he said in his light, cadenceless voice.

"Sì," we said. Don took out the cigarettes. The man lifted his hand in a slight, deprecatory gesture. Don insisted. The man bowed formally, sitting, and fumbled at the pack. The woman took the cigarette from the pack and put it into his hand. He bowed again as he accepted a light. "From Milano," Don said. "It is far."

"It is far," the woman said. Her fingers rippled briefly. "He has been there," she said.

"I was there, signori," the man said. He held the cigarette carefully between thumb and forefinger. "One takes care to escape the carriages."

"Yes," Don said. "Those without horses."

"Without horses," the woman said. "There are many. Even here in the mountains we hear of it."

"Many," Don said. "Always whoosh. Whoosh. Whoosh."

"Sì," the woman said. "Even here I have seen it." Her hand rippled in the sunlight. The man looked at us quietly, smoking. "It was not like that when he was there, you see," she said.

"I am there long time ago, signori," he said. "It is far." He spoke in the same tone she had used, the same tone of grave and courteous explanation.

"It is far," Don said. We smoked. The mule cropped with delicate, jerking tinkles of the bell. "But we can rest yonder," Don said, extending his hand toward the valley swimming blue and sunny beyond the precipice where the path turned. "A bowl of soup, wine, a bed?"

The woman watched us across that serene and topless rampart of the deaf, the cigarette smoking close between thumb and finger. The woman's hand flickered before his face. "Sì," he said; "sì. With the priest: why not? The priest will take them in." He said something else, too swift for me. The woman removed the checked cloth which covered the basket, and took out a wineskin. Don and I bowed and drank in turn, the man returning the bows.

"Is it far to the priest's?" Don said.

The woman's hand flickered with unbelievable rapidity. Her other hand, lying upon the basket, might have belonged to another body. "Let them wait for him there, then," the man said. He looked at us. "There is a funeral today. You will find him at the church. Drink, signori."

We drank in decorous turn, the three of us. The wine was harsh and sharp and potent. The mule cropped, its small bell tinkling, its shadow long in the slanting sun, across the path. "Who is it that's dead, signora?" Don said.

"He was to have married the priest's ward after this

harvest," the woman said; "the banns were read and all. A rich man, and not old. But two days ago, he died."

The man watched her lips. "Tchk. He owned land, a house: so do I. It is nothing."

"He was rich," the woman said. "Because he was both young and fortunate, my man is jealous of him."

"But not now," the man said. "Eh, signori?"

"To live is good," Don said. He said, *e bello.*

"It is good," the man said; he also said, *bello.*

"He was to have married the priest's niece, you say," Don said.

"She is no kin to him," the woman said. "The priest just raised her. She was six when he took her, without people, kin, of any sort. The mother was workhouse-bred. She lived in a hut on the mountain yonder. It was not known who the father was, although the priest tried for a long while to persuade one of them to marry her for the child's—"

"One of which?" Don said.

"One of those who might have been the father, signor. But it was never known which one it was, until in 1916. He was a young man, a laborer; the next day we learned that the mother had gone too, to the war also, for she was never seen again by those who knew her until one of our boys came home after Caporetto, where the father had been killed, and told how the mother had been seen in a house in Milano that was not a good house. So the priest went and got the child. She was six then, brown and lean as a lizard. She was hidden on the mountain when the priest got there; the house was empty. The priest pursued her among the rocks and captured her like a beast: she was half naked and without shoes and it winter time."

"So the priest kept her," Don said. "Stout fellow."

"She had no people, no roof, no crust to call hers save what the priest gave her. But you would not know it. Al-

ways with a red or a green dress for Sundays and feast days,
even at fourteen and fifteen, when a girl should be learning
modesty and industry, to be a crown to her husband. The
priest had told that she would be for the church, and we
wondered when he would make her put such away for the
greater glory of God. But at fourteen and fifteen she was
already the brightest and loudest and most tireless in the
dances, and the young men already beginning to look after
her, even after it had been arranged between her and him
who is dead yonder."

"The priest changed his mind about the church and got
her a husband instead," Don said.

"He found for her the best catch in this parish, signor.
Young, and rich, with a new suit each year from the Milano
tailor. Then the harvest came, and what do you think,
signori? she would not marry him."

"I thought you said the wedding was not to be until after
this harvest," Don said. "You mean, the wedding had already
been put off a year before this harvest?"

"It had been put off for three years. It was made three
years ago, to be after that harvest. It was made in the same
week that Giulio Farinzale was called to the army. I remember how we were all surprised, because none had thought his
number would come up so soon, even though he was a
bachelor and without ties save an uncle and aunt."

"Is that so?" Don said. "Governments surprise everybody
now and then. How did he get out of it?"

"He did not get out of it."

"Oh. That's why the wedding was put off, was it?"

The woman looked at Don for a minute. "Giulio was not
the fiancé's name."

"Oh, I see. Who was Giulio?"

The woman did not answer at once. She sat with her
head bent a little. The man had been watching their lips

when they spoke. "Go on," he said; "tell them. They are
men: they can listen to women's tittle-tattle with the ears
alone. They cackle, signori; give them a breathing spell, and
they cackle like geese. Drink."

"He was the one she used to meet by the river in the
evenings; he was younger still: that was why we were surprised that his number should be called so soon. Before we
had thought she was old enough for such, she was meeting
him. And hiding it from the priest as skillfully as any grown
woman could—" For an instant the man's washed eyes
glinted at us, quizzical.

"She was meeting this Giulio all the while she was engaged
to the other one?" Don said.

"No. The engagement was later. We had not thought her
old enough for such yet. When we heard about it, we said
how an anonymous child is like a letter in the post office:
the envelope might look like any other envelope, but when
you open it . . . And the holy can be fooled by sin as quickly
as you or I, signori. Quicker, because they are holy."

"Did he ever find it out?" Don said.

"Yes. It was not long after. She would slip out of the
house at dusk; she was seen, and the priest was seen, hidden
in the garden to watch the house: a servant of the holy
God forced to play watchdog for the world to see. It was
not good, signori."

"And then the young man got called suddenly to the
army," Don said. "Is that right?"

"It was quite sudden; we were all surprised. Then we
thought that it was the hand of God, and that now the
priest would send her to the convent. Then in that same
week we learned that it was arranged between her and him
who is dead yonder, to be after the harvest, and we said it
was the hand of God that would confer upon her a husband
beyond her deserts in order to protect His servant. For the

holy are susceptible to evil, even as you and I, signori; they too are helpless before sin without God's aid."

"Tchk, tchk," the man said. "It was nothing. The priest looked at her, too," he said. "For a man is a man, even under a cassock. Eh, signori?"

"You would say so," the woman said. "You without grace."

"And the priest looked at her, too," Don said.

"It was his trial, his punishment, for having been too lenient with her. And the punishment was not over: the harvest came, and we heard that the wedding was put off for a year: what do you think of that, signori? that a girl, come from what she had come from, to be given the chance which the priest had given her to save her from herself, from her blood . . . We heard how they quarreled, she and the priest, of how she defied him, slipping out of the house after dark and going to the dances where her fiancé might see her or hear of it at any time."

"Was the priest still looking at her?" Don said.

"It was his punishment, his expiation. So the next harvest came, and it was put off again, to be after the next harvest; the banns were not even begun. She defied him to that extent, signori, she, a pauper, and we all saying, 'When will her fiancé hear of it, learn that she is no good, when there are daughters of good houses who had learned modesty and seemliness?' "

"You have unmarried daughters, signora?" Don said.

"Sì. One. Two have I married, one still in my house. A good girl, signori, if I do say it."

"Tchk, woman," the man said.

"That is readily believed," Don said. "So the young man had gone to the army, and the wedding was put off for another year."

"And another year, signori. And then a third year. Then

it was to be after this harvest; within a month it was to have been. The banns were read; the priest read them himself in the church, the third time last Sunday, with him there in his new Milano suit and she beside him in the shawl he had given her—it cost a hundred lire—and a golden chain, for he gave her gifts suitable for a queen rather than for one who could not name her own father, and we believed that at last the priest had served his expiation out and that the evil had been lifted from his house at last, since the soldier's time would also be up this fall. And now the fiancé is dead."

"Was he very sick?" Don said.

"It was very sudden. A hale man; one you would have said would live a long time. One day he was well, the second day he was quite sick. The third day he was dead. Perhaps you can hear the bell, with listening, since you have young ears." The opposite mountains were in shadow. Between, the valley lay invisible still. In the sunny silence the mule's bell tinkled in random jerks. "For it is in God's hands," the woman said. "Who will say that his life is his own?"

"Who will say?" Don said. He did not look at me. He said in English: "Give me a cigarette."

"You've got them."

"No, I haven't."

"Yes, you have. In your pants pocket."

He took out the cigarettes. He continued to speak in English. "And he died suddenly. And he got engaged suddenly. And at the same time, Giulio got drafted suddenly. It would have surprised you. Everything was sudden except somebody's eagerness for the wedding to be. There didn't seem to be any hurry about that, did there?"

"I don't know. I no spika."

"In fact, they seemed to stop being sudden altogether until about time for Giulio to come home again. Then it began to be sudden again. And so I think I'll ask if priests serve on the draft boards in Italy." The old man watched his lips, his washed gaze grave and intent. "And if this path is the main path down the mountain, and that bicycle turned off into that narrow one back there, what do you think of that, signori?"

"I think it was fine. Only a little sharp to the throat. Maybe we can get something down there to take away the taste."

The man was watching our lips; the woman's head was bent again; her stiff hand smoothed the checked cover upon the basket. "You will find him at the church, signori," the man said.

"Yes," Don said. "At the church."

We drank again. The man accepted another cigarette with that formal and unfailing politeness, conferring upon the action something finely ceremonious yet not incongruous. The woman put the wineskin back into the basket and covered it again. We rose and took up our packs.

"You talk swiftly with the hand, signora," Don said.

"He reads the lips too. The other we made lying in the bed in the dark. The old do not sleep so much. The old lie in bed and talk. It is not like that with you yet."

"It is so. You have made the padrone many children, signora?"

"Sì. Seven. But we are old now. We lie in bed and talk."

II

BEFORE WE REACHED the village the bell had begun to toll. From the gaunt steeple of the church the measured notes seemed to blow free as from a winter branch, along the wind. The wind began as soon as the sun went down. We watched the sun touch the mountains, whereupon the sky lost its pale, vivid blueness and took on a faintly greenish cast, like glass, against which the recent crest, where the shrine faded with the dried handful of flowers beneath the fading crucifix, stood black and sharp. Then the wind began: a steady moving wall of air full of invisible particles of something. Before it the branches leaned without a quiver, as before the pressure of an invisible hand, and in it our blood began to cool at once, even before we had stopped walking where the path became a cobbled street.

The bell still tolled. "Funny hour for a funeral," I said. "You'd think he would have kept a long time at this altitude. No need to be hurried into the ground like this."

"He got in with a fast gang," Don said. The church was invisible from here, shut off by a wall. We stood before a gate, looking into a court enclosed by three walls and roofed by a vine on a raftered trellis. It contained a wooden table and two backless benches. We stood at the gate, looking into the court, when Don said. "So this is Uncle's house."

"Uncle?"

"He was without ties save an uncle and aunt," Don said. "Yonder, by the door." The door was at the bottom of the court. There was a fire beyond it, and beside the door a bicycle leaned against the wall. "The bicycle, unconscious," Don said.

"Is that a bicycle?"

"Sure. That's a bicycle." It was an old-style machine, with high back-swept handlebars like gazelle horns. We looked at it.

"The other path is the back entrance," I said. "The family entrance." We heard the bell, looking into the court.

"Maybe the wind doesn't blow in there," Don said. "Besides, there's no hurry. We couldn't see him anyway, until it's over."

"These places are hotels sometimes." We entered. Then we saw the soldier. When we approached the table he came to the door and stood against the firelight, looking at us. He wore a white shirt now. But we could tell him by his legs. Then he went back into the house.

"So Malbrouck is home," Don said.

"Maybe he came back for the funeral." We listened to the bell. The twilight was thicker inside. Overhead the leaves streamed rigid on the wind, stippled black upon the livid translucent sky. The strokes of the bell sounded as though they too were leaves flattening away upon an inviolable vine in the wind.

"How did he know there was going to be one?" Don said.

"Maybe the priest wrote him a letter."

"Maybe so," Don said. The firelight looked good beyond the door. Then a woman stood in it, looking at us. "Good day, padrona," Don said. "Might one have a mouthful of wine here?" She looked at us, motionless against the firelight. She was tall. She stood tall and motionless against the firelight, not touching the door. The bell tolled. "She used to be a soldier too," Don said. "She was a sergeant."

"Maybe she was the colonel who ordered Malbrouck to go home."

"No. He wasn't moving fast enough when he passed us up yonder, for it to have been her." Then the woman spoke:

"It is so, signori. Rest yourselves." She went back into the house. We slipped our packs and sat down. We looked at the bicycle.

"Cavalry," Don said. "Wonder why he came the back way."

"All right," I said.

"All right what?"

"All right. Wonder."

"Is that a joke?"

"Sure. That's a joke. It's because we are old. We lie in the draft. That's a joke too."

"Tell me something that's not a joke."

"All right."

"Did you hear the same thing I think I heard up there?"

"No spika. I love Italy. I love Mussolini." The woman

brought the wine. She set it on the table and was turning away. "Ask her," I said. "Why don't you?"

"All right. I will.—You have military in the house, signora?"

The woman looked at him. "It is nothing, signor. It is my nephew returned."

"Finished, signora?"

"Finished, signor."

"Accept our felicitations. He has doubtless many friends who will rejoice at his return." She was thin, not old, with cold eyes, looking down at Don with brusque attention, waiting. "You have a funeral in the village today." She said nothing at all. She just stood there, waiting for Don to get done talking. "He will be mourned," Don said.

"Let us hope so," she said. She made to go on; Don asked her about lodgings. There were none, she answered with immediate finality. Then we realized that the bell had ceased. We could hear the steady whisper of the wind in the leaves overhead.

"We were told that the priest—" Don said.

"Yes? You were told that the priest."

"That we might perhaps find lodgings there."

"Then you would do well to see the priest, signor." She returned to the house. She strode with the long stride of a man into the firelight, and disappeared. When I looked at Don, he looked away and reached for the wine.

"Why didn't you ask her some more?" I said. "Why did you quit so soon?"

"She was in a hurry. Her nephew is just home from the army, she said. He came in this afternoon. She wants to be with him, since he is without ties."

"Maybe she's afraid he'll be drafted."

"Is that a joke too?"

"It wouldn't be to me." He filled the glasses. "Call her

back. Tell her you heard that her nephew is to marry the
priest's ward. Tell her we want to give them a present. A
stomach pump. That's not a joke, either."

"I know it's not." He filled his glass carefully. "Which
had you rather do, or stay at the priest's tonight?"

"Salut," I said.

"Salut." We drank. The leaves made a dry, wild, continuous sound. "Wish it was still summer."

"It would be pretty cold tonight, even in a barn."

"Yes. Glad we don't have to sleep in a barn tonight."

"It wouldn't be so bad, after we got the hay warm and got
to sleep."

"We don't have to, though. We can get a good sleep and
get an early start in the morning."

I filled the glasses. "I wonder how far it is to the next
village."

"Too far." We drank. "I wish it were summer. Don't
you?"

"Yes." I emptied the bottle into the glasses. "Have some
wine." We raised our glasses. We looked at one another. The
particles in the wind seemed to drive through the clothing,
through the flesh, against the bones, penetrating the brick
and plaster of the walls to reach us. "Salut."

"We said that before," Don said.

"All right. Salut, then."

"Salut."

We were young: Don, twenty-three; I, twenty-two. And
age is so much a part of, so inextricable from, the place where
you were born or bred. So that away from home, some distance away—space or time or experience away—you are always both older and eternally younger than yourself, at the
same time.

We stood in the black wind and watched the funeral—
priest, coffin, a meager clump of mourners—pass, their gar-

ments, and particularly the priest's rusty black, ballooning ahead of them, giving an illusion of unseemly haste, as though they were outstripping themselves across the harsh green twilight (the air was like having to drink iced lemonade in the winter time) and into the church. "We'll be out of the wind too," Don said.

"There's an hour of light yet."

"Sure; we might even reach the crest by dark." He looked at me. Then I looked away. The red tiles of the roofs were black, too, now. "We'll be out of the wind." Then the bell began to toll again. "We don't know anything. There's probably not anything. Anyway, we don't know it. We don't have to know it. Let's get out of the wind." It was one of those stark, square, stone churches, built by those harsh iron counts and bishops of Lombardy. It was built old; time had not even mellowed it, could not ever mellow it, not all of time could have. They might have built the mountains too and invented the twilight in a dungeon underground, in the black ground. And beside the door the bicycle leaned. We looked at it quietly as we entered the church and we said quietly, at the same time:

"Beaver."

"He's one of the pallbearers," Don said. "That's why he came home." The bell tolled. We passed through the chancel and stopped at the back of the church. We were out of the wind now, save for the chill eddies of it that licked in at our backs. We could hear it outside, ripping the slow strokes of the bell half-born out of the belfry, so that by the time we heard them, they seemed to have come back as echoes from a far distance. The nave, groined upward into the gloom, dwarfed the meager clot of bowed figures. Beyond them, above the steady candles, the Host rose, soaring into sootlike shadows like festooned cobwebs, with a quality sorrowful and triumphant, like wings. There was no organ, no music, no human sound at all at first. They just knelt there among the dwarfing gloom and the cold, serene, faint light of the candles. They might have all been dead. "It'll be dark long before they can get done," Don whispered.

"Maybe it's because of the harvest," I whispered. "They probably have to work all day. The living can't wait on the dead, you know."

"But, if he was as rich as they told us he was, it seems like . . ."

"Who buries the rich? Do the rich do it, or do the poor do it?"

"The poor do it," Don whispered. Then the priest was there, above the bowed heads. We had not seen him at first, but now he was there, shapeless, blurring out of the shadows below the candles, his face like a smudge, a thumb print, upon the gloom where the Host rose in a series of dissolving gleams like a waterfall; his voice filled the church, slow, steady, like wings beating against the cold stone, upon the resonance of wind in which the windless candles stood as though painted. "And so he looked at her," Don whispered. "He had to sit across the table from her, say, and watch her. Watch her eating the food that made her change from nothing and become everything, knowing she had no food of her own and that it was his food that was doing it, and not for him changing. You know: girls: they are not anything, then they are everything. You watch them become everything before your eyes. No, not eyes: it's the same in the dark. You know it before they do; it's not their becoming everything that you dread: it's their finding it out after you have long known it: you die too many times. And that's not right. Not fair. I hope I'll never have a daughter."

"That's incest," I whispered.

"I never said it wasn't. I said it was like fire. Like watching the fire lean up and away rushing."

"You must either watch a fire, or burn up in it. Or not be there at all. Which would you choose?"

"I don't know. If it was a girl, I'd rather burn up in it."

"Than to not be there at all, even?"

"Yes." Because we were young. And the young seem to be impervious to anything except trifles. We can invest trifles with a tragic profundity, which is the world. Because, after all, there's nothing particularly profound about reality. Because when you reach reality, along about forty or fifty or sixty, you find it to be only six feet deep and eighteen feet square.

Then it was over. Outside again, the wind blew steadily down from the black hills, hollowing out the green glass bowl of the sky. We watched them file out of the church and carry the coffin into the churchyard. Four of them carried iron lanterns and in the dusk they clotted quietly antic about the grave while the wind leaned steadily upon them and upon the lantern flames, and blew fine dust into the grave as though all nature were quick to hide it. Then they were done. The lanterns bobbed into motion, approaching, and we watched the priest. He crossed the churchyard toward the presbytery at a scuttling gait, blown along in his gusty black. The soldier was in mufti now. He came out of the throng, striding also with that long-limbed thrust like his aunt. He looked briefly at us with his bold surly face and got on the bike and rode away. "He was one of the pallbearers," Don said. "And what do you think of that, signori?"

"No spika," I said. "I love Italy. I love Mussolini."

"You said that before."

"All right. Salut, then."

Don looked at me. His face was quite sober. "Salut," he said. Then he looked toward the presbytery, hitching his pack forward. The door of the presbytery was closed.

"Don," I said. He stopped, looking at me. The mountains

had lost all perspective; they appeared to lean in toward us. It was like being at the bottom of a dead volcano filled with that lost savage green wind dead in its own motion and full of its own driving and unsleeping dust. We looked at one another.

"All right, damn it," Don said. "You say what to do next, then." We looked at one another. After a while the wind would sound like sleep, maybe. If you were warm and close between walls, maybe.

"All right," I said.

"Why can't you mean, all right? Damn it, we've got to do something. This is October; it's not summer. And we don't know anything. We haven't heard anything. We don't speak Italian. We love Italy."

"I said, all right," I said. The presbytery was of stone too, bleak in a rank garden. We were halfway up the flagged path when a casement beneath the eaves opened and somebody in white looked down at us and closed the shutter again. It was done all in one movement. Again we said together, quietly:

"Beaver." But it was too dark to see much, and the casement was closed again. It had not taken ten seconds.

"Only we should have said, Beaverette," Don said.

"That's right. Is that a joke?"

"Yes. That's a joke." A wooden-faced peasant woman opened the door. She held a candle, the flame leaning inward from the wind. The hall behind her was dark; a stale, chill smell came out of it. She stood there, the harsh planes of her face in sharp relief, her eyes two caverns in which two little flames glittered, looking at us.

"Go on," I said. "Tell her something."

"We were told that his reverence, signora," Don said, "that we might—" The candle leaned and recovered. She raised the other hand and sheltered it, blocking the door with her body. "We are travelers, en promenade; we were told—supper and a bed . . ."

When we followed her down the hall we carried with us in our ears the long rush of the recent wind, like in a sea shell. There was no light save the candle which she carried. So that, behind her, we walked in gloom out of which the serrated shadow of a stair on one wall reared dimly into the passing candle and dissolved in mounting serrations, carrying the eye with it up the wall where there was not any light. "Pretty soon it'll be too dark to see anything from that window," Don said.

"Maybe she won't have to, by then."

"Maybe so." The woman opened a door; we entered a lighted room. It contained a table on which sat a candle in an iron candlestick, a carafe of wine, a long loaf, a metal box with a slotted cover. The table was set for two. We slung our packs into the corner and watched her set another place and fetch another chair from the hall. But that made only three places and we watched her take up her candle and go out by a second door. Then Don looked at me. "Maybe we'll see her, after all."

"How do you know he doesn't eat?"

"When? Don't you know where he'll be?" I looked at him. "He'll have to stay out there in the garden."

"How do you know?"

"The soldier was at the church. He must have seen him. Must have heard—" We looked at the door, but it was the woman. She had three bowls. "Soup, signora?" Don said.

"Sì. Soup."

"Good. We have come far." She set the bowls on the table. "From Milano." She looked briefly over her shoulder at Don.

"You'd better have stayed there," she said. And she went out. Don and i looked at one another. My ears were still full of wind.

"So he is in the garden," Don said.

"How do you know he is?"

After a while Don quit looking at me. "I don't know."

"No. You don't know. And I don't know. We don't want to know. Do we?"

"No. No spika."

"I mean, sure enough."

"That's what I mean," Don said. The whisper in our ears seemed to fill the room with wind. Then we realized that it was the wind that we heard, the wind itself we heard, even though the single window was shuttered tight. It was as though the quiet room were isolated on the ultimate peak of space, hollowed murmurous out of chaos and the long dark fury of time. It seemed strange that the candle flame should stand so steady above the wick.

III

So WE DID NOT see him until we were in the house. Until then he had been only a shabby shapeless figure, on the small size, scuttling through the blowing dusk at the head of the funeral, and a voice. It was as though neither of them was any part of the other: the figure in blowing black, and the voice beating up the still air above the candles, detached and dispassionate, tireless and spent and forlorn.

There was something precipitate about the way he entered, like a diver taking a full breath in the act of diving. He did not look at us and he was already speaking, greeting us and excusing his tardiness in one breath, in a low rapid voice. Still, without having ceased to speak or having looked at us, he motioned toward the other chairs and seated himself and bowed his head over his plate and began a Latin grace without a break in his voice; again his voice seemed to rush slow and effortless just above the sound of the wind, like in the

church. It went on for some time; so that after a while I
raised my head. Don was watching me, his eyebrows arched
a little; we looked toward the priest and saw his hands writhing slowly on either side of his plate. Then the woman spoke
a sharp word behind me; I had not heard her enter: a gaunt
woman, not tall, with a pale, mahogany-colored face that
might have been any age between twenty-five and sixty. The
priest stopped. He looked at us for the first time, out of weak,
rushing eyes. They were brown and irisless, like those of an
old dog. Looking at us, it was as though he had driven them
up with whips and held them so, in cringing and rushing
desperation. "I forget," he said. "There come times—"
Again the woman snapped a word at him, setting a tureen on
the table, the shadow of her arm falling across his face and
remaining there: but we had already looked away. The long
wind rushed past the stone eaves; the candle flame stood
steady as a sharpened pencil in the still sound of the wind.
We heard her filling the bowls, yet she still stood for a time,
the priest's face in the shadow of her arm; she seemed to be
holding us all so until the moment—whatever it was—had
passed. She went out. Don and I began to eat. We did not
look toward him. When he spoke at last, it was in a tone of
level, polite uninterest. "You have come far, signori?"

"From Milano," we both said.

"Before that, Firenze," Don said. The priest's head was
bent over his bowl. He ate rapidly. Without looking up he
gestured toward the loaf. I pushed it along to him. He broke
the end off and went on eating.

"Ah," he said. "Firenze. That is a city. More—what do
you say?—spirituel than our Milano." He ate hurriedly,
without finesse. His robe was turned back over a flannel
undershirt, the sleeves were. His spoon clattered; at once the
woman entered with a platter of broccoli. She removed the
bowls. He reached his hand. She handed him the carafe and

he filled the glasses without looking up and lifted his with a brief phrase. But he had only feinted to drink; he was watching my face when I looked at him. I looked away; I heard him clattering at the dish and Don was looking at me too. Then the woman's shoulder came between us and the priest. "There come times—" he said. He clattered at the dish. When the woman spoke to him in that shrill, rapid patois she thrust his chair back and for an instant we saw his driven eyes across her arm. "There come times—" he said, raising his voice. Then she drowned the rest of it, getting completely between us and Don and I stopped looking and heard them leave the room. The steps ceased. Then we could hear only the wind.

"It was the burial service," Don said. Don was a Catholic. "That grace was."

"Yes," I said. "I didn't know that."

"Yes. It was the burial service. He got mixed up."

"Sure," I said. "That's it. What do we do now?" Our packs lay in the corner. Two packs can look as human, as utterly human and spent, as two shoes. We were watching the door when the woman entered. But she wasn't going to stop. She didn't look at us.

"What shall we do now, signora?" Don said.

"Eat." She did not stop. Then we could hear the wind again.

"Have some wine," Don said. He raised the carafe, then he held it poised above my glass, and we listened. The voice was beyond the wall, maybe two walls, in a sustained rush of indistinguishable words. He was not talking to anyone there: you could tell that. In whatever place he was, he was alone: you could tell that. Or maybe it was the wind. Maybe in any natural exaggerated situation—wind, rain, drouth—man is always alone. It went on for longer than a minute while Don held the carafe above my glass. Then he poured. We began to eat. The voice was muffled and sustained, like a machine might have been making it.

"If it were just summer," I said.

"Have some wine." He poured. We held our poised glasses. It sounded just like a machine. You could tell that he was alone. Anybody could have. "That's the trouble," Don said. "Because there's not anybody there. Not anybody in the house."

"The woman."

"So are we." He looked at me.

"Oh," I said.

"Sure. What better chance could she have wanted, have asked for? He was in here at least five minutes. And he just back from the army after three years. The first day he is home, and then afternoon and then twilight and then darkness. You saw her there. Didn't you see her up there?"

"He locked the door. You know he locked it."

"This house belongs to God: you can't have a lock on it. You didn't know that."

"That's right. I forgot you're a Catholic. You know things. You know a lot, don't you?"

"No. I don't know anything. I no spika too. I love Italy too." The woman entered. She didn't bring anything this time. She came to the table and stood there, her gaunt face above the candle, looking down at us.

"Look, then," she said. "Will you go away?"

"Go away?" Don said. "Not stop here tonight?" She looked down at us, her hand lying on the table. "Where could we stop? Who would take us in? One cannot sleep on the mountain in October, signora."

"Yes," she said. She was not looking at us now. Through the walls we listened to the voice and to the wind.

"What is this, anyway?" Don said. "What goes on here, signora?"

She looked at him gravely, speculatively, as if he were a

child. "You are seeing the hand of God, signorino," she said. "Pray God that you are too young to remember it." Then she was gone. And after a while the voice ceased, cut short off like a thread. And then there was just the wind.

"As soon as we get out of the wind, it won't be so bad," I said.

"Have some wine." Don raised the carafe. It was less than half full.

"We'd better not drink any more."

"No." He filled the glasses. We drank. Then we stopped. It began again, abruptly, in full stride, as though silence were the thread this time. We drank. "We might as well finish the broccoli, too."

"I don't want any more."

"Have some wine then."

"You've already had more than I have."

"All right." He filled my glass. I drank it. "Now, have some wine."

"We ought not to drink it all."

He raised the carafe. "Two more glasses left. No use in leaving that."

"There aren't two glasses left."

"Bet you a lira."

"All right. But let me pour."

"All right." He gave me the carafe. I filled my glass and reached toward his. "Listen," he said. For about a minute now the voice had been rising and falling, like a wheel running down. This time it didn't rise again; there was only the long sound of the wind left. "Pour it," Don said. I poured. The wine mounted three quarters. It began to dribble away. "Tilt it up." I did so. A single drop hung for a moment, then fell into the glass. "Owe you a lira," Don said.

The coins rang loud in the slotted box. When he took it up from the table and shook it, it made no sound. He took the coins from his pocket and dropped them through the slot. He shook it again. "Doesn't sound like quite enough. Cough up." I dropped some coins through the slot; he shook the box again. "Sounds all right now." He looked at me across the table, his empty glass bottom-up before him. "How about a little wine?"

When we rose I took my pack from the corner. It was on the bottom. I had to tumble Don's aside. He watched me. "What are you going to do with that?" he said. "Take it out for a walk?"

"I don't know," I said. Past the cold invisible eaves the long wind steadily sighed. Upon the candle the flame stood like the balanced feather on the long white nose of a clown.

The hall was dark; there was no sound in it. There was nothing in it save the cold smell of sunless plaster and silence and the smell of living, of where people have, and will have, lived. We carried our packs low and close against our legs like we had stolen them. We went on to the door and opened it, entering the black wind again. It had scoured the sky clear and clean, hollowing it out of the last of light, the last of twilight. We were halfway to the gate when we saw him. He was walking swiftly back and forth beside the wall. His head was bare, his robes ballooning about him. When he saw us he did not stop. He didn't hurry, either. He just turned and went back beside the wall and turned again, walking fast. We waited at the gate. We thanked him for the food, he motionless in his whipping robes, his head bent and averted a little, as a deaf man listens. When Don knelt at his feet he started back as though Don had offered to strike him. Then I felt like a Catholic too and I knelt too and he made the sign hurriedly above us, upon the black-and-green wind and dusk, like he would have made it in water. When we passed out the gate and looked back we could still see, against the sky and the blank and lightless house, his head rushing back and forth like a midget running along the top of the wall.

I V

THE CAFÉ was on the lee side of the street; we sat out of the wind. But we could see gusts and eddies of trash swirl along the gutter, and an occasional tongue of it licked chill across our legs, and we could hear the steady rushing of it in the high twilight among the roofs. On the curb two musicians from the hills—a fiddler and a piper—sat, playing a wild and skirling tune. Now and then they stopped to drink, then they resumed the same tune. It was without beginning and seemingly without end, the wild unmusic of it swirling along the wind with a quality at once martial and sad. The waiter fetched us brandy and coffee, his dirty apron streaming suddenly and revealing beneath it a second one of green baize and rigid as oxidized copper. At the other table five young men sat, drinking and ringing separately small coins onto the waiter's tray, which he appeared to count by the timbre of the concussion before tilting them into his waistcoat in one motion, and a long-flanked young peasant woman stopped to hear the music, a child riding her hip. She set the child down and it scuttled under the table where the young men sat, they withdrawing their legs to permit it, while the woman was not looking. She was looking at the musicians, her face round and tranquil, her mouth open a little.

"Let's have some wine," Don said.

"All right," I said. "I like Italy," I said. We had another brandy. The woman was trying to cajole the child from under the table. One of the young men extracted it and gave it back to her. People stopped in the street to hear the music, and a high two-wheeled cart, full of fagots and drawn by a woman and a diminutive mule, passed without stopping, and then the girl came up the street in her white dress, and I didn't feel like a Catholic any more. She was all in white, coatless, walking slender and supple. I didn't feel like anything any more, watching her white dress swift in the twilight, carrying her somewhere or she carrying it somewhere: anyway, it was going too, moving when she moved and because she moved, losing her when she would be lost because it moved when she moved and went with her to the instant of loss. I remember how, when I learned about Thaw and White and Evelyn Nesbitt, how I cried. I cried because Evelyn, who was a word, was beautiful and lost or I would never have heard of her. Because she had to be lost for me to find her and I had to find her to lose her. And when I learned that she was old enough to have a grown daughter or son or something, I cried, because I had lost myself then and I could never again be hurt by loss. So I watched the white dress, thinking, She'll be as near me in a second as she'll ever be and then she'll go on away in her white dress forevermore, in the twilight forevermore. Then I felt Don watching her too and then we watched the soldier spring down from the bike. They came together and stopped and for a while they stood there in the street, among the people, facing one another but not touching. Maybe they were not even talking, and it didn't matter how long; it didn't matter about time. Then Don was nudging me.

"The other table," he said. The five young men had all turned; their heads were together, now and then a hand, an arm, secret, gesticulant, their faces all one way. They leaned back, without turning their faces, and the waiter stood, tray on hip—a squat, sardonic figure older than Grandfather Lust himself—looking also. At last they turned and went on up the street together in the direction from which he had come, he leading the bicycle. Just before they passed from sight they stopped and faced one another again among the people, the heads, without touching at all. Then they went on. "Let's have some wine," Don said.

The waiter set the brandies on the table, his apron like a momentary board on the wind. "You have military in town," Don said.

"That's right," the waiter said. "One."

"Well, one is enough," Don said. The waiter looked up the street. But they were gone now, with her white dress shaping her stride, her girl-white, not for us.

"Too many, some say." He looked much more like a monk than the priest did, with his long thin nose and his bald head. He looked like a devastated hawk. "You're stopping at the priest's, eh?"

"You have no hotel," Don said.

The waiter made change from his waistcoat, ringing the coins deliberately upon the table. "What for? Who would stop here, without he walked? Nobody walks except you English."

"We're Americans."

"Well." He raised his shoulders faintly. "That's your affair." He was not looking at us exactly; not at Don, that is. "Did you try Cavalcanti's?"

"A wineshop at the edge of town? The soldier's aunt, isn't it? Yes. But she said—"

The waiter was watching him now. "She didn't send you to the priest?"

"No."

"Ah," the waiter said. His apron streamed suddenly. He fought it down and scoured the top of the table with it. "Americans, eh?"

"Yes," Don said. "Why wouldn't she tell us where to go?"

The waiter scoured the table. "That Cavalcanti. She's not of this parish."

"Not?"

"Not since three years. The padrone belongs to that one beyond the mountain." He named a village which we had passed in the forenoon.

"I see," Don said. "They aren't natives."

"Oh, they were born here. Until three years ago they belonged to this parish."

"But three years ago they changed."

"They changed." He found another spot on the table. He removed it with the apron. Then he examined the apron. "There are changes and changes; some further than others."

"The padrona changed further than across the mountain, did she?"

"The padrona belongs to no parish at all." He looked at us. "Like me."

"Like you?"

"Did you try to talk to her about the church?" He watched Don. "Stop there tomorrow and mention the church to her."

"And that happened three years ago," Don said. "That was a year of changes for them."

"You said it. The nephew to the army, the padrone across the mountain, the padrona . . . All in one week, too. Stop there tomorrow and ask her."

"What do they think here about all these changes?"

"What changes?"

"These recent changes."

"How recent?" He looked at Don. "There's no law against changes."

"No. Not when they're done like the law says. Sometimes the law has a look, just to see if they were changed right. Isn't that so?"

The waiter had assumed an attitude of sloven negligence, save his eyes, his long face. It was too big for him, his face was. "How did you know he was a policeman?"

"Policeman?"

"You said soldier; I knew you meant policeman and just didn't speak the language good. But you'll pick it up with practice." He looked at Don. "So you made him too, did you? Came in here this afternoon; said he was a shoe-drummer. But I made him."

"Here already," Don said. "I wonder why he didn't stop the . . . before they . . ."

"How do you know he's a policeman?" I said.

The waiter looked at me. "I don't care whether he is or not, buddy. Which had you rather do? think a man is a cop and find he's not, or think he's not a cop, and find he is?"

"You're right," Don said. "So that's what they say here."

"They say plenty. Always have and always will. Like any other town."

"What do you say?" Don said.

"I don't say. You don't either."

"No."

"It's no skin off of my back. If they want to drink, I serve them; if they want to talk, I listen. That keeps me as busy as I want to be all day."

"You're right," Don said. "It didn't happen to you."

The waiter looked up the street; it was almost full dark. He appeared not to have heard. "Who sent for the cop, I wonder?" Don said.

"When a man's got jack, he'll find plenty of folks to help him make trouble for folks even after he's dead," the waiter said. Then he looked at us. "I?" he said. He leaned; he slapped his chest lightly. He looked quickly at the other table, then he leaned down and hissed: "I am atheist, like in America," and stood back and looked at us. "In America, all are atheists. *We* know." He stood there in his dirty apron, with his long, weary, dissolute face while we rose in turn and shook hands with him gravely, the five young men turning to look. He flipped his other hand at us, low against his flank. "Rest, rest," he hissed. He looked over his shoulder at the young men. "Sit down," he whispered. He jerked his head toward the doorway behind us, where the padrona sat behind the bar. "I've got to eat, see?" He scuttled away and returned with two more brandies, carrying them with his former sloven, precarious skill, as if he had passed no word with us save to take the order. "It's on me," he said. "Put it down."

"Now, what?" Don said. The music had ceased; from across the street we watched the fiddler, fiddle under arm, standing before the table where the young men sat, his other hand and the clutched hat gesticulant. The young woman was already going up the street, the child riding her hip again, its head nodding to a somnolent rhythm, like a man on an elephant. "Now, what?"

"I don't care."

"Oh, come on."

"No."

"There's no detective here. He never saw one. He wouldn't know a detective. There aren't any detectives in Italy: can you imagine an official Italian in plain clothes for a uniform?"

"No."

"She'll show us where the bed is, and in the morning early—"

"No. You can, if you want to. But I'm not."

He looked at me. Then he swung his pack onto his shoulder. "Good night. See you in the morning. At the café yonder."

"All right." He did not look back. Then he turned the corner. I stood in the wind. Anyway, I had the coat. It was a shooting coat of Harris tweed; we had paid eleven guineas for it, wearing it day about while the other wore the sweater.

In the Tyrol last summer Don held us up three days while he was trying to make the girl who sold beer at the inn. He wore the coat for three successive days, swapping me a week, to be paid on demand. On the third day the girl's sweetheart came back. He was as big as a silo, with a green feather in his hat. We watched him pick her over the bar with one hand. I believe she could have done Don the same way: all yellow and pink and white she was, like a big orchard. Or like looking out across a snowfield in the early sunlight. She could have done it at almost any hour for three days too, by just reaching out her hand. Don gained four pounds while we were there.

V

THEN I CAME into the full sweep of the wind. The houses were all dark, yet there was still a little light low on the ground, as though the wind held it there flattened to the earth and it had been unable to rise and escape. The walls ceased at the beginning of the bridge; the river looked like steel. I thought I had already come into the full sweep of the wind, but I hadn't. The bridge was of stone, balustrades and roadway and all, and I squatted beneath the lee of the weather rail. I could hear the wind above and beneath, coming down the river in a long sweeping hum, like through wires. I squatted there, waiting. It wasn't very long.

He didn't see me at first, until I rose. "Did you think to have the flask filled?" he said.

"I forgot. I intended to. Damn the luck. Let's go back—"

"I got a bottle. Which way now?"

"I don't care. Out of the wind. I don't care." We crossed the bridge. Our feet made no sound on the stones, because the wind blew it away. It flattened the water, scoured it; it looked just like steel. It had a sheen, holding light like the land between it and the wind, reflecting enough to see by. But it swept all sound away before it was made almost, so that when we reached the other side and entered the cut where the road began to mount, it was several moments before we could hear anything except our ears; then we heard. It was a smothered whimpering sound that seemed to come out of the air overhead. We stopped. "It's a child," Don said. "A baby."

"No: an animal. An animal of some sort." We looked at one another in the pale darkness, listening.

"It's up there, anyway," Don said. We climbed up out of the cut. There was a low stone wall enclosing a field, the field a little luminous yet, dissolving into the darkness. Just this side of the darkness, about a hundred yards away, a copse stood black, blobbed shapeless on the gloom. The wind rushed up across the field and we leaned on the wall, listening into it, looking at the copse. But the sound was nearer than that, and after a moment we saw the priest. He was lying on his face just inside the wall, his robes over his head, the black blur of his gown moving faintly and steadily, either because of the wind or because he was moving under them. And whatever the sound meant that he was making, it was not meant to be listened to, for his voice ceased when we made a noise. But he didn't look up, and the faint shuddering of his gown didn't stop. Shuddering, writhing, twisting from side to side—something. Then Don touched me. We went on beside the wall. "Get down easier here," he said quietly. The pale road rose gradually beneath us as the hill flattened. The copse was a black blob. "Only I didn't see the bicycle."

"Then go back to Cavalcanti's," I said. "Where in hell do you expect to see it?"

"They would have hidden it. I forgot. Of course they would have hidden it."

"Go on," I said. "Don't talk so goddamn much."

"Unless they thought he would be busy with us and wouldn't—" he ceased and stopped. I jolted into him and then I saw it too, the handlebars rising from beyond the wall like the horns of a hidden antelope. Against the gloom the blob of the copse seemed to pulse and fade, as though it breathed, lived. For we were young, and night, darkness, is terrible to young people, even icy driving blackness like this. Young people should be so constituted that with sunset they would enter a coma state, by slumber shut safe from the darkness, the secret nostalgic sense of frustration and of objectless and unappeasable desire.

"Get down, damn you," I said. With his high hunched pack, his tight sweater, he was ludicrous; he looked like a clown; he was terrible and ugly and sad all at once, since he was ludicrous and, without the coat, he would be so cold. And so was I: ugly and terrible and sad. "This damn wind. This damn wind." We regained the road. We were sheltered for the moment, and he took out the bottle and we drank. It was fiery stuff. "Talk about my Milan brandy," I said. "That damn wind. That damn wind. That damn wind."

"Give me a cigarette."

"You've got them."

"I gave them to you."

"You're a goddamn liar. You didn't." He found them in his pocket. But I didn't wait.

"Don't you want one? Better light it here, while we are . . ." I didn't wait. The road rose, became flush with the field. After a while I heard him just behind me, and we entered the wind. I could see past my shoulder his cigarette shredding away in fiery streamers upon the unimpeded rush of the mistral, that black chill wind full of dust like sparks of ice.

Divorce in Naples

I

WE WERE SITTING at a table inside: Monckton and the bosun and Carl and George and me and the women, the three women of that abject glittering kind that seamen know or that know seamen. We were talking English and they were not talking at all. By that means they could speak constantly to us above and below the sound of our voices in a tongue older than recorded speech and time too. Older than the thirty-four days of sea time which we had but completed, anyway. Now and then they spoke to one another in Italian. The women in Italian, the men in English, as if language might be the sex difference, the functioning of the vocal cords the inner biding until the dark pairing time. The men in English, the women in Italian: a decorum as of two parallel streams separated by a levee for a little while.

We were talking about Carl, to George.

"Why did you bring him here, then?" the bosun said.

"Yes," Monckton said. "I sure wouldn't bring my wife to a place like this."

George cursed Monckton: not with a word or even a sentence; a paragraph. He was a Greek, big and black, a full head taller than Carl; his eyebrows looked like two crows in overlapping flight. He cursed us all with immediate thoroughness and in well-nigh faultless classic Anglo-Saxon, who

877

at other times functioned in the vocabulary of an eight-year-old by-blow of a vaudeville comedian and a horse, say.

"Yes, sir," the bosun said. He was smoking an Italian cigar and drinking ginger beer; the same tumbler of which, incidentally, he had been engaged with for about two hours and which now must have been about the temperature of a ship's showerbath. "I sure wouldn't bring my girl to a dive like this, even if he did wear pants."

Carl meanwhile had not stirred. He sat serene among us, with his round yellow head and his round eyes, looking like a sophisticated baby against the noise and the glitter, with his glass of thin Italian beer and the women murmuring to one another and watching us and then Carl with that biding and inscrutable foreknowledge which they do not appear to know that they possess. "*Èinnocente*," one said; again they murmured, contemplating Carl with musing, secret looks. "He may have fooled you already," the bosun said. "He may have slipped through a porthole on you any time these three years."

George glared at the bosun, his mouth open for cursing. But he didn't curse. Instead he looked at Carl, his mouth still open. His mouth closed slowly. We all looked at Carl. Beneath our eyes he raised his glass and drank with contained deliberation.

"Are you still pure?" George said. "I mean, sho enough."

Beneath our fourteen eyes Carl emptied the glass of thin, bitter, three per cent beer. "I been to sea three years," he said. "All over Europe."

George glared at him, his face baffled and outraged. He had just shaved; his close blue jowls lay flat and hard as a prizefighter's or a pirate's, up to the black explosion of his hair. He was our second cook. "You damn lying little bastard," he said.

The bosun raised his glass of ginger beer with an exact

replica of Carl's drinking. Steadily and deliberately, his body thrown a little back and his head tilted, he poured the ginger beer over his right shoulder at the exact speed of swallowing, still with that air of Carl's, that grave and cosmopolitan swagger. He set the glass down, and rose. "Come on," he said to Monckton and me; "let's go. Might as well be board ship if we're going to spend the evening in one place."

Monckton and I rose. He was smoking a short pipe. One of the women was his, another the bosun's. The third one had a lot of gold teeth. She could have been thirty, but maybe she wasn't. We left her with George and Carl. When I looked back from the door, the waiter was just fetching them some more beer.

II

THEY CAME into the ship together at Galveston, George carrying a portable victrola and a small parcel wrapped in paper bearing the imprint of a well-known ten-cent store, and Carl carrying two bulging imitation leather bags that looked like they might weigh forty pounds apiece. George appropriated two berths, one above the other like a Pullman section, cursing Carl in a harsh, concatenant voice a little overburred with *v*'s and *r*'s and ordering him about like a nigger, while Carl stowed their effects away with the meticulousness of an old maid, producing from one of the bags a stack of freshly laundered drill serving jackets that must have numbered a dozen. For the next thirty-four days (he was the messboy) he wore a fresh one for each meal in the saloon, and there were always two or three recently washed ones drying under the poop awning. And for thirty-four evenings, after the galley was closed, we watched the two of them in pants and undershirts, dancing to the victrola on the after well deck above a hold full of Texas cotton and

Georgia resin. They had only one record for the machine
and it had a crack in it, and each time the needle clucked
George would stamp on the deck. I don't think that either
one of them was aware that he did it.

It was George who told us about Carl. Carl was eighteen,
from Philadelphia. They both called it Philly; George in a
proprietorial tone, as if he had created Philadelphia in order
to produce Carl, though it later appeared that George had
not discovered Carl until Carl had been to sea for a year
already. And Carl himself told some of it: a fourth or fifth
child of a first generation of Scandinavian-American shipwrights, brought up in one of an identical series of small
frame houses a good trolley ride from salt water, by a
mother or an older sister: this whom, at the age of fifteen
and weighing perhaps a little less than a hundred pounds,
some ancestor long knocking his quiet bones together at the
bottom of the sea (or perhaps havened by accident in dry
earth and become restive with ease and quiet) had sent
back to the old dream and the old unrest three or maybe
four generations late.

"I was a kid, then," Carl told us, who had yet to experience or need a shave. "I thought about everything but going
to sea. I thought once I'd be a ballplayer or maybe a prize
fighter. They had pictures of them on the walls, see, when
Sis would send me down to the corner after the old man on
a Saturday night. Jeez, I'd stand outside on the street and
watch them go in, and I could see their legs under the door
and hear them and smell the sawdust and see the pictures of
them on the walls through the smoke. I was a kid then, see.
I hadn't been nowheres then."

We asked George how he had ever got a berth, even as
a messman, standing even now about four inches over five
feet and with yet a face that should have followed mon-

strances up church aisles, if not looked down from one of
the colored windows themselves.

"Why shouldn't he have come to sea?" George said.
"Ain't this a free country? Even if he ain't nothing but a
damn mess." He looked at us, black, serious. "He's a virgin,
see? Do you know what that means?" He told us what it
meant. Someone had evidently told him what it meant not
so long ago, told him what he used to be himself, if he could
remember that far back, and he thought that perhaps we
didn't know the man, or maybe he thought it was a new
word they had just invented. So he told us what it meant.
It was in the first night watch and we were on the poop
after supper, two days out of Gibraltar, listening to Monckton talking about cauliflower. Carl was taking a shower (he
always took a bath after he had cleared the saloon after
supper. George, who only cooked, never bathed until we
were in port and the petite cleared) and George told us what
it meant.

Then he began to curse. He cursed for a long time.

"Well, George," the bosun said, "suppose you were one,
then? What would you do?"

"What would I do?" George said. "What wouldn't I do?"
He cursed for some time, steadily. "It's like the first cigarette
in the morning," he said. "By noon, when you remember
how it tasted, how you felt when you was waiting for the
match to get to the end of it, and when that first drag—"
He cursed, long, impersonal, like a chant.

Monckton watched him: not listened: watched, nursing
his pipe. "Why, George," he said, "you're by way of being
almost a poet."

There was a swipe, some West India Docks crum; I forget his name. "Call that lobbing the tongue?" he said. "You
should hear a Lymus mate laying into a fo'c'sle of bloody
Portygee ginneys."

"Monckton wasn't talking about the language," the bosun said. "Any man can swear." He looked at George. "You're not the first man that ever wished that, George. That's something that has to be *was* because you don't know you are when you are." Then he paraphrased unwitting and with unprintable aptness Byron's epigram about women's mouths. "But what are you saving him for? What good will it do you when he stops being?"

George cursed, looking from face to face, baffled and outraged.

"Maybe Carl will let George hold his hand at the time," Monckton said. He reached a match from his pocket. "Now, you take Brussels sprouts—"

"You might get the Old Man to quarantine him when we reach Naples," the bosun said.

George cursed.

"Now, you take Brussels sprouts," Monckton said.

III

IT TOOK US some time that night, to get either started or settled down. We—Monckton and the bosun and the two women and I—visited four more cafés, each like the other one and like the one where we had left George and Carl— same people, same music, same thin, colored drinks. The two women accompanied us, with us but not of us, biding and acquiescent, saying constantly and patiently and without words that it was time to go to bed. So after a while I left them and went back to the ship. George and Carl were not aboard.

The next morning they were not there either, though Monckton and the bosun were, and the cook and the steward swearing up and down the galley; it seemed that the cook was planning to spend the day ashore himself. So they had to stay aboard all day. Along toward midafternoon there came aboard a smallish man in a soiled suit who looked like one of those Columbia day students that go up each morning on the East Side subway from around Chatham Square. He was hatless, with an oiled pompadour. He had not shaved recently, and he spoke no English in a pleasant, deprecatory way that was all teeth. But he had found the right ship and he had a note from George, written on the edge of a dirty scrap of newspaper, and we found where George was. He was in jail.

The steward hadn't stopped cursing all day, anyhow. He didn't stop now, either. He and the messenger went off to the consul's. The steward returned a little after six o'clock, with George. George didn't look so much like he had been drunk; he looked dazed, quiet, with his wild hair and a blue stubble on his jaw. He went straight to Carl's bunk and he began to turn Carl's meticulous covers back one by one like a traveler examining the bed in a third-class European hotel, as if he expected to find Carl hidden among them. "You mean," he said, "he ain't been back? He ain't been back a-*tall*?"

"We haven't seen him," we told George. "The steward hasn't seen him either. We thought he was in jail with you."

He began to replace the covers; that is, he made an attempt to draw them one by one up the bed again in a kind of detached way, as if he were not conscious, sentient. "They run," he said in a dull tone. "They ducked out on me. I never thought he'd a done it. I never thought he'd a done me this way. It was her. She was the one made him done it. She knew what he was, and how I . . ." Then he began to cry, quietly, in that dull, detached way. "He must have been sitting there with his hand in her lap all the time. And I never suspicioned. She kept on moving her chair closer and closer to his. But I trusted him. I never suspicioned nothing. I thought he wouldn't a done nothing serious without asking me first, let alone . . . I trusted him."

It appeared that the bottom of George's glass had distorted their shapes enough to create in George the illusion that Carl and the woman were drinking as he drank, in a serious but celibate way. He left them at the table and went back to the lavatory; or rather, he said that he realized suddenly that he was in the lavatory and that he had better be getting back, concerned not over what might transpire while he was away, but over the lapse, over his failure to be present at his own doings which the getting to the lavatory inferred. So he returned to the table, not yet alarmed; merely concerned and amused. He said he was having a fine time.

So at first he believed that he was still having such a good time that he could not find his own table. He found the one which he believed should be his, but it was vacant save for three stacks of saucers, so he made one round of the room, still amused, still enjoying himself; he was still enjoying himself when he repaired to the center of the dance floor where, a head above the dancers, he began to shout "Porteus ahoy!" in a loud voice, and continued to do so until a waiter who spoke English came and removed him and led him back to that same vacant table bearing the three stacks of saucers and the three glasses, one of which he now recognized as his own.

But he was still enjoying himself, though not so much now, believing himself to be the victim of a practical joke, first on the part of the management, and it appeared that he must have created some little disturbance, enjoying himself less and less all the while, the center of an augmenting clump of waiters and patrons.

When at last he did realize, accept the fact, that they were gone, it must have been pretty bad for him: the outrage, the despair, the sense of elapsed time, an unfamiliar city at night in which Carl must be found, and that quickly if it was to do any good. He tried to leave, to break through the crowd, without paying the score. Not that he would have beaten the bill; he just didn't have time. If he could have found Carl within the next ten minutes, he would have returned and paid the score twice over: I am sure of that.

And so they held him, the wild American, a cordon of waiters and clients—women and men both—and he dragging a handful of coins from his pockets ringing onto the tile floor. Then he said it was like having your legs swarmed by a pack of dogs: waiters, clients, men and women, on hands and knees on the floor, scrabbling after the rolling coins, and George slapping about with his big feet, trying to stamp the hands away.

Then he was standing in the center of an abrupt wide circle, breathing a little hard, with the two Napoleons in their swords and pallbearer gloves and Knights of Pythias bonnets on either side of him. He did not know what he had done; he only knew that he was under arrest. It was not until they reached the Prefecture, where there was an interpreter, that he learned that he was a political prisoner, having insulted the king's majesty by placing foot on the king's effigy on a coin. They put him in a forty-foot dungeon, with seven other political prisoners, one of whom was the messenger.

"They taken my belt and my necktie and the strings out of my shoes," he told us dully. "There wasn't nothing in the room but a barrel fastened in the middle of the floor and a wooden bench running all the way round the walls. I knew what the barrel was for right off, because they had already been using it for that for some time. You was expected to sleep on the bench when you couldn't stay on your feet no longer. When I stooped over and looked at it close, it was like looking down at Forty-second Street from a airplane. They looked just like Yellow cabs. Then I went and used the barrel. But I used it with the end of me it wasn't intended to be used with."

Then he told about the messenger. Truly, Despair, like Poverty, looks after its own. There they were: the Italian who spoke no English, and George who scarcely spoke any language at all; certainly not Italian. That was about four o'clock in the morning. Yet by daylight George had found the one man out of the seven who could have served him or probably would have.

"He told me he was going to get out at noon, and I told him I would give him ten lire as soon as I got out, and he got me the scrap of paper and the pencil (this, in a bare dungeon, from among seven men stripped to the skin of everything save the simplest residue of clothing necessary for warmth: of money, knives, shoelaces, even pins and loose buttons) and I wrote the note and he hid it and they left him out and after about four hours they come and got me and there was the steward."

"How did you talk to him, George?" the bosun said. "Even the steward couldn't find out anything until they got to the consul's."

"I don't know," George said. "We just talked. That was the only way I could tell anybody where I was at."

We tried to get him to go to bed, but he wouldn't do it. He didn't even shave. He got something to eat in the galley and went ashore. We watched him go down the side.

"Poor bastard," Monckton said.

"Why?" the bosun said. "What did he take Carl there for? They could have gone to the movies."

"I wasn't thinking about George," Monckton said.

"Oh," the bosun said. "Well, a man can't keep on going ashore anywhere, let alone Europe, all his life without getting ravaged now and then."

"Good God," Monckton said. "I should hope not."

George returned at six o'clock the next morning. He still looked dazed, though still quite sober, quite calm. Overnight his beard had grown another quarter inch. "I couldn't find them," he said quietly. "I couldn't find them nowheres." He had to act as messman now, taking Carl's place at the officers' table, but as soon as breakfast was done, he disappeared; we heard the steward cursing him up and down the ship until noon, trying to find him. Just before noon he returned, got through dinner, departed again. He came back just before dark.

"Found him yet?" I said. He didn't answer. He stared at me for a while with that blank look. Then he went to their bunks and hauled one of the imitation leather bags down and tumbled all of Carl's things into it and crushed down the lid upon the dangling sleeves and socks and hurled the bag out onto the well deck, where it tumbled once and burst open, vomiting the white jackets and the mute socks and the underclothes. Then he went to bed, fully dressed, and slept fourteen hours. The cook tried to get him up for breakfast, but it was like trying to rouse up a dead man.

When he waked he looked better. He borrowed a cigarette of me and went and shaved and came back and borrowed another cigarette. "Hell with him," he said. "Leave the bastard go. I don't give a damn."

That afternoon he put Carl's things back into his bunk. Not carefully and not uncarefully: he just gathered them up and dumped them into the berth and paused for a moment to see if any of them were going to fall out, before turning away.

IV

It was just before daylight. When I returned to the ship about midnight, the quarters were empty. When I waked just before daylight, all the bunks save my own were still vacant. I was lying in a halfdoze, when I heard Carl in the passage. He was coming quietly; I had scarcely heard him before he appeared in the door. He stood there for a while, looking no larger than an adolescent boy in the halflight, before he entered. I closed my eyes quickly. I heard him, still on tiptoe, come to my bunk and stand above me for a while. Then I heard him turn away. I opened my eyes just enough to watch him.

He undressed swiftly, ripping his clothes off, ripping off a button that struck the bulkhead with a faint click. Naked, in the wan light, he looked smaller and frailer than ever as he dug a towel from his bunk where George had tumbled his things, flinging the other garments aside with a kind of dreadful haste. Then he went out, his bare feet whispering in the passage.

I could hear the shower beyond the bulkhead running for a long time; it would be cold now, too. But it ran for a long time, then it ceased and I closed my eyes again until he had entered. Then I watched him lift from the floor the undergarment which he had removed and thrust it through a porthole quickly, with something of the air of a recovered drunkard putting out of sight an empty bottle. He dressed and put on a fresh white jacket and combed his hair, leaning to the small mirror, looking at his face for a long time.

And then he went to work. He worked about the bridge deck all day long; what he could have found to do there we could not imagine. But the crew's quarters never saw him until after dark. All day long we watched the white jacket flitting back and forth beyond the open doors or kneeling as he polished the brightwork about the companions. He seemed to work with a kind of fury. And when he was forced by his duties to come topside during the day, we noticed that it was always on the port side, and we lay with our starboard to the dock. And about the galley or the after deck George worked a little and loafed a good deal, not looking toward the bridge at all.

"That's the reason he stays up there, polishing that brightwork all day long," the bosun said. "He knows George can't come up there."

"It don't look to me like George wants to," I said.

"That's right," Monckton said. "For a dollar George would go up to the binnacle and ask the Old Man for a cigarette."

"But not for curiosity," the bosun said.

"You think that's all it is?" Monckton said. "Just curiosity?"

"Sure," the bosun said. "Why not?"

"Monckton's right," I said. "This is the most difficult moment in marriage: the day after your wife has stayed out all night."

"You mean the easiest," the bosun said. "George can quit him now."

"Do you think so?" Monckton said.

We lay there five days. Carl was still polishing the brightwork in the bridge-deck companions. The steward would send him out on deck, and go away; he would return and find Carl still working on the port side and he would make him go to starboard, above the dock and the Italian boys in bright, soiled jerseys and the venders of pornographic postcards. But it didn't take him long there, and then we would see him below again, sitting quietly in his white jacket in the stale gloom, waiting for suppertime. Usually he would be darning socks

George had not yet said one word to him; Carl might not have been aboard at all, the very displacement of space which was his body, impedeless and breathable air. It was now George's turn to stay away from the ship most of the day and all of the night, returning a little drunk at three and four o'clock, to waken everyone by hand, save Carl, and talk in gross and loud recapitulation of recent and always different women before climbing into his bunk. As far as we knew, they did not even look at one another until we were well on our way to Gibraltar.

Then Carl's fury of work slacked somewhat. Yet he worked steadily all day, then, bathed, his blond hair wet and smooth, his slight body in a cotton singlet, we would see him leaning alone in the long twilight upon the rail midships or forward. But never about the poop where we smoked and talked and where George had begun again to play the single record on the victrola, committing, unrequested and anathemaed, cold-blooded encore after encore.

Then one night we saw them together. They were leaning side by side on the poop rail. That was the first time Carl had looked astern, looked toward Naples since that morning when he returned to the ship, and even now it was the evening on which the Gates of Hercules had sunk into the waxing twilight and the River Ocean began to flow down into the darkling sea and overhead the crosstrees swayed in measured and slow recover against the tall night and the low new moon.

"He's all right now," Monckton said. "The dog's gone back to his vomit."

"I said he was all right all the time," the bosun said. "George didn't give a damn."

"I wasn't talking about George," Monckton said. "George hasn't made the grade yet."

V

GEORGE TOLD US. "He'd keep on moping and mooning, see, and I'd keep on trying to talk to him, to tell him I wasn't

mad no more. Jeez, it had to come some day; a man can't be
a angel all your life. But he wouldn't even look back that
way. Until all of a sudden he says one night:

" 'What do you do to them?' I looked at him. 'How does
a man treat them?'

" 'You mean to tell me,' I says, 'that you spent three days
with her and she ain't showed you that?'

" 'I mean, give them,' he says. 'Don't men give—'

" 'Jeez Christ,' I says, 'you done already give her something they would have paid you money for it in Siam.
Would have made you the prince or the prime minister at
the least. What do you mean?'

" 'I don't mean money,' he says. 'I mean . . .'

" 'Well,' I says, 'if you was going to see her again, if she
was going to be your girl, you'd give her something. Bring
it back to her. Like something to wear or something: they
don't care much what, them foreign women, hustling them
wops all their life that wouldn't give them a full breath if
they was a toy balloon; they don't care much what it is. But
you ain't going to see her again, are you?'

" 'No,' he says. 'No,' he says. 'No.' And he looked like he
was fixing to jump off the boat and swim on ahead and wait
for us at Hatteras.

" 'So you don't want to worry about that,' I says. Then I
went and played the vic again, thinking that might cheer
him up, because he ain't the first, for Christ's sake; he never
invented it. But it was the next night; we was at the poop
rail then—the first time he had looked back—watching the
phosrus along the logline, when he says:

" 'Maybe I got her into trouble.'

" 'Doing what?' I says. 'With what? With the police?
Didn't you make her show you her petite?' Like she would
have needed a ticket, with that face full of gold; Jeez, she

could have rode the train on her face alone; maybe that was her savings bank instead of using her stocking.

" 'What ticket?' he says. So I told him. For a minute I thought he was crying, then I seen that he was just trying to not puke. So I knew what the trouble was, what had been worrying him. I remember the first time it come as a surprise to me. 'Oh,' I says, 'the smell. It don't mean nothing,' I says; you don't want to let that worry you. It ain't that they smell bad,' I says, 'that's just the Italian national air.' "

And then we thought that at last he really was sick. He worked all day long, coming to bed only after the rest of us were asleep and snoring, and I saw him in the night get up and go topside again, and I followed and saw him sitting on a windlass. He looked like a little boy, still, small, motionless in his underclothes. But he was young, and even an old man can't be sick very long with nothing but work to do and salt air to breathe; and so two weeks later we were watching him and George dancing again in their undershirts after supper on the after well deck while the victrola lifted its fatuous and reiterant ego against the waxing moon and the ship snored and hissed through the long seas off Hatteras. They didn't talk; they just danced, gravely and tirelessly as the nightly moon stood higher and higher up the sky. Then we turned south, and the Gulf Stream ran like blue ink alongside, bubbled with fire by night in the softening latitudes, and one night off Tortugas the ship began to tread the moon's silver train like an awkward and eager courtier, and Carl spoke for the first time after almost twenty days.

"George," he said, "do me a favor, will you?"

"Sure, bud," George said, stamping on the deck each time the needle clucked, his black head shoulders above Carl's sleek pale one, the two of them in decorous embrace, their canvas shoes hissing in unison: "Sure," George said. "Spit it out."

"When we get to Galveston, I want you to buy me a suit of these pink silk teddybears that ladies use. A little bigger than I'd wear, see?"

Carcassonne

AND ME ON A BUCKSKIN PONY *with eyes like blue electricity and a mane like tangled fire, galloping up the hill and right off into the high heaven of the world*

His skeleton lay still. Perhaps it was thinking about this. Anyway, after a time it groaned. But it said nothing. *which is certainly not like you* he thought *you are not like yourself. but I can't say that a little quiet is not pleasant*

He lay beneath an unrolled strip of tarred roofing made of paper. All of him that is, save that part which suffered neither insects nor temperature and which galloped unflagging on the destinationless pony, up a piled silver hill of cumulae where no hoof echoed nor left print, toward the blue precipice never gained. This part was neither flesh nor unflesh and he tingled a little pleasantly with its lackful contemplation as he lay beneath the tarred paper bedclothing.

So were the mechanics of sleeping, of denning up for the night, simplified. Each morning the entire bed rolled back into a spool and stood erect in the corner. It was like those glasses, reading glasses which old ladies used to wear, attached to a cord that rolls onto a spindle in a neat case of unmarked gold; a spindle, a case, attached to the deep bosom of the mother of sleep.

He lay still, savoring this. Beneath him Rincon followed

its fatal, secret, nightly pursuits, where upon the rich and inert darkness of the streets lighted windows and doors lay like oily strokes of broad and overladen brushes. From the docks a ship's siren unsourced itself. For a moment it was sound, then it compassed silence, atmosphere, bringing upon the eardrums a vacuum in which nothing, not even silence, was. Then it ceased, ebbed; the silence breathed again with a clashing of palm fronds like sand hissing across a sheet of metal.

Still his skeleton lay motionless. Perhaps it was thinking about this and he thought of his tarred paper bed as a pair of spectacles through which he nightly perused the fabric of dreams:

Across the twin transparencies of the spectacles the horse still gallops with its tangled welter of tossing flames. Forward and back against the taut roundness of its belly its legs swing, rhythmically reaching and overreaching, each spurning overreach punctuated by a flicking limberness of shod hooves. He can see the saddlegirth and the soles of the rider's feet in the stirrups. The girth cuts the horse in two just back of the withers, yet it still gallops with rhythmic and unflagging fury and without progression, and he thinks of that riderless Norman steed which galloped against the Saracen Emir, who, so keen of eye, so delicate and strong the wrist which swung the blade, severed the galloping beast at a single blow, the several halves thundering on in the sacred dust where him of Bouillon and Tancred too clashed in sullen retreat; thundering on through the assembled foes of our meek Lord, wrapped still in the fury and the pride of the charge, not knowing that it was dead.

The ceiling of the garret slanted in a ruined pitch to the low eaves. It was dark, and the body consciousness, assuming the office of vision, shaped in his mind's eye his motionless body grown phosphorescent with that steady decay which had set up within his body on the day of his birth. *the flesh is dead living on itself subsisting consuming itself thriftily in its own renewal will never die for I am the Resurrection and the Life* Of a man, the worm should be lusty, lean, hairedover. Of women, of delicate girls briefly like heard music in tune, it should be suavely shaped, falling feeding into prettinesses, feeding. *what though to Me but as a seething of new milk Who am the Resurrection and the Life*

It was dark. The agony of wood was soothed by these latitudes; empty rooms did not creak and crack. Perhaps wood was like any other skeleton though, after a time, once reflexes of old compulsions had spent themselves. Bones might lie under seas, in the caverns of the sea, knocked together by the dying echoes of waves. Like bones of horses cursing the inferior riders who bestrode them, bragging to one another about what they would have done with a first-rate rider up. But somebody always crucified the first-rate riders. And then it's better to be bones knocking together to the spent motion of falling tides in the caverns and the grottoes of the sea.

where him of Bouillon and Tancred too

His skeleton groaned again. Across the twin transparencies of the glassy floor the horse still galloped, unflagging and without progress, its destination the barn where sleep was stabled. It was dark. Luis, who ran the cantina downstairs, allowed him to sleep in the garret. But the Standard Oil Company, who owned the garret and the roofing paper, owned the darkness too; it was Mrs Widdrington's, the Standard Oil Company's wife's, darkness he was using to sleep in. She'd make a poet of you too, if you did not work anywhere. She believed that, if a reason for breathing were not acceptable to her, it was no reason. With her, if you were white and did not work, you were either a tramp or a poet. Maybe you

were. Women are so wise. They have learned how to live
unconfused by reality, impervious to it. It was dark. .

and knock my bones together and together It was dark,
a darkness filled with a fairy pattering of small feet. stealthy
and intent. Sometimes the cold patter of them on his face
waked him in the night, and at his movement they scurried
invisibly like an abrupt disintegration of dead leaves in a
wind, in whispering arpeggios of minute sound, leaving a thin
but definite effluvium of furtiveness and voracity. At times,
lying so while daylight slanted grayly along the ruined pitch
of the eaves, he watched their shadowy flickings from obscurity to obscurity, shadowy and huge as cats, leaving along
the stagnant silences those whisperings gusts of fairy feet.

Mrs Widdrington owned the rats too. But wealthy people
have to own so many things. Only she didn't expect the rats
to pay for using her darkness and silence by writing poetry.
Not that they could not have, and pretty fair verse probably.
Something of the rat about Byron: allocutions of stealthful
voracity; a fairy pattering of little feet behind a bloody arras
where fell *where fell where I was King of Kings but the
woman with the woman with the dog's eyes to knock my
bones together and together*

"I would like to perform something," he said, shaping his
lips soundlessly in the darkness, and the galloping horse filled
his mind again with soundless thunder. He could see the saddlegirth and the soles of the rider's stirruped feet, and he
thought of that Norman steed, bred of many fathers to bear
iron mail in the slow, damp, green valleys of England, maddened with heat and thirst and hopeless horizons filled with
shimmering nothingness, thundering along in two halves and
not knowing it, fused still in the rhythm of accrued momentum. Its head was mailed so that it could not see forward at
all, and from the center of the plates projected a—projected a—

"Chamfron," his skeleton said.

"Chamfron." He mused for a time, while the beast that did not know that it was dead thundered on as the ranks of the Lamb's foes opened in the sacred dust and let it through. "Chamfron," he repeated. Living, as it did, a retired life, his skeleton could know next to nothing of the world. Yet it had an astonishing and exasperating way of supplying him with bits of trivial information that had temporarily escaped his mind. "All you know is what I tell you," he said.

"Not always," the skeleton said. "I know that the end of life is lying still. You haven't learned that yet. Or you haven't mentioned it to me, anyway."

"Oh, I've learned it," he said. "I've had it dinned into me enough. It isn't that. It's that I don't believe it's true."

The skeleton groaned.

"I don't believe it, I say," he repeated.

"All right, all right," the skeleton said testily. "I shan't dispute you. I never do. I only give you advice."

"Somebody has to, I guess," he agreed sourly. "At least, it looks like it." He lay still beneath the tarred paper, in a silence filled with fairy patterings. Again his body slanted and slanted downward through opaline corridors groined with ribs of dying sunlight upward dissolving dimly, and came to rest at last in the windless gardens of the sea. About him the swaying caverns and the grottoes, and his body lay on the rippled floor, tumbling peacefully to the wavering echoes of the tides.

I want to perform something bold and tragical and austere he repeated, shaping the soundless words in the pattering silence *me on a buckskin pony with eyes like blue electricity and a mane like tangled fire, galloping up the hill and right off into the high heaven of the world* Still galloping, the horse soars outward; still galloping, it thunders up the long blue hill of heaven, its tossing mane in golden swirls like fire.

Steed and rider thunder on, thunder punily diminishing: a dying star upon the immensity of darkness and of silence within which, steadfast, fading, deepbreasted and grave of flank, muses the dark and tragic figure of the Earth, his mother.

WILLIAM FAULKNER, born New Albany, Mississippi, September 25, 1897—died July 6, 1962. Enlisted Royal Air Force, Canada, 1918. Attended Universiy of Mississippi. Traveled in Europe 1925-1926. Resident of Oxford, Mississippi, where he held various jobs while trying to establish himself as a writer. First published novel, *Soldiers' Pay*, 1926. Writer in Residence at the University of Virginia 1957-1958. Awarded the Nobel Prize for Literature 1950.

VINTAGE FICTION, POETRY, AND PLAYS

VINTAGE CRITICISM: LITERATURE, MUSIC, AND ART

VINTAGE BIOGRAPHY AND AUTOBIOGRAPHY

VINTAGE POLITICAL SCIENCE AND SOCIAL CRITICISM

VINTAGE WORKS OF SCIENCE AND PSYCHOLOGY

VINTAGE WOMEN'S STUDIES